JACOB'S LADDER

JACOB'S LADDER

Ludmila Ulitskaya

**TRANSLATED FROM THE RUSSIAN BY
POLLY GANNON**

FARRAR, STRAUS AND GIROUX

NEW YORK

Farrar, Straus and Giroux
120 Broadway, New York 10271

Copyright © 2015 by Ludmila Ulitskaya
Translation copyright © 2019 by Mary Catherine Gannon
All rights reserved
Printed in the United States of America
Originally published in Russian in 2015 by AST/Elena Shubina Publishers,
Russia, as *Лестница Якова*
English translation published in the United States by Farrar, Straus and Giroux
First American edition, 2019

Library of Congress Cataloging-in-Publication Data
Names: Ulitskaia, Liudmila, author. | Gannon, Mary Catherine, 1953– translator.
Title: Jacob's ladder / Ludmila Ulitskaya ; translated from the Russian by Polly Gannon.
Other titles: Лестница Якова. English
Description: First American edition. | New York : Farrar, Straus and Giroux, 2019.
Identifiers: LCCN 2018050162 | ISBN 9780374293659 (hardcover)
Subjects: LCSH: Families—Soviet Union—Fiction. | Soviet Union—History—Fiction.
Classification: LCC PG3489.2.L58 L4713 2019 | DDC 891.73/5—dc23
LC record available at https://lccn.loc.gov/2018050162

Designed by Abby Kagan

Our books may be purchased in bulk for promotional, educational, or business use. Please
contact your local bookseller or the Macmillan Corporate and Premium Sales Department at
1-800-221-7945, extension 5442, or by e-mail at MacmillanSpecialMarkets@macmillan.com.

www.fsgbooks.com
www.twitter.com/fsgbooks • www.facebook.com/fsgbooks

1   3   5   7   9   10   8   6   4   2

Published by arrangement with ELKOST International Literary Agency, Barcelona, Spain

The shadows of my world extend beyond the skyline of the page, blue as tomorrow's morning haze— nor does this terminate the phrase.

—VLADIMIR NABOKOV

Contents

The Ossetsky Family Tree

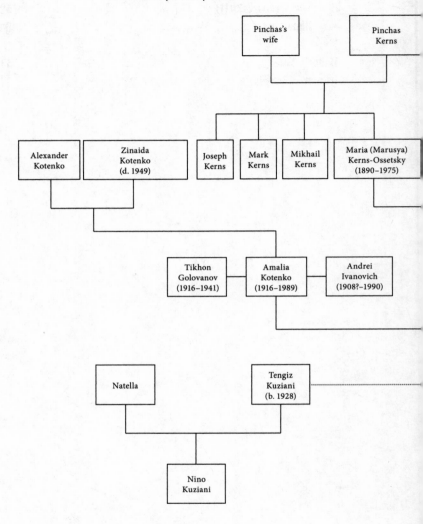

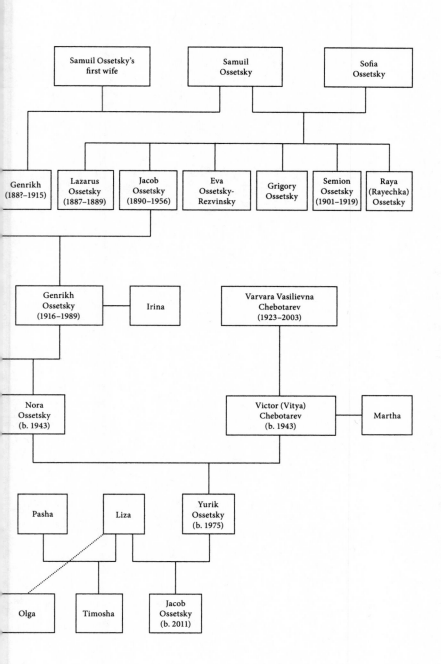

JACOB'S LADDER

1

The Willow Chest

(1975)

The baby boy was lovely from the start. He had a pronounced dimple on his chin and a neatly formed little head, as though fresh from a visit to a good barber. His hair—just like his mother's—was cropped short, though it was a shade or two lighter. Nora fell in love with him on the spot. She had been uncertain about it before; she was thirty-two years old, and believed she had learned to love people on their own merits, not simply because they were related to her. The baby turned out to be fully deserving of her unconditional love, however. He slept soundly, didn't bawl, and nursed punctiliously. He examined his own clenched fists in wonder. He didn't keep to a strict schedule. Sometimes he would sleep for two hours, and sometimes for six hours straight, after which he would wake up and start sucking at the air—and Nora would put him to her breast. She didn't like schedules either, and she made a mental note that they had this in common.

Her breasts underwent a remarkable transformation. During her pregnancy, they had begun filling out nicely. Before then, they had looked like flat saucers with nipples. Afterward, when her milk began flowing, they made her feel like a preening bird. Nora studied her chest as it blossomed and derived a peculiar satisfaction from the changes. Physiologically speaking, of course, they were somewhat unpleasant—what with the constant heaviness and pressure, and the inconvenience of it all. But nursing itself brought with it a sweet pleasure not directly related to the purpose at hand . . . It had been three months since the little one had made his entrance into the world, and already they called him Yurik instead of "baby."

He was installed in the room that had once been considered her mother's. It had become nobody's after Amalia Alexandrovna moved for good to Prioksko-Terrasny Nature Reserve, where her new husband, Andrei Ivanovich, worked. Two weeks before Nora went into labor, the room had been hastily whitewashed. When she brought him home, Yurik was snuggled into the white crib that had been a prop for the second act of *Three Sisters*. By now it was irrelevant, but during the previous theater season the whole troupe had been convulsed by the scandal that erupted when the play was shut down. Nora was the set designer; the director of the play was Tengiz Kuziani.

Before he flew back to Tbilisi, Tengiz vowed never to return to Moscow. A year later, he called Nora to tell her that he had been invited to Barnaul to stage Ostrovsky's *Without a Dowry*, and that he was considering the offer. At the end of the conversation, he suggested that she come with him as the set designer. He seemed not to know that Nora had had a baby. Or was he just pretending not to know? That would have been surprising—was it possible that the backstage grapevine had faltered all of a sudden? The theater world was a fetid swamp, where private lives were turned inside out and the most insignificant details were broadcast far and wide. Whoever loved, or failed to love, whom; whoever got tangled up with whom in the bedsheets of provincial hotels while on tour; whichever actress had had to have an abortion because of which actor—it all immediately became common knowledge.

This had no bearing on Nora, however. She was not a star. The only thing that could be said of her was that she had had a serious comedown. And that she now had a baby, of course. The silent question on everyone's lips was: whose? Everyone knew about her affair with the director. But her absent husband was not part of the theater. He belonged to "the audience"— and she herself was just a young set designer, at the beginning of her career. Which was also, evidently, the end of it. For these reasons, the theater riffraff paid no attention to her. There was no whispering behind her back; there were no covert glances. None of it mattered now, anyway. She had quit the theater.

Yurik was already awake by eight o'clock. Nora was expecting the nurse, Taisia, to arrive at nine, to give him a vaccination. It was past eleven, and she still hadn't arrived. Nora went to do some laundry, so she didn't hear the doorbell right away. When she did, she jumped up and ran to open the door. Taisia started babbling even before she stepped inside. She

4

wasn't simply a nurse from the children's district polyclinic, but a woman with a mission: to educate foolish young mothers. She imparted to them the age-old secrets of nurturing babies—and, while she was at it, shared with them her pearls of feminine wisdom. She edified them on the subject of the family unit, including how to get along with "mamas-in-law" and the husband's other relatives, not least his former wives. She was a cheerful gossip, a lively rumormonger, who was certain that without the benefits of her patronage (her official vocation was "Home-Visit Nurse-Patron") all these little babes would fail to thrive. She did not acknowledge any methods of upbringing but her own, and the mere mention of Dr. Spock shattered her composure.

Nora was the kind of young mother she liked best of all—a single parent, her first child, with no help or support from her own mother. Nora was simply ideal. Because of her postpartum weakness, she needed to rally all her strength merely to survive, and she put up no resistance to Taisia's science and its applications. Moreover, Nora's experience in theater, where actors, like little children, were given to endless squabbling and fits of jealousy, had taught her to listen to all kinds of nonsense with polite attention, holding her tongue when necessary, and nodding sympathetically.

Nora stood next to Taisia, absorbing her chatter and watching the snowflakes on the needlelike ends of her fur coat turn into tiny droplets and roll off.

"I'm sorry, I was held up. Can you imagine, I stopped by the Sivkovs'— you know, Natasha Sivkov, in apartment fifteen? Her little Olya, eight months old, is just precious; she'll make a good match for your little fellow. I walked in right in the middle of a family quarrel. The mother-in-law, who had just arrived from Karaganda, claimed that Natasha wasn't taking proper care of her precious son, and that the baby had developed allergies on account of poor nourishment. Well, you know me—I gave her a piece of my mind and set things to rights."

While she was washing her hands in the bathroom, Taisia chided Nora: "How many times do I have to tell you—use children's soap for washing clothes! That washing powder is no good. I'm not just making it up . . ."

Yurik had gone back to sleep, and Nora didn't want to wake him up just yet. She offered Taisia some tea. Taisia settled down at the head of the table in the tiny kitchen. It was a fitting place for her. She had an imposing head, with loose curls gathered up in a clawlike hair clip, and the space she occupied seemed to organize itself around her deferentially—the teacups and saucers arrayed themselves like a flock of sheep around a shepherd. Nice composition, Nora noted to herself.

Nora placed on the table a box of chocolates sporting a picture of a flying deer. Guests sometimes brought them to her, but Nora was indifferent to sweets. The supply of chocolates piled up, waiting for their chance to be eaten, meanwhile growing a thin white veneer.

Inadvertently spraying droplets from her hair around the tabletop, Taisia reached out her hand to pluck the confection of her choice from the expensive box of sweets. Suddenly, her hand still hovering in midair, she said, "Hey, Nora, are you even married?"

She's inducting me into the secrets of baby care, and now she wants my secrets. In exchange for her tip on children's soap, Nora thought. Tengiz had taught her to analyze dialogues between characters, to grasp their internal workings, in just this way.

"Yes, I'm married."

Don't divulge too much; you might spoil everything. The dialogue has to unfold, it has to suggest itself.

"A long time?"

"Fourteen years. Since graduating from high school."

A pause. It was falling into place nicely.

"Then how come you're always alone when I come over? He never helps out, and you always come to clinic appointments by yourself."

Nora stopped to think for a moment. Should she say that he was a ship captain, off sailing the seven seas? Or that he was doing time?

"He comes and goes. He lives with his mother. He's an unusual person, very talented, a mathematician. But as for survival skills in life, he's about on a par with Yurik." Nora told the truth—about a tenth of it.

"Oh, I know of another case just like yours!" Taisia said, animated.

Just then Nora's keen ear picked up a slight noise, and she went to check on the little one. He woke up and looked at his mother as though in surprise. Taisia was standing right behind her, and he stared at her.

"Yurik, sweetie, have we woken up?" Taisia said in melting tones.

Nora picked up her son. He turned his head toward the nurse, watching her expectantly.

Nora didn't have a diaper-changing table. She used an old-fashioned desk with a folding top, which Yurik was already outgrowing. And Nora didn't put him in regular diapers. She had two special romper suits made for him at a sewing-and-alterations workshop, where the seamstresses had

6

"overhauled" some foreign model. Taisia grumbled about the capitalist underpants lined with rubber that chafed his little rumples of fat when they were wet. Then she kissed the baby on his bottom and ordered Nora to spread a clean sheet on the divan while she got the vaccination ready.

She mixed something from one vial with another, drew the liquid up into a syringe, and jabbed him gently with the needle. The baby screwed up his face and was about to bawl, but then changed his mind. He looked at his mother and smiled.

What a smart little fellow; he understands just what's going on, Nora thought in delight.

Taisia went out to dispose of the cotton wad. From the doorway, she bellowed, "Water! Nora, the bath is running over! It's a flood!"

The bathtub had indeed overflowed, and water was streaming down the hallway, reaching nearly to the kitchen. They plumped Yurik down in his crib, evidently in too much haste, and he started to cry. Nora turned off the tap, threw a towel down on the floor, and began sopping up the water. Taisia helped her with dexterous alacrity. Just then, amid the howls of the child abandoned in the crib, the telephone rang.

It's the neighbors; their ceiling is already leaking, Nora thought, and ran to pick up the phone to tell them it was all under control.

But it wasn't the neighbors. It was Nora's father, Genrikh.

Bad timing, as usual, Nora just had time to think. Yurik had set up an indignant wail for the first time in his life at full volume, and water was no doubt already gushing down into the neighbors' apartment . . .

"Dad, the apartment's flooded, I'll call you back."

"Nora, Mama passed away," he said, with slow, decorous solemnity. "Last night . . . at home . . ." Then he added, without any trace of solemnity, "Hurry over, please, as fast as you can! I don't know what to do."

Nora, barefoot, flung the still-dripping towel onto the floor. Again, bad timing. Why did her relatives always choose the most inconvenient moment even to die?

Taisia grasped the situation in an instant.

"Who?"

"Grandmother."

"How old?"

"Over eighty, I should think. She lied about her age her whole life. She even managed to change it on her ID. Will you take over for a few hours while I'm gone?"

7

"You go ahead. I'll stay here."

Nora went to wash her hands again, quite unnecessarily, after the flood. Then she rushed over to Yurik and gave him her breast. At first he refused the nipple haughtily, but Nora coaxed him by putting it to his lips. Then he began to suck and gulp, and went quiet.

Meanwhile, Taisia had stripped off her skirt and blouse. She deftly sopped up the water and emptied it into a bucket, and afterward dumped it into the toilet down the hall. Her pink slip and short white cotton camisole, and thick streams of hair that had escaped from the clasp, flashed into view at the end of the murky hallway. Nora couldn't suppress a smile at her agility, her beauty, and the precision of her movements.

"I don't know how long I'll be gone. I'll call you. She lives nearby, on Povarskaya Street."

"Go on—I'll call off my next two visits. But express some milk, just in case. You might be a long time. When things like this happen . . ."

Well, what do you know, Nora thought. You've only seen her a few times in your life, but she jumps right in, at a moment's notice, when you need her. What a godsend!

Ten minutes later, Nora was rushing down the boulevard. She turned the corner at the Nikitsky Gates, and in another ten minutes was ringing the doorbell of a communal apartment under which hung a small copper plate with the inscription "The Ossetskys." The names of the other seven families were written on plain cardboard.

Her father, the chewed-up end of his now extinguished cigarette dangling from his lips, gave her a weak embrace, and began to cry. Curbing his emotions, he said: "Can you believe it? I called up Neiman to tell him Mama had died, and it turns out that he's dead, too! I already have the death certificate from the doctor, and now I need some other paper from the polyclinic. And we have to decide where to bury her. Mama said it's all the same to her, as long as it's not next to Jacob."

All this he told Nora as they were walking down the long corridor. A fat neighbor, Grandmother's enemy Kolokoltsev, poked his head out the door of one room, and the squat Raisa looked out of another. Walking toward them down the corridor was Katya "Firstonehere" (as she had baptized herself). Her mother had lived here as a servant since the building was new. Katya was born in the little room off the kitchen. She knew everything about everyone, and to this day wrote ungrammatical, barely legible letters denouncing the other residents—which was no secret to any of them. In fact, she was so artless and ingenuous that she had warned them all beforehand, "Watch out, I'll rat on all of you!"

Grandmother's dusty room reeked of tobacco—Nora's father had been smoking there—and of the eau de cologne her grandmother had sprayed around her with an atomizer her entire life. This procedure took the place of tidying up. Now she lay on the rustic, hand-built divan in her white nightgown, its oft-mended collar covered with a maze of tiny stitches. She looked small, her head thrown back proudly, her eyes not completely shut. Her jaw was slack, her mouth hung open slightly, and the shadow of a smile hovered on her face.

Nora's throat constricted in pity. She looked around her and saw the bitter dignity of her grandmother's life. Poverty by choice. Bare windows. Curtains, according to her grandmother, were a petit-bourgeois affectation. The enfilade doorways on either side of the room, no longer functional, were blocked with a bookcase on one wall and a buffet on the other. There was as much dust in the bookcase as there were books. Since childhood, Nora's allergies had always kicked in when she spent the night here—during those years when she still called her grandmother Purr-Purr and adored her with passionate, childlike intensity. Every single book was familiar to her. They had been read and reread, over and over again. To this day, Nora battled all forms of ignorance with the weapon of culture, and culture in its entirety originated for her in these several hundred tomes, pored over like books on a desert island, their margins swarming with tiny pencil marks and notations. From the Bible to Freud. Well, the island was not exactly deserted. It was densely inhabited: flocks of bedbugs grazed in these parts. They had feasted on Nora in childhood, but Grandmother hardly noticed them. Or maybe they had hardly noticed her?

The remnants of a decorative coverlet hung in front of the entryway. It had never been laundered or dry-cleaned since the day it had arrived. A bare incandescent lightbulb—"Lenin's Lamp," as it was called back in the day—dangled from the ceiling. And Grandmother had read him—earnestly and fearfully. Indeed, she was personally acquainted with Lenin's widow, Krupskaya, and People's Commissar of Education Lunacharsky. She had engaged in cultural work—she had once mentioned something about founding a drama studio for homeless children . . . What a strange, unlikely world, in which Karl Marx and Sigmund Freud, Stanislavsky and Evreinov, Andrei Bely and Nikolai Ostrovsky, Rachmaninoff and Grieg, Ibsen and Chekhov, went hand in hand. And, of course, her beloved Hamsun. The starving journalist who had already begun gnawing at his leather shoelaces, and saw lovely visions while hallucinating from hunger, until he was struck by an astonishing idea: why not go out and find work? And he hired himself out as a ship's boy.

Grandmother had practiced some form of esoteric dancing, then the forgotten and maligned science of pedology, and in her later years referred to herself as an "essayist." And she lived a spiritual life, as far removed from present-day reality as the Jurassic period. These thoughts washed over Nora like a sudden storm as she stood there, not even taking off her coat, looking at her grandmother, who was gone forever.

How much Nora had learned from her! Grandmother had played on this piano, and Nora had "danced the mood" of the music. Here, on the corner of the table, Nora had drawn a blue horse, much to her grandmother's delight: it reminded her of Kandinsky's *Blue Rider*. They visited the Pushkin Museum together, they went to concerts and plays. How passionately Nora had loved her then—and how cruel Nora had been later, when she grew disillusioned with her and coldly rejected her. Grandmother hated anything that smacked of the bourgeois. She detested philistinism in all its forms, and called herself a "nonpartisan Bolshevik." Eight years earlier, they had quarreled once and for all—Nora was ashamed to admit it—about politics. How petty and ridiculous . . .

Nora and her father moved the stiff body onto the table. It was not heavy. Her father went out to the kitchen to smoke. With a pair of scissors, Nora cut through the fabric of the ancient nightgown. It seemed to fall apart in her hands. Then she poured some cool water into a tub and started washing the body. It looked like a narrow boat and surprised her by its physical resemblance to her own: long, thin legs, the high arch of the feet, big toes extending beyond the line of the others, with nails long left unclipped, small breasts with their pink nipples, a long neck and narrow chin. The body looked younger than the face, its skin milky white and hairless.

Her father smoked in the huge communal kitchen crammed with small individual tables, one for each resident or family. Now and then, he went out to the corridor to talk on the ancient telephone, to inform the relatives. Nora picked up the strains of his mournful voice, repeating the same words over and over: "Mama died last night . . . I'll call you about the funeral when I know more."

When the body had been washed and rubbed dry with a torn duvet cover, Nora felt a stream of warm liquid running down her belly. It seemed to shock her awake—how could she have forgotten about Yurik? It was his milk flowing down, useless. She wanted to sit down on the divan, but she noticed that there was a damp spot on the sheet—the last juices and residues of the dead body. Nora ripped off that part of the sheet, crumpled it up, and threw it into the corner. She found another place for herself, in the armchair next to the window, where Grandmother used to sit and read those same books from the bookcase; she had never acquired any new ones for as long as Nora could remember. Under her breast, Nora placed a large mug with a broken handle—she remembered it well from childhood—and expressed milk until it filled the mug almost to the brim. She poured it out into the tub—impossible even to consider carrying those three hundred grams of milk home with her from here. She wiped off her chest with her T-shirt. Everything in the room seemed contaminated with death, including the hapless mug.

She got dressed again and went out into the corridor. Her father, wearing a woolen jacket and a hat, was smoking in the kitchen again. He had just returned from the polyclinic, which wasn't far away, just over on the Arbat, with the required paperwork.

"I can't get through to the crematorium; the line's always busy. I'll just go there myself. As soon as possible, I want to get all of this . . ." Here he made some vague circular gesture with his hand, which meant "over and done with." And he went to make another phone call.

Then Nora dialed her own number. Taisia picked up immediately.

"Don't you worry about a thing, Nora, honey. I've already called home. Sergei can manage on his own, and I can stay here till evening. Yurik's fine; he's fast asleep."

Nora made her way over to the "closet"—a corner behind the buffet. All Grandmother's things were hanging there on three hangers. What humble poverty: a winter coat with a shawl collar made of lambskin, worn threadbare in spots; a blue skirt and jacket, refashioned from a man's suit; two blouses . . . Nora could remember each item from childhood. Judging by the cut, they were all from the late 1920s. Nora picked out the least shabby blouse. You could study the history of costume from these relics of the past. Traces of some pseudo-Egyptian motif were still visible on the sleeves.

The body had grown cool and stiff, like plaster, and she realized she would need to cut through the back of the blouse to get it on. She laid it out next to the body.

We'll have to be careful moving her into the casket, Nora thought. But I'll dress her now, so she's not lying here naked.

Suddenly she felt that the room was cold. Wishing to dress Grandmother in something warmer, she took the jacket down off the hanger. She didn't have to cut through the skirt—she pulled it up over the legs. Grandmother was a child of the Silver Age—its product and its victim. Two photographs, dusty with age, featuring a young beauty, hung above the piano. Lovely. She had been very lovely.

Nora dragged out a suitcase of old shoes that had been stuffed under the divan. They were now museum pieces—straps on leather buttons, goblet-shaped heels. Grandmother had worn these during the New Economic Policy period. Nora couldn't put them on her grandmother's stiff feet.

She did all of this as though she had been doing it every day of her life. In fact, it was the first time. Nora was only six when her other grandmother, Zinaida, had died, and she didn't remember it. And she had hardly known her grandfathers. It was a matriarchal family. The only man was her father, Genrikh. Had he lived with them on Nikitsky Boulevard for a long time? Amalia had divorced him when Nora was thirteen.

It was too late now to mend things with Grandmother Marusya. It was too late to make peace with her. Now Nora was washing her, getting her dressed, and an old sense of irritation against the entire order of the world, against this awful shell of someone who had once been urgently, deeply loved by her, rose up from the depths of her being. A sarcophagus. Every dead body was a sarcophagus. You could stage a play in which every character occupies a sarcophagus. When they die, they stand up and step out of them. In that sense, everything alive is already dead. She would have to tell this to Tengiz.

Her milk started running again, forming a dark spot on her T-shirt. What captives of physiology they were—Grandmother Marusya had been the first to tell her this, of course. The biological tragedy of women . . . Her grandmother, the poor, timid fighter for women's dignity, for justice. A Revolutionary. How frightened she was when Nora had been expelled from school. She refused to let her come home. So solemn and haughty. Then they had reconciled. But about three years later, they quarreled for good—like a black cat, the Soviet regime had run across their paths and come between them. And their mutual trust, their closeness, came to an end. And later there was Czechoslovakia . . . Now all she could do was smile about it. So silly.

Nora looked out the window. The glass was filthy; it hadn't been washed in years. She saw gray snow outside the window, turning into gray rain. Why didn't I do anything for her? How foolish I was to be angry at an old woman. I'm a heartless bitch.

But Nora had once loved her more than anyone on earth. Nearly every day after school, she rushed along the familiar route past the rerun movie theater, crossed the street by the Nikitsky Gates, then passed the Konservy store and ducked into a maze of small lanes—Merzlyakovsky, Skatertny, Khlebny, Skaryatinsky—to surface on Povarskaya Street by Grandmother's house. And her heart skipped a beat when she ran up the stairs to the third floor and buried her nose in Grandmother's tummy.

Still, how white her skin was. Her eyes were peeking out from under her eyelids and staring at Nora with indifference. Nora cut apart the back of the blouse and pulled one half of it on, beginning with the left arm, and the other half starting with the right. For the past twenty years, it seemed, Marusya had not brought home a single new object. Was it because of poverty? Or obstinacy? Or some sort of ineffable principle?

Someone tapped on the door timidly; it was her father, who had been afraid to see his mother naked. He walked in with a businesslike, satisfied expression on his face.

"Norka, I've ordered the casket. They're delivering it tomorrow morning at ten. They didn't even request a certificate. They just asked about the deceased's measurements. I said she was five eight."

"Five six," Nora corrected him. "And don't call me 'Norka.' My name is Nora. Your mother named me. Haven't you read Ibsen?"

The sun peeked out for a moment, briefly illuminating the room so that the mother-of-pearl button under Grandmother's chin gleamed; then the sun retreated again into the gray drizzle.

Nora tucked the jacket under either side of the body, after she had cut it through the back, as she had cut the blouse. The jacket, which had a round bronze brooch on the lapel, was the one Marusya had worn to meetings of some union or other, of journalists or of playwrights.

"Are you staying here overnight?" Nora asked her father.

"No, I have to go home," he said, alarmed. He hurried to add, "I'll be here by nine tomorrow, though." Then, hesitating, he said, "Will you come back to the apartment tomorrow, too, sweetie? I still have to go to the crematorium. I hope I can manage to do everything tomorrow."

"It can wait until the day after tomorrow."

"True, but I'd like to get it done as soon as possible. I'll do my best. I'll call you tonight." Genrikh Yakovlevich had suddenly become a wonder of efficiency.

"I'll be here at nine," Nora said dryly, nodding. She felt she couldn't leave her deceased grandmother alone for the night, but it was also unthinkable for her to stay here overnight with Yurik.

Nora went out into the corridor leading to the kitchen and walked down it, turning the two corners she had known since childhood. In the kitchen, Katya Firstonehere stood with her back to Nora, slicing something at the table, her elbows working energetically.

"Katya, we need to talk."

Katya turned around, swiveling her entire torso. She had no neck to speak of: her head was planted directly on her shoulders.

"What's wrong, Nyura?" This is what the charming idiot had called her her whole life.

"Will you sleep in Marusya's room tonight?"

"Sleep there yourself, why don't you? What are you asking me for?"

"I have a small baby; how can I manage it with him?"

"You had a baby?"

"Yes."

"My Ninka had a baby, too! So Genrikh won't stay overnight?"

"He has to hurry home. I'll pay you."

"Oh, I'll take the buffet, then, Nyura. I like it."

"Fine," Nora agreed. "Take it. Only it won't fit in your room."

"Well, I'll just move into her room, too. Nobody will refuse me. Ninka lives at her husband's place, but she's registered here."

"All right, all right," Nora said, nodding indifferently, imagining how Katya would rummage around in the room searching for loot.

"Ten rubles, Nyura! I can't do it for less," Katya said, though she winced at her own temerity.

"Ten—that's for staying the night *and* for cleaning up," Nora said, making sure.

That was how they left it.

The next day, Taisia volunteered to babysit Yurik again, so Nora didn't have to worry about making other arrangements. She had two friends she could call on to help out—Natasha Vlasov and Marina Chipkovskaya, nicknamed Chipa—whom she had known since their years in theater school. They were both reliable, but Natasha had a five-year-old son, and Chipa worked three jobs to support her disabled mother and her younger sister.

Back in Grandmother's room, she found several people: her father; Valera Bezborodko, his assistant; Katya and her daughter Ninka; their neighbor Raisa; and a woman from the Housing Management Committee, who wore a crooked red wig. The women were engaged in quiet but lively conversation. Nora guessed they were deliberating material, as opposed to spiritual, matters.

"It's sad about Marusya," Raisa said, with a subtle shake of her head. "For fifty years, we lived side by side like this, with only a wall between us. I've never said a bad word about her in my entire life . . . I'd just like to have . . . to remember her by . . ."

"Raisa, what did you say you wanted?" Genrikh said abruptly, in an unexpectedly sharp tone.

"No, no, never mind, Genrikh. I'm just saying that for fifty years we lived here, you might say, soul to soul, heart to heart . . ." And she backed toward the door.

The vultures are already here, thought Nora, and sent them all out the door, one by one. Her father looked at her gratefully. He had lived in this apartment as a child, and he had known these old women when they were still in the prime of life, but he had still not learned how to talk to them. He was never consistent, either speaking down to them or trying to ingratiate himself. Nora knew that he was unable to deal with people as equals. There was always a ladder—higher, lower . . . Poor guy, she thought. She felt sorry for her father, even a certain warmth. And he understood, and put his hand on her shoulder. Awkwardly. In Nora's earliest years, he believed that, merely because she was his daughter, he was superior to her. He spoke commandingly to her, issued orders. Then she grew up and put everything in its proper place. She was about eighteen when she visited him in his new home, with his new family. He took her aside and began reproaching her for visiting so infrequently, saying that it was, no doubt, the influence of her mother, who didn't want them to spend time together. Nora cut him off: "Dad, can you really not understand that if Mama didn't want me to, I wouldn't come? She just doesn't care, one way or another." After that, he never tried to lord it over her again.

They delivered the casket at ten. Two undertakers, working with consummate skill, placed the casket on the table next to the deceased. Deftly, even artfully, they lifted the body up and dropped it gently into the casket, where it landed in just the right place with a hollow thud. Her father went out of the room with the undertakers, leaving Nora alone. He paid them their fees in the corridor, at the door, and Nora heard them thanking him. Her father had no doubt given them more than they expected.

The flaps of the garments she had cut through the back had shifted and come apart, and Nora tucked them in on either side of the body again. She combed her grandmother's wispy gray hair and parted it the way she liked it, then gathered up the loose strands and pulled them to the back. She admired her grandmother's slightly sloping forehead and elongated eyelids. Her grandmother's silhouette was defined by several basic lines—the outline of her cheekbones, the transition from her neck to her shoulder, the line that ran from the knees to her toes. Nora even had the urge to pick up a pencil to sketch her. The deceased seemed to have grown more attractive overnight. Her face could not have been described as pretty; rather, it was beautiful, slender and luminous, and the excess aging skin that had hung down under her chin had melted away. She had become more youthful. Too bad Nora's own face hadn't turned out to resemble her grandmother's.

"Nora, the neighbors are saying that we should organize a meal . . . There should be a funeral repast." Her father looked at her expectantly.

Nora thought for a moment. Grandmother had objected to having neighbors barge into her room her whole life. It didn't make any difference now, though.

"Tell Katya to set the table, and give her some money for shopping. Have her set it up in the kitchen. But don't let her buy a lot of vodka, or she'll drink too much. We can't *not* have a repast, of course . . ."

Her father agreed. "Before the war, there weren't as many tables in the kitchen. We always set the table there. There were a lot of old men here back then. They're all dead now, of course. But I never went to the wakes, and Mama didn't go, either. Strange as it may seem, my father was the one who attended them."

This was one of the first times Genrikh had ever mentioned his father. Nora noted this with surprise. In fact, no one had ever told her anything about Jacob Ossetsky. He was just a hazy recollection from childhood. She did remember him, though: he had been at their house on Nikitsky Boulevard once. A few traces remained in her memory—a bushy mustache, long, large ears, and a self-fashioned crutch made from a single piece of wood, with a crook in the branch that served as a handgrip. She never saw him again after that.

Her father went to find the recently banished Katya. She was glad to be charged with the task, and glad about the money, and said that she would go to the store and buy everything. Nora's father nodded in assent. It was all the same to him, but to Katya it was an exciting prospect. Nora and Katya left at almost the same time, one to the florist's on the Arbat, the other in the direction of Revolution Square. Katya was happy. She had money, an amount that was one and a half times her monthly wages, and she was estimating how to cut down on the cost of the necessary purchases so there would be something left over.

In the florist's on the Arbat, Nora came across something that filled her with wonder: enormous hyacinths, a whole bucketful of them, which she was seeing for the first time. She bought all of them—the lilac-blue ones, and the white, and the rosy pink. She spent all the cash she had. They wrapped the flowers in multiple layers of newsprint, and even threw in the bucket for good measure.

Lugging the garden bucket, she walked along a short stretch of Trubnikovsky Lane. Then she crossed Novy Arbat, and again found herself on Trubnikovsky, now on the longer section of it. It was drizzling—rain or snow, she couldn't distinguish. The light was pearly gray; the bucket was heavy. Her boots were completely soaked through, and her milk had already started up. But she had stuffed folded diapers into her bra, and on top of this layer of rigging she had bound an old kerchief. Early in the morning, Taisia had kicked up a fuss, demanding that Nora bind up her breasts and threatening that if she refused, Taisia would put her foot down and forbid her to go to the funeral. Nora had laughed and complied.

She arrived back at her grandmother's apartment at the same time as the hearse. She went upstairs first, ahead of the undertakers. A few downcast figures, distant relatives, were standing around. One or two vaguely familiar people came up to Nora and her father and kissed them, uttering stock phrases, with varying degrees of warmth. One tiny elderly woman in a white scarf and beret wept silently; someone in the corner offered her a few drops of valerian in Grandmother's "medicine glass," to soothe her. Nora didn't recognize the woman.

Nora threw the flowers into the casket. There was no need to arrange them in any special way—the flowers had their own magic, which transformed everything around them. The paucity of the surroundings acquired splendor, like Cinderella. It nearly took Nora's breath away—Nora, a professional with years of experience in theater set design, whose mastery consisted in transforming the stage through artifice. It was like the magic lantern that had been used long ago in *The Blue Bird* at the Moscow Art

Theatre, in the scene when Tyltyl and Mytyl arrive in the land of the dead to find their grandmother and grandfather. Of course, it had been Marusya who took her, when she was five years old, to see this play. It seemed to Nora that she could discern, in the thin strip between Marusya's imperfectly closed eyelids, sympathy and approval. The hyacinths possessed some sort of uncanny power. They filled the room with their pungent scent, over-whelming the smell of her grandmother's eau de cologne, and the dust, and the valerian. Nora even felt that, with just one touch of a magic wand, this room would become a palace, and her poor grandmother, with her large ambitions, would become what she had always wanted, but was unable, to be . . .

Then all four of the undertakers picked up the casket and carried it down to the street. The hearse (which resembled an ordinary small bus; it accommodated the coffin and about ten of the mourners), took off, and her father followed behind it in his Moskvich.

It was only a short distance to the Donskoy crematorium. They arrived earlier than necessary, and milled around for a half hour, waiting their turn. Then the casket was loaded onto something resembling a baggage trolley, and Nora and Genrikh were allowed to proceed ahead of the others. Nora was again in charge of the flowers. It seemed to her that since the time she had bought them the flowers had opened further, and were now fully bloomed. This time she chose not to cast them chaotically into the casket, but to lay them down deliberately, with foresight: the rose-pink blooms closer to the yellowed face, the lilac ones in an unbroken line around her head and along her arms. And all those inappropriate carnations that the mourners were now bringing in—Nora decided to toss these at her feet.

Then the mourners entered, all of them dressed in heavy black coats with red carnations, and surrounded the coffin in a horseshoe formation of relatives and friends. Everything looked a bit shimmery, but she could see with perfect clarity. In the midst of this clarity of vision, she realized that all the relatives fell into two different breeds: her father's cousins, who reminded her of hedgehogs, with their coarse hair growing low on the forehead, long noses with a snout on the end, and shortish chins; and her grandmother's nieces and nephews, who had slender, elongated faces, large eyes, and triangular fish-mouths . . .

And I'm from the hedgehog breed, Nora thought, feeling hot and queasy all of a sudden. At that moment, Chopin's "Marche funèbre" began to play,

18

disrupting her strange vision. The march had long ago become an aural impropriety, fit only for comic scenes.

"Hold my hat," whispered Genrikh, who was standing near her, thrusting his Astrakhan sheepskin cap into her hand. Then he rummaged through his briefcase to make sure he had remembered to bring his passport. Nora immediately caught the smell of his hair, which had permeated the cap, a smell that she had found unpleasant since childhood. Even her own hair, if she failed to wash it every day, gave off this same acrid scent, an admixture of coarse fat and some sort of disgusting plant.

A woman functionary read some official nonsense from a piece of paper. Then her father uttered some commonplaces, equally bland. Nora felt more and more disheartened by the triteness and vulgarity of the event. Suddenly, out of the blue, her despondency was dispelled by that same tiny old woman who had wept in Grandmother's room. She went up to the head of the casket and, in a surprisingly resonant voice, made a genuine speech. She began, it was true, with the official phrase, "Today we are saying farewell to Marusya," but what followed was passionate, and anything but predictable.

"All of us standing here now, and many who are already in their graves, buried in the ground, were shaken, shaken deeply, when Marusya came into our lives. I don't know of anyone who was acquainted with her just in passing. She would turn everything upside down, then set it all back on its feet again. She was so gifted, so vibrant, even eccentric. You can take my word for it. Because of her, people learned to feel surprise; they began to think with their own minds. Do you think Jacob Ossetsky was such a genius merely through his own merits? No, he was a genius because he had known a love like hers from the age of nineteen, a love they only write about in novels."

A whisper started moving through the dark clump of relatives, and the old woman noticed this: "Sima, you hold your tongue! I already know what you're going to say. Yes, I loved him. Yes, I was with him during the last year of his life, and this was my joy, my happiness—but not his. Because she left him. And you don't need to know why she did. I don't know myself how she was capable of such a thing . . . But here, by her coffin, I want to say, in front of everyone, that I am not guilty before her. I would never have so much as looked Ossetsky's way. He was a god and Marusya was a goddess. And who was I? A registered nurse, that's what I was! I am not guilty before Marusya; and only God knows whether Marusya was guilty before Jacob . . ."

At this point, Genrikh grabbed the old woman, and her ardor ceased.

She brushed him aside with a flutter of her dry hands. Then, hunching over, she left the hall with a brisk tread.

Everything faltered. The functionary rushed up to restore order, strains of the unbearable music struck up again, and the coffin was lowered, sinking slowly down to where it would be consumed by the unquenchable fire, and sulfurous rains, and fiery Gehenna . . . although worms were unlikely to survive down there. She'd have to ask her father who this old woman was, and whether he knew her story.

Throughout the entire painful and distressing event, Nora had not given a single thought to the repast. Her father reminded her. "Shall we go?"

The relatives piled into the funeral bus in an orderly manner. Nora got into her father's Moskvich. Along the way, without taking his eyes off the road, he said, "Looks like your mother didn't think it necessary to come and pay her respects."

"She's sick," Nora fibbed. In fact, Nora hadn't even called her. She'd find out soon enough. After Genrikh's divorce, Marusya had stopped seeing Amalia.

The door to the apartment was wide open, and the smell of pancakes from the kitchen wafted through the corridor. The door of Grandmother's room was open, too, allowing the scents of her eau de cologne and the scrubbed floors to mingle with the kitchen smells. The window in the room was flung open, and the white pillowcase that had been hung over the mirror billowed slightly in the breeze. Nora went in, took off her coat, and threw it on the armchair. She sat down on the coat, peeled off her woolen cap, and glanced around. Even the age-old dust on the piano top had been wiped off. When she was about five, Grandmother had seated her on top of two pillows and begun teaching her to play on this instrument. At that time, though, Nora had more fun playing with the piano stool than playing on the piano. She had turned the stool on its side, sat on the stem, and tried to turn the seat like a steering wheel. Now she touched the stool—at one time shiny with lacquer, now covered in dull patches. Maybe I should take the piano for Yurik? she thought. But she immediately rejected the idea. Movers, a piano tuner, shifting furniture around . . . No, no way.

Then the whole busload of relatives, in the same order in which they had been sitting, entered in pairs: her father's hedgehog-cousins, four of them, took off their black coats and placed them on the divan. Then the women's brigade, the fish breed, swam through the door like the school of fish that they were. They were all wearing fur coats—Grandmother's three nieces with two young daughters, Nora's second and third cousins, all of them with sharp little chins pointing downward—very charming. And another pair of ladies she didn't recognize. Nora had met her cousins in childhood at parties that her grandmother had organized for them. But they were all younger than Nora, and thus bored her. Nora hadn't liked younger children—she had always preferred people who were older than she was. There was one person in the women's brigade who stood out—the tall Mikaela, a brunette with a faint dark mustache, who was about sixty. Nora tried hard to remember whose daughter or wife she was, but she couldn't; she had forgotten. She saw these people only once every decade, at other such family gatherings or events. The last time was a celebration in honor of her father, when he had defended his doctoral dissertation. Lyusha, Nyusya, and Verochka were the older cousins, and their daughters were Nadya and Lyuba. Then there was this solitary Mikaela.

The women stamped their feet on the rug by the door, shook off the dirty snow that had stuck to their boots, and threw their coats on the divan. Nora noticed that a puddle had formed on the clean floor around her own shoes.

Then, in a whirlwind, they all made their way into the kitchen, where the neighbors were waiting for them. The awkward absurdity of what was under way didn't escape anyone's notice. In the middle of the large communal kitchen, two tables had been pushed together and covered with newspaper. A mountain of pancakes towered in the center. Galia, an old actress, a former bosom buddy of Grandmother's to whom she hadn't spoken in more than twenty years, was cooking the rest of the pancakes in three different frying pans. Katya was pouring warm fruit compote out of a saucepan into Grandmother's washstand pitcher. It was covered with a web of tiny cracks. The estranged washbowl, the other half of the set, contained a spartan beet salad made of ingredients that Katya had been given by her sister free of charge, which she had chopped up fine with her own two hands.

There was nothing to drink but vodka.

On Grandmother's tiny table—she never cooked, but preferred to eat in public cafeterias or eat convenience foods at home—there was already a shot glass full of vodka, covered with a piece of rye bread. Nora felt a surge of sharp annoyance. It was all a farce, a sham! Grandmother had never taken a drop of vodka in her life. To her way of thinking, even drinking wine was verging on decadence. Again, the absurdity of the situation gripped her, and Nora felt personally responsible for what was happening here. How hard would it have been to announce, with grim finality, "No, you won't have any funeral dinner"? But the neighbors were running the show here, and now this communal repast would just have to play itself out.

Katya felt she was the hostess of this celebration, and the relatives and mourners were her guests. Genrikh looked complacent—all the unpleasantness was behind them now. They poured out vodka, raised their glasses, and drank it all in one go, without clinking glasses, according to the unspoken rules of a funeral repast. "May she rest in peace."

Genrikh threw himself at the food hungrily, and Nora felt the usual irritation at her father—irritation that had evaporated while he was rushing around making the funeral arrangements. He chewed energetically, and Nora, who had always eaten very little, and always slowly, recalled how, when he had lived with them, she had also watched with annoyance as he wolfed down his food.

How heartless I am, Nora thought. He just has a good appetite.

She plucked a beet out of the salad. Though the beets were delicious, she could hardly force herself to swallow anything. And her breasts were sore; it was time to express her milk.

Old Kolokoltsev, dressed in his at-home attire, his jogging pants, sat on a tiny stool, his bottom hanging over the sides. Raisa led in her daughter, Lorochka, an old maid with an unaccountably intelligent, refined face. Katya's Ninka also took a seat at the table. Marusya had been on good terms with Ninka. Marusya, who considered herself to be a great expert on child rearing, had helped her in her schoolwork all five years she attended school. When she was small, Ninka had received hand-me-downs from Nora; but by the time she turned eight, she was already bigger than Nora, though she was two years younger. Then some bad girls had taught Ninka to steal, and everything went awry. Marusya had grieved when Ninka was sent off to a correctional institution for juvenile delinquents; she believed Ninka had real potential.

Ninka and her potential sat on a stool, resting her ample bosom on the table. She wanted to talk to Nora about babies: about labor, about breastfeeding. She had given birth recently, too, but she had almost no milk and fed her newborn on baby formula. He bawled nonstop.

As it turned out, all the relatives had gravitated to one side of the table, and all the neighbors to the other. Face-to-face, wall to wall. Nora was already starting to see a play unfold, which could be staged right here. With this very scenery, just as it was. A play with a compelling social critique as a subtext. How they all suddenly start remembering the deceased, and eventually it comes to light that . . . But what exactly was revealed, Nora didn't have time to consider, because that woman in the crooked wig from the Housing Management Committee who had been conferring with the neighbors yesterday tapped her on the shoulder: "Nora, just for a moment. Come into the corridor. We need to talk."

Her father was already there. The woman said that the room would revert to the ownership of the state. Tomorrow they would seal the door. "Whatever you need, you should take today." Her father was silent. Nora didn't speak, either.

"Let's go take a look," the woman suggested.

They entered the room. Someone had closed the window, but it was still cold. The pillowcase gleamed on the mirror like a cataract. The overhead light had burned out, and the desk lamp cast a meager light.

"I'll go get a new one," her father said—this had always been his task—and off he went to fetch a new bulb. He knew where they were kept. He screwed it in. The light blazed, sharp and intense. Grandmother didn't have a lampshade; that would have been a bourgeois extravagance.

A stage set, Nora thought again.

Her father took a spherical clock, about the size of an apple, off the piano—as a memento of his grandfather, who had been a watchmaker. "That's all I need," he said. "Nora, you take whatever you want."

Nora glanced around. She would have liked to take everything. Except for the books, though, there was nothing here one really needed for life. It was a tough decision. Very tough.

"Can't we decide tomorrow? I'd have to sort through things," she said hesitantly.

"Tomorrow the district police will come over to seal it. I don't know whether it will happen early in the morning or later in the day. I'd advise you to finish with the business tonight," she said, and tactfully retreated, leaving Nora alone with the nagging thought that this woman and the neighbors might be in some sort of conspiracy together, wanting to get rid of Nora and Genrikh as soon as possible so they could make off with the spoils.

Genrikh surveyed the room sadly—his first home. He no longer remembered his grandfather's apartment in Kiev, where he had been born. But in this long room, two windows wide, he had lived together with his mother and father until 1931, his fourteenth year, when his father was arrested.

There was nothing, nothing among these meager belongings, that

Genrikh needed. And what would his current wife, Irina, say if he dragged any of this junk home with him?

"No, Nora, I don't need any of it," he said, and stomped back to the kitchen.

Nora closed the door gently and even fastened the small brass latch. She sat down in Grandmother's armchair, and for one last time let her eyes roam about the room, which was still alive, though the person who had inhabited it was not. On the walls hung several small pictures, the size of large postcards. Nora knew them all by heart. A photograph of her grandmother's brother, Mikhail; an autographed picture of Kachalov, the famous actor; and a photograph—the smallest of all—of a man in a military jacket, with the inscription "To Marusya" grazing his cheek. She didn't know who it might be. For some reason, she had never asked her grandmother who this gentleman was. She'd have to ask Genrikh. Nora looked at her watch; she needed to get home. Poor Taisia had spent her entire day off at Nora's house, watching the baby.

Under the window stood a chest woven from willow branches. Nora lifted the lid. It was full of old notebooks, writing pads, piles of paper scrawled all over. She opened the one on top. It looked like a manuscript or diary of some sort. There was a stack of postcards; newspaper clippings . . .

That settled it—she'd salvage the books and this willow chest. Still looking around, she took the pictures from the walls and stuffed them in the chest, too, along with the slender silver goblet in which Grandmother kept her hairpins, and another one she used for her medicine, as well as a single faience saucer without a cup, which Nora herself had broken at some point in her childhood. Then, from the buffet, she rescued a small sugar bowl, with tiny pincers for lump sugar. Her grandmother was diabetic, but she adored sweet things, and from time to time would break off minuscule pieces of sugar, no bigger than a match head, with these pincers. She then remembered about the washstand pitcher and bowl; but they had already begun a new life in the old kitchen—as common property. Damn it all.

An hour later, when the relatives had all gone their separate ways, Nora and her father together took the chest and the books down to the car. The chest fit into the trunk, and the books were piled up like a small mountain filling the whole back seat and blocking the rear window. Her father drove Nora home and helped her carry all the stuff up to her apartment. He didn't come inside, but stopped in the front hall. Nora didn't invite him in. He had been there about two months before, to see the baby. At one time, in these three smallish rooms, he had lived with his family of four: he and his wife, their daughter, and a mother-in-law. Now there were only two living in it.

It's a nice, comfortable apartment. Good thing they don't "densify" anymore, forcing people to forfeit space to accommodate strangers, he thought. And, out of nowhere, it occurred to him that it was too bad Mama's room would revert to the state.

With that, he left for his new home, in Timiryazevka, where Irina was waiting for him.

In a flurry, Taisia gathered up her belongings, kissed Nora on the cheek, stepped over the piles of books strewn about, and left the apartment, looking back to say, "Oh yes, someone named Tusya called, and Vitya called twice, and some Armenian—I didn't catch his name."

And off she ran.

Finally, it was over . . .

On the kitchen table were three shiny, clean bottles. The baby had drunk twenty ounces. Nora peeped into his room. He was sleeping on his tummy, his legs tucked under him. His little face was hidden; all she could see was a round cheek with an earlobe stuck to it. Without taking off her hat, Nora took a piece of paper and a pencil and, in several deft motions, made a sketch that came out just right the first time. It was a good drawing. For many years, this was how Nora had lived. Something would catch her eye and gladden it, and she would immediately reach for the pencil and paper. They would pile up and pile up, those sheets of paper, until she would throw them all away. But her memory seemed to require this method of taking a snapshot of a moment with the physical movement of her hand.

The pencil moved mindlessly, automatically . . .

Then she looked at the big pile of books by the front door and realized she wouldn't be able to sleep until she had found a place for them and put them away. The smell of dust bothered her most of all. She took a damp rag and began wiping off the books, one at a time, not even looking at their spines or covers. She recognized them just by touch—they were so familiar to her. She filled up the gaps in two large bookcases, then started to make piles in the walk-through room that served as her studio. By four in the morning, she had finished putting the books away; now only the chest remained. But she was exhausted. She perched on a creaky bentwood chair to catch her breath. Then Yurik turned over. She took off her dusty clothes, got into the shower, and while he was fussing indignantly, unable to comprehend why his food hadn't appeared, she dried herself and ran to him naked, her breasts overflowing with milk. He smiled at her with his bright eyes and opened his mouth. While he sucked, she drowsed, and when he fell asleep, she woke up. She put on her pajamas, then collapsed onto the divan in the next room.

She fell asleep like a stone—and started awake, feeling as if she were on fire. She looked down to see a line of bedbugs marching across her, leaving in their wake marks where they had bitten her. She shook her head and looked at the clock; it was just after seven. She hadn't even slept for two hours. She leapt up, rushed to the door, and realized what had happened— the bedbugs had warmed up and emerged from the cracks between the branches of the chest to go out hunting. Nora pulled off the top of the chest. It was full of paper, and there were nests of many generations of the insects. She recognized the familiar bedbug stink. What an inheritance she had received! Disgusting.

She grabbed hold of the chest by one of the two remaining handles on its sides. The balcony was in Yurik's room. She lugged it past his little white crib, opened the balcony door, and, letting in a bracing stream of cold air, shoved the chest outside. Let the bastards freeze to death! Then she locked the balcony door behind her.

Yurik woke up, smiled blissfully, and stretched. On the child's blanket, a bedbug, parched from lack of nourishment, sat meditatively. Nora brushed it to the floor in horror, then picked it up and flung it out onto the balcony. The baby laughed. He was already learning to play and have fun, and his mother's sweeping gestures seemed to be an invitation for a game. He began to wave his arms around, too.

Nora rubbed kerosene along the entire path from the door to the balcony, shook out her bedding, and waited to see whether reinforcements would arrive. But the bedbugs, it would later become clear, had all met their death on the balcony. For a time, Nora forgot about both the chest and the bedbugs.

The next day, there was a late hard frost, followed by torrential rains. In May, Nora moved to a rented dacha in Tishkovo and lived there for the next three months with hardly a break.

When she returned and began cleaning the apartment, grown dusty during those months, she noticed the abandoned chest out on the balcony. The woven surface had swollen up with water. Washed by many rains, the chest now looked much cleaner than it had been immediately after the rescue.

She removed the top and discovered a solid mass of limp paper, covered in smeary traces of ink. The notes in pencil had washed away completely.

It's for the best, she thought. Now I won't have to dig around in that maudlin past. She brought a garbage pail out from the kitchen and began stuffing the foul-smelling paper mush into it. Only after taking four loads of the stuff out to the dumpster did she discover, at the very bottom of the chest, a parcel, carefully wrapped in pink oilcloth. She opened it up and found bundles of letters bound together with ribbon. She pulled out the first letter. The address on the envelope read 22 Mariinsko-Blagoveshchenskaya Street, Kiev. It was postmarked March 16, 1911. The addressee was one Maria Kerns. The sender was Jacob Ossetsky, 23 Kuznechnaya Street, Kiev. It was a very bulky correspondence, carefully arranged by year. Interesting, very interesting. There were several notebooks, filled with diminutive old-fashioned script. She examined the package carefully—she didn't want to encourage another bedbug infestation of the house—but everything was clean. Marusya had put the bundles of letters, together with the oilcloth, in her theater archives, which had already existed by then. And forgot about them for many years.

The papers lay ripening in darkness year after year, until all the people who could have answered any questions prompted by reading the old letters had died . . .

2

The Watchmaker's Shop on Mariinsko-Blagoveshchenskaya Street
(1905–1907)

Maria, later known as Marusya, was born in Kiev. Her father, Pinchas Kerns, had moved there in 1873, seventeen years before her birth, from a small town in western Switzerland called La Chaux-de-Fonds. Her father was a third-generation watchmaker, and he intended to open his own branch of a Swiss watch works that by that time had already begun its victory march around the world. Pinchas was on good terms with Louis Brandt, his employer and the owner of the watch works that would later become known as the Omega Company. Pinchas was a first-rate watchmaker, and, given his assiduity and conscientiousness, he could have begun importing Swiss watch parts to Kiev and reaped a rich harvest and hard cash in his new home. Louis Brandt even contributed to financing the initiative.

His noble mission as one of the promoters of Western capitalism gradually fell apart, although he put down roots in the new place, marrying a local Jewish girl and fathering three sons and his daughter, Marusya. In time, he learned both of the official Slavic languages (Russian and Ukrainian). He was used to such linguistic pairings, since in his native La Chaux-de-Fonds German was also spoken, along with French and nearly on equal footing with it. To this bilingual mix were added the two reigning tongues of his Jewish community—Yiddish, which was spoken at home, and Hebrew, which every educated Jew knew how to read.

The Swiss money he invested in the move and in basic amenities did not slip entirely through his fingers, however. Quickly realizing that commerce did not come to him as easily as craftsmanship, Kerns started a watchmaking-and-repair shop that dealt primarily in homegrown, nonpedigreed specimens on Mariinsko-Blagoveshchenskaya Street. He placed a high value on his craft, and viewed commerce almost with contempt, considering it to be a variety of swindling. Although Marx's *Das Kapital* had already been written by this time, and the soon-to-be world-renowned genius mentioned Pinchas's birthplace, La Chaux-de-Fonds, in a flattering light, considering it to be an exemplar of capitalist specialized production, the watchmaker never read this bible of communism. He remained a craftsman all his life, and never quite grasped the finer, or even cruder, points of communism, much less capitalism. His children, however, assimilated from an early age the progressive ideas of humanity, and, though adoring their kind, cheerful father, with his multifaceted goodness, they continually teased him about his archaic habits, his French accent, and his old-fashioned Swiss frock coats, which he had been wearing upward of forty years.

All the Kerns children could chatter away in French, and this circumstance made them rare birds in the neighborhood—their local tribespeople spoke a different idiom. The watchmaker's descendants, although they spoke their mother tongue perfectly, loved to bandy words about in aristocratic French, which was never otherwise heard on their street. They were all educated at home. The tutor of Mark and Joseph, the older boys, was engaged when the family was still relatively prosperous. After their financial ruin, the older boys taught the youngest brother, Mikhail. And he, in turn, taught Marusya, when he grew a bit older. In the early years, when they still lived comfortably, they even received music lessons from a teacher, Mr. Kosarkovsky, who eventually became a family friend. Marusya had always shown a keen interest in learning. The Kerns children were close-knit and fond of one another, but Marusya, as the youngest, was an object of adoration. Her confidence in the love of those around her, in particular men, betrayed her from time to time in her adult life; but in her youth, it only added to her charm.

The preparatory school, because of the quota system for Jews in place at the time, was off-limits for the Kerns children. Joseph, the eldest, had joined the proletariat early on. The second brother, Mark, didn't make the cut for the quota. Mikhail didn't even try. Both Mark and Mikhail completed the preparatory-school academic program at night school.

Pinchas's business plans with the company owner, Louis Brandt, had long before ground to a halt, but their good relations continued in epistolary form, now with the heir of the firm, Louis, Jr. Pinchas had paid off his debt on time, and now and then he would order watch parts from Omega. Slowly but surely, the family lost all their wealth. Nevertheless, in spite of their poverty, their home remained a hospitable one, with constant tea parties and musical evenings that attracted assorted youth of every stripe and color. They were freethinkers. Their gatherings in the warmer months of the year, when they would set up a samovar in the little yard behind their building, were especially popular. Poverty did not cancel out amusement.

In October 1905, a pogrom against Kiev's Jews raged through the city, hastening the ruin of the family. The watchmaker's shop was completely destroyed, and the family's property plundered. What the marauders didn't take away, they smashed. They even managed to render the samovar unfit for use.

Kiev's Jewish tradespeople and craftsmen had been ruined, but the consequences of this pogrom were not only material. The Jews who lived through it felt that there was just a thin barrier between them and their utter demise. Talmudic teachers and scholars, living repositories of divine texts and thousands of years of history, sank into sorrow and desperation. Zionism came into vogue, promoting the return of the dispersed Jewish exiles to the Holy Land to establish the historic Israel. But the ideas of socialism had no less appeal for Jewish young people. The 1905 Revolution failed, but the idea of a new, purifying, and liberating revolution took hold of them and troubled their hearts. Politics was all the rage. Only Pinchas Kerns, who had always loved reading newspapers in all the languages available to him, had lost the taste for dispute and argument carried on by journalists and politicians. He abandoned his habit of reading newspapers, and instead took to repairing an old music box left crippled by the pogrom thugs. He only sighed, listening silently to the endless conversations of his sons and their friends about the rebuilding of this unjustly ordered society, about the coming changes, and the struggle, from which old Pinchas didn't expect anything but trouble and new pogroms.

Fifteen-year-old Marusya, whom their good neighbors, the Yakovenkos, had sheltered from October 18 to 20, during the pogrom, hiding her in their bedroom and, during the most dangerous moments, in their cellar, emerged from this experience as an ardent Christian radical. Her character had matured completely during those dark, shameful days of Kiev's history. The formerly hospitable, affable world now divided itself into two halves, without shades or nuances. On the one side were the fighters for human dignity and freedom; on the other, their enemies, exploiters and the Black Hundreds.*

The Yakovenkos, who had sheltered Marusya, who fed her and protected her throughout those horrific days, belonged to neither one side nor the other. To simplify matters, she counted them as relatives, for whom you feel an affinity dictated by nature.

While Pelageya Onisimovna Yakovenko was removing the small icon of the Holy Mother and Child from where she had placed it between the two window frames, Marusya looked at the piece of painted wood and felt a confused sense of gratitude to both of them—to the statuesque Ukrainian neighbor, with her tiny eyes and fake crown-braid, and to Miriam (Maria) the Jewess (who bore the same name as Marusya), holding her little Christ Child. Together they had defended her from the screaming crowd of wild beasts who called themselves Christians. In this place, her thinking underwent some sort of turbulence. Her inner certitude faltered, and the world no longer divided itself into two parts, with bad people and good people, but in some other, more complex way. Pelageya Onisimovna and Uncle Taras were monarchists. They owned two apartment buildings and a tavern, and so they were exploiters. But they were good people, even heroic. Rumors were making the rounds that, during those awful days, a Russian family that had sheltered an elderly Jewish woman had been killed. The Yakovenkos had certainly risked a great deal by taking Marusya into their home. None of this accorded with the terms of her understanding, and one thought unsettled another. There was neither clarity nor order in her mind—only agitation, disturbance, and the feeling that drastic changes would be necessary before life could continue. And, with or without Marusya's help, things were already changing. Her elder brother Joseph, a member of the Jewish Self-Defense Organization, was banished for three years to the Irkutsk region in Siberia, like all those who had taken up weapons during the days of the pogrom. Mark had left the family even earlier. After graduating from the Faculty of Law at St. Petersburg University, he stayed on in the capital to take up an insignificant position with a law firm. To his father's bitter disappointment, Mark received his "higher" education at a shamefully low cost: he had become a Lutheran. The family refused to talk about it, as though it were some kind of shameful disease.

---

* The Black Hundreds was an ultranationalist movement in Russia in the early twentieth century that supported the House of Romanov and opposed any challenge to the autocracy of the emperor.

Old Pinchas, who had read newspapers his whole life, never became a religious fanatic. He did attend the synagogue now and then, however, and never broke off relations with his religious brethren. He did not approve of his elder son's choices; he simply remained silent, and mourned. Mark put a great deal of effort into trying to help his younger brother join him in Petersburg to study. Soon Mikhail left Kiev, to enroll in St. Petersburg University as an auditor.

Although none of them had perished during the pogrom, the family's circumstances were still dire. But life began improving of its own accord. The Jewish Relief Committee, which had been set up to aid victims of the pogrom, sent them money and clothes, somewhat the worse for wear, but still in perfectly good condition—though, unfortunately, several sizes too big. Mother sat down at the sewing machine with one of the garments, then ripped out the seams, cut off the excess fabric, and took it in. The result was the most beautiful dress Marusya had ever worn—chestnut-colored flannel wool, trimmed with silk lace. They bought her some little button-down boots with small heels—the first time she had ever worn boots that weren't made specially for children. Marusya had become a young lady.

When her brothers scattered and went their separate ways, Marusya, spoiled by the attentions of the numerous boys and young men, and used to stormy discussions and to domestic amusements, joking, and games, discovered that she had been feeding on other people's lives. She herself had meant nothing to them, and now no one visited their house except rather boring distant relations, Mikhail's friend Ivan Belousov, his former classmate, and Bogdan Kosarkovsky, the erstwhile music teacher, who was now a clarinetist at the opera theater.

Ennui, ennui . . . Music was no longer heard in their house. The old piano had been smashed to smithereens by the pogrom thugs, and there could be no thought of buying another. In place of lively shared meals, there were infrequent letters from her older brothers, and many postcards from Mikhail, describing the colorful, exciting life of the capital. Marusya only felt more despondent after reading them.

Her father replaced the shattered windows in the shop and in the apartment, whitewashed the walls, and repaired his box of watch parts, full of wonderful little rods and springs. Then he attached it to the wall next to his desk. Her father spent most of his time here in the shop, though there weren't any customers to speak of. Instead, he busied himself with repairing the music box. Pinchas lovingly restored the crumpled cylinder that played the roll of sheet music. The task was finicky and arduous: he had to replace the missing pins on the cylinder and align it with the tuned teeth of the comb, which had sustained damage.

Marusya, who had always preferred the silent company of her father to that of her constantly fretting mother, made herself a little nest in a corner of her father's workroom and, drawing herself up into a ball in an armchair, read, one after another, the books her brother Mikhail had miraculously acquired. This gift, an entire library of two hundred tomes, had been sent to their home by the writer Korolenko when he learned that all the books that belonged to the Jewish student had been destroyed during the pogrom.

Who could have imagined that these very books would accompany Mikhail to the end of his life, and form the basis of the collection that to this day has been preserved by his granddaughter Lyuba, Nora Ossetsky's third cousin, in the apartment on Tverskaya Street in Moscow?

Marusya, grown thin, with large blue moons under her eyes, had buried her nose in an issue of *The New Journal for Everyone* from the year 1903 with a blue stamp on the cover: "From the library of Vladimir Galaktionovich Korolenko." For the third time in a row she was reading Chekhov's story "The Betrothed." How could he understand so much, not only about the main character, who had escaped the wretched dullness of provincial life into a new, elevated form of existence, but about her, Marusya, who also wanted to break out of this boredom and ennui, into a life of freedom, meaningfulness, and inchoate beauty?

Her mother called her to dinner. Marusya refused to budge. Her father, wiping the metal dust off his hands with a clean rag, called her, too, but she shook her head. Just looking at the chicken soup brought on nausea. The smell alone, which wafted in from the back room, made her feel sick.

"Fine, just stay here, then. If someone stops in, call me." Her father sat in the shop nearly without a break, afraid to miss a customer.

As soon as her father left, the bell over the door tinkled. Marusya put her journal down on the pile of books that had amassed around the armchair over the past week and opened the door. A woman in a heavy wool coat trimmed with velvet stripes entered. She wore an elegant hat that looked like a cylinder with wings, something that wasn't worn in Kiev, or in any other city as far as Marusya knew. Marusya let the woman in and invited her to sit down and wait for a moment so she could call her father.

While Marusya was gone and her father was washing his hands, the lady examined the pile of books lying on the floor next to the chair. She wasn't interested in *The New Journal for Everyone*; but the cover of another book caught her eye. Was it possible that this frail young girl was reading, in French, the recently published book by the fashionable author Romain Rolland, *La Vie de Beethoven*?

The woman directed this question to the aging watchmaker, who appeared a few minutes later.

"That is my daughter, a book lover."

The clock the woman had brought in for repair was of course that round gold Omega, one of the first models, so familiar to the watchmaker. They struck up a conversation. Madame Leroux turned out to be Swiss herself. Her parents were from the Upper Jura. Like Pinchas, she had left her native parts long ago; but just the mention of the names of rivers and valleys gave them both pleasure. During their lively conversation, the watchmaker opened the back panel of the clock and, placing a round piece of glass in a frame made of bone on his eye, like a monocle, extracted a trifling screw with his tweezers. Then he rummaged through his desk drawer and found one just like it. The watch face was missing a single tiny stone. Pinchas asked what color the stone had been.

"It was red," the woman said. "They're all red."

Pinchas nodded. He'd have to order the stone from Switzerland; he didn't have a supply of ruby splinters on hand.

The book lover who had shunned chicken soup glided into the workroom like a silent shadow. The visitor, losing all interest in her clock, turned to the young lady.

"Do you read French? Do you like the book?" she asked in French.

"Yes, very much."

"Do you like Beethoven?"

Marusya nodded.

From this moment began that new life Marusya had been longing for. After conversing with her for ten minutes, Madame Leroux, secretary of the local Froebel Society, director of a public kindergarten under the society's guidance, invited her to visit their exclusive organization. In January, a week after her birthday, Maria (Marusya) Kerns started her first job—as an assistant teacher in a recently opened school for children of poor parents and domestic workers. In the autumn of the same year, she entered the newly opened Froebel Courses at Kiev University. She became a Froebel Miss, a "children's gardener," as they were called.

3

From the Willow Chest
The Diary of Jacob Ossetsky
(1910)

JANUARY 6

I was sick for more than a week, sicker than I've ever been in my life. For several days it felt like it was all a dream. Suddenly Mama would show up with a cup of tea, and Dr. Vladimirsky and some others I didn't recognize, some of them very nice. But always, in back of them, was someone very dangerous, even terrifying. I can't describe it; even recalling it is unpleasant. From time to time, I felt like I was in some sort of dark, flat space, and I realized I had died. I feel that if I don't write this down it will all evaporate, disappear into oblivion. But there was something enormously important there—about my life in the very distant future. I envy writers; I just can't find the words.

JANUARY 10

I've started reading again. Voraciously. I was starving for books the whole time I was sick. Now I'm reading the biologists. I've read all the Darwin that Yura brought over for me.

(Karl Snyder, *Picture of the World in Light of the Natural Sciences*. Troels-Lund, *Cosmology and Worldview*.)

Thoughts on Darwinism: The theory of the evolution of organic life suggests to me a kind of fundamental axis, surrounded by myriad bifurcated branches. Representatives of the existing animal world are arranged around the tips of the branches. We don't know all of them from the central axis, since the transitional species don't live long. Having fulfilled their purpose (so to speak)—i.e., having served as a phase toward another species—they disappear.

The most intriguing problem is to place the human being in this scheme. Is he just a transitional step on the way to something else (for example, Nietzsche's *Übermensch*), or does he occupy a place on the tip of the branch, which would account for his relative youth as a species?

Just now an answer to this problem has occurred to me. If we breed some animal that reproduces very quickly—for example, one of the lower organisms or protozoa, or bacteria—then, after a time, we may have hundreds of generations, and according to the law of evolution, the last ones may differ radically from the first. Observing how many generations must pass to produce a distinction, knowing how much time is necessary for one generation to become extinct and succeed in passing on its life to another, we might deduce the relationship between the origins of life and the stage when distinctions will emerge.

This relationship may be applied to humans, to discover when such distinctions could have emerged, or might do so in the future, thus making it possible to determine a person's place in the taxonomy of existing and previously existing species.

This little theory of mine follows from the fact that I presuppose a direct correlation between the age of the human species and the culmination of a phase after which he can pass on life to something else.

Now, having written this, I am already questioning it. Even as I was writing the last page, I already knew that when I finished the "theory" I would have to refute it. Darwin proved only the law of evolution of organic life, attaching to it an explanation: natural selection. Darwin stopped short of including humans in this process. It was Thomas Huxley who did that, acknowledging that the closest relative of the human being is the ape.

As a matter of fact, this isn't true. Darwin often repeats: "The origin of humans from some species of lower animal is irrefutable. The monkey evolved from the same ancestor."

The biogenetic law of Ernst Haeckel states that the "ontogeny, or the growth of the embryo, schematically recapitulates phylogeny, or the history of development of the species."

Asexual reproduction, or parthenogenesis, or reproduction without participation of males and their spermatozoa, is widespread in nature (drones, for example).

If the spermatozoa could be artificially emulated, their role, most likely, would come down to a shove, a push, given to the female egg. Both artificial coercion and chemical manipulation work in this way.

On the other hand, we also know of several cases of so-called merogony, or the independent development and reproduction of the spermatozoid. Thus, the process of fertilization turns out to be only one of the ways nature achieves the goal of reproduction, including in higher animals. If I didn't want to study music, I would study biology. It's the most fascinating branch of science I've read for a long time.

But music is more important to me!

JANUARY 15

By now, I've already started to love my journal and the pleasure of writing.

I'm already finishing my first volume of the *Complete Works of J. Ossetsky.*

I'll begin the second volume with even greater enthusiasm than the first. It's quiet around me . . .

I opened the window a crack—the sparrows are chittering away, and my heart feels calm, a bit sad—I have a feeling of satisfaction after making notes in my journal. And, somehow, sadness about the unknown future . . .

Today I went outside for the first time since my recovery.

FEBRUARY 1

How weak man is! I have, it would seem, principles, my own worldview, and some notion of freedom, and of sexual morality. But it only takes a single glance at the décolleté of a washerwoman and I feel a rush of blood to my heart (yes, my heart), I can't see or think straight, and something draws me to her . . .

When she disappears, I am well again, except that my hands tremble slightly. It is outrageous that I can't keep myself under control. I'm sure that a woman would just have to wink at me and I'd run after her like a puppy; I'd forget Ellen Key, and Tolstoy, and Jules Payot.

What contrasts! After this, I sit and read Ellen Key. To fortify my nature—most likely that same nature that tomorrow will start chasing after a washerwoman.

FEBRUARY 15

Today I decided to speak to Papa about my further studies. I'll graduate from the Commercial High School in the spring, and want to study music. I was too impassioned about it last time; I understand that now. Papa listened to me with complete indifference, as though he had made up his mind long before, and it was final. He said I had to enter the Commercial Institute, and agreed to pay for my further musical studies only if I enrolled in the university. This conversation was very unpleasant to me. Precisely because of the money. Whatever he talks about, it all comes down to materialism, to money.

APRIL 7

I read *The Chronicle of My Musical Life* by Rimsky-Korsakov. It made a strong impression. Now I desperately want to perform with real talent, to go to Petersburg to be around talented people. I want to be a talent myself. While I was reading, I started believing I could embark on that path. Maybe in five or six years I'll laugh at these dreams of mine . . .

APRIL 11

Music lessons. A new teacher, Mr. Bylinkin. It feels as though I didn't know anything before. It's ANOTHER kind of music altogether! I began to hear it completely afresh. Up until now I've been playing all WRONG!

APRIL 19

Beardsley has an illustration for Chopin's Ballade (op. 47).

APRIL 20

Today I discovered something that I have already managed to disprove.

Because of how a piano is tempered, the same notes in the higher and lower registers are not in unison. Thus, for the C in the contra-octave, C-sharp will be in unison in the four-line octave, not C. Just now I hit upon the following idea: continuous C octaves played in the contra-octave.

On top of it, a short melodic pattern played around the C in the four-line octave—a consonantly sounding chord. Then the pattern—without change—moves downward toward the three-, two-, one-line octaves. Then it continues down to the small, great, and finally the contra-octave.

The small error grows, and in the contra-octave already turns into dissonance.

One might call it "the gradual transition of consonance into dissonance." Very interesting idea!

You can actually do all kinds of "tricks" with piano temperament.

APRIL 24

I could never live alone. I love company. Only in company do I feel alive, happy, witty.

I cannot imagine myself without society around me. I dream about a group of people, a society, where I am at the very center.

In my heart of hearts, I dream of being raised up on a stage, to the people's cries and applause. All around there are frock coats, ribbons, bare shoulders . . . seas of flowers . . . But without society?

"Gentlemen, you cannot imagine how hard it is when a man has nowhere to go. A man needs to have someplace to go to." Even Dostoevsky, the gloomiest, darkest of writers, speaks about the pain of loneliness, through the words of Marmeladov. Even such a giant among men as Dostoevsky feared the horror of loneliness!

I become afraid. The picture of a man sitting alone in a dark room— this is what fills me with fear. Now I'm writing in a comfortable room after my lessons. I'm thinking about how I'm going to visit some girl students from the women's college. My heart warms at the thought. Yet someone else might be sitting in a room, alone with his thoughts . . .

I'd like to go to him, to take him gently by the arm and lead him into society, to make him start talking. I would tell him how he makes his own life difficult and absurd . . . but I have no skill, no dexterity, no strength to accomplish this . . .

MAY 11

Why don't they write études, exercises, for the orchestra? It is especially necessary for "melding" all the sounds to form a particular "orchestral" tone.

Ilya just proposed that I join his circle and present a piece on art. I still don't know whether I'll accept the invitation, but I am considering it. I have a very interesting idea for such a piece: "Description of the Contemporary Musical Moment." It seems to me that what characterizes the current moment is a longing for strength, for power . . . And, when it comes right down to it, not only in music . . .

JUNE 19

Listening to Glière's quartet. In a sense, there is a parallel between newer trends in visual art—pointillism, impressionism—and modern music. In painting, there is haziness, lyricism, and, the main thing, something ineffable, a lightness. A picture covered in points and strokes seems to be covered

39

with a light veil of air. In music, there is polyphony, complexity, also an indistinct lyricism, as well as that same elusiveness.

It is, naturally, a good thing that these parallels exist.

This means there is an idea, a theoretical basis, common to all art forms.

Now I want to write, to write a great deal.

They are playing vivace, the third movement . . .

They finished the scherzo, a small, elegant part.

But, altogether, it's complex. I like this composer, Glière.

He creates a heady mixture of the Russian style with modernism.

The Russian melody alternates with its striking absence.

The fourth movement begins with an Oriental theme.

This quartet develops in the most complex possible way.

A decadent treatment in the Eastern theme, on the violin.

Here is something strange. Some sort of new, sinister touch or flavor.

And again the Russian melody.

AUGUST 4

"Where words fall short, music begins. Impotent in conveying an act of will, music can, with deep intensity, reveal the inner state of a human being, expressing pure emotion."

AUGUST 20

I haven't written in over two weeks. Many things have come to pass. I started the Commercial Institute, and, most important, the music conservatory! My dream came true! I managed to do it.

I've got so many plans for this year—they would fill an abyss!

I'll study music very hard. At Christmas there will be five exams to pass, and in May another four. I'll also take some classes in German. I'll be at the university for four whole years. Everything I need for "real life," with a residence permit. After that, it's goodbye to music, and pedagogy, and to travel . . . All I'll have to look forward to is working as a lousy bank clerk— with an annual bonus. Little by little, you plod away, until you realize it's too late to quit your post . . . If I give up music as well, I'll die. There are times when I live completely in dreams, when I retreat from everyday reality altogether. There is a great deal of Rudin and Peer Gynt in me . . .

I'm afraid that, through my own weakness, I'll never realize a hundredth part of my dreams.

A terrible day. Tolstoy has died. I'm now completely calm, and I even feel comforted to recall how, half an hour ago, I was standing in the darkened entrance hall, sobbing into my handkerchief, and terrified that someone would notice me. After the tears, my heart was less heavy. Truly, one pours out grief through tears.

They're selling little pamphlets on the streets. My chest constricted; somehow I felt scared, and I walked past the people reading the pamphlets with a sinking heart. The rain pours down, slow, stupefying, inexorable.

In the window of a store was a large portrait of Tolstoy, and a little piece of cardboard next to it: "Died November 4, 1910."

I came home. Shall I tell them? No, I won't.

Whenever you get a piece of news, your first thought is: I have to hurry and tell others! But I won't say anything at home.

Even though the world, the whole world, is grieving, I'm constantly thinking of myself. I heed my own thoughts, sympathize with my own grief, think about the sad expression on my face.

In Odessa, Genrikh is probably crying, too. Lying in bed, crying. My closest friend, my elder brother. It's a pity that he's not here with me.

I'm standing by the table, and the rain is pouring down. I can't hold it back: "Mama, Tolstoy is dead." I couldn't stop myself from crying, and I ran out into the dining room, into the front hall, and cried my heart out . . . But they understand nothing.

I wonder to myself: Is this a general law of some sort? Or is it our personal family tragedy? Why can't my parents—good, loving people—understand how we live, what we live by? Why do they understand neither my feelings nor my ideas? Will I really be the same way when I grow up? And will my children look at me with indignation and think: "Father is so good and loving, but I have nothing to talk to him about. He's buried in his own concerns, his own world, boring and dull"? No, that can't happen to me! I have given my word that I'll try to understand my children's lives, even share a common life with them. But I still don't know—is it even possible?

Tolstoy isn't dead! He's alive! A message was sent to the whole world by telegraph that he had died, but it turns out the message was false!

Yes, Tolstoy has died; only it happened today, November 7, at 6:00 a.m. I (again, I!) received the information with absolute calm. My grief was already spent beforehand . . .

At one time, I said the following: Death is such a terrible thing that it's best not to think about it at all. Someone who thinks constantly about death will probably see no meaning in life, not just in the larger sense of life, but in the sense of our small, day-to-day matters. A person like that might as well go hang himself.

But people don't hang themselves, so that must mean that there is sense in our day-to-day matters. So you ought not to think about death.

These thoughts seemed so resonant, so well constructed in my mind, but when I put them down on paper they sound naïve and half formed, simply childish. But I know what I want to say. A person has died—so, right away, everyone should just forget about that person. I once said that when I am on my deathbed I will tear up all my photographs, my papers, and I'll ask my children not to talk about me. I'll forbid them to wear mourning garments.

We must hasten and push forward the processes that time sets in motion anyway.

In general, the entire past, everything you can't bring back, is terrible and oppressive. Life rushes by at an extraordinary pace.

"Life is but a moment." This is why we can't allow memories to poison the present, the only thing that has meaning. What could be more fleeting than time?

There are times when I positively can't stand my parents. It usually happens when I talk seriously to them. When I don't see them for a while, I start to miss them. Once, I was telling an acquaintance about my father, and I talked so much that I almost started weeping; I was choked with tears. But now it's even unpleasant to me that I have to have dinner with them. We are complete strangers, yet I am for some reason dependent on him for my survival. When we have to go somewhere together (which I try always to avoid), I begin to jabber and to spew all kinds of nonsense so as not to say nothing at all. He takes no interest in me whatsoever; he doesn't respect me, or my convictions and habits, at all. Yet he loves me all the same, most likely. A strange kind of love!

I feel that I get angry and annoyed with them, for the most part because of trivial things. A lot of the time, my only fault is that I tell them things I shouldn't; I goad them into discussions that don't convince them. Now I find I talk to them less and less.

I sometimes love Mama, but I don't respect her at all. It's terrible, in fact. Like strangers coming together and nagging at each other, spoiling one another's lives, and all the time living at someone else's expense. And Papa works like an ox. But from the outside it looks like life as "a happy family." The worst thing of all is that I'm starting to feel that, sooner or later, I'll end up with the same sort of life, the same sort of family.

No, it's not true, that can't happen to me! I firmly believe this.

NOVEMBER 9

Rodenbach. *Bruges-la-morte.* Art that feeds on death, rooted in death. It's horrible. I shouldn't think about it.

Two years ago, Grandfather died. His death didn't affect me in the least.

Recently, I was holding little Rayechka on my knee. She's weak, sickly; her pale, pretty face is sensitive and thoughtful. I thought about her dying. It seemed to me that I was walking through the room, holding the dying Rayechka in my arms. Suddenly I understood that moment when you press a cold little corpse to your chest and you feel an overwhelming powerlessness to stop the life that is ebbing away.

As I write this, I get a lump in my throat, just remembering . . . Rayechka is in the other room now, singing a little song about a mosquito.

The best thing would be to yank out the whole place in your heart that belongs to the dying, to cross it out of your memory, to forget about love. To forget! . . . Impossibly difficult; but necessary!

On the other hand, why should a person force his feelings? Time itself will smooth out all the bumps and wrinkles of experience. A person wants to weep, to grieve, to complain about the unjustness of fate. Wants to give himself over to memory, like he wants to dream about tomorrow . . .

Something in my soul is restless. I have a vague feeling of oppressiveness, that something has to happen . . .

And in Astapovo, Tolstoy is lying peacefully, washed and dressed in a clean shirt. His face is full of peace, absolute peace.

Probably solemn, as well. Listening to the babble of the whole world around him.

In church. A funeral service. Thoughts about religion visit me these days, and about glory and fame—fame, in particular. Reason suggests its uselessness, but with my emotions I passionately, intensely desire fame. Fame, the most paltry of all things, devoid of all inner meaning. Andrei Bolkonsky—that is, Tolstoy—pondered this. The vanity and insignificance of "human love." But I want people to shout my name at the crossroads; I want them to praise me, to admire and adore me.

I know very well that if I achieved this, I would soon be disillusioned. All famous people attest to this. Tolstoy, Artsybashev, Chekhov, etc. I know that fame is about external trappings, but inner emptiness. It is accompanied by deprivation, unpleasantness, and bitterness, in particular the hardship of a lack of solitude, constant company. And I know that fame is nothing before the largest thing in life—death (as Artsybashev put it). He spoke so warmly and eloquently about the poet Bashkin: "Before the dying face, before the chest growing ever stiller, the last spasmodic breaths—how paltry, how trivial my own fame seemed, my name, my literary merits."

My reason accepts all of this, but my heart wants to see "J. Ossetsky" printed in bold letters above an article in the newspaper. It's trivial and pathetic, but I still want it.

Evening of the same day. Study some music theory.

I ride in the trolley, standing on the back platform, staring out at the road.

Evening. The trolley races along, and the tracks, gleaming and spinning swiftly away, lay themselves down neatly in two strips. This is a moment I recall very vividly.

It was then that I felt especially urgently the rush of time, the leap of seconds . . .

Just now, you were on that particular spot—you look back, and it's several feet, several blocks, finally several versts behind you.

What a chatterbox I am! If there's someone to listen to me, I'll talk till the cows come home, only to regret it later. Why should I tell everyone how I dream of a career as a conductor?

Tolstoy says . . . Oh, apropos of Tolstoy: today the newspapers are reporting on the hundredth anniversary of the birth of Pirogov. And about Tolstoy, there were only two articles. Tomorrow there will be just one, and the day after tomorrow, just a chronological note—and on the first page of the news there will be a piece on the anniversary celebration of the Kiev railroad stationmaster.

Yes, this is how it will, and should, be. Time smooths out all memories and ushers in new events.

Newspaper articles bring this into sharp focus.

It's a bit sad . . .

I think that Osip Dymov describes dreams better than anyone. He knows how to talk about that elusiveness, and that feeling you have in the morning in bed when you feel sad after a dream you've already forgotten.

Sometimes after you've just woken up, there's an inkling of something you can't quite recall, something you dreamed about.

I'm studying German now. I finished reading a story and leaned back in my chair, realizing that I just finished the lesson. A pleasant sensation . . . a light dream . . . I wake up and remember that it had several different scenes, with different characters, different events, but I remember only one scene, in the lobby of a theater, a woman is unbuttoning several buttons on her bodice . . .

I don't remember any of the rest—no details, not a single word, nothing in specific . . .

I remember only that it was very pleasant . . . I found a description of gymnastic exercises for two-year-old children: throw a few pillows on the floor and force the children to roll around on them. The children will expend a great deal of effort trying to get off of them. I have to play this game with Rayechka. I think she'll like it. It's movement as an educational approach. Movement is a natural part of learning, but this exercise develops the capacity.

Recently, I've been very productive. Like never before. I'm now studying many subjects and doing well in almost all of them. A month from now (it's November), I will take three exams at the Commercial Institute: statistics, political economy, and the history of political economy. I already know the statistics; I'm studying now for polit. econ. I study German for one hour every day, and am making great progress. Every day, I play for about three hours. Twice a week, I attend music lessons (two hours each time), and twice a week, lessons in music theory. The only thing I don't get to do is read every day.

. . . Things are actually very fine at the moment . . . so fine it almost feels strange—I don't know what else I might need.

I have everything I need, I'm studying what I want to study . . . except for the lack of someone who would be as happy about everything as I am myself. That's true enough. Right now I don't have a real friend (age, ethnicity, "sex" are immaterial).

DECEMBER 1

I've just come home from the theater, from *Khovanshchina*. I came home and wanted to write . . . I listened to the first act with great attention; I nearly always listen closely to the first acts in performances. I paid attention to the unfolding of the plot, to the different performers, and especially to the orchestra, the conductor.

It seems to me that the Russian style in music is monotonous and wearisome. But Glinka is unsurpassed. Even Rimsky-Korsakov, who has written heaps of Russian opera, called himself a "Glinka-ist." Still, *Khovanshchina* is quite middle-of-the-road . . . though there are a lot of dramatic episodes in it. The music is always calm and unhurried, even monotonous . . . One wants to hear some outburst of energy, some tragic passion, but that is lacking.

During the intermission, I noticed a young girl. She was sitting near me. I liked her very much. I couldn't concentrate on the last act; I was thinking about her. I felt sad that I liked her so much, and that she didn't even know, that I would never see her again, and—this was the worst thing—that I would soon forget what she looked like. I stared at her, trying to memorize her face. In the middle of the act, she started coughing uncontrollably. This alarmed me. I had already suspected she might have weak lungs. I became very sad. She had such a nice face, even beautiful. She wore a blouse with a large white collar, and a blue tie. It suited her very well. There were two disgusting students with her.

When I try to resurrect the image, I see that it's already very pale and blurry, and will soon fade away altogether.

On the way home, I felt angry with myself. I remember dozens of faces I see in passing, on the street, on the trolley, but I am already forgetting this particular sweet face.

Just now I started dreaming: I'm walking down the street, and I run into

46

her. She is alone (definitely alone). I go up to her and introduce myself; then we go together to the theater . . . I just imagined what I would say to her at that moment . . .

If I see her on the street . . . I'll immediately recall her face and remember it for a long time. If only I could run into her.

I sat down to write about something else, and saw the last line I had written: "If only I could run into her." The thought already seemed stale and old. Today I've only thought once about that young lady, in the morning. That was the only time.

Recently, I've started being aware, truly aware, of my own happiness. Truly, I have everything I need. I have music, my studies, a clean room, a new suit, a good coat to wear, Beethoven's sonatas . . . What else do I need?

If someone were to give me twenty rubles right now, I wouldn't know what to do with it. Of course, I could spend it: I'd buy sheet music (which I can't play), I'd buy a harmonium, or something. I could "make an effort" to spend it. But I have no strong urge, no strong desire—just small desires, bordering on vulgarity (and I have money—enough to go to the theater, at least).

I'm sitting in my room now, studying German.

I brought a cup of tea into the room for myself. When I drink tea, I am enveloped by a feeling of peace, comfort, and . . . domesticity.

The nickel-plated lamp reflects a small figure drinking tea. And it seems to me that, from somewhere up above, I'm watching the miniature person, J. Ossetsky, watching his life. He's as tiny as can be.

Quiet . . . Calm . . .

DECEMBER 5

I read some of Chekhov's stories. He writes a great deal about women. And for the most part, it seems, pejoratively. Like someone who had suffered a great deal at the hands of women might write. I have to think more about this. "Anna on the Neck"! How Anna, sensing her power, drives Modest Alexeyevich away: "Be off, you blockhead!" It just takes your breath away. In a split second, such a reversal of character! And how she rides down the street, and her drunken father, her brothers, are described with such sympathy, but she drives right on past . . . "Slime" is especially horrible. What a terrifying woman. As though he is taking revenge for the fact that he himself can't refuse her! And with a touch of anti-Semitism, too. But after Tolstoy, Chekhov is our greatest writer! There is something here I don't understand—as though all the charm of a woman, her elegant hands, her white neck, and the curls that escape from her hairdo, are created just to awaken the basest instincts in a man. But this is not at all the case!

Strauss's Sonata for Violin and Piano.

The muted violin, the piano passages, pianissimo.

Very pretty! Lately, because of my busy days, I've almost stopped dreaming. And it's for the best! Good riddance! I think only about the most useful way to spend the day, about music lessons, about German.

They finished the second movement—"improvisation."

Now for the finale.

My most distant dreams reach only to the end of this summer, which I'm hoping to spend productively.

The last few days have been frustrating in terms of my music. Quartet in E-flat minor.

I read about Brahms. He died in 1897. That means that I was already seven years old when he died.

On symmetry:

There is no symmetry in nature. Nature is neither symmetrical nor asymmetrical. Nature transcends it.

Symmetry is found only where there is a human being who notices it. Only a human being notices such a phenomenon in nature: two halves that seem to resemble each other.

Aesthetics don't exist in nature, either. Physics, chemistry, especially mechanical physics, do exist, but aesthetics (and several other disciplines) do not. Nature has no classification, nothing significant or insignificant. All this is created by the human being.

DECEMBER 19

I'm sad . . . I'm also sad because I will now write about ordinary sensations in ordinary words.

I just finished a book by Dymov, the saddest, the tenderest poet I've ever read. Even more tender than Chekhov. Why am I so sad?

I listen to music—I feel sad because I can't play that way, because I can't even play my own pieces as well as I'd like . . .

I look at people who are strong, and people who are beautiful, and again my heart protests: why?

While I write this, I'm remembering Dymov's story "Evening Letters."

UNDATED (LAST ENTRY OF THE NOTEBOOK)

Perhaps it is precisely art that must proclaim what is unsubstantiated, groundless.

There are no criteria, there is no theory of art. There is just an artist; there is no history of art, but a catalogue of paintings.

Every person takes what he likes from art. There is no objectivity, only subjectivity.

The art of Isadora Duncan.

One can manage to capture the basic characteristics of modern art, but to delineate a theory that fits all epochs and media is completely impossible.

Tannhäuser (all of Wagner).

1. An artist's creative output depends on his personality, his epoch, and his milieu. And the artist does not mimic his milieu, but creates an ideal version of it.
2. The lack of criteria in art. However hard this may be for artists, and particularly critics, and the public.
3. The character of modern creativity: longing for might, the urge to power. Rodin, Vrubel, Wagner, Bryusov, Böcklin, Roerich.
4. The reflection of Art Nouveau in architecture.
5. The methods and technical means available to modern art.
6. Modern art as a whole does not reflect what I have just described. It is only the outlines of these tendencies that are visible.
7. The urge in modern art toward archaism, toward the Renaissance. Roerich, Somov, Benois, Borisov-Musatov.
8. The inadequacies of this urge.
9. Art must be contemporary. We must remember that history will understand the incomprehensible.
10. The weak reflection of modernity in our art.
11. The weak dissemination of art in its applied forms.

Artists don't like to serve industry. But this is the truest path. The Old Masters.

In *The Queen of Spades*, at the moment when the old countess appears, there is a spectrum of whole tones in the orchestra.
Faust

6 *petits préludes pour les commençants*
12 *petits préludes*
   ou exercices pour les commençants
Vrubel, Botticelli
Rodin, Böcklin, Beardsley
Riehl, Baumbach
Dominant chord (fifth, sixth, third, fourth)

Read:

Taine, Readings on art
Jean-Marie Guyau, *Art from A Sociological Perspective*
Lessing, *Laocoön*
Lieber, *The History of Western Literature*
Yudin, *Art in the Family*
Vasnetsov. *Art*
Andrei Bely, Vyach. Ivanov, *The Book on the New Theater*
Wilde
Hanslick, *On the Beautiful in Music*
Woermann, *The History of Art from Ancient Times*
R. Muther, *The History of Modern Painting*
Gnedich, *History of Art*
The New Journal for Everyone (1902)
Chekhov, "Betrothed"

Time! There's not enough time! Sleep less! Somewhere I read that Napoleon slept only three hours a day.

Closing Chekhov

(1974)

They had been together for eleven years. Tengiz said it was time to close Chekhov. Nora was surprised: Why all of a sudden, why now? What was a Russian theater without Chekhov? But Tengiz said that he had wanted to for a long time already. And he began picking apart *Three Sisters*, scene by scene, line by line, with unexpected, pitiless trenchancy. He raised his beautiful, very beautiful hands, held them up in the air while he talked, and Nora didn't hear his speech as single, separate words, but soaked it up whole, in strings of words, strange phrases it would have been impossible to recount. His Russian wasn't quite perfect, it must be said, but he spoke with intense, expressive eloquence. He had a rather strong Georgian accent, which sometimes garbled the meaning. And sometimes even deepened it. Though Nora could never understand why this should have been the case, she always felt glad that it wasn't only about the language, but about the whole cast of thought of a person from another place and culture . . .

"Just tell me one thing, why did they shut down Efros? He staged *Three Sisters* the way it should be performed! Poor things, it's so unfortunate. I feel so sorry for them, it brings me to tears. Since 1901, they've been elevating this play to the skies, higher and higher it goes. Right? I just can't bear to see it anymore! Enough is enough, right?" His drawling, ascending "right" wrapped around Nora and drew her in.

"Nora, Nora! Tolstoy said about *Three Sisters* that it was a 'dreary bore' of a play! Did Leo Tolstoy know a thing or two, or not? Everyone is bored, full of gloomy longing! No one works! No one works in Russia; actually, in

Georgia it's no different, no one wants to work. And if they do, it's reluctantly, with disdain. Olga is the director of a school. This is an excellent position at the beginning of the century: they've started teaching the women students science, and not just embroidery and Holy Writ, and they are educating the first professional women. But Olga's bored, and her strength of will and her youth desert her, drop by drop. And, out of pure boredom, Masha falls in love with Vershinin, very noble, but very stupid. He's pathetic! What kind of man is he? I don't understand.

"Irina works in an office—at the telegraph, or God knows where. Her work is dull, tedious; everything is bad. She doesn't want to work; she wants to go to Moscow. They complain—all they do is complain. And what are they going to do in Moscow when they get there? Nothing! That's why they're not going!

"Andrei is a nobody. Natasha is a coarse animal. Solyony—a real beast! And poor Tusenbach—how can you marry a woman who doesn't even love you? It's a rotten life, Nora! Do you understand who the real hero is? Do you? Think—it's Anfisa! Anfisa is the true protagonist! The nanny who goes around cleaning up after everyone. She is the one with a meaningful existence, Nora. She has a broom, a mop, rags; she washes and wipes things down, she picks things up, makes things smooth and shiny. All the others—they're just layabouts, idiots who sit around twiddling their thumbs. They're bored! And what is it that's all around them? The turn of the century, right? The industrial revolution is under way, capitalism. They're building roads, factories, bridges. But they want to go to Moscow, and they can't even make it to the station! You understand me, right? Right?"

Nora was already way ahead of him: she already knew what she would draw now, how she would design the set. She knew how glad Tengiz would be that she had immediately hit upon it without even moving an inch from the spot—the entire play! She already saw the Prozorov home, open, exposed, pushed far out into the foreground—and on the left and on the right, everywhere, building sites, cranes rising to the sky. Freight trains are carrying goods, and life is on the move; there are loud screeches (of metal), and some whistles and signals . . . But in the Prozorovs' house they don't notice a thing; the activity and transformation completely pass them by. They wander around the house drinking tea, conversing. Only Anfisa is busy, lugging around buckets, rags, pouring out basins . . . Excellent. Excellent! All the characters are shadows, shades; only Anfisa has substance. They are all dressed in muslin, like smoky mist, and the military men also seem to be only half there. Anemia. A suspended space. A garden of nearly insubstantial souls. And she will clothe everything in sepia, like the faded, colorless garments in old photographs. True historical antiquity. Yes, of course, Natasha Prozorov is plump; she inhabits her body. A deep-rose dress, with a green belt. The background will be sepia all over, drained of color, beiges and browns . . . Brilliant!

And Nora said, "Right." Tengiz put his arms around her and crushed her to him. "Nora, we'll do something that no one has ever seen before! And never will! They'll destroy us completely, of course, but we'll do it anyway. It will be the best thing we've ever done!"

For two months, they were together constantly. Tengiz rehearsed the play. Chekhov's text, mundane, down-to-earth, laconic, always packed with subtle directorial subtexts, heightened significance, was transformed into mechanical chatter. The viscous familial space became dreamlike, as though the dreams and unrealized plans were the reality of life—the transparent patterns of the imagination. Theater of shadows! Shadow puppets. And in this illusory, volatile space, only two people do any real work—Anfisa with her rags, and Natasha, taking in hand all the substance of life—the rooms of the sisters, the house, the garden, the local municipal officials, all the world available to her.

Tengiz did not divulge his killer plan to the actors, and over and over again they repeated the hackneyed text with bored indifference. Which was precisely what Tengiz wanted of them.

Tengiz lived with his Moscow aunt, Mziya, a widowed pianist who worshipped him. Nora, at Tengiz's request, moved into her apartment, which was a strange, two-story structure in back of the Pushkin Museum that had by some miracle been spared demolition. Mziya gave them two tiny rooms on the second floor, and lived herself on the first, in a large room with an ancient, cavernous ice cellar under the floor. At one time, ice from the river had been kept there for the entire summer. Now it held only a damp, hollow, ringing emptiness, covered with a lid of wooden slats.

Yet again, Nora was carrying out this ritual, mounting this celebration with Tengiz, as she had countless times before. All ordinary boundaries and routines were swept away by the pressure of work and love, and by an astounding surge in their strength and capabilities. The fullness and intensity of life were remarkable. Nora lost all sense of the past and future, and all other people—relations and friends—seemed to evaporate completely. She called her mother only two or three times during those two months.

Calling her was complicated. It was usually done through the post office, where she had to order the call, then wait for the call to be returned, most often with a poor connection. Amalia had to trudge three kilometers to the post office to receive it. Inevitably, she would be offended that Nora called her so seldom, and chide her timidly.

In fact, everything had fallen into place long ago. Since the moment he entered her life, Amalia Alexandrovna had adored her Andrei Ivanovich, and she had pushed her daughter away. This passion of old age, as Nora viewed it, was a fire that consumed the entire world around it. The couple had left for Priaksko-Terrasny Nature Reserve, the birthplace of Andrei Ivanovich, where he began working as a park ranger. They bought a house, and started building their own little paradise, which Nora found unendurable. This time, her mother invited Nora to come to visit them in the countryside "with that director of yours," and Nora promised they would. She usually didn't stoop to lying, but now she didn't feel like wasting time on superficial conversation.

It took Nora a week to make her preliminary sketches and to assemble a maquette of the stage. When he saw the building cranes, hanging virtually over the roof of the Prozorovs' home, and the structures drawn on the backdrop resembling skyscrapers or Gothic cathedrals, Tengiz moaned with delight. The play seemed to stage itself. Anfisa enters and walks along in front of the closed curtain, wiping the floor; then the sounds of the construction site start blaring. The curtain opens, and the entire stage is thrown into an exaggeratedly industrialized mode of existence: the screech and thunder of metal, of pneumatic hammers, ring out, and the cranes start to sway. Then the commotion dies down, evaporates into air, and the Prozorovs' home seems to materialize from behind a curtain of light. It is morning . . . The table has been set . . . "Father died exactly one year ago, on this very day, the fifth of May . . ."

Everything unfolded of its own accord, naturally, like grass growing in the yard, only very swiftly. Svistalov, the arrogant and influential production manager of this hallowed, distinguished theater, treated Tengiz with uncharacteristic respect, getting him a bit confused with Temur Chkheidze. He gave the green light to all the theater workshops and departments, and they got right down to work—there had never been a light so green! Everyone knew Svistalov's character; he loved to throw his weight around. He had argued with Borovsky, had put obstacles in the way of Barkhin, and had even set the dogs on Sheintsis—in other words, he had played dirty and interfered with all, all of Nora's favorite set designers . . . A miracle, it was just a miracle! Perhaps the administrator really was touched by Tengiz's appearance, by outward considerations; for some reason, people in Russia did like Georgians, in contrast to Jews, Armenians, or Azeris . . .

They floated arm in arm, the two of them in a cloud of love, through the staff-only entrance. The doorman and the buffet servers smiled at them, and their happiness wove such a lovely cocoon around them that Nora felt, as they moved along in harmony with each other, that they were like figure skaters, or ballet dancers, and they were flying, flying . . .

The play was shut down on the eve of the premiere. They managed only to perform the dress rehearsal, all the sets in place. When their own people in the audience, relatives and close friends, began to disperse, and only the administrators and Party bigwigs, thirsting for blood, remained (they had come intentionally one day earlier than they had promised), it became clear that a scandal was brewing, and Tengiz went out onto the stage and requested that the dear members of the audience stay for a discussion of the play. But the ministerial special forces, the Party hacks, only grew more incensed at this, and it took them just fifteen minutes to kill the play.

Tengiz mounted the stage again, together with Nora, whom he led, very respectfully, by the hand, and said, in a loud voice livid with rage: "Respected guests! You allowed Efros to play his *Three Sisters* thirty-three times! Is our *Three Sisters* really that much better?"

Nora accompanied him to the airport. A gloomy spring, without a single sunny day, and a gloomy Tengiz. He seemed not to see Nora at all; no one smiled at them anymore; the love cloud had vanished. He was flying to Tbilisi, back to his wife and daughter, in a heavy metal airplane. He stood there dejected, unshaven, graying at the temples, with his sloping Neanderthal forehead, reeking of stale alcohol, sweat, and, surprisingly, tangerines. He took a tangerine out of his pocket, thrust it into her hand, winked, gave her a peck on the cheek, and hurried to the boarding area.

5

A New Project

(1974)

From the airport, Nora went straight to Mziya's and collapsed onto the bed that still smelled of Tengiz. She didn't budge from the little second-floor room for two weeks. For about ten days, all her bones hurt; then they stopped. Mziya brought her tea in the mornings. Nora pretended to be asleep, and Mziya would put the cup on top of a checkerboard tabletop next to her. Then she left, closing the door behind her. Almost every day at around noon, the sound of scales being played would drift upstairs: piano students had arrived. There were beginners, who played Czerny's études; several advanced students; and one boy who came in the evening twice a week and played wonderfully well. Mziya devoted longer lessons to him. He had learned some Beethoven sonata, but Nora couldn't recall which one it was. Definitely not the *Tempest*, and not any of the three final ones . . . Nora had quit music school when she was in the sixth grade. Though her abilities weren't exceptional, she had inherited a good ear for music from her father.

Mziya's instrument was adequate, but the sound was weak and muted. Nora didn't feel the pain so much when she could listen to music. When she woke up, she told herself, Today I can't get up; maybe tomorrow I'll manage. But the next day she couldn't make herself get out of bed, either. Sometimes Mziya came to the door and invited her to have something to eat. On the fifth day, Nora went downstairs. Mziya didn't ask anything, and Nora was very grateful to her for that. Only now did she really perceive the cultivated expression on Mziya's face, which was covered in tiny lines, her cheeks rouged. Her hair was dyed in the Caucasian style with thick henna and gathered into a bun at the back of her neck; her tiny feet, in their slender high heels, tapped out rhythms. While Tengiz was here, Nora had barely noticed his silent aunt. She hadn't even paid proper attention to Mziya's idiosyncratic, fancifully adorned apartment. Now she sat downstairs, at the table covered with wine-colored velvet, and Mziya put a plate before her with two sandwiches and an apple, peeled and sliced into small pieces.

"Since my husband died, I have never cooked a real meal," Mziya said apologetically, and Nora felt that they were, most likely, kindred spirits.

I've *never* in my life cooked anything for my husband, Nora thought. She smiled for the first time in all those days and said, "Forgive me, Mziya, for dumping myself on you like this."

"You can stay for as long as you wish, child. I'm used to living alone. I've been alone for a long time. But you don't disturb me in the least."

"I'll just stay a few days longer, if that's all right with you."

Mziya nodded, and they didn't talk anymore. About anything.

Nora lay around on Tengiz's sheets until his scent had nearly faded away; only sometimes the pillow would still yield a hint of his body, and Nora would feel convulsed with pain.

It's simply a molecule, a molecule of his sweat, Nora thought. And I have some sort of illness, a hypersensitivity to his smell. What is this unfortunate condition? Why do such momentary chemical transmissions leave such long, deep traces, such scars? What if he were just an ordinary lover, the sort you go on vacation with to the Crimea for a week, or an affair you have while you're on tour? There was that wondrous young boy last year in Kiev, or even old Lukyanov, the actor, a skirt chaser, a connoisseur of niceties and detail, nearly twenty years her senior. Would I hurt just the same? But there was no answer.

This was the sixth time Nora and Tengiz had parted, and each time it was worse than before.

She sniffed the pillow, but his scent had disappeared; it was redolent of dampness, dust, and whitewash. She dozed off, then woke up. From downstairs she heard scales and Mziya's voice: "Misha! It's a third! The right hand begins with E! When it's a tenth, the right hand begins with the E, but an octave above! Misha!"

The scales ran up and down. Nora dozed off, started awake, then dozed off again.

I can't fall out of love with him; I have to bury him. I just have to think how to do it. So that it happens suddenly, right now, not after a slow decline from illness! Let him drown, or tumble down a mountain. Better yet, die in a car crash. No, we'll die together in a car crash. Two closed caskets side by side. His wife will come from Tbilisi, wearing black. My mother will be sobbing. Vitya will come with his crazy mother, Varvara. And Varvara will weep, too! At that point she smiled, because her mother-in-law couldn't stand the sight of her, and would most likely be thrilled on the occasion of Nora's funeral. Poor, poor things . . . Both of them mad . . . Oh, this is all horrible. I'm being ridiculous.

Half asleep, Nora imagined receiving a telegram about Tengiz's death, or tearing up his passport, or she saw herself taking his jacket out to the garbage and stuffing it into the dumpster—and she was free of him. During the second week, she began inventing a new life for herself. She had to leave the theater; that was the first thing. The second was to hit upon something completely new—not teaching drawing to children, which they had been urging on her for a long time, but something unprecedented in her life. Getting another degree of some sort: becoming a chemist, or a biologist. Or becoming an ace dressmaker. No, she didn't want to be that kind of woman. In short, for the time being, she couldn't quite find what she was looking for. But one amusing thought came to her all of a sudden, and she began to get used to it, very gingerly. This would definitively be all her own . . . Nothing like this had ever occurred to her before . . .

Three days later, Nora crawled out of her now finally deserted bed and went downstairs to say goodbye. Mziya kissed her, told her not to forget about her and to come back to visit. The aunt was a marvel. She didn't say a single word about Tengiz. Nora was grateful for this.

From the closed yard, she went out and crossed over Znamenka toward Arbat Square. Everything was nearby. Nora walked slowly, because, as she discovered, she was extremely weak. A rainy mist hung in the air. She crossed Arbat Square, then turned toward her home. At the entrance, she met a neighbor, Olga Petrakov, pushing a baby carriage, which she helped her squeeze into the elevator. The neighbor was no longer young, certainly over forty, and she had a fairly grown-up daughter, about fifteen years old—and here she had a new baby.

"Why do you look so surprised? This is my granddaughter. My Natasha had a baby. You didn't know? The whole building knows."

Oh, so that was the story. The slutty schoolgirl got knocked up. In ninth grade, was she? Curious. In ninth grade, I found a superman, too. Nikita

Tregubsky. Because I was shameless and daring. And proud. But having a baby? No, back in those days I would have had an abortion.

Nora glanced into the baby carriage at the offspring; only the nose poked out of a little pink cap.

"Cute!" Nora said approvingly. She nudged the carriage into the lift. "You go on ahead. I'll take the stairs."

"What's so cute about her? Spit and image of the father. Look at that nose! It's Armenian!" And, propping the door open with a hand, she added, "The baby's got the whole family wrapped around its little finger. That's Armenians for you."

Nora went up the stairs to the fourth floor. By the time she reached her apartment, she knew for certain that she was going to set her life to rights, and that it would be more interesting than she could ever have imagined before.

The door to the apartment had two locks, and both were locked. Her mother must have been here: Nora usually only locked the lower one. Mama and her husband, Andrei Ivanovich, rarely came to Moscow. There was a note on the kitchen table: "Nora, you got calls from Anastasia Ilyinichna, Perchikhina, and Chipa. Call me. We'll be here on Friday evening and leave again on Saturday. Hugs, Mama."

The only thing she couldn't figure out was which Friday she meant—last Friday, or the Friday before that. The days of the week, and the dates, had all run together for her.

Without even stopping in her room, she went to take a bath. She soaked for a long time, even drifted off for a bit. Tengiz kept trying to break into her semi-sleep, to let her know he was still there, but Nora chased him away. Then he sent Anton Chekhov, with his sepia sisters—and that was his mistake, because the three sisters, doleful and unhappy, pushed her toward life, with all its harshness, without sentiment, life with its problems and solutions. She hurried to get out of the water, which was cooling off quickly, and to turn on a steaming-hot shower.

I have a new project, she told herself. She sprang from the bathtub and wrapped herself in a terry cloth robe, because she had forgotten to bring in a clean towel. She suddenly felt famished.

It can't possibly be Friday. It must be Wednesday. I'm going to run down to The Gut (a nearby grocery store by the Nikitsky Gates that had a long hall lined with food counters) to get some food, and then I'll call Vitya. Good old Vitya. A joke of a husband she had not lived with for a single day.

And it would have been impossible, anyway. He was a genius—autistic and crazy. They had married right after high school. And there was no love in it—only calculation. To take revenge. But on whom, and why? Nikita Tregubsky. She had run into him five years later, in a café, the Blue Bird. He had walked up to her, swinging his shoulders nonchalantly, with a rangy, athletic gait, as though they had just parted ways yesterday, as though nothing at all had happened. My God, what an idiot! A plastic mannequin! Was this the person she had been in love with? What a fool she was! But she couldn't seem to change her ways: Tengiz also looked like a superhero! Just a different one. Damn hormones. A new project! Vitya!

She called him. Varvara Vasilievna picked up and handed the phone directly to Vitya, without bothering to talk to her. Nora's mother-in-law hated her with blunt intensity. They were both quite mad—mother and son. Just in different ways.

"Could you come over, Vitya? This evening?"

"Okay."

Maybe it wasn't such a good idea? But I married him for something, didn't I? I'll give it a shot. It is the right thing to do; maybe my baby will be a genius. And it will redeem that childhood mistake.

The rain grew stronger toward evening. Nora put on a jacket with a hood and ran to The Gut to buy frankfurters. For her husband.

More than a year had passed since Tengiz had left. Nora had changed everything in her life, turning it upside down and setting it right again. She didn't want a trace of the past to remain. She didn't want any more conflagrations, or floods, or earthquakes, because she had to live. She had to survive, and Tengiz was always going away, going away for good, with his unshaven face, his sculptural hands that resembled the hands of Michelangelo's *David*, with his overbite, his smell of cheap country tobacco, with his narrow hips and his lanky, doglike legs. Tengiz was gone; and their own magnificent smash-hit show for two would never be performed again . . .

They were not in the habit of writing letters to each other. There were just one-way phone calls from time to time—from Tengiz to Nora. This could have been because he wanted to protect his Tbilisi life from her, or because their long-term relations were put on hold, bracketed off, like something especially valuable that wouldn't mix with the quotidian flow of

Tengiz's Tbilisi life, which Nora didn't know, the life in which he had women, and family ties with some big-shot criminal who sometimes rescued him when he was in trouble . . . The only letter that Nora had received from Tengiz came a year and a half after he had left her, after his monthlong stay in Poland at the Laboratory Theatre of Jerzy Grotowski. The letter was clumsily written on what seemed to be a piece of wrapping paper, brownish and old-looking. He informed her that he had converted, changed religions, that everything from the past was shattered, and that the shards were better than the original whole had been . . . "We need to talk," he had scrawled across the bottom. But it would be two whole years before she would see him again.

Yurik was already walking, tottering around, and falling down on his little bottom.

6

Classmates

(1955–1963)

They were supposed to beat up Vitya Chebotarev. It wasn't a choice; it was an obligation. But he was lucky—they beat up Grisha Lieber instead. And they didn't mess him up too much—just enough to display their contempt for the wunderkind Jew. They were both wunderkinder, in fact, but Grisha was a half-pint Jewish kid, chubby and pink, whereas Vitya was a strapping lad who disarmed people by his obliviousness to society's dissatisfaction with him. Vitya's upper lip protruded slightly, the consequence of too many tightly packed teeth, and this gave him a good-natured expression. He was somewhat autistic—"a bit odd," as his mother, Varvara Vasilievna, described him. She was from the country, unpretentious but smart. She had worked her way up the ladder from housekeeper to administrator in the Housing Maintenance Committee.

Even before he started school, she sought advice about her little Vitya from an elderly professor, an acquaintance from her former housekeeping days, who told her that the boy was in no sense a moron, more likely even a genius, but one with peculiarities. Such children were what you might call rarities, and must be handled with care. With proper nurturing, children like this could grow up to become great scientists; otherwise, they could end up on the margins of society. Varvara received this news with delight, and she never so much as laid a hand on him, but protected him and expected great things of him. She was someone who had raised herself high above the place where she had begun in life. Working for good employers, she was able to graduate from primary school, then trade school for housing-maintenance workers, and finally to get assigned a private room for herself. Afterward, when she was already working at the HMC, she became eligible for a separate apartment in the city center—albeit on the ground floor, as they deferentially called the cellar of the building, located in close proximity to Gogol's last apartment.

Such was the career of Varvara Vasilievna; it was as though she had made the transition from plumber to academician in a single leap. Thus, she had high hopes for her son, born of a not entirely successful union. And her maternal hopes were not disappointed. Varvara stoically endured the first years of Vitya's education, when the teacher complained about his inattentiveness, his absentmindedness and inability to blend in with the other children and take part in their activities. But in the fifth grade, when simple arithmetic was replaced by algebra and geometry, Vitya blossomed. The math teacher immediately singled him out from the other students, and began sending him to the Math Olympiad, where he excelled and enjoyed his first faint glimmers of fame.

The elderly professor had been right. Vitya was inattentive to what didn't interest him, but when something engaged his mental capacities, he was quick, sharp, and hungry for knowledge. Despite his unusual memory and his innate abilities in logical thought, he was emotionally rather backward, and had not an iota of a sense of humor. There seemed to be some sort of short circuit in his head that allowed him to exist happily in the most abstract realms of mathematics, whereas any literary text, from "Little Red Riding Hood" to *King Lear*, which he read as an adolescent, filled him with indignation at the lack of logic, the contrivances, and the flouting of causal connections and motives in the behavior of both characters and authors.

His classmates, with their soccer and their paper airplanes, did not interest him; only Grisha Lieber proved to be a satisfactory interlocutor. They made a funny pair: little Grisha, who was much shorter than his classmates but far exceeded most of them in weight, rolled around the rangy, lanky Vitya like a ball, constantly trying to prove a point to him. Vitya would listen silently, nodding and scratching his prominent forehead. He received a great deal of interesting information from Grisha, whose father was a physicist and discussed such matters with his son. Grisha was by nature sociable and talkative, so they were an odd couple—a garrulous little ball and a taciturn beanpole. When the classmates had to read *Don Quixote*, they started calling Grisha Sancho Panza. And he did indeed play the same role.

Thanks to Grisha, Vitya finally even got to know some of their other class-mates, who up until then had been so unimportant to him he didn't even know many of them by name.

In the fifth grade, the boys' and girls' schools joined together, but even this momentous event went practically unnoticed by Vitya. The girls paid no attention to him, either, it must be said. The only girl he sometimes talked to was Nora, and their relations were not spontaneous, but thanks to the promptings of the literature teacher and class adviser, Vera Alexeyevna. She appointed Nora (a book lover with an innate grasp of grammar) to help Vitya bring up his grades in that subject. During their sessions, they didn't become friends, but they did at least get to know each other. And Nora helped him pull up his grades until the ninth grade. He intrigued Nora with his critical reading of any work put in front of him, which he analyzed with unwavering precision, pointing out the glaring inadequacy of any metaphor taken on its own merits, and the fundamental logical inconsistency and lack of rigor of the humanities as a whole. His grades never rose above a C in Russian language and literature, but the teachers were quick to pardon this star of the Math Olympiad for many years running.

Vitya was not popular with his classmates, and the girls dismissed him because they thought he was a smarty-pants who imagined himself to be more intelligent than everyone else. In fact, he imagined no such thing, since his imagination was restricted to very specific tasks and orders of knowledge where girls rarely ventured, so there was barely a whiff of them around him.

In the seventh grade, they were laid low by an epidemic, something akin to chicken pox: everyone fell in love. The girls quarreled and wept, the boys got into fights more often than usual, and a weak electric charge hovered in the air. Vitya himself never fought. Nor did he express any interest in girls.

A cloud of tension grew thick around Nina Knyazeva, a budding beauty, and Masha Nersesyan, who had developed early and was already in full bloom at fourteen. There were a few other pretty girls who turned the boys' heads, but not as dramatically. Nora was not one of them. She did have one admirer, however—funny, sweet Grisha. Nora ignored Grisha entirely. Though she had been independent and idiosyncratic from an early age, this time she traveled the general route.

Nikita Tregubsky was the embodiment of all the girls' notions of mas-culine perfection. He moved confidently, had a nice smile, and was affec-tionate and impudent, both at once. He had virtually no rivals. The other boys had not achieved enough manliness to meet with any kind of success. At the very sight of Nikita, half the girls in the class went into preservation-of-the-species mode. Nora was not spared this fate. She fell desperately in love with Nikita in the sixth grade, and in the eighth, she fearlessly, without shame, offered him her love in the most literal sense. Nora was taken by surprise at the wondrous world that awaited her between the sheets, and she happily explored it at every opportunity over the course of several months. Later, Nikita would stay overnight at Nora's, to the silent consternation of Amalia.

The young lovers kept their secret to themselves for a whole year. At the beginning of the ninth grade, rumors began circulating. Most likely, Nikita had boasted of his conquest to the other boys, and it had finally reached the staff room. Vera Alexeyevna, the class adviser, undertook to have a heart-to-heart pedagogical talk with Nora, with the noble purpose of nipping the brewing scandal in the bud.

Scratching her head nervously, Vera Alexeyevna, who was deeply agitated, broached the ticklish subject by referring to moral principles. Nora didn't even allow her to finish. She informed her coldly that she had no intention of discussing her personal life, that her relations with men—that's what she said, "with men" (and here Vera Alexeyevna started scratching her head with redoubled energy)—were no one's business but her own and one other person's, whose existence she was not going to broadcast. In short, mind your own business!

Vera Alexeyevna was offended and kicked up a fuss. The Party organizer of the school, Elena Azizovna, suggested convening a PTA meeting after school devoted exclusively to the crimes of ninth-grade minors. The criminals' parents were invited. Romeo made a poor performance, publicly repenting his love affair and offering a version of events whereby he was not the initiator but, rather, the victim of her machinations. Dark with fury, the father of the "victim," a hockey coach the size of a double-door refrigerator, made a testimony denouncing Amalia Alexandrovna. He seemed to be well informed about the family life of the mother of the juvenile delinquent. At that time, Amalia Alexandrovna was still not married to Andrei Ivanovich—that is, she was in a relationship with a married man, which Tregubsky *père* announced to a rapt audience. When Nora glanced at her mother, who was sitting in a corner of the classroom looking crushed, she was suddenly filled with a rage that surpassed anything she would ever again experience. How dare this old goat insult her mother! She saw a dark-crimson mist before her eyes, and suddenly she exploded. Later, she couldn't remember the content of her retort to old Tregubsky and the PTA members, but most of the words she used could not be found in a standard dictionary. Taking her mother by the hand, she left the room, slamming the door behind her. She was immediately expelled from school, without further deliberation.

The next day Nora, her eyes red and swollen from weeping, as composed and collected as a parachutist before a jump, went to school and collected her records. Then she wept for three days straight. Amalia Alexandrovna tried to comfort her, but Nora rejected any involvement of her mother in the unpleasantness that had befallen her. Poor Amalia was no less traumatized than her daughter by the public execution. Nora was offended more on her mother's behalf than her own, and resented Andrei Ivanovich with renewed vigor for putting his beloved in such a compromising position. She hated Nikita with a passion, and at the same time wanted to engage in criminal action with him again as soon as possible, which would go a long way toward mitigating the state-sponsored unpleasantness.

These events brought with them important lessons in life. First, she decided that she would never in her life have an affair with a married man, as her mother had. Second, she understood that love made a person defenseless and vulnerable, and that sex had to be kept separate from human emotions and relationships for reasons of personal safety. And, third, as she told herself: I don't want anyone to pity me. Nor will I ever pity myself.

On the day when the announcement of Nora's expulsion from school was pinned on the official notice board, and rumors about the scandalous PTA meeting were making the rounds among the upperclassmen, a fight—or, more accurately, a skirmish—broke out at the entrance to the school. Grisha Lieber stopped Tregubsky, who was running late, as usual, and uttered, with grim solemnity, these words: "You, Tregubsky, are scum."

Grisha had planned to give him an aristocratic slap in the face, but, though he swung his arm out, the theatrical gesture fell flat. Nikita forestalled the blow, and punched Grisha's soft little face with his hard fist. The duel never got off the ground. Grisha slumped down, hitting his face on the iron door handle, and, without breaking stride, Nikita rushed in through the wide-open door and up to the third floor. He lived almost next door to the school and was the only one who always arrived without a hat or coat in any kind of weather. The school nurse took the bloodied Grisha to the nearest emergency room, where they gave him stitches over his cheekbone.

He explained what had happened by saying he had tripped and fallen, knocking his cheek against the door. This scar—in a faint V-shape, like a checkmark in a box—stayed with him his entire life, a memory of his first, secret love for Nora.

A week later, Vitya learned that Nora had been expelled, from Nora herself. He had come over to her house and sat down; without saying anything about it or asking any questions, he just pulled out his literature notebook. They were studying Goncharov.

"Here's *Oblomov*," he said.

"You want me to study with you? Don't you know they kicked me out of school?"

Somehow he had managed to remain oblivious to the event, which had been hotly debated in the men's, not to mention the women's, bathrooms. At this point, Nora finally had to laugh. She told him what had happened between her and Tregubsky. Vitya stayed for about fifteen minutes. They didn't feel like discussing *Oblomov* and the Oblomov syndrome, but there wasn't anything else they could talk about. He drank a cup of tea, which he took with five spoonfuls of sugar; ate all the food that was set before him, emptying out the refrigerator completely; and headed for the door. Walking right behind him, Nora, who had cheered up considerably after this unexpected visit, invited him to drop by any time he needed to write an essay. One reason his visit was nice was that he was the only one of all her classmates who had visited her. In fact, she was not really friends with anyone in the class. There was Chipa, Marina Chipkovskaya, though they hadn't met in school, but in the art studio she had started attending that year.

Vitya visited Nora after that on a regular basis, albeit not very frequently. He would appear at her door, but for the life of her she couldn't figure out what drew him to her—certainly it wasn't for a cup of tea. He himself couldn't have explained it. Most likely, it was just out of inertia, a conditioned reflex he had developed: literature, Nora, essay . . . He visited Nora now and then in this manner until the end of the school year. In the summer, the visits stopped, which was only natural—classes were over.

During the summer, Nora breezed through the entrance exams for the Theater Arts Institute, and when the new school year began, she rode the "B" trolleybus to Sretenka Street every day to attend classes. She found everything interesting, from the trolley ride to the subjects she was studying there. Her most important new acquisition, however, was her teacher, Anastasia Ilyinichna Pustyntseva—or Tusya, as she was called—a true theater artist and set designer, teacher, and the embodiment, according to Nora's notions, of the ideal modern woman. Studying to become a set designer and theater artist was interesting, and Nora was glad that she had been kicked out of school; otherwise, she would have had to languish in the back row for two more years.

The only thing that cast a shadow over her life was her own appearance, which had never satisfied her, and now even less so. But the theater offered her a new approach to life. Nora began to experiment, searching for a new image. She used a lot of makeup, cut off almost all her hair, lost weight—inadvertently, it must be said, but she liked it. Plump cheeks made her look like a little pink doll, but with hollows under her cheekbones she felt very sharp and stylish. She began to watch her weight seriously, forbidding herself to eat sweets—a ban she held herself to for the rest of her life, having once told herself, I don't like sweet things. And it seemed she really did not. She picked up smoking—heavily, without deriving any pleasure from it whatsoever. Amalia could hardly keep from crying as she threw out the butts from the ashtray: "Nora, even drinking is better than smoking. It goes without saying that it's bad for you, but the smell is also disgusting! Chekhov said that kissing a woman who smokes is like licking an ashtray!" Nora dismissed her with a wave of the hand and said, laughing, "Mama, Chekhov and I will never have to kiss anyway."

But she really did want to kiss someone, she needed some small love conquest—or, better yet, several. She coldly examined the horizon of possibility and discovered that the most attractive young man was in the third year, from the design department. His name was Zhora Beginsky, and although his appearance was nothing like Nikita Tregubsky's, there was something in his manner that did remind her of him. No, no! Please, no! She didn't need that again. She had no intention of ever falling in love again. Not now, not ever. Especially with another superhero. Subjects of average quality, or of no quality at all, among the future stagehands, lighting designers, and sound operators were a dime a dozen. Fairly soon thereafter, Nora had won her first minor victories. They had not cost her much, and she understood perfectly well that at this period in her life she was interested only in the technical aspects of love; she practiced her new skills on every possible occasion, with every more or less suitable partner. With each new victory, her womanly self-respect increased.

Vitya became unwitting prey in this long line of victims, and as prey he was grateful. He fell into Nora's clutches somewhere in the vicinity of an essay on *And Quiet Flows the Don*. For him it was completely unexpected that there could be something in the world that afforded so much pleasure unrelated to calculus. He was prepared to lose a portion of his valuable mathematical time for the sake of these new joys, even though he was in the tenth grade, and entrance exams to the Faculty of Mathematics and Mechanical Engineering of the university were on the horizon—a challenge even for him, winner of the Math Olympiad year after year. They began to meet again, reviving their old custom but dramatically altering the content.

Vitya didn't have an ounce of playfulness in his nature. Honesty, earnestness, and conscientiousness were present in everything he undertook. The question of whether she was pretty or not ceased to worry Nora when she was around him. He simply didn't notice any of her experiments in search of beauty, style, and success. He noticed only that the way she cut her hair was different from the way other women did.

The presence in Nora's life of the solid and dependable Vitya in some sense freed her from concern with her appearance. Even the question of whether men liked her or not lost its poignancy. Both of them were busy like never before with their studies. They met at Nora's whenever there was a gap in their schedules; the time they spent together was light and carefree, and things always went without a hitch. There was nothing to talk about, but, then, that was not why they were meeting.

Toward the end of the school year, Nora began thinking about how funny it would be, after her scandalous expulsion from school, to show up at the graduation party in a white dress and a veil, as Vitya's bride. It would be very, very funny! Let the old bags chew on that, let Nikita eat his heart out, while I look on! And she proposed to Vitya, suggesting they get married for a laugh. He did not consider the idea to be particularly funny, but marriage would not pose a threat to his plans in life. Moreover, his notions about society in general had their genesis in his mother's perpetual dissatisfaction and suspicion of others, and through her he had formed a conviction that intimacy outside marriage was virtually criminal, or, at the least, very wrong.

They went to the municipal marriage registry, not telling anyone, and submitted their application for an appointment to tie the knot.

Their application was accepted, though not automatically. Nora, hanging her head solemnly and folding her hands over her belly, whispered to the woman official that she had reason to want to hurry things up. The woman smiled—it wasn't the first time she had seen this in her line of work. She took the bait, and, full of tenderhearted patience, explained the process to them. Soon, through Nora's efforts, all the bureaucratic obstacles facing the underage newlyweds were removed—with the active participation of one of the senior students from the arts college, who earned his living by preparing falsified certificates, IDs, transport passes, and other fairly simple documents—and at the beginning of June, both their internal passports were adorned with the necessary stamps attesting to their union.

Nora later ditched the idea of the white dress, realizing that there would be a lot of girls dressed in bridelike white at the graduation festivities. Instead, she conceived of something that was far more theatrical and extravagant.

Nora turned up at the school graduation with Vitya in tow and, as they entered, announced to the whole school that they had gotten married. She was dressed in a devil-may-care manner—that is, with extreme impropriety. In the midst of the girls in their white finery, she looked like a crow in the snow: she wore ragged black shorts and a black, completely transparent blouse, on top of which she wore a white satin whalebone corset that she had borrowed from the Stanislavsky Theater costume department. Her getup had the desired effect. The teachers, who keenly remembered the scandal from two years before, startled to life: Should we ask her to leave? Or let her kick up her heels at the event that she had deprived herself of the right to celebrate? Nora's reputation as a libertine and hooligan was solidified.

This dramatic performance—the wedding and Nora's appearance at the graduation—made a very strong impression on Grisha. He never even suspected that the quiet Vitya had been so successful in the romance department. Grisha's crush on Nora had long since evaporated, leaving only the scar on his cheek. What impressed him far more was the way Vitya had kept secret from him, his only friend, his relationship with Nora. Not to mention the marriage.

Vitya, whom the teachers viewed as Nora's next victim, didn't even notice Nora's outrageous attire. He was only waiting for one thing—for the official ceremony to end, so he and Nora could go home to her house, close the door, and engage in that fascinating activity that he sometimes found even more interesting than solving mathematical equations.

Nora never even glanced at Nikita Tregubsky. He was so dumbfounded that he couldn't bring himself to approach her. He hovered at a respectable distance from her and blinked his ramlike eyes, adorned with thick eyelashes. The whole marriage charade was for Nikita's benefit, and yet Nora derived no pleasure from it.

Both Nora and Vitya quickly forgot about this one-off graduation performance. The parents of the young couple didn't find out about the strange marriage—which was neither exactly fictitious nor conventional—until two years later. Varvara Vasilievna was beside herself when she discovered this prank, and fumed in indignation for a long time afterward. Then that passed, replaced by a real hatred of the daughter-in-law, whom she had never yet laid eyes on. When they finally met, by chance, she didn't like Nora one bit, and, it seemed, never would. Amalia, when she found out about her daughter's secret marriage, threw up her hands and said, "Well, Nora, it's impossible to know what you've got up your sleeve."

Vitya called Nora now and then. They did see each other, but she forgot all about him between one visit and the next. A few times, she brought out her marriage license to show one of her girlfriends, more for a good laugh than anything else; and her marital status freed her from the anxiety of unmarried girls that reigned all around her.

In her third year of marriage, Nora embarked on a feverish romance that lasted for a full two weeks. This was her first affair with someone other than a fellow student her own age. He was a grown-up man, a theater director, who had dropped by Tusya's studio to wish her a (belated) happy birthday. On the first evening, the director tried feebly to fend her off, but Nora all but turned somersaults around him. Used to women's advances, he gave in through sheer laziness. He had always been attracted to fleshy women with large breasts, hair, and legs. Young girls with delicate, slender legs, transparent ears on an almost bald head, and eager lips frightened him. Recently, many girls of that description had appeared in actors' circles, and up until then he had managed to steer clear of them. But on this particular evening, he was tired and not as vigilant as usual. He'd had a bit to drink, felt soft and mellow from conversation, and surrendered without resistance. A Moscow romance in no way fit into his plans, but the girl wouldn't let him out of her clutches; for two weeks, they were inseparable. Then he left, taking with him a heightened respect for himself and gratitude toward Nora, who, with her fierce love, had awakened in him hidden powers that he intended to use, of course, for something else altogether.

Nora remained in Moscow, bereft, trying to stop up a hole that felt bigger than she was herself. It turned out that the affair with Nikita Tregubsky, which she thought had left her older and wiser, had not taught her anything. She had fallen in love again. By now, she already understood that you have to fight fire with fire—she mobilized all her admirers, and tumbled around with them in various positions and situations—but the memory of this infernal Tengiz would not fade. At that time, she still hoped that she could get along without him. Neither he nor she could have supposed that what they had begun would last a lifetime.

That year, Nora hardly saw Vitya at all. Just by accident, near the metro station, they ran into each other, and their relationship flared up again for a while. It was during this time that Andrei Ivanovich finally managed to get divorced, Amalia resigned from the design bureau where she had worked as a draftsman for twenty years, and they went to live in the country, at Prioksko-Terrasny Nature Reserve. At first, they would travel back and forth to Moscow, but then they renovated a house, adding almost all the modern conveniences, took in pets, and came back to the city less and less often.

Vitya again started coming over to see Nora now and then, and sometimes stayed the night. Varvara Vasilievna's hatred for her invisible daughter-in-law grew more and more intense, but Nora was oblivious to it, a cause for more annoyance to Varvara Vasilievna: What kind of an attitude was this? She was just waiting for the chance to give Nora a piece of her mind, and to quarrel to her heart's content; but the chance eluded her. It eluded her for a long, long time. In fact, Nora never did give her mother-in-law the opportunity to air her grievances on the subject once and for all for the rest of her life.

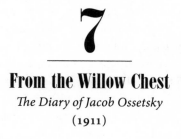

7

From the Willow Chest

The Diary of Jacob Ossetsky

(1911)

JANUARY 1

I woke up this morning fairly early, suddenly recalling with vivid clarity a memory from early childhood. Thirteen years ago. I'm not yet seven. Mama helps me with my lessons. Every day I write two pages to practice my penmanship. I sit in the dining room of our tiny little house (our "own home") in Rtishchevo. It's evening already. I have copied out a whole story, and there are still two pages left. I write on them: "Jacob Ossetsky, January 1, 1898." Mama says that there are two hours to go, it's still December. I answer, "But I'm already going to bed."

And in the morning a manservant came over, and another man, a peasant who was a stranger to me. And they wished us a Happy New Year, and showered us with rye and barley. The newspaper *Life and Art* was extra fat, with pictures in it. Then Genrikh, my older brother, came—what joy! I felt such love for him! He is still the most interesting and well-read person in the family. His mother died in childbirth, and he was taken in by his aunt; she also had an infant, so she nursed both of them at once. And he stayed in that family to live. When Father remarried, to Mama, they wanted to take him back, but his aunt wouldn't agree to it. I missed him terribly when I was little. I still do when I don't see him for a long time. It's been a whole year and a half since he went to Germany to study in Göttingen. His adopted family is wealthy, but Father doesn't have the means to send me to Germany. I'm sure that in time I will earn enough myself to pay for my studies and go to Germany, like Genrikh. To Göttingen or Marburg.

It means so much to have an elder half-brother, even though I rarely see him. The little ones are another matter altogether. They are wonderful, but I love Eva most of all, and feel the most for her. And I mean the most to her. It will be this way our whole life—an eternal bond. She's no longer a child, but a young lady. She has developed a womanly figure, real breasts, and she has started feeling embarrassed about it. She's a charming creature. It's strange to me to think that some man will love her, that the carnal world will claim its due, and there will be children. For some reason, it's unpleasant for me to think about. In three weeks I'll be twenty, and I still can't figure it out—am I already grown up, or still an adolescent? When I study music or mathematics, or read a serious book, I always think I'm completely grown up; but as soon as I'm around my younger siblings, I seem to shed five or six years. Yesterday we were horsing around and playing, and I was galloping around like a madman, until Rayechka fell and bumped her nose. Is it possible that I'll have kids, a lot of them? First, though, a wife. It's hard for me to envision her. I think I'll recognize her, though. But it's unlikely to happen anytime soon.

JANUARY 10

Yesterday Yura told me that Rachmaninoff was coming to Kiev. Two concerts! January 21 and 27. The main thing now is to get hold of tickets. They haven't gone on sale yet, but I'll run over to see Radetsky today and ask him to ask his aunt, who has been secretary of the Kiev Musical Society for many years, to get a ticket for me. I'll go down on my knees and beg—only I don't know whom to kneel before, Radetsky or his aunt!

JANUARY 22

Yesterday I didn't have the strength to write. I don't know about today, either. But I always feel that if I don't write down everything that happens to me, from the first to the last, it will all disappear. I have never experienced such a storm of emotion, and the main thing is that I feel I never really lived before yesterday—up until now, it was all practice, just études of some sort. Scales, nothing but scales!

First—Rachmaninoff. In the first half of the concert he conducted the orchestra. The Second Symphony. I had never heard it before. Modern genius. But I will have to listen to it a lot; there is much in it that is new for me. He didn't wear a tuxedo, as is customary, but a frock coat. His hair is cropped short, and he looks more like an aviator or a scientist, a chemist, than an artist. And he looks so powerful that from the first moment you lay eyes on him you know he's a colossus, a giant! For the entire first half of the concert, I had no idea where I was—in paradise? I could have been anywhere, except on earth. Still, it was not a divine realm, but a human one— an exalted human realm. The melodic principle is very strong in it. It takes another direction altogether from Scriabin's, and it is more in keeping with my nature. I even had the feeling that all the organs inside me, each individually—heart, lungs, liver—were rejoicing at these sounds. My ticket, moreover, was for a seat in the orchestra, not for a cheap upper-balcony seat. Father gave me ten rubles for my birthday. Eva probably told him that I was longing to be able to attend this concert. I would have been happy even to stand on the stairs, but I was in the orchestra. And this had important consequences. At the end of the first half of the concert, the audience gave a standing ovation, for ten minutes. I have never seen such a successful performance in my life. During the intermission, I went out to the lobby. Everyone was enthralled; the atmosphere was electric, and rapturous exclamations filled the air. Then I saw her. Standing by a column was a slender girl, pale, her delicate neck rising from a large white collar, like a white stem growing from it. I saw her from the side, and recognized her immediately. It was *her*! The very same girl! With the blue tie under the white collar. I hardly saw her face—I simply rushed up to her and said: "What luck! I knew I was sure to meet you again! And at a concert like this, a concert like this!" She looked at me calmly and said, surprised, "I beg your pardon, there must be some mistake. We aren't acquainted." "No, no, of course we're not! But I saw you at a performance of *Khovanshchina*. You were with two students. Very unpleasant ones!" That just burst out of me, and I was horrified that it had slipped off my tongue so easily. And she looked at me with enormous surprise, then laughed such a wonderful, girlish laugh, like Eva.

"What didn't you like about those young men? One of them was my brother, and the other his close friend! You have a funny way of beginning an acquaintance!"

Still smiling, she stepped to the side a bit, and I understood she was not there by herself, but in the company of a formidable woman, no longer young, wearing a queer-looking net over her gray hair—by all appearances, a schoolmistress.

I was terribly afraid that everything would fall through, that she would leave and I would never see her again. I clutched at her sleeve like a madman and held her back. She was not in the least alarmed, just brushed away my hand and said she had to go back up to the top balcony, and she hoped I would get even more pleasure out of the second part of the concert.

It's over, it's all over—now she will go away, forever, and that will be the end of it! "I beg you, I beg you, don't go upstairs to the balcony. My father gave me a ticket in the orchestra seats, for my birthday, you see . . . I beg you, change seats with me; it's the fifth row, in the middle, seat number eleven."

She looked at me with great sympathy and began nodding her head: "Please, don't worry yourself, I'll gladly take your seat—especially since not only can I not see anything from mine, but the sound is also bad there. I am very grateful to you for your kindness."

She waved to her companion and said, in French, "Madame Leroux, I've just run into an acquaintance who offered to exchange his seat for mine. It's in the orchestra."

The girl clutched the ticket a bit uncertainly, as though offering it to the Frenchwoman, but the woman became very animated, pushed her hand away, raised her eyebrows, and said, laughingly, something along the lines of "Run along, Marie . . . And keep your eye out for another acquaintance of yours in the orchestra."

And we exchanged our tickets, and I led her to my place and seated her, and she nodded to me gratefully, but without constraint. She was no doubt a girl of exceptionally good upbringing—that kind of simplicity of behavior is only common among well-bred people.

By the time I rushed up to the balcony, Rachmaninoff was already seating himself behind the piano. He played the first chord—and I was lost! I have already managed to get hold of the musical score from Filimonov, a clarinet player. I looked it over, and will study it for a long time to come, but I am left with the feeling that the first part is simply unattainable. It is the principle of conversation in a higher and middle register, and the lower F in the contra-octave, the very beginning, and the mighty theme, and the introduction of the strings and clarinets . . . The concert was enormous in its content and meaning; there was not a single empty phrase, nothing merely decorative, only the essence itself! The audience was in a state of nervous rapture, but Rachmaninoff himself was calm and unflappable, a giant among men, a giant! Everyone applauded rhythmically, then got out of phase, then picked up the rhythm again!

Oh my God! I forgot, I completely forgot about the marvelous girl. When the audience had grown tired of the ovations and started to disperse, I remembered about the girl and realized that I had lost her. She had already left, never to be found again. I practically flew down the stairs, and, truly, the crowd was already departing. I rushed to the coat check for my things, and although the magic of the music had still not left me and I was still happy, I was sad at the same time, because I understood that I had lost what I would never again find. I grabbed my coat and, pulling it on as I walked, made a beeline for the exit, so that I might, if I was lucky, run into her on the steps or at the trolley stop . . . Then I stepped on the hem of a coat belonging to some lady who was sitting on the velvet bench, putting on her boots. I apologized—and it turned out to be her! Her face looked both solemn and troubled by the music, and also radiant. She had, of course, forgotten all about me, and didn't even recognize me at first.

I walked her home—she lives on Mariinsko-Blagoveshchenskaya Street, a five-minute walk from our house. Her name is Maria. Maria. Maria.

8

The Garden of Magnitudes

(1958–1974)

When they were still in the eighth grade, Grisha Lieber and Vitya Chebotarev went to the Department of Mathematics and Mechanical Engineering at the university to enroll in study clubs. About twenty boys and two (chance) girls began to live there in a unique, highly rarefied atmosphere. But even in this hothouse of young talent, Vitya stood apart. That year, he took first place among all the Moscow school-age children, and, what was most surprising, he also came in first among the ninth-graders. One year later, he won a prize at the first Math Olympiad of schoolchildren in Bucharest—true, only second place. This was more of a surprise than a disappointment to him. By that time, he was already used to being the best and the brightest in his age group. But he was not conceited, because he was a natural-born scientist, and there was no greater reward for him than solving a task or problem.

In the autumn of the ninth grade, Grisha took a book over to Vitya, who was home sick with tonsillitis. The book was Hausdorff's *Set Theory*, a prewar edition, somewhat battered and dog-eared, which had passed through many hands and minds before coming to Vitya and changing his life in the most profound manner.

In the evening, after he had taken his prescribed pills and gargled before going to sleep, Vitya sprawled out on the divan, picking up the little book Grisha had brought over with instructions to guard it carefully—it was valuable. He had never seen anything like it! His sleep, and his tonsillitis, and his very sense of reality deserted him. He was hooked. With every page he read, he felt he changed, even physically. For several years, he had been trying to solve the most disparate and intricate problems, thinking he was doing mathematics; but it wasn't until this night that he felt he had set foot in the realm of true mathematics. It was a whole new world of wondrous and varied sets. In the morning, he looked out the window and noticed that the world had not changed a bit, and it was incomprehensible to him how buildings could even remain standing, and not collapse in a heap, when there were such wonders in the world as he had discovered in this little book.

Vitya had never read the well-known lines of Mandelstam, but he experienced the same emotion the poet describes in his obscure, redolent, pulsing words:

> And I step out of the space of the world
> and into the garden of magnitudes
> and I rend the illusory permanence
> and self-evidence of reasons.
> And your very own primer, eternity,
> I read all alone, in solitude—
> Wild, leafless book of medicinal lore—
> problem set of enormous roots.

In short, he had ended up in that garden. It was impossible to imagine anything more wonderful.

By the tenth grade, Vitya had become a real mathematician. His massive, somewhat convex forehead—like that of a child with a mild case of hydrocephalus—contained the brain in which the expanding universe moved, breathed, bubbled, and frothed. All other natural functions of the organism—eating, drinking, sleeping, etc.—were mere obstacles to the constant working of the rest of his highly functioning mind. Very little interested him apart from mathematics, and even his friendship with Grisha waned a bit. Grisha no longer satisfied him as an interlocutor. To be more precise, the pleasure he got from the music of mathematics so exceeded all other joys, including that of spending time with other people, that he began avoiding everything "extraneous." Even physiological growth into manhood was an inconvenience or a malady to him, something like tonsillitis, which prevented him from studying. During that period in adolescence when young people are in the throes of hormonal revolution, Vitya found a simple method for releasing the tension that gripped him: overtaxing his mind.

Nora, who inhabited the outskirts of the world of Vitya's interests, took the initiative at this timely moment to change her status from tutor in literature to friend and companion in sexual activity, and readily accepted his newfound manly maturity. She was a premature, illegitimate offspring of the sexual revolution, of which she knew nothing—if you didn't take into account Marusya's bold but old-fashioned pronouncements about the full emancipation of women in the socialist world, spoken in a whisper for fear the neighbors would overhear her.

Vitya was grateful to Nora for liberating him from the yoke of his hormones, a relief he experienced immediately after each one of their short, stormy meetings. Business meetings . . . The marriage prank they staged for the graduation ceremony had no effect on their relationship. Sometimes Vitya went to see Nora, with a friendly but purposeful aim; sometimes Nora would call him. They would come together, then part ways, without discussing when they would see each other again. Sometime or other . . . Vitya devoted all his energy to another romance—mathematics. Nora did her artwork with supreme pleasure, attended lectures on the history of theater, and read books.

Vitya was admitted to the Department of Mathematics and Mechanical Engineering, and from the first year of his studies dived headlong into set theory, a field of mathematics that had arisen relatively recently, in the mid-nineteenth century—a field that seemed to appeal greatly to madmen and suicides. It also beckoned to Vitya. Human fates, characters, and biographies did not yet stand behind the names of theories. It wasn't until a few years later, when the Russian translation appeared of a multivolume work on mathematics and its history written by a group of mathematicians who had adopted the pseudonym Nicolas Bourbaki, that Vitya found out about the founder of the entire field. Georg Cantor, born in St. Petersburg, was the originator of the notion of actual infinity. A philosopher, musician, and Shakespeare scholar, he lost his way in the world of his own creation and died in a psychiatric clinic in Halle. He left behind (in addition to all of the above) what is known as Cantor's Problem or the Continuum Hypothesis, which, as the next generation of mathematicians would claim, was possible neither to prove nor disprove. Vitya learned about the death of Felix Hausdorff, who took his own life in 1942 before he could be sent to a concentration camp, about Hausdorff spaces and the Hausdorff Paradox, which were his legacy to his descendants, and much else besides, concerning not so much mathematics as mathematicians.

Vitya spent the entire fourth year writing about computational functions, which thrilled his department chair, who was also quite an eccentric fellow.

The university administration, forced to consider the outstanding achievements of the department head, a world-renowned scholar, forgave his eccentricity; but Vitya, his student, did not get off so lightly. In those days, the Communist Party representative called the shots, and the dean's office was beholden to him. The students were kept on a tight leash—mandatory Komsomol meetings, political briefings, "volunteer" social work. From time to time, Vitya was taken to task for disregarding the laws of existence. Once, he was barred from taking an exam for skipping PE classes. Another time, he was nearly expelled from the university for what became known as the "potato-carrot incident."

Every September, all the students were sent "potato-picking" on communal farms. Those who were best suited to the conditions of Soviet life managed to procure medical exemptions beforehand. As secretary of the Housing Management Committee, Varvara Vasilievna had connections all over the district, and getting hold of the desired certificate would have been a breeze for her; but Vitya hadn't even thought to ask for one, and now he had to fulfill his Komsomol obligations.

The students worked with great enthusiasm this time, since Dennikov, the Komsomol organizer in their class, promised that they would be released as soon as they dug up all the potatoes from the immense field. Inspired by this promise, the young people worked from sunrise to sunset, took in the entire harvest in two weeks, and were glad that they had earned fifteen extra days of free time. Toward the end of the harvest, however, Dennikov disappeared. He had been recalled on important Komsomol business, and the Party comrade who replaced him announced that now they would pick carrots. The rains started the same day.

The students howled and went into the carrot fields. Not all of them, however—some of them refused on principle, and left for home. Vitya also left—not out of principle, but because of illness. He had a terrible cold and a fever, so he took to his bed and gave himself over to mathematical dreams. He experienced what in later years he would call "intuitive visualization." He even attempted to describe this experience of the world of sets as forests or lacework of profoundly beautiful ties and nodes, moving in space, and having no connection whatsoever with crude reality, where the teakettle boiled, and sometimes all the water boiled off; where the indestructible cockroaches persecuted by Varvara Vasilievna roamed the kitchen; where the exhaust fumes from Nikitsky Boulevard came in through the window and filled up his ground-floor basement room. The attempt failed.

Misty visions the mind couldn't comprehend alternated with a semiconscious state in which the shadow of Nora was present. She offered him amazing objects on a large flat plate made of bright metal, and these objects were algorithms, and they were alive—they stirred slightly and interacted with one another. Vitya felt that there was some exquisite idea he had to write down, but something was missing, something was always missing. A tall man was walking down a long corridor with a shining hole at the end and carrying the same dish that Vitya had seen in Nora's hands, and on the dish were the same creatures—which were the theory of functions and functional analysis. The man's name was Andrei Nikolayevich, and Vitya desperately needed to have this man notice him, but because of some unspoken law he didn't dare call out to him, so Vitya had to wait until the man noticed him first. Then the scenery changed, and the tall man went away; the dish with the algorithms ended up in Vitya's hands, only they were all dead and didn't stir any longer, and horror engulfed him.

He was sick for a long time, and there were complications. Just at the time he returned to the university, there was a meeting at which the students who had abandoned the potatoes, or, rather, the carrots, were expelled from the Komsomol. Their fate was predetermined: after expulsion from the Komsomol, expulsion from the university followed automatically. Vitya Chebotarev's case was considered separately. He had a medical certificate attesting to his illness, but it was dated two days after the exodus from the carrot fields.

Logically, he was guilty and did not deserve pardon; but from a humane perspective, he really had been ill. Moreover, there were other factors of a purely medical nature that had bearing on the matter: the two days prior to the issuing of the certificate could have been the incubation period of the illness, when the symptoms had not yet manifested but the infection was already hard at work trying to undermine the host organism.

In short, taking into account the above-mentioned circumstances, they gave Vitya a break in the form of a reprimand, though all the other offenders were kicked out of the Komsomol.

While he was sitting in the Komsomol meeting, he made an effort to remember why he had ever joined. This detail had completely vanished from his memory. Then he remembered—his mother had insisted. Yes, Varvara Vasilievna considered it necessary. She herself was a Party member, and knew there were certain matters in which you had to be like everyone else, and even a bit better—so as not to violate the laws of life. Vitya, who had never objected to his mother's trivial demands, had submitted his application for acceptance to the Komsomol in the eighth grade with the same insouciance with which he applied for a marriage certificate two years later.

In matters that did not interest him, Vitya never made a show of principle. This time, however, he suddenly sensed the injustice of it all: they had been deceived. They were promised that if they dug up all the potatoes, they would be allowed to leave, but they were prevented from leaving. So in what way were they to blame? For believing what they were told? This was fraud!

"What do you think you're doing, you idiot? Stuff it!" Slava Berezhnoi, a friend and fellow student, whispered. "You won't help us, you'll only make things worse for yourself."

And that's just what happened: Vitya was expelled, too. Shocked and shaken to the core, he went home and lay down on the divan. And refused to speak. Varvara Vasilievna wasn't able to ferret out the facts from him, but she put two and two together and decided that Nora, her mythical daughter-in-law, was the culprit in Vitya's depression. By this time, she and Nora had already met, and Varvara Vasilievna managed to get hold of her telephone number, which wasn't all that difficult for someone who worked in the Housing Management Committee. She called Nora, but wasn't able to get a straight answer from her. She believed Nora was beating around the bush.

A week later, Slava Berezhnoi came to visit him and explained everything to Varvara Vasilievna. But Vitya refused to discuss anything with Slava, either, and was taciturn the whole evening. Nevertheless, Varvara Vasilievna, now that she understood everything, went to the university and straight to the Party committee, where she spoke with the department representative heart to heart, communist to communist. He understood the situation on a human level: it's hard for a single woman, a soldier's widow, to raise a son by herself . . . It must be said that Varvara Vasilievna embellished the truth somewhat, elevating the rather unseemly circumstances. She wasn't exactly a soldier's widow, and not really a widow at all, but she did say things that were perfectly true: Vitya had fallen into a depression, and Varvara Vasilievna had managed to pull him out of it with good medication, an effort that took her three whole months. Vitya was reinstated in the Komsomol, and they didn't expel him from the university. The head of his department also weighed in on the matter: though frightened, the old crank didn't want to lose an outstanding student. "The future of Soviet mathematics"—those were his very words.

Though Vitya remained enrolled at the university, he was granted a leave of absence; he had been traumatized by the whole affair. He had discovered that life consisted of more than a roll with salami for breakfast, mathematics, and the episodic Nora. These heretofore unknown difficulties were something he had wanted neither to notice nor to know about. He had developed no immunity to hardships like this, a fact that would cause him no end of suffering later in life.

Unlike her son, Varvara Vasilievna was adept at handling the everyday contingencies of life, and it was not for nothing that she worked for the Housing Management Committee. She acquired a valuable certificate from the Neuropsychiatry Clinic attesting that Vitya Chebotarev was subject to fits of depressive psychosis, though he was otherwise absolutely healthy. And, as later life would prove, she had not done this in vain.

Everything fell into place. Vitya successfully defended his honors thesis and was admitted into the graduate program. Three years later, he was ready to defend his doctoral dissertation on an absolutely new subject: "Computable Operations on Sets." It is impossible for a nonmathematical mind to grasp, and even for some mathematical minds, but at the preliminary defense, Professor N, a brilliant proponent of the newest branch of "constructive mathematics"—not yet widely accepted, but very highly regarded in the Department of Mathematical Logic—advanced sharply critical views, reproaching the defendant for failing to follow the principles of this very constructive mathematics. Vitya did not accept his premises, and calmly held forth, insisting that the most constructive objects, including his beloved algorithms, could be viewed within the framework of classical logic and mathematics, a framework that was accepted in all the other departments. This unleashed a dispute for which Vitya's dissertation was only a pretext, because underlying the scholarly issues was a discord in personal relationships that Vitya was not privy to. Vitya listened to the noisy quarrel and couldn't make heads or tails of what either his defenders or his opponents were arguing for or against. When he tried to interject something, he couldn't get a word in edgewise—so he quietly stood up and left the auditorium.

The argument dragged on for a long time after he left; the preliminary defense was aborted. Vitya followed the well-worn path to the divan, where he lay for another three months.

Varvara Vasilievna also followed the beaten path—to the Neuropsychiatry Clinic, where medication was prescribed for her son, after which he gradually recovered.

Meanwhile, the year 1968 had come and gone. Vitya was not aware of a single event rocking the socialist world. When his buddy Slava Berezhnoi, who dropped in from time to time to talk about important things, discovered the absolute political infantilism of his friend, he said, "You are simply another Luzin."

Vitya's feathers were somewhat ruffled, since he held Luzin in very high esteem as a mathematician.

"What do you mean by that, Slava? What does Luzin have to do with anything?"

Slava related an anecdote that Professor Melnikov had told during a lecture. After the war, the eminent Luzin took part in a seminar, at which he said, "In 1917, the greatest event of my life took place. I began to study trigonometric series."

"And? What did he say next?" Vitya said, his curiosity piqued. (He also had a great deal of respect for Melnikov.)

Slava was astonished by his naïveté. "Nothing. Everyone associated the year 1917 with another event!"

"Which one?" said Vitya.

Slava waved his hand, exasperated. "Vitya, 1917 was the year of the October Revolution!"

"Oh . . . Oh, I see."

Vitya's dissertation adviser, who was also the head of the department, paid him a visit at home two weeks after the preliminary defense fell through. By this time, Vitya was already coping with his new trauma, and had started thinking about the future again. The two specific criticisms made by his opponent that had ultimately prevented the defense from passing, which concerned Lemma 2.2 and Theorem 6.4, contained a kernel of thought that Vitya began mulling over deeply. He himself had already discerned a few defects, or, rather, inconsistencies, in his dissertation. This disturbed him, and he plunged into the debris of variable and branching sets, which reached far beyond the boundaries of the poor three-dimensional world.

The head of the department spent two hours in the semi-basement apartment by the Nikitsky Gates, and left, saddened that his student had abandoned the actual (according to his notions) field of mathematics and leapt into a realm where those damaged by the burden of highly developed intellectual capacities grazed. These were the professional risks of being a mathematician, and the professor had already witnessed two such breakdowns in his life. Regrettable. A very capable young man, perhaps even with a dash of genius, Vitya had completed all his coursework but now refused to defend his dissertation. No job, of course. No means of subsistence. What could the professor do for him? No, there was no way he could help him.

But in this case the professor was at least partly mistaken. For six months, Vitya gnawed at the lock and bars of the theorem, and managed to wriggle out of the seemingly hopeless situation in an unexpected, almost miraculous way. He sat down and wrote a paper. Then he called Nora. She received him, somewhat bewildered but quite glad. He spent three days with her, and a glimmer of tenderness even appeared in their relations.

As he was leaving, he asked Nora, "Maybe we ought to get married for real? Things are going so well."

"But where are they going? We're already married," Nora said, laughing. "Live together, you mean? At your place?"

"Well, no," Vitya said, imagining life with Nora and Varvara under the same roof. "Perhaps if we live at your place?"

"Here? I'm sorry, that's not going to work."

Nora was surrounded by people of all stripes and colors—a most varied assortment of artists, actors, people with one foot in the theater or none at all, gifted, fascinating people who adored being on display. Not one of them was truly unique, or free of at least a touch of vulgarity and superficiality. They all aspired to be geniuses; but geniuses they were not. Vitya came closest of all of them to being a genius. Nora had already guessed this when they were still in school, and required no evidence or proof of the fact. But she couldn't very well keep him in the house!

Vitya had a few mathematician friends who knew his worth—his trusty friend Grisha Lieber, and Slava Berezhnoi. Who needs lots of friends, anyway? Vitya was not fine-tuned emotionally, and was incapable of conversation on subjects of general interest, so he was condemned to a life of strictly mathematical friendship.

It was Slava Berezhnoi—who had been expelled from the university over the "carrot affair," afterward graduating from evening courses at the Moscow Higher Technical University and taking up computer programming in the early days of the field—who found a position for Vitya in the computing center. The work suited Vitya down to the ground. From the theory of algorithms to programming was just a short leap. Mathematics had never promised to be of any practical use to Vitya; it was a captivating mental game. On the other hand, algorithms written in an artificial, simple, and logical language facilitated the solution to the most various problems, problems that were actually not connected to mathematics at all.

The directors of the center valued him, and Slava took more pride in Vitya's achievements than in his own. For the first time in his life, Vitya received a salary, which he spent on books about mathematics and on expensive sweets. He had more than just a sweet tooth—he was addicted to glucose. Couldn't live without it.

His work left him some spare time. He moved away from the strictly defined tasks of programming, solved several problems that he, in part, created, and even wrote two papers for a scholarly journal. One of them, however, the one Vitya considered to be the more successful, was returned to him with a negative review, very rude in tone. This offended him, and he took back both articles. Faced with this unfair criticism, Vitya, after a moment's consideration, sent the papers off to an American mathematical journal. He only found out they had published them a year later.

At the same time, thanks to Vitya's blunt honesty, he became embroiled in a conflict with the director of the center, Bogdanov. By the standards of the day, Bogdanov was a decent man, but a careerist. Not long before, he had received a secret award from the government—part of the work of the computing center was classified, involving sensitive military matters—for a new program that was intended to put the West at a disadvantage, with the aim of not merely catching up to it but outstripping it altogether.

Bogdanov was the nominal head of the project, but he took no part in developing or implementing it. He could not have done so even if he wished to, because he understood almost nothing about computer programming. A Party man, not a scientist, he compensated for his inadequacies by insisting on adding his name to the collection of authors.

A group of five people were involved in the project, including Vitya as the senior member, and, as the junior member, Amayak Sargsyan, who was a student intern from the Moscow Institute of Physics and Technology. He had a fine mind, it must be said.

There was a great deal Vitya did not know about the administrative organization of the computing center. The computer itself took up an entire building. It was filled with punch cards and young women, who were in charge of delivering them from point to point, so computations, among other things, involved their rushing energetically between floors to the rhythmic clip of their high heels. Vitya did not even suspect the existence of another, invisible level, that of relations between people. In short, at a certain moment, when the program was ready to be sent to the higher-ups for final approval, Vitya noticed that the name of Bogdanov, who had made no contribution to developing the program, headed the list of authors, while the name of the highly competent student, who had helped Vitya a great deal, especially in debugging the program, was missing altogether.

Vitya went to see Bogdanov during his office hours. Perhaps if he had begun the conversation more diplomatically the matter would have had a different outcome. But Vitya began by saying that it was unjust for Bogdanov to put his own name first on the list of authors, since he didn't have a clue as to the merits and faults of the program, whereas the name of Sargsyan, who had taken part in the project and made a genuine contribution, for some unknown reason was absent. Bogdanov answered dryly that he would look into it.

After this meeting, Vitya could no longer gain admittance to Bogdanov's office. He showed up at the weekly office hours time after time, until the secretary whispered to him that he should just give up—it was pointless. Vitya then forced his way into the office and caused a bona-fide scandal. He even shouted something about the interests of the state, which the director wasn't taking into account. Poor Amayak Sargsyan was immediately fired from the computing center. He was not permitted to defend his honors thesis, and, being an exceptionally thorough and conscientious person, he wasn't able to write a new one in time. Vitya's hunger for justice resulted in a great deal of misfortune for Amayak, but it strengthened his faith in humanity.

A month and a half later, Vitya himself lost his job. He felt both indignant and dejected—not so much because his name was also removed from the list of authors as because he did not understand the first thing about this whole predatory and cruel operation.

Vitya lay down on the divan again without a word. He did not intend to search for a new job, and he refused to answer his mother's questions. Varvara Vasilievna, who still continued to hope that her son was a genius, began to doubt the wisdom of that elderly psychiatry professor who, shortly before his death, had predicted for Vitya a unique and outstanding role in life. Where was it, then? Where was it?

Vitya himself was completely oblivious to the idea of any unique mental endowments or gifts he might have had. After he was dismissed from the computing center, he continued, through inertia, to think up new programs. When he had been lying in bed for a long time, he realized that his initial program could be improved. He began elaborating something that he could no longer have presented to anyone. Such was the program that his own mind was running: his brain could not live without intellectual activity, just as an ordinary person cannot live without food. He would have been glad to do something else, to live in some other way, but he knew not how. He sank deeper and deeper into a sleepless depression, until Varvara Vasilievna realized it was time to call in the doctors. This was the same trap that had snared him before his defense of the ill-starred dissertation.

It was cold and rainy, an autumnal spring. Tengiz had gone away forever. Again. Nora intended to start a new life. She called Vitya and invited him over. He came. While he was eating frankfurters he told Nora about what a bastard his boss had turned out to be. He explained to her how a good computer program differed from a bad one. Nora listened to him with half an ear, then made a beeline for the bedroom.

Vitya fulfilled the task entrusted to him seriously and honestly. And a new life began: for Nora, a pregnancy; and for Vitya, ever deeper depression.

Yurik was born early in the year 1975.

Admirers

(1975–1976)

A ndrei Ivanovich had been ill with pneumonia for the whole autumn and into the winter, and Amalia Alexandrovna spent that time nursing him back to health. Thus, it turned out that the first family member to visit the newborn was Genrikh. He came over with his wife, the kindly, talkative Irina. They came bearing presents and provisions. Irina's name did not suit her in the least. In Nora's estimation, an "Irina" should be fragile, slender, and slightly angular. This woman was a sort of gentle, unbridled bear, with a somewhat bulbous nose and a soft pouch instead of a chin. She could have been a Domna, or a Xavroniya—or so thought Nora.

This time, the presents were all the very things she needed: a miniature swing set, and a squishy, oversized teddy bear that resembled Irina just a bit. Yurik, in fact, adored the teddy bear, and two years later began calling it Bearfriend. It was one of his first words.

Nora's father usually gave her things that were exceptional in their uselessness—a set of baking forms for making cookies of various shapes, or a set of knives that could only have been wielded by the market butcher. Once, completely out of the blue, he gave her a hat made of silver-fox fur, which Nora immediately donated to the theater.

The food that her father brought from the delicatessen shop at the Prague Restaurant was, as usual, delicious. Grandmother Marusya herself had loved to indulge in treats from this delicatessen, and surprised her granddaughter with pâté in tiny fluted pastry cups, or fish gleaming under a coat of aspic, transparent as ice. Irina desperately wanted to tickle and squeeze the baby, but she pulled back her hands under Nora's cold gaze, and cooed at him from afar. Yurik looked at her, astonished, but Nora was glad: Clever boy! Blood is thicker than water.

Genrikh didn't venture to touch, but examined the child attentively, with obvious approval: "He definitely takes after our side of the family—round head, big ears. And such a tiny little mouth."

Nora, somewhat disappointed, was forced to agree. Some of Genrikh's features revealed themselves like the play of shadows in Yurik's tiny face.

Amalia showed up a month and a half after that—with Andrei Ivanovich, of course. Even before she had taken off her coat, she hugged Nora and immediately started crying. She wept openly, with childlike tears.

"Forgive me, daughter! I'm so sorry. We couldn't make it until now. But I know you understand; you always do, my clever one."

Nora understood. From the moment Andrei Ivanovich had appeared in their lives, Nora had understood, though she was not yet ten years old. When he visited them at home for the first time, she had felt that his face was already familiar. She had noticed him when he stood on Nikitsky Boulevard, observing her and her mother going out for a stroll, or when he was there to rush her to Filatov Hospital after an attack of appendicitis, or when he met her and Mama coming out of the theater and walked home behind them like a shadow, so that he could spend twenty fleeting minutes with his beloved Amalia. Her mother only rarely turned back and smiled at him—and for the sake of this brief smile, he would tell his wife a little lie, break free, and fly to the theater to catch a glimpse of them as they left to go home. What other lover was capable of such devotion?

Growing up, Nora experienced a multitude of emotions toward this stern, serious, wiry man—jealousy, deep irritation, admiration, and confused love. He stood behind her mother in his customary stance of protector, prepared to intervene at a moment's notice, to beat off any attack, to fend off anyone who dared insult her. Even when she embraced her mother, Nora couldn't shed her sense of having been betrayed, her feeling that her mother had abandoned her, her only daughter. Amalia so loved her Andrei that she damaged her other great love—her daughter.

And now Amalia was crying. So she, too, understood. It wasn't right. Not during the last weeks of Nora's pregnancy or during the first days after Nora brought the tiny creature home with her had Amalia been there. The old scores, never yet revealed, were poised in her mind as she stroked the back of her mother's woolen coat. Andrei Ivanovich stood behind her with a look of guilt. Throughout his illness, he had urged Amalia to go to Moscow, but she couldn't bear to leave him behind, alone and sick, in the country. Now Nora's mother was shedding hot tears, and Nora passed her palm over her mother's knitted cap again and again and felt sadness, and envy, and was filled with a sense of superiority, because she was not that way—she would not have cried.

Nora helped her mother unbutton her coat, but Andrei Ivanovich dashed over, grabbed the coat, and, crouching down on his knees, unbuckled her boots and placed house slippers on the floor in front of her. While he was doing this, Amalia mechanically smoothed down the sparse hairs on top of his bent, balding head. His hands moved up one of her calves and stroked her knee surreptitiously. Nora saw this out of the corner of her eye.

There were times when indignation at the impropriety of this constant fondling scorched Nora like fire. This attraction, this unwaning passion for each other of people no longer young, irritated her.

It's jealousy speaking in me, Nora thought, bringing herself up short. I should be ashamed.

Nora was pitiless to everyone, not least to herself.

Her mother wiped off her tears with the back of her hand. "Well, then, show me my grandson."

Nora led the way. From the doorway of the room they could see a little white crib and a baby, lying on his tummy, face turned toward the people entering.

"Oh my goodness! What a beautiful little boy," Amalia said.

She lifted him deftly from the crib, pressed him to her chest, and began snuffling him, patting him gently on his little back.

"What sweetness, Nora! When you stop breast-feeding him, we'll take him, won't we, Andrei? Shall we? Clean air, goat's milk, freshly picked berries from the forest. The new apple trees in the orchard have started bearing fruit," she began exultantly, confidently, but then she slowed down, anticipating Nora's reaction. "Well, Andrei, here we are, already old enough to have our own grandchildren."

Andrei Ivanovich was a man of few words; moreover, he stuttered. The only one he didn't stutter with was his beloved Amalia. She passed the little fellow over to her husband. He held him in one arm, his other arm circled around his wife.

They aren't even that old; they look like they're still in their forties. Strange, strange person—very attractive, a man's man, and he's blushing; I can understand why my mother fell for him. What a couple. They were meant for each other; it was almost fated. Just like Tengiz and me. Only Tengiz isn't Andrei; they're cut from different cloth altogether. This one looks youthful; his light hair doesn't show any gray. Tengiz turned gray early, and he's aging early. Andrei Ivanovich almost looks younger than Tengiz, though he's at least twenty years older. And they're both from the country. They grew up on the land, Nora thought.

They resembled a sculptural composition: Mama and Andrei with the baby between them, their eyes fixed on the little one. Well, after all, why not? She could actually send the boy to live with them for the summer when he got a bit bigger.

This was the first time Nora allowed herself to consider the possibility of leaving her son with her mother. Then she recalled something she had long ago forgotten—what a lively and cheerful companion Amalia had been in her childhood! She was funny and animated, and all Nora's friends envied her. Mama had been the best of friends to her. Later, of course, it was Grandmother Marusya, but in a completely different way. Though a boy needs a man around most of all . . . And Andrei Ivanovich would be just the sort of man he'd need: a former soldier, a woodsman, a handyman, whether building a house or digging a well. Yes, a boy needs a father, of course. Or at least some sort of man in his life. Well, Vitya would never do, that was obvious.

After they left, Nora made a sketch of them. It turned out well. While she was drawing them from memory, she realized that when they had first met they had still been quite young—not much older than Nora was now. Thirty-eight? Thirty-nine? They could have had their own child. Something hadn't worked out. At first Amalia had thought about the pros and cons of having a child without a husband. Andrei Ivanovich couldn't get divorced for a long time, waiting for his children to grow up. When the children did grow up, they didn't want to see him again after the divorce; they couldn't forgive him his treachery. Yes, they might try to grab Yurik now and take him away from her. Nora felt a surge of jealousy again—she was not going to give up what was hers—and again she stopped herself. You're being possessive, Nora; that's not a good thing. A child needs to have lots of people around who love him. Let them love him.

By the time he was one year old, Yurik had met all his close relatives. It was only then that Vitya managed to visit him for the first time. By this time, he had grown used to the fact that Nora had given birth to a child, and that the child was his son. It was difficult for Vitya to accept this fact, partly because, while their child was changing from a clump of cells into a disc, stretching out, elongating, growing new tissue and the rudiments of organs, Vitya himself was sunk into depression. When Nora's belly became convincing, she invited her husband over to announce the imminent advent of the child. Vitya responded to this information with deep inner protest: he was categorically and irrevocably against it. His own life seemed to him to be so tormented and tangled up that he had no wish to bring another suffering creature like himself into the world. Moreover, he considered Nora's behavior to be morally objectionable. How could she have taken such a step without warning him beforehand?

He was right, but she had no intention of taking his objections seriously. She had cured herself of the illness of love, which had been, moreover, barren in the biological sense. The birth of a child seemed to her to be a reasonable solution to the problem, and she simply didn't take Vitya into account in the matter. She did not count on him to be a father in the fullest sense of the word—just a seed bearer.

Vitya was offended and hurt. These were perhaps the strongest emotions he had felt for Nora during the long history of their sporadic relationship. That entire year was singularly difficult for Vitya. He spent three months receiving treatment in a psychiatric clinic. When he left the clinic, he was even less sociable, and considerably plumper. The doctors, however, considered the period of danger to have passed.

The call from Nora inviting him to his son's birthday took him by surprise. He was so taken aback that he informed his mother about it. Varvara Vasilievna, with her complicated and wholly negative feelings about his "so-called wife," immediately jumped to conclusions: Nora had given birth to another man's child, and she now wanted to collect child support from Vitya. Nevertheless, she did express a desire to go with Vitya to see her "so-called grandson."

Vitya did not accept Varvara's hypothesis, but they went together to see Yurik anyway.

Vitya himself was incapable of deception. His weighty cognitive apparatus, in many ways exceeding the endowments of ordinary people, was unable to register certain simple things—lies, cunning, self-interest.

Nora prepared well for the visit of her husband and mother-in-law. She washed the floors in the apartment, bought Vitya's favorite cake, and dressed Yurik in velvet trousers that she had refashioned from a cast-off garment of her own. Varvara Vasilievna had contemplated for a long time whether to go see the baby—wondering whether or not it would be good for Vitya. She took out her tarot deck to help her decide, and the cards read a resounding yes.

Nora was forewarned that Vitya would be coming with his mother. She did not anticipate that any good would come of the visit, but decided that, in and of itself, a visit signified the victory of her indifference over poor Varvara's long-standing hatred of her.

The relatives were about an hour late. Yurik stood in the doorway of the nursery and swayed slightly, preparing to toddle over toward the guests in greeting. Vitya almost completely blocked the doorway, so it was hard for Varvara Vasilievna to see around him. Nora was shocked by Vitya's appearance: the unhealthy pallor of his immobile face, his heaviness, his withdrawn demeanor. A sense of pity rose up in her: Poor thing, he really is ill . . . Awful. Could she be partly to blame for this? Like Varvara, she had for many years dismissed the idea that Vitya suffered from mental illness; but now it seemed obvious.

"Allow me to introduce myself," Vitya said slowly, and held out a large, plump hand. Yurik started crying; he had never seen such huge hands, or such huge people. Vitya, no less frightened than Yurik, took a few steps backward. Varvara came to the rescue and held out a little red fire engine to Yurik. Nora had not yet given Yurik any cars. This was the first one he had seen in his life—and it was such a beauty! Nora kept her surprise to herself; she hadn't expected her mother-in-law to make such an entirely brilliant choice.

Yurik calmed down immediately. He clutched the toy, banged it against the floor, and very soon discovered its wonderful metal wheels. He made them spin, then tried to stick the toy in his mouth. Varvara was alarmed: "Nora, he wants to eat it!"

"Oh, that's all right," Nora said soothingly. "He's cutting teeth. He keeps trying to scratch his gums. Give him some time to get used to you; then he'll come up to you by himself. Coffee? Tea?"

Varvara glanced around her daughter-in-law's apartment, taking it in little by little. The apartment seemed none too clean by her standards, but very cultured. Throughout all these years, she had only seen her daughter-in-law two or three times, and she had been under the impression that her family was not well off. Now she realized that Nora's family was most likely gentry. She always made this distinction: either ordinary people, or gentry.

Tea was served not in the kitchen but in the living room, which resembled a dining room, with its small oval table and closed sideboard. A real one, not Czech-manufactured . . . The tea set was old porcelain; the spoons were silver. The cake was removed from its cardboard box and placed on a round plate, with a serving utensil lying beside it. In the next room, the baby banged away with the toy fire engine and gurgled with pleasure.

They ate cake and drank tea. Nora put another piece of cake on Vitya's plate. He ate it impassively, if rather quickly. Nora took Yurik by his little hand and led him to the table. The boy looked cautiously at Vitya, but Vitya paid no attention to him. Varvara began to get nervous: This wasn't the way it was supposed to happen. They shouldn't have come. And she shouldn't have let Vitya come. But she still hoped that the boy would be able to penetrate Vitya's leaden indifference. Alas, it was no use.

For almost the first time in her life, Nora was thinking the same thing as her mother-in-law. How Vitya had changed! He was, of course, a genius—but he was a sick one. This could not be denied. What guarantee was there that her son had inherited his genius and not his illness? Or both at the same time? But what could she do? It hadn't happened with Tengiz, and with Vitya it had happened at the drop of a hat, without any grueling, long-term practice.

Vitya finished all his cake. By now, Yurik had taken an interest in Vitya's shoe and was trying to drive the fire engine along it. Varvara pushed the plate with the cake on it away from her son. He didn't take the hint.

Varvara began to get ready to leave. She thanked Nora, and praised the little one: "He's a fine baby."

When they were descending the stairs, she repeated it, to her son this time.

"He's a fine baby. Too bad he's not ours."

"What do you mean by that?" Vitya asked.

"Well, just that Nora has a fine baby, but it isn't yours."

After a long pause, Vitya said, "What difference does that make, Mama?"

Varvara stood still, astonished. "What do you mean, what difference does it make?"

"Theoretically speaking, it doesn't matter to me. Practically speaking, there are methods of determining paternity nowadays."

And Vitya didn't say another word until they reached home. As they were entering the building, he said, "I liked the cake."

10

A Froebel Miss

(1907–1910)

Marusya didn't look back. She completely forgot those two sad years when she had sat in the watchmaker's shop near her father, reading chaotically, unsystematically, and longing for real life—which kept eluding her—to begin. Finally, it did. Now she woke up early and performed her morning ablutions—in cold water, in the Swiss manner. She dressed in the working clothes, somewhat resembling a nurse's uniform, that all the employees of the kindergarten for the children of poor domestics and wage laborers were required to wear. Then she dashed off to work.

This daytime shelter had been established, and was now run, by fine ladies who were, for the most part, no longer young. They were the wives and daughters of the wealthy exploiters of the same poor workers. The head inspector of this shelter was Madame Leroux, sent by the Lord God to minister to the needs of proletarian children, and to set Marusya's fate to rights. Marusya really did do everything at a run, since the children arrived at seven in the morning, and it was her duty to greet them. In addition, when she finished her singing lessons with the youngest and lunched on bread and soup in the small dining room for employees, she took to her heels again—to her classes in the Higher Froebel Courses.

She had been accepted to the Courses solely thanks to the influence of Madame Leroux—Jacqueline Osipovna, as the employees called the Swiss lady. She was an important figure. She had been sent by the Froebel Society to organize their affairs in Kiev. For five years, she had worked tirelessly and was held in high esteem by the local government heads and their wives.

Marusya passed the required examinations without exceptional distinction, but satisfactorily. Most of the other prospective students were preparatory-school graduates, and Marusya had a hard time keeping up with them. There was, in fact, very little real competition; they accepted almost everyone who wished to attend, and who could pay the tuition fees. The fees were not insignificant: fifty rubles a year. Marusya's brother Mark sent her the necessary sum. The money arrived by a circuitous route—"Jewish" post, as it was called. Some friends of relatives or relatives of friends delivered the money, too late, by which time Marusya was already sick to death of her poverty and of her unhappy fate. On the very day she received the money, she went to the bursar of the Froebel Society, Varvara Mikhailovna Bulgakov, who kindly accepted the money even though classes had already begun.

Varvara Mikhailovna—a perspicacious woman, a widow with a family of her own, seven children and two nieces, and a paltry pension from her husband—never tired of telling her children, among whom was a future writer, that she could not leave them an inheritance; the only thing she could provide them with was an education. It was not only considerations of a higher order—promoting the education of women—that inspired her to take a job as bursar of the Froebel Society, but also material privation.

Now Marusya no longer envied either the Petersburg successes of her brother Mikhail, or Ivan Belousov, who had been expelled from the History of Philology Department and had devoted himself completely to illegal revolutionary activity. He sent her subtle hints, vague suggestions, that she should follow the only true path, but she was not tempted. She already had what she had dreamed about—the opportunity to study.

Her health, never very strong, was restored not by the sanatoriums her parents had wanted to send her to, but by the intensely busy life that she herself had chosen. The migraines, nervous attacks, and minor ailments she had been prone to disappeared of their own accord. The rest of her life confirmed that her health always suffered when she was idle, and instantly improved as soon as she busied herself with a grandiose scheme, such as improving humanity.

Her studies in the Froebel Courses afforded her such pleasure that the difficulties of daily existence seemed insignificant to her. Many years later, she recalled this time as the happiest in her life. That random, chaotic reading she had engaged in before she entered the Courses proved to be very useful: all the book knowledge she had gleaned from the wonderful ency-clopedia or from reading literature found its proper application in the new disciplines. And what disciplines they were! Marusya went to lectures every day: the history of literature, philosophy, psychology, diction and declama-tion, as well as physiology, zoology, and botany. There was even a class in gymnastic exercises for children. The lectures were read by the best profes-sors, whose names Marusya would recall with pride, or with horror, or be afraid to mention at all, for the rest of her life—but not one of them would she ever forget.

This information, which she hardly managed to digest, had no value in and of itself, however. It was only valuable insofar as it served a larger pur-pose, a greater goal—the education of a marvelous, free, new human being. Madame Leroux did not abandon her protégée. Now and then she invited Marusya to her home, questioned her about the teachers, and shared her own plans with her. Several times, she invited her to the theater, to concerts. She gave her books to read on pedagogy, the most novel and recent trends from Switzerland and Italy. It never occurred to Marusya that Madame Leroux was grooming her to become her assistant.

Meanwhile, Marusya was becoming ever more interested and involved in her work in the kindergarten. Now she was not only teaching singing, but also putting on little plays with the older children. Jacqueline Osipovna encouraged her in these activities. Marusya had no more doubt that ped-agogy was the only worthy undertaking; the revolutionary ideas of her elder brother Joseph, who was stuck in Siberia, were no longer so attractive to her. The ills of society would wither away and disappear by themselves if children were given, according to their abilities, moral guidance and a proper education.

Ivan Belousov's educational work was, of course, socially useful; but Marusya's work with children of the same proletariat that Ivan was trying to enlighten was much more in keeping with her own notions of the social good.

When he returned home for Christmas, Mikhail found that his little sister had grown up into a young woman, both intellectually and physio-logically, and he was somewhat abashed. His former teasing, playful de-meanor toward her was no longer appropriate, and there was even some tension in their relations at first. He was used to having his sister hang on to his every word, but now she showed an independence of thought and judgment, and a discomfiting sharpness he was seeing for the first time. He was no longer her idol. She didn't go into raptures about his poetry, which he no longer wrote for domestic amusement, but with unremitting earnestness.

She insulted her brother with concise, withering critiques of his poetry: It's not Blok. It's not Nadson. It's not even Bryusov. It was also vexing that this provincial girl, whom he had coached and tried to instruct since childhood, was studying, in his absence, without his guidance, the most important science of all—learning itself.

With Mikhail's arrival, the house livened up. Even old Kerns—who was deeply affected by the banishment to Siberia of his eldest son, from whom they received only smatterings of news—grew more cheerful. He was a silent presence at the evening gatherings of friends, and was visibly pleased at the young people's arrival. In addition to Mikhail's old friends Ivan Belousov and Kosarkovsky, there were new faces, too. A guitar came to replace the all-but-destroyed piano. It was a poor substitute, but the musical repertoire of the guests sitting around the table changed with it, and there was more singing. There was nothing they didn't sing—Jewish songs, Ukrainian songs, Russian love songs . . .

Mikhail bought Marusya tickets to the theater and the philharmonic, five tickets at a time—balcony tickets, it must be said, but this made Marusya very happy, because she could invite her cousins or her girlfriends. Mikhail's generosity was lavish, and every one of his visits home was like a holiday. Perhaps the only thing that put a damper on these visits was a sense of injured annoyance that arose in her each time: in the capital, Mikhail was moving in social circles that seemed to be populated by semi-celestial beings, and he was in ecstasy over them. For many years, Marusya kept one of his letters from that period. She showed him the letter only years later, during one of their deep ideological disputes, as evidence of his vanity and propensity for idle chatter and name-dropping.

Self-impressed and opportunistic. That's what he is! Marusya thought angrily. My brother is just like Khlestakov, in Gogol's play, *The Government Inspector*. The letter was preserved in the willow chest, together with the other correspondence that Marusya had intended to sort through. But she never got the chance.

11

A Letter from Mikhail Kerns to His Sister, Marusya

(1910)

NOVEMBER 25, 1910

8:00 A.M. (ACTUALLY, P.M., BECAUSE WHEN I WAKE UP AT 7:00
I HAVE TO LIGHT THE LAMP FOR THE NEXT TWO HOURS, UNTIL IT
GETS LIGHT. OUTSIDE, IT'S STILL NIGHT.)

My dear Marusya,

You write me with indignation that the letters I write other people are
more serious and filled with more details than the ones I write you. So that
I can feed your curiosity and your demands (fully justified) in at least one
letter, I will begin with . . . a description of my daily life. (Don't be surprised
by the change of ink: I've just managed to walk down the whole of Liteiny
Prospekt, cross Semyonovsky Bridge over the Fontanka River, walk down
Karavannaya Street, and along a section of Nevsky Prospekt. I'm now sitting in the offices of G. Block and Partners and continuing this letter.)

That explanation makes it seem like I must have walked five versts, but
the whole trek only takes eleven or twelve minutes by foot. There are bridges
everywhere you look, and many of them are terribly grand; you'll see for
yourself. (It often happens that you think you're walking down a very broad
avenue, and suddenly you realize, Oh, it's Troitsky or Liteiny Bridge.) But
to continue: until the end of October, there was sunlight—some clear, sunny

days, etc.—but now I'll be hanged if there's a single clear patch of sky anywhere in sight! And it will stay this way till the end of February. Not one clear day to look forward to! As for the "daytime nights"—it only really gets light at 9:30 in the morning. Anyway, when it's winter at home, is it easy to rise at 7:00 to read or write? It gets dark here at 3:00 or 3:30 in the afternoon. Well, what of it—at home we have dark, gloomy days sometimes, too. In short, it's wrong to slander our Petersburg.

I continue: After I rise at seven in the morning (night), I light the lamp and begin my morning toilet. I have to shave regularly in S. Pb., since I want to look interesting and young (at least for the editors—there's no one else I want to impress here). Then, at eight o'clock, Marya brings in the samovar (all this by lamplight). Marya is a sweet old grumbler who spends most of her time talking to inanimate objects: to the stove, the samovar, the lamp, the oven, the broom, etc. A slice of life—here's a monologue. Marya (with heartfelt tenderness): "Poor little thing! Why aren't you burning? Oh Lordy! The wick! The wick is too short. What do we do now? Eh? Oh, my little sweetie! Well, never mind, I'll go out and buy a new wick—and then you'll burn. You'll burn nice and strong!"

When the doorman calls me to the telephone and stumbles over the surname, she is quick to say: "I know, I know. Since you can't pronounce it, it has to be one of ours!"

I continue: I'm in the office at nine o'clock sharp. I used to sleep until two in the afternoon. Now I work, keep records, write verse, relate anecdotes to all the other employees—there are about fifteen of them—until five o'clock in the afternoon (evening), with a short break for two glasses of tea and a chunk of ham (quarter-pound). At exactly five, I leave to eat dinner. Now I take my meal in the renowned restaurant Kapernaum's. I'm sure you've come across the name of this restaurant in literature, because it has been celebrated by many of our best-known writers. The whole of literary Petersburg eats here. (At the restaurant called Vienna, people only dine late.) Everyone frequented Kapernaum's in their time: Dostoevsky, Griboyedov, Pushkin, Lermontov, Zhukovsky, Saltykov-Shchedrin, Sheller, Turgenev—the list goes on. I have seen Kuprin, Potapenko, Barantsevich, Poroshin, Gradovsky, Skabichevsky, Artsybashev—all the modernists, the naturalists, the catskinners; in short—everyone who's anyone! I am there every day from five-thirty to seven o'clock.

Starting at seven, I begin to live with my whole heart and soul. I visit editorial boards, lectures (I never miss a single literary or scholarly talk, because the learning must go on). On Friday I was at a closed literary gathering (i.e., the public was not invited). Vladimir Sergeevich Likhachev read about sixty of his poems. They were very fine. To acquaint you a bit with the circles I now move in, I'll mention the names of the new acquaintances I like to converse with: Batyushkov, Ovsyaniko-Kulikovsky (the very same), Bogucharsky, Vengerov, Linev (Dalin) (remember his *Not Fairy Tales?*), Brusilovsky, Andruson, Poroshin (the last three visit me at home), Merezhkovsky (Dmitry Sergeyevich, he's brilliant), Likhachev, Gradovsky (my protector and friend—thrice my age; he presented me his book *Two Plays* with a warm inscription in it). Also I. A. Poroshin, Chyumin, oh, and I almost forgot: our darling, whom we all adore—dear Nadezhda Alexandrovna Lokhvitskaya (Teffi)—is now my interlocutor. She's heard all about you, too. I won't go on enumerating all my acquaintances; otherwise, you might explode with envy!

I'm blossoming like an aromatic country burdock. I now read my poems only to other writers and poets, the literati. I have only read once to the public at large—"In the Watchmaker's Shop" and "Night Visions" (news—"enormous success," as they write sometimes on posters). I write a great deal, and talk, and feel I'm sprouting wings in the region of my ribs. My poems have been accepted in: *The New Journal for Everyone, Education, The Lively Word, The World,* and *The Dale,* among others. Not bad for a start. Some editors give me the same honorarium they give Roslavlev and Dyadya Fedya: forty kopecks a line. I'll be a millionaire by February. For now, I'm in debt. I don't know whether I'll get clear of it by New Year's. And fifty rubles of my current salary is nothing to sneeze at . . . But don't worry, Marusya, I will earn the money for your tuition with my literary labors. It's not all for Mark. Oh yes! "At the Mirror" will appear in *Theater and Art.* I moonlight now and then for Averchenko (*Satyricon*). A ruble here and a ruble there—it all adds up.

You say Mama is angry that I don't write. If only she could put herself in my shoes, she'd understand—I'm so busy I don't even have a spare second. Besides, when I write to you, I see everyone before me and I'm talking to all of you. Explain this to them, please!

I think that with this letter you'll be "pleased" for the time being.

Write to me on thin paper in small script. I'll send you stamps at some point. What's going on at home? Are you freezing to death? Lord, it's so painful to me to think about the daily hardships, about the frost in the rooms, etc., etc.

On Friday, I will go to the Society of Writers and Scholars, where Gradovsky is reading (he was supposed to read last Friday but took ill, so Likhachev read instead). I'm always there on Fridays.

In fact, Friday is the best day of the week for me, because on that day I float in clouds of "chimera-like propensity" (as dear Ivan Ivanovich Marzhetsky says) and bask in the presence of my radiant literary family. I think I already told you that I received a personal pass to the St. Petersburg Literary Society, and it was suggested I put myself up for nomination. I hemmed and hawed (for show), but my heart was singing. Toward the New Year, I will be selected—for my name is printed (this is the custom) and distributed to all members, to find out whether anyone can point to any of my sins. Then they "announce" me at two consecutive meetings, and only after that is it put to the (secret) vote. It's something like the ancient feudal custom of bestowing knighthood on someone. I am somewhat timid and apprehensive about the whole thing, because I haven't made any special contributions yet to literature. Nevertheless, the future is cloudless and bluey! (I think this is a neologism . . . "bluey"!) I love new words—"speedupping," "twinx," "itaksigranstal," "pokomopstkzhopaktotepel . . ." I love the "sonorous and impure spirit." In short, I am a modernist. (I have a dramatic poem called "I am a Modernist" for which I would have myself flogged. In any event, I'll send it to you.) As a companion piece to the poem "Book," I wrote a poem called "Newspaper." It will pass. Where it will end up I don't know, because I have to think long and hard about it first. I only know that not a single newspaper would ever print it.

How's Mama? Is it possible that even now she's bustling about the stove? This makes me so unhappy. You can't imagine how much I want you to be able to live well, to be warm and carefree. Oh, how I long to be a leading light! If not for the fame, then for money. It's all one! I have one poem called "To the Gourmet." You must read it. You'll see how much truth it contains.

Go to Ms. Nelli and give her my regards; kiss Anya-Asya-Basya-Musya-Dusya-Verusya, and all our cousins, who don't rhyme. Greetings to Boomya. Don't forget. Why didn't she respond to my letter? Now I don't remember; I think I wrote her. Tell Nelli that I've become good friends with a Polish writer named A. Nemoyevski. Has she read him? Tell her that a certain gentleman who was sitting with us at the Editorial Board and didn't say a word to anyone for three days (I thought he was a Brit) turned out to be a Pole, and when I started talking to him in Polish, he nearly threw himself on my neck and kissed me (he's our Warsaw agent) and wouldn't let me out of his sight after that. Here I don't hesitate to speak Polish like a natural-born . . . Turk! I make tons of mistakes, of course.

I still have a lot to tell you, but that's all for today. I do everything in extremes!

If need be, write me at *poste restante*, or c/o G. Block and Partners, 62 Nevsky Prospekt.

I receive several newspapers and journals. I buy books.

There are many pretty blue eyes here—but none of them are dear to my heart.

I have spent four hours writing this letter! I'm exhausted. That's enough.

12

One-of-a-Kind Yurik

Yahoos and Houyhnhnms

(1976–1981)

At least a whole year passed after the child was born before Nora realized what profound changes were taking place in her as well. Besides the obvious things, things that were to be expected—that she was destined for lifelong servitude to Yurik, that she was intimately, physiologically dependent on whether her child was hungry, healthy, or in good spirits—she discovered that her perception of the world had become doubled, as though it had acquired a stereoscopic property. A pleasant puff of wind blowing through the window became both frightening and alarming, because Yurik turned over in his crib from the stream of air on his cheeks. The tap of a hammer in the apartment above, which she wouldn't even have noticed before, was painful to her ears, and she responded to these blows from the depths of her body, just like the baby. Moderately hot food now burned her mouth; the tight elastic of her socks irritated her. These and many other things she now seemed to measure with two different thermometers—one for adults and one for children.

The habit of constant analysis so quickly took root in her that she became a bit frightened for herself. She hadn't expected motherhood to alter her entire biochemistry so thoroughly. She hoped that when she stopped breast-feeding him her familiar world would re-establish itself. But this never happened. On the contrary, it was as though, together with the baby, she was learning to know what was soft, hard, hot, or sharp; she looked at the branch of a tree, a toy, any object at all, with primordial curiosity. Just like him, she ripped pages of newsprint and listened to the rustling of the paper; she licked his toys, noting that the plastic duck was more pleasing to the tongue than the rubber kitten. Once, after she had fed Yurik, she was wiping the sticky cream of wheat off the table with her hand and she caught herself thinking that there was indeed something pleasurable about smearing it on the surface. Yurik was thrilled when he saw his mother doing what he liked to do, and started slapping his little palm in the mess of porridge. Both of them were rubbing their hands around on the tabletop. Both of them were happy.

Nora shared fully in the surprise and excitement of the baby the first time he saw snow falling from the sky and the cold white carpet on the ground. He stamped around in his little boots, examining the ribbed footprints and tracks they made, caught snowflakes, put them in his mouth and wanted to chew them (but they melted, and he didn't understand where they had gone—he stuffed his mitten into his mouth and licked it). Nora stood beside him and tried looking around through his eyes: a huge dog that towers a head above you, a giant bench you can neither climb up on or sit on, a statue of Timiryazev with only the pedestal visible, the rest of the monument stretching up to the clouds.

With her son, Nora became reacquainted with the feeling of water—she filled up the bathtub, crawled in with the baby, and enjoyed watching him splash the water with the palms of his little hands, trying to drink the flowing streams and grabbing hold of the water to lift it up, indignant and unable to understand why it ran through his fingers.

Sensing that the child and his remarkable world were leading her into a volatile, uncertain region, she decided to put down anchor—she acquired a once-a-week lover, youthful Kostya, one of the recently matured young men who had studied under her several years before in the classes for young people. "Dialysis" was how she referred to these hasty evening visits. She didn't bother to invite Vitya for this purpose: he was angry at her and couldn't forgive her callous use of him to fulfill her biological needs. Kostya was easygoing, frisky, and nearly mute; he demanded nothing of Nora. Sometimes he even brought her flowers. Once, Nora put these abstract, meaningless carnations into a vase in the evening, and in the morning, when she woke up, she saw something very amusing: Yurik had climbed up onto the table and yanked the flowers out of the vase, and was stuffing a whole flower into his mouth with a frown. Nora snatched him off the table, then slowly and deliberately ate a flower herself. It wasn't at all tasty, but it was edible. That is to say, if you were certain it was food, you could learn to like it.

Yet even Yurik wasn't enough to fill the gaping hole Tengiz had left in her life, and she tried to patch it up with any available material. Once-a-week Kostya didn't plug the gap; he was just a little bandage on a big wound. The best caulking for the hole was work; she was eager for any task or job that didn't require her to leave home.

She bought several watercolor pads of twenty pages each, and every evening, after she put the baby to bed—if she didn't have visitors from the theater, who had grown fond of her home as a hub on various Moscow walking routes—sketched his fingers and toes, his ear, his back, his folds and fat rumples, and tried to capture his gestures. Only one other body in the world was that intimately familiar to her: a head, slightly flat in back; round, delicate ears, much softer than the rest of him; a broad forehead; deep-set walnut-colored eyes; long clefts along his cheeks; an aquiline nose with a delicate bridge at the top; a neat little mouth with a somewhat protruding lower lip; and a number of missing teeth.

With the tips of her fingers, with her lips, she had explored that body so thoroughly that she could sculpt it in clay. She knew by heart the slightly sagging skin on his neck and in places surrounding the muscles—on his chest and his arms. She knew all the skin folds on his stomach that formed when he sat cross-legged, slightly stooped over.

Tengiz had grown older through the years she had known him, immersing herself in the most intimate details of his body and mind (with long pauses, though deeper and deeper every time); but her child developed more and more wonderful details with each passing month. As he grew, the soft plumpness gradually turned into his first, barely defined shapes—the soles of his feet flattened and roughened up, his teeth came in (slightly crooked on his upper jaw), and the shape of his mouth began to change.

Nora tried rebuilding her life in a way that would free her from Tengiz. Or, rather, from the absence of him.

He appeared again, as always, at the moment when Nora had already begun to think that she had parted with him for good and was already reconciled to the idea that the movie that had been in vivid color with him, and was black-and-white without him, was nevertheless interesting. Just then, he called her and asked whether it was convenient for him to drop by in about fifteen minutes.

"Sure, come right over," Nora said casually. It had been two years since she had last seen him.

She hung up the phone and began rushing around. The doorbell rang almost immediately, even before she managed to control the cold sweat that made her shiver. He stood in the doorway, dressed in an old sheepskin coat that still carried the acrid stench of living creatures. He was carrying a stuffed bear in his arms—exactly the kind of bear that Genrikh had given Yurik—and the ancient duffel bag that he always traveled with.

"You won't send me packing?" Tengiz said, sloughing off the sheepskin.

You bet I will, Nora thought to herself; but out loud she said, "Come right in!"

The shivering stopped. Nora realized that, in the space of one moment, she had re-entered the basic condition of her existence—being together with Tengiz. This was, perhaps, the best thing she knew—talking to him, sitting with him at the table, sleeping and sharing her silences with him.

"I want to chase you away and go to bed with you, both at the same time, Tengiz. I'm a Capricorn. For a Capricorn, the world ceases to exist when she is doing what she most loves. And what I love most in the world is you."

"I adore you, Nora. And I, as it turns out, am a Dragon! Natella has grown keen on astrology, and it's the best madness she's ever suffered from."

"Wait a minute—the Dragon is from another astrological calendar. According to the Chinese, I'm not a Fish . . . a Goat, I think."

"For Dragons everything is good! They're brilliant and wise, and lucky in everything! Like me!"

The dialogue continued, but their clothes already lay in a heap on the floor next to the coatrack. Nora breathed in his smell, the only one in the world that all her receptors were attuned to—sheepskin, the crude country tobacco he liked to smoke, and Tengiz's body. He noisily expelled a breath of air, like a runner coming in to the finish line.

"Don't pay any attention to me; it's just that I haven't been here for a while."

But now he was back, and he was still the same, whole and undamaged. Was such a coincidence possible? Inhale, exhale, pulse, blood type, what have you . . . Nora spat out a piece of the wool that had immediately found its way into her mouth. Tengiz laughed and removed it from her lip. The last time he was in Moscow, it was also winter, and the sheepskin coat had served them trustily in all kinds of unpredictable adventures.

One-and-a-half-year-old Yurik woke up, crawled out of his crib, and toddled up to them. Right away he noticed the bear lying next to the door and grabbed hold of it. He paid no attention to Tengiz. Nora, hopping on one foot, struggled to put on her trousers, which had turned inside out. Tengiz shook out the sheepskin, releasing a cloud of the acrid fragrance, and hung it on a hook on the coatrack.

"Now, where were we?" he asked Nora, and took out a handful of tangerines and a bottle of Cognac from his duffel bag.

"Right here, at this very place," Nora said, laughing. No, they hadn't parted ways. They hadn't parted in any sense whatsoever.

Nora picked up Yurik along with the bear and started dressing him.

While Yurik was introducing the new bear to the old one, Nora went out to the kitchen. "Are you hungry?"

Tengiz nodded. "I haven't had a bite to eat since yesterday."

"Buckwheat porridge. Sauerkraut. That's all there is."

"Excellent."

He ate slowly, almost reluctantly, as though he wasn't even hungry, like all well-mannered Georgians. Nora sat across from him, her chin resting on her interlocking fingers, not feeling anything but his nearness, while he ate silently; but her entire body, still full of his presence, glowed with happiness.

He placed his fork on the empty plate and said, "Let's start on a new project, Nora. Puppets—this time we're going to work with puppets. They will be large. Architectural. With actors inside, and they'll be able to emerge from them. A real actor will play Gulliver."

"Wait, wait, I've never worked with puppets. What's the play? And where will we perform it?"

"Oh, Nora, Swift, of course!"

"Gulliver in the Land of the Lilliputians?"

"Yes, only now it will be about the Yahoos and the Houyhnhnms. About people who've lost the semblance of humans, and the horses that are superior to the people. And Gulliver is also an instrument for taking temperatures by this standard of measure."

"And the play?"

"What play? There isn't one."

"But some sort of script?"

"We have to come up with the idea first; and I know someone I can ask to write it." Tengiz was in top working form, in a white heat of excitement and inspiration, and this enthusiasm was already communicating itself to Nora, though she had only read Swift as a child, in an adapted, abridged version, and didn't remember it very well.

Tengiz took a dilapidated book out of his duffel bag. "Here!"

Nora held the tome in her hands and began glancing through it. The book was in Russian, with a blue library stamp in Georgian script. It was a 1947 edition.

"Did you steal this from the library?"

"I took it for business purposes."

"I'll have to reread it."

"Well, sit down and read."

"I have to walk Yurik before it gets dark."

"No problem. Get him dressed, and I'll take him out for a walk. You read. Read!"

While Nora was getting Yurik dressed, he made a bit of a fuss, because he wanted to take both bears with him on the walk. Nora tried to distract him by giving him a little shovel.

"What's the big deal? We'll take the bears for a walk, too. Come on, little fellow! Let's get going," Tengiz said.

Nora was absolutely sure that Yurik would refuse to go with Tengiz, but he went willingly. When they were already on their way out the door, Tengiz was still pulling on his sheepskin coat. Yurik hugged his stuffed animals to his chest. Nora watched as they slowly shuffled to the elevator, half a flight of stairs down, and felt an unprecedented churning in her heart—here were the two men, the most important men in her life, together; but it was impossible for that to last longer than an hour's walk down Nikitsky Boulevard.

In the evening, after Yurik was in bed, they continued their conversation.

"Okay, I like the premise, but why puppets? All our puppet theaters are for children. Who will we perform the play for? Plus, you haven't said a word about where you plan to perform it."

Tengiz brushed her objections aside.

"For children? What gave you that idea? As you know, in the seventeenth century, when Shakespeare was already gone, the British Parliament outlawed dramatic theater. A bill, an edict, whatever it was called—I don't remember. But that was when puppet theater started flourishing. They performed in markets, on city squares. It was theater of the highest order. Nothing childish about it. So—any objections? Look, there's this Yahoo, a lumpen, a boor, and next to him a noble animal, the horse. Have you ever ridden on horseback? Do you know anything at all about horses? And the theater is a good one! In the provinces, as usual. In Altai. They've made me an offer. I haven't signed on to it yet. If we can agree on it, you and I, I'll fly out there right away. Generally speaking, I have to tell you that puppet theater is where the most interesting things are happening right now. That's where there is freedom. Well, for the puppets, anyway."

Nora shook her head. Tengiz was waiting for her response, her objections. This was their little game: it was precisely on the foundation of her queries, her objections, that he would construct his directorial arguments. No one knew how to play this role better than she did.

"I don't know anything about horses. We didn't have horses. We didn't even have cats. We have allergies. And I don't know anything about puppet theater. I need to finish the book. I can't commit to it just like that, out of the blue."

Nora finished reading toward morning. She read quickly—but not all of her time had been spent with Swift. Afterward, Tengiz embraced her and said, "Now, read, read. Don't get distracted."

But distracted she was. Then Yurik woke up and started crying. It seemed to Nora that he had a bit of a fever, but he went back to sleep very quickly, before she had time to give him any medicine.

The men slept late. Nora finished Swift and closed the book. It contained so much, it required contemplation. She cooked some porridge and put the pan under a pillow to keep it warm, then took a soft pencil and began sketching a horse. The first horse in her life. She kept thinking about how the Houyhnhnms differed from horses, and the Yahoos from people. Yurik woke up completely healthy. He ate his porridge. And Nora said yes.

As soon as Nora agreed, Tengiz hopped on a plane to Altai to sign the contract and discuss details. The general director of the theater had studied with him at the Moscow Art Theatre school, where he had spent two years in the now-distant past. Everything was falling into place. Three days later, he returned, happy; he had found an actor who was, in his word, brilliant.

The happiest time in Nora's life now began—the three of them together, Nora, Yurik, and Tengiz.

The play was born out of wrangling over sketches and hashing out the basic question posed by the piece: What was the point at which a human being becomes an animal, and an animal a human being? What does this distinction consist in, and how can it be expressed in dramatic form? When she read the book more attentively, Nora concluded that the society of

Houyhnhnms was hardly exemplary; they were rather dull, limited, and overall boring beasts. Here Nora became a bit despondent, because her thoughts about the society of horses and humans were hard to translate into the idiom of puppet theater. In time, however, this sorted itself out. Tengiz set her mind at rest: for their work, it was enough to recall Swift's/Gulliver's pronouncement about humanity, "Upon the whole, I never beheld, in all my travels, so disagreeable an animal, or one against which I naturally conceived so strong an antipathy."

"To work with this material, we just have to set aside our surmise that the noble Houyhnhnms are dullards with no emotional intelligence. They don't know love or friendship, anxiety, or sadness. The hatred and wrath they experience is reserved for the Yahoos, who in their world occupy about the same position as Jews did in Nazi Germany."

Nora accepted these premises. The boundaries had been laid out. Tengiz and Nora went to pay a visit to an elderly playwright, the widow of an avant-garde director who died before the war in a lucky accident that saved him from being arrested. The widow, a faded butterfly of the Silver Age, lived in a dilapidated one-story house on Mansurovsky Lane. She served them weak tea and was abundantly kind and sympathetic to them, immediately understanding what they needed from her. She wrote the script in a week. It worked very well, and required only a few adjustments during the rehearsals. Unfortunately, she never managed to collect the fee for her work. The theater had negotiated the contract with her, and had submitted the request for approval from the Ministry of Culture, but while they were awaiting a decision she died.

Nora worked conscientiously. By way of beginning her project, she decided to spend time with living nature, and she took Yurik to the zoo to see all sorts of ungulates. Yurik showed most interest in the sparrows and pigeons roaming at large, which were not exhibits at all, but were, if anything, service workers. Even the elephant himself failed to impress him: the scale of the creature was simply too large for Yurik to notice it. Nora made several sketches in her notebook, and realized she was pursuing the wrong path. She rejected the idea of studying from nature, and immersed herself in visual art. She sat in libraries and contemplated all kinds of artists' depictions of horses. The library of the All-Russian Theater Association allowed her to bring Yurik along; she had known the librarians there for nearly twenty years and was on good terms with them. She had to enlist Taisia's help when she went to the other libraries. Sometimes her friend Natasha

Vlasov took Yurik under her wing and brought him home with her, where her son, Fedya, was happy to look after and amuse the little fellow.

Soon Nora knew precisely which horses she needed. And which Yahoos.

Tengiz, who had gone to Tbilisi to sort out some domestic affairs, returned, and announced that rehearsals would begin in a week.

Nora placed a stack of sketches in front of him. He took the first one and examined it. Gulliver occupied one side of the page, an observer, and in the center were two trusslike horses that appeared to be constructed out of the metal rods and bars of a child's construction set, held together by crude bolts, articulate, hinged, with huge bellies that contained a small platform for the actors. Their faces were vaguely human, smiling, with bared teeth—but fearsome nonetheless.

"You're a genius, Nora! You did it."

In the second sketch, Gulliver was crawling out of a tiny house with a ring on the roof, squeezing through a swing door. All around, hairy, unkempt creatures with wild but recognizably human faces were frolicking. All of them were bound together with a single net.

"Excellent. The masses," Tengiz said. Then he took the next drawing.

He was sitting down, and she was standing in front of him; they were at eye level with each other. He scratched the gray stubble on his cheek, smacked his lips now and then, frowned, and said, in a mock mournful tone, "You've thought of everything. The whole thing can be staged without me."

"Without *me*, Tengiz. Without *me*."

"What do you mean?"

"I can't go with you. I have no one to leave Yurik with."

"We're not leaving him; we're taking him with us. I rented a two-bedroom apartment. There weren't any three-bedroom apartments in the entire town. It's spacious, though. We'll all fit."

Nora shook her head. "No, I'm not going."

"You've lost your mind! I can't work without you! I know it! I've tried! How can you abandon me like this? Our flight is in three days, and the boy's going, too. They already bought us the tickets."

At that moment, Yurik shuffled up and held out his hand to Tengiz. Nora realized that she would go. She would fly and she would crawl on her hands and knees. Anywhere. Anywhere at all. To Altai. To the back of beyond. To hell and back.

"Want to go for a walk?" Tengiz said. Yurik hurried into his room to fetch the two teddy bears.

"What about a shop to work in there? Even here the construction would be fairly difficult. I consulted one of the best Moscow puppeteers, and he said that not every craftsman would be up to it."

"They've shut down some sort of military factory there. Two of the craftsmen used to work there. Not only can they build you a horse—they'll build you a rocket if you need one!"

Then Amalia came over. She said that she would take Yurik to the nature reserve. Fresh, clean air, goat's milk, homegrown vegetables . . . Andrei Ivanovich, too, thought it would be a mistake to drag the child off to such a remote region.

She should never have mentioned Andrei Ivanovich and the "mistake." More than once, tempers had flared on this subject.

"Mama, please let me make my own mistakes. I wouldn't be me if I didn't make them. I'd be you."

"But think of the child! Who has ever shown you such . . . cruelty?" The question was rhetorical and should have been left hanging, but a quick retort followed: "You."

At this point, Amalia began to cry, and Nora got upset: she could have kept her mouth shut. Nora put her arms around her mother and whispered in her ear: "Mama, I'm sorry, I won't say that anymore. But don't pressure me. Please don't try to make me do things I don't want to."

By the time they parted, they had made peace. Things were even better than before; each of them felt she was guilty.

And another happy chapter in her life began—in a provincial Altai town with a large river, doing work that felt like a celebration. Nora discovered that puppeteers were a special breed of actor, who hadn't veered very far from the old Punch and Judy shows in market squares of yore. Such playful, entertaining folks could never be satisfied with ordinary theater. The director of the puppet theater, a former Party official, turned out to be a marvelous woman, exceptionally so, for which she was subsequently fired from her job—luckily, not for *Gulliver*, but for the next one. For *Gulliver* she only got a reprimand.

The Altai episode in their lives turned out to be very important for Yurik, too. He was late learning to talk, but here he began speaking in complex sentences that were both striking and funny. Many years later, it became evident that his prodigious memory had begun working here as well. His earliest memories were about the theater, the construction workshop, and Tengiz, whom he decided to adopt as his father.

The opening night was September 15. On the morning of that day, Tengiz received a telegram that his mother had died. He left for home the moment the play reached the end. The premiere went off without a hitch. The audience was in raptures, but Tengiz was not present to take a bow. He was already flying on a flimsy local airplane to the big city of Novosibirsk, from where he would fly to Moscow, then on to Tbilisi.

Nora hardly had time to say goodbye to him. She stayed on at the theater for three days, and even managed to catch a thrillingly scathing review by the deputy head of the local department of culture, someone by the name of Shortbread (you couldn't make it up if you tried!), who detected in the play "bourgeois avant-gardism and Picassoism." The second critical notice took a more substantive approach: "From whence this disregard for the human being? Does the director really imply that people are worse than animals? Does this not cast aspersions on the Soviet people?"

Nora and Yurik returned to Moscow in the second half of September. It had rained all July and August, and now, by way of compensation, a true Indian summer had set in. Tengiz didn't call. He had told her that he had plans to go to Wrocław in the fall to work in Jerzy Grotowski's Laboratory Theatre. Poland was the most liberal of the socialist countries, and Georgia was the most liberal of the Soviet Republics, and Tengiz received ideologically supportive permission from the Georgian Ministry of Culture for the trip. He sent no letters, either about Grotowski or about anyone else. Nora had to go through a final parting with him yet again. This time it was easier for her, though—perhaps because of Yurik?

The three of them had spent half a year together, the happiest half year of her life thus far. After that, another life began, in which she had to get used to Tengiz's absence and fill up the yawning hole. Now, however, she had the feeling that he might show up at any time, walk in with his duffel bag and his sheepskin coat, wearing a hand-knit sweater or a baggy T-shirt, and the holiday would start all over again.

Taisia, who had remained "on call" to help out and was now almost a member of the family, thought that Yurik was behind in his development. But when Yurik met her after the two-month sojourn in Altai with the words "Hairy Taisia came to see Yurik, and brought him candy," she stopped insisting for a time that Nora take him to a neurologist, a speech therapist, or a child psychologist.

Nora felt that she had finished her work on Yurik's babyhood. She still drew him, but now, on the same large pieces of Whatman paper, she wrote down his little utterances. She had to jot them down immediately. Sometimes they were so strange and unintelligible that Nora had a hard time decoding them.

One day, when he was washing his hands in the bathroom, he turned on the faucets over and over again—first the cold, then the hot, then again the cold. Nora waited patiently.

"Nora, why does the cold water have a man's voice, and the hot water a woman's voice?"

Nora thought for a bit. She didn't hear any difference, she told him. Then he waved his hand as if to brush off his disappointment, and said, "Well, tell me where the very middle of the water is, then."

Nora felt that she was the one who was lagging behind her son in his magical absorption in the world, his unfolding within it.

"There's a little bit of fire in each thing," the boy said while he was playing with a piece of twine.

"I don't understand what you mean," Nora said, leaning over him.

He clutched the twine in one hand and pulled hard on it with the other. "See? There's a little bit of fire in the rope, and it stings."

He unclenched his fist. There was a red mark on his palm.

"Mama, does the twine have a round face?"

When he was about five, Yurik developed a new infatuation. A friend of Nora's, the puppeteer Sergei Nikolayev, gave him a real African drum, a *djembe*, and tapped out a simple rhythm: "Baby Avocado, Baby Avocado, Baby Avocado went to bed." This straightforward, no-frills toy became his favorite for months to come. Yurik would beat on the drum for hours—with his palm, with a spoon, with a stick, with his fingertips—galloping around it in a circle all the while. Nora was exhausted by the constant pounding and tried to distract him with less noisy activities. Once, she complained to Sergei that he had ruined her life. Sergei brushed her comment aside, but took it to heart—his next present, a xylophone, rectified the situation somewhat. Now Yurik was captivated by a new musical instrument—and the sound was considerably less jarring than the pounding of the *djembe*, it must be said.

I should have taken Grandmother's piano, Nora thought. Maybe he has an ear for music? It's too bad I left the piano behind with the neighbors. She remembered perfectly how her grandmother had tried to give her piano lessons, and what a torment it was to her. And for her grandmother as well . . . She had no inclinations in that direction whatsoever. Maybe her hearing wasn't sharp enough? Genrikh had a wonderful ear for music, and Nora remembered how he used to sing long operatic arias at any holiday gathering, after downing his first glass. Amalia was always humming some Soviet song or other under her breath. Nora's maternal grandfather had been a precentor, so he must have been musical, too. Perhaps Yurik took after Genrikh or after that great-grandfather . . .

When he gets a little older I'll send him to music school, Nora decided.

Then he learned to read. All by himself. Nora discovered it by chance. He couldn't get to sleep, so he asked her to read to him. When it was already after eleven, and Nora was getting tired herself, she closed the book. "That's all. Now go to sleep."

He resisted, saying, "Okay, then. I'll read myself."

Nora always tried not to contradict him. She agreed to his demand. "All right, only you have to read out loud. I read to you, now you read to me."

And he started reading—not very confidently, stopping here and there, but reading whole words, not just sounding out the letters. It was a story about a rejuvenating apple tree, and he couldn't have memorized it, since it was the first time they were reading it. Nora didn't say anything; she didn't ask him how he had learned to read. But she thought: Well, that's that. Another childhood milestone passed. He's got Vitya's head. He'll probably be a mathematician. Or a physicist. And she didn't believe any good would come of it.

Yurik constantly surprised Nora. Once, he sat on his haunches for a long time, studying the grass.

"What do you see there?" Nora said. Without taking his eyes off the grass, he said, "Nora, am I growing headfirst or feet-down?"

Then, suddenly, he hugged a tree, pressing his ear to the trunk and caressing the bark. He made a fist and pounded softly on the bark, still listening. When Nora asked whether he heard something, he shook his head. "I don't hear anything. I'm wondering why people don't have such nice shapes as trees. You don't know? It's because they stand still and be pretty. But people are always running and running and running." And he stood next to the tree again, threw out his arms, and froze. A little boy in a red jacket with a pocket on the front.

Tengiz didn't stay away for long. Now he would summon Nora to collaborate with him, sometimes in the Baltic Republics, or in Siberia. The country was huge, stretching from Brest to Vladivostok. They began to get invitations as a team. The couple enjoyed great success, sometimes even notoriety. They received awards and warnings in turns. Tengiz was offered a theater in Kutaisi. He considered it, then rejected the offer, primarily because of Nora. The position of head director would not allow him to travel about the country so freely, and he couldn't invite Nora to Georgia. And she wouldn't have gone, anyway. He visited Nora at home now and then, but tried not to stay overnight, preferring to check into a hotel. The boy had chosen him to be his father, would cling to his leg every time he saw him, and it was cruel to create the illusion that they were a family. And things were getting harder and harder for Tengiz.

When he was nearly six, Yurik started asking about his father. Nora had prepared for this question beforehand. Vitya, who had only seen Yurik once, when he was a year old, had completely disappeared from the child's memory. Vitya had visited Nora two or three times since, but each time the boy had been asleep. Vitya had already grown used to the idea that Nora had deceived him in giving birth to a child without consulting him about it, and was reconciled to the fact of the child's existence. This was why, when Nora called him and asked if he wanted to see his son, he agreed, albeit without much enthusiasm. Without taking his mother's point of view into consideration, he agreed with Nora that she and Yurik would visit him at his house.

Nora, yet again, smiling to herself, bought a cake and set out to visit the relatives. Vitya and his mother had moved from Nikitsky Boulevard to an apartment near the Molodezhnaya metro station, and this shift in geography added another dot to the long ellipsis of their sporadic and artificial relations.

The visit was a short one. Varvara, torn by conflicting feelings—hatred of Nora and curiosity—went to see the neighbors. Vitya set up the chessboard and showed Yurik how the pieces moved.

"Is this a game of war?" Yurik said. Vitya thought for a while and said that it was.

"Why are there so many pawns? They're all the same."

"Well, they're like the foot soldiers. They need to protect the king and queen, and to attack." Vitya moved first. "The first moves of the game are called the opening."

"Can you do it another way?" Yurik asked.

Fifteen minutes in, Yurik got the hang of the game, and said that he wanted to start again. Vitya refused, saying that it wasn't fair to stop a game in the middle, and very quickly won. They began another game. In the middle of the third game between her son and her half-acknowledged grandson, Varvara returned. Curiosity had triumphed. She pretended she hadn't expected to see them, but the ingenuous and uncompromisingly honest Vitya unmasked her with his blue-eyed astonishment: "But I told you they were coming, Mama."

She waved her hand dismissively. "Oh, Vitya, I never know what you mean."

Yurik lost the third game in a row, and was about to start howling, but Vitya said, "My friend, you play very well. I couldn't play as well as you do at your age. Now I'll show you one more move, and no one will ever be able to beat you in the game again."

Vitya set out the pieces again in order to show Yurik a "fork." Yurik caught on immediately and laughed, asking Vitya to show him another trick like that. After this, Vitya liked the boy so much that he had no objections to seeing him from time to time.

"Wonderful!" Nora said. "You can come and see us. You can play chess together. Just call beforehand to let us know."

While they were riding on the metro to go home, Nora kept thinking about what she would say the next time Yurik asked about his father. She herself didn't bring it up. A week and a half later, Yurik asked a question out of the blue, which, at the same time, prompted a satisfactory answer.

"Mama, is there such a thing as a cousin-papa?"

Which of Nora's men was the papa-papa and which the cousin-papa was never determined with absolute certainty. Vitya began coming over now and then. He didn't really stand out among the other numerous visitors to the "crossroads." All Nora's friends loved and spoiled Yurik—both those who considered him to be smart and wise beyond his years, and those who were wary of his eccentricities. Among the latter was Taisia, who continued to urge Nora to take the child to a children's neurologist and other specialists. Nora, however, was reluctant to consult the specialists, until she realized that Yurik could distinguish colors only by their intensity. First she went to see an ophthalmologist. After studying a chart for ten minutes, the doctor announced that Yurik suffered from color blindness, and a rare form of it at that. They were referred to a neuropathologist, and from there made the rounds of all the specialists at the children's polyclinic. Finally, they gave her a referral to the Institute of Defectology, where Yurik was examined by a whole brigade of doctors. Nora, who was present at this council of physicians, was astonished by the imprecision of the doctors' questions, and the accuracy of Yurik's answers. To begin, they asked whether he knew the names of the basic geometrical forms—triangle, circle, square. Then they asked, "What shape is a Christmas tree?"

"Round," Yurik said without missing a beat.

They presented the geometric shapes again, and then asked the same question.

"Round," he said. Another explanation followed, and the question was put to him again.

"But I'm looking at it from above!" Yurik said, agitated. Nora could hardly suppress a smile. She knew about his ability to look at things from his own perspective.

The doctors exchanged glances and presented him with the next task. On a piece of paper divided into four sections, there were pictures of a horse's head, a dog, a goose, and a sled.

"Which picture doesn't belong here?" an older woman with a braid encircling her head asked him in a sugary voice.

"The horse."

"Why?" all the doctors said in a chorus.

"Because the other ones are all whole, and there's only one piece of the horse—his head."

"No, no, that's wrong, think again," the lady with the braid said.

Yurik thought for a while, and examined the picture with great concentration.

"The goose," Yurik said confidently.

And again they were taken by surprise.

"Why?"

"Because the horse and the dog can be hitched to the sled, but not the goose."

The women in the white robes exchanged significant glances again and requested the mother to leave. By now Nora had guessed that the correct answer was "sled," since it was the only inanimate object in this menagerie. She left the room.

When she was in the corridor, she no longer found it amusing, and felt angry at herself. Why had she dragged her bright child here to be examined by these idiots? They didn't even realize how much better organized his mind was than their own. Nonetheless, they made a diagnosis: retardation of psychological development. In addition to giving Nora the paper with the diagnosis, they also directed her to a special live-in school for children with psychological aberrations.

Not on your life! Next year, when he turned seven and was ready to go to first grade, she would enroll him in the same school that Nora's parents had attended. She herself had not been able to attend because of new zoning rules requiring that she go to another school, which she still shuddered to remember. But there was still a year to go before he entered first grade, and Nora decided to start him in music school in the meantime.

The closest one was the Central Music School, curated by the Moscow Conservatory. It was one of the best schools in the city, a rather refined and snobbish place that had been evacuated for a time for refurbishment but had just begun to function again in its home premises. Everything was institutional green-and-tan and smelled strongly of paint. Yurik inhaled the thick air through his nose. The interview was conducted by a plump middle-aged woman with an impressive tortoiseshell comb in her wispy gray hair, held back in a small bun.

The woman first asked Yurik to sing, but he outright refused, and made a counteroffer to the woman—he suggested they play a game of chess. The lady raised her eyebrows slightly and declined the offer. She tapped her fingers on top of the piano and asked him to tap out the same rhythm. Yurik put his hands on the lid and beat out a rhythm that was long and complex, but in no way resembled what he had just heard; he was remembering his African *djembe*. The woman turned out to be needlessly persistent, and, bending over him, urged him to repeat the simple passage. Again he beat out a rhythm of his own. The teacher opened the lid of the piano and played do-re-mi. Yurik, standing next to her, held his nose and said, "It really stinks in here."

Perhaps if the woman had not doused herself with the old-fashioned Red Moscow scent, and had sprinkled the more modern Silver Lily-of-the-Valley or Carmen, Yurik's life would have taken a different turn.

They walked home. Yurik was quiet the whole way, contemplating something deeply. Next to their entranceway, he stopped, took his mother's hand, and said, "Nora, why am I me?"

Nora took in a gulp of air. How could she answer a question no one could answer?

"Well, you know about yourself that you're your own person, one of a kind, that you're . . . 'I.' Other people are not you, but they all have their own 'I.'"

"But how do you know that I'm a one-of-a-kind person?" As they stood at the front door to the building, Yurik fiddled with Nora's hand. She felt helpless with confusion. Then he said, "We're all one-of-a-kind. Me, Grandmother Amalia, and Taisia. But I thought I was the only special one."

"Well, you were right," Nora said, unsure what else to say.

"And Vitya is also one-of-a-kind," Yurik added, after thinking about it a bit.

Nora froze. He's right, she thought. They are both as different from other people as the Houyhnhnms are from the Yahoos.

13

A Major Year

(1911)

The year 1911 was wonderful from the start. Marusya spent Christmas with her brother Mikhail, who had arrived from Petersburg laden with presents and was dressed in the latest style of the urban capital, fashionably coiffed, with a small, neat beard and a waxed mustache. He had always been handsome, but now his appearance was almost provocative. Marusya felt a certain kind of ambivalence: It was exciting to walk down the boulevards with him. He piqued the interest of the ladies they encountered on their strolls. She found it pleasant that they looked at him, and at the same time at her, but there was some discomfort mixed into it. Her overcoat was old, a cut that had long gone out of fashion, and, added to that, it was too big for her. What embarrassed her even more than the unfortunate overcoat, however, was that she, a sophisticated and educated young woman, suffered for such a banal, unworthy reason.

Still, my hat is pretty, Marusya thought, brightening up—and then brought herself up short. What idiotic vulgarity! So the hat suits me. What does that matter? What significance does that have? What truly mattered was that Mikhail now talked to her about serious and weighty questions, as an equal, and not as if she were an empty-headed young lady.

Their house was filled with Mikhail's friends every evening. All of them admired Marusya's beauty: her gray eyes fringed with thick lashes so dark they looked tinted—never! how trivial and coquettish it would be to paint them!—and her delicate, graceful hands. Her coat may have been old and ugly, but a new dress had just been made for her out of wonderful woolen cloth bought at the manufactory of Isaac Schwartzman. It was purchased at a reduced price because the cut was undersized—only enough for a girl. But it was just enough to make something for Marusya, and Mama accompanied her, not forgetting to bring the tape measure. They figured out how to lay the pattern just so, to use the least amount of fabric, and she said she would manage to cut it. Mother deliberated for a long time, afraid to cut into the expensive material, pinning it on Marusya this way and that, but at last it became a dress that was both elegant and modest, and not at all coquettish—with a tie! Marusya now lacked only one thing—her own ample bosom that would fill out the bodice a bit and be somewhat visible from above. Her solicitous mother, who was endowed with her own impressive bosom, suppressing a smile, made some gathers here, and some tucks there, concealing the faults and enhancing the virtues (a small, neat waist) of her figure.

The month of January was like one long celebration. Marusya's birthday was glorious; everyone came to congratulate her on her special day, even Jacqueline Osipovna. It was the first time in her life that Marusya had enjoyed such popularity. Every evening, someone invited her to the theater, or to a party, and—the crowning event—Jacqueline Osipovna invited her to a Rachmaninoff concert. Marusya had never attended such a momentous concert, and didn't realize she would remember it to the end of her days, because such an event happens only once in a lifetime.

One more event took place—and again fate took a decisive turn with the help of Madame Leroux—in the middle of February. On the invitation of Jacqueline Osipovna, the legendary Ella Ivanovna Rabenek came to lecture at the Courses. A graduate of the Grunewald School established by Isadora Duncan, favorite of the great barefoot dancer and founder of one of the first schools of movement in Moscow, an actress who went onstage without shoes or stockings, scantily clad, a teacher of movement and rhythm in the Stanislavsky Art Theatre, she made her first appearance at the Froebel Courses in a formal man's suit devoid of any feminine baubles or details, and wearing a flowery silk scarf, more suitable as upholstery fabric than as a lady's garment. The audience was breathless with expectation. Marusya, who by this time had become a teacher in her own right and no longer rushed to meet the kindergarten children at seven in the morning but arrived at nine o'clock to lead her group in simple, unpretentious music lessons, had a revelation, as early as the first lecture, about why she was studying all this history and literature, anatomy and botany, why she listened to semi-incomprehensible discussions among adults and clever people, and why she went to theaters and concerts—it was to be able to study with the marvelous Mrs. Rabenek as soon as possible.

The lecture inspired her with awe. The names alone—Nietzsche, Isadora Duncan, Émile Jaques-Dalcroze—the rhythms of the world, the rhythms of the body . . . All these rhythms were encoded in music, which itself is the expression of the pulse of the universe. Marusya had not yet had time to learn about the creation of the "new human being" by listening to and perceiving these cosmic rhythms, but soon . . . soon . . . Of course, this was what Marusya dreamed about—becoming a new, free-thinking and -feeling human being, the New Woman, and helping others along this path. Oh, the presentiment of marvelous changes to come!

Still, what would become, perhaps, the most important event in her life occurred on the day Ella Ivanovna read her final lecture and gave a demonstration, with music. She changed her menswear suit for a short white tunic. There was nothing in her movements reminiscent of ballet. They were charged with freedom and energy, authenticity and daring. "This is me! This is utterly me!" Marusya felt with her whole body. After the lecture, she flew home as if on wings. Her posture and gait changed within a single hour— her back straightened out, her shoulders relaxed, her long, graceful neck seemed to grow even longer, and her feet seemed to glide over the ground as though on ice.

Mama was already asleep, and her father was sitting by the kerosene lamp in his nightcap, reading an old book in French. She had no one to whom she could communicate her newfound joy, her delight, her sense of light intoxication. She lay down in her angular room, a former pantry, and thought it would be impossible to fall asleep; but she fell asleep instantaneously. She rose early, easily, made her Swiss ablutions, adding a few drops of the Brocard eau de cologne that Mikhail had given her as a present, and put on her new pantaloons. She held her corset in her hands, then cast it away, determined never again to squeeze her body into the disgusting thing, the outmoded, disgusting thing, because since yesterday her body had wanted to be free—not constricted, bound up, but supple and lissome, Grecian . . .

She put on her old walnut-colored dress. Then, instead of the abhorrent overcoat, she put on a worn-out man's double-breasted jacket, and a round fur hat with a shawl tied over it. When she looked into the mirror, liking very much what she saw, she thought, How charming that Marusya is! She laughed, because she remembered perfectly well which of Tolstoy's marvelous heroines had said these words, delighted with the springtime and with her own youth.

It was after nine o'clock when she left home. The weather was sunny, but fairly cold. The air was clear and pure, and the feeling of lightness and freedom from yesterday returned to her; she smiled thinking about it. It turned out, however, that she was not smiling at her recollections from yesterday, but at a young man who was standing in front of the window of the watchmaker's shop. He had curly reddish-brown hair and was wearing a student's cap and overcoat. His face, not quite familiar to her, beamed with the same joy that filled Marusya.

"Maria! I despaired of ever seeing you again! Remember me? We met at the Rachmaninoff concert."

Although nearly a month had passed, Marusya remembered. She immediately remembered the student who had given her his seat in the orchestra, and then walked her home. He had impressed her then as a very well-brought-up young man, and now, too, he behaved with deferential respect toward her.

"Will you allow me to accompany you?" he said, offering her his arm for her to lean on. The sleeve of his coat was made of delicate, expensive fabric.

"Where are you going?" Marusya herself didn't know where she intended to go. She had no lessons today with the children, and there were still two hours before her lectures at the Courses began.

So they walked in the direction their feet carried them. Mariinsko-Blagoveshchenskaya Street, long and hilly, meandering up and down. Life still unfolded serenely, at a measured pace, on that street; but the peaceful days of the street, and indeed of the whole city, graced with its intricate, fanciful architecture, were numbered. Underground, the Revolution was already brewing, to be followed by civil war; and the near future—some weeks, at most—would bring with it the murder of the boy Andryusha, a murder committed "from personal motives" by who-knew-whom. If only he could have lived; but he was murdered, and the Beilis Affair was about to cover the local world in a poisonous, stinking fog. Nor had the assassination yet taken place of Prime Minister Stolypin by the terrorist Bogrov, who lived not far from here, on Bibikovsky Boulevard, though it was already being plotted. Lukyanovskaya Prison was expanding in all directions; the new buildings were all full, and countless people were incarcerated there, people still unknown to Jacob and Marusya: the Ulyanov sisters, and their brother Dmitry, and Dzerzhinsky, and Lunacharsky, and Fanny Kaplan. Very soon,

127

through a little caprice of life, they would learn all these names, and many other names, and they would read books and play music together—for four hands, in unison—and all the novelties and discoveries in science and art they would breathe together, and this would fortify and deepen their impressions and sensations many times over.

They walked along the peaceful Mariinsko-Blagoveshchenskaya Street and conversed for the first time. In some strange way, their talk unfolded almost without verbs, a single recitation of names and sighs, inhales and exhales, and occasional interjections: Tolstoy? Yes! *The Kreutzer Sonata?* No, *Anna Karenina!* Oh yes! Dostoevsky? Of course! *Demons!* No, *Crime and Punishment!* Ibsen! Hamsun! *Victoria! Hunger!* Nietzsche! Yesterday! Dalcroze? Who? No, never heard of him! Rachmaninoff! Ah, Rachmaninoff! Beethoven! Of course! Debussy? And Glière? Magnificent! Chekhov? Dymov? Korolenko! Who? Me, too! But *The Captain's Daughter!* What happiness! Lord! Unbelievable! Never before anything like it! Jewish? Sholom Aleichem? Yes, the house next door! No, Blok, Blok! Nadson? Gippius! Never read her! Oh, but you must, you must! Ancient history! Yes, the Greeks, the Greeks!

This was how they walked to the Botanical Garden. Then Marusya remembered that she had to go back soon, that she needed to go to Bolshaya Zhitomirskaya, because her lecture was starting soon and she would be late. He laughed and said that it was already too late for him, he had missed his altogether, and that today was the happiest day of his life, because what he had only guessed at had come to pass, and a thousand times better than he had guessed it might be . . . They didn't part until evening. They walked around the entire town, and came out at the Dnieper, and passed some time in St. Sophia Cathedral.

Yet again there was the same recognition, the coincidences in the very depths of their souls, of their most secret and elusive thoughts. And where? In church! Who can you tell about it? It's a mystery! Maria! The Child! Yes! I know! Be quiet! Impossible! Yes, my Nikolai! Nikolai! I sometimes turn to him! Oh yes! No, what baptism! No! Why? It's a connection! Well, naturally! Never! Abraham and Isaac! Horrible! But the cross! But the sign! But blood! Yes! Me, too! And the fresco? It's my favorite! Very favorite! Musicians! Yes, but the bear! Of course! Of course! The hunt is marvelous! And these musicians! Minstrels and clowns! This dance! King David?

He was handsome in a special way—not a way that appealed to everyone, but he was handsome to her. She liked his heavy chin with its dimpled cleft, and his neat mouth, determined, without any youthful plumpness, and you could see that, though he shaved closely, if he let his beard grow it would be coarse and thick. His eyes were clear; his face was pink with health; and even in his uniform you could tell he was broad-shouldered and narrow-waisted, with no extra flesh anywhere, absolute masculine clarity and definition.

She was more than beautiful—infused with spirit! Her lacy wool shawl barely concealed her sunken cheeks; there was nothing superfluous in her features, carved by a gifted sculptor, or, rather, etched by an engraver or an artist—Beardsley, perhaps. Slightly muted tints, pastel, lighter than air. Air— that was her element! No flesh and bones, nothing weighty—angels are made of such stuff as she is! Yes, angels . . .

The next day, they met again. Marusya told him that soon she would be graduating from the Froebel Courses, and she already knew what she wanted to continue studying. She told him everything she knew about the great dancer and her protégée, and about the rhythm that no one hears, in which is the key to everything, because outside this rhythm there is no life. You have to know how to catch the rhythm, and you can learn how to do it. It doesn't matter what path you choose, but without this pulse, without the grand metronome, nothing is possible. And these years of study were only a preparation for what she was now ready to devote herself to . . . Precisely, only this!

Yes, yes, I understood that very well when I was still a child. I was sick with tonsillitis, and I was standing by the window with a bandage around my throat, and I was counting the falling autumn leaves, and I knew that the pain was echoed by each falling leaf that touched the ground. I couldn't explain it to anyone, and you're the first one I've ever known who is able to understand it . . . Not Mama, of course . . . Oh no, not Mama . . . She's not at all . . . Yes, yes . . . They'll never understand . . . Although their love, yes . . . But such understanding . . . Such oneness . . . And music? Music! That's where the metronome of life is! The pulse! The meaning!

Every day, they walked through the city hand in hand, spending every spare moment together, and Jacob was happy and somewhat overwhelmed by this abundance of happiness. Marusya was happy, too, but also scared that it might all suddenly disappear. They discussed this as well, but he assured her that they would hold on to it, preserve it, and that she could count on him, put her faith in him, because he had had everything he might need in life except her. Now that they had found each other, it was all so simple. They lived on neighboring streets . . . Yes, Rachmaninoff, of course, Rachmaninoff! . . . It would be criminal not to hold on to the golden fish, the firebird, because everything had acquired meaning, a significance that was missing up until now. Now it had become clear why the world needed music, and all the sciences, and all the arts, because without love everything loses all meaning. Now the meaning was obvious, and not limited, but general, and pedagogy wasn't isolated from life, it was invented precisely for the purpose of teaching people to be happy—and statistics, and political economy, and mathematics, to say nothing of music, were meant for one thing only, and that was to generate happiness.

Several days later, having covered versts of city streets in the town where they were both born, while walking along the beautiful river in which they had both gone swimming as children: Do you not agree, Marusya, that the word "river" should be masculine, as it is in German: *der Fluss*? Well, like our word "stream" . . . "Dnieper"—even the name is masculine, is it not? Not like "Volga," which is feminine . . . They skipped up the hills and down through the flats of the ancient city, showing each other their favorite places, growing so intimately acquainted with one another that there didn't seem to be any more room for delving into each other's souls. And this was such an unequivocal preface to a supremely happy future life that even kissing was frightening, as though it might scare away the still greater happiness that awaited them. Nonetheless, at night, Jacob, sprawled out on his bed, hugged his pillow tight and promised himself that tomorrow he would kiss Marusya. But tomorrow he backed down, afraid to shake her trust in him, to offend her by introducing something lowly into their high-minded, noble friendship. Marusya waited and prepared herself for this new step in their relations, but did nothing to hurry the event.

It was still early in the year 1911; the end of February arrived. Their happiness was undiminished, and even put out new shoots, fresh green leaves. This major year, 1911, picked up definition and speed at a dizzying pace. At the beginning of March, Jacqueline Osipovna said that she had exchanged some letters with Ella Ivanovna Rabenek, who was inviting Marusya to come to Moscow for an audition, for the classes in *plastique danse flore*—movement and dance. Marusya, feeling a lump forming in her throat—her whole life, this lump appeared at moments of strong emotion, through the heightened functioning of the thyroid gland, as a doctor would explain to her many years later—said she would go, no matter what.

Afterward, things happened as though in a fairy tale. Her brother Mark arrived from Petersburg to visit his family. Mikhail visited more often, so his visits seemed less momentous. Mark was only home for four days, and Marusya, from his very presence in the house, noticed how much everything had changed since he had left home. The whole apartment seemed to have shrunk, and, most surprising, her parents themselves seemed to have become more diminutive. They had never been large people, but when Mark, tall and broad, stood next to his father and bent his head down to him, and his father craned his neck, lifting his handsome head up to Mark, Marusya almost cried, realizing how much older her parents had grown in the last five years. Mark moved in an aura of prosperity and success. He announced that he was moving to Moscow, where he had been appointed to a new position. Now he would be working as an attorney in an insurance company; it was a challenging job, and they were offering him a large salary. He had already rented a furnished apartment in Moscow, and, by the way, the apartment had two bedrooms, so Marusya could come whenever she wished to stay with him. She gasped and said she was ready to leave immediately. There was no "let's wait and see"—everything simply took off—and the next day he bought the train tickets. He put them on Marusya's desk—two long, stiff cardboard tickets, and two pale-green slips of paper, the reservations for the sleeping car.

On the evening of the same day, Marusya met Jacob and, beaming, told him she would be going to Moscow for an audition with Rabenek herself. Jacob was not glad. He took her hand, held it, then pressed it hard—not so that it hurt, but the gesture was charged with meaning.

"You're leaving for Moscow? We have to say goodbye?"

"It's only for a few days," she said, and realized that she wasn't telling the truth. If Ella Ivanovna accepted her, if she could find the money for the classes, she would stay in Moscow. It had never even entered Marusya's mind before that her departure would mean she wouldn't see Jacob for a long, long time.

"I will wait for you to come back, if you ever decide to return," he said with a somewhat theatrical gesture, himself aware of the theatricality, and wincing at his own hypocrisy.

"No, no, don't say that! After all that binds us together"—she didn't say what "all" was, because they were bound both by spiritual discussions and by a deep attraction, which seemed somewhat shameful to both of them—"we will never lose each other."

They sat in the Royal Garden. Marusya was in a hurry—she needed to pack her traveling bag and run to say goodbye to Madame Leroux. Jacob struggled, because he had still not been able to carry out his intention—to kiss Marusya. He said to himself, It's now or never, turned to her, moved his face close to hers, and kissed her . . . cheek. It was not at all what he had been dreaming about all those weeks. She laughed and said, "Later, later . . . Now please walk with me."

The next day, Marusya was sitting in a second-class compartment, in a window seat, next to her brother Mark, with a respectable married couple sitting across from them, older Kievans on their way to Moscow for a family celebration. They talked deferentially to her brother. The conversation was inconsequential, completely vapid, but very genteel. Marusya watched her brother silently, with the same merry spite that had been so characteristic of her in her childhood, but which had diminished somewhat during the years of her studies and her pedagogical activities.

Thus, Marusya and Jacob parted for the first time. Although she regretted every day spent apart from him, the trip to Moscow, a city she had never visited before, and the opportunity to experience the highest achievements of world culture (which is how she envisioned this trip for herself), was something she wasn't willing to pass up. Poltava was as far as she had ventured beyond Kiev, and the dreams and visions she and Jacob shared about traveling together to Germany, to Italy, to France, paled in comparison with this first real journey. In short, her great life plans had already begun to be realized. It was a pity that Jacob could not be with her this time, but this was nonetheless the start of that great and serious shared life that they had summoned up so quickly in their minds and hearts. It was the first way station on the road they had mapped out in such great detail in their imaginations.

Marusya looked out the window, intoxicated by the breathtaking speed at which the train moved, almost flying over the ground, and feasting her eyes on the sights flashing by. She thought of it as a humble prelude to the enormous adventure of life, in which she had already found love, and her studies. Learning to understand the world, and active, exciting creative endeavor, all lay ahead.

At the station in Moscow, her brother hired a cab, and soon they arrived at an enormous building on Myasnitskaya Street, unprepossessing by Kiev standards, with a gloomy aspect and no intriguing architectural details or flourishes. It had towering entrance doors that looked like they were made for a giant. Inside was a vestibule, a mirror, and an elevator, behind a severe wrought-iron door of simple design.

Her brother was immediately waylaid by a huge gentleman in a fur coat, who slapped him on the back amiably and began talking in a voluble, lisping stream of words. Marusya turned away tactfully so as not to disturb their conversation. Mark nodded to her gratefully, called out, "Just a second," and stepped aside with the gentleman. They talked for quite a while, but Marusya was not at all bored. She watched the people entering and leaving. Some people got into the elevator; others chose to walk up the broad, shallow staircase. This building made the first and most lasting impression on Marusya during her visit to Moscow: the men and women who bustled through the lobby dressed differently, rushed headlong, with purpose and confidence, and spoke rapidly, animatedly, as though they were all actors. The house itself was "modern," and the people who lived there were "modern," and the whole of life in Moscow was also "modern." From the very first, it was clear to Marusya that Moscow was where she had to live, not in provincial old Kiev, stuffy and second-rate. Jacob should finish his studies and come live here. Both of them would live here together, in a house just like this one, and they would have a "modern" life, not a vulgar, pokey existence among Jewish relations, craftsmen, merchants, and bankers.

Her brother finished his conversation with the man in the fur coat, ending it in a strange way, with some sort of double handhold and a clap. Mark grabbed Marusya under the arm and guided her not to the lift but to the stairs, saying, "Hurry up, hurry up, Marusya. The elevator is too slow, and we're just on the second floor."

The apartment was wonderful, and also, in keeping with the whole building, unique, with an enormous alcove, and wood paneling—but no kitchen, just a stovetop in a small recess. There was, however, a real bathroom. Mark took some papers out of a desk drawer and whistled under his breath while he perused them. Then he picked out a clean handkerchief and said, "Marusya, I've got to rush. I'll be home in the evening; here's a key, here's some money; don't do anything foolish."

When she was alone, Marusya stood for a while in front of the window, which was protected by wrought iron in a simple, stylized pattern. She imagined how she would look, with her upswept hair held by a velvet ribbon, if someone outside could see her. On the opposite side of the street, there was an identical gloomy building, but the snow that had just started to fall obscured the view into the windows. That meant no one could see her, either. Marusya fixed her hair, securing it more firmly under the ribbon. She exchanged her old dress for a skirt and a roomy blouse cut in the latest fashion, put on her little boots and an unseasonably light coat. She had left the despised winter coat at home; there was no place in her new life for that frightful old thing.

She hadn't had time to ask her brother how to find Maly Kharitonievsky

Lane, so she asked the doorman downstairs. He told her it was nearby and explained how to get there. Marusya was not even surprised at the coincidence that her brother's apartment was just a stone's throw from the Courses. In five minutes, she had reached an imposing house with huge windows on the first two floors; that was where the Courses were held. She had arrived right on time—the students were getting ready for their class, and Ella Ivanovna herself was standing by the door to the room, dressed in a light-colored tunic, with her hair swept up, like Marusya's. It was usually painful for Marusya to talk to people she didn't know, but this time she approached the teacher without any timidity, surprising even herself. She mentioned the recommendation from Madame Leroux.

"Yes, yes, I remember." Rabenek let Marusya go ahead of her into the room, and she followed. "You sit and watch the class for now. We'll talk afterward."

The room was fairly large, with a raised stage and enormous windows lining one entire wall. There was a rug on the floor, and the walls were covered with white fabric. A small black piano was pushed up almost against the wall. Then a young lady with a powerful build came in and moved the instrument out into the room. She pulled out the round swiveling stool, opened the piano, and began playing some quiet music that was unfamiliar to Marusya. Jacob would have recognized the piece and known the composer, of course.

Marusya looked around unsuccessfully for a chair, then went out into the hallway to search for one. She didn't find one there, either. While she was wandering through the hallway, a flock of young girls appeared in the room, barefoot, wearing short tunics. Ella Ivanovna began to address them, but they seemed not to be listening to her. They milled aimlessly about, over the stage, stretching their arms and legs casually, spontaneously, without any coordination with one another. The musical accompaniment continued quietly.

"Now, then; here we are . . . Natasha, Natasha, I'm saying this again for your benefit—every movement is made with the least expenditure of energy. You lift your arms beginning from your wrists, from the elbows; you need only a slight tension of the shoulder muscle, and all the other muscles are completely relaxed. This is the foundation of all foundations. Free your arms from unnecessary tension and your movements will become fluid, natural. Stop. Freeze. You must feel the weight of your arms, of your body, the weight of its extremities . . . Natasha, look at Eliza . . . Yes, like that . . . In this way, the unity destroyed by our unnatural clothing and absurd customs is restored. The *plastique* that we observe on antique vases, in Greek sculpture, returns to us. We have lost it. Raise your arm, lift your knee, twist your torso! Better, that's better already . . . Fine, now everyone stop. The rope, please!"

Marusya, who never found a chair, stood by the door at first. Then, so that she could better hear Ella Ivanovna's words, which were muffled somewhat by the music, she moved along the wall and sat down on the floor, tucking her legs up under her. She already knew about antique sculpture from Ella Rabenek's lecture, about bas-reliefs, and about the inner logic of gesture. Now her whole body ached, so urgently did her arms, her legs, and her back long to respond to the music, to skip and jump, to express themselves without words.

Meanwhile, they tugged on the rope, and Rabenek herself ascended the stage. She waved her hand at the accompanist and called out a single name, unfamiliar to Marusya: "Scriabin, please!" The pianist began to play some other music, different from any she had ever heard before. Ella Ivanovna jumped over the rope with a strange, slow movement, as though she were rolling over it. Then everyone began to jump, but not ignoring the still-resounding music. Now the teacher requested that the music cease, and each one carried on according to her inner rhythm.

"Search for your own rhythm, your very own rhythm."

They all pranced about the stage, together, and individually, and Marusya took off her little boots and went up to prance with them.

"Excellent! Excellent! Here's true artistic talent!" Ella Ivanovna said, praising Marusya. Marusya, filled with lightness and strength, galloped about with all the girls until the break.

During the break, Ella Ivanovna came up to Marusya.

"One of the girls will give you a tunic in the changing room, and you may continue the lesson with us."

That evening, Marusya wrote a letter to Jacob. She told him that she had passed the test, that in the fall she would begin training in the Rabenek studio, and that they had to do everything possible to move to Moscow, because she was sure of it: their future life was bound up with this city.

This was the first letter of that long correspondence that continued for twenty-five years—the correspondence, carefully tied up in a bundle, that had lain on the bottom of the willow chest in the communal apartment on Povarskaya Street until Marusya's death, and had then migrated to Nikitsky Boulevard, to the home of her granddaughter, Nora, where it waited to be read.

14

A Female Line
(1975–1980)

Yurik was growing up. Nora grew up with him, always aware how indebted she was to her son for so much. When the other "playground" mothers and grandmothers talked about child-raising in her presence, she only smiled. She understood early on that the child was raising her to a much greater degree than she was raising the child. The child demanded a patience that she was completely devoid of by nature; but each new day required her to exercise this indispensable ability. The hardness of her own character, her resistance to the imposition on her of someone else's will, and even someone else's opinion, had complicated her relations with her mother during her adolescence. Now she had learned to see everything from Yurik's perspective, as a two-year-old, a five-year-old, a first-grader . . .

From his first days of life, Nora had shared hers with Yurik, which the baby sling that Marina Chipkovskaya had given her greatly facilitated. In it the baby traveled with Nora to exhibits, to the theater, to visit friends. At that time, this blue baby sling had been an imported novelty, but in later years, throughout the entire world, it became one of those objects that fostered a new relationship between mother and child. Now the child was not left at home with a babysitter, a grandmother, or a neighbor, but was brought along to places and events to which one would never have thought to bring a child in former days. The sling allowed for a certain freedom of movement, making the connection between mother and child yet more profound. Nora thought about this when Yurik started walking. Even after he was sure on his feet, he was still reluctant to stray too far from his mother. Nora devised a new strategy, diametrically opposed to her earlier practices: when Yurik took one step away from her, she would increase the distance between them by one step in the other direction. This was how she encouraged his independence. Fully aware of the dangers inherent in their double introversion, she made a conscious effort to establish some distance, baby step by baby step. It didn't take long for him to develop a taste for freedom.

Taisia spent more and more time with Nora, to their mutual advantage. She had been working for time-and-a-half pay at the polyclinic, but Nora asked her to cut back her hours and to come to relieve her two days a week. Taisia agreed. Nora's child-rearing methods seemed too harsh to Taisia, however, and she spoiled her charge with all the means at her disposal. Nonetheless, Yurik was learning to be very independent and self-reliant. Sometimes Nora detected signs of Vitya's self-absorption, his introspective unwillingness to engage with his surroundings. Yurik had a hard time accepting new people. Sometimes it took him a long time to call by name another child he played with every day on the playground. He knew how to amuse himself, and didn't necessarily need someone else to play with.

During the first years of Yurik's life, Nora thought a great deal about her own family history. Only now had she come to understand why she had so wanted a son, and had rejected even the possibility that she might give birth to a girl. The thought alone had frightened her. Her memories of her maternal grandmother, Zinaida Filippovna, were vague. She had died before Nora turned seven, and had been bedridden the last two years of her life, growing weaker and weaker. She always wore a woolen cap and lipstick, and from time to time she shouted at Amalia—vociferously if rather indistinctly, though the individual curse words were completely audible.

Much later, after she had grown up, Nora asked Amalia to tell her about her mother. Her story was quite short. Zinaida had had an unhappy life. Her parents, former merchants whose finances had been ruined, threw their daughter onto the street when she was only sixteen. Though Amalia didn't know exactly why, she suspected it was because her mother had had a secret lover. Zinaida left for Moscow and worked as a servant in various homes. She married the last master she worked for: Alexander Ignatievich Kotenko. He was much older than she was, a widower, and half blind. In his younger years, he had been a precentor in a choir, and continued to sing in the choir in a deep, booming bass, for which Zinaida called him the "Trumpet of Jericho."

The marriage was difficult. Her husband drank too much and beat her from time to time. Not to be brutal with her—just to teach her how to be-have. Into this joyless marriage, Zinaida's daughter, Amalia, was born. Kotenko claimed that the child was illegitimate, that he had not fathered it, but he didn't throw his wife out. He was indifferent toward Amalia, but for the most part treated her well. True, Kotenko, who remained in doubt of his own paternity, insisted on having her christened as Magdalena; but she later changed the name to Amalia on her official ID. This was Zinaida's life, putting up with silent battering and verbal abuse at the hands of her husband, now completely blind, until he died, in 1924.

"I remember the funeral service at the church where he sang in the choir, somewhere in the neighborhood of Dolgorukovskaya Street, on a small lane. If Mother ever knew any peace in her life, it could only have been after her husband's death; but she was never happy. She was afraid of everything, es-pecially her husband. I felt so sorry for her. And she was very beautiful; everyone turned around to look at her when she walked by. Perhaps her beauty annoyed your grandfather—I don't know. Sometimes I think that there was someone else she loved. She was aware of her own beauty—she curled her hair, used lipstick. She didn't pay too much attention to me. At the end of her life, she was senile, and she cursed up a storm. At the end, I put up with a lot of grief from her, but all in all, no, there was no love lost between us . . ." Here Amalia ended her brief account.

In her childhood, Nora had been very attached to her mother, in part out of protest against her father, and the hostility she had felt toward him from an early age. Her relations with her mother were uneventful and calm: no childhood passions or conflicts. The alienation between them occurred later, when Andrei Ivanovich entered their lives.

In her adolescence, Nora considered her mother's relationship with him to be a betrayal. The way her mother shone in his presence, the way her voice changed, and the coquettishness and tenderness that appeared when her mother looked at him filled Nora with fastidious irritation. This was exacerbated by the fact that her mother took Nora, not very wisely, into her confidence, extolling the high moral virtues of her chosen one. Finally, Nora remarked very sharply that it was impossible for one and the same person to be an exemplary husband and family man, and at the same time someone's devoted lover. Amalia sighed sorrowfully. "You're too young to understand, Nora, that such a thing is possible. Andrei doesn't want to cause his wife and children pain, and I am prepared to put up with the equivocality of my situation for his sake. You realize that he would have left his family long ago if I wanted him to. But I know how much he would suffer."

"What about you? Don't *you* suffer from this ambiguity?" Nora said hotly.

Here Amalia started to laugh, her pretty face beaming.

"Ambiguity? Don't be silly! It's a very small price to pay for love."

"Well, I find it humiliating. I would never stand for that kind of relationship. I would break it off. You have no character, you're just weak! It should be one way or the other." And Nora lifted her chin, proudly and defiantly.

Amalia laughed again. "You silly girl! I've left two husbands. I didn't love either Tisha, my first husband, or Genrikh. I didn't even know what love was. I only began to understand it with Andrei. And you're still too young to understand."

Their secret love affair lasted for years. Until he finally decided to leave his family, he stood next to the entrance of their apartment building every morning at quarter to eight, waiting for Amalia to come out, so he could walk her to work. She had already divorced Genrikh long before . . .

At exactly five in the evening, she would rush home and make dinner for Andrei. Nora never got home before seven. This was their agreement— don't disturb. If Andrei was working the second shift, Amalia met him by the sound-recording studio where he worked; now it was she who accompanied him, to the train station. He lived out of town and took the commuter train to work, until he bought a car in the late sixties.

This was their routine, every day except Sundays and national holidays, for many years. The lonely New Year's and May Day holidays were only a small sacrifice for Amalia. She never visited other people on these days. Society viewed single women with hostility; they made married women uneasy. Amalia had no desire to spend time in the company of other single women, sharing in their complaints, their gossip, and their wounds and hurts. She spent these holidays at home. She put on her nightgown, smeared her face with cold cream, and went to bed with a good book and the telephone (which she had moved into her room). Sometimes Andrei called her from home; when she picked up, he either remained silent or said, "Excuse me, I must have dialed the wrong number."

Chicken; silly goose—this was how Nora dismissed her mother. But these judgments were in fact about herself, herself alone . . . As the years passed, a peaceable alienation set in. There was one other curious angle to

Nora's relations with her mother. When she was about fifteen, Nora discovered that in one sense she was more mature than her mother. Amalia acknowledged this seniority with a cheerful equanimity. She had a simple, open heart, but she was no fool. She sensed in her daughter a maturity that exceeded her age, and she surrendered without a struggle. Not only did she stop trying to manage Nora; she even stopped trying to guide her with advice, especially after the scandalous school episode.

After Yurik was born, Nora realized that the entire female line to which she belonged suffered from some general defect—an illness, as it were—the daughters didn't love their mothers, and protested against the model of behavior their mothers represented. Nora herself inherited this deep-seated negativity, this mistrust and concealed enmity. Where did it come from? About such matters, Grandmother Marusya would have said, "It's all in the genes."

How glad I am that I have a boy, Nora thought with satisfaction. At the same time, however, she realized that this perpetuation of familial female hostility had to be stopped. It seems that I know a thing or two about what Freud was saying . . . Actually, I need to find out more about the Oedipus complex. She recalled that among her grandmother's books rescued from Povarskaya Street were some well-worn copies of Freud's work, with notations in the margins. She would have to read them. What had he written about Oedipus? Who wanted to kill whom, and for what? The boy struggles with his father, and the girl—with the mother? Was that it? No, no, it was a horrible idea.

The practical result of these confused, inconclusive meditations was that Nora decided to invite Amalia and Andrei Ivanovich to share in her own narrow, cramped family life, in order to give Yurik the chance to develop emotionally. He was, beyond any doubt, emotionally immature. She would let him visit Prioksky. There were lots of animals and plants there, growing things, and other delights completely unknown to a city boy. Moreover, she imagined how wonderful Andrei Ivanovich would look in his sweatshirt, with an ax or a pitchfork in his hands, and how appealing that would be to a small boy. She already felt a bit jealous, scared that they might commandeer the boy and smother him to death with love.

In the summer after Yurik had just turned five, he was "set free" for the first time. Andrei Ivanovich came to pick them up. Amalia had stayed behind in the country, and was waiting for them with freshly baked pies and goat's milk; there were still no berries at the beginning of June. Nora spent a day and a night there, then left, feeling a bit sad that Yurik was happy, and that he would now long to go see his grandparents. She admitted to herself that her mother's happiness annoyed her—that she displayed a kind of inappropriate childishness, as though she were twelve years old and not sixty-four, that there were too many pies, and too many puppies, of some rare Chinese breed, by means of which the happy couple were trying to earn extra income. And there was too much kissing—they lavished kisses on each other when they were only parting for an hour and a half, while Andrei Ivanovich drove Nora to the train station, where she would catch the commuter train.

For half the journey back to Moscow, Nora contemplated her own intolerant temperament, her inability to forgive her mother her silly, girlish happiness. Then she opened a volume of Sukhovo-Kobylin.

The play *Tarelkin's Death* had intrigued her for a long time. The device of a sham death offered a wealth of possibility. Last year, she had been the stage designer for *Sleeping Beauty* in a provincial children's theater. She had turned the plot over and over in her mind, trying it out this way and that, finally coming up with what seemed to her to be a nice twist—at the end of the play, the Prince wakes up, and Sleeping Beauty turns out to be a dream within a dream. But *Tarelkin's Death*—she could really do something unprecedented with it. If only she could find a director to work with. She would direct it herself, if they gave her half a chance. Tengiz, Tengiz . . . An empty summer, a completely empty summer, stretched out before her. It was the first time she hadn't rented a dacha, the first summer she would spend without Yurik. She arrived home late in the evening. When she opened the door, she heard the last trills of the telephone, before it went silent. She undressed and took a bath. Just as she was getting out of the bath, the phone started ringing again. This time, she was able to answer it.

"Where on earth have you been, my dear? I've been trying to get hold of you all day." A Georgian accent. Tengiz.

15

Unaccommodated Man

(1980–1981)

N ora, today we're starting a new life," Tengiz said.

"I know. I took Yurik to Mama's, and I was thinking it the whole time. Today's the day."

In fact, it was already night, and today was already yesterday. Tengiz was the same as always, and even better. Damn him. "Like antimony-washed iron," to quote Pasternak. They hadn't seen each other in two years. Not a single phone call. Nora knew from other sources that he had even been in Moscow, but hadn't called her. She had a lump in her throat, which made it impossible for her to talk, so she swallowed hard and said nothing.

"You and I are going to Poland to stage *Lear*."

Nora didn't speak.

Tengiz went on. "*King Lear*. It's the apex. The highest you can reach. For a year and a half, I read and reread it. I taught myself English so I could read it. I know it by heart now—almost. You and I are going to stage it. Before, I never understood what it meant to be satisfied with staging just one thing. How is that possible? A single author, a single play, a single thought. But now I understand—you need to do just one single thing, one thing alone. It's very powerful when it's the only thing in the world that exists. I understood—you have to stage it so that the world ends when your play ends. That's what theater is. One thought, but played out in such a way that there is nothing else left. Do you understand me?"

Nora still couldn't swallow the lump in her throat; moreover, there was nothing for her to say. The fire in her veins that had blazed up of its own accord had begun to go out. Deep sadness and perplexity: words, empty words. Were they on different wavelengths now? Were they so out of sync? She should probably have gone to bed with him first, and then let words follow. All the same, he touched her deeply, in some wild inner place. He was so . . . There was more talent in him than intellect. Yes, as though he were made of iron . . . scorching . . . hot. Was it all gone now?

"No, listen to me. You're not really hearing me, are you? *Lear* has been staged a hundred times, a thousand times! But we're going to stage it for the last time! We'll do it so that there isn't any point in staging it again. It will be about freedom, about happiness, about taking leave of the world, the world of the elements, passions, the flesh, about the transfiguration of the flesh—that's what it will be. And I know how. Gordon Craig! You'll see! Well, Nora? What? You still don't hear what I'm saying?"

Nora heard every word. Everything Tengiz was telling her now she already knew. Certainly about Gordon Craig. Grandmother Marusya had managed to tell her quite a bit. And everything with a light touch, in a few powerful strokes. Marusya had adored Ella Rabenek, Isadora Duncan's pupil, and Rabenek had told Marusya many things about her—about the terrible car accident in which Isadora's two children perished. The older, a girl, was Gordon Craig's daughter, and it was this particular detail, passed down by word of mouth, that had long ago made Gordon Craig almost a distant relative of the larger theater family, in which there was undoubtedly a system of transference of sacred knowledge. And Nora, recalling all Marusya's rapturous stories about her youth, when she had first studied rhythm and movement, and then taught and practiced some new kind of pedagogy (which was later officially disavowed by the authorities, like genetics and cybernetics), felt that she was an active participant in world culture. And Tengiz was a provincial—that's what he was. Reinventing the wheel. But I'm urbane, cosmopolitan. I already know about the wheel.

She swallowed the lump in her throat and said, "You know, it's your business how you regard Gordon Craig's theories, and what you do with them. But, as for Shakespeare, I won't take him on. I personally don't have the guts."

Tengiz blinked at her like an A student who has just gotten a D.

"Nora! What's happened to you? You would never have talked like that before. You can manage Chekhov? Goldoni? Swift? And what about Aeschylus? The important things that happen before death—that's what's at stake here. You can't refuse, Nora. *Lear! King Lear!* It's about the transfiguration of the flesh; that's the question it poses. About metamorphosis! Just listen to me. Look here. What are you looking at? Yes, that's a bicycle for Yurik; it's first-rate," he said, gesturing toward the big box by the door.

He had indeed come in carrying a big box, which he left in the entrance hall. Nora hadn't thought to ask him about it. She smiled—how funny! The bicycle had come to life, materialized out of the metaphor about reinventing the wheel, as soon as it had occurred to her.

"Look here." Tengiz put his hands on his chest, showing her where to look—at him. "I can't pull it off without you. Just listen. 'Thou art the thing itself. Unaccommodated man is no more but such a poor, bare, forked animal as thou art. Off, off, you lendings!'"

Nora even winced, but she suppressed a smile. She didn't know English very well, but what Tengiz had managed to pronounce was some sort of linguistic parody which had nothing to do with English. Nora caught three words: "art," "man," and "poor."

"What is it in Russian?"

"In Russian, it goes like this . . ."

At that point, Nora covered her eyes with her hands. She knew these lines. She knew them perfectly well. But now the words "Off, off, you lendings," seemed very significant to her. It always happened like this: you live, see, read something a hundred times, and suddenly, as though the scales have fallen from your eyes, you find right under your nose what you have been searching for all these years.

"I can't do it, Tengiz. I'm not ready. Find another set designer."

Tengiz struggled out of the deep armchair and rose to his full height, looking even taller than he really was.

"Nora, half our lives we spend accumulating things, and the other half of our lives we spend casting them away. Every year is like a brick. By the time you're fifty, the burden is so heavy you have no strength to carry it. I get it! It's a crisis! You have to cast things off. I looked through everything, and threw away half my life, half the people I knew and loved—relatives, teachers, everyone who was superfluous, not absolutely essential. But you— you're a part of me. Perhaps the best part of me."

The conversational prelude of the evening ended here, abruptly; only when it was near morning did they again pick up the conversation they had abandoned.

"Give me two weeks to think about it."

Tengiz, as was his wont, disappeared. Nora didn't waste a minute in her deliberations. She visited Tusya and laid out all her doubts. Tusya was her only older friend. Her virtues were many and varied, including the fact that she had been acquainted with Marusya even before Nora was born. Tusya was well aware of the story of Nora's relations with Tengiz, and also of the history of stagings of *Lear*, in Russia and elsewhere.

With a toss of her head, Tusya whisked her gray bangs aside like a horse. "You have to separate one thing from the other, for heaven's sake. What are we talking about here? Your relationship with Tengiz or with *Lear*?"

Nora pondered a bit. She wished she knew. Tusya went out to the kitchen and put the coffeepot on the burner. Neither of them spoke. Then Tusya took out two stained cups and poured the coffee. They drank, still not talking.

"First, I don't see any basis for such a surge of emotions. You have several very successful pieces of work under your belt. Several adequate ones. You aren't a novice. *Lear* has been poorly staged many times. It's easy not to stage it well. And it can be done adequately. But at GOSET, the Moscow State Yiddish Theater, Mikhoels staged it with true genius. My father was a friend of Alexander Tischler's—the set designer for *Lear*, among other things. And he knew Mikhoels, too. I thought I told you, I saw one of his last performances, in Moscow. I never told you? I thought I always regaled my students with this story. I was already working as a set designer, just starting out. I was twenty years old. Younger than you are. Mikhoels invited my father to the opening night at GOSET, on Malaya Bronnaya. My father was a lapsed Jew. He did everything in his power to distance himself from his Jewishness. He was a Soviet writer—and not completely without merit, or the basest of them.

"The play was performed in Yiddish. He had grown up speaking Yiddish, though he wanted to forget it . . . I was the one who didn't understand a word. But I couldn't tear my eyes from the stage. It turned out that the script wasn't important. That's when I realized it. Well, I only realized it once and for all much later, but at that moment I saw that the power of theater doesn't lie in the script; it's in the actor who is charged by the power of the script. Gesture, movement, mimicry . . . Marusya knew this very well. Did you know that Gordon Craig was in Moscow for one of the performances of *Lear* and said that in England there was no real Shakespeare in the theater, because there was no actor of Mikhoels's stature? Imagine that! Gordon Craig, who knew every word of that play by heart, made that remark after watching it performed in Yiddish! It was an actors' theater. Tischler worked there, a marvelous set designer; Chagall worked at GOSET, too. He didn't understand the nature of theater—instead, he created his own theater, on canvas.

"It was Les Kurbas who was responsible for that play. He was a stellar director. A Ukrainian, but world-class . . . His theater had been forced to disband by that time. I think it was in 1933. And he rehearsed with Mikhoels for three months. During that production, Mikhoels had quarreled with Radlov, the official director. Mikhoels received his inspiration directly from Les Kurbas. It was Kurbas's idea that Lear would become younger and younger onstage as the play progressed. And Mikhoels carried it off. But Kurbas wasn't the director of the production, although I'm sure many of the ideas and decisions originated with him.

"The actors were, of course, brilliant: Mikhoels himself, Zuskin, the wonderful Sara Rotbaum. But nowadays theater doesn't rest on its actors. To a far lesser degree, anyway . . . Now the director and the production artist have to conceive the play so that the script doesn't just take over. Who doesn't know those words? They're familiar to every school-age child. All the responsibility rests with them these days, with the director and the artist. The actor today is more a performer than a creator. There are a few geniuses—but you can count them on the fingers of one hand. The directorial decisions are paramount in any production of a classic these days. You managed with Chekhov; you passed the exam ascertaining your professional skills. *Lear* requires the same abilities. If you and Tengiz can figure out what your play is about—beyond the commonplaces of the script, of course—it makes sense to undertake it. But Kurbas's idea about living an inverse trajectory from old age to youth—that could be a point of departure. He has been forgotten, completely forgotten. He was imprisoned in 1933, and they killed him not long after. It was the time of the famine in Ukraine, you see. He staged *King Lear* during the famine, a genocide. Tischler was good, but he was no match for Kurbas. Tischler had his own theater. To make up for not having enough interesting projects for the stage, he created theater in painting, in sculpture.

"Something very funny happened to me with Tischler later on. I had known him since childhood; he was a friend of my father's. Alexander Tischler was a wonderful, very unaffected, happy man. Everyone around him had been taken down, but by some miracle he remained alive. Very handsome, always wearing a cravat (which no one wore in those days). Once, at the beginning of the sixties, I visited him in his studio. I had some question to ask him; I can't remember what it was. During those years, he liked to carve wood into sculptures—remarkable sculptures, it must be said. His entire small apartment was filled with them—figures of different dimensions, mainly of women. I guess that time I must have been visiting him at home, not far from his studio. The conversation was a long one, about everything—life, work, everything. Things weren't going well for me at the time. My father had died; I had divorced my husband; my work was a failure, or so it seemed to me. I went to visit him, and he was so welcoming, so hospitable. His father was a joiner, a backwoods craftsman, and with these sculptures in wood he seemed to have returned home . . . The wood shavings, all the same smells . . . Well, he gave me one of the female figurines as a gift: a small figurine, about ten inches tall. I held it in my hands, warming my hands on it—it seemed to be a source of warmth.

"I said goodbye, and went out to the entrance hall, clutching the figurine to my chest. And his wife came to see me out—a pretty lady, with large, plump hands. 'Goodbye, all the best,' she wished me, and snatched the present out of my hands, pushing me out the door with a supercilious smile on her face. I wasn't able to say a word. Some story, hmm? But you—don't suffer needlessly. Keep working, Nora. Romances are very useful for creative people. God forbid that they're happy. I seem to remember that your grandmother Marusya worked with Kurbas in Kiev in 1918 . . . She didn't tell you?"

"She didn't tell me everything. She only confided in me on occasion. I don't remember hearing anything about Kurbas. I know that during the war she worked as a literary director in some Moscow theater. She spoke about some famous writer about whom she wrote some essay. I don't remember the name."

"I think I know who he was. She may not have mentioned the name to you at all. He was executed in 1937." Tusya waved, brushing away the bad memories. "I'll tell you the rest of the story one of these days. Not now. Marusya was an extraordinarily vibrant and extraordinarily contradictory person."

Tusya was a treasure trove—she knew everything, she remembered everyone. All you had to do was ask. It was her calm equanimity, her deep commitment to her profession and to her students' lives, in which she invested her unrealized maternal affection and instincts, that distinguished her from the common run of theater artists, who were already a breed apart. They were, it could be said, more humane, with more refined sensibilities, than their colleagues—easel painters, draftsmen, graphic artists.

Were they freer? Nora wondered. Unlikely. The censor laid a heavy hand on all of them indiscriminately. The Khrushchev persecutions, particularly intolerable because of the boorish ignorance of the leader himself, had ended. The underground was stirring, coming to life, and Polish magazines were bringing news from the distant West. In the theater world people began searching for what had been lost long ago. But Tusya was someone who had never lost anything—she herself guaranteed the continuity and linkages of time. This was why her art-school students, past and present, continued to gravitate toward her and seek her out. And this Les Kurbas . . . Nora would have to find out more about him.

"Not much has survived, Nora. Even I have had to destroy my theater archives, twice over. I'll take a look, though; maybe I still have something at the dacha."

Nora knew that Tusya had singled her out among the many who clamored for her attention, accepting her as an intimate. Her mood improved. She went home and made herself comfortable on the divan—to read. She knew that this was how the process began: you read, you go for a walk, then you start to draw. That was just what happened this time, too. It was a strange time, unprecedented—no Yurik, no work, the children's art class she taught on summer break, her theater friends gone, some on tour, some on holiday trips—a void. Happiness. Even thoughts about Tengiz didn't disturb her. He had arrived this time with *King Lear*, and *Lear* turned out to be more important . . . It was a question of "unaccommodated man." As Tengiz said, half your life you accumulate things, and then you begin to cast them off. It wasn't just about Lear. It was about everyone. You start going backward, to finish the cycle: You're born, you acquire a multitude of qualities and traits, possessions, fame, knowledge, habits. You become a person, and then you slough it all off. And, finally, you abandon personhood itself. You reach absolute, primordial nakedness, the condition of a newborn baby, the aboriginal state.

Tengiz had put in a brief appearance, then left. Nora quickly threw a few things together and went to Prioksky. Yurik was glad to see her, but five minutes later he was fussing around the puppies again. Their mother was weak, and the pups had to be bottle-fed. It was impossible to drag Yurik away from them; he held the bottle for hours on end. Nora went for a walk in the neighboring forest, a bit apprehensive, since it was a real forest, where you might lose your way. She spent two days with her mother. Amalia had positively bloomed from country life, and she laughed constantly, a high, ringing laugh, about everything and nothing. Andrei Ivanovich walked around with a contented smile on his face.

"What are you smiling about?" Nora asked.

"About everything," Amalia answered, suddenly very serious, her smile gone. "Learn how, Nora, before it's too late."

"Learn what?"

"How to be happy."

"To be happy about what?" Nora said sternly, sensing all of a sudden that her mother was trying to tell her something important.

"Oh, come on," Amalia said, with a wave of her hand. "There's every reason to be happy! I can't explain it, and I can't teach it to you. You just have to be happy." Her face looked very young—perhaps not so much young as childlike.

"Mama, what age do you feel?" Amalia was already past sixty.

"You'd laugh if I told you," said Amalia, laughing herself.

"Don't be coy with me—I'm not Andrei. Tell me the truth. We all have our own sense of how old we are."

Amalia stopped laughing. She thought hard, as though weighing something in her mind.

"I can't say exactly. But not more than twenty-three. Maybe a bit less. Between eighteen and twenty-three. What about you, Nora? How old do you feel?"

"I don't know. I'll think about it. But definitely not twenty-three."

It's a good question, Nora thought. Sometimes maybe even thirteen. On the other hand, she had always felt that she was older than her peers, until she was at least thirty. Then she discovered that they had become older, and she had remained young. Her friends became boring and put on weight. By forty, they had acquired a stolid respectability. I most likely stopped developing, Nora thought. Forty is certainly not the age I feel. But it's just around the corner. Yes, maybe thirty is what I feel. I was always thirty. And then it's understandable why at a certain moment I discovered I was older than Mama. She's between eighteen and twenty-three.

"You're so intelligent and wise, Nora. How did I ever manage to give birth to such a brilliant daughter?" And again her girlish laughter rang out.

Andrei Ivanovich drove Nora to the station, but this time Yurik came with them. He sat in the front seat, next to the driver. They talked together quietly, so quietly Nora could hardly hear. She had the unpleasant suspicion that they were talking about her. And, indeed, they were. When they got out of the car, Yurik went up to Nora to say goodbye, and handed her a little man made of wood chips. His hat was three tiny pinecones stuck together, and he had large feet and pawlike hands.

"Nora, I made this myself. Sort of. He's a jester. Grandpa helped just a little. He's funny, isn't he? It's for you."

So that's what they were whispering about. The jester. Very apropos . . . And that silly conversation with Amalia was very much to the point. It was also connected to what Tengiz had said.

The whole way home, she dozed, dreaming lightly, feeling the rocking of the train, which sped along sometimes, then slowed down, and sometimes halted altogether. She had that strange feeling of suspension, of being in some indeterminate temporal dimension. She held the wooden jester in her hands, and from time to time he ended up in her dream. This was how her work on the project began.

She still had to read a bit more—about the Transfiguration. First, Mount Tabor. The disciples fall down in a faint, because they can't bear the light of Transfiguration; it plunges them into a sleeping dream. Not a dream, of course, but a sort of narcosis. It's impossible for a human being to withstand, like leaping into the fourth dimension. That's what I need. This is the finale, when Lear emerges into another dimension, beyond human cares and concerns, but is not yet dead—he's in another, transformed state. The people who surround him, still alive, cannot perceive this state. They, and the audience with them, are agitated and shaken, and cannot comprehend what has happened.

Then Tusya gave her a book by the philosopher Berdyaev. There, too, Nora found what she needed. It was articulated in somewhat complex language, but, simplified to the level that suited Nora's needs, it came down to the idea that everything is infused with spirit, though the spiritual content of human beings is more capacious than that of animals; trees and other plants also partake of the spiritual principle, but to a still lesser degree. Even inert matter, such as a rock, is not completely dead; it also contains a trace of spirit. Which is very important in this case, since the storm in *Lear* is a mutiny of living elements—water, wind, fire. This is where Lear has his epiphany about naked man. Precisely here. And with this insight he begins to grow younger and younger as the play progresses. It begins as a story of an old man, and ends—through Transfiguration—with Lear casting everything off. Well, he begins to divest himself even before. And the first thing he casts off is power. But he still doesn't understand what will follow from this.

The first drawing that Nora made was Lear in the first act. He is dressed in multilayered garments. They hang from him as though on a standing coatrack, with extended hooks and arms, and over all the layers is draped his royal mantle. He takes it off, announcing that he is ceding his power to his daughters. His gnarled, emaciated hands, with their enormous swollen joints, are, possibly, trembling. His face is covered with deep wrinkles, folds of sagging skin, with hanging lips and jowls, and two tendons in his neck, between which a flaccid sack of skin hangs down under his chin.

I'll make a mask out of latex, Nora thought. I can try, at least. And old-man's warts with tufts of hair growing from them. And overgrown shaggy eyebrows that hang down, nearly covering his eyes. After his rejection of Goneril and his flight to take refuge with Regan, he is wearing less clothing. Part of it he threw off in rage. His face looks younger, sterner, and more defined—let's say he looked ninety before, and now he has become younger by twenty years. And after the storm—we'll simply rely on good old-man's makeup, without any of the extras. We'll remove all the facial molding . . . And now he's wearing only his undergarments. And in the final act, at the very end, he's a young man, with the young Cordelia in his arms—they are the same age. No makeup at all. A young face, a young body. And let Lear be played by a young actor, in his early thirties. So here there must be complete transformation—no clothes whatsoever, absolutely naked. Well, in a flesh-colored bodysuit, without any hair, without any visible sexual traits— because sex is also cast off. Denuded man!

The set will be spare in the extreme. Only the cliffs. But in the first act, the cliffs are covered with rugs, priceless tapestries, and fabrics; then, with the first banishment, and the second, the rugs and tapestries disappear. During the storm, only rags blow across the stage. And in the finale, there is not a scrap of anything left. Corpses, the sentries pressed against the cliffs, are strewn somewhere below. Lear carries the dead Cordelia in his arms and climbs up one of the cliffs. Naked, without any covering at all.

Edgar, the Jester, and Kent watch them from below, like Jesus' disciples at the moment of his Transfiguration. The light is unbearable. The cliffs begin to light up. That's what we'll do. And Lear and Cordelia remain, standing in the rays of light. The End. Applause.

16

A Secret Marriage
(1911)

Marusya spent just a few days in Moscow, but when she returned home, it seemed to Jacob that she was now older than he was. She was, indeed, older than he was—by eleven days. Jacob, with all his inclination to philosophize, had not yet stumbled on this notion—the incommensurability of the flow of time and age, and, especially, the disparate rhythms and cycles of age in men and women. That note of condescending tenderness that he had acquired through the years of interacting with his younger sisters, and which he at first transferred to Marusya, seemed misplaced or insufficient. Marusya's unexpected maturation forced him to grow up, too. He wrote an entry about it in his diary soon after her return:

Everything that has happened to me up until today was simply a puppy's ecstasy at the sight of a pretty young woman. Even our wonderful conversations are meaningless, because they are just the dreams of underdeveloped, puerile young people. Now I understand that only manly behavior, powerful masculine action, can correct this. If not, I'm lost. I remember with shame how we stood by the ravine in the Royal Garden, and the moment was perfect, but even then I didn't dare kiss her. Even writing the word "her" makes me uncomfortable. Our relationship has formed on the basis of interests we share, and the fact that we belong to different sexes, that there is something between us that is purely "sexual," should not be that important. It's almost a kind of captivity, and it can only be overcome through unity, through wholeness and integration. Indeed, if I understand Plato correctly, this is the idea behind the "androgyne"—to be such an integrated being that sex doesn't undermine the unity.

Jacob, following his tried-and-true custom of sharing his deepest thoughts with Marusya, outlined his notions for her in a less coherent form. Yes, she also thought about the subject of sex, and the biology lectures in her studies had made a strong impression on her. From them, Marusya had gleaned that women pay a high price for their childbearing capacity, and the inequality of the sexes derives directly from the divergent biological functions of the male and the female. But this view led her in the opposite direction—not toward androgyny, but in the direction of the authentic emancipation of women in the psychological, intellectual, and spiritual realms. There could never be any equality on the level of biology, since nature had assigned women the role of the continuation of the species, the birth and nurturing of children. This inhibits the full development of her capacities. Jacob completely shared Marusya's views on emancipation, and even pointed out to her that men were obliged to share these views; otherwise, an intelligent, rational partnership would become a competition, and no good would come of it.

These conversations brought them closer and closer together, and Marusya's thoughts in some way fed his courage. They finished their exams in June. Jacob qualified to enter the second year of the Commercial Institute, he passed his *in absentia* exams in the program of music theory at the conservatory, and Marusya received a certificate of completion of the Froebel Courses. Jacqueline Osipovna offered her the chance to work in the Froebel Society as an assistant until autumn. Now Marusya and Jacob met nearly every day; he came to see her at home, and got to know her parents and her brother Mikhail, who had just arrived from St. Petersburg. On July 12, having been detained in town for two weeks because Rayechka was ill, the Ossetsky family left for a dacha in Lustdorf, near Odessa, where they had rented a spacious house for many years running.

Jacob stayed in town. Both he and Marusya understood that it was written in the stars—the ineluctable, long-desired, and frightening moment of reckoning had arrived. The day after his parents' departure, Jacob brought Marusya, trembling with horror and determination, home with him. On that day, her own parents were traveling to Poltava, to the funeral of a distant relative on her mother's side. This only intensified the sense of criminality about what they were doing. The Ossetsky apartment was on the third floor of one of the most beautiful homes on Kuznechnaya Street. In the entrance hall, Marusya already felt oppressed and irritated by the dark-red carpet runner on the stairs and the gleaming chandelier on the landing.

"What a bourgeois house," Marusya said with marked disapproval.

"Yes, I know," Jacob said absentmindedly.

"I could never live in a house like this!" She felt like arguing a bit with Jacob; she was scared to go inside.

"Of course, Marusya, you and I would choose a very different kind of apartment to live in."

"You can be sure of that," Marusya said.

Jacob opened the door with his key, slammed it behind them, then pressed Marusya against the door in a rough and awkward embrace.

She knew why they had come to this empty apartment. Now his strength and passion, his urgency, his insistent embraces, the smell of his man's cologne, the smoothness of his shaven cheeks, and the brushlike mustache he had recently grown left her no escape. It could not have been called capitulation, and it was uncertain whose victory it was over whom.

The details of this night were unforgettable. For many years, they smiled when they recalled their first fumbling attempt and their mutual disappointment, and how they wept, burying their heads in each other's necks in shame for what didn't happen. How they fell asleep hugging each other, having cried out all their tears over their unfulfilled lovemaking, and how, toward morning, waking up together at the same time, they discovered that everything had happened for the best, just as they had imagined it, and even better.

"My wife," Jacob said, placing her small foot on his head.

"My husband," Marusya answered, trying to kiss his hand. When he tried to pull the hand away, she quickly turned it over and kissed his palm. "Jacob, dear heart, my Jacob!"

Then they kissed for a long time.

"Let's go take a bath," Jacob said, and she followed him down the long hallway to the bathroom. It was only the second bathroom—after the one in Moscow—that Marusya had ever seen. Luxury upon luxury—a white bathtub on cast-iron legs. A bourgeois bathtub, a bourgeois life, but—devil take it—how lovely it was! The water was cold, because the boiler had been turned off while the family was away. They splashed around in the frigid water until they couldn't take the cold anymore, feeling like young animals, puppies or beavers, completely unashamed of their nakedness. Then Marusya washed the sheet, on which there was a small oval patch of blood. It didn't hurt—she just stung a bit inside.

Morning came. They were terribly hungry.

"What do you eat for breakfast?" he said.

"Bread and butter. With milk."

"There's no milk. Shall I prepare tea?"

He went to the kitchen. A loaf of white bread wrapped up in a kitchen towel, slightly stale, lay in the bread basket. He took some butter out of salted water and put it in the butter dish. Wanting everything to be nice, he fetched two of the best china teacups from the cupboard, boiled water on the kerosene burner, and prepared the tea in a teapot, which he placed on a tray with the two cups. Then he took it to his room.

Marusya, wearing a light-blue blouse, her hair gathered up in a velvet ribbon, was standing by the window. Jacob nearly dropped the tray in surprise—a stranger, a completely unfamiliar young lady, turned around to look when the door to the room opened. But she smiled, and became herself again.

They breakfasted at Jacob's desk—the only table in the room—moving the books and papers aside to make room for the tray in the middle.

"What beautiful cups," Marusya said, raising hers.

"Papa gave them to Mama when their first son was born. He died of diphtheria when he was only two. Grandmother says that Mama nearly lost her mind from grief, and even tried to drown herself."

Marusya was quiet, holding her tongue though there were words clamoring to be said.

"She was already pregnant with me at the time, and her depression went away when I was born. Papa sent her to a sanatorium in Germany, and I was with her when she came back. And she was all better."

Here Marusya couldn't restrain herself, and she said what was on her mind. "Rich people can afford to take cures abroad. You should see how simple women laborers live. If a child dies, they go to the factory the next day after the funeral and work ten hours—no depression or sanatorium for them. Rich people don't even want to know this."

Jacob spread some butter on a piece of bread with a blunt knife, then put it on a small plate with fluted edges and placed it in front of Marusya. "Well, we didn't invent social inequality. That's just how the world is made," he said in a conciliatory manner.

Marusya pushed away the plate in fury. "I hate this entire capitalist world! It's unjust. This beautiful cup costs as much as a woman factory worker earns in a month!"

Jacob was bewildered. Such a wonderful morning, such a special day in their lives . . . The general unfairness of the world turned on its head, so that he was the child of fortune, of a happiness so great he could hardly contain himself. He didn't want to think that his own happiness meant someone else was deprived of it.

"Marusya, why should we think about injustice today? What does it have to do with us? What makes you think something like justice exists anywhere in the world?"

"Have you read Marx?" she asked. "A peasant or a worker can't eat a piece of bread and butter because they're exploited by capitalists!"

"Marusya, I'm an economist. We study Marx," he said stiffly. The echoes of their physical intimacy and happiness were still with him, and he had no wish to discuss political economy.

"We have to get some things clear between us, Jacob, so that there won't be any misunderstanding about it later. For a whole year, I attended a study group where we read the works of Marx. It was an illegal group, as you might imagine. But I can't conceal it from you anymore—I'm a Marxist."

It wasn't true that Marusya had been part of the group for a whole year; Ivan Belousov took her a few times, but it had bored her.

"Marusya, why conceal it? Nowadays there isn't a single course in political economy that doesn't deal with Marx. I've covered everything, from the *Economic and Philosophic Manuscripts of 1844*, his early work, to the last. Why do you need to go to a study group? I have his basic works, by the way, in German; the Russian translations are poor. But I can get them in French. I know they exist. I've read them very carefully—from Marx's early works, it's evident that he was a humanist, and his goal was to liberate the human being from the strictures of capitalist relations. In the human will he saw only the reflection of historical conditions, though. He subordinated the value of individual existence, freedom of the personality, to the ideals of justice in some future society. But it seems to me that subordinating the needs of the individual to social interests in this way can lead to suppression of the personality—and that troubles me. No, no, I could never be a Marxist. And why would you need a study group, in any case? Group efforts like that are always a waste of time, I'm convinced."

At this point, the whole conversation ceased to interest Marusya. She took a bite of her bread and swallowed the still-warm tea. "You simply don't understand. You can't, because you yourself are from a bourgeois family. Let's not talk about it anymore."

But now Jacob was wounded to the quick. He was indeed from a bourgeois family. His father owned a mill, a ferry that plied the Dnieper, some sort of grain trade, a banking office . . . and it was his father's wish that he would eventually manage all these eggs, distributed among so many baskets, in order to provide for the family and ensure its continued prosperity. Jacob was bored by it, and even, for some reason, ashamed of it. Music was what truly interested him, it was the life he yearned for; but his father's condition was that he only pursue music as a caprice, a whim, a diversion. Jacob saw no way of escape from these paternal demands and prejudices.

Jacob took away the tray, and Marusya was left alone. She was overcome with despair. Why had she talked that way, why did she think she had to bring up Marx? Why this outburst at such an inappropriate moment? She had ruined everything! Everything! What must he think of her now? She stood by the window, her forehead resting against the pane.

He returned quietly, making sure the door didn't give him away, and put his arms around her, kissed the back of her neck, then turned her around and kissed the place on her throat where the clavicles meet. All the wounding words and thoughts disappeared in both of them. They gave themselves over to the joy of touch, and they built their house of love in the darkness and depths of the body.

When it was almost evening, Jacob walked her home. They walked in silence, because what they had experienced couldn't be put into words. Jacob embraced Marusya next to the entranceway to her house.

"Husband and wife?" he asked, to make sure.

"Husband and wife," she replied. "But for now it's our secret."

"But I feel like telling everyone I meet. That you're my wife."

"Not now. Why should we? We know, and that's enough."

In the intimate shared language that nearly every couple indulges in, they called this night, the first night of their marriage, "Lustdorf" for the rest of their life together.

Their honeymoon lasted until the end of August. The Ossetskys returned from the dacha in Lustdorf on the 29th, and on the same day Marusya boarded a train for Moscow. This time, she was traveling alone, with a small suitcase given her by her cousin Lena and a basket of provisions prepared by her mother for her to eat along the way. Jacob, slender, handsome, and nattily dressed, accompanied her to the station. Marusya felt proud that she had such a wonderful husband, and that the passengers were staring at them, most likely thinking, What a lovely pair! They exchanged a protracted grown-up goodbye kiss. Write me! Write me!

17

From the Willow Chest

Jacob's Notebook

(1911)

I came back home from the station. The house was filled with a hubbub and din, children racing around, sunburned and pretty, things being cleaned and put away everywhere. In the kitchen it smelled like food cooking; something sizzled in the frying pan. For a month and a half, the house had been ours—Marusya's and mine—we were so used to being here together, just the two of us. Every moment was so weighty. Now it has ended, and today the house has returned to its noisy existence, so far removed from my own. No, it's not really alien to me—but I have witnessed a rehearsal of my own future together with Marusya, and it is wonderful. Rayechka and Eva pushed two armchairs together to make a bed. Rayechka put her favorite toy dog and doll in it; but I see Marusya sitting in the armchair reading a book, by the green light from the lamp. Marusya looked pale, but it suited her. My wife.

Today, at the station, she was so poised, so lovely, that I almost felt flustered. I looked at her as though through someone else's eyes—this young woman in a light, loose-cut blouse, with an elegant neck and facial features, a supple figure, harmonious, her cheeks a bit hollow, long shadows, huge eyes, gray, stern. Such perfect slenderness, so womanly, without a drop of artificiality—my wife.

It's good that she's going away. I need time to process my emotions and experiences so I can make new plans for my life. Papa is paying for my studies at the Institute, and at the conservatory. I've already finished my

German classes, so that expense is gone. I can't tell him I have a wife yet, while I'm in this position. I will be forced to continue to accept help from him, but I'll have to provide Marusya with her most basic needs. I'll advertise my services as a tutor in the newspaper. I can help pupils prepare to enter the gymnasium: mathematics, geography, history, German. Piano lessons—for beginners. I have to think up an announcement that doesn't sound like the cry of a drowning man. If I get even three private students, I'll be able to send at least twenty rubles to Moscow; forty if all goes well.

I'll speak with Yura, Verzhbitsky, and Filimonov about tutoring.

I have to admit that my intentions to do independent reading and study this summer came to naught. I didn't manage to read even half of what I set out to do.

Papa brought me a letter from Genrikh from Heidelberg. He describes his summer trip through Switzerland and Italy. It is mainly addressed to Papa, just a few lines to me, but very important ones. He completely affirms the ideas I expressed in my letter to him. He says he'll help me. He's the noblest person I've ever known in my life.

SEPTEMBER 2

Yesterday something horrific happened. The terrorist Bogrov wounded Stolypin in the municipal theater, in the intermission of the opera *Tsar Saltan*. It was Mordka (Dmitry) Bogrov, an anarchist. Papa is acquainted with his whole family; his father is a barrister. They live on Bibikovsky Boulevard. I know where their house is, since Papa once took me with him to deliver some German documents, to help translate them. I've seen this Mordka-Dmitry on several occasions. A pathetic man. He graduated from the First Gymnasium. He was good friends with my cousin David. It's hard to predict what kinds of political consequences will follow if Stolypin dies from his wounds. Most likely, the authorities will become harsher and more punitive toward all sectors of society. Reforms will be halted immediately, and the economy may also react to the event by ceasing to develop. I don't see a single positive outcome of this in the near future.

SEPTEMBER 12

Stolypin died of his wounds a week ago. Today they announced that Bogrov was executed. I'm not sorry for him—such a public murder at the opera is an outrage, an abomination! How can one kill in the presence of music! But one is filled with horror that in the twentieth century, in an enlightened empire, an execution by hanging can be carried out, like in the Middle Ages. That's what is most horrifying! Undoubtedly.

Marusya's letters affect me perhaps even more strongly than her presence. Each time a letter arrives, I want to rush to the station and take the next train to Moscow. I close my eyes and it's easy to feel her near me physically, right here, where she really was not so long ago. I fall asleep, and wake up right away. And can't get to sleep again. From longing. Tonight I reread Chekhov. Poor, poor thing! What unhappy relations he must have had, one would think, with women. How clearly that is revealed in his stories. I couldn't fall asleep for a long time, because I kept trying to devise other plots, contrary notions—about the courage and decisiveness of women, about their sacrificial nature. Nekrasov was the only one in Russian literature who was able to describe this, when he wrote about the Decembrist wives. But not even in Tolstoy can one find a positive image of the modern woman. There are a number of charming young ladies, but no truly active women. Strangely, Pushkin sensed this better than anyone. During a time when education for women simply didn't exist—they learned the ABC's from the local priest, along with household management—Pushkin envisioned the character of Tatiana Larina, who had only this scanty education but had such a strong sense of her own worth! This is what Pushkin wanted to say, I think.

The other day, I read *Women and Ladies*, by Mr. Amfiteatrov. Yura brought it over, it's brand-new. And it's a pathetic excuse for literature. Lightweight feuilletons, sketches, anecdotes. Every single woman he describes in this collection is a nonentity. What has happened to that sense of self-worth that Pushkin ascribed to women? If we elaborate this further, we see that only Pushkin wrote about personal self-worth, about the dignity of the human being—male (Pyotr Andreyevich Grinev) and female (Masha Mironova and Tatiana Larina). This is the foundation of foundations. From the artistic point of view, Amfiteatrov's writing is lively, but the style is journalistic, unrefined. Again, I can't help noticing that Dina, a Jewish female character-type, deals in contraband, and resembles Chekhov's Susanna Moiseyevna. It's astonishing, but all the Jewish girls I know, like Marusya, Beti, Asya, are students—some study pedagogy, others medicine. Verochka Grinberg works in a library. Yet in the stories of Mr. Chekhov and Mr. Amfiteatrov, they all seem to be pawnbrokers. Dostoevsky's old woman pawnbroker inspires less intense disgust than these Jewish pawn-brokers. Maybe it's because the old woman is Russian, and not Jewish?

The woman question will become more and more important, I think. This is only the beginning of the process, and in a hundred years everything will change—women will be different. Doctors, senators, even government ministers, will be women. And these young ladies, girls who plunge into education and learning, are just the beginning of the process of development. Turgenev, fragile, refined Turgenev, created a single, integrated type, the "Turgenev woman." But he chose a formidable woman, a singer, a world-renowned figure, as his lover, as his own companion. Emancipated, in other words? Or am I judging the matter incorrectly?

I even had two ideas for stories—fairly good ones, if I do say so myself.

One is about a young girl who falls in love with an old man and meets with him in secret, even bearing his children, two or three of them. She conceals from everyone else who the father is. Everyone looks down on her and judges her; not even her mother understands where these children have come from. The old man dies and leaves her a small fortune in his will. She leaves the children and goes away to study. Like our Beti, for example, to Switzerland. She becomes a dentist, or maybe a gynecologist, then returns home to her children. She works, and gives them a good education. And the whole time she is studying, the children stay with her mother, their grandmother, and everyone thinks she has abandoned them. I'll have to ask Beti about her studies in Switzerland to give the story verisimilitude.

I also thought of another story, in the vein of Sholem Aleichem—about a tailor, very famous and sought-after, someone like our Meyerson, for example, who is gradually going blind, and his daughter begins to work for him, and no one knows that she has taken his place. Her father is dying, and she becomes . . . I have to think a little more about how her life will take shape, independent of men. And she herself is not pretty, not married, yet she is content with her life, and feels fulfilled.

Marusya is right: world culture suffers without education for women. Truly, these are revolutionary times.

SEPTEMBER 16

I have completely adapted to my new regimen. I need to observe strict discipline. I rise at 5:30. Hygiene. From 6:00 to 7:30, I study science. Then I drink tea and have breakfast and go to the Institute (three versts). I go on foot, so I can exercise my limbs and pass Marusya's house on the way, rather than taking a trolley. I'm at the Institute by 8:30. I have classes until 2:00. Then I teach a lesson (one lesson in piano; another, starting next week, in mathematics). Three times a week, I have classes at the conservatory. I play regularly, but I can't manage more than an hour a day. (My education in music theory doesn't require me to be a first-rate performer, but I consider mastery of an instrument to be mandatory.) I have a late lunch at home. After lunch, I copy Solovetsky's or Kononenko's lecture notes (if the lectures are essential), which I missed on the previous day, so that I have no gap in my knowledge of statistics or political economy. At 7:00, we have dinner, and after that I play with the little ones until about 8:00. From 8:00 until midnight is my time for reading, when I don't go out to a concert. I usually attend concerts at least twice a week. I try to go to bed by midnight, but I don't always manage. What bliss—the house is asleep, it's quiet, I roam through the world of science and art in my reading. I borrowed a book on movement and exercise. I read about Isadora Duncan's school, which borrows from traditions of antiquity; it appeals to me greatly. But—and this I have not said to Marusya—her pedagogy classes, especially concerning education for women, seem to me to be more socially useful than all the recent enthusiasm for *Bewegung* (contrapuntal motion).

1. New play by Leonid Andreyev
2. *The Way to Live: In Health and Physical Fitness*, by George Hackenschmidt. On physiological degradation of the modern man despite the advances of medicine in the areas of combating infectious diseases and improvements in nourishment. Increased life expectancy??? Now, that's a perfect application for statistics!
3. Sigmund Freud, *Die Traumdeutung*. It *hasn't* been translated into Russian. It's a pity, the book is exceptionally compelling, but not convincing. A hypothesis!
4. Sigmund Freud, *Eine Kinderheitserinnerung des Leonardo da Vinci*, 1910
5. Boethius—on music—I have to look for sources. Does it exist in Russian? In German? Is it really the oldest tract on music theory?

OCTOBER 1

I've taken on so many activities and commitments, and this saves me. Letters from Marusya. I acquired a special box to store my letters and postcards in. I hide it among the books. It's the most secret part of my life. I can't even imagine what would happen if these letters fell into the wrong hands. Poor thing, she's so busy that she can't always find time to write a letter to me. We agreed to write every other day. I finish my exams on January 15, and on the 16th, I'll be on the train! The letters stimulate me enormously. Sometimes I think, How is it possible that only four months ago I lived without Marusya? No, this question is disingenuous. How is it possible I lived without a woman? I'm suffering terribly now from the absence of a woman, and I fully understand those young men who go to prostitutes. It's not a matter of love, only of physiological needs. True, said physiology is so simple you can easily get by without a prostitute, relying on your own means. The aversion one feels, I think, is the same.

NOVEMBER 2

The weather has taken a turn for the worse. Rain. I no longer want to go to the Institute on foot. I take a horse-drawn tram and this saves me half an hour of morning time. But these morning walks gave me energy, and I miss them. Marusya writes that it has been raining in Moscow for a whole month, and it's cold on top of that. She's always freezing in her little room at home. Yesterday I sent her twenty rubles that I earned teaching my two classes. I haven't seen her in so long, sometimes it seems that she never existed—I just imagined it all, it was some kind of hallucination. But on my desk there is a receipt from the post office, as proof that, in some room I've never seen on Bogoslovsky Lane, a fire is burning in the stove, and it will be warm.

NOVEMBER 21

If it's not one thing, it's another. I've been working on statistics for two weeks. I lack the mathematical means for processing the statistics. I've consulted several textbooks on differential calculus. It seems to me that there must be more precise means of working with data than we were presented in Savenko's lecture. And Marxism, which one simply can't get around these days. It isn't just by chance that Marusya took it up. It's the main intellectual current. It makes many important claims that are hard to dispute, but it inspires some sort of aesthetic antipathy in me. I have to consider why this might be. Maybe it's more ethical than aesthetic. But he is a serious scholar. He has many fundamentally important ideas—not just empty words. It's fascinating. In the meantime, I missed a whole week of classes at the conservatory. But I can't live without music, and I can get along very well without economics. Although I have changed my views somewhat in the past year. Before, I went to the Institute because I didn't wish to disappoint Papa, who relied on me to take over his business and secure the family fortune. Now I see that my studies have scientific meaning and value. No history of civilization exists without a consideration of economics. You can't examine a civilization without taking into account this factor. Economics has its own laws that are bound up with the laws of the world order. You can't achieve anything without it. And I also spent a whole week reading Adam Smith. And I realized that, without a deep understanding of the history of the Middle Ages, nothing that came afterward makes any sense. And that's how it always is—you think you're pulling at one little thread, and it turns out that everything is attached! But as for what lies closest to my heart—it's music. Only music matters!

18

Marusya's Letters

(DECEMBER 1911)

DECEMBER 26

I received your letter at the studio, on Kharitonievsky Lane. It's better to write to Bogoslovsky. I've lived here for two months already. It's a nice room. I share the apartment with two women, one an actress, the other a teacher. We all work hard. There is only one servant—provided by the landlord.

It's three in the morning, and I'm only now sitting down to write you. I can't sleep. A button popped off on my shoulder, and I encountered my own body underneath, which made me long for you . . . Oh, and your last letter . . . Your words, tenderness, your wonderful manly sensibility shape me. I feel myself becoming more and more of a woman, blossoming, growing more flexible, softer, and more beautiful, with every letter you write me. It's strange, but until now I was not much of a woman at all. And I'm glad that I'm growing into one. And this is your doing; I've become more formal, more rational, even in my dreams. Just as you wish. Everything you wish for is wonderful. And your thoughts immediately become mine. It feels as though that was what I always felt, what I always wanted. I don't think I'll ever say (at night) anything that would make you stop and say reproachfully, "Come, now, Marusya."

On the other hand, maybe we'll just laugh about everything, it will all seem funny.

Remember how we sometimes laughed? I love remembering that.

Good night! I'm going to bed now . . . I'm going to kiss you a long, long time, to caress your lips, your body.

The twilight has ended. I turned on a lamp. Now I feel good: it's cozy and clean. Only it's very cold. I rocked in the armchair.

There is a performance under way at the studio. It has been very well received. Ella Ivanovna praises me. I'm glad. There is a rumor making the rounds that they'll accept me into the troupe next year, and my apprenticeship will be over. Time will tell. Anything is possible. Both bad and good. What I need now more than anything is money. I was given some lessons to teach by the Froebel Society. I managed to earn fifty rubles. I'm not able to take on a permanent position—I take too many classes at the studio. Lessons are another matter.

Yesterday B. came to the studio and gave me a "Christmas present"—a porcelain dish with sweets—which I found so touching.

Soon it will be evening, time for the performance. My head feels a bit dizzy, and I don't want to go. I want to keep writing and writing this letter to you. About how I spent Christmas Eve, and about Jacobson the musician. I'll write you later. Goodbye for now.

DECEMBER 28

So—your arrival has been delayed for one more week. I just closed my eyes. I felt your presence so strongly, you felt so near. It's difficult for me. I never thought I could feel so much longing. I walk and walk, marking the minutes—I don't know where to stash my heart. Whenever will I get used to you?

You help me, you support me, you have strong, gentle hands and a good heart. I'm afraid of you, my husband, I'm afraid with a wondrous fear.

Study, study well. Don't postpone your exams, whatever you do. Otherwise, all our suffering will have been in vain. No—study hard. Don't give up. You won't regret it. But come as soon as you can. Oh, I'm waiting, I'm waiting . . . Well, sleep, then, dear one, my precious one and only.

I kiss your head, your lips. Sweetly, over and over, all night long.

DECEMBER 30

This letter has been lying here for two days. Yesterday I had no time to send it, and today is a holiday—the post office is closed. These are just trivialities. I don't want to write with a pencil. The words fade away with time, and the letter will die.

This is better . . . Lena says that love letters should be written in pencil, so the letter won't outlive the feelings. "My feelings have died, they're gone, but the letter written in ink is alive." No—she's wrong about this. Could Hamsun ever renounce *Pan*, or *Victoria*? *Pan* outlived Hamsun, his youth. Hamsun is an old man, but Johannes is still young, still in love. And thank God for that. A love letter, my letter to you, is the purest, the most chaste thing I have created. Because it has no form, no strained effort—you know that yourself. Sometimes there is not even any content. But every line I write is inexpressibly dear to me. This is why it is still so galling to me that your letter went missing. Several pages of your thoughts, your caresses, your love, were stolen from me. And one reason it is so painful is that they belonged to me, only to me. Someone stole what was mine, mine alone. And I am very possessive, only my possession is so very far away from me.

Where is Boris Neiman these days? In Kiev? Why haven't you written anything about him to me? What about Konstantinovsky?

Have you told your Yura that I'm an actress? How strange it must sound to him—your fiancée, an actress. I sense that you want to talk to him about me. I have an intolerable need for an interlocutor, too. I urgently need to talk to someone about you. And I do talk. You can tell Yura that we are already acquainted, he and I. Without knowing me, he most likely feels some unconscious hostility toward me—a woman who is a complete stranger to him. Who knows whether she is worth knowing . . . Just ask him—you'll see that's how it is. That's probably what he thinks. Well, so be it. May God give him happiness and the best of wives.

It's time for me to go to sleep. My life will go back to normal on January 1, and I'll take better care of myself—for you. If only it weren't so cold! Good night. That's all.

Here, take me! My lips, my entire self . . .

19

First Grade
Fingernails
(1982)

Nora bought a bouquet of asters next to the Arbat metro station. It was the last one the old flower-vendor had—a bit wilted, too big, and too bright. Nora looked at it disapprovingly and calculated that the two dangerously red blooms she could toss out, the three yellow ones she would take home for her own enjoyment, and the white and purple ones she would give to Yurik. Tomorrow she was taking him to school: his first day in the first grade.

She was trying to prepare him for this profoundly life-changing event as though it were both a serious and a joyous occasion, but she herself was full of dark presentiments about it. It was already clear that his skills and his abilities were in part insufficient, and in part exceeded the basic requirements. He read fluently, but didn't know how to hold a pencil or a pen correctly. He couldn't write at all. He gripped a pencil tightly in his fist, and Nora had been thus far unsuccessful at teaching him to hold it differently. He wasn't left-handed; rather, both hands showed an equal lack of dexterity. A good doctor, whom Taisia had recommended, said that a defect in the abductors in his hands was preventing him from learning to write properly. He was sedentary and patient when he did something he liked: he would play chess with Vitya for hours on end, until Vitya was too tired to continue.

Yurik hated new clothes. He didn't like to change them. He didn't know how—or didn't like—to tie his shoelaces. He sobbed when he had to put a hat on; he couldn't bear anything to touch his head. Cutting his fingernails was a herculean task for Nora. He loved any kind of construction set, from the metal planks with holes fastened together by nuts and bolts to the wooden blocks meant for younger children; he could busy himself with these things for hours. But it was impossible to force him to do something he didn't want to do. He refused point-blank to engage in any sports, to draw, or, recently, to play music; though when he heard music being played, he would freeze, with a strange, dreamy look on his face expressing rapt attention mixed with suffering. Nora's attempt to enroll him in music school the previous year had turned into aversion to the very word "school," and she had a hard time persuading him that the school he would begin on September 1 was another kind altogether, and that he would like it.

"It stinks there, it's really stinky!" he insisted. Nora couldn't understand how he knew about school smells, since he had never been there. In her heart, however, she had to agree with him. She had completely forgotten about the experience of taking Yurik to music school, and she was oblivious to the smell of the music teacher's perfume, which had so distressed him. Her olfactory experience of school was associated with food smells from the cafeteria, chlorine, and the sweaty stench of the gym, which hung in the air constantly.

Two days before the first day of school, Nora tried to trim Yurik's fingernails. She did everything she could, maneuvering this way and that. She told him that germs were living under his long, broken nails. She drew multi-legged and multi-horned monstrosities on a big piece of paper to illustrate her argument; he laughed, but refused to let her cut his nails.

She tried bribing him—it went so far that she promised to let him bring back Chura, his favorite Chinese crested chihuahua mix, from Grandma's. Yurik looked down at his nails and said with a sigh, "No, only for a German shepherd."

Honest Nora shook her head no; she would only allow him to keep a small dog. She wouldn't agree to anything bigger than a cat. But Yurik didn't want a cat. In the evening, after he had gone to bed, Nora managed to trim two nails on his left hand; but while she was working on the third, he woke up and began to howl.

On the evening of August 31, Nora put Yurik in the bathtub. He played and splashed around in the water for a long time. Then Nora, tense and ready for battle, said in a firm, bitter voice, "And now we are going to cut your nails."

Yurik clenched his fists. Nora tried to pry them open. Yurik spat in her face. She lost control. She dragged the screaming child out of the water, clamped his left arm under her armpit as if in a vise, and somehow or other, with great difficulty, managed to cut his nails. Both of them were bellowing. He: "No! No! Don't cut them!" She: "Yes! We have to! We have to cut them!"

When she had twisted his right arm around, he began to weaken and give in. The operation was completed. At first Nora even felt a sense of triumph. Yurik, pale and wet, his fists balled up, left the bathroom and walked slowly, his body hunched, to his room. And then Nora felt the horror of loss. Their relations would never be the same again. He would never forgive her this violence.

Her moment of triumph—a pile of nail clippings on the floor—in fact signaled her defeat. She placed these paltry scraps in front of her, and began to weep. She wanted to hug the boy tight, to ask his forgiveness, but she was afraid to enter his room. She lit a cigarette. Thinking that she had never felt so wretched, she lay down on the floor on her back, her arms spread out like a cross, and moaned: "God, oh God, help me! I've done something terrible! What should I do now? Help me!"

Then she stood up and smiled. I'm losing my mind . . . I've never done anything like this before. She finished another cigarette and opened the door to Yurik's room. He lay on a striped rug in the middle of the room, just as she had been lying a moment before—his arms outspread like a cross. He was small, naked, and very white in the dusky twilight. Nora sat down beside him, but he seemed not to notice her.

"Yurik, I'm sorry."

"You wrecked my life," he said quietly.

Nora realized that he was right. And she had nothing to say. "Forgive me."

"Nora, I don't love you anymore," he said solemnly, in a grown-up voice.

No, no. We are not equals. I am thirty-nine, and he is seven. I am responsible for him. What to do?

"What can I do? I love *you*."

"I don't know."

"Well, all right, then. This is how we'll live from now on. I'll love you forever. I love you more than anything in the world. And you don't love me. But you're still my son, and I'm your mother."

Last year, he had asked, "Nora, when did you born me?"

"At night," she said.

"Mama, I'm sorry I woke you up." And also, "When I was in your tummy, I wanted so much to sing."

"Why didn't you?"

"It was very tiny in there, and there was nothing else besides me—no plates and dishes, nothing . . . But it was nice."

"I'm going to run away," the boy said now, not looking at her.

Nora gathered him into her arms. "Of course you will. All children go away when they grow up. But we still have a long time to live together."

"I really don't want to live with you anymore."

"Fine. We'll decide later. But now I'm going to make you some custard."

"Are you trying to butter me up?"

"Yep. Here's a towel. Dry yourself off, and I'll go make the custard."

Then Yurik ate the scalded-cream delicacy—still warm, without waiting for it to cool off. It didn't taste as good as it usually did. But both Yurik and Nora had cooled off, and he came to sleep with her in her bed, as he did when he was sick. They hugged. Nora kissed his still-damp hair. His hair was so thick that it always took a long time to dry. Then, when he was already falling asleep, he said, "Nora, good things always come to an end. And after that, things aren't nice at all. At first it's really, really nice, but just when it's really, really nice, you fall from heaven into hell."

How does he know that? Nora thought. He can't possibly know that already . . .

The next morning, it seemed all was forgotten. Dressed in his new blue uniform, his bright, thick hair shining on his large head, holding a bouquet of asters, he mingled with the crowd of other seven-year-olds on their first day of school. Nora watched them attentively, musing that inside each one of them was a secret being, wise beyond its years, who knew things that grown-up people could no longer remember.

20

From the Willow Chest

Jacob's Letter to Marusya
Volunteer Ossetsky
(1911–1912)

SEPTEMBER 6, 1912

My sweet wife! My treasure! Instead of the tender words that are heaped up inside me since our parting, I'm going to pour out my heart to you. Being together is the only natural and right situation for us. The scrutiny of family members, my parents, relatives, and acquaintances was always dispiriting to me. But our relations exist somewhere beyond all the stuff of daily life, the trivial bickering and disputes, mutual annoyances that are so unpleasant to me. It's different with us—such banality is impossible. Never before has fate put such a hard choice in front of me as the one I face now; but without your approval I can do nothing. Our future depends on this.

Perhaps you are not aware that the Kiev Commercial Institute is the first of its kind in Russia, very advanced. When it was established as an institution of higher learning six years ago, quotas were not observed. As a result, almost 60 percent of the current students are of Jewish descent. We have to keep in mind that the Kievan Jewish community donates large sums to the Institute, which is why the administration agreed to educate Jewish young people. This little historical sketch concerns me, too, because I am one of these 60 percent. In a word, this shortcoming in the regulations is being redressed this year, and the usual quota for educational institutions, a Jewish enrollment of not more than 5 percent, has been introduced. Jews are faced with a choice—either convert to Christianity or enroll merely as auditors.

Last year, I came out first in my department, and transferring my status to that of auditor, going to lectures and waiting to see whether there is an opening, and competing for this with Jewish students like myself, would be degrading. It's especially painful now, when I have a good chance of getting a master's degree in commercial studies upon graduation. I had a talk with Professor Pogorelsky about the possibility of teaching in the future, which appeals to me much more than the practical application of the degree that my father favors.

The other option, that of conversion, is even more humiliating. You and I have touched on this subject many times before—how living in an Orthodox country, surrounded by its culture, we have come to love Orthodoxy, to sympathize with it. I have spoken to you about my basic religious views. The Ten Commandments passed down by God to Moses are also the foundation of Christianity. The figure of Christ inspires even more sympathy, as one of the most revered heroes of history, of culture. But I do not accept his divine origin. The Son of Man—this is how he referred to himself. As are all the rest of us, Jews first and foremost, and through them all others who have accepted the Commandments in some form or other. The prospect of being baptized is still more humiliating than transferring my status from student to auditor. Formal philosophical and religious considerations aside, there are many issues I haven't been able to resolve concerning my worldview; but no religion, neither Judaism, nor Christianity, nor the Chinese religion, has played a major role in building it. This kind of coerced baptism would be pure opportunism.

As for my own personal views, I am most likely agnostic. Although these notions (gnosticism and agnosticism) are rather confused, they are not diametrically opposed. If gnostics consider the world to be ultimately knowable, and agnostics think the world is not, I choose Gnosis itself as my God, which undoes the contradiction. This means that I am prepared to pursue knowledge and wisdom my whole life without hope for the possibility of attaining it. Of course, all these ideas are far more sophisticated than the practical decision I now face, but it's impossible for me not to take them into consideration. And the price one pays for one's education, even such a practical branch as I have chosen, cannot be subject to compromise. I have already made my decision. I am withdrawing from the Institute.

I have written about my decision to Genrikh. The opinion of my elder brother is far more important to me than that of my father in this matter. But his response will not arrive anytime soon, and the decision has already been made. I don't know whether he will support me in it. This year Genrikh's younger sister Anyuta was sent to Switzerland to study in a medical college in Zürich. I can't even dream of the possibility of going to Germany to study.

But about my withdrawal. I can't make my final decision without your input, because you are my wife, and if my long-term plans don't coincide with yours, I have to find another solution. Such a long-winded forewarning was due to the fact that I am afraid of revealing my plan to you, knowing beforehand how hard it will be for you to reconcile yourself to it. I have decided to enlist in the army as a volunteer. Don't be upset, don't faint, don't despair. I'll explain: This one-year (or two-year) term of military service will allow me to re-enroll in the Institute. Then I will be able to complete my studies in economics, to support a family, and to enjoy all the advantages of a happy marriage. The final decision rests with you alone. I give you the Roman right of veto.

I've already devised a plan for the coming months, and taken the first steps in preparation for my withdrawal. I took my German exam, fulfilling the requirements for the whole course. I also took my exams in trade and industrial law in advance. I am getting ready to take my English exam ahead of schedule. I'll pass it easily. It's not as hard as German, although the pronunciation is difficult. I read *King Lear* for the exam. Shakespeare's language is archaic, so I had to make a glossary; but the differences between the original English and the Russian translations are enormous! It's very satisfying to examine the differences. Kanshin's version is the best; it's a prose translation. Compare Kanshin's translation with this passage in English: "Thou art the thing itself. Unaccommodated man is no more but such a poor, bare, forked animal as thou art. Off, off, you lendings!"

In short, the original is stronger, more energetic, than the translation.

I would translate it like this: "You, abject man, are but a poor, naked two-legged animal! Begone, begone, superfluous attire!"

You see? Whenever I talk to you about pragmatic matters, I always have the urge to share my literary musings.

One or two years in the army—that's exactly what it's about. I'll be living among "poor forked animals"—not "bare," however, but wearing army coats. I must admit that I feel oppressed by my dependence on Papa, who is paying for my education. After two years of army service, I will most likely achieve financial independence.

I understand the sacrifices that you will have to make. It means that we will not be united for another one or two years. I will understand if you say no. I can't demand that you agree to this delay. But I am also sacrificing what I have always considered to be the most sacred thing for me—music. My musical education is in a bad state. The history of music, music theory, the foundations of composition—all this I can work through on my own. I have a knack for learning from literature. But reading books is a poor substitute for making real music, listening to music, and interacting with others in a musical environment. And this will not be available to me in the army.

The final decision rests with you, Marusya. If you object to my serving in the army, I will abandon the idea. Going to work in a commercial office would be an even greater trial for me than spending two years in the army. I leave the decision in your hands. I kiss those incomparably wonderful hands, and do not dare to encroach any further.

—Jacob

21

A Happy Year
(1985)

I n the fall of 1984, disaster befell Taisia—a disaster that became an unexpected boon for Nora. Taisia's husband, Sergei, a quiet, henpecked man, left her. No one could have expected such an audacious step after such a long, harmonious, and uneventful marriage. He left her without warning or regret, having stuffed his pants and instruments into a gym bag. He did not intend to return. Taisia was still trying to recover her composure after her initial bitter indignation when her listless, indolent daughter, Lena, a student in her final year at the Agricultural Academy, announced that she was getting married to a classmate, an Argentinian exchange student, and leaving with him for Argentina. While they were going through the bureaucratic rigmarole that attended such a move, her daughter brought the pushover husband home to live with them. They settled into Taisia's orphaned bedroom, and instead of Sergei, this disgusting "black-ass," as Taisia referred to her son-in-law, now frolicked in her bed. Her sagging, unattractive Lena suddenly straightened out and bloomed, fully liberated from her indisputable dependence on her mother. Taisia, who had spent her whole life teaching quotidian domestic wisdom to young mothers, now witnessed the complete destruction of her personal universe. She came to Nora and, sobbing, recounted both stories. She ended by saying she couldn't bear living under the same roof with a "black-ass." What should she do?

Without even considering the new possibilities that would open for her, Nora invited Taisia to move in with her until the newlyweds moved away, and Taisia gladly accepted the invitation. They began reorganizing the household right then and there. They moved Nora's desk into the room she called the "living room," and covered the divan with her bedsheets. Grandmother Zinaida's ancien-régime boatlike bed was put at Taisia's disposal. When Yurik got home from school and discovered Taisia, whom he had always considered to be some close relative, in Nora's room, he was delighted.

Not until that evening, when they were sitting over dinner together, did Nora realize that Taisia's constant presence in her home offered her a freedom she had never even dreamed of. Taisia had immediately taken early retirement when she moved in with them, and now picking up Yurik from school and feeding him dinner had become her sacred duty. Nora paid her the difference between her pension and what she had earned at the polyclinic, and both of them were happy with the arrangement.

Nora didn't manage to take advantage of the new opportunities right away, because, a couple of weeks after Taisia had moved in, Tengiz appeared again—without warning, without so much as a phone call.

They hadn't seen each other in a year. Their last meeting, in Tbilisi, had been short and accidental. Nora had arrived in Tbilisi with a theater company to stage a play—a rather weak one, a detective story with a set that resembled the labyrinth of a child's pocket maze puzzle. Nora had no intention of seeking out Tengiz. The unwritten rule of their relationship had never changed: they took it up again at any moment, in any place, that he wished; then he disappeared, as though he had never been. Nora had never taken the first step to contact him.

It was the first time Nora had ever been to Tbilisi, Tengiz's city. In the evening, she left the hotel to take a walk through the unfamiliar town by herself. She walked along Rustaveli Avenue, then wandered into the oldest part of town, down a crooked, deserted lane. She kept expecting him to appear from around a corner, waving to her. She walked along, enjoying both the sights of the city and her own fearlessness. He didn't appear from around a bend in the road or stepping out of a taxi; but his name popped up in a conversation the next day.

The director with whom she was working invited her to visit a local celebrity. They went in a large group to the dreary outskirts of Tbilisi, to a gray nine-story apartment building, where an Armenian artist about whom Nora had heard from some mutual friends lived. They were welcomed by someone who resembled a soothsayer or conjuror. She had a nose like a beak, and bright violet-plum eyes, and wore a strange, threadbare, dove-colored

177

garment made of silk and some sort of intricate turban on her head. Nora immediately wanted to draw her.

Nora didn't say a word, but looked at the paintings that covered every available space and stood three rows deep against the walls. It was impossible to know where the artist in her silks slept, because every surface was covered with easels, stretchers, pads of paper, and jars. Among all this painting paraphernalia was a small burner with two long-armed Turkish coffeepots and a few cups and saucers. There wasn't a single hint of daily routine, of daily life, of a bed. All the paintings depicted imaginary mythological beings—fairy-tale beasts, snakes, goddesses, and virgins. Colorful Oriental madness, executed with great talent and skill. In the middle of the room, on an easel, stood a large portrait of Tengiz, very academic, painted with a strong hand, and without even a touch of whimsical Orientalism. He was looking out from under his brow. The artist had grasped some precise crease of the lips, and the coloring of the portrait was so accurate, heavy, and above the head it seemed there was an explosion of sky—a desperate blue . . . The portrait was large and as yet unfinished. Nora imagined she could even smell his homegrown country tobacco . . . He was just here, sitting for the portrait, she mused.

She spent the entire next day at the theater, but after the first act she slipped away with David, a sweet young Moscow-Georgian actor who had grown up in Tbilisi. They killed him in the first act, so by the second, when the plot was unfolding, he was already as free as a bird. They were good companions, and he offered to show her around town. First they went down to the Kura River, then walked along the embankment. When they got hungry, they stopped at the first little wine cellar *cum* restaurant they came to. There was some sort of celebration under way. One half of the rather small room was occupied by a long table, and at the head of the table sat Tengiz. Next to him was a large Georgian woman with a drooping lower lip, who looked like a Gypsy. They were celebrating Tengiz's birthday.

He saw Nora and her companion as soon as they walked in. He stood up and announced: "Oh, we have guests from Moscow! Now, this is a real birthday present! Nora Ossetsky, my favorite artist! And her friend . . ." Tengiz faltered.

With a tender smile on her face, Nora said her friend's name to fill in the awkward pause.

"Sit down, sit down!"

Nora and David sat down on the chairs they were offered. For an hour and a half, Nora sat as though onstage, in the midst of the happy din of the Georgian feast, after which she and David stood up to go, thanking them all for their hospitality. Then they left, holding hands like lovers. She felt heartsick—Tengiz might think that she had planned this.

They went to the hotel without talking. Nora had a private room, like a VIP; the actors were all assigned shared rooms. David stayed in her room until the morning. He was wonderful, very young and shy. And it was good that he stayed. He probably wouldn't have if Nora had not invited him in. She had never discovered a better way of curing the wounds that Tengiz inflicted on her.

This time, Tengiz arrived with the words "You won't chase me away?" He was carrying the same duffel bag, and under his arm he had a case with a guitar for Yurik: a nearly full-fledged instrument, three-quarters of the size of a grown-up's guitar. Yurik grabbed hold of the instrument and immediately started strumming all six of the strings at once.

"Wait, we need to tune it first." And they went off to Yurik's room. Tengiz turned the tuning pegs deftly with his sensitive fingers and demonstrated the first five chords.

"Learn these chords and you'll already be able to play something," he said, and they strummed for a whole hour. With the movements of a sculptor, Tengiz arranged Yurik's fingers on the strings, and he got results almost immediately.

After dinner, Tengiz told Nora that he had come for half a year or a year, depending on how things worked out. He had gotten an interesting offer from Mosfilm, and in a few days, after the details were decided, he would be moving to a rented apartment that the studios had promised to provide him with. Then he went quiet, mumbled something, and went quiet again. Nora didn't say anything, either; but both of them were thinking about the same thing.

"There have been some changes in my life, you see. Nino got married, and her husband has a house outside Tbilisi. Natella decided to move in with our daughter—they're living there now. Natella left me, right? I'm a lone wolf now."

"I see," Nora said, nodding. He did have a trace of the wolf's gauntness about him—his eyes glittered with fierceness, or perhaps hidden fear. And he wants to stay here, with me!

Tengiz's hands had always been stronger than his head. He even said this about himself: "especially when my hands are you," he told Nora. But that wasn't quite what he meant. What he wanted to say was that Nora could put into words what he was unable to express. Russian was not his first language, of course, but even in Georgian he didn't know how to articulate his thoughts with precision. He relied on circumlocutions, gesticulations, howls and groans, and other forms of body language to get things across, but he ultimately succeeded in making the actors submit completely to his will. And not just the actors. It was a gift. He knew how to motivate people, and they did what he wanted them to. It was probably some ancient power of suggestion. There was possibly only one person on earth who didn't succumb to his power—his wife, Natella. He was in thrall to the primordial but insurmountable female power she wielded. For almost thirty years they had been locked in constant battle. Both of them felt doomed to continue this struggle, which neither of them could win.

"You're a witch, Natella, a witch," he would say in despair when he couldn't bear the sight of her any longer. "Just kill me outright. Why do you suck my blood, like a bird?"

Why a bird, he couldn't explain in ordinary, daytime language. He had a recurring dream, a nightmare: He was lying naked on the warm ground, in a pale-grayish-brown light, and someone seemed to be poking needles into his veins. And then he saw that they were actually filthy birds, covered in dirt, sucking his blood through their thin beaks—one on his neck, another on his stomach, and a third in his groin . . .

Nora gave him what Natella took away from him; this was the secret of their enduring relationship. Nora was the ideal receiver and retransmitter of his will, and working with her on a play was a pleasure for Tengiz. She was adept at translating his intentions, his mumbling and bellowing, into material language—a dark-red wall imitating brickwork, sepia-colored dresses, a white backdrop that had been spattered by a hail of artillery fire . . . And she kissed his hands, and licked every one of his fingers, like a puppy that nuzzles its mother's belly, looking for a nourishing teat.

"My clever girl," he whispered to her, surrendering his hands to her moist lips, her hard tongue.

What precisely she was licking off cannot be captured in words, but after each new episode, after each new performance, Nora became stronger and more sure of herself. Later, when Nora herself proved her mettle, transforming herself gradually from an artist and a set designer into a director, even an author, and staged her first plays in provincial theaters, she told him, "Tengiz, my directorial skills were sexually transmitted."

That first night, Tengiz slept on the floor, on a quilted cotton comforter spread out in the living room. The next day, they moved the furniture around again: Grandmother's boat bed sailed into the living room, the divan was passed on to Taisia, and the former population of the apartment (Nora and her son) was doubled, much to Yurik's delight.

Several days after Tengiz moved in, Yurik whispered in Nora's ear, "It's even better this way than with a German shepherd." It wasn't about the dog, of course, but about the guitar. He took it in his hands and began to like himself more. When no one else was home, he went out into the hallway, where there was a full-length mirror, and played, watching his reflection out of the corner of his eye. The happiness he experienced at this moment wasn't completely unprecedented. He suddenly remembered feeling the same thing when he was five years old, beating out rhythms on the African drum, and then on the xylophone. But he was also learning to read at just that time, and he had traded the xylophone for Kipling: first there was a cat who walked by himself; then Mowgli, who for many years was his favorite character from a book; and after that, four other books, which Nora thrust under his nose in short order, one after another. Now all that he had forgotten came rushing back to him. The guitar seemed to contain the rhythm of the drum, and the xylophone, and sounds, sounds from which phrases emerged in some mysterious fashion—though the phrases were different from those in books.

Tengiz shared his rudimentary theoretical knowledge of music with Yurik, and no new information inspired him like the ideas of modes, major and minor keys, intervals, and chord changes. He listened attentively now to the sounds of the world around him, evaluated them in the light of his newfound knowledge, and discovered every day anew that all the sounds of the world could be described with these new rules, and that there was music playing everywhere, at every moment, even in your sleep, getting louder or dying down. Now he heard a complex rhythm in the patter of the first raindrops, the dangerous pauses in the rumbling of the iron sheeting on the roofs of sheds; in the trill of the doorbell he caught the sound of a minor third . . . Tengiz had no idea what a powerful mechanism for perceiving the soundscapes and aural structures of the world he had unlocked. He was just happy about the boy's rapt attention, and the eagerness with which he absorbed this new information. Not that everything he discovered in this new aural universe was radiant and blissful: sometimes his new capacity for hearing filled him with anxiety, even torment.

Yurik now came straight home from school, not dawdling, and not getting distracted by the ways and habits of cats, which he used to follow for hours on end in their meanderings through the courtyards, over the roofs of sheds, and into basements. Nora was now teaching a children's drawing class—her only source of regular income during that year—so twice a week she was unable to pick Yurik up from school. Taisia wasn't always able to catch the boy at the school door. Sometimes Nora rushed home after her classes and found no sign of either Yurik or his book satchel. Then she would wander around the neighborhood for hours, looking for him. But after acquiring the guitar, Yurik no longer roamed the streets and court-yards, and when Nora got home she could already hear him strumming from the stairwell.

Tengiz met the screenwriter every day to discuss the grandiose project Mosfilm had offered him—the film version of *The Knight in the Panther's Skin*. They were trying to collaborate on the first draft. Nora read *The Knight* and tried to find something in it that spoke to her, to untangle the endlessly complicated story of the relationships between the sovereign, his knights, and their beloveds; it all seemed to her to be extremely ornate and fussy, mannered, and convoluted. When she tried to convey this to Tengiz, he brushed it off, saying it was only the preliminary material. The script they were writing would be very different from the original source. It would be about something different altogether.

"Just read it, and then we'll talk about it. When the script is finished, we'll do our own thing with it."

Tengiz never doubted for a minute that he could arrange Nora's confirmation as art director of the future film. But she had never worked in film before, and she understood that they had their own close-knit professional community, which would hardly welcome an outsider, with no experience in film, into their midst. This didn't worry Tengiz in the least. "We'll make you assistant director in that case," he said. In the meantime, Nora drew sketches that had been commissioned from her in Tashkent for *The Snow Queen*, feeling amused by the likely disparity in temperatures between the auditorium and the scenes unfolding onstage. But, for the time being, they were leading a happy and unusual life, visiting friends almost every evening, often taking a delighted Yurik along with them, or inviting friends over to their place. Natasha Vlasov came most often, with her eccentric husband, Lyonchik, and sweet Fedya, their son, who was connected to his parents by two umbilical cords. Yurik latched on to Fedya; at Yurik's age, an older friend was a valuable possession.

The only thing that remained unchanged for Nora was the need to oversee Yurik's daily homework. By this time (he was already in the fourth grade), it had become very clear that Yurik couldn't manage it on his own. Actually, even under Nora's supervision, he did it every which way. The main problem was his penmanship—a misnomer, since it was more like chicken scratch. Every time Nora sat him down to do his homework, the most agonizing task was getting him to do his lessons in Russian. He wrote as if he were seeing a pen for the first time in his life and his goal was to invent some new, nonstandard way of depicting familiar letters. He had a whole pile of unfinished notebooks, abandoned efforts to write legibly. It was seldom that Yurik managed to complete the third page of an assignment well enough to present it to the teacher, though the first and second were more or less acceptable. The teacher, Galina Semyonovna, was horrified by his handwriting, which she conveyed to Nora with inexhaustible zeal, hinting from time to time that Yurik belonged in a remedial school. Now Nora had a lever of influence: "You can play the guitar only after you do your homework." But the results weren't very impressive; though he started doing his homework more quickly, it was no better. Maybe this really was the best he could do?

Tengiz, observing Nora's frustration, shrugged and said, "Leave him alone. Can't you see? He's a wonderful boy."

Whether it was because Tengiz had been able to nudge awake the boy's slumbering memory of their trip together to Altai, or because Yurik had simply decided to assign the role of father to Tengiz, Yurik stuck to him like a burr. Tengiz responded to the boy's love with all his heart. Yurik discovered that Tengiz had a great many virtues. To Yurik's ear, he played the guitar beautifully; he taught him new chords, new tunes, and introduced music into their home that Yurik never knew existed. Tengiz ate with his hands, dexterously and with graceful ease, as only people who grew up in the Caucasus Mountains knew how to do. In his presence, Taisia stopped making remarks about how Yurik should be holding his knife and fork. Tengiz knew how to whistle. Not only that, but Yurik played chess better than Tengiz. At least, when he played against Tengiz, Yurik finally got to know the sweet taste of victory. Vitya very rarely lost, but Tengiz conceded defeat cheerfully and easily, which only added to his merits.

On Sundays, when Taisia gave in to her newfound urge for churchgoing and wasn't there to restrain Yurik in the hallway by Nora's bedroom door, Yurik burst into the room and crawled into their bed. Yelping like a puppy and poking them with his knobby knees and elbows, he dived under the covers and nestled his way between the still-sleeping Nora and Tengiz. Yurik, so sensitive to smell, didn't seem to notice the mixture of sweat and lingering vapors and traces of love, which the lovers had had no time to wash away. At first, Nora tried to discourage her son from these Sunday incursions, and even wanted to put a lock, or at least a latch, on the door. But Tengiz wasn't in the least shy or embarrassed. He hugged the boy to his chest and tickled him, laying his mouth against his belly and blowing noisily, which sent Yurik into gales of laughter. The game was, of course, an infantile one, but Yurik had evidently not outgrown the need for it.

The punctuated romance between Nora and Tengiz had lasted for more than twenty years, but they had never been completely alone. There was always a third party between them: the play they were staging together. This time, they had no common project, only indefinite plans. Now the third party was Yurik. It was genuine family life, a new arrangement of power, in which, fairly often, Tengiz and Yurik stood together against Nora in deciding the small issues that arose from one day to another. These were mostly trivial matters—potatoes or pasta for dinner, where they would go on Sunday, what to give Taisia for her birthday. But it was life as a threesome, family life, something wonderful and new in their shared experience; and they were happy in it.

Not long before the New Year, Genrikh came to visit. He had already met Tengiz, and liked him; and Genrikh wanted Tengiz to like him, too. From the first moment of their acquaintance, Genrikh had plied him with jokes and stories, laughing and slapping Tengiz on the back, very hail-fellow-well-met. He usually stayed a long time, and didn't want to leave. This time, though, he was uncharacteristically despondent. Still standing in the doorway, he told them he had contracted some strange illness called narcolepsy. From time to time, he would just fall asleep, all of a sudden, without warning—during a conversation, at a meeting, even while driving. Twice he had nearly crashed, and now he had come to the decision to part with his favorite toy, his trusty blue Lada, polished and gleaming inside and out, his Valya. He was in the habit of giving names to all his automobiles—the previous one had been called Marusya. Genrikh had even made a graph to keep track of all his inadvertent sleeping spells—from the first incident, a year and a half before, when he fell asleep during a meeting of the Academic Council, during a talk by one of his graduate students, right up to the most recent, very dangerous spell, on the road to the dacha, with his wife's daughter and grandson in the back seat. It was lucky he had ended up in the ditch, and not in the lane of oncoming traffic. In short, this time he was not full of jokes and fun. He looked defeated and doleful, and Nora pitied him.

He's still a kid—a kid, just like Yurik, Nora thought. Then Genrikh said, "If Yurik weren't so young I'd give the car to him, rather than try to sell it." Yurik, who had been preoccupied with fishing out the longest, juiciest strips of Taisia's home-fried potatoes from the serving dish, suddenly said, without missing a beat, "You could give it to Nora and she'd drive me around," and went back to eating his favorite meal.

"Now, that's a thought!" Genrikh said, brightening up. "I'll teach you to drive myself. I'll use my own method, and you'll become a pro in two weeks. All those driving instructors take the wrong approach, you know, like they're teaching you to read, letter by letter, syllable by syllable. But driving is like swimming, much closer to swimming than reading. You have to feel the movement! When you understand that it's about the movement of the car, or yourself in it, you're already a driver. What do you say, Nora? You do want to learn to drive, right?"

Now Genrikh, who had been so gloomy when he arrived, was beaming.

He's basically so kind, Nora thought. It wasn't often that she thought good things about her father, but now he was making her feel happy. A kind sort—he really is. He's showing off a bit, naturally, for Tengiz and Yurik. He wants them to like him. Actually, he wants everyone to like him . . . But he *is* a good man.

"Of course I want to. I always did. But listen, Dad, are you sure about this? You won't miss the car later?"

Tengiz poured Genrikh some wine. They drank to Nora's new automotive future. She hadn't thought about cars at all before this, but after Genrikh's suggestion, she suddenly realized that she wanted very, very much to shut the car door and step on the gas, to tear off down the road. And to steer! To steer!

The following Sunday, Genrikh stopped by to pick up Nora and fairly quickly taught her the essentials of driving. Much faster than she would have learned in driving school.

Two months later, Nora got her driver's license, after passing the exam on her first try. Genrikh signed the car over to her as a gift, and it became official: she was the driver of her own car. And it came in very handy indeed.

By spring, *The Knight in the Panther's Skin* had ground to a halt. Tengiz had quarreled with the screenwriter; launching the film at the beginning of the following year was out of the question, so either the director or the screenwriter had to go. The film studio decided to get a new director. They invited someone else, also a Georgian, who lived in Moscow; but, as they later found out, that arrangement didn't work out, either. Then the funding for the film was withdrawn, and it was never made.

While both of them were trying to cope with the fallout from this fiasco, all their money suddenly dried up: both Tengiz's advance and Nora's small savings. Without telling Tengiz, Nora first borrowed twenty rubles from Tusya, who had played the role of older friend her whole life. Nora didn't want to ask Amalia—although the puppy business was thriving, and the "dog money" was constant—because Amalia would start to worry, to pity Nora and Yurik, and to bemoan Nora's unfortunate life-choices. As for Taisia, who understood the complications of the situation, not only did she turn down her pay, but she spent her whole pension on food and considered going back to work at the polyclinic part-time.

Tengiz grew gloomier with every passing day. He had worked to support his family since childhood, had done all kinds of odd jobs in his college years . . . But he had forgotten, during this half a year of living with Nora, that a man is responsible for the upkeep of the family. He stayed in Nora's home like a guest, bringing home food and drink, extras they didn't really need, without thinking about providing sustenance day in and day out. Tengiz was already considering capitulation—going back to Tbilisi. Not only out of humiliating penury, but also out of fear, fear of losing his self-respect. Nora could understand this.

They were driving home after visiting friends on the outskirts of Moscow late one evening when a nicely dressed older man with a briefcase hailed them on a street in the Belyaevo-Bogorodskoe neighborhood. He asked whether they could give him a lift to Razgulyai. Nora was just about to tell him it was out of their way, when Tengiz intervened; he told her to take the passenger's seat next to him, and he himself got behind the wheel. The passenger got into the back seat. They drove to Razgulyai in silence. When they arrived, Tengiz took the five-ruble note the passenger proffered to him. The passenger got out.

"Let me earn money this way, Nora. I used to moonlight using my uncle's car when I was a kid. I can still do that, can't I? Until some work comes our way."

That night, while Zinaida's bed was still sailing over to dry land, Tengiz asked Nora: "What do I mean to you, Nora? Who are you to me?"

"Do you really want me to put it into words, an exact description?" She was delighting in the protracted moment of blissful emptiness.

"Yes, tell me."

Nora pondered for a minute, then said, "However shameful it is to admit, I'm prepared to be whatever you want me to be—an artist and set designer, a lover, a girlfriend, service personnel—even a floozy or a doormat, I guess. The fact is that you're the largest and best part of my life."

"But that's terrible. I have no way to repay you. There's not enough of me for that."

"For the time being, what you are is enough," Nora murmured. "Shh, shh . . ."

She was terrified that she would scare away the happiness that swept her up and held her afloat. And the better it was, the more terrified she felt.

The next day, Tengiz brought home a record that changed Yurik's life. Tengiz called him over and turned on the record player in the living room. It was a single by the Beatles: "I Want to Hold Your Hand." In those days, Beatles songs were still in the air, and although the group was already a thing of the past, Yurik was hearing their music for the first time. He sat with his eyes fixed to one spot, his fingers tightly clenched, swaying his head and shoulders back and forth like a Jew during prayer. Then Tengiz noticed that his feet were tapping out the rhythm. He said something, but Yurik didn't seem to hear him. They listened to the song till the end.

"Tengiz, what was that?"

"The Beatles. You've never heard of the Beatles?"

Yurik shook his head and put the record on again. It was impossible to drag him away from the record player until evening. When Nora took the record away, Yurik asked Tengiz whether he would buy him more Beatles.

"It's easier to get tapes. There are tons of them. The band doesn't exist anymore, you know—John Lennon was killed some years ago."

"What? Someone killed him? That's impossible!" Yurik wailed.

"But the band broke up before his death. Some years before."

Yurik began to cry.

"Why are you so upset? Only this morning, you didn't even know this John Lennon existed."

"Did they really kill him?" he sobbed. "I didn't know they killed him! And the drummer? Did they kill him, too?"

"Come, now. The time for all those tears has passed. He managed to accomplish in his life what few people even dream of doing," Tengiz said to Yurik, trying to comfort him. "But the drummer—his name is Ringo Starr—is alive and well, and plays with other people."

"With other people? How could he! What a bastard!"

"Never mind, he wasn't the best drummer in the world; they invited other musicians to take his place on their studio recordings."

Yurik banged his fist on the table, so hard that the record player jumped slightly, and ran into the other room, howling. In a single day, he had experienced, both at the same time, unbearable love and unbearable loss. Nora, who only caught the second part of this rather protracted scene, couldn't understand what had happened. Yurik had shut himself up in his room. Tengiz couldn't quite grasp what had happened to the child, either, why he had dissolved in grief.

But for Yurik, it was all as clear as day: Someone killed John Lennon. It was a terrible misfortune, because now there was no one to write that sublime music, music he needed from the first moment he heard it, as he needed air to breathe; music he would need, it went without saying, for the rest of his life. But no one, no one, understood. Not even Tengiz.

From the Willow Chest

Letters from and to the Urals

(OCTOBER 1912–MAY 1913)

ZLATOUST–KIEV

23 KUZNECHNAYA STREET, KIEV

JACOB TO HIS PARENTS

OCTOBER 31, 1912

I'm now in the barracks. The journey here was supposed to take four days, but we were delayed in Penza for eighteen hours. In Kuznetsk, where I sent you the telegram, we were delayed for twenty-two hours because of drifting snow. So, instead of four days, it took us six to get here.

They assigned me to the barracks, and I won't budge from here, since you aren't allowed to live in an apartment. But this doesn't pose any problem. In the training detachment I've been assigned to, the people seem to be nice enough, and everything will be fine. I'll most likely have to spend very little money, and I'm extremely happy about that.

Zlatoust is not a large city, but it's extremely spread out. It's situated on tree-covered mountains. We live near the train station, which is about six versts from town. For the time being, I have plenty of books. I am eager to study as much as time will allow.

Now I'm sitting in the well-heated room of the sergeant major, and I have no idea where I'll be sleeping tonight. Perhaps here, in the sergeant major's room. Don't laugh—it's a great honor for a soldier.

What I'm afraid of is that when you read my letter you'll moan and groan from worry. Poor thing, what a life! etc. It's not at all what you might think. There's nothing squalid about it, it's not a hard life. In all the places I've been so far—the adjutant's regiment, the senior doctor's, the junior doctor's—I've been treated very well. They invited me to sit down—which is the greatest honor they can pay a soldier.

My letters will surely take a long time to reach you. After I drop a letter in the regiment mailbox, it will not leave Zlatoust until the next day. And from the station, it will take at least five days to get to you. So there may be times when you won't get a letter for six or seven days.

Write me at the following address:
Zlatoust, Ufimskaya Guberniya
196th Infantry, Insarksy Regiment
Training Detachment
To: Volunteer Jacob Ossetsky

NOVEMBER 3, 1912

My duties have not yet begun. For the time being, I'm just observing my surroundings. I spend all my time in the office, together with one other person. I take my meals in the Officers' Assembly. The food is quite tasty and cheap. I buy my breakfast in the regiment store. Now I can even read the newspaper. They will give me *The New Times* every day in the Officers' Assembly. For the time being, I wear my own clothes. The accoutrements will be ready in a week. You must order two uniforms. One of them you give to the armory for safekeeping (for parades, celebrations, and campaigns), and the other is for everyday wear.

It's a good thing I arrived in my student uniform. Everyone noticed it, the officers inquired about it, and today some soldier even saluted me. My superior in the training detachment asks: "Where are you studying? Are you in college? What grade are you in?" (That's how much they understand about higher education.)

I'm so glad I brought books with me to read. I should have taken more, not just on specialized subjects. I've already done some studying today. There isn't even a regiment library here, and the town is six versts away. The Officers' Assembly only subscribes to *The New Times* and *Russian Invalid*. And that's in an officers' club, of all places. Maybe in the General Assembly there are a few more newspapers and periodicals.

The first day, I was very circumspect and cautious. I looked around me anxiously. I kept thinking they would grab me and send me to the guardhouse (military prison). In the evening, I sighed in relief and said my prayers—I'm joking, of course.

An officer I was conversing with said this to me: "There may be worse regiments than this one, but I doubt there are better ones." Maybe he's right.

THE NEXT DAY . . .

I got leave to go to town today. While I'm still not in uniform, I have a great deal of freedom. I don't take part in training yet. I just walk around among the soldiery and observe. And I come across many things that interest me. Now I'm going into the city. I'll send you this letter from there. If I mail it directly from the station, you'll receive it a day earlier. Letters don't leave the regiment mailbox until the following day . . .

SEPARATE PAGE, TO THE KIDS

NOVEMBER 3, 1912

Dear kids! I got your letter in the mail. It made me very glad. Use my paper and ink wisely! Form a committee, choose a chairman, and make your own decisions. You have my approval, in advance.

You know that this place is called Zlatoust—meaning "Goldmouth." But if you think that Zlatoust is full of golden mouths and that the soldiers ride around on cannons all day long, think again. So far, I haven't even noticed any golden mouths, or even any golden mustaches. The mouths you see here are the kinds you'd never want to kiss! And the soldiers don't ride around on cannons, because there are no cannons in sight either. Poor soldiers! If only they could!

They haven't made me a general yet, and they haven't entrusted me with a golden sword. But in time, God willing, both things will come true. You'll see!

For the time being, though, I'm just a soldier. But you probably don't know what this means. Let me explain. I open the manual for young soldiers, and this is what I read (page 16): "The word 'soldier' is a common one, familiar to all. Every subject who has sworn allegiance to the Tsar and who agrees to carry out the sweet and heartfelt obligation to defend the Faith, the Imperial Throne, and the homeland is given the name 'soldier.' He must do battle with both internal and external enemies." That's me. Attention! I'm everyman, and famous! I'll defeat enemies, internal and external, with my gun! (Senya, I have a rifle, a real rifle. And it shoots.)

Perhaps you're interested in my economic situation and domestic affairs, Mama?

I bought thick woolen socks in Zlatoust. I also got a mattress. That's about all. I have need of a small basket—after one change of clothes, I keep my dirty linen in a large basket. When it comes time for a second change, I have things laundered. You aren't allowed to keep more than two changes of linen in the basket.

I can't wait for my uniform to arrive. It puts me in an awkward situation not to have it. When I meet an officer from my detachment in the street, I still have to salute. Yes, sir; No, sir; Good morning, sir—I already have that down pat. But it's somehow a shame for my student uniform. In any event, I should be getting the uniform tomorrow or the next day.

SEPARATE PAGE, TO THE OSSETSKY KIDS

Wait a bit and I'll be sending each of you your own letter. But for now, this is how it has to be. I'm writing to the whole flock!

Senya, what books on the history of Russian literature are you talking about? You have to tell me the name of the author, not the color of the cover. What if you colored it yourself? Grisha, you haven't written a word to me. And I'm so interested in your studies.

The city of Zlatoust is high in the mountains. The mountains are so high that you can't even see the top. And they're covered with forest, thick pine forest. You can't collect rocks and minerals here, because the snow is very, very deep. In the summer, I'll search for them, though, and by the first of November, you'll receive them.

There are many Tatars living in this city. But they don't sell old things; and some of them even sell very new things. So they aren't called "rag-and-bone men" here. All the people here (Tatars included) walk down the middle of the street, not on the sidewalk. I don't know why myself. Maybe you can guess? Could it be because there aren't any sidewalks to walk on?

There are lots of soldiers here. So many that Rayechka wouldn't be able to count them all. Or has she already learned to count to a hundred? Eva, write me about what you're reading now. Who chooses books for you to read? And what Senya is reading, too.

A big hello, from Zlatoust all the way to Kiev and back. And that's no small hello! It travels a thousand versts.

Slowly but surely, I'm settling into military life. It's a very special field of activity, which you civilians have no inkling of. The soldier's life has its own particular hardships and its own particular joys. And you can't avoid any of them.

When I take a good hard look at the people who surround me (and they are all officers and soldiers), I have to consider myself to be the happiest of them all. The officers here are bored in the extreme. They curse both the service and Zlatoust. Soldiers are downtrodden, browbeaten creatures. They all suffer, and make one another suffer. What does it matter to me? In a year, I will have fulfilled my term of duty, and I'll wipe it all from my memory. I'll go home—and goodbye, Zlatoust. But they will all be staying right here.

Our regiment is stationed in four places: a unit in Zlatoust, one in Chelyabinsk (six hours away), and two in factories not far from Zlatoust. Small towns. My own Twelfth Company is stationed at the Katav-Ivanovsky Ironworks (three or four hours away). After I complete my "training course" in the detachment, they'll send me to the company. But this will happen only after the summer camps. For the time being, you can write to me at the Training Detachment, 196th Infantry, Insarsky Regiment. The camps take place in different locations every year. In recent years, they took place near Chelyabinsk, another time near Samara . . .

Change is afoot in my life. It seems I'll be leaving for my company very soon. In the company, it will be a lot better than in the detachment. The crème de la crème of the soldiery is found in the detachment. They choose the best people, who go through a special school and, after finishing the course in one year (with a "diploma" in hand), are assigned as teachers to the young soldiers. And they get the highest soldiers' ranks: corporals, junior and senior noncommissioned officers, and sergeant majors. They study for the entire day in the detachment. And the discipline is much more stringent than in the company. Of course, this does not affect me at all. I sit around doing nothing all day. I go to bed and get up whenever I want to. I even have time to study! To my great disappointment, all roads to promotion in the ranks are closed to me. A Jew can become a corporal—but nothing higher. The way is barred. My career as a soldier is over. This is why they are transferring me from the training detachment to the company. All the volunteers (Russians) envy me.

The conditions of barracks life are quite decent, but when I enter the company, they will improve.

If I were from this area, they might even let me live at home. But barracks life is not as terrible as you might think. It's spotlessly clean. No sign of bedsheet fauna. They are very strict about cleanliness. You're punished for even the most minute spot of dirt. For a torn shirt, dirty hands, toenails, mud-stained legs and puttees, an unmade bed, dust on surfaces, a cigarette smoked in the barracks—punishment! It's extremely effective. The ventilation is good. I had to sleep for a few nights in a common barracks. Can you imagine that in a place that houses twenty-five people (soldiers, at that!) the air is as fresh in the morning as it was during the day? It's quite incredible, but it's true.

The walls of the barracks are lined with pine boughs.

I'm eating well. I go to the Officers' Assembly to eat. I eat both lunch and dinner there, and drink my tea.

ZLATOUST–MOSCOW
JACOB TO MARUSYA

NOVEMBER 19, 1912

I write my parents about the everyday details of my life. They aren't really interested in anything else. The longing I feel here I can describe only to you. What I lack here is—You, Music, Books. There is simply no cultural life whatsoever. Even the officers are poorly educated. Among them are, of course, some wonderful and sincere people. I must learn to survive this year without all of those things that are the very stuff of life for me. Even, it seems, without study. It is very difficult to find time here during the day. Envy is an ugly feeling, but something like it has taken hold of me. Somewhere in Kiev, in Moscow, in Paris, the life that intrigues me, the life I can participate in, is going on without me. How marvelous it is, Marusya, that you are able to study, and you have your school, and the courses, and a life filled with both intellectual and physical activity. In an article by M. Voloshin, which I happened to read last year, he describes in a very compelling way your *Bewegung*, but he also discusses the artistic side of things and holds in high regard the performances of Mrs. Rabenek's troupe. And, poor me, I have yet to see them! I have never once witnessed you onstage! And when will I get the chance? My imagination paints a sublime but dim spectacle for me.

My longing is only augmented by the constant sense of your absence. I think that a romantic lover would put it differently: I am always aware of your presence! Alas, I feel only absence. And the complete absence of letters. Only one postcard in all this time!

NOVEMBER 19, 1912

This is one of the rare moments of silence in the barracks. The troops have gone to the city for a scheduled review. It's nice and quiet. I received your letter yesterday. It didn't take long at all to arrive here—just five days. Four days and six hours en route. Thus, 102 hours altogether. As long as it takes to get from Kiev to, say, London.

About clothing and the climate. The winter here is not terribly harsh. It rarely gets colder than fifteen or twenty below (Fahrenheit). And, in general, I love the cold. In spring, it's worse. There are mists and fog from the mountains, dampness . . . But it doesn't pose a problem, since I don't catch cold very often.

The overcoat lined with quilted cotton batting—your advice, Mama!—isn't permitted, and it would be inconvenient, because I couldn't roll it up and wear it over my shoulder. Moreover, it would be extremely hard to carry out the manual of arms. If it gets terribly cold, I'll wear more layers of underwear. That will suffice. Actually, it's only on their feet that soldiers feel the cold. I'll have to think about what to do. I was advised to buy government-issue boots (the best ones cost three or four rubles). They are very roomy, so you can wrap many layers of puttees around your feet. That's what I'll do. I bought some woolen socks, and they've already worn through. Puttees are better. So I advise you not to worry, Mama. It's obvious that if it's cold, or if something's uncomfortable, unpleasant, I'll try to get warm and comfortable and feel better as soon as possible, in any way I can.

I received my uniform—that is, the order for it arrived at the company. Tomorrow the order will be delivered to the tailor, and they will take my measurements. It will be ready in about six days. That means I won't be a full-fledged soldier until after November 25. All this time, I have been idle, from the point of view of a soldier's duty. I don't attend training, or take part in formations. I practiced gymnastics for a few days, and rifle disassembly; but then they sent me to the office unit, where I have nothing to do.

On the other hand, I can spend some time with my books. Many thanks for the Kiev newspaper. I can't subscribe to it here, however. I often read *The New Times* in the Officers' Assembly, where I take my meals. And sometimes I buy *The Russian Word* at the train station.

You tell me that business is good this year, Papa. I'd love to know about it in more detail: about the mill, the hay transport, and the "Berlin" barges— whether navigation is still possible . . . Before I left, you said I would be your assistant after I finish the Institute. Well, an assistant has to know the details! This will be my main activity, rather than music. Perhaps you were right. There are places on this earth where music simply doesn't exist.

Yesterday I was sitting on my bunk and reading a book in German. Some soldiers came in and asked me to read it aloud to them. I read, and they listened attentively.

Once, in a lesson on Divine Law, one of them answered, very confidently, "Moses was born in a basket"!

A SEPARATE PAGE

Dear kids! Your letters make me so happy! So write me as much as you can. I want to know about everything, everything interests me. About Ivan the Terrible, and about stamps, and about your new pencil.

Yesterday I took a walk in the woods and was very sad you weren't with me. The forest is thick, fir trees everywhere you look . . . It's quiet, there's no one around. The snow is deep. And the road in the forest is narrow. When I met an oncoming wagon and had to step out of the way, my legs sank into the snow past my knees! That's how deep it is. Now everything is covered with snow. And the river Ai and the river Tesma look like big snowy plains.

MOSCOW–ZLATOUST
MARUSYA TO JACOB

Postcard

NOVEMBER 20, 1912

I have three postal receipts—for Zlatoust . . . I've sent three letters: on the 8th, the 10th, and the 16th. I can't even remember how many postcards I've sent. I don't understand it. If the letters have gone astray, I'll complain in no uncertain terms! Devil take it! It's so frustrating and unpleasant. I'm furious!

ZLATOUST–MOSCOW
JACOB TO MARUSYA

NOVEMBER 20, 1912

My Sweet Marusya! Your postcard arrived! I thought I'd never get a letter from you. I'd much rather fault the postal system than look for another reason. And the reasons that occurred to me I won't even bother telling you. After writing three letters to you and not getting an answer, I was almost convinced that I had only dreamed Marusya, the one and only Marusya. And our summer strolls through Kiev, and our secret Lustdorf, and my wife—they were all a mirage. And our trip to Moscow (which I hardly noticed) was enveloped in Marusya's shadow, like a hallucination or psychological aberration of some sort. And introducing you to my family—how worried I was that you wouldn't like them, or they you. Only I didn't worry about the kids, I knew they would love you. All of these memories were like a theater of shadows. Had they ever happened? But now I look at your postcard, and it's proof that you exist. You write that you are furious, and that means you are you. I'm furious, *ergo sum*! Furious, therefore I am. Ah, I never learned Latin, and you won't find a dictionary around here for miles. For three weeks already, I have been trying to persuade myself that life here is interesting nevertheless, that I have to delve into it, to make something of myself within this strange term of duty—in a word, that I have to accept all the gifts life brings, even the fact that you shimmered in my sky, then flashed on past, as shooting stars have a habit of doing.

ZLATOUST–KIEV
JACOB TO HIS PARENTS

DECEMBER 6, 1912

Today is a holiday. The Feast of St. Nicholas, the patron saint of our Tsar. Would you like me to describe to you, my dear ones, how the barracks celebrates this holiday? In complete idleness. People read the drill regulations manual and do exercises, while five accordions are playing and everyone is spinning yarns and playing the fool. The first platoon is singing songs. You don't believe me?

Here's a soldier, asleep. A noncommissioned officer and a few soldiers sidle up to him. The officer swings his belt above his head like an incense censer, and intones, "Remember, O Lord, the soul of the deceased soldier so-and-so!" The chorus chimes in, "Lord, have mercy on him." They sing in harmony. Someone opens the drill regulations manual and recites it out loud, like the Gospels.

It ends with the "deceased" sitting bolt upright, then leaping up and chasing around the "priest" and the "choirboys." There's a friendly tussle, which then escalates into a war. Platoon against platoon. The platoon commander himself serves as the banner flag. They capture him, and he shouts from the other room, "Boys, rescue me, give it all you've got!"

The boys give it all they've got; with a loud "Hooray!" they storm the room and save their "banner." It really is a lot of fun!

A deputation comes up to me:

"Mr. Volunteer, we're having a disagreement among ourselves. How much does a little whip with a rabbit's foot cost?"

. . . These are my last days with the detachment. My uniform is ready. The overcoat is being made now.

On Sunday, most likely, I'll be leaving for my ironworks. My Twelfth Company is stationed not in Zlatoust, but at the Katav-Ivanovsky Ironworks—eight hours away from there, it turns out. It will be much better there than in the detachment. There is very little supervision from above. Much more free time.

KATAV-IVANOVSKY IRONWORKS–KIEV
JACOB TO HIS PARENTS

DECEMBER 9, 1912

I'm in Katav already. As predicted, it's much better here. I think things are going to be fine.

Before I left, the head of the Training Detachment pestered me with questions about what I intended to do in Katav, where I would eat. I was a bit worried about that myself. Katav is in the middle of nowhere, and it's very hard to get anything.

"Listen, Ossetsky, send the commander of the Twelfth Company my personal regards and ask him whether it would be possible for you to take meals at his place with him."

"Of course. I'm grateful to you."

The company commander listened to my request and promised to ask his wife. But today he told me that it would be awkward for a company commander to accept money from someone in the ranks. Therefore, he recommended that I take meals with one of the officers. Ensign Biryukov has accepted the duty to "nourish" me. Today I ate with him for the first time. I'm going there to take my evening meal now. Biryukov and his wife are sweet people; they treat me with great courtesy. I'm happy overall with the higher-ups here.

Oh, and another thing! The company commander ordered me to wear my soldier uniform. At the transfer station (where we were held up for seventeen hours, waiting on a military troop train!), I changed into my student uniform. I decided it would be better to report for duty for the first time in that attire. I was wearing civilian dress when I went to the Biryukovs', but now I'm already wearing my soldier uniform.

It's quite well made. A fitted waist, cinched with a belt. Red piping, double-breasted buttons, Rifle No. 152525, Personal No. 83, Second Platoon, Volunteer Private Jacob Ossetsky. Picture-perfect!

Perhaps you're interested in where I'm writing this letter? I'm sitting in the company office. "Mr. Ensign" is reading the orders for the regiment. A twenty-inch lamp is burning on the table. The light is steady and bright. The papers I have just begun to write up are lying on the table. Lists of names in the lower ranks eligible for allowances from the Twelfth Company of the 196th Insarsky Infantry Regiment on December 1, 1912. I'm writing you on official government paper. By my own calculations, this theft could get me two years in a disciplinary battalion, but I'm too lazy to walk over to the other stack of paper. You see the problem? So write me, all of you! Relieve me of this boredom!

Write me, Papa; write me, Mama! Siblings one and all, write me! Otherwise, I might forget you.

I just found out that in the Kazan region some reserves who had already finished their term of duty were detained. I feel terribly sorry for them. They've already served for two extra months. Their three years of duty probably went by faster than these last two months. In the event of war, they will most likely send us to the interior, to guard the region. Although, if war breaks out between Russia and China, they'll send us there immediately. I don't think there will be any war, though. It won't come to that.

DECEMBER 15, 1912

I'm close to despair. It's like beating my head against a wall. I've sent five letters already! Two registered letters and one ordinary mail. The registered letters were sent on December 1 and 8. So you should have gotten the first one on the 5th. Dancing devils, what's going on? Tomorrow I'll make inquiries about the letter from the 13th.

How stupid and annoying it is—you write and write, and your words disappear into the ether. Am I going to disappear somewhere along the way, too? I have to leave soon. In two months and fifteen days. The time will fly by, and you won't notice.

I'm feeling mournful—mainly because of the postal situation. Mikhail is coming over on Christmas. He's become a true bon vivant, a dandy and a man of the world! Mark will probably invite us over for New Year's. It seems he'll be moving to Riga next year. I've never been as close to him as I am to Mikhail, but I'll miss him very much. Is there a place in your life for music now? Someone probably has a piano there. Ask around. Is it possible that you haven't been able to play for all this time?

DECEMBER 20, 1912

I dream of music. Last night, before I woke up, I heard Tchaikovsky's Piano Concerto No. 2 in its entirety. From the first note to the last. I really do know it by heart. I love the first concerto more, though. But in my dream, it was even fuller and more alive than I was aware of. Richer and more resonant. But I long for music. I went to church. The singing was unbearably flat. Remember when your ridiculous friend Vanya Belousov took us to Blagovesh-chenskaya Church? What sublime singing! Breathtakingly beautiful.

I try not to let myself think about you coming here. I won't indulge my hopes—otherwise, I might drift off into daydreams, and that would be a luxury I can't afford here. Before I know it, I see your lips, with a sweet, childish expression, your hands, and the lovely little bones of your wrists, the little blue veins under your pale skin . . . No, spare me! I transfer my gaze to the crude, rough fabric of my existence here. I feel that from the contrast alone I could explode like a cold glass touching boiling water.

That's all; I kiss you, a very formal kiss, on the white part on the top of your head, and on your neck, in the back, where the hair starts to grow . . . It's impossible . . . and all of you, all of you . . . Lustdorf.

DECEMBER 21, 1912

Ah, Marusya! I can't keep silent! The company is getting ready to perform a Christmas play. A real soldiers' play, in which the men's and women's parts are all played by heavyset soldiers with mustaches. I have been asked to be the prompter. If only you could see what awkward, ridiculous figures they cut, not knowing what to do with their hands, their feet. At first they stood facing the audience for the entire act, not moving a muscle. When the sergeant major ordered a bit more dynamism, they began running around like chickens with their heads cut off, waving their arms aimlessly.

It was hilarious! It inspired laughter—but only in me. No one else sees anything comical in it. What bumpkins!

Marusya, I've made a discovery. Coming here was like going deaf—I'm completely deprived of music, and miss it terribly. A barrage of shouts, curses—these are the sounds that surround me. I went to church. The choir is wretched, but fairly large—about a dozen choristers, with a precentor hailing from true peasant stock, creaking, aged voices singing any which way. Do you remember the singing in the church in Kiev, what a joy it was to listen to? One hears the crudest sounds in the world here; even the sound of the church bells is somehow off. My God, how musically moribund it is here! And I believed that music was banished completely from these parts.

But yesterday one of the soldiers grabbed the accordion, a barbaric instrument, and started playing. Two other soldiers took up the tune and started singing something so wonderful, the likes of which I've never heard before in Ukraine. It was as though my ears opened up to these heartrending sounds. The folk music here is a delight, every bit as wonderful as Ukrainian music. Now I walk around listening for it whenever and wherever I can. I seem to have missed a huge piece of musical education, which was only slightly familiar to me through Russian opera. Only now do I understand where it originated, the wondrous Russian love songs, and Varlamov, and Gurilev, from whom both Glinka and Mussorgsky borrowed a great deal. Goodness, how could I have missed it . . .

DECEMBER 22, 1912

Getting ready for the holidays. Yesterday we cleaned, scoured, decorated the whole day long. Actually, cleanliness in the barracks is always maintained. Every Saturday, all the bunks are stripped and turned out to air, the floors are scrubbed and strewn with pine shavings, and the rooms fill up with the lovely scent of pine tar. The kitchen is equally clean. There is a large marble-topped table, on which rations are sliced and divvied up—although the rations are then placed by hand on dirty scales to weigh out the allotted hundred-gram portions. After lunch, cleanliness reigns again. The samovar boils the whole day long. This beverage is the soldier's constant helpmeet. Soldiers live for the most part on tea, porridge, and sleep.

Yesterday was the soldiers' steam bath, *banya* day. I enjoyed it immensely, because it was the first time in my life I had ever been in a real Russian *banya*. I thoroughly and deliciously steamed myself. I lay down on the top bench, where it is hottest, and beat myself with birch branches in the customary fashion. A soldier kept crying out: Make more steam! Harder, thrash me harder! In the dressing room, now fully relaxed, and without an ounce of strength left in me, but extremely satisfied and content, I lay down on a bench and gave myself all the time I needed to gather my strength and wits about me. Now, that's what you call a *banya*! First-class. I'll never take a bath again at home.

I'm learning a great deal from the soldiers here. I already take steam baths and play the accordion. Well, what of it—it's also a musical instrument, is it not? Who knows what the future holds?

Yesterday I read in the papers that the Dnieper is already ice-free and open for navigation. That's never happened before, has it? It's also very warm here—around twenty-six or twenty-eight degrees Fahrenheit, and never colder than about twenty-three. I was already used to fifteen or twenty below. Well, I can live with it.

Addendum

Children! You haven't written me in a long time. I'm not happy about this. Write me about the play you saw (Andersen's fairy tale). I received a letter and a playbill. I'm delighted about both of them. I'd like to know more about it. But—I'm sorry—my eyes are closing.

KATAV-IVANOVSKY IRONWORKS–MOSCOW
JACOB TO MARUSYA

JANUARY 15, 1913

Today I received your first letter sent directly to Katav! And right after that came three more, which had been written earlier and were lost along the way. What a rich man I am today! I arranged them all by date, and didn't unseal them for a long time. Impatience, and anticipation, and reassurance that there is another life, in which my wife is alive, in her blouse I love, with her hair bound up in a ribbon, with sunken cheeks, only an outline of flesh . . . What nonsense I'm writing you, my mind is wandering. It seems I live only in the world of my imagination!

You ask what Katav is like. It's a small settlement that lives solely from the large cast-iron foundry and factory. From the time when there was a strike, the factory stopped working. For this reason, Katav became impoverished, and the population of the village dwindled. Only parts of the factory are functioning now. There's a sawmill and a locksmith's—that's all. The huge factory halls are locked up and empty; the tall chimneys belch no smoke. A railroad was built here especially for the ironworks, and a huge pond was dug. The barracks stand on the far side of the pond, in the village of Zaprudovka. Why am I telling you all of this?

No, no, we won't be together in Katav. I'll meet you in Chelyabinsk. Although I still can't imagine that I will see you in the flesh, dressed in your gray hat and wearing your white felt boots, and that you will descend the steps of the train car, right into my arms . . . I'm trying to get furlough for those days, and if they don't grant it, I'll just up and head for the hills! Of course, they'll let me off on leave. Imagine how all the officers would surround you and stare at you here in Katav. No, no! We are meeting only in Chelyabinsk, and that's final. I can wait two and a half months to see you—but I'm willing to wait two and a half years if I have to! Though even two and a half hours is unbearably long. March 1 is the day!

Life in the army is going well. There's only one cause for complaint. And it's something very, very unpleasant. The company commander reads all the soldiers' letters. He hasn't opened my letters yet, and it seems he doesn't intend to. But, in any case, be aware that it might happen at some point. At the first sign a letter has been tampered with, I'll let you know. I sent a letter to my fellow student Korzhenko, asking him about the exams. I've already begun studying for them.

I'll send you more details about my furlough when I know more myself.

Yesterday evening, the sergeant major and I were lying in bed in the barracks. The conversation turned to the subject of conjugal life. He spoke very seriously, earnestly—my God, the things he told me! His manner was such that I started asking probing questions. Soon it turned into a question-and-answer session. I listened and I learned, and eagerly. Truly, Marusya, life itself, not just books, must be a source of learning.

I was only anxious about one thing—whether he would start asking questions, too. But it all turned out well. After I discovered what was most important for me to know, the discussion became less serious and lost its sense of urgency, and I said good night.

There was just one thing that struck me as strange—he thought that he was talking to a very experienced person. He didn't notice, by my questions, how ill-informed I really was. Actually, I tried to appear very canny about everything. And, apparently, I pulled it off.

5:00 a.m. I've just returned. I was at the "Wednesday," and afterward a large, fascinating group of people came over to talk. Four interesting men, very intelligent, hovered around me for a long time. They like me. Do you understand, my Jacob, they like me! And I'm happy. It pleases me to hear about my lovely arms and hands, my eyes, that I'm divinely inspired, etc., etc. They say I have remarkable eyes, and I want to shout with joy, Jacob! It's me, your wife, who has lovely eyes, and lips, and hands! I'm desired by all these elegant, refined men—and it makes me happy, simply happy—because you desire me.

Jacob, my dearest and best—there is no success or joy that can tear me away from my dreams for so much as a second. It makes me want you even more intensely. My God! My faith in you is so strong, so deep, it frightens me. You are my most profound, and everlasting, faith. So much so that I am scared by it.

It's already daylight. I'm going to bed. I embrace you. No need to kiss my hand today.

Well, goodbye, beloved. My Jacob . . . Don't think badly of me—I'm not drunk! Only I miss you terribly.

KATAV-IVANOVSKY IRONWORKS–KIEV
JACOB TO HIS PARENTS

JANUARY 20, 1913

What will become of my studies at the Institute? This disturbs me even more than the war. Through my friend Korzhenko, I found out that I must take furlough immediately and pass a minimum number of exams. Don't mention this in your letters, though. The company commander mustn't know that I'm planning to take a leave. Just to be on the safe side. The only thing that really worries me is that they won't grant me furlough. Oh well, I'll just drop out of the Institute in that case. Without any hopes of being readmitted. And the obstacles before me are formidable: first, they may refuse to give me leave—it's not at all unlikely; and second, if they grant me leave, I still might not satisfy the minimum requirements for passing the exams. It's hard for me to find even three hours a day to study. And how can I work in a tiny room packed with people? And there's nowhere else to go.

JANUARY 23, 1913

... There are moments when I am filled with jealousy and longing, thinking about you onstage—wearing your tunic, your arms and shoulders bare, your wondrous feet—you dance in a circle with other actresses, and still the spectators are staring only at you. And I feel anguish and suffering, that strangers' eyes can gaze at your body. The greedy gazes of men. I feel these thoughts will suffocate me! I banish them, realizing that I shouldn't be thinking them, much less writing them. But we made a pact about mutual honesty.

JANUARY 25, 1913

... "My dream is that you will abandon the theater or at least leave it temporarily and come 'home.'" Every other year! I am so sad. Does this mean that you in fact don't approve of my being onstage? Why?

Jacob, I can't abandon the stage, I can't and I shouldn't. Every other year would be impossible. In one year, the public forgets an actress's name! They would even forget Komissarzhevskaya if she left for a year! And a young actress all the more! I believe in myself, and I believe in this opportunity I have. It will allow me to become what I can and must be. This is not ordinary theater. It's an intricate and complex life, in which dance is only one way of grasping it, its great mysteries. We have spoken so much about this. I've only been onstage for one year. And I have accomplished a great deal in this year. You must also take into account the fact that I have not fallen victim to anyone's embraces or touched anyone's lips. By ignoring male protection, I know that it will take me three times longer to achieve what I wish. How can you speak about "greedy gazes" to me? I feel these gazes constantly, even on the tram, or in the library. I won't abandon the theater. Unless it abandons me. I can't imagine that you would ever issue an ultimatum—"me or the theater." It would be doubly hard for me—to lose you for this reason, or to lose the theater?

Horrible! Did you really talk to that sergeant major about me?

KATAV-IVANOVSKY IRONWORKS–MOSCOW
JACOB TO MARUSYA

JANUARY 25, 1913

The degree to which a man is capable of adapting to his circumstances is simply remarkable. I think that, if I end up in hell, within a month I'll be feeling right at home, after I've found out where the library is, the opera, and whether some sinner might get hold of a piano for me. In a few months' time, I'll be so comfortable there that I won't want to move to another apartment, even one in heaven.

At first, especially in Zlatoust, it was very hard to make myself get up in the morning. I would dream about home, and when I woke up I couldn't figure out where I was, how these strange walls that surrounded me had sprung up. Then, in a flash, it all comes back to you, and reluctantly, lazily, you start getting dressed. Now it's not like that at all. I've completely adjusted to life inside these new walls, and to my dirty room. I'm as contented as a cat here. And, in time, I may get used to spitting on the floor, blowing my nose in my hand, and using my own handkerchief as a napkin and a tea towel.

The transition back to being a gentleman promises to be long and painful.

You will teach me, Marusya, as you taught the little children when you were still a Froebel teacher—to hold a fork and knife, not to wipe your nose on your sleeve, not to make improper noises.

"Jacob, don't eat with your fingers. Use your napkin to wipe your face. How many times do I have to tell you not to spit in the dining room!"

It's hard for me even to imagine you'll be here soon! Not counting today, since it's already evening, there are thirty-nine days left until March 5. I can't wait until you get here—and at the same time it's hard to believe in your visit. Every day, I draw a portrait of my wife in my notebook; but there are fewer pages in the notebook than days before your arrival. Still, I remind myself constantly that it's all some kind of game. No one's coming to visit me. It's just a subject in a novel in the spirit of Bunin. With a tragic ending, it goes without saying—just like in "Antonov Apples."

Telegram

FEBRUARY 1, 1913
THE STAGE IS YOURS I'M SORRY FORGIVE ME ONLY 32 MORE DAYS HUS-
BAND JACOB

MOSCOW–KATAV-IVANOVSKY IRONWORKS
MARUSYA TO JACOB

FEBRUARY 10, 1913
Here's a story for you apropos the incident with the sergeant major, which so irked me. Only mine is better, because it's not a conversation between men about women, which I hate, but about humanity.

Lena came from Kiev for a recital. It was organized by Goldenweiser. The very same—friend of Leo Tolstoy's. I happened to be free that evening, and I went to hear Lena. I was nervous and excited for her, but it all went smoothly. Lena played beautifully—she was the best of all of them. Goldenweiser (a plain man with an unpleasant voice) praised her.

But this is how the story goes: The concert hall was very far away. It was late, and I had to take a cab. The first cabbie I came across didn't ask for too much money—so I agreed, and we talked along the way. The cabbie had been married for six years, and had two children. "Is your wife here? In Moscow?" "Of course! I couldn't exist for a single day without her." That's what he said—"exist." "You wouldn't believe it—my kids are dressed like little lords. I got them boots, new lambskin winter coats, little mittens, the very best quality." He went on and on, talking very happily. Then he turned to me and said, "You know, miss, I loved my wife before, too, but when the children came, my love for her felt sweeter than ever. I wonder why that is?" Loving his wife became even sweeter . . . If you could only have heard him say those last words—"I wonder why that is?"—words filled with quiet reflection and happy surprise.

He told me many things, and expressed things I can't really convey in words at all. His intonations, in his ruddy, cheery, smiling face, the jaunty way he cracked his little whip—it was all charged with meaning for me. When I left him, I asked him to give my regards to his wife. He was very pleased, glad. Glad to have an attentive listener. It is just as necessary for us to express our joy as it is to express our sorrow. And I listened to him with such eagerness.

I like my cabbie much more than your sergeant major; you can be sure of that!

KATAV-IVANOVSKY IRONWORKS—MOSCOW
JACOB TO MARUSYA

Telegram

FEBRUARY 13, 1913
20 MORE DAYS

Telegram

FEBRUARY 18, 1913
15 MORE DAYS

Telegram

FEBRUARY 28, 1913
5 MORE DAYS WE MEET IN CHELYABINSK ON THE 5TH

MARCH 11, 1913
Today I tidied up the room where we lived so happily together. I found your hairpin under the bed. An ordinary, sturdy hairpin. I wanted to kiss it. It's not the right kind of object for kissing. Not romantic in the least. Gloves are another thing altogether. But luckily you didn't forget your gloves— otherwise, you'd have frozen on the train on the way home.

The third move is easier than the first two were. I'm already accustomed to gathering my things together, even though the household effects have now increased. A soldier has almost no possessions, so any extra thing is precious.

My wondrous wife! I love you. That's all I can say. There is nothing more to add.

My dears! I haven't written you in a long time—but there were reasons why I couldn't, very serious reasons. Marusya was here visiting me. I didn't tell you about it, because I was so afraid it wouldn't happen if I talked about it too confidently beforehand. She stayed here for five days, and I was supremely happy. This fragile young woman undertook the whole difficult journey alone, without any companions. I'm writing this for you, Mama, since I know you think that an actress is not a suitable partner for your son. You see how courageous and decisive Marusya is in her undertakings?

I have news about my army service. I'm writing you before a departure. I'm now attached to the Battalion Office as a military clerk. It's an important position—I'll have to salute myself.

Things will be incomparably better for me now. I'll give you the details in a few days.

Well, I send you kisses, dearest ones. I have no time just now—there's not even time to blow my nose properly.

This is my new address:
Yuryuzan Factory, Ufimskaya Guberniya
Ninth Company, Insarsky Regiment
To me.

Report

I declare that from this date I have entered the employ of the Battalion Office, Third Battalion, 196th Infantry of the Insarsky Regiment, and I hereby convey this information to my wife. Thunder of triumph, resound!
Commander of the Battalion Office
Lieutenant Colonel (crossed out)
Private of Volunteers
Jacob Ossetsky

Dear Marusya! I walked around in a daze for a whole day after your departure. I kept dreaming about our future, which I anticipate will be beautiful. Then I gave myself a good shake and threw myself into the fray to make up for lost time. My motor kicked in, and I studied a long time. I left only three hours for myself to sleep. And what satisfaction can sleep give if you're not here with me? For three whole days, I sat with my books during every spare minute. And suddenly, yesterday, I was informed about an appointment I could never have dreamed of. It turned out that the previous clerk was promoted for some deed or other. Or a service? And he was sent to Kazan!

From the attached report, my dear wife, you can see that I have received a much better appointment than my previous one. Better by orders of magnitude. Before I was just a run-of-the mill private; but now I'm Mr. Clerk.

"Mr. Clerk, may I come in? Mr. Ossetsky, please give me a reference! Mr. Ossetsky, call Chelyabinsk on the telephone, please! Mr. Volunteer, please convey such-and-such to Battalion Commander So-and-so."

That's what I've become. Now I have to salute myself and issue commands—attention, eyes right and left.

New address:
Yuryuzan Factory, Ufimskaya Guberniya
Ninth Company, Insarsky Regiment
Volunteer Ossetsky

MOSCOW–KATAV-IVANOVSKY IRONWORKS
MARUSYA TO JACOB

MARCH 16, 1913
I'm lying on the divan, thinking about the future, thinking, longing, for you.

The physical pain that I experienced when we parted I now feel constantly. I think about you—your lips, your hands—and I feel orphaned. There is no place for me to go. Nothing is the way it should be. Everything is partial. Nothing is complete.

MOSCOW–YURYUZAN
MARUSYA TO JACOB

MARCH 20, 1913
Here is my report. I have classes in Rabenek's studio three times a week, and studio performances one or two times a week. Ella Ivanovna is

satisfied with my progress. I have received an invitation to a *real* theater, as a replacement for another actress. Once a week, I have a class in the Froebel Society in pedagogy. One morning (Tuesday), I give lessons in movement in a private school for girls. And I read, read everything you recommend to me and much, much more. Mikhail is finally moving permanently to Moscow.

MARCH 20, 1913

The living conditions here are by far the best. I have my own room, where I'm completely free from obligations, and a lot of time for my books.

My duties are the following: at nine in the morning, I sort the mail from the post office, write dispatches and reports, orders, and memoranda. At ten o'clock, the battalion commander arrives and signs everything, and then leaves at twelve. After that, I'm completely free. In the evening, I go to his apartment with a report, and that is the end of it until the next morning.

He gets all the mail first, then sends it to me. I sort it through and send it on to the company commanders. So you can rest easy. The battalion commander never opens anyone's mail, of course, not least mine.

In short, my duties are light. It will continue like this until the summer training camps, and then we'll see.

I received the Yiddish and German books.

I read the books in Yiddish with enormous pleasure. In particular Sholem Aleichem. It's amazing how fluently I can read Yiddish. I opened it to the first page—not confident at all that I could. I read it through, then the second page, and the third, and the whole book; and then the next book. In short, thank you, Papa, for making me take lessons for two years with that unbearable Reuben. He actually taught me a thing or two, despite boring me to death. I haven't been able to open the German books yet. They'll have to wait until next week.

Here everything is very conducive to writing letters. I'm not joking. I don't have to write on a footlocker, but I get to write at a real desk. I don't have to sit on my bed pushed up against the wall, but on a real stool.

I can actually complete all my tasks in the Battalion Office in a good two hours. Yesterday, however, I sat until five-thirty with an intelligent expression on my face. No one asked me what I was doing, though, and I just carried on with my own affairs.

MARCH 22, 1913

This has nothing to do with real soldiering. A clerk is a blue blood. Illiterate soldiers (and they do exist in our fatherland) come to me and ask me to write them a nice letter. At first I thought they were talking about the handwriting. No, they want it to sound beautiful and expressive. The poor human soul—it wants beauty, but has received no training in it. It's very touching, really. Maybe I should go to a country school and work as a teacher . . .

I've gotten into the swing of things here now. I am very much the clerk: I take an interest in the affairs of the regiment, and I never talk to anyone about my wife. And it seems that I'll soon begin to study seriously. I'm in the mood for it now. It's often that way—suddenly you feel confidence in an action you have yet to take.

My life as a soldier is better than it has ever been. The only thing I lack is my wife. After reflecting on that thought, I changed my mind. My wife is an actress. Her place is in the acting studio and on the stage, and not leading a dull life with a clerk in the Ural Mountains.

MARCH 23, 1913

The battalion commander is very kind to me. I teach a lesson at his home (I'm helping his son prepare to enter the officers' corps). I "nobly" refused payment for the lesson. The fact of the matter is that Mitya (the son) is so ill-prepared, I have to cover the material for the entire curriculum at a regular school: mathematics, Russian, and German. I'm not sure whether he'll be accepted into the corps. In addition, the requirements for the program are not entirely clear to me.

After the lesson with Mitya last week, I was waylaid. The lieutenant colonel came into the nursery, where we were having the lesson, and invited me to stay to dine. I considered declining, then accepted the invitation out of curiosity. I went downstairs into the large dining room—like a banquet hall, but decorated and furnished in a provincial country style. It was a dinner party, and there were many guests. The twelve chairs they had were not enough, so they had to fetch two kitchen stools to accommodate everyone. The guests were the local *beau monde*—mostly officers and their wives, the director of the gymnasium, not a pleasant sort, and one more person, who appeared to be quite cosmopolitan. This turned out to be Mr. G. Papas, and it was the first time since I left home that I have conversed for a whole evening with a European, of the caliber one doesn't even come across that often in Kiev. He is a highly educated economist. And it would have been interesting for you to talk to him as well. He has very original ideas, something in the spirit of Taylor, whom I've told you about. They subject management itself to scientific study and discover the laws that govern it and must be taken account of in managing it.

YURYUZAN–MOSCOW
JACOB TO MARUSYA

MARCH 30, 1913
I received the bundle of newspapers (including *Footlights*, and the postcards—they all arrived). The parcel took ten days to get here. There is a lot written about your studio. A startling cacophony of opinions. Some brilliant, others weak and incompetent. And, of course, the latter are wrong. Besides, one should always keep in mind the old adage: It's far better when critics diverge in their opinions; it means an author has been consistent with himself.

In what does the freedom of theater lie? In the absence of a consistent method of staging. For *The Fair at Sorochyntsi* they chose naturalism, for *Beatrice* they choose, for instance, decadence. Perhaps this is possible—not having one consistent personality. The individuality of an actor consists in the absence of any individuality. Today Shylock, tomorrow the Mayor.

I've struck up an acquaintance with the local priest, and very fine person, Father Feodosy. He's interested in music. He's a widower raising two sons, and he asked me to tutor his elder son in German. I wouldn't have felt confident enough in English or French, although I know them pretty well. Reading is very good for developing language skills. I agreed to the lessons,

214

and received compensation I wasn't counting on. I've already been to their home twice, and got to play the harmonium after the lessons. It made me very happy, and very sad. I'm lagging so far behind. How hard I'll have to work to catch up!

I'm reading *Childhood and Adolescence*. Sometimes I was overcome with terrible longing for you—I wanted to talk to a true friend, the only true friend of my life. I recalled some memories from childhood, dreams I had—all those things you can only confide in the person you feel closest to.

Why do we so love Tolstoy, you and I? Besides all his other merits, Tolstoy has taught both of us the importance of sincerity. There is nothing more difficult; that's my belief, which I have formulated for myself definitively over the past few days. Carlyle considered sincerity a hallmark of genius.

No one surpasses Tolstoy in this regard, it would seem. And in this lies his pedagogical significance. The next logical premise is that this is why he brings people together. What unites people, if not sincerity?

It seems that you didn't receive my last letters. Some of them I sent without registering them (with only one stamp, that is). Evidently, they went missing. Well, I kiss you. I kiss your hands tenderly.

I have a strange relationship to human hands. It's a feature in a person that means a great deal to me, because I prize them so highly. People I love have many beautiful traits and features that I would forgo—but not the hands. The eyes, brows, hair can all change, as far as I'm concerned, as long as the hands remain the same. And provident nature agrees with me. It guards this feature carefully. The hair falls out, eyes grow rheumy and dim, the body ages—but the hands stay the same. They get covered with tiny wrinkles, but the shape remains constant.

MOSCOW–YURYUZAN
MARUSYA TO JACOB

MARCH 31, 1913

Nighttime. I've just come back from the Zimin Theater, where I saw *Sadko*. I suffered because you weren't with me to enjoy it. It's all so wonderful, so intriguing. All of the costumes designed by Egorov. Every single costume was a miracle. The conductor was Palitsyn.

I want to sleep. I hardly slept at all last night. Good night, Jacob, my love. Oh, how tired I am! And I always feel this exhaustion lately.

Still, it's hard to make myself stop writing. There's so much I need to tell you.

Once, Mikhail said to me, "If you write Jacob, don't forget to send him my greetings—double greetings, in fact." That's what he said. Yes, Jacob, we already have a big family. You already have three new brothers. Well, good-bye, then, my dear. And now I'll go to sleep and kiss you all night long.

Telegram

APRIL 15, 1913
ILL DETAILS TO FOLLOW IN LETTER YOURS

YURYUZAN–MOSCOW
JACOB TO MARUSYA

APRIL 16, 1913
What kind of illness is it? Are you confined to bed? It's almost impossible for me to imagine you sick; sometimes I don't want to believe anything. You have too much theoretical health to fall ill! Get well, Marusya! If I were there I would make you some tea with lemon and Cognac, and it would take all your exhaustion away, just like that. But I'm going to bed. It's evening here, and already late for me (ten o'clock). I did some domestic chores before bed. I laid out my linen, sprinkling it with the cyclamen you love. Why did I do it? You're not here! I also washed a handkerchief.

I'm going to get undressed. But you're not here.

APRIL 18, 1913
Good day, Marusya! Are you feeling better today?

It's evening here, and my eyelids feel heavy and want to stick together. I've said hello to you, kissed your hands, and now I'm bidding you good night again.

I'm going off to dreamland.

"My wife is ill, her bed is two thousand versts away."

How terrible it sounds. I can't imagine you ill.
Goodbye, little one, be a good girl and get well soon!

APRIL 23, 1913

It's so strange, and just not right—you are sick, and I want to talk to you more than ever, but I can only write about myself. You are sick, and I'm writing about my worries, my thoughts, my hopes.

Well, never mind. Let it be this way, then. Please refrain from writing me, or at least don't send me anything longer than a postcard, so as not to exhaust yourself.

Telegram

APRIL 25, 1913

TELEGRAPH ME HOW IS HEALTH I'M WORRIED JACOB

MOSCOW–YURYUZAN
MARUSYA TO JACOB

MAY 4, 1913

My sweet husband! My Jacob! I am beside myself. I have real reason to suspect that my life is going to change, in such a way that your secret wish—that I leave the stage—will come true. And our dreams that we spun and believed were still far away are already here, now, when I am not at all ready to change my life, to abandon the theater and become the respectable wife of a respectable husband. It's terrible. And this is what constitutes the tragedy of a woman's existence, her slavery to nature. You and I have talked about how we will have a big family and many children, and how our children will be happy, with parents who raise them to be free and well-adjusted people. But this will mean that my artistic life must end before it has really begun. Now I can't help seeing my mother in myself—buried in her humdrum everyday existence, frying pans, collars, sewing, and anxieties. I hate all of that! And my mother (you don't know this) wrote poetry in her youth, and has kept her journal with lyrical jottings commemorating her unfulfilled life.

MAY 12, 1913

My little one! Pride, and fear, and ecstasy, and much more I can't name! I found out about the possibility of getting married officially here, although you would have to travel for four days by train again. Perhaps I could try to talk them into granting me furlough? But try to find out, in any case, if among your "high-society" friends there is a lawyer who can tell you about the consequences of having a child out of wedlock. Also about children out of wedlock who are legally assigned to the mother and then adopted by the father. I have some thoughts about this myself. I studied all of this at one point, and passed an exam on it, but I've forgotten it all. I have no volume ten of the Legal Code here.

Do not feel anxious and overwhelmed by all of this. You have a husband, and he will take all the burdens onto his own shoulders.

23

A New Direction

(1976–1982)

I t wasn't the doctors who finally healed Vitya's psychological ailment, or whatever one might call it, but Grisha Lieber, his former schoolmate. Rotund, bald, and satisfied with life, Grisha resurfaced out of the oblivion of the past, after a long absence. He was married, had a son, and was brimming with plans, including that of emigration. But this was something he did not share with Vitya.

During the year when Vitya entered the Department of Mathematics and Mechanical Engineering, Grisha was admitted to a chemistry institute, where there was a strong mathematics department and a relatively lax policy on accepting clever Jewish students. He graduated with high marks, and began working as a junior researcher in a laboratory that practiced and researched a real science whose precise name had not yet been determined.

The researchers in the laboratory were reluctant to describe to outsiders what they were doing. In particular, they were trying to establish the difference between living and nonliving matter, to grab the elusive secret of the structure of the world by the tail. Discussions about this subject inspired perplexity and doubt among the majority of scholars who were not involved in these audacious speculations. Their activities concerned the quivering, volatile forefront of scientific knowledge, a frontier whose existence most people didn't even suspect. But those who did suspect—who acknowledged that it was precisely here that a new breakthrough in science was under way, a stunning flowering of consciousness—numbered only ten or so on the planet, roughly half of them in Russia: Kolmogorov, the world-renowned academician; the underrated Gelfand, who was highly regarded in narrow circles; and two or three others.

Scientific thought of truly global significance boiled and seethed around these chosen few. Grisha was lucky enough to be stewed in this remarkable cauldron, and it was Gelfand who tended the fire. Grisha was among the devotees, but devotees of the very lowest degree. He accepted with resignation that the level of his devotion was determined by nothing more than the speed of neurons, the capacity of the brain to acquire and process information—that is, measurable biological parameters still to be discovered and named. Grisha guessed that, because of his ethnic origins, Gelfand had had to have read the Bible at some point; but he had been barred from the right to secular higher education. It was unbelievable, but he didn't even have a higher degree. Still, Grisha was sure for some reason that Gelfand's origins alone predisposed him to share the idea that so preoccupied Grisha: in science, modern man was doing the same thing that Adam had done long ago when he bestowed names on nameless creatures; he was calling by name the first things he encountered and took to be living facts of life. Grisha was canny and gifted enough to appreciate this project, and the proximity to genius was the source of happiness and meaning of his life.

Grisha spent three hours with Vitya, telling him about his work. Vitya listened rather listlessly at first, but when he heard the words "universal language," he sat up and took notice.

"What do you mean by that?" Vitya said. Grisha gave him an answer that amounted to a whole lecture on the subject: from Darwin to Mendel to Pasteur to Mechnikov to Koltsov, Timofeyev-Resovsky, and Morgan. He finished with Watson and Crick. "The double helix of the DNA is the alphabet on which the entire history of the world is written. And it's not only a collection of genes, but a program for molecular computers of the living cell."

"Fascinating," Vitya said, nodding. "I've never thought about that. You're saying that this chemical molecule, as you call it, can be a program?"

Grisha opened the battered briefcase of his late grandfather, a famous doctor, with a silver clasp that read *"Für liebe Isaak Lieber,"* and, with a mysterious expression, took a book out of it. Vitya looked at the book attentively. Grisha's expression was the same one he had worn fifteen years ago when he gave Vitya Hausdorff's *Set Theory*, which changed the course of his life. The book he was holding now was dog-eared, rather small, and was called *What Is Life? The Physical Aspect of the Living Cell.* The author's name on the cover he didn't read until the next morning, after he had read the whole book from start to finish: Schrödinger.

The simple, mundane law of duplexity, by which similar events occur twice in succession—first roughly, approximately, and next, definitively—familiar to all observant people, especially women, was unknown to Vitya. For the second time in his life, Grisha was the bearer of news of such magnitude it could alter Vitya's fate. This little book, though unprepossessing in appearance, gripped Vitya and held him fast. That night, his usual insomnia was transformed from tormenting bondage into complete bliss. His clear head delighted in its activity. It was as though a veil had fallen from his vision, and the world was transfigured, illuminated by a thought that was absolutely novel to him: mathematics, the highest stage of human reason, did not exist separately from the rest of the world, but was itself an auxiliary science, a part of a whole, a part of a more general and higher stage. A part of what, though? The word "Creation," which slipped off Grisha's tongue so easily, was not a notion that Vitya was conversant with, and Vitya felt a combination of envy, desire, and haste. He wanted to enter this world which only the day before he had had no inkling of, and no interest in discovering. The vestiges of his depression lifted, as though it had never been.

The next morning, Vitya set out for the Lenin Library and started reviewing all the material about those things of which he had no inkling. Quantum mechanics and calculus posed no problem; their language of description was self-evident. With chemistry and biology he was on shaky ground—he had to begin with the high-school textbooks. Three days later he was delving into the college-level textbooks. This was far more interesting stuff. Like most mathematicians, he took a rather dim view of physics. Biology he didn't consider to be a science at all; rather, he saw it as a refuse heap of facts. It was all like unplowed land, experiments performed higgledy-piggledy, uncoordinated data that demonstrated the researchers' inability to manage and process the results it yielded. On top of all this, there was the complete absence of a mathematical foundation. Chemistry, about which he had the vaguest notions of all, seemed to him a somewhat more rigorous science than biology.

Schrödinger looked at this plethora of disparate facts and decided that Darwin's theory of evolution was the only structure capable of maintaining and organizing this avalanche of information. Most important, he noted that the phenomena connected to space and time, which physicists observe, also apply to living organisms. Thanks to Schrödinger's book, Vitya discovered that mathematics is not the highest achievement of human reason, but only an instrument for grasping the workings of the world, a world that is far greater than mathematics. This was a revelation to him.

From that point on, Vitya started to revive. Within the space of three months, he lost ten kilograms. He spent every day in the library, from the time the doors opened to when they closed again, in a state of eager impatience. At a certain moment, he realized that his English, adequate for reading articles on mathematics, was completely insufficient for reading articles on biology. He called Nora to ask her whether she could help him study English, as she used to help him in Russian. Nora refused, but recommended a good teacher she knew, whose rates were reasonable. Vitya had no money at all at this time; but he didn't really need it, either. Meals were always on the table, ready for him. The library was ten minutes away by foot, and the one ruble he needed for a lunch snack with tea at the library he took from his mother's wallet, with no feeling of compunction whatsoever. It was only through conversations with Nora that he came to understand that money might come in handy. It remained unclear, however, how he would get it. Certainly not by teaching mathematics: his inability to communicate with other human beings rendered that impossible. He asked Nora, "How does one earn money?" She just laughed and said she'd like to know the answer to that question, too. Their relations had solidified with time. Vitya even graced her with his presence for an overnight stay a few times; they remained an unconventional family.

To give this out-of-the-ordinary family its due, the idea of alimony never entered the minds of either one partner or the other. Vitya had to scrap the English lessons because of financial insolvency, but he began to study independently, with the help of an old English textbook that had been languishing on Nora's bookshelf since the time when Genrikh had still lived with his first family. This was a slim volume published before the war for rapid acquisition of "basic" English—*Step by Step*, by Ivy Litvinov.

Three months after Grisha's visit, Vitya called him. They met. Vitya returned to him Schrödinger, about which he had a number of questions. Grisha answered them to the best of his ability. But—and it was essential to keep this in mind, he told Vitya—the book was published in 1943, the year they were born. Science had advanced so much since then that Schrödinger himself was no longer as relevant as he had once been.

Grisha told him fascinating things about the cell membranes he had been studying for several years. He shared with Vitya his brilliant (in his own estimation) idea that the future generation of computers would be quantum computers—maybe not tomorrow, but in fifty years—and that this was the main current in scientific development. Vitya understood everything almost intuitively, and began asking such sophisticated questions that Grisha felt a bit flustered: Vitya was able to grasp the essence of matters that it had taken Grisha five years to get to the bottom of. But Grisha was a creature of preternatural nobility, and, shrugging off the petty jealousy that stirred in the depths of his soul, he invited Vitya to have a conversation with the head of the laboratory a week later. The conversation lasted for four hours, and at the end of it, Vitya had been offered a staff position. True, it was the lowliest position in the laboratory—senior lab assistant—but it came with special privileges for him. He wasn't required to come in to work, and he would have a weekly meeting with the head of the lab to discuss concrete problems assigned to him. He was now occupied with building a model of a living cell as a computer. It was connected to what he knew best of all—computer programming.

Vitya's trained mind worked in overdrive, and the pleasure his work gave him spurred him on still more. He was completely consumed by his task, and had no interest in any events or processes that didn't feed the fires of his devotion. He simply didn't notice them. He attentively followed the computer revolution that was advancing day by day before his eyes, and understood the degree to which the creation of a computer model of the living cell depended on the development of the general idea of the computer and on new technologies, and that the idea of a cell computer was a function of technological progress.

Grisha, who didn't know much about programming, assured Vitya that from the stuff of our world (atoms, molecules, the entire periodic table) it was impossible to create a more perfect computational machine than the living cell. And he kept harping on quantum computers—the possibility of which was oh so remote.

Artificial intelligence was still in its infancy at the end of the seventies. Vitya's finely honed mind lived at its usual fevered pace, but the tasks that confronted him compelled him to examine, in a not yet formally described manner, the chaos of biological life and yoke it to the strict order of mathematics. But is it possible to construct a computer on the basis of biological analogues?

The deeper Vitya delved into his work, the closer he came to answers to the particular questions, the more he felt he was on a treadmill and not getting anywhere. It seemed he was nowhere near a definitive answer, and that finding one was in fact impossible. But nothing in the world was more important. Grisha more and more often took him aside to assure him that it was mandatory to concentrate on studying the living computers of the cell. Vitya believed that Grisha was veering off into the realm of science fiction, and that the practical and realizable goal of contemporary scientists was to create "thinking" computers that would be more intelligent than their creators. This was to be a source of profound disagreement between himself and Grisha.

24

Carmen

(1985)

After the *Knight* fiasco, Tengiz went around gloomy and depressed for several days, slept on a pallet on the floor, and ate almost nothing. He didn't hit the bottle, as one would expect a Russian man to do in such a situation. They had already discussed the matter of drink and concluded that a Russian drinks from grief and joy, a European with meals, and a Georgian from the pleasure of company. On about the fifth day, bright and early, he woke up and started whistling that most famous of all melodies from Bizet's opera *Carmen*. He reached up to Nora's bed and pulled her down onto the floor with him, saying, "Tell me, woman, why are you in the bed while I'm down here on the floor?"

On the floor, in bed, on a park bench, on a train, on the damp ground—many were the places they had found themselves in each other's arms over the years.

Tengiz leaned back slightly so he could look at her face. "I'll say one thing. I've had many women. Actresses love directors—they gravitate to you like bees to honey. But afterward you always feel shame and raw regret. A kind of deadly boredom, Nora. It was always that way with me. You're the only one I've never felt this deadly boredom with after copulation. Do you know this feeling, or is it unique to men?"

"I'm not sure," Nora said, musing on what Tengiz had said. It was the best thing he had ever told her. Actually, he never talked about anything related to the horizontal position. This was a very heady confession. There was nothing to add to it.

Nora reached out to grab a pack of cigarettes, lying conveniently within reach.

"I'm really not sure, Tengiz," she said. "By the time I was fifteen, I was already adept at keeping sexual matters separate from anything one might call love. So as not to confuse what were inherently different things. This freed me from a lot of emotional unpleasantness. Only once did I mix those things up, and I have yet to extricate myself from the result. No, I've never felt deadly boredom; ordinary regret, to be sure. My sexual revolution happened back when I was still in high school."

"Good, let's get back to love. To this, I mean." And again he started whistling "Habañera."

"Oh, that," Nora said, laughing. "But Mérimée actually didn't write it at all. That somewhat vulgar and banal story—the libretto of the opera, I mean—was written by Meilhac and Halévi, a couple of French hack writers."

"You astonish me, Nora! You're the most literate person I know. You know everything about everything."

"That's a strange statement, coming from the friend of a philosopher like Merab Mamardashvili. I didn't even graduate, Tengiz. The only education I got was in trade school. Well, it was a solidly respectable trade, of course. But you know my background. I even dropped out of the Moscow Art Theatre studio. That's where my miserable regret has been spent . . . I simply have a good memory. I remember everything I read. And I read a lot. And my grandmother, of course, was pushing good books under my nose from early childhood."

"You're lucky you had an educated grandmother. Mine was a peasant. Illiterate. She only knew how to sign her name."

Nora held an unlit cigarette in her hand. Tengiz reached for his jeans, lying in a heap on the floor. He took a lighter out of the pocket to light Nora's cigarette.

"Well?"

"Mérimée was a genius," she said. "He was the first person in Europe to appreciate Pushkin. Everyone ignores the last chapter of *Carmen*, believing it to have been tacked on gratuitously. They all rack their brains trying to figure out why he introduces such a scholarly discussion willy-nilly at the end of the book—but it's very important."

Here Tengiz interrupted her. "Hold on. Do you know why I suddenly came back to life? I realized how lucky it was that *The Knight in the*

Panther's Skin fell through. I hate it, that's what I realized. And Tariel and Avtandil, his minions, too. They can all go to hell, with their adoration of beautiful women and their subservience to authority. If we have to speak of love, let it be about your *Carmen*. Go on, tell me more about Mérimée! And let me read it, to see why it's so brilliant."

Now, this was happiness. True *happiness*. They took it apart bit by bit, this unwieldy, hybrid admixture—a traveler's notes, jottings of a fictional scholar, the literary games of an extraordinary writer. Tengiz's enthusiasm grew, and hers was fired by his, as always happened when they worked together. She read the book out loud, and from time to time he would raise his finger in the air and say, "That's exactly what I need." After two days of slow and painstaking reading, Tengiz told Nora, "Now get some paper and start writing."

"Are you crazy? I do costumes, and I have the temerity to do set design and décor, too. One time I worked on a play with Sergei Barkhin himself; I did the costumes, and he just watched what I was doing—I learned everything from him. But writing a play? Even Tusya would never take that on. I know that for a fact. I've been learning from her my whole life. Barkhin doesn't write plays, either. And his hand is present in everything I have done."

"Oh, and I was thinking it was my hand that was present in everything you have done."

"Pinocchio knows best who his Papa Geppetto is. I can't argue, though—you honed me still further."

"Hmm, you're starting to make me suspicious . . ."

Nora immediately put him straight: "Stop right there!"

But he understood that he had transgressed an unspoken rule. When they were together, occupying the small islands of life they claimed only for themselves, neither past nor future existed. Tengiz had reprimanded Nora harshly for her trip to Tbilisi—he considered their chance meeting to have been deliberately planned. Their open relationship would have been impossible to maintain if they didn't observe these sacred boundaries. Tengiz had established these boundaries many years before. It was difficult and painful for Nora to accept them, but with time it seemed that the boundaries were symmetrically enforced, and just as necessary to her.

"Write, Nora, write!" Tengiz said. "We've already hammered everything out. We just need to write the play."

"I'm not a writer," Nora said.

"How do you know? Have you ever tried it? A writer is someone who takes up a pencil and writes."

Nora took a pencil and Yurik's cast-off notebook. After two pages of her son's childlike scrawl, a new text started to emerge, written in Nora's certain hand—perpendicular, occasionally left-leaning letters. She wrote down snatches of conversation, dialogues, repartees, conjectures.

They agreed on the lines of demarcation. They'd forget about Bizet, forget about Shchedrin. No musical allusions whatsoever. They'd sound the death knell for the entire surface layer of the narrative, anchored firmly in the history of opera.

"Well, first off, I'd put Mérimée on the stage, making him a character in the play. The author is of course present—the author himself, or the Englishman, or the traveler, but in any case a scholar, an observer. It creates so many possibilities."

"It's crucial to decide on the point of departure, as well as the ending."

"The line of tension runs between Mérimée and Carmen, you understand? Not between Carmen and José."

They interrupted each other, and got rid of the ballast, and put on the table everything that was indispensable.

"Right, but it's Carmen who holds sway over the other characters. She makes the Cigarette Girls and the men, and all the others, dance to her tune."

"Exactly! Mérimée, the author and god of this story, holds the thread of life and death in his hands."

"No, Carmen is the one who's in control of everything!"

"But Carmen vanquishes Mérimée's logic . . ."

"I don't know. She's the one José kills, out in the bushes, or by the side of the road."

"No, she kills *him*!"

"I would want there to be objects. Objects that play a role in themselves."

"You don't have to look too far to find them; they're right there for the taking. Gold watches, playing cards—no, cards are rubbish, a garrote is better."

"Yes, what does it look like, this strangulation wire? We'll have to look it up. It can't be just some plain old wire. It must have handles of some sort, right? Or an entire mechanism?"

"I so love the cabbage she doesn't want to plant! And if there are flowers and little nosegays, we have to think of how to make those work, too."

"Okay, the cabbage might come in handy. But I somehow don't want to nod in that direction. I wouldn't put a flower in her teeth, but a big gold coin."

"No, it should be a cigar."

"Hey, she could have gold teeth! Nowadays all Gypsies are supposed to have gold teeth; but back then?"

"No actress is going to agree to come out onstage with gold teeth."

"What about Fellini? Remember the scene in Fellini when the Gypsy laughs, reading some lady's palm?"

"Oh, fortune-telling! Yes, of course. A fortune-teller! Obscure, portentous words. An old woman tells Carmen's fortune: Beware of the soldier. 'To fear a soldier—in our trade? . . . What nonsense!' 'The soldier will kill you! Beware of the soldier.' And Carmen knows beforehand that he will kill her. She makes him kill her! To fulfill the designs of fate."

"Dangerous, very dangerous. We're straying into the domain of the opera again. And we have to strip away that layer of associations. So there is no trace of that perfumed surface."

"We could introduce Death as a character, too. We should! An affinity between Carmen and Death. The other side of her freedom is—Death."

"I don't get it."

"You will, though."

"Our Carmencita isn't really interested in love at all. She doesn't even want to hear about it. For her, love is just the manifestation of her will—her willfulness, as it were. And an instrument."

"And what about him? Who is he?"

"José? He's nobody. A nobleman who has a fiancée in the village. He became a robber, a brigand, out of stupidity. He's actually a stupid fellow. Well, not stupid—just a simpleton. There could even be a scene with his fiancée. A conversation between them about 'our beloved village.' A tête-à-tête between idiots. He's a victim, of course, but ultimately his behavior is not too shabby. He just ended up in someone else's story. When all is said and done, his fate is to plant cabbages; and Carmen glanced his way quite by chance."

"He would be difficult to love. Except for his ideals—a pure, clean life, white curtains that open onto a white garden—and, in fact, he dreams in white. But he ends up in a life of black-and-red."

"We'll have to think about the toreador. Although I'm more interested in the bull, to be honest. The story here would be that whoever she looks at follows her obediently—resisting at first, of course, but ultimately giving in.

And in this respect, all the men are the same: José, Matteo, the toreador—even the bull. Not to mention the Englishman. Like they've drunk a love potion."

While Nora was writing the play, trying to cleave to Mérimée and avoid falling into the gravitational field of the opera, Tengiz was negotiating the staging of *Carmen* in a theater nestled in one of Moscow's old clubs, the beating heart of the city. Tengiz didn't work very often in Moscow, but people knew him and held him in high esteem. Moreover, their names were now often yoked together.

Carmen was written over the course of two weeks. Tengiz was responsible for much of how it came to life and cohered internally, but the finale was Nora's handiwork: the author—Mérimée, that is—brings a cigar into the cell of the hero, José, and José is led off to be garroted with a cigar between his teeth. A long, slow procession follows behind him . . . The executioner, wrapped in a cloak and wearing the mask of Death, carries out the execution by strangling. The mask falls away. The executioner is Carmen.

On the cover of the notebook, Nora wrote in large, plain script: "Mérimée. Carmen, José, and Death," and prepared to place the notebook in the desk drawer "until further notice." At that moment, Tengiz announced that he had already reached an agreement with the theater. The play was included in the repertoire for the following year.

25

The Diamond Door

(1986)

Years passed. His mother aged. His son was growing up. Summer replaced winter. Vitya ate bread and sausage for breakfast. His mother traveled by metro from the Molodezhnaya station, where they had been resettled, to the Arbat, to buy her son his favorite kind of sausage. Once a month, Vitya visited Yurik, and they played chess together. Political events happened in the world that Vitya didn't so much as notice. He didn't see any connection between the computer modeling of cells and the placement of mid-range missiles in Europe, meetings between Gorbachev and Reagan in Reykjavik, or negotiations in Geneva. The prospect of nuclear war had been temporarily suspended, but Vitya failed to notice even this. He was unable to comprehend the degree to which the fate of the scientific developments carried out in the lab, with its brilliant laboratory head and researchers passionately committed to science, as well as his own personal fate, depended on whether the Russians and Americans would come to an agreement.

Vitya didn't even notice something that was happening right under his nose, in his own apartment. Varvara Vasilievna had been carried away by cheap esoteric teachings and preachings. She visited various underground meetings of like-minded enthusiasts, groups of healers and magicians. She was determined to improve her karma, which she imagined as something hefty and substantial, like a piece of meat or a new armoire. This was accompanied, of course, by spiritually charged water and a burning interest in UFOs, mixed in with a fear of devils and all manner of unclean spirits.

Varvara Vasilievna began her activities by cleansing Vitya's karma remotely, which she prudently refrained from informing him about. At around the same time—the rapprochement of the Soviet Union and the United States, and Vitya's karmic cleansing—the laboratory received an invitation to a conference in the United States on the modeling of biological processes. The invitation was for the head of the laboratory, Vitya, and one other assistant, who was Jewish. The head of the laboratory was banned from leaving the country, because he had been required to take part in some secret military scientific councils or other; the Jew fell under suspicion by definition; and so the only more or less unsullied person was Vitya Chebotarev. By this time, Grisha was no longer associated with the laboratory. He had emigrated as early as 1982 to Israel, and Vitya's interactions with him were limited to reading articles he published in the world's leading scientific journals.

The invitation was examined in detail, and it was decided that Vitya Chebotarev should be sent to give a lengthy paper summarizing the work the laboratory had carried out during the past years.

The year 1986 was the year of political thaw. Flights from Moscow to New York were packed, and Vitya was lost in the crowd of Jewish émigrés leaving the Soviet Union for good. Vitya received permission to leave for his ten-day business trip to deliver his lecture. Before he left, Yurik gave him a list of LPs without which his life was incomplete. Varvara Vasilievna accompanied her son to the airport, filled with conflicting emotions that tore her apart from within: pride and fear. She was afraid that in America her son would be the victim of some horrific psychotropic attack perpetrated by the imperialists, but at the same time she felt a vain satisfaction that he was going on a business trip, not to some musty, fusty Hungary or Poland, but to the one and only U.S. of A.

Before they left home, she had put a sandwich wrapped in waxed paper into his suitcase. In the airport, she realized that the suitcase, along with the nourishment it contained, would be relinquished at the baggage check, and she began demanding that the suitcase be returned. Vitya couldn't understand what she was so agitated about. Varvara sensed her profound impotence in the face of a world in which the suitcase was flying over the ocean with a sandwich inside it, and not a single one of the important problems in life was amenable to resolution, on either the material or the spiritual plane. She began to cry. Vitya comforted her vaguely.

"You are so heartless," she told him, wiping away bitter tears, as they parted.

She still wasn't sure whether her son was a genius or an ordinary guy down on his luck. True, a friend of hers who was a clairvoyant informed her that Vitya was now standing before three doors—one made of silver, one made of gold, and one made of diamonds—and that, whichever one he opened, it would all turn out well.

The plane took off. Varvara Vasilievna watched the airfield and murmured a prayer to herself: May it be the diamond door . . .

At Kennedy, Vitya was met by Grisha, who was wearing a brightly colored skullcap; Vitya didn't recognize this as a yarmulke. They hadn't seen each other in four years. Grisha had flown in from Israel two days earlier. By this time, he had begun working at the University of Haifa, doing research not only on cell membranes but also on the Bible. The meeting between the friends was the most cordial that Vitya was capable of.

They sat in a cramped hotel room—Vitya, who was dead on his feet after the nearly ten-hour flight, and the exuberant, freshly groomed Grisha, hungry for conversation. The question that had been exercising him for many years concerned what took precedence in the world—the idea of the living cell, or the computer?

"Computers emerged first. Every living cell is a computer, a quantum computer," he said.

Vitya winced. Either his head had not completely shifted to American time, or Grisha was talking nonsense. "No, what you say is absurd. The molecular computer of the cell works with DNA. DNA programs its activity. What does a quantum computer have to do with it?"

"It results from considerations of energy; the capacity of a molecular computer is insufficient. Not only that, but the quantum computer must be acoustic. Enormous texts. Divine Writ is enormous! And biological computers must be very, very powerful."

Vitya just shrugged and interrupted Grisha's inspired religio-scientific pronouncements: "You've lost me. What divine texts? You want to read the entire process of evolution as a divine text? It's unfalsifiable."

Grisha was upset. He felt a bitter taste in his mouth, and started to perspire, but was unable to draft Vitya into the cause of his faith. Finally, their differences of opinion went so far that Vitya announced that he personally had in all these years of work never needed the concept of the Creator and Divine Writ. One could easily get by without them.

With the fervor characteristic of him, Grisha objected: "It's self-evident that the original text is God-given, and that what we are in fact doing is decoding it in our research."

"No, no, no. I am carrying out a concrete task—I write computer programs, and these are fairly simple texts, and the biochemists examine the degree to which they correspond to actual synthesis in the cell. It is completely unrelated to the plan or design of your Creator. Okay, I'm going to sleep now," Vitya said, and, leaning his head back on the armchair, was out for the count.

The next two days were a whirl of activity. Vitya spoke English fairly fluently, but it was hard for him to understand his interlocutors, and Grisha was always by his side to assist. Even more now than during their school years, they resembled Cervantes's heroes. Grisha was rosy and rotund, and Vitya was lanky and rather absurd-looking in his formal suit, its sleeves and trouser legs slightly too short: when she was shopping for the suit before his trip, Varvara Vasilievna couldn't find the right size. The primitive shaving-bowl haircut had been replaced by a cap of shapeless curls that were also Varvara Vasilievna's crude handiwork.

In spite of the technical shortcomings of his sartorial gear, however, Varvara Vasilievna's prayers to the Lord God had evidently been heeded. After Vitya's impressive lecture, the diamond door really did open before him.

It looked like an ordinary, unprepossessing wooden door at Stony Brook University, on Long Island, and led to a wonderful university laboratory, where he had been invited to work. He would most likely have declined such a risky offer, but Grisha, who had acted as translator during Vitya's conversation with the famous American scientist, groaned, clapped his hands, and threw them heavenward. "Vitya, this is your chance! And what a chance! It's amazing! What a lab! There are a hundred people waiting in line for this opportunity, all of them deserving. You'll be up for a Nobel before you know it. Whereas in Moscow they'll just sweep the floor with you."

Grisha was more excited about his prospects than Vitya was. When he was leaving, he whispered to Vitya: "First I gave you the Old Testament in the form of Hausdorff, and then the New Testament in the form of Schrödinger. By now, you can't fail to see that we are all engaged in a single common task—decoding the language without which no living thing would exist on earth. Holy Writ, Vitya! The Divine Text! There is nothing more important on earth."

Vitya thought about the offer and accepted it. He had his reasons—the laboratory was state-of-the-art, and he understood that he would be able to work much more effectively here than in Moscow. It occurred to him that he wouldn't see his mother for a long time, or his son, but this thought didn't hold him back. At first they gave him a place to stay on campus; a month later, he found an apartment to rent that was a ten-minute walk from the campus. Someone from the university assisted him in finding it, an extremely large unmarried woman of Irish extraction named Martha.

In the Soviet Embassy, they were offended at first, and balked; then, by some miracle, they backtracked. They didn't even stamp "unreturnable" in his passport. Instead, they retroactively granted him the status of participant in a "scholarly exchange."

26

From the Willow Chest
The Correspondence of Jacob and Marusya
(MAY 1913–JANUARY 1914)

MAY 8, 1913

Give me your word, Jacob, that we will never, ever mention this again. Only on that condition will I tell you everything that has happened. It was terrible! In the middle of the night on the 5th, I woke up, not from pain, but from a sensation of hot trickling down below. I discovered that I was covered with blood. I was terrified. I couldn't get up. Three o'clock in the morning! All alone, no one else around. I knew I was dying. But I managed to stand up and, somehow, make it to Nyusha's attic room. I woke her up. During the day, I can telephone from Mrs. Malygin's, one floor below. But not in the middle of the night! And I sent Nyusha off to alert Mikhail, who had arrived from Petersburg the day before and was staying on Sytinsky Lane. He arrived in forty minutes—very drunk, as he told me later; he was coming from some sort of banquet. After that, I don't remember anything. I woke up in the hospital. Now I'm home again. Weak. But alive. We lost the child. And I beg you—bury the memory about what might have been, but now can never be. Perhaps for the best.

YURYUZAN–MOSCOW
JACOB TO MARUSYA

Telegram

MAY 14, 1913
LITTLE ONE DEAREST IT PAINS ME THAT YOU SUFFER AND I'M NOT THERE
ALL WILL BE WELL HUSBAND JACOB

MAY 14, 1913
Little one, dearest treasure, I am in despair. I rushed to see Lieutenant Colonel Yanchevsky without thinking and didn't choose my words carefully—who was sick, with what, why it was urgent. In short, my request for leave was denied. There is another clerk here, on rotation, but he happens to be on leave for his father's funeral. So I'm unable to come to you right away. It wasn't me but Mikhail who was by your side, and this pains me. It's as though he stole that moment from me when I needed to be with you. I will honor your wishes, and not inquire further about it. I just prayed to the God I'm not sure I believe in. And felt nothing but distant emptiness. I recall all the miracles that take place, even in our time—remember the stories my cousin told about John of Kronstadt? But I'm willing to pray to all the gods, even John of Kronstadt! Only I don't know how.

I retreated to my little corner, sat down, and was suddenly overcome with a boundless sense of gratitude, to whom I'm not sure, that you are alive, and well, and that nothing happened from which you can't recover.

MOSCOW–YURYUZAN
MARUSYA TO JACOB

Telegram

MAY 16, 1913
I'M FULLY RECOVERED JUST TIRED MARUSYA

237

MAY 17, 1913

Hello, my love. I got your telegram yesterday—it crossed in the mail with mine. You write that you have recovered, but that you're tired. How is it possible to have already recovered? After such a serious condition, you can't get well all of a sudden like that. You may feel better, but all the same you have to take care of yourself. Eat well, look after your health. All those things you aren't fond of doing. And take your temperature—if it goes up, it could be dangerous. Yesterday evening, I stopped by to talk to a doctor, a Pole, who settled here a long time ago. He treats everyone around here. He said that if you don't have any fever, and if there are no discharges, the danger has most likely passed. He said that anemia can sometimes result from this, and that you should have it checked. And, the whole evening, he regaled me with stories about some other Pole from Petersburg, who discovered some substance or crystal contained in the blood, and I spent two and a half hours listening to him. I'm usually interested in scientific subjects—but this time, not in the least. I couldn't wait to get back to the barracks, to my bunk, to write you and tell you to take your temperature immediately! And if you're anemic, you must eat meat, cooked rare. Beefsteak. And lemons. In the morning, I'll send you some money. I'm very worried about you, so look after your health. If not for your own sake, then for mine. And put aside your studies for the time being, I beg you. Write me openly, little one, and include all the details.

MOSCOW–YURYUZAN

MARUSYA TO JACOB

MAY 24, 1913

There are things that you want to erase from your memory forever. I asked you never to write me about this subject again. When the first sense of alarm had passed, I realized that I didn't want to have the child at this moment, and the baby felt that. We will not have a little Elga. I feel profound guilt toward her, and I don't want any reminders. I told Mikhail, too, not to dare speak of it again. If you want to anger me, you can continue to pester me with your questions and worries.

MAY 31, 1913

The greatest gift is confidence in your own future. For the past few days, I've been very downcast, God knows why. Perhaps you'll think it's because I doubt myself, doubt you, doubt life and all higher things. Not at all. I've only been thinking about my future earnings. Oh, how much I need to earn, to maintain a wife who deserves to dress like the famous actress she is, and to feed the fragile creature she happens to be, and to shower her with presents to make her happy.

MOSCOW–YURYUZAN
MARUSYA TO JACOB

MAY 31, 1913

Headache. Weariness. Bad temper. My soul is asleep—there is nothing I want, nothing! Suddenly everything has become dreary, a burden. Perhaps your unspoken desire that I leave the stage is bearing fruit. Our studio is preparing a new performance, to a new composition called "Leaves in Autumn." I began the rehearsals, then abandoned them; and now I'm unable to take part in the performance. The performance is very interesting. The dancers are in thrall to the wind, which blows them hither and thither, sweeps them around, throws them down, and picks them up again. And every figure is stripped of her own strength and will, and submits to the whirlwind motion, the intricate but random interactions of the figures, and a gust of wind sweeps them off the stage one by one, defeated, helpless bodies of the leaves and forlorn souls. After my absence, I came to the class and saw this piece finished, in its final form—without me. And the winter tour abroad, which I wasn't eligible to take part in last year, will go on without me. London and Paris. It seems to me that I won't have the strength to return to my studies after the troupe comes back from abroad. You are probably glad to hear I will be exchanging my old life for a more "respectable" one, and that I will devote myself to the subject of pedagogy, so dear to your heart, that there will be one more Froebel Miss on the planet, or, even better, one more housewife.

JUNE 10, 1913

Little one, nice as can be, I love your dancing, your art! Marusya, I have never had the privilege of seeing you onstage, but when I do, I'm sure it will bring me enormous pleasure. And it will happen, without fail. Your despondency can be explained by the weak state of your health. Your dance troupe will return, and you will continue your studies. I can take care of things myself; I can do everything around the house. I've learned how in the army.

JUNE 15, 1913

Sweet Marusya! More than half my term of duty is over! In two weeks, I was supposed to go to a four-month training camp, but suddenly I got lucky—they decided to let me stay in the office, because they couldn't find another clerk like me anywhere. And they didn't look very hard, because they foresaw that I would surpass everyone else in skill and dedication. True, I had to learn to write in a special "clerkish" script, so that the page looks decent and slightly legible. I can address an envelope with flourishes and curlicues that even Akaky Akakievich would be proud of! I even thought, Hmm, I'm a kindred spirit of Gogol's character with the pen and the overcoat . . . my penurious friend!

I'm spurring myself on. My studies have me chomping at the bit, and the books are good. In four months, you can accomplish a lot. It's too bad I postponed taking my exams. After I read something, it gets fixed in my memory, but I've never tested its longevity.

JULY 6, 1913

I'm in a foul mood again. I was just about to go to a restaurant, but I decided not to. I have promised myself that, from this month on, I have to live at a calmer pace. I don't sleep well; I'm nervous. I don't think I can be away from you much longer. I can't, I don't even want to, get close to other people when you aren't here. And I'm lonely.

I received an unexpected letter from Paris. Someone from the past wrote me. We haven't seen each other or corresponded for many years. And now there's a long letter. It was so strange to see a forgotten but familiar script all of a sudden. Sweet, strange life . . . There is so much sadness in memories of the past, and, true, profound happiness. My Jacob! My Jacob—you are the most important thing, the largest thing in my life. My young husband, dearest to me, closest to my heart. My own happiness; my own life. Good night! I kiss you.

YURYUZAN–MOSCOW
JACOB TO MARUSYA

AUGUST 12, 1913

Write me, Marusya, and tell me whether you have begun your studies at the Rumyantsev Museum. You had intended to read something there, if I recall correctly. And about the planes of dynamic composition, if that's what it's called.

I did read the books you sent me. *The Voice of the Blood* is quite good, but the others—oh, how weak and uninspired. Really, to cool your ardor, find the article by Chukovksy in the June issue of *The Russian Word*. Don't be afraid. You'll admire him afterward—but his halo will fade just a bit.

Now, *Little Wars* by H. G. Wells is something I understand. How could there be a parallel, though? I simply read one book after another. It intrigued me for a long time.

Ask someone who knows the English language and literature to read Barrie's play *Peter Pan* to you. It's a wonderful children's play in which the characters talk to the audience, and the very memorable finale depends on the last answer given by the audience.

AUGUST 23, 1913

I'm reading *Myths in Art—Old and New* by René Ménard. I'm not so much reading it as looking at it, and I can't get enough of it. Sculpture from antiquity—if it truly captures the structure of the modern human bodies—emphasizes a fact that I have never noticed before. A woman's body does not differ so much from that of a man. There are many, many sculptures and statues in which the breasts are the only distinguishing feature between man and woman. But there are figures in which this sign communicates nothing. The majority of the male gods have a soft, rounded build, with somewhat full hips, shoulders, hands, and breasts that are too small for a woman but slightly too large for a man. The face does not always convey features typical of one sex or the other, especially if the face is very young. The width of the hips is misleading in the extreme. In modern man, the hips are considerably narrower.

Dress is the most unreliable sign of all. *Apollo Musagetes* is wearing a pleated robe with a train and a high waist. *Apollo Sauroctonos* has a typical woman's body, with delicate, slender legs. *Venus Genetrix* has a typical male body.

One could cite many examples on this subject, but there's no reason to do so. It is enough just to visit a museum or examine a cultural atlas to be convinced of it. Is it possible that the sexes back then didn't differ so much from each other, that their ways of life, habits, ways of thinking, were more similar? They lived together, danced, studied, swam, practiced gymnastics, and loved together. Life was much simpler, more naïve. And that marvelous "unashamedness."

It's difficult to love Egyptian stone sculpture, with dead figures and one-dimensional profiles. But the graceful figure of Isis is lovely. She wears a tight sheath that ends at her breasts. And on another bas-relief she is depicted with the head of a cow, feeding Horus, a youth who already stands shoulder-high.

And about something that is of special interest to you, a good subject for your dynamic compositions: dance with theatrical masks. They are easy to create from papier-mâché. A tragic mask, laughing and crying. The possibilities are myriad.

Isadora Duncan's dancing, in which the only material is her own body, demands a special degree of talent, for the added richness of visual means of expression is lacking.

There will come a time when you and I will read these books together—the history of art, music, a bit of medicine and pedagogical theory. The sooner the better.

Goodbye, little one. I await orders for maneuvers. And then—freedom. It's unlikely that I'll be given early discharge, though.

Write me sometime. I shower you with kisses—many of them, and often.

—Your Jacob

Addendum
Look in the library for a handbook for reading the authors of antiquity, and for interpreting poetic allegories and symbols in works of art. Publisher-

editor of *The New Journal of Foreign Literature*, richly illustrated. You might also need Stoll's valuable work, *Myths of Classical Antiquity*. I highly recommend it.

I received *Footlights* and for several minutes was transported there, to your world. It's a pity it contains none of your notes! I enjoyed the article about Bogolyubov and the pictures of Reinhardt. I'm extremely interested in Western theater arts. Back home, I read a good book by Georg Fuchs— about the Munich Art Theater. And there's still Dresden and Nuremberg to visit.

If I were an opera director in the present moment, I would adopt Reinhardt's views on it. Reinhardt is made for opera, with its palpable conventions, its heightened theatricality. Of course, all art has its conventions, but drama is still somewhat closer to life. Opera, with its enormous scale, needs large-scale directorial decisions. The architectural-sculptural manifestations can change from opera to opera, but the main thing is that the "spectacular" dimension, the "staginess" or "showiness," is particularly evident in opera, in extravaganzas, in ballet, as well as in tragedy.

The Munich Art Theater (drama) attempts to minimize the dimensions of the stage. On a large stage, the actors, characters, words dissolve and disappear. A large stage always requires many people, which artistic necessity does not always call for. But Reinhardt works with thousands of people, whole circuses, hundreds of torches, thousands of colors.

I read the papers and the magazines. I scour them for news about the Rabenek studio. And I read about the Free Theater, and about the Moscow Art Theatre.

MOSCOW–YURYUZAN

MARUSYA TO JACOB

A few days ago, I was bathing in the kitchen. Nyusha was there, puttering around at her chores, and talking all the while. She recalled how, as a girl, she had liked to play outside, splashing around in puddles. And then about her family, how the matchmaker called and brought her together with her husband (she's married). Then she started remembering her wedding night. I listened, quiet as a mouse. With a kind of agitation, and some other feeling

I couldn't quite describe. This is what Nyusha told me: It was very painful for her. She couldn't bear it, and screamed at the top of her lungs. But no one responded to her call—everyone knew that that was how it happened. "Rivers of sweat were streaming down me. I started pounding him with my fists, then grabbed him by the throat, by his hair. I even pulled out clumps of his hair. I swear, madame, my heart starts pounding every time I remember it. For a whole week afterward, I felt as if I was ill. I thought I didn't want to see a man again." There were many other graphic details, but I'll leave them out. And while I listened, I leaned low over the water basin, washing my feet carefully.

This story soothed me.

Jacob! Maybe I shouldn't have written this to you? Should I cross it out? If it's wrong, cross it out yourself, and tell me I was bad. That's how it is now. If I'm ashamed before you, I cover my face with your hands. If I'm afraid of you, you are the one I look to for protection at the same time. You are everything to me. This scares me. But it seems it's just the way it is.

YURYUZAN–MOSCOW
JACOB TO MARUSYA

SEPTEMBER 25, 1913

I remember my words about Christianity in a recent letter. They were absolutely right, and don't think it was the first time I wrote something like this. Only the exterior, the outside, very attractive, is accessible to us. It holds out the prospect of warmth, peace, hope. It's childish in its popular manifestation: if you behave well, you will receive praise; if you're bad, you'll be punished.

The Christian Gospels are terribly dogmatic. Christ's words: "They say this, that, and the other, but I say unto you . . ." etc. Dogma, commands—and if you don't carry them out, you will be doomed to Gehenna for all time. Forgiveness for the one who repents is no surprise; but forgiving the cruel brigand or robber? It's a pity I don't recall the texts from memory.

The Gospels themselves are not a religion, but material for creating one. There are as many religions as there are people. From the same texts, you can derive a great deal of real love.

I don't wish to talk about such a large matter, because it's nonetheless alien to me. Religion is something that completely passed me by. Perhaps I'll have to return to it someday.

And do you have enough money? Tell me the truth, little one.

CHELYABINSK–KIEV
JACOB TO HIS PARENTS

OCTOBER 1, 1913

Dear Papa, I've finally arrived in Chelyabinsk. I sent you a postcard saying that the doctor here exempted me from exercise, without even examining me. He just came up to me and said, "Aha, a volunteer! You're relieved." The next day, I was sent here in a military train with a detachment of feeble soldiers to be housed in apartments for the winter. Now I only await discharge!

I was very happy about this, of course. The exercise will not be difficult, they say; still, walking thirty-five versts on the first day, carrying upward of thirty-five pounds on your back, is hard work.

The nights here are already cold, very autumnal, and it's easy to catch cold at night, because you sleep in the field in tents, on the hard ground, covered with your coats, with a knapsack for a pillow.

And suddenly, instead of sleeping in a field, in a flimsy tent with a knapsack under my head, I'm in the city, in a hotel, writing you at a desk, drinking tea from a samovar (and not from a dirty teapot). The ceiling here doesn't leak as it does in the barracks, there are no superiors, and I am completely free until the troops return from exercise. All this instead of mud, filth, camp chores.

I feel I have literally revived since yesterday evening. Not to mention the modern conveniences, the soft mattress, electric lights, a clean room.

. . . I'm just sick of the loneliness I lived in for so long. I want people, books, theater, music, but, more than anything, a free life, not having to deal with superiors, not having to depend on them.

CHELYABINSK–MOSCOW
JACOB TO MARUSYA

OCTOBER 1, 1913

Good morning, Marusya! I'm writing you from a hotel. I absolutely love writing lying down. It's morning now. I woke up long ago, and thought

245

about you, then fell asleep again (dreamed), then read a story by Kuprin, and now I'm coming back to you. Although things are so nice at the moment, I can't help reproaching you. You know, Marusya, I was already thinking . . . In your last letter you said something about losing each other in our correspondence, becoming more distant from each other.

My dear wife! As is always the case in life, in illness, in turmoil, when you reach the very top, the apex of growth or development, there's a break, a turning point. And you find new strength. (Look how bold I am to quote Kuprin's idea here.)

I wanted to say something about illness. If it isn't a serious illness (I'm speaking generally here), it can even bring a certain amount of satisfaction or pleasure. I would gladly be sick for a time if you were there to take care of me. But a serious illness, an illness that goes on for a long time, drives out all poetic thoughts and feelings, and is just plain bad.

Someday when illness strikes I won't have to leave your side. I alone will be your nurse. We will live a long life together, until old age, until illness takes us both. And we will take care of each other.

I have terrible plans for winter: burying myself in my books day and night. We'll read lots of books, and a bright, beautiful life will open up before us, won't it, Marusya? I'm not thinking about music as much as I'm thinking about scholarly research at the Institute these days.

Fly, time, fly by! If I could drive it with a whip, I'd crack it all day long.

OCTOBER 15, 1913

What am I going to do with you? I received another letter in the spirit of "So-so. Not so good." You write about being a wife, a lover—what can I say? Do you wish to be my wife or my lover? I don't understand the difference, God help me! You will be the closest person in my life, the person most needful to me—and that's all. You would be a lover if I was already married. Then I would leave my wife for you. But this would never happen. If I marry, it will be forever.

Marusya, my good girl, I don't ask you for much—only to believe my fidelity. Yes, you can recall bad things I've said or done—but you've never heard lies coming from me! I have said many bad things about myself, said too much—but it's only because I don't know how to protect you, and it's often difficult—but I have always told you everything!

Why, oh why, all this sadness in the subjunctive mood—"If only this, then that would . . . or could . . . or should . . ."? And if you believe me, why

246

don't you remember my words, my constant refrain: "No, never, not for the world"?

Yes, you are my wife, my first wife, my remarkable, wonderful lover; and I don't care what will happen in twenty years. We need only to be sure of the present moment for our marriage.

This is the formal, official part of my conversation with you. The unofficial part I'll whisper in your ear. And not just today, but forever and ever.

Oh, what a happy ending it would be if we were sitting side by side. I would kiss your hands, and say: "It doesn't mean anything, it's unimportant. You're imagining it." And right away you would see that I was right, and it would comfort you for a long time.

Don't be sad, my heart. Soon. Very soon now!

Don't worry about the money. It's not from Papa. No one knows about it. I teach private lessons here. And I'm very happy that I can help you in some way. You have to spend all of yours on getting fitted out.

When a woman's dress is shabby, she becomes self-conscious. But when she is dressed well, we don't even notice it! (There's a proverb there.)

OCTOBER 17, 1913

Good evening, good dusk to you, Marusya! I'm so glad you're fine. I'm also exceptionally fine—fine "squared." Perhaps you'd like to know whence this exceptional state? Why "squared"? Because Private Volunteer Ossetsky has been thrown in the guardhouse for ten days, for insulting an officer. And in recognition of his record of good behavior, with no prior infractions, another five days were tacked on. I hope that it will be possible to reduce the sentence, because the volunteer in question has fewer than fifteen days remaining to serve in the army. In addition, unfortunately, there is no suitable place for arrestees in the barracks. The best-beloved superiors (Commander-Fathers) would never have expected to find such unruly specimens in their midst, of course.

Recently, all my superiors have literally taken a dislike to me. Eternally nitpicking.

Today is the 17th—there are fourteen or fifteen days to go. There are already fifty weeks behind me, only two short weeks left. When you get this letter, there will be only ten days or so.

The entire year, the most difficult year of my life, has brought me everything I have. There will never be a worse year. If I had lived this year in Kiev, it would have been otherwise. Worse, and otherwise. How will it end? Is it really true that everything is for the best in this best of all worlds? Is it possible that the boorishness of this officer was a necessary step along the way of my path in life?

Good day, my good girl! The door has just banged shut behind me, and I am alone with my loneliness and my thoughts. The task before me: that my arrest become an interesting way of passing the time. I will write down everything, every single thing—and you will read it when it is all in the past, and perhaps my recollections will appear sweet and vaguely poetic by then.

And so—I am in prison. Excellent. Let Tolstoy be my mentor in the circumstances of my present life. I am referring, of course, to the story "The Divine and the Human." My life should now turn into a burst of will, a single absolute, unremitting aspiration. I don't want to pace desperately from corner to corner, tear at my hair, and weep.

I wrote my schedule on a piece of paper. At the bottom is a large inscription: "Our Lady, Holy Virgin Mary, give me strength!" In the severe and comfortless Hebrew monotheism there is no such warm corner. We'll see. Now it's time to make myself comfortable.

The military guardhouse resembles, most likely, an ordinary prison. The difference is that your own soldiers are the ones guarding you. At the end of a watch, this sentry might himself become a prisoner. If your own company is on duty, all the better. We are very dependent here on the sentry superiors—noncommissioned officers. Prisoners consider twelve noon, when the new watch appears, to be the beginning of a twenty-four-hour day.

At 6:00 a.m.—prisoners' reveille—the door opens, and you go to wash. You fold back the plank bed and go out. It's still completely dark. Up by the ceiling, a tiny window covered by a grate lets in a meager light. Not until eight o'clock is the twilight bright enough for reading. Right now it's eight o'clock.

After washing, you sit in the dark, waiting for the guard. Finally, you hear him call out, "Tea." He comes up to the door and thrusts the spout of the teapot through the "spy hole," filling the cup you hold under it. All day

248

long, you hear nothing but "Guard! Take me out to relieve myself!" The keys jangle, and they lead someone out.

By five o'clock, it's already dark. They don't give you any light. At this time, I practice music—I do ear training, recall various pieces, whistle, and sing.

My neighbor on the right, a Jew (he's in for theft), sings Yiddish songs and prayers the whole day. My neighbor on the left sings, too—military marches, waltzes, and yesterday he suddenly broke into "O Sole Mio"!

I hear a woman's voice in the sentry room. What does it mean? It turns out that in one cell there is a twelve-year-old boy, a pupil from a martial-music school. They "gave him up for music" when he was seven years old. For his schooling, he is required to serve for five years. He's awaiting trial now. He's being tried for escaping service for the sixth time. This lively, intelligent boy is learning to be a first-class criminal, of course. One soldier was discharged on leave to Sevastopol. This boy tampered with the ticket, to make it valid for two, and went with him. He worked as a musician on a naval vessel: "I dreamed of sailing on a boat like that my whole life." A few months later, inquiries were made about him, and he was sent back to his company under military guard. He was held in many guardhouses along the way. He happened to pass through Voronezh, where he was from. He saw his mother there. "She came and brought me some sausage, and started to cry. I don't like that, so I went back to my cell. She stopped crying, and then I went out to see her again."

This cruel military atmosphere puts the mind to sleep once and for all, and hardens the hearts of the majority of grown-up people who come into contact with it. So you can imagine, Marusya, how devastated the soul of this young boy is after all these years.

He is facing pretrial imprisonment, a trial, and sentencing—to a (child's) disciplinary detachment of music pupils, for the duration of his punishment—and serving three more years in his company.

The nights are tormenting. The bed hardly deserves the name. I roll up my uniform and put it under my head, put on my overcoat, and go to sleep. The hard planks chafe your sides, your shoulders, your legs. You fall asleep for an hour, then wake up and turn over. It's very uncomfortable. Although I'm not terribly particular about creature comforts, I've never had to adjust to conditions like this. It's not easy to sleep on wooden planks.

I remember that during my training I had to spend one night sleeping on the ground. I slept beautifully the whole night long. But this isn't unbearable, either. Now it's day, and night doesn't terrify.

Today I am almost happy and satisfied with myself. In the morning I worked on French, and during the day I studied my economics textbook. Tomorrow my studies will be wonderful. Today, before-lunch passed seamlessly into after-lunch, because my entire lunch consisted of a few hunks of contraband cheese. I asked the sentry, and he ran to the store to get it.

Dusk, dusk at four o'clock. My day is ending. There are still five hours left to pace around. My neighbor sings mournfully. I hear music in my head—Rachmaninoff. If only I could look at you for just a moment and kiss your hands quietly. I can't see a thing! Goodbye, little one.

Baratynsky's verse is going round and round in my head. I remember it well. I remember Lermontov well. And Pushkin very well.

NOVEMBER 5, 1913

My imprisonment experience is over. I'm in a rented apartment, awaiting the discharge orders.

Masses of reserves—about one and a half thousand bearded, strapping peasants—joined the company. Now they are in formation outside the window to go to lunch. There weren't enough copper and aluminum cooking vessels. They fetched black tin washtubs from the baths and poured the cabbage soup into them.

In the evening, I walked through the barracks for the reserves. People sleeping on straw, not getting undressed, snoring; someone cries out in his sleep, cursing. Simple folk. I've been living among them for a whole year. So close together that our differences get erased. They feel that I'm one of them—so there is no question of mutual misunderstanding. A sluggish, uninteresting mass of people. In most cases, crude and slovenly; they love winning and forgive everyone who wins. They're nasty, not very smart, sometimes gratuitously violent and cruel (hooliganism), and all of them respect science for its profitability.

There will always be exceptions. But, alas, I've come across precious few. In fact, there weren't real exceptions, only exceptional deeds. Sometimes I scrutinize them and wonder—who will remain in my memory in the new life that's about to begin for me? There are no exceptions, and the exceptional deeds are easily forgotten, and all that remains is a monotonous gray background. Without people, without souls, without bright spots. Gray, colorless—like butcher paper.

I even start feeling indignant. Where is Platon Karataev? Where are the people who inspired characters in *The Snow Maiden*, or in *Boris Godunov*, people who built the Kremlin, people who told such remarkable tales, sang such memorable songs? Where is the tiniest fragment of Mikula Selyaninovich, the folk hero, or someone who bears even the slightest resemblance to Ivan Tsarevich? Where are the turbulent, impassioned figures from Malyavin's paintings?

Is it only because we're in the Orenburg province? True, it's impoverished, dreary. But is it really that different in Penza, or in Riga? The only thing they know how to do well is go to war and die without thinking. Without a murmur—they'll do whatever you ask them to. Sorrowful thoughts.

CHELYABINSK–KIEV
JACOB TO HIS PARENTS

NOVEMBER 5, 1913

I received everything—the money and the letter. But I'm still waiting for discharge orders. I'm also tired of writing letters. I'm glad it will all be over soon. This year has seemed like ten. I still can't believe everything that has happened. Until I see you at the station, I won't believe it. This year has had a bad influence on me—I've been cut off from people, theater, music. I wasn't able to study properly. I've grown wild . . . And I've never wanted to study as much as I do now. I am aware of the difficulties that await me. I've completely forgotten how to focus. It will be a long time before I can really catch up in my classes. I'm especially concerned about finance law. I don't have the books I need, but it's not easy to find them in Kiev, either. On the other hand, I'm well versed in political economy. Unfortunately, I'll have to take an exam in statistics again. This irks me, because I already passed it in the second year; but now the volume of required information has increased, and I'll have to take it again.

Oh, if you can, get me a subscription to the symphony concerts for the month of December. I desperately need music. Now my only comfort and amusement are motion pictures. I go often. And my favorite reading matter now is the book of train schedules.

CHELYABINSK–MOSCOW

JACOB TO MARUSYA

NOVEMBER 6, 1913

Still no discharge orders! This is my plan: as soon as they discharge me, I'll go directly to the station, take the train to Moscow, where I'll stop for a day or two, and then on to Kiev. I'll take my exams (some, at least) and in two or three weeks I'll travel to you in Moscow and stay for a long time. I won't tell anyone at home about Moscow. They are tired of waiting. But I am even more tired—I've dreamed about you several nights in a row. Oh my, how hard it is without a wife . . . It hits me from time to time. You know what it's like, too. I kiss you deeply, dear one!

Never mind. I'll be patient. "But he that shall endure unto the end, the same shall be saved." The end will come soon. And what a brilliant ending it will be! Just released from prison to Bogoslovsky Lane, fourth floor, just below the heavens—is heavenly bliss not in store? I will arrive in paradise soon. And you will be my wife!

KIEV–MOSCOW

JACOB TO MARUSYA

NOVEMBER 21, 1913

Well, Marusya, I have something to tell you that I think will interest you. Prick up your little ears (which I kiss in passing). Yesterday Papa was taking his usual postprandial walk through the living room. The twilight was approaching, Mama was sitting in the rocking chair, her sewing in hand. I enter, take Papa by the arm, and start walking in step with him.

"I need to speak with you, Papa."

"Proceed."

I launched into a long conversation about you, about me, about our future. By the way, he said, "With a wife like that, life is not a daunting prospect. If you are in straitened circumstances, she will bear up under them and help you do the same." You see? I was surprised and glad that he didn't insist we live in Kiev. He said, "In May, you will pass the qualifying exams, and in August, you can finish the state examinations. Then you can move to Moscow permanently. I have some connections there who may be able to help you find a position. At the same time, I am willing to send you money for living expenses for the first year, which should help you out. You don't need to live in luxury at first—a single room is probably sufficient."

I'm hurrying now, because Papa made an appointment for us at the tailor's. We're ordering two new suits (one for him and one for me) and two overcoats.

DECEMBER 31, 1913. EVENING.

The year is ending, my very best year—the happiest, most promising year. 1913. This will set the standard for the rest of my life. I have learned to understand myself. And I have understood you, and decided how to live my life. I can't put it into words, but there seems to be a solid grounding under me now, something to take root in.

I'm not a seeker of truth, not a fighter, a poet, a scientist. But I will try to be more sincere, to live justly, always to study and learn, and to respond if someone near me is crying out in pain. And I will also always be strong and love my wife and companion.

It's almost midnight. Are you in a noisy crowd, having fun? May all the gods conspire to send you heaps of joy and mountains of flowers today.

It doesn't matter that I'm alone. As soon as I shut the door, there are already two of us, until morning.

I'm going out for a walk now. Have fun there, my Marusya!

MOSCOW–KIEV
MARUSYA TO JACOB

JANUARY 5, 1914

As I write you, I'm surrounded by deep silence. Everyone is asleep. I am very tired, and want to sleep, too. There are constant matinees and evening performances. The holiday season is the busiest time for an actor. But I don't mind it. Work is not a burden for me. Except that today I injured my leg during a performance. It's painful and swollen.

I want to be strong and healthy, to be beautiful. I want fine clothes. And to be free of the studio and the theater for a few days. Free from all obligations. I think when you come I'll feign illness for three days or so. Yesterday I was at a party with Beata. Today someone called me on the telephone and told me, "Yesterday you were not only interesting, you were beautiful. Your eyes were sparkling, your cheeks were rosy, etc."

I have a new hat that truly becomes me. New shoes. One new blouse, and new pantalettes made of tricot. Very warm and pretty, with elegant black ribbons that lace up the sides. But they won't be new anymore by the time you arrive! It's too bad.

You must come. Leave on either the 25th or the 27th. No, I don't want you to arrive on the 27th. Let it be the 28th! It's silly, but I'm terribly superstitious. I can't help it. Seven has always been an unlucky number for me. And if you come a bit later, it might turn out better: from the 20th to the 22nd, I'll probably be ill, but by the 26th–28th, I'll be right as rain.

Jacob! My love of loves, best beloved . . . mine! I'm getting ready for your arrival. A bride should be dressed in all new things on her wedding day. Everything I wear will be brand-new. And there will be flowers.

I have become so silly. It'll be just us. No friends or parental advice (a mother always has something to say to her daughter), just me and you. Only the two of us at our own wedding. It's frightening, and it's good, and my head is spinning and spinning. I'm already thinking like you, exactly like you . . . that we should have many children, and the first one will be Genrikh, as you suggested, or Elga, as I would want her to be called, if it's a girl. Does that make you happy? You'll have a silly, completely silly, wife. That won't stop you, will it?

27

Nora in America
Visiting Vitya and Martha
(1987)

Nora and Tengiz were very successful in their collaborative work. Working separately brought good results, too, sometimes—but when they worked together, the air around them grew brighter, lighter, the actors surpassed themselves, the music rang out more clearly, everything played and shimmered, and luck was always with them. That is, if you left out of consideration the fact that their relationships with theater higher-ups did not always run smoothly, and that fine productions were shut down on occasion the day after the premier. Such was the case with Chekhov, and with Saltykov-Shchedrin. The audience and the critics were often ecstatic about their work, especially Western audiences. They were invited to perform in Yugoslavia and in Poland, and once Tengiz even took part in the Edinburgh Theatre Festival, albeit without Nora.

This time, they had brought down the house in Moscow. Gogol ensured their success. They staged *Viy*. Nora wrote the adaptation herself, with great confidence—after *Carmen*, she had gained sufficient courage and daring to tackle it. She was both the scriptwriter and the set designer. The play ended up being more comical than frightening. They inserted a subplot into the action—an unspoken rivalry for the "philosopher" between Pannochka the Witch, and a more youthful Khveska in a walk-on part. Which of the rivals wins in the end remained deliberately vague. Tengiz was satisfied with the finale: On the last night, Khoma, protected by a circle of magic, reads out a prayer over the dangerous female corpse. They lift up the Viy's eyelids, which droop all the way down to the ground, and a deafening chorus strikes up a wild din. With the first rays of the sun, the rooster crows, the icons plunge to the ground, and in the empty eye sockets of the iconostasis, devils and evil spirits of all kinds, along with peasants who are nearly indistinguishable from the devils, struggle to break out. All of them are trying to get to the windows to escape before the rooster's third crow; but Pannochka the Witch and Khveska continue to pull each other by the hair in their final skirmish. In short, a gothic novel.

The music for the play was written by a young composer, and it ended up being a heady mixture of the avant-garde with ethnographic flourishes. Tengiz invited a choreographer from Perm, an elderly connoisseur of folk traditions and a master in tap dancing, a dance form that was only semilegal. The dances he choreographed for the play were a sensation.

One of their friends from the theater community brought along a visiting American, the Broadway producer Felix Cohen, to see the play. He waxed ecstatic about what he had seen.

After the performance, the wrinkled old man with dyed hair and sporting crocodile shoes invited Tengiz and Nora out to a restaurant. They spent a pleasant evening with him, dining on borscht, dumplings, and vodka, and at the end of their late supper, he invited them to bring their "very Russian" production to the American stage.

Tengiz and Nora forgot about the proposal as soon as they left the restaurant, but that wasn't the end of it. A month and a half later, they received an official invitation from Felix Cohen, offering to pay their travel and living expenses for the duration of the trip.

The multistage process of forging an agreement with the directorial board of the All-Russian Theater Organization and acquiring a visa lasted about eight months. The arrangements did eventually fall into place, however, and Nora and Tengiz got ready to take their production to New York's Broadway Theater District. Russia was again just coming into fashion, and a "Russian" play, as Cohen understood it, was very much in keeping with such Russian souvenirs as nesting dolls, military caps, wooden spoons, and floral headscarves.

Tengiz and Nora were dumbfounded by the ironies of this new situation. It was clear to both of them that they belonged Off-Broadway—beyond the bounds of the world's center for commercial, although high-quality, theater. Nevertheless, such offers come your way once in a lifetime, and for the first few days, Nora brainstormed about how to adapt the play to the reigning local fantasies. To start with, they thought up an English title for the play, *The Phi-*

losopher Thomas Brutus, which Tengiz found very amusing. Let them rack their brains about who the philosopher was, whence this Thomas, and what Brutus had to do with anything, he thought. The fact that Ukrainian and Russian folk songs were not quite the same thing never occurred to anyone.

Nora and Tengiz flew to New York. They checked into a hotel on Forty-second Street, between Sixth and Seventh Avenues. The first evening they arrived, Marina Chipkovskaya, "Chipa," who had been living for a long time in Upper Manhattan, rushed down to see them. For two days, some lower-ranking administrators showed them around the theater. Cohen himself appeared on the third day, apologizing that he had just flown in from Europe. The negotiations lasted for exactly one hour. Nora and Tengiz handed over the Russian version of the play so it could be translated, gave him a tape of the musical score, and took their leave. They were somewhat nonplussed by the meeting—the Americans had spent tons of money on their trip—but the unprofessional and awkward way they were handling things was their own problem. Cohen gave the impression of being a man beset by problems, whether in business or in his personal life.

Three days later, they moved from the hotel to Chipa's and continued their explorations of the city. It was the most alive city in the world, but also somewhat unreal. Even though Chipa adored New York, she was so busy these days with work, and with her twins, that she couldn't take them around, showing them her favorite places. She gave them some tips instead.

Together, Nora and Tengiz walked around the city, in which everything was in excess—the multihued people in an endless grid of streets, the stupefying plethora of colors, smells of unfamiliar food and powerful deodorants and disinfectants, the captivating sounds of street music—all of it strange and incomprehensible to them. In the evenings, Chipa offered her commentary on things, but her observations did not shed any light on American life; it remained a variegated, bustling mystery.

One day before their departure, after leaving Tengiz in the Metropolitan Museum, Nora went to Penn Station to catch a train to visit Vitya on Long Island. She wanted to take a look at his American life. Besides, Yurik had requested that she be sure to see his father while they were in New York. He had asked Vitya to buy him a few records that were vital to his survival.

When Vitya met her on the platform, he was not alone. Standing next to him was an enormous woman with a smile on her rosy face that stretched from ear to ear. This plump stranger exuded sympathetic warmth, and it was clear at first glance that Vitya was in good hands. Nora's dry little hand was enveloped by a fleshy, freckled paw. "Welcome to Long Island, Nora!" the woman said in English.

Vitya hadn't changed one bit, though he was now suntanned and dressed American-style, in shorts and a baggy sweater. They all piled into a big old car and drove off. Martha was behind the wheel. Vitya sat next to her, with a look that seemed to say this was the only way he had ever gone around from place to place. Nora sat in the back seat. Vitya was silent. Martha spoke rather quickly, and not always very clearly. Nora made out from her words that Martha wanted to show her some "light house." They drove for quite a long time, passing through the city, with its massive, tall buildings, and through towns and suburbs with their smaller (lighter?) houses, and everything sparkled and gleamed. The somewhat showy, somewhat tawdry beauty of America spread out before them, dropping off to the right and the left as they drove through the miles. Finally, they arrived at the ocean, and Nora understood at last what lighthouse Martha meant.

"Do you want to go up to the top?" Vitya said. Martha again said something Nora didn't quite catch.

"Martha's not going up; her legs hurt," Vitya interpreted.

Next to the lighthouse was a museum, but they didn't go inside. There were very few people around. The tourist season was over, though it was still warm at the end of October. At the entrance to the lighthouse was an exhibit of lamps and lenses of some sort. They passed these antique technologies without investigating them, and instead started the long climb up the narrow stairway. The ascent was long and exhausting, and even Nora, agile and light on her feet, got winded. But when they reached the observation deck at the top, they were rewarded with a view worth any amount of strain and effort.

"This is Montauk. They say it's the oldest lighthouse in New York State," Vitya told her. "I've been here before with Martha."

The ocean was enormous, and the edges curved in such a way that even the naked eye could see that the earth was round. Whether it was a disc or a sphere was another question. Most likely a sphere, judging by how the shore of Rhode Island sank away in the distance. And there was no perspective—linear, reverse, or curvilinear—that could depict this vision, because space organized itself by a law completely unknown to the human eye or reason. The wind at this height moved in circles, too. Nora felt she was standing on the top of the world, and it surrounded her, as if she were a kernel hidden in its fleshy fruit.

258

"Nora," Vitya said, touching her shoulder, "I need a divorce. Could you divorce me, you know, without me, so I won't have to go to Moscow?"

"What? What do you mean?" Nora didn't understand immediately.

"Martha doesn't know I'm married. She knows I have a son, but she doesn't know I'm married."

"What did you tell her?"

"That you were my classmate, a friend."

Nora forgot about the ocean all of a sudden. She forgot about the round world, in which she had just now been a tiny seed buried in the middle.

"You lied, Vitya? You? Lied? The first time in your life?"

Vitya smiled slowly. Vitya laughed. Then he bent down to Nora.

"Nora, you know what Grisha Lieber says? He says that women force men to lie. He reads the Torah now, you know, what we call the Bible, and he tries to reconcile modern science and the God of the Old Testament. And he says that lies were invented by woman."

"And there I was, thinking my whole life you were openhearted and simple," Nora said, with what was almost a moan.

"You never knew Martha before. That's who is openhearted and simple."

"Are you thinking of getting married?"

Vitya didn't say anything. He rubbed the railing with his finger. He scratched his ear. He sighed.

"I think Martha wants it. You know how Catholics are. She'll feel more comfortable. Well, and, frankly speaking, it wouldn't get in my way, either."

Wouldn't get in your way! Oh, Vitya, Nora thought. They were still standing on the observation deck, and Nora had already stopped noticing all the beauty around her, as though it had never been. Vitya, always a paragon of equanimity, a man without expectations, as upright as a column, as honest as wood . . . Or was I mistaken about him? Has he changed so much in the last year and a half?

"All right, all right. I'll send you the divorce papers. Only, you must tell Martha that I'm your wife, not a classmate."

"But you are a classmate," he insisted.

They descended a few more steps, and entered the glass room from which the light was beamed. A gigantic lens, about the size of a hefty watermelon, sent out its light nonstop. By the light of day it didn't seem so powerful, however. The lighthouse had ceased to interest Nora, and they went out of the glass room and began the long descent down the steep staircase.

"Will you tell her yourself, or do you want me to?" Nora said.

"It's all the same," Vitya mumbled.

Martha was waiting for them at the bottom. They went down to the ocean shore. Huge stone slabs were piled up around the lighthouse. A powerful surf washed over the pebbles on the shore.

"You know, Martha, I was his first wife," Nora said, poking Vitya with her finger.

"I guessed." Martha smiled and blushed, making her already red face even redder. "I've seen a picture of Yurik. He looks a lot like you."

"Looks like you've just proposed on my behalf," Vitya said.

"How do you mean?"

"Well, you said 'first wife.' She can count to two. She'll be the second."

"You said yourself that it wouldn't get in your way."

"You're very decisive. I only started thinking about it."

"What's there to think about? She's a very good match for you."

They got in the car and drove to Vitya's house. It was a little three-room rental, shabby and comfortable. Two bedrooms and a large dining room. In the dining room there was a portrait of James Joyce and some old mustached policeman, who turned out to be Martha's grandfather. So she had already put down roots here some time ago. For dinner, Martha had made Irish stew, slippery pieces of overdone meat with potatoes and onion; it stuck in Nora's throat.

Martha and Vitya resembled each other—both of them large and rosy, and both of them with an appetite for fatty meat, washed down with sweet beer. Moreover, Martha never took her eyes off Vitya.

"Well, come on, come on. Propose!" Nora urged, trying to hurry along Vitya's still half-baked decision. "Right now, while I'm here. I'll send the divorce papers as soon as I can."

After dinner, Martha took Nora to the station. Nora smiled all the way to New York, as though something very good had happened. She had been in this ridiculous platonic marriage for twenty-six years, and it was unclear why she hadn't divorced him earlier. It hadn't meant anything at all. They were already at Penn Station when she realized that she had forgotten the records Martha had bought, which Yurik had ordered from his father.

The next day, sitting in the plane waiting for takeoff, Nora said to Tengiz, "I think I have just given my husband away in marriage."

Tengiz lowered his glasses down to the end of his nose and stared at her over the rims. "Is that a threat?"

"Take it easy, Tengiz. You're not in any danger."

As for *Viy*, it never made it to Broadway.

The Left Hand

(1988–1989)

Nora, who had chosen the profession of theater set designer and artist at the age of fifteen, was aware that she could have done other things—directing, perhaps scriptwriting, she could even have acted or become a teacher—but never could she have become a doctor or an engineer or a mathematician. Tengiz? Tengiz could have been anything—a winemaker, a psychologist, even a hawker at the market. Anything at all, except for a profession that demanded strict discipline—a soldier, for example, or an electric-locomotive driver. Vitya could never have been anything but a mathematician. With Yurik, however, from early childhood, it was unclear. He could do anything at all, as long as he was inspired to do it, but as soon as the inspiration left him, he abandoned the pursuit. It was impossible to make him do anything he didn't want to. Something had to occupy him fully, heart and soul. The interest had to consume him completely. As mathematics consumed Vitya.

By the time Yurik was twelve years old, such an all-consuming interest had taken root in him. It was music. Not music in general, but a particular kind—the music of the Beatles. He learned how to play song after song by ear, and Nora was exhausted by his maniacal commitment. She made several attempts to pull Yurik out of his Beatlemania—she tried to enroll him in a regular music school, where scales, Goedicke's études, ear training, and choir practice reigned, but nothing came of it. Each time he started taking lessons, he dropped them soon after for a variety of reasons: either the teacher was mean, or he didn't like the instrument anymore, or he objected so strongly to the other pupils that he refused to attend the class.

Several years passed, but he didn't advance beyond the Beatles. On the other hand, he knew their music by heart, each of them separately and all of them together. Yet, the further music was from that of his idols, the less interesting it was to Yurik. Every one of their records, every recording that came his way, was a major event in his life. They became his only teachers, and over the course of several years, he wouldn't accept any other kind of music but this universal language of youth, to which Nora was by then nearly allergic. She tried introducing him to some other kind of music: she took him to the conservatory, to the opera, she acquainted him with Arsenal. Alexei Kozlov, Arsenal's band leader, himself a devoted Beatles fan, made some impression on Yurik. All the musical vibrations that reached his ears fell into two categories: "them" or "not them." Tengiz, who dropped in from time to time, was a good interlocutor, because he also loved the Liverpool four, and always brought Yurik some "new old" record.

"You can't make a profession of Beatlemania!" Nora objected. But Tengiz just winked at Yurik, shrugging his shoulders. Then he shook his head and replied: "Why not? You can drive a taxi, can't you? Become a plumber? Or a policeman? But not a Beatlemaniac? Why, Nora? Why can't the boy be a Beatlemaniac?" He continued: "Nora, it's very amusing, but, for Lennon, Elvis Presley was a god. Rock and roll was his universe. It was as though nothing existed before Elvis. Culture is by its very nature a mass of citations; we have many of them at our disposal, but for him the world was born out of a single quotation." Then he laughed and said, "We know too much."

Yurik had no interest in school whatsoever. His grades were low, and he got by from grade to grade only with Nora's prodding and assistance. But this didn't bother him in the least. He didn't find it especially irksome to have to sit in lessons all day, since he could drift off into his musical dream-world during geometry or chemistry classes. Though he had no close friends and was completely indifferent to his classmates personally, or to what they thought of him, he was almost popular in school—with both boys and girls alike. Even the teachers, who considered him to be a lazy underachiever, were kindly disposed toward him. He was good-natured, open and unassuming, and physically appealing, with his bright face, curly hair, and average height. Even his slightly protruding incisors were attractive, giving him the expression of a cute, furry little animal.

From the moment the guitar came into his life, almost all his innocently wise questions and riddles, which had once thrilled Nora, ceased. When he was eight years old, he had told Nora, his spoon frozen in midair between plate and mouth, "Mama, life is like a chink between the skin and the spirit." Another time, brushing his teeth, his mouth still full of both toothbrush and toothpaste, he had said, "Nora! I know! Life is the space between hell and heaven." Nora would swell with pride, but she didn't let it show, saying instead, "Great. Now if only you could learn to wipe your own bottom . . ." To which he answered, "Mama, you can see yourself where my bottom is. It's hard to reach back there." Eventually, however, he did learn to cope with the task.

Only a few years had passed, but now music seemed to have unburdened him of existential angst about eternity, time, freedom, God, and other abstract conundrums. He "played them out" on the guitar, with the help of the Beatles. He played with abandon, and rather awkwardly, with a vaguely beatific smile on his face, the corners of his mouth drawn slightly upward. Nora saw all of this and despaired: yet another artistically inclined person in the family, without an iota of talent. And the boy had reached the age when he should be deciding on a direction in life.

Nora recalled Vitya at that age—his complete absorption in mathematics, and a corresponding absence of interest in anything else. She was glad that Yurik got along with his classmates. His Beatle-inspired strumming made him a center of gravity for all the adolescent cliques and groups, and his less-than-stellar academic record didn't jeopardize his reputation at all. In the general ambience at school, A students were not exactly sought after: an athlete, a musician, or a hooligan was far more attractive. This reverse stigmatization of social outcasts meant that being one of the good students carried less prestige than passing as a hooligan.

The times when Yurik read voraciously, and went to the theater and to museums with Nora, had ended on the day when Tengiz brought the guitar over. The guitar steadily increased his popularity among the school marginals, and from that moment on he abandoned the company of "well-brought-up children" for many years to come. Nora understood this perfectly. She couldn't object, either: during her school years, she, too, had been drawn away from the "good girls."

In the beginning of December, at the birthday party of Sergei the Cyclops, one of Yurik's "hooligan" classmates, he received an unexpected party favor—an army firecracker in a cardboard sheath. Sergei, who had flunked a year, had been very solicitous toward Yurik, even protective, warning him that although the firecracker was only for training purposes, it could explode like the best of them.

The firecracker lay in the desk drawer for several days, and Yurik's hands were itching to set it off. On the first evening he was alone at home, he took the firecracker out of the drawer and to the kitchen. Then he lit the end of the tantalizing, twisted fuse, about six inches long, which dangled from the cardboard tube. It caught fire eagerly, then burned with a cheerful confidence, showing no intention of going out. When only about an inch of the fuse remained before it reached the smoldering kernel inside the capsule, Yurik began to feel uneasy, and decided to end his experiment. He turned on the faucet and tried to douse the burning string with a gush of water. It turned out that the fire was of some unique kind that water couldn't extinguish. He rushed around the kitchen, and wanted to throw it out the window, but the old window was stuck fast and wouldn't open. Now the fuse was very short, and Yurik made a dash for the bathroom, where he planned to throw it down the toilet. But he never made it. The firecracker exploded with such force that the whole kitchen shook, and the glass pane in the window, standing its ground till the bitter end, blew out. The bang was glorious.

My hand blew off, Yurik thought mournfully, his eyes shut, and froze, for some reason expecting another explosion. But there wasn't one. He opened his eyes. It was dark and smoky; it stank of war. His hand was right where it was supposed to be; but in the triangle between his thumb and his index finger a fiery wound gaped, a piece of flesh indistinguishable from the meat sold in stores: red, streaked with white . . .

"No, not the left hand!" Yurik shrieked. "Not the left hand!"

Goodbye, guitar! It was not at all painful, but it would have been better to have his head blown off. He howled and raced around the apartment, waving his bloody hand and spattering the walls, the floor, even the ceiling, with fresh bright-red droplets.

He ran around in circles, deafened and crazed, unable to hear the wild knocking on the door—the neighbors from across the landing. But he rushed over to the door of his own accord, goaded by fear for this unfortunate left hand, without which what kind of guitarist could he be? When he unlocked the door, he saw three neighbor ladies and an old man. Yurik kept crying, "My left hand, my left hand!" and they gaped at him silently, moving their mouths and not making any sounds. There was a whistling in his ears, and a metallic taste in his mouth. He was experiencing a post-concussion syndrome. The most adroit of the neighbors ran to call the ambulance, but the most intelligent wrapped his hand in a towel, looking for his hat, and at the same time commanding her husband to run downstairs on the double to start the car. Then they drove to the hospital.

It was already after one in the morning when Nora got home. Coming into the lobby, she noticed spattered blood by the entryway, and then in the elevator. She froze, anticipating disaster. The traces of blood led directly to the door of their apartment.

A note was hanging on the door: "Nora, drop by apartment 18." Nora had a ticket to fly to Warsaw the next day, where she was supposed to meet Tengiz at a theater festival. They were performing a play by Alexander Gelman, a production-worker drama with a human face . . .

Yurik was operated on that very night. The signs and symptoms were such that sweet Dr. Medvedev insisted that the boy be transferred from the post-op to the neurology ward. When he examined the damage from the concussion, he determined that the trauma was mostly psychological. Yurik's hearing began to return on the third day, but the young man wept without ceasing, and to all questions he replied: "Left. Why the left? If only it had been the right!" And he shook his bandaged hand in despair.

Tengiz called from Poland the following night. "Why didn't you come? It's a success!" Nora told him about the accident. Astonishingly, Tengiz cried out, "No, not the left one?!"

Dr. Medvedev called in a psychiatrist for consultation. The psychiatrist prescribed pills. Nora was shaken by this turn of events. Damn heredity!

Ten days later, the bandages were removed. His fingers looked like sausages. Yurik's thumb was numb for several months. It was painful for him to play, but he managed. On his first day at home, he began exercising his hand so he could recover his guitar-playing skills and former agility.

"When does he turn seventeen?" Doctor Medvedev asked Nora when Yurik was being discharged.

"He'll turn fifteen in a month. There are still two years," Nora said, catching his drift immediately.

"I suggest you take care of his military service. He should be exempt from the draft. Guard this discharge paper carefully: it says 'moderately severe concussion with partial loss of hearing.' It may come in handy."

The war in Afghanistan was already over by this time, but the fear of military conscription ran deep. Nora already knew that she would do everything in her power to prevent Yurik from having to serve in the army, and that trying to extricate him from the clutches of compulsory military service would be an ordeal. The draft board made a living from such pacifist parents, and Nora was prepared to offer all manner of bribes in a subtle, impeccably artistic manner. Suddenly the indispensable piece of paper seemed to fall from the heavens. The prospect of a legitimate exemption from military service beckoned.

Yurik had just been let out of the hospital when Tengiz showed up again.

"How's the boy?" he asked from the doorway.

"He's home."

"Congratulations!"

From Yurik's room, they heard the soft strumming of guitar strings. Tengiz hugged Nora. Then he hung his sheepskin coat on the coatrack. He had a present for Yurik in his duffel bag—the Beatles album *Let It Be*. After the album came out in 1970, Paul McCartney left, and the group ceased to exist. But Yurik continued to live in their world, and had no intention of leaving it.

29

The Birth of Genrikh
(1916)

In the spring of 1914, Marusya finished out the Moscow theater season and returned to Kiev. Living in Moscow had been difficult for her. Jacob did everything within his power to overtake time, trying to finish his work at the Institute a year ahead of schedule by taking early exams, but it was already clear that he would still be bound to the Institute in the coming year. He implored his wife to come back to Kiev.

War broke out in the summer, and the prospect of being parted was frightening. Marusya quickly found herself a job, though only part-time. The Froebel Institute opened up its arms to her. They gave her a class in dance movement for workers' children, and she began teaching rhythm and movement in a theater studio not far from home. The work was poorly paid, but during wartime it wouldn't do to set one's sights too high.

They lived in Jacob's room. Having their own lodgings was unthinkable, for a number of reasons: overcrowding in the city because of the war, the high cost of living, the difficulty of arranging an independent domestic life and household, which would have told on Marusya's weak health. Yet, in the prosperous home of Jacob's parents, in spite of the burdens imposed by the war, the level of comfort remained undiminished. In the bathroom, which appealed more to Marusya than all the other bourgeois niceties, there was still running water.

All conversations revolved around the war, its incompetent management, and the base ruses of the Allies. By this time, the losses of the Russian army were already so great that many families had suffered the loss of loved ones. The Ossetskys, too, were in mourning. Jacob's elder brother, Genrikh, a student at Heidelberg University and his father's pride and joy, was captured while trying to return to his homeland. He was interned by the authorities in a concentration camp for displaced persons in the village of Talerhof near Graz, where he died of dysentery in January of 1915.

A good friend of Genrikh's sent his family news of his death, along with a murky photograph of an unattractive young man with large ears. For Jacob, it was a devastating loss. He had idolized his brother as a child, and when he was older, trusted Genrikh's judgment, his opinions, and his views unquestioningly. Genrikh played the role of the older friend Jacob had dreamed of having in his youth.

In 1915, the situation on the front deteriorated day by day. There were fierce battles on the Western front, and on the Eastern front it was not much better: Russian troops were pulling out of Galicia, Poland. Just then, at this most inconvenient time, Marusya got pregnant. The first weeks of her pregnancy were very difficult. She was overcome with nausea and could hardly eat, and, in addition to this, was terribly fearful about the future. She had complicated feelings about being a mother of a newborn, whom she would have wished instantly to be five years old—a charming little girl or a handsome lad. Mixed in with these feelings was irritation that, even before the baby was born, it was already destroying many of her plans. She had to give up teaching and her classes in the studio. She couldn't continue with her German classes, which she had begun at Jacob's urging, because she felt so unwell all the time. He insisted that even now, during the war, Germans had the highest technological and scientific potential; and in the field of pedagogy and psychology, German was indispensable. And, generally speaking, a person had to strive continually to raise her level of cultural proficiency; otherwise, degeneracy would set in. But the future child demanded sacrifices, and she offered them.

Jacob spent all his free time with his wife. He didn't have much of it, however: he had finished his coursework and was writing his thesis, and had been promised a position as a teaching assistant immediately upon completing it.

Marusya was made ill by her pregnancy, as though protecting herself from being overcome by a more general sense of grief. The Ossetsky family treated her with gentle reverence as her belly grew visible. Sofia Semyonovna smiled to herself at this kid-glove treatment. She was one of seventeen children, the last child of her prematurely old mother, and had herself given birth eight times, of which only five children had survived to grow up; and she had lost track of the number of miscarriages she had suffered. She didn't know about Marusya's miscarriage two years before, and was surprised by Jacob's anxiousness; he seemed to consider Marusya's pregnancy to be some sort of dangerous illness.

Marusya's parents didn't often visit their daughter, and preferred that she herself visit them at home. Jacob's family really was very wealthy, and to Pinchas Kerns, a struggling master craftsman, the Ossetsky patriarch appeared haughty and overbearing. As for Marusya's mother, she was shy by nature, and visiting the grand apartment where her daughter lived was a trial.

Seeing how solicitous everyone was toward her, Dusya, the servant, began calling Marusya "Princess." But after the exaggerated burdens of pregnancy followed a truly difficult birth, which almost cost Marusya her life. She was in labor with her firstborn for two days. Professor Bruno, the head of the Faculty of Gynecology and Obstetrics, and the best surgeon in town, performed an operation that saved the life of both mother and child. After the operation, she began to hemorrhage, however, and her life hung in the balance for several more days.

Jacob spent those terrible days in the public library on Alexandrovskaya Street. To try to understand what his wife was going through, he borrowed a volume of *Surgical Obstetrics* by Fenomenov. Here he encountered many unfamiliar words and horrifying pictures. He empathized and suffered with her, barely thinking about the child—the precious life of Marusya overshadowed the rest of the world, which seemed to be quaking under his feet.

Sofia Semyonovna, cursing herself for her dismissive attitude about what she had thought were the exaggerated sufferings of her daughter-in-law during her pregnancy, now sat in her room with the woman's prayer book in Yiddish, wept over it, and prayed, not according to the book, but as her own heart moved her to pray. Dusya ran to the Mariinsko-Blagoveshchenskaya Church, ordered a service for Marusya's recovery, and lit a fat candle for her.

Marusya was still suffering, but the esteemed Professor Bruno assured her that her current pain was only to be expected, that her life was no longer in danger, and that the best thing she could do now was to return home. The heating in the hospital was inadequate, and he felt she would recover more quickly amid the comforts of home. They did not show the baby to Marusya until the third day. She had never seen newborn babies, and was upset, having expected a pretty little child; this wrinkly bit of a thing, with its crumpled little face, inspired only pity in her. She began to cry.

A week later, Jacob brought his growing family home with him, but here there were new difficulties to contend with. Though Marusya's childlike breasts were swollen with milk by this time, her flat nipples refused to open, and seemed to want to lock in the milk for good. Expressing the milk was painful, and the newborn was too weak to suck the milk out of her breasts for himself. Mastitis set in, followed by fever. Breast-feeding was out of the question. During the first days, the child was saved by a precious can of Nestlé powdered milk, which they managed to get hold of in the impoverished city through their combined efforts. Sofia Semyonovna, with the help of her extended family, found a wet nurse—a young village girl with a seven-month-old soldier's son named Kolya. She and Kolya were settled in Eva and Rayechka's room, and they moved into the living room. The baby, named Genrikh, stopped crying. Now he spent most of his time next to the ample breast of the wet nurse, and started squealing whenever he was removed from her. Kolya, the nurse's own child, didn't object. He clearly preferred the porridge of milk and white bread crusts that the experienced Sofia Semyonovna cooked for him.

Then Asya Smolkina, a relative of Marusya's who was a certified nurse, showed up at their home. Always ready to offer medical assistance to her relatives, friends, and acquaintances, she worked as a surgical nurse in Kiev Hospital, where the wounded were transferred to undergo complicated operations that were impossible to carry out in the field hospitals. She rushed over to Marusya either early in the morning or late in the evening and made her compresses, applied lotions, gave massages, always wearing an expression that suggested it was an honor for her to be invited to their home. A week later, Asya managed to express the rest of the standing milk—it was excruciatingly painful—and bind Marusya's breasts with a long linen wrapper, to kill the milk. She also massaged and manipulated her stomach, from navel to pubis, admiring the precise, evenly spaced stitches, which were Professor Bruno's masterful handiwork. Asya idolized Marusya and was prepared to offer her medical services to her until the end of her life, if Marusya would permit it.

For the first six months of Genrikh's life, Marusya was sick and in pain much of the time. Little Genrikh had brought her many new difficulties. In the evenings, when Jacob returned home from the library (he couldn't study at home any longer), they brought the baby to them. Jacob and Marusya put him on display, examining his tiny little hands and feet; they felt surprised by, and gradually grew accustomed to, the new member of their little family. The three of them passed the time in one another's company until the little one began to cry. Then Sofia Semyonovna took him back to the wet nurse.

After that the two of them were alone. Tenderness gave way to passion. Their mutual desire was as strong as ever, and fear of causing pain spurred the discovery of new ways of touching, new kinds of intimacy. Marusya, despairing at how disfigured her stomach was, covered it with her nightgown; but Jacob said that the stitches were particularly dear to him. He told her that the stitches not only did not spoil her looks, they bound the two of them together. They were a mark of her heroic deed, and she meant even more to him with them than without them. The dream of a family with many children had been foolish and empty: he would never again allow her to undergo such suffering.

Jacob kissed the wound that was suddenly right next to his lips, his fingers touched the moist forbidden depths, and for the first time in their relations they discovered not only the smell but also the taste of each other . . . They again began to talk about things that were in no way related to their ever more complicated domestic life. They made plans, and more plans for the future.

When the future arrived, it was not at all the one they had envisioned or hoped for. Things were going from bad to worse on the front. In the fall of 1916, after he had secured his teaching position at the Commercial Institute, Jacob was called up, and transferred from the reserves to active army service. He was sent to Kharkov, to the Second Sappers Reserve Battalion, in which there was a company orchestra. This was not the kind of music he longed for, but a rifle was even less enticing. He was stranded in Kharkov for a long time. The war turned into revolution, and revolution into civil war. Now frontiers and fronts lay between him and his family, and their communications were sometimes disrupted for many months.

30

Endings

(1988–1989)

Nora had known for a long time already that no year ever ended uneventfully. The last weeks of December always brought surprises—both good and bad—as though all the events that were supposed to happen during the course of the year ran out of time and piled up in a heap during these pre–New Year's days. On December 16, Taisia came over with a box of chocolates and a huge bale, out of which she pulled a checked blanket clearly of Scottish provenance. While Nora was still blinking in astonishment, Taisia dexterously put the teakettle on to boil.

It had already been two years since she left Nora's and returned home. After two years of red tape and other ordeals, Lena had finally received a visa to go to Argentina and was now living in a small town in Mendoza Province, where her swarthy husband worked as an engineer in a winery—something his impoverished family in Buenos Aires couldn't even dream of. Taisia had received twelve letters in two years from her daughter—strange, incomprehensible letters, from which she could derive only one thing: that Lena wasn't dancing the tango in Argentina. Six months earlier, a letter arrived that made things absolutely clear: Lena was expecting a baby, and she wanted her mother to come help her out in the first months. It was astonishing that Taisia, who was usually a chatterbox, had never said a word to Nora about this invitation. Taisia had received her visitor's visa, printed on fancy paper covered with official stamps, from the Argentinian consulate, had bought a ticket without saying a word, and two days before her departure had come to inform Nora about it. The chocolates and the blanket were,

thus, goodbye presents, and Nora, bewildered, ate two sickly-sweet chocolates in a row; they seemed to stick in her throat. She couldn't wrap her head
around the fact that Taisia, whom she considered to be a straightforward,
trustworthy person, had so deceived her. It was as though she had now discovered a hidden layer in Taisia, some inexplicable insidiousness in her
behavior, a completely unwarranted furtiveness.

Nora still couldn't bring herself to ask the question that most perplexed
her: why did Taisia conceal her plans for so long, why did she wait until two
days before the departure to tell Nora about it? Afraid she would start to
cry from hurt and confusion, Nora got up and went over to her desk, where
she began rooting around in a drawer. She took an unattractive gold ring
with faceted alexandrite that had belonged to Grandmother Zinaida out of
a little wooden box and placed it in front of Taisia—a memento. Taisia put
it on her finger and burst into tears.

"Oh, Nora . . . But it's gold! And it fits perfectly. You won't regret it? But
I shouldn't really take it . . . It's so valuable!" She took it off, and put it on
again. And smiled, and wiped her nose, and went to kiss Nora.

"I don't know what I'll do without you and Yurik, Nora."

Get lost, Nora thought. You're such a fake.

Out loud she said, "When are you coming back?"

"Soon, soon. I'll only be gone for three months," Taisia said.

Nora's project with Tengiz was pending; all her plans were falling
through.

Maybe I should have Mama come stay for a few weeks, Nora thought.

She didn't have time to ask her. Not two days had passed since Taisia's
departure when Andrei Ivanovich dropped by. He was alone, without Amalia. Nora immediately sensed something was amiss. And it was worse than
she could ever have suspected.

Amalia had cancer.

"Where is the tumor?"

"It's . . . everywhere. They didn't find just one tumor. It's all over. She's . . .
she's on her way here. She just went to the hairdresser."

Andrei Ivanovich choked up. He was pale, and his hands trembled. Nora
sat silently, designing a set for the immediate future in her mind. She would
prepare Amalia's old room for her and drag in the old bed, call the plumber
right away to repair all the faucets and the toilet tank, free up the one-door
wardrobe for her mother's belongings, buy some potted plants—the way
Mama loved it. She didn't get any further than that in building her plans,

because an indescribable nightmare loomed. She would have to tell Yurik. Poor thing, he loved both of them so much. Sometimes it seemed he didn't love anyone but them. Nora thought about the dogs that her mother would probably want to bring here with her. Then she stopped herself.

"Andrei Ivanovich, maybe they made a mistake?"

"No, there's no mistake. It has already—what's it called?—metastasized. I can feel myself that things are bad with her. Not a day goes by when I don't wonder: Why her? Why not me? I would give anything if I could trade places with her."

Soon Amalia arrived, with a traditional flowery shawl over her head, her nails painted red. Nora stared at her in astonishment: it was the first time in her life she had ever seen her mother wearing nail polish. She was a first-rate draftsman; long fingernails were considered inappropriate in her profession. Amalia started laughing.

"Nora, I realized that I couldn't appear before the doctor with hands looking the way they did. They'd think I was a cook or a housepainter and not offer me the proper treatment."

Was this a case of extreme self-possession, or simple incomprehension?

"Mama, move back home with me. You are officially registered at this address. The municipal hospitals are better, after all. Tusya's cousin runs the department at the Herzen Institute; we can arrange for you to get treated there."

"I've already thought about it. I understand the situation, of course, dear. They were about to suggest I get treated out where we live, in the country, not here where I am registered. But we've already been to the municipal oncology clinic, and they gave me a referral." Amalia began to rummage through her purse, but Nora stopped her.

"How do you feel, though? Are you in pain?"

"You won't believe it, but I just had a sore throat—I thought it was tonsillitis. I kept gargling, and gargling. I felt it on one side, as usually happens with tonsillitis. But it kept hurting and wouldn't get better. I thought maybe it was my tooth; I've had problems with it on that side of my mouth for a long time now. Then my glands swelled up—here, take a look." And she moved aside her scarf, which had been tied in a jaunty bow.

How sweet and youthful she was! But she was already over seventy. The hair at her temples had only just started turning gray, and it was growing out in tight little ringlets. She was still pretty; she had almost no wrinkles on her face. Only her neck betrayed her age—it was crepey and lined. She had lost weight in the last half year, and this suited her. Nora was suddenly overcome by such a strong rush of love for her—she had never felt anything like it. It was like water bursting out of a tap. Or fog covering a mountain. Or a downpour on a quiet day.

"Did Andrei tell you? Today the doctor told me an operation wasn't necessary. I thought they'd just cut it out and that would be it. She says that I have to consult some professor or other, and that chemotherapy is the best way to go. It's more effective, you see."

Amalia stayed overnight, and Andrei Ivanovich went home to feed the dogs.

And so Amalia returned home, to the place she had lived since she was born. For Nora, a new life began. She spent a lot of time with her mother, but now things were different from before. Amalia was like an honored guest at Nora's house. Andrei Ivanovich came every day and stayed for an hour or two, having spent six or eight hours on the road.

Nora drove her mother around to her doctors' appointments. Amalia was quiet and submissive. Her eyes looked anxious, and her movements were uncertain. She no longer laughed out loud at the slightest provocation. Nora missed this almost gratuitous laughter, which had so irritated her before.

A month later, Amalia was admitted to the hospital. Now Nora brought her soup and pomegranates, watching her mother grow weaker and more diminished from one day to the next, becoming more and more like a frightened child. Andrei Ivanovich found homes for the dogs, got rid of the horse, and moved in with Nora.

Now Nora spent less time at the hospital. She saw how her mother perked up when Andrei Ivanovich entered the ward, and felt the old jealousy that she had experienced as a child. Then the doctors sent Amalia home—to give her a break from the treatment, as they said. She started feeling better. It turned out that the chemotherapy had not helped at all; her blood was destroyed, but the doctors insisted that she continue with this sadistic treatment. They prescribed a very expensive foreign drug called vincristine, which Tengiz managed to get hold of in Germany. He was in Düsseldorf to stage *The Death of Tarelkin*, a production Nora had dreamed up and designed, though she had been unable to accompany Tengiz.

The love fest between Amalia, dying of a fatal disease, and Andrei Ivanovich, helpless to do anything to prevent it, played out in the next room, behind a tightly closed door. The door to the second bedroom was also constantly closed, but from it escaped snatches of melodies that Nora was already sick of—Beatles, and more Beatles. She already knew every song by heart, both text and melody, because Yurik sang them all, imitating now Lennon, now McCartney. Fairly accurate renditions. Nora asked her mother one day whether the music disturbed her.

"What music?" she asked, and Nora realized how far she had already traveled from this world.

For three and a half months, Andrei Ivanovich held fast to Amalia's arm. For three and a half months, he carried her to the bathtub, washed her, wiped her dry, dressed her again, put her to bed, and lay by her side. If he was absent, she began to cry, and there was nothing Nora could do to comfort her. But when Andrei Ivanovich returned, Amalia took his hand and held it, and calmed down immediately. Then she fell asleep. Like a nursing child who was given the breast.

From time to time, the doctor from the polyclinic came, measured her blood pressure, and ordered blood tests. Then the nurse came. When the nurse came for the last time, Andrei Ivanovich happened not to be at home. Nora took her into her mother's room. Amalia lay on top of three pillows, sitting almost upright. She held out her withered hand trustingly, and the nurse stabbed her finger with the needle. From the incision it made oozed a transparent reddish-yellow drop. Nora started in horror—the red blood cells had died.

When the nurse left, Nora returned to her mother. She was smiling the smile of a child. Her teeth were the same as Yurik's—bright white, a bit uneven at the sides. They were the most alive thing in her dry, diminished little face.

"What do you think, child—if they give me an invalid's pension, will it increase by much? Because, the way it is now, we can't raise dogs for money anymore."

On the evening of that same day, she went into a coma, and only woke up once, in the middle of the night. Seeking Andrei Ivanovich with her eyes, she said, "Have you had your dinner, Andrei?"

For another whole day her breathing was labored, spasmodic; then it stopped. It was in the predawn hours. Andrei Ivanovich held her hand until it grew cold. Nora's tears poured down her face, and from Yurik's room came strains of "Yesterday." For some reason, she felt there should be silence. She opened her son's door and said, "Yurik, Grandmother died."

He kept on playing the song. When he finished it, he said, "I sensed it."

And so he played his Beatles until morning, and for the first time in years, these sounds were not jarring to Nora's ears. They didn't irritate her in the least. In his breaking, thirteen-year-old voice, at the top of his lungs, he sang "Your Mother Should Know," "I Want to Hold Your Hand," "She's Leaving Home." The music suddenly seemed appropriate and necessary. It was astonishing: he didn't say a word, but the music that had irritated Nora a hundred times over sounded bitterly sad, and even exalted.

Andrei Ivanovich remained by Amalia's side, holding the hand of his beloved wife, and Nora had no desire to make practical decisions and plans: requiem service–funeral repast . . . It was all meaningless and in vain . . . What a pity that I didn't love her as I should, that I couldn't forgive her her love, that I didn't understand her giftedness, her genius and uniqueness, which she invested almost solely in this love . . .

Nora sat next to Andrei Ivanovich, feeling empty, completely empty, then gradually filling with tenderness and a sense of guilt and repose that it was over, this sad suffering of Amalia's parting from the world—her world, which consisted almost entirely of her love for this balding old man. Andrei Ivanovich held Amalia's dead hands in his own. She had broad palms; short, triangular fingernails; strong, confident fingers. How self-assured and precise, even elegant, the movements of her hands were when she sat at the drafting table, Nora thought, recalling a memory from childhood. She was the one who taught me to hold a pencil. And wasn't able to teach Yurik.

How is it I never realized this before? My hands, which resemble Marusya's so much outwardly, are actually Mama's, in their grip, in their feeling for pencil and line, in their innate confidence of movement.

Genrikh came to the requiem in the church with a bunch of red carnations, and stood at a distance from the others. There weren't a lot of mourners: a few former friends and colleagues, neighbors from Nikitsky Boulevard, and one or two from Priokso. Next to Nora stood Andrei Ivanovich and Yurik, with his guitar, and Nora, glancing at Genrikh, sensed the kind of abandonment and loneliness he must have been feeling.

When the service ended, she went up to him and asked whether he would go to the cemetery with them. He hemmed and hawed, and mumbled something along the lines of "I don't know if she would have wanted it . . . if he would like it." But he got into the funeral bus with everyone else and went to Vagankovo Cemetery, where Amalia's parents, Zinaida Filippovna and Alexander Ignatievich Kotenko, were buried under an enormous wooden cross erected by the Church of St. Pimen in 1924 for its former precentor.

Then Genrikh came to the funeral repast in the house where he had once lived with Amalia, sat at the same table with Andrei Ivanovich, and kept looking at him, wondering why Amalia had left him, a fine fellow, for this scraggly, balding man who looked so simple and ordinary. Andrei Ivanovich didn't even notice that he was there.

That evening, Nora could never have imagined that her respite from misfortune would be so brief. Three months later, it was Genrikh's turn. He was diagnosed with cancer, too. Lung cancer. He needed an operation. Genrikh's wife came to see Nora—the fat Irina, in her fat boots, shedding fat tears as Nora poured her some tea. While Genrikh was in the hospital, undergoing his examinations and tests, Irina's daughter gave birth to her second child, and now her daughter, her daughter's two children, and her husband had all moved in, and were staying in Irina's living room.

"What was I to do? I couldn't chase my own daughter out!" It was impossible for Irina and Genrikh to occupy the tiny bedroom together, because of the cancer, because he smoked, because the children cried. "You take him, Norka. They've promised my son-in-law an apartment, and as soon as he gets it, they'll move out. It will definitely happen this year—they promised him. Then I can take Genrikh back."

This will be the end of me, Nora thought. She was filled not with pity but with rage. And complete helplessness. Not because Genrikh had paid for their apartment, and this banishment would be a severe blow. She felt she just didn't have the strength to bear up under another illness when she had just traveled that road. There were no two ways about it, she had loved her mother; but her father? To be honest, absolutely honest, she didn't love him. She didn't like him. She knew, she understood, but it was still hard to love him. She wouldn't say it out loud, of course. Not to this cow, in any case. Nora was allergic to him. And she didn't want to do it. Out loud she said, "When should I pick him up?"

Irina cheered up, not expecting such an easy victory. "Oh, Norka, Norka!"

At this point, Nora lost her composure. "Don't call me Norka; I'm Nora! You know, Ibsen has a play called *A Doll's House*. Nora is the main character. Nora Helmer. And my highly cultured grandmother Marusya named me after her."

"Yes, that's what I said, Norka. Nora, I mean!" Irina said, correcting herself.

Nora decided not to move the boat bed. She changed the curtains, replacing the dark-green linen curtains with a piece of unbleached canvas she had taken from the theater. She dragged Yurik's larger bookcase into the room, and put the desk in Yurik's room. Irina had left the negotiations about the move to Nora: "It will be easier for you."

Nora visited her father in the hospital. He was in a good academic hospital, and was rather proud of his privileged situation. When Nora came, he was walking down the corridor with a squat, rotund man wearing silk pajamas and a ski cap. Her father introduced him to her. "This is my daughter, Nora, a theater set designer and artist. Nora, this is Boris Grigorievich, a well-known physicist, winner of the Stalin Prize," and the ski cap rolled away down the corridor.

"Do you know who that is?" Genrikh whispered to her conspiratorially.

Nora had been preparing herself for this meeting with her father the whole way—cancer, cancer, not certain how far it had gone, control yourself, the situation is hopeless, he's vain, garrulous, but he's a good man, he's good, and so certain that everyone will like him, that everyone loves him . . . He's not to blame, it's not his fault, I know that, I know that . . . Nevertheless, she could hardly restrain her irritation with him.

"Who, then?"

"The director of an academic research institute, the big boss! An inveterate bastard, they say," he told her in a cheerful voice, and she laughed. Still, there was something charming about him, the old blabbermouth.

"Well, how are you?"

"Wonderful, dear, wonderful! The food is good. Well, Irina does her bit, too—yesterday she brought over a whole bucket of borscht. There's a fridge in the ward. Would you like some? There's even a kitchen here for the patients. And the staff is simply exceptional. Oh, the nurses!" And he clicked with his tongue, as though he intended to enjoy their charms without delay. Nora was very sensitive to nuance and intonation, and his response made her shudder. It's horrible, how distasteful he is to me. Still, I can't do anything about it.

"Do you want to go for a walk?" Nora suggested.

"Gladly. I took a walk the day before yesterday, too."

Nora helped him get dressed—it was hard for him to move his left arm. His left lung had been removed. The doctors didn't tell him what they had told his wife and daughter: with lung cancer, you had about five years to live, at most. Judging by the X-rays, four of those years had already elapsed. "You can have an operation, or you can choose not to. Makes no difference," a famous surgeon had told them. "The operation is difficult for the patient, and rather pointless, since the second lung has already been affected. But miracles do happen. The disease does sometimes stop on its own."

Irina took the decision upon herself: operate. She didn't consult Nora about it.

Now they walked around the hospital grounds. He had been here five weeks already, and already knew half the hospital. He greeted everyone.

Sociable, Nora thought, wincing inwardly. Then she steeled herself and said, "Dad, I have a suggestion. You know that Ninka and her children have moved in with you for a while."

"Yes, yes. Ninka's a great girl; I can't see any problem. Let them stay until they have an apartment of their own. They promised to give it to them soon."

"Right, but you know yourself . . . A small baby will cry at night. And after your operation . . . Why don't you move in with me for a while? Until the apartment issue gets sorted out."

And then something she never could have imagined happened. Genrikh's mouth twisted, his face crumpled, and he began to cry.

"Daughter, my dear daughter . . . I didn't expect . . . Do you mean it? For this . . . For this it was worth getting ill. My good daughter . . . I . . . I don't deserve it." He wiped his eyes with a soiled handkerchief, and Nora looked at him, looked at him for a long time, then kissed his forehead.

My God, she thought, but he's really very unhappy, and all the cheerful camaraderie, the jokes and funny stories, his clowning, are a front. They're the mask of an unhappy man. My God, how could I not have seen it? I'm such an idiot.

Four days later, Nora moved Genrikh to Nikitsky Boulevard, and prepared to take up her sorrowful duty for a second time.

Several days before he died, his exhausting cough disappeared. He stopped talking about how they would all go to the Crimea in the spring. He couldn't smoke anymore, but from time to time he took a cigarette between his yellowed fingers, rolled it back and forth gently, then set it aside. Just before he slipped into unconsciousness, he asked Nora to bury him with Mama. He spoke so softly she had to ask him to repeat himself, just to make sure.

"With your mother," he said, very clearly. "With Amalia."

Nora was unable to carry out his wishes because of Andrei Ivanovich, who rushed to the cemetery nearly every weekend to sit with her by her grave. But Nora didn't say anything.

After he was cremated, Nora placed the urn with her father's ashes in the columbarium niche reserved for the ashes of his parents, Jacob Ossetsky and Marusya Kerns. While the attendant removed the marble slab in front of the boxlike niche in order to squeeze the new urn into the narrow space, Nora recalled Marusya's wish, which she had expressed to Genrikh not long before her death: "You can bury me anywhere, as long as it's not with Jacob." Genrikh hadn't wished to remain for all time in intimate physical proximity with his parents after his death, either. What complex, confused feelings and relations they had . . .

Not long before Genrikh's death, when he only had a few weeks to live, Nora asked him to write down the family tree and to describe what he remembered from his Kiev childhood and relatives. Resting his elbows on the desk, his muffled cough coming and going, he wrote something down for her.

When Nora opened the desk drawer after his death, she found a single sheet of paper covered with her father's right-leaning handwriting. It read:

I, Genrikh Ossetsky, was born on March 11, 1916, in Kiev. I moved to Moscow in 1923 with my parents. I graduated from the eighth grade at the United Labor School No. 110. I worked as a tunneler in the Metro Construction Project. In 1933, I entered the instrument-making technical school. I graduated in 1936. In 1938, I entered the Machine Tool Institute, from which I graduated in 1944. In 1945, I became a member of the Party (crossed out). In 1948, I defended my Candidate's Degree thesis and became head of a laboratory at the same Institute.

Here the report ended. Nora read it with sadness. He was just the candidate any personnel department was seeking—but why hadn't he recorded a single true memory about his own family? What had happened that prevented him from recalling anyone? It was an enigma. A mystery.

Now they would have to tolerate one another in death till the end of time . . . or love one another.

31

A Boat to the Other Shore

(1988–1991)

The war in Afghanistan, which lasted for years and then burned itself out, hardly touched the lives of Muscovites who were not involved in politics, in particular artists and nonconformists, who had their own reasons not to see eye to eye with the government. The radio droned on and on about the duty to internationalism and the dangers of American imperialism. After a short stint in a training unit, eighteen-year-old conscripts were sent to Afghanistan, where they fought; and then came back—though not all of them. Some of those who did come back were badly crippled. But all of these soldier-internationalists without exception were knocked off balance, traumatized; they carried monstrous memories inside them, which they would have to outgrow in order to return to a normal life.

Yurik's friend Fedya couldn't cope. He was unrecognizable when he got out of the army. Yurik rushed over to the Vlasovs' during the first week after Fedya was demobilized. He wanted to invite Fedya to a New Year's Eve party where he had been asked to play, but Fedya refused to get up off the divan. He answered Yurik's questions with inarticulate mumbling, and Yurik left feeling angry and hurt, thinking that Fedya no longer wanted to spend time with him. But Fedya didn't want to spend time with anyone, even his parents. He lay on the divan for two and a half months without speaking, his face turned to the wall. Suddenly, while his parents were temporizing, wondering whether it was time to consult a psychiatrist or a psychologist, he disappeared. Without saying a single coherent word . . . They found him a week later in the attic of their dacha. He had hanged himself.

This happened during that same "lethal" year when Nora buried her parents and discovered that, with their deaths, the wall separating her from her own demise had collapsed. She had to grow accustomed to a new sense of her own personal chronology—*I'm next in line.* The fact that this chronological order could be broken, and that children could die first, Nora realized only now.

All the friends of the Vlasovs knew Fedya. From the time he was a young child, his parents had taken him everywhere with them, beginning with the Bulldozer Exhibition* during the Khrushchev era, where he was probably the youngest witness of the infamous battle between tractors and paintings; the Izmailovo exhibit; and all the exhibits in private apartments and in the basements of the Municipal Committee for Graphics on Malaya Gruzinskaya. Sweet-natured Fedya, emotionally attached to his parents, charming, rather sickly and physically stunted, and not yet matured into manhood. The war in Afghanistan destroyed him from within. For Yurik, who had just been forced to accept the deaths of his grandparents and become reconciled to the idea that old people ultimately die, the death of Fedya, his friend and nearly his peer, was unbearable. Moreover, it was suicide, which left all those who had been close to him with a sense of guilt.

The funeral was attended by a large crowd of people, and was particularly gloomy. The entire Moscow underground art scene, and other friends and acquaintances of the Vlasovs, gathered at the Khovanskoye Cemetery, which was forlorn and desolate, like all the new cemeteries surrounding the city.

Tengiz, who had arrived in Moscow at just this time with indefinite plans, would not let Nora go to the cemetery alone; he accompanied her. Yurik didn't go to the funeral. He stayed in his room, weeping. He was badly shaken. Nora didn't try to persuade him to change his mind. She saw terrible confusion and despair in his eyes.

Tengiz stood by the grave, behind Nora, with his hand on her shoulder. His brow was furrowed. It was painful to look at the Vlasovs—they looked like two black shadows. Natasha's head was shaking . . . and in the past few days Lyonchik had aged visibly, and was so bent over that he looked older than his own father, who was holding him by the arm.

---

* The so-called Bulldozer Exhibition was an infamous, unofficial open-air art exhibition held on September 15, 1974, in Moscow. The exhibition was broken up by the police, using bulldozers and water cannons.

On the way home, Tengiz drove. They were silent the whole way. When they were approaching their house, he said, "The boy was murdered."

Two days later, Tengiz flew back to Tbilisi.

Nora couldn't stop thinking about Fedya Vlasov.

Yurik was already fifteen. His grades were poor. Getting into college, which would exempt him from the draft, was out of the question. It was very unlikely he would even be accepted at the conservatory, since he didn't have a certificate of completion from an ordinary music school. In any case, a music college wouldn't disqualify him from military service. The concussion that was described in his medical records provided no guarantee of exemption, either.

It was strange, but the recent deaths of her parents were less devastating to Nora than Fedya's. She lived in a state of quiet, unrelenting, veiled horror. The image of his closed coffin haunted her during the daytime, and she dreamed about it at night. She looked at Yurik, and she saw Fedya, as she remembered him long before his death, when he was probably fourteen—a stooping posture, with a sweet, pimply face and a side part in his sleek hair.

She had to get Yurik away, before he got snatched by the army. One war had ended, but they could easily start another one.

There were two possibilities. One, the less realistic, was Israel. But what would she do, a half-blood, in a foreign country, with a son who didn't even know he was one-fourth Jewish? The other one, more reliable but even less acceptable to Nora, was to send Yurik to America to live with his father. At this point, Nora fell into a stupor, paralyzed with indecision.

There were still two more years, but she needed to sort the problem out now. She couldn't stop thinking about it. Soon she took the first step: she wrote a long letter to Vitya, expressing her worries about Yurik's future. A reply came two months later. And it was written not by Vitya but by Martha, in English. This rather absurd woman—or so she had seemed to Nora, after their only meeting—was thrilled about the idea of Yurik's coming to live with them. She wrote: "We will be happy . . . We will do everything we can for him . . . We await Yurik's arrival, today or any day."

Huge, shapeless, wearing a jogging suit and sneakers, with a pink face and unrefined features, and a smile that stretched from ear to ear . . . She moved as though she were carved out of wood—not a log, however, but a huge trunk of soft linden. And her squeaky voice, like that of a cartoon character . . . And madly in love with Vitya. Martha seemed to see merits and qualities in him that were invisible to Nora. Nora pondered the matter.

Vitya's life was evidently undergoing a profound shift. Now it was not Varvara Vasilievna who governed his behavior, but Martha. Whether Vitya himself had changed, whether he was ready to take on day-to-day decisions, whether any emotional movement was under way in his heart, was unclear from the letter. What was clear, however, was that there was a good woman at his side. She loved him. From the moment Nora received the letter from Martha, her soul felt less heavy. Her plan to send Yurik to live with his father had taken on weight and definition. Nora answered the letter. They struck up a correspondence. Martha had clear handwriting and a straightforward style.

When Yurik entered the tenth grade, Nora asked Martha to send Yurik a "visitor's" invitation for a visa. It arrived fairly soon. Only at this point did she ask Yurik whether he would like to go visit his father and stay there to study, if it all worked out.

"To America? Really, to America? To live with Vitya? Hooray!"

During the years when they hadn't seen each other, Yurik had thought about his father about as much as his father had thought about him. But he was over the moon about the idea of going to America to live with him. Music! American music!

Nora covered her face with her hands and shook her head. How old was her son, judging by this behavior? Six? Ten, at most? They were both immature—like father, like son. Infantile . . .

"Yurik, you understand that it might be for a long time. I'm worried about the army."

"Well, sure, I understand. But you don't. America is where it's at! I can learn a kind of music there that they don't even teach here."

Thereafter, things unfolded at a fevered pace—and, as it turned out, none too soon. From January 1, boys who were born in 1975, Yurik's year of birth, were to be registered for the draft. After this date, it would be mandatory to ask permission from the draft board to travel abroad. But for Yurik, acquiring documents, a visa from the consulate, and the departure itself—all fell into place with remarkable, almost magical ease.

The final step—buying the ticket—happened with lightning speed. There were no plane tickets available; they were sold out for the next two months. It was always difficult to come by tickets of any kind—to the skating rink, to the theater, or to the conservatory. Everything was in short supply; but people learned the art of procuring things by hook or by crook. The well-trained Soviet citizen used circuitous means, and if he didn't know how, he wouldn't be able to make it to Leningrad, say, to attend his grandmother's funeral. Nora had her own resources, her own currency of exchange—her connections in the theater. People approached her for tickets, and her connections were such that she could get tickets to the Bolshoi, to the Theater on Malaya Bronnaya, or to the Taganka.

This network offered her the possibility to barter, and when she needed a ticket to New York—before the New Year; it had to be before January 1—Nora issued a call, and it worked. A day later, armed with Yurik's passport and the American visa, she went to meet a cashier from the Aeroflot office, who charged her exactly two times the normal price for a ticket to New York. Nora hadn't counted on having to pay such a steep rate, but, out of habit, she had taken with her every last bit of money she had before she left home. After she paid, there was just enough left, not a kopeck extra, to pay for a ticket on public transportation to get home. Nora took this as a good omen.

Yurik, an adolescent whom it was nearly impossible to consider a young man by any stretch of the imagination, had slipped out of the clutches of the army, skipped out, flown the coop: he was on a plane headed for New York on December 29. Just under the gun.

Nora was approaching fifty, an age at which it was similarly not possible to consider a woman young by any stretch of the imagination. She stayed behind, alone. However things worked out in America with Vitya and Martha, there would be no Afghanistan in his life.

A time to stop and reflect had arrived for Nora. She returned in her thoughts to the depths of despair she had felt, dragging herself back to her empty apartment after her sojourn in the strange, wonderful home of Mziya, Tengiz's aunt. After parting from Tengiz again, after countless such partings—when she had understood that only a child would save her. And he was born—kind, amusing, with a wonderful sense of humor, a supremely original human being, with difficulties. And now he had grown up and gone to live with his father, another original human being, with difficulties of his own. Perhaps he had gone there forever. Perhaps it was for the best if it was forever. And she remained alone.

Maybe it was even worse for her now. She was in the same place, with the same Tengiz, who was again far away from her. Yurik hadn't solved any of her big problems. For so many years, she had been going round and round in circles, along the very same path. Maybe she had been gaining altitude? Maybe she was falling down deeper each time? How could she live without

Yurik? No, that was the wrong question. Forget about yourself. Yurik will get along fine without me. There's no need to live under illusions: Yurik loves me very much, when I'm right there in front of him. But when I'm not there—I'm not so sure.

Nora boiled coffee for one in a small long-handled Turkish pot, as she had learned to do long ago from Tusya. She spread out a cloth napkin, got a blue Chinese ashtray, and put her cigarettes and lighter next to it. She fetched a coffee cup from the shelf. She got everything ready for her morning ritual. The way it turned out, after Yurik's departure she resumed her old life. And what was that?

She had always done what she wanted to do. She had wanted a child—there he was. He grew up and left home. She hadn't expected it to happen so quickly. But, fine, this was what she wanted. All right. But I remember Fedya Vlasov, she thought. And that won't happen in this case. It's so obvious that Yurik doesn't fit into the mold of life here; he's more likely to find himself elsewhere. Yurik's music is all from over there. He can stay there if he wants to; if he doesn't, he can come back here. In any case, he has a choice. I didn't want to send him away. Yes, I did. I'm afraid for him. It's not selfishness on my part. He never got in my way; on the contrary, he deepened and broadened my life. Motherhood. I haven't been the best mother, of course. But I'm afraid for him here. Now I have to fill up the emptiness. I have to try to arrange my life without Tengiz, without Yurik. Look at Tusya. Now, there's a wise older woman. She's an inspiring example of both freedom and female virtue. No, that's a silly thought. What do I know of her younger years? A pregnant silence. An all-encompassing silence.

Nora hadn't seen Tusya in more than a month. She hadn't even called her. Actually, Tusya didn't like the telephone, and trained all her close friends to use the phone like a telegraph—for short messages, not for lengthy conversations.

After her coffee ritual was over (her version of morning meditation: Everything is fine, Nora, all is well, above, below, here and now), she called Tusya to agree on a time to meet.

"So—did you send the boy off?" Tusya said, greeting her in the doorway to her studio. Tusya had two homes—one in the country, a dacha, in a settlement of old Bolsheviks, most of whom had died out, and this studio, in the center of the city, rather small, with an alcove in which she could sleep if she wished.

"Yes." Nora nodded. "I feel empty, somehow."

"What do you think about that folkloric play? It's not really drama—more like an experimental piece," Tusya said.

Just then, Nora remembered that at their last meeting Tusya had suggested she work with some choral ensemble. In all the confusion surrounding Yurik's departure, Nora had completely forgotten about it. Besides, the idea of a folklore ensemble was itself rather dubious.

"To be honest, it completely slipped my mind. Tusya, I just don't like musicals. I don't like taking on music—music is so much larger than theater, it makes it hard for theater to compete. Impossible, in fact."

"Yes, I know. But in this case it's just about assistance. The director of the ensemble is very talented, maybe even a genius. He deserves our support. He wants to get away from the folkloric-costume kitsch. He wants minimalist set design. Perhaps you know him? No? Go talk to him, listen to what he has to say. It will be interesting, I guarantee you."

Nora and Tusya sat talking for hours, until well after midnight. There had been many such evenings over the past thirty years of their friendship. Tusya's unique gift was that she treated her students as equals, and, in some wonderful way, this elevated her interlocutors above themselves. These interactions inspired them to grow into their future selves, and afterward they felt more confident and certain.

When Nora left Tusya's, she had a large volume of Frazer's *The Golden Bough* under her arm. This book, which she had been unaware of, pushed her thinking in new directions, and not just because of its study of magic, its myriad facts about the development of religion and the byways of human thinking; the book confronted her with the abyss of her own ignorance. She had missed so much during those years when she was blindly following all Tengiz's initiatives.

Now she sat in the Theater Society library from the moment the doors opened until it closed, researching the aquatic spaces that appeared before the human soul just after death in the mythologies of all peoples. They were small rivers or streams, sometimes underground, sometimes oceans, enormous, bleak waters of all peoples, extinct and still living: the ancient Egyptians, Scandinavians, Indians, Native Americans, Mongols. But for Nora it was important to figure out how the Slavs envisioned this river. The practical task of set design was only a pretext for this captivating reading. Although Nora had a prodigious memory, she made small notebooks in which she jotted down the names of rivers and the names of ferrymen, sometimes even the names of the vessels that were charged with enacting this great passage, as well as vestiges of rituals that had been preserved. The boats themselves were extremely diverse—from rickety rowboats to winged sailing ships.

It was clear that the vision and scope of this small folkloric ensemble and its director were vast, in addressing one of the most forbidden and impenetrable questions of human experience: the fate of the soul after death. The view seemed to be universal in all cultures—the human world, earthly and concrete, is surrounded by great waters, and after death one must undergo a passage through the waters in order to reach the other shore. Nora already saw in her mind how, from backstage, on both the left and on the right, the shores of all these worlds would float into view, and in the center, amid the dark waves of the waters that washed them, a boat full of rowers, a crew, a captain, and a boatswain would be plying its way forth, as described in all world mythologies, in all books of the dead. It could be any river—let it be the Volga.

Then the memory of an event that Nora only knew from her mother's account rose up from the depths of her past. When she was just four years old, they rented a dacha in Tarusa, on the banks of the Oka River. The summer was hot, and the children splashed in the shallows of the water. Nora wandered a bit too far from shore, beyond the drop-off. Without a sound, she sank to the bottom. When she lost sight of Nora, the little girl she had been playing beach ball with called out to her, and set up a howl when she couldn't find her. Nora was pulled out of the water and revived with great difficulty. She hadn't remembered any of this, but she still had a fear of water—which she loved very much in measured quantities, from the faucet. She never learned to swim.

Now, sitting over her books in the library, she could clearly remember this river in Tarusa, and herself, lying on the shore, on an old flannel blanket, which they had used as a stretcher; she saw the four-colored beach ball, and a young man with wet hair leaning over her. Everything matched up: Amalia had told her that the son of the landlady, a medical student, had saved her and administered mouth-to-mouth resuscitation. She associated this distant memory with a recurrent dream she had, also involving water: She was swimming in some terrifying inky moisture, heavier and more viscous than ordinary water, to the shore. The shore was getting closer, but when Nora was already crawling out of the water, she realized that she had swum not to dry land but onto an enormous monster. She was filled with an indescribable horror, which jolted her, panting and drenched in sweat, out of the dream like a cork popping out of a bottle. The stench of her own sweat was awful, but it was in fact the stench of that awful water . . .

She finished her reading and put the books aside. From the time she had been able to formulate the question of religious belief in her life, her answer had been a flat-out no, and she had considered herself an inveterate materialist. Neither the turbid pantheistic views of her grandmother Marusya, nor the touching, childlike, superstitious faith of Amalia, and even less the bookish pronouncements of her friends, newly converted Christians with ecumenical inclinations, appealed to her in the least. Now, however, after this essentially archaeological reading, she felt that another shore did exist, and, consequently, death—as she had envisioned it, observed it, touched it— did not. Instead, there was something of far greater importance and complexity, something far more fascinating, and music was what affirmed this best of all. Perhaps those primordial yelps and cries that the brilliant director of the folklore ensemble collected, making the rounds of dying villages to record the rasping, quavery voices of already half-dead old women, provided the best evidence of all. In fact, Nora had had the impression that this genius, with the overbearing mien of a provincial actor, with his heavy jaw and tiny eyes drowning in dark folds of skin, was a self-absorbed egotistical crank.

Nora prepared for the meeting, bringing a sheaf of drawings with her. On the turquoise fabric that rose up to the horizon, representing water, was a large, elegant boat with its prow facing the audience. This was where the first scene took place—though there were no scenes in the conventional sense, since the action would unfold without intermissions between scenes and acts. Changing the sets would be a rather formidable task, and Nora decided to employ various lighting effects to accomplish it. Then the ship shed the decorations on its prow, its elegant sails unfurled, its chorus-crew turned into oarsmen, and at the culmination of the extended act, two dark, looming cliffs moved onto the stage—Scylla and Charybdis, say. The ship split into pieces, and the actors came out on the proscenium to sing the thundering finale.

The genius, who was both the artistic director and the choirmaster, studied the sketches for the sets with sullen attention, then requested to see the costume designs. Nora placed a pile of drawings in front of him. The first ones resembled nearly true-to-life folk attire of the Russian north. He shuffled through those without even pausing to take a closer look. The second series, which Nora had dubbed "X-rays," depicted faded gray smocks, with only minimal differences between the men's and women's garments, overlaid with the hastily dashed-off outline of skeletons, corresponding fully to human anatomy. This series of drawings caught his attention, and he tapped them several times with a discolored fingernail, murmuring "um-hmm, good." In the third group of drawings, which Nora called the "peacock's tail," the shape and cut of the traditional peasant costumes—the apronlike *sarafan*, blouses and vests, the *povoinik* and *kokoshnik* headdresses—were preserved, but the usually somber northern colors were replaced with orange-red-lilac and blue-green tints. Pure India, Africa, Mexico . . . These he immediately pushed aside, then rested his chin on his hand and seemed to reflect on what he had seen.

"You've hit on something here. Yes, there's a great deal in them. Perhaps too much. I'll need to think about it. But, to be honest, I'm inclined to the most banal, denuded approach—making everything from black broadcloth. So as not to distract the audience."

He never called back. Tusya, much later, told Nora, "You aimed a bit too high for him."

Nora was not in the least distraught. While she was exploring these mythical watery spaces, Yurik's life across the ocean had completely sorted itself out. Martha—wonder of wonders!—wrote Nora weekly letters that arrived in a desultory fashion; it took them a week or even ten days to cover a distance that took ten hours of flying time. Once in a while, Nora called to America from the Central Telephone and Telegraph office. Yurik sounded well. He was going to school, had learned to speak English fairly quickly, and, most important, was playing in the school jazz band. That was all he needed to be happy.

Nora had crossed a new Rubicon, and life continued.

From the Willow Chest
Family Correspondence
(1916)

MIKHAIL KERNS TO MARUSYA
I. D. Sytin Company
Editorial Offices
The Dawn Weekly Illustrated Journal
48 Tverskaya Street, Moscow
Tel.: 5–48–10

OCTOBER 16

Dear Marusya,

I was very worried when I didn't hear from you, and only found out today that my worries were not groundless: Jacob has been drafted. I'm sure that my strong and courageous little sister will endure this trial with dignity. I also believe, unconditionally, that everything will turn out well. I know that we will all one day be together again, joyful and proud. Listen, Marusya, you must prove my hopes in your own life. Do not be anxious or afraid. All will be well. I think that your family has already paid its debt to this war—with the death of Genrikh, whom I never met. But I witnessed what a blow it was to Jacob. They are all very talented, your Ossetskys; but Jacob said that Genrikh could have become a truly great thinker. I believe that this war will soon end and we will be together again, and little Genrikh will live up to his name.

I'm feeling half crazy, not knowing what is going on in your life right now, which only adds to Shura's and my sense of alarm. I'm writing from the editorial offices; Shura is in the sanatorium. She is feeling much better. She sends you kisses.

Marusya, please, send us word that you've received this letter. Otherwise, if the already infrequent correspondence doesn't arrive, I'll be at my wits' end.

As I'm writing, we've heard the most wonderful news about the war. They say that the major Allied powers have decided to surround Wilhelm and bring him to his knees once and for all. So Jacob is sure to return home soon.

What does Genrikh say? Wah-wah?

Write me about everything. I send you endless hugs. Papa, Mama, write me!

Have everyone write me.

Your Mikhail

GREBENKA, POLTAVA GUBERNIYA–KIEV
JACOB TO MARUSYA

OCTOBER 8

The train car had no coal or flour. It was an ordinary freight train, like 400,000 others. Cold. No one was there to hold me close, and the person sleeping next to me stank. I got up, found a spot near the single dim lantern (only one for the whole car), and started to do some calculations. We have been married for thirty-four months, and how many days out of these months have we spent together? Half of them? No, even fewer! We can count them up by our letters. But, without engaging in such petty accounting, we can say that for twenty-seven months the two of us were together, and for the last seven of those months there were three of us. It's a miracle of miracles to see that Genrikh's little ear is mine, and his gray eyes are yours, and his hair grows like mine, in a spiral on the top of the head, and his fingers are yours, long, with short nails . . . Over time, other traits will emerge— of your brothers', and mine, in particular my dear brother Genrikh, whom no one on earth will ever be able to replace for me.

I kiss all the Ossetsky lips. J.

OCTOBER 12

Hello, little one. We'll begin this new period in our lives with this Letter No. 1. And so—a separation again; and again letters and more letters . . . The one good thing in all of this is that there are pen and paper within reach. You and I will write a lot of them now. It's the best kind of self-reflection, catching all our weakly flickering thoughts in passing. If we can't kiss each other, the only thing left is this self-reflection—and the thoughts we can share provide some comfort.

. . . In the reading room at the Public Library.

I kiss you, little one, on your hands and forehead. And Genrikh—on his little foot! October is here, and the steady, needlelike rain outside soaks you through and through. Yesterday I wandered around town, and spent piles of money. I came back to the barracks loaded down with purchases, which the other soldiers viewed with deferential curiosity. When I laid all the shining, pretty objects and leather supplies out on the clean bed, I felt like an accomplished household manager.

The other day I bought Rubakin a new book, apples, and shoe polish for kid-leather boots.

The library I'm now writing from is large and comfortable. There are many books, including books in foreign languages. The subscription fee for the library is merely five kopecks a month. In the library, a lady asks me: "Are you borrowing the books for yourself? Aren't they sending you off to war soon?" There are only women working in the library—old women, young ladies, girls.

One day, I had quite a "woman's day." In the morning, I saw a crowd of prostitutes on Banny Lane. During the afternoon, I read a feuilleton by Doroshevich about women (I even shed some tears). And in the evening, there were the wholesome, pure ladies in the library, and the stories Garkovenko tells me that awaken horror.

My little one, I am filled with such pity for the poor bodies of women, I have no words to express it. What they do here with this work of art I cannot begin to describe to you. I have strong nerves, I have grown accustomed to many things in military service—but I couldn't bear what I heard in these stories.

Doroshevich wrote about a woman who was visiting a soldier. It's not an unusual story, but it was difficult to read about this class of people who are so united by common work, trust, and a common bed.

The ladies in the library represent another social layer, united not only by love, but by their common intellectual commitment. I immediately felt like writing a story about such a marvelous aging "girl" who lives her life in books, since she has nothing else to call her own. I'm determined to write it one of these days.

I'm writing you about myself, and more about myself, but all the while I'm thinking of you. You remember that I don't like to make inquiries about things in letters. You know best what to tell me—about the state of your health, about your emotional state, about our baby boy. Who is my hope . . . I am here, but my fragile life is in Kiev. Remember that I always repeat this phrase, and I am always afraid. My sweet one, my own little life, be strong, keep well! I kiss my own little family. Jacob

JACOB TO MARUSYA
From the Field Forces
Military Clerk Detachment
Second Reserve Sappers Battalion

OCTOBER 19

Good day, little one. Again, the days rush by, as they always do when we don't cherish them, value them fully. I am now indifferent to the passage of time.

I'm hurrying to tell you good news: the day before yesterday, I was summoned to the battalion headquarters, where the commander-elders had learned about my musical inclinations from my files, and ordered me henceforth to join the regiment band in the capacity of flautist. Tell the others, especially Father, that my musical pursuits were not in vain—they are even required in the army. It's not the kind of music I dreamed about before; but I never dreamed at all about a rifle and a clerk's pen, so you might say that it's better than nothing.

My day is organized like this: Today I got up at 6:00 a.m. The rest of the detachment gets up later. My morning ablutions are finished by 7:00. My glass is washed, and my boots are cleaned. Practice begins at 8:00. Each one takes up his instrument and plays exercises. The result is an earsplitting cacophony. The basses roar, the clarinets squeak, the French horns quack. I'm studying French. My flute is being repaired, and I'm using my time wisely. I've already learned not to pay attention to my surroundings. I'm making good progress, and speak much more fluently.

This is the unexpected surprise that military service has given me! But you, Marusya—watch out! In a few months, I'll write you a letter full of compliments in French.

I like your *Tartarin*. After I've finished a lesson I read aloud, savoring every nuance of the pronunciation. I'm very happy about my studies. In the library, I borrow books on three subjects: war, history, and literature. The other day I bought Rubakin—an excellent book. Strange to think that in the field of library science there is a branch that is concerned with lively ideals, happy pastimes, and creative undertakings. He's a good person, even though he works and writes permanently in Switzerland.

Marusya, if my letters are delayed by a few days, please don't worry. It may happen, since it's not easy to get them out of the barracks.

KHARKOV–KIEV

JACOB TO MARUSYA

OCTOBER 21

I wanted to write about the people who surround me. Today I thought about how many scoundrels there are among ordinary people. Every person has some stain on his conscience, of course. Bezpalchin, my neighbor in the barracks, laughed today when he told me how, many years ago, after spending the night with a fashionable Moscow prostitute, he stole the five rubles he had paid for her services from her stocking, and, at the same time, her silk handkerchiefs. This fat animal was so proud of his fine pranks he didn't even blink when he told me. "We frolicked and rolled in the hay, and I still came out ahead! Ha-ha-ha!"

Another one, Garkovenko, also told me about himself (three-quarters of it lies), but I was astonished by how his strange head works, his mad cruelty and torment, the dregs of his soul.

Many of their actions are simply criminal. Others are crimes in miniature, shadows that will eventually assume concrete form. Nearly every one of them is a candidate for shackles. At the same time, they are free. They are the masses.

I thought about how prison society, the community of convicts, is no different from what we have here. It's just that the people who are behind bars or in shackles are not so lucky. Life obligingly arranged to put favorable circumstances in their way, to supply them with a knife that was conveniently within reach. But perhaps Garkovenko will be lucky, and there will be no knife. And Bezpalchin will acquire a fortune, and will wear a bowler hat and vote for candidates to be elected to the State Duma.

But there, behind bars, it's the same society, the people are just the same. They lose their wits once—and then continue as before. They are the same ordinary fellows they were before they got down on their luck.

All of these people are from the city's lower strata, the petite bourgeoisie. In the detachment there is another category of people—peasants who are fresh from the land, who do the dirty work. They are simpler, more honest, have stronger morals.

My first sergeant is particularly amusing. He received another letter from his wife, and read it to me in full. "My Dear Kuzichka," she writes, "I kiss your lips fervently." Then she makes observations about running the household, very sensible and detailed. He is proud of her, her efficiency, her good grammar, her ingenuity. They correspond frequently. They have a warm, understanding, healthy relationship.

I'm writing during band rehearsal. We're learning to play a medley from Glinka's *A Life for the Tsar*. Our band has improved somewhat. We have taken on new musicians.

I'm going into town today, and I hope to find a letter from you . . .

I'm having a suit turned. They say it will work very well. The tailor suggested I unpick all the seams myself. Today I took the trousers apart. I wasn't making much headway on my own, so I invited Aleyinikov to lend me a hand. After that, it went faster. He said, "Doing things together is always better than doing them alone—working, even sleeping." My ears are greedy for that folk wisdom about the bed.

I kiss you, my little Marusya.

OCTOBER 24

In the past few days, I have been quite busy with domestic affairs. Now my boots have been repaired, my cap altered, and my suit turned. I look very snappy and spiffed up; everything fits well. I want you to look neat and tidy, too. Have you bought yourself a dress, or a new hat yet? Hurry up!

I'm reading many interesting things. In *Russian Notes*, No. 8, I found the next installment of a fascinating women's novel. I read several lines over and over again. It's *The Horsewoman* by Brovtsyna. There are many observations about love. Some of them coincide with our own experiences, and others are curious in the ways they contradict our relationship.

I received perfumed letters from you, but I send one to you that reeks of kerosene. Someone is always coming up and grabbing the lamp in order to smoke, and one of them spilled kerosene on the letter.

Two weeks from now, our band will start to play for a cinema house, and on Sunday, twelve people are invited to play for a wedding. The musicians will be sitting in an entrance hall, and will play all night long. Toward morning, they'll get to eat the leftovers from the table. It's a good thing the entrance hall is tiny and cramped; only twelve musicians will fit into it, and I won't have to be among them.

Now I'm going to write about what interests you most of all—the woman questions. As one might have expected, this concerns me deeply. Two and a half years of married life has trained my male body to expect certain things. It's not a trial, and not at all painful, just a small, constant inconvenience—but it's as though my entire psyche is tied to a leash, and that is the worst thing.

The mind doesn't follow its well-trodden path of scholarly interests and logical thought, but keeps turning back on itself. Out of habit, I rush to read a new issue of a magazine, and note with surprise that I impatiently seek out stories with tempting descriptions of women, that what I look for in literature reflects the preoccupation of my heart. For the first time, I neglected to read a scholarly article on economics. And the other soldiers' stories only concern illicit street-corner love. When a lady of the night approaches me on the street, I hasten my steps.

I'll tell you one more thing. In a moment of frustration and impatience—well, you know what happens next. You know all about it. And it felt disgusting and unclean. Love shouldn't have to stoop to this! Please don't be angry about my frankness. I always tell you everything.

Because it's true that a woman is monogamous; that's the way it should be. But why should a man be allowed to do whatever he wishes, at any time? Why is he endowed with so much superfluous energy and all-enveloping ambition? All-enveloping in both the figurative and the literal sense. I know that I'm speaking about one of the fundamental and more mysterious incongruities of nature. Nature was mistaken in arranging things this way. Your body has already gone through so much pain, and will be subject to more. Your body is constructed in a rather inconvenient and messy way; and my body does not take account of its own soul, and sets out boldly in any direction it wishes. It shouldn't work that way! God should have employed a better architect and adviser.

Marusya, my life has become as hectic as it is around exam time. I'm awfully busy, and always have more work than I can ever finish. I haven't studied my French in a week. But I have news: I'm organizing a choir among the musicians of our detachment, and the conductor is—me! I've been dreaming about the conductor's baton for many years now, and it has fallen into my hand, just by chance. The choir will be large—about thirty people. They have a great deal of artistry, though little experience or knowledge. But I am very hopeful that self-assurance and equanimity on my part will help. I thought up a strategy the day before yesterday. I bought some sheet music and a tuning fork, just to keep up appearances. For two days, I couldn't get them together at the same time to rehearse, but you should see how impatient the detachment is: Why is there no rehearsal? We get out of the baths at nine o'clock; can we sing at night? They snatched up the sheet music and started to study it on their own. This evening is my debut. We're beginning with "Come On, Boys!," "The Broad Dnieper Roars and Moans," "Heave Ho, Lads!"—both Ukrainian and Russian songs . . . "A Life for the Tsar."

My work with the band is giving me marvelous training in music. It develops the ear, and increases, deepens, my grasp of music. I write now in spurts. Now they're playing "When They Killed the Little Bird's Mother," and I have some free time. So I'm using it to write you. The band has achieved a lot already, and the repertoire is large. They play much better than before. Still, sometimes the band sounds like an organ—all the instruments sounding at the exact same volume. Every day they learn some new part. "The Peasants' Chorus" from *Prince Igor*. I think when the band has learned it I'll study it with "my" choir as well. Today is my debut! What will it be like?

. . . Now I lead the rehearsals like an experienced precentor. I'll quote Pevsner, who didn't sing but watched from the sidelines: "I was absolutely struck not by how the choir sang, but by the appearance and bearing of an 'authentic' conductor that you had. When you raised the baton, both you and they looked as though at any moment now a choir of angels would begin to sing." It's impossible to imagine a greater compliment than this.

Something as trivial as getting the choir to prepare to begin singing demanded careful consideration. Our conductor let the choir get out of hand—before beginning, he tapped the baton many times, until they grew quiet. I took a different tack. I didn't strike the baton unnecessarily. When it was time, I tapped it three times, quickly raised both my hands, and watched them expectantly, until I knew I had commanded their attention. At that very moment, the electrical current of the baton is released, and we begin. Yesterday I made several mistakes, but I didn't let it show; on the contrary, I railed at the bass singers! Until I have established a solid reputation, I can't afford to make mistakes.

In short, it was marvelous. I kiss you, my darling, again and again.

You know, Marusya, I often kiss you in my letters; but passing them on through you to Genrikh seems awkward. They're different kisses . . .

NOVEMBER 10

In the Chrysanthemum Cinema, there is a poster announcing a moving picture with an accompanying brass band. The brass band is us. The foyer is long, empty, cold. Cinema posters line the walls, one after the other, advertising films with names like *The Bloody Batiste Handkerchief*, *The Wheel of Hell*, *The Capture of Trebizond*, *The Dashing Merchant*, and *Hurricane of Passion*.

We sit at the end of the foyer and play in the intermissions, as well as to comedies and travelogues. For five minutes we play, then have a break for ten minutes. And on and on. By about nine, you begin to feel a bit tired. By ten, you start looking at your watch. The last march—and everyone begins to pack up the music and the instruments. Weary and irritable, we hurry home as fast as we can to a dinner of cold soup, and then to bed.

Twice a week, I'm free. When you come to see me, I probably won't have to perform at the cinema at all.

Here, not far from the barracks, there is a second-class hotel. I'm afraid you'll have to stay there. Don't forget to take care of your passport. But when . . . ?

Name a day—it will be easier for me to wait. It would be most convenient either before Christmas, or after. We have a busy playing schedule during Christmas, and it's harder to get away.

I keep forgetting to write you about the diaper you packed with my clothes. When I was unpacking the things, I thought it was a scarf, but then

I recognized it and suddenly got very excited. How is he now, our Genrikh? I won't recognize him at all when I come home.

Today I'm not playing. I'm resting, and every second, I'm aware that I'm not playing in the cinema. The day before yesterday I played there as well—piano accompaniment to the films. Finally, I've become something of a cinema pianist.

NOVEMBER 16

I received your letter. I'm very happy to hear about your new job, but also a bit anxious. How unpleasant it could be if they refuse you! The fee was quite a sprightly one. My compliments. I just want to advise you on one point. Besides knowledge and skill in a subject, you must know how to "shine." In your case, you should do some smart advertising. Make journals, calendars, weather reports, and hang them on the walls, pasting things to huge pieces of paper, etc. This not only decorates the room, but inspires more respect for your profession. This is not only necessary for the child: you need to talk to the mamas and stress how important it is. They are frequently not very far ahead of the children in their development.

Have you seen how a wise doctor behaves when they call him in to minister to a dying person? They no longer believe in his scientific knowledge, but only in his wizardry, his scientific wizardry. This is why people love doctors with eccentricities. A wise doctor issues a long list of petty instructions. Move the bed, put the head of the bed thus and the foot of the bed so, cover the patient with a different blanket, take the clock out of the room, and many other things. Everyone attending the patient is busy. Little by little, the doctor accomplishes his main goal: to raise the sinking spirits of the patient and the patient's loved ones, and to assure himself that he is powerless to do anything else.

There, now! Try to do the same, Marusya. And your attire! You must deck yourself out, Marusya. Unkempt, unclean clothing has a dispiriting effect, which we're sometimes not even aware of. And don't skimp on money.

I kiss you—everything, everywhere. I kiss your knees (on the sides, and in back, where it tickles).

NOVEMBER 22

My dearest, has Papa already told you everything he could about me? I was so happy to see him. In the first moments when he came to the cinema to see me, I turned around and tried to recollect this familiar face. I stared at him for several long seconds. I only recognized him when I had reviewed everything in my thoughts—who he was, how he could have appeared at this moment, and why he might have come. We very soon finished sharing the most urgent matters with each other, and switched to exchanging random information. The conversation became somewhat stilted after that.

I was so glad he visited, and had to fight back the tears when we were parting the next evening in front of his hotel. We embraced heartily, started to walk away, then turned back for another hug. I felt his soft mustache against my face, and that in particular made me want to cry. My throat was tight the whole way home.

I inquired about everything, but I somehow couldn't formulate any sensible questions about you.

"So—is Marusya cheerful, does she laugh?"

"Yes, yes . . ."

"And . . . does she look pretty in her new hat?"

"Yes, very pretty."

Papa talked about Genrikh with such affection and sweetness. Always resorting to the same words and expressions, he tried to describe how he plays and has fun, how he walks, how Genrikh recognizes him already, how he's afraid of the bath . . . He only betrayed the depth of his sadness and loss one time, when he said, "Your Genrikh will be just like mine." These were the first words about his son I have heard him utter since Genrikh died. I thought Papa was a dry, sober-minded man. In fact, he's just not used to sharing his feelings with other people. But you and I convey every little thing to each other. About you he said, "I wouldn't advise Marusya to take on a second (morning) lesson; it will exhaust her."

On occasion, your letters make me especially proud and happy—when you tell me how well your teaching is going, about your self-control and endurance. There's no better feeling for me than knowing that you respect yourself. It seemed like your lot in life that although most of the people around you hold you in high esteem, you constantly underestimate yourself. Apparently, you are outgrowing this moral malady. I congratulate you and am glad for you.

I think nonstop about you and your visit. These are my feelings about it: I can't endure being apart from you until May. I await your arrival, not for Christmas, but before the holidays. I no longer have any shame. I think only about my love for you, endlessly, over and over again.

I love you, Marusya. Even when I turn fifty, I will love you just as deeply as I do now. I have thought about how, for loving spouses, love is limitless. Until the very end of their conjugal life, their shared path, their spiritual and emotional intimacy can be amplified physically. (Maupassant understood this very well. No one is as sympathetic toward older women as he is in his writing.)

This seems to me to be completely healthy and normal. When we reach this age, we will love each other and treat our bodies, bearers of our love, with the same tender solicitousness. The beauty of line and silhouette, the suppleness of muscles and skin, and our youthful health will all be gone. But we won't mind!

So, Marusya, did you take on the morning lesson after all? If you did, please let me know—is it too exhausting for you? You promised me you would take care of your health; what are you going to bring me? Will I really be hugging the same little slip of a thing? I want more of you. Promise me there will be more of you for me when you visit.

Kisses for Marusya, good woman and love of my life.

I await your arrival impatiently.

J.

DECEMBER 2

It gladdens me when our correspondence gets out of whack because of your upcoming visit. I'll try to write often, but please don't worry. I know all your silly thoughts, and I often love those even more than your wise ones. You can't sleep at night, you have visions of me in penal servitude, at war, in prison . . . I promise that when we see each other I will infect you with my calm equanimity and composure. First I will prove to you that all is well, and then I'll show you how calm I am about it.

I'm looking for a better hotel nearby. If they won't allow me to spend the night, I'll have to settle you in a dubious furnished room among people who are colorful but not very pleasant.

And, please, do not be afraid, ever. I will write often before you come, so that you don't start to expect you'll find me shaven-headed, with shackles on my hands.

Instead of worrying, please bring me some sheet music, anything that takes your fancy. That's the entire list for you. (And also Händel's suite.)

I have just finished reading Rolland, and I wanted to share a few thoughts with you about him, and about you and me. He is a Frenchman, and all those devastating generalizations about the French hold true in part for him, too. That spirit of cultural prostitution and senseless destruction has affected him to no small degree. He dethroned Paris, but it was necessary to build something in its place. I paid close attention to how he took apart the great buildings stone by stone. When the eternal city lay in ruins like a dismantled house, I thought: Now, perhaps, he'll begin to construct a new, more magnificent, more profound work of art out of the same stones. He says (and I remember the words clearly) that France lives, and, somewhere, those primordial streams of popular consciousness that feed an entire nation must exist. That they do exist, no one knows better than Rolland; but that he has not found his way to them, no one knows better than Rolland's reader.

All you see are crude features and unsightly mugs everywhere in his work. For God's sake, where are the people? This is why I felt bereft and unsatisfied after I put down the book. I hope I'll find what I was seeking in the subsequent volumes. He looks for real people in the lower orders of the urban population. This is still a thorny issue, by the way. I believe very strongly in his statement that "people live by something." I would call this idea "historic-statistical religion": when many people, a whole nation or group, believe in something for a long time, or have been occupied with a common task, you can be certain that this common task has not been harmful, that it is benign, and that things are as they should be. When I heard this idea expressed for the first time, I was astonished by its exceptionally wise attitude toward life. And you are the one who expressed it! During a romantic meeting, in the first moments of heady delight of two souls approaching each other.

Those were delightful moments (Marusya, in our old age we will certainly have something to recall about our youth). From that moment, that bond that is worthy of as much admiration as love, but is much more difficult—the bond of sincerity, the complete melding of two thinking minds and two feeling hearts—was created between us.

Do you remember what you said? Simple but wise words—if that's the way it is, that means it's needful, it's some sort of human mending of a divine mistake. From that day, I began developing the idea I now call "historic-statistical religion." To rise above our epochs, to rise above people who surround us, to observe how these people live according to the generalizations they have created, and then to derive laws of life and morality from these observations.

But the main thing is not to stop respecting oneself. You taught me this, and now I'm teaching you. This is the fundamental law of our happiness. Fate has bestowed a unique happiness on us. To love and at the same time to respect each other is a rare and fortunate combination, don't you agree?

Evening, in the barracks. I've just taken a moment's rest from the score I'm writing. I think I've already told you that I'm orchestrating "The Northern Star" by Glinka for our brass band. Today I showed it to the conductor. He found a few mistakes and inaccuracies, but ultimately praised it. My musical development is proceeding by leaps and bounds. I am very proficient in the brass band; it's a pleasant enough ensemble, but not easy to play with. When I get to work with a symphony orchestra, I will know all the brass instruments to perfection. And they are the most difficult part of the orchestra.

When the score is finished, I'll write you about how the rehearsal goes. I'll still have time to send you a letter before your departure.

The news in the papers about the offer of a truce made me excited at first, but I soon calmed down and recovered my ability to think soberly. And thinking soberly means schooling yourself in pessimism. There will be no peace now.

I finished the new issue of *The Modern World* magazine. In this issue, No. 9, there is an article that I want us to read together. It was written by someone, a very intelligent person, most likely an eminent scholar, who signed his name with just one letter: S. It expresses my own thoughts in a scholarly and cogent manner. The way my worldview takes shape is strange. Things seem to transpire somewhere in the depths of my soul, at the boundaries of consciousness, almost unnoticed. A process is under way that seems to be completely independent of my brain. I ponder, and my thoughts rearrange themselves there, and sooner or later these deep thoughts rise up out of obscurity, and it seems that I have known them all along. These are thoughts about aristocracy and elitism, about the liberal bourgeoisie, about slavery, about the historical development of the idea of freedom.

I'm impatient for your train to arrive. Soon, soon, my little one, I will embrace you.

Your letter made me so happy, so glad that in an instant I forgot about the long wait and about my weariness. In it I read the joy of life, the joy of creation, and the joy of a person who receives the appreciation she well deserves. I am happy about your clever work. (You've always been my clever girl!) Don't forget to buy the sheet music for all the dances you performed in the Courses. It's so strange and sad that I (who so believe in you) have until now never seen you dance in captivating, passionate abandon. I only saw you in the children's dances, *The Lament of the Grecian Girl*, briefly in *Pierrette*, and *Poem of Ecstasy*.

But I am patient. Our hour has not yet come. It still awaits us, as does that home where our boundless happiness has already been prepared for us. This home will be comfortable and warm, with a large library. The doors won't squeak when you open them, and the bathtub will be covered with enamel bas-reliefs, and the bed will be wide.

And creativity must reign everywhere . . . in the study, in the nursery, in the bedroom. Every corner of the house is good. And a remarkable woman walks around from room to room—one of only ten in the whole of Europe.

Marusya, buy me some English books in Kiev that I can't get here. *English Books for the Russian Reader*, published by Karbasnikov, second series—all the books except Wilde's *The Happy Prince and Other Tales*. Now I have to hurry to play. Marusya, please spoil me some more with more happy, smiley letters like the last one.

DECEMBER 7, 2:00 A.M.

I have just returned from the officers' club. We played for the gentlemen officers and their ladies. It was interesting to observe from a distance. The girls who waited to be asked to dance, the "wallflowers," were very touching. You should have seen how one of them bloomed, how her eyes shone, when some scrawny specimen of an officer finally invited her to take a turn on the dance floor. He may not have been much to look at, but he was still a man, for all that. I felt very sorry for the girls.

At the beginning of the evening, there was dancing for the soldiers. That was where it was fun to play! You know that every note pierces the soul of the dancers, and shakes them down to their toes. There were chambermaids, cooks, fine ladies "in hats." In a soldier's slang, a "hat" is a lady with pretensions. On the one hand, he is attracted to her; on the other, he is critical of her airs and graces. He can't choose between the hat and the headscarf.

I so want to read with you, to study the world together.

Yesterday I read a bit of Maupassant in French, and decided to postpone my studies until we are together again. Will you help me work on my pronunciation?

I'm going to bed. I'm sleeping away my last bachelor nights . . . I kiss your shoulders. Jacob

DECEMBER 20

Dear Marusya! I'm writing from the barracks, where I've come to get chocolate and bread.

You will be leaving in a few hours. My heart is aching, but I'm trying to keep myself in check.

We do make a curious pair, don't we: the happiest and the unhappiest on earth. In happy moments we believe in the first part of the formula, and in unhappy moments the second.

Today we're unhappy, and there isn't a drop left of the happiness we've been feeling.

JACOB TO MARUSYA

DECEMBER 30

Everything is as it was, but a
Strange silence reigns . . .
And at your window, the dark
Mist of the street sows fear.
—*Alexander Blok*

Here, no strange silence reigns. Everything is as it was. I received your letter, and so the sweet old papery bond between us has sprung up again. You—a letter; me—a letter; a letter—a vessel of joy; a letter—a tear of sorrow. Everything as it was.

Still, I feel better—I've become calmer and more self-assured, like I was in the good old days. I don't hurry to get anywhere, I have no expectations (since I don't have your arrival to look forward to anymore). I'm motivated to work. I hope all of this holds true for you as well, my dearest friend.

Immaturity is having a serious attitude toward trivial matters, and to those sincere concerns that trivial matters awaken. Immaturity is an unconscious feeling by definition. As soon as an adult becomes aware of his childishness and tries to continue playing the role, he instantly turns into an affected, unpleasant creature. But unconscious childishness is enchanting. When you see an adult ice-skating, or peering at the ornate handle of an umbrella (your father), or simply smiling all of a sudden, without rhyme or reason (my father), you begin to understand that you have stumbled upon some extraordinarily precious feature in the chaos of everyday life, and you take delight in it.

Today we had another military outing. It's very cold outside, but there is no greater pleasure than these happy processions. In the letter that got lost, I wrote that the outing is like a whole symphony of experiences in a mass of healthy young bodies. The mood gets transferred from one person to another, and conquers even the most solemn and cheerless souls. When music plays (we are the ones playing it; I play it), the whole mood takes on a rhythmic embodiment. Children rush out from all the court-yards; kitchen maids with galoshes pulled up over their bare legs exchange smiles and laughter with the soldiers, who look at them like a pack of hun-gry wolves.

Today, during the outing, I had some thoughts about Chekhov. They ran like this. The newspapers bemoan the fact that Moscow is losing its authen-tic Moscow character because it is overrun by refugees (read: Jews), who are corrupting the Russian language. The paper claims that people regularly mispronounce words, speak with rising intonations when they should be falling, and vice versa . . . I think that all this nostalgia and mourning for the past, what we read about in *The Cherry Orchard*, has no basis in real life. All that remains is a vestige, a sort of aesthetic mist enveloping everything.

I am no Lopakhin, but Lopakhin is closer to me than all the other dying people. He's the only character who is truly alive. But he was conceived as a comic hero! And it is, in fact, a comedy. Chekhov sees the inhabitants of the manor as satirical archetypes. But if that is the case, then Lopakhin is the only person with real agency among them. It's the death knell of the past, but in mild, comedic form. Yet Stanislavsky staged it as drama: the beauti-ful manor house with columns, the beautiful suffering of its starry-eyed inhabitants. Chekhov doesn't laugh; he smiles wanly at the cozy world, the world he himself belongs to, and this is his parting smile. Not because he knows that he will die soon, but because he knows that this world won't out-live him by very long. Let them hack down the flowering trees—I know that poor, flimsy houses will spring up on crooked little lanes and alleys sur-rounding the factory. Suffering will increase, the family structure will crumble, but there will be one more step toward consciousness, toward con-scientiousness. Whether the next step in the struggle will be taken doesn't interest me. The greatest evil is impoverished humanity, filthy, uncultured, uncomprehending. And the price we pay for acquiring consciousness is usually centuries of suffering and bloodshed. But it is worth the price.

It seems to me that Chekhov anticipated this. He felt contempt for the old world, but he feared the new one. The suffering of the cherry-orchard keepers is precious, prettified. The other kind of suffering—naked, anguished, hungry, but active, dynamic—transforms itself into something unprecedented and new, which will surpass all the utopias of the first socialists, from Sir Thomas More to Tommaso Campanella, which were conceived and elaborated long before Marx. I think that a hundred years from now, when human culture will have achieved an unprecedented level, theaters will view Chekhov as the greatest monument to a vanished world. But his plays are an indispensable step for achieving something higher, something better.

These days are very busy for me, though the company has holidays back-to-back. The officers invite their ladies, and the soldiers invite theirs. The soldiers seat their best girls and are particularly proud of the fine dresses their beloveds wear. The officers' ladies survey the kitchen girls with disdain and seat themselves in the front rows with a show of refined dignity. One of the cooks utterly charmed me. She was wearing a white blouse with a very low neckline and a blindingly blue skirt, which might even have been a petticoat. How pleased she was with herself! One sees such characters only among cooks—my goodness, what she managed to do with her bust! Hilarious! The gallery, where the soldiers without girlfriends were sitting, was in very high spirits.

My English studies are proceeding apace. Today I finished "The Happy Prince" by Oscar Wilde. I liked it extremely well. I'm no enemy of apropos moral maxims. I highly recommend the story to you. It's quite suitable for children's classes. I'm sending along two stories for you ("The Beast Tree [The Tibetan Statuette]" by Remizov and "The Unforgiven Tree" by Teffi), for the following reason. In order to compose stories yourself, you must familiarize yourself with the folktale elements and features, turns of phrase, examples, stereotypes, allegories, and conventions that are universal for all folk or fairy tales. Ideas, plots might vary, but the core elements remain the same. In these stories, one comes across some new features. The features of Oriental tales, as well as those of exotic peoples such as Negroes, Chinese, or the Hindus, are particularly interesting. But for the most part, stories can embody their own unique laws of existence, which the author creates out of combinations of these familiar conventions.

Write me and tell me what you manage to do with these stories. (The Tibetan one can be used in its entirety, I think.)

I kiss you, my dear one!

Hello, Marusya! The soldiers may have holidays every day now, but for us it's double the work. But it's pleasant work, watching, observing everything, letting my eyes wander where they will. And occasionally I see something amusing. Dmitrenko's *The Good Miller, or Satan in a Barrel.* A comedy with dancing, song, and vodka. Vodka is prohibited here, but there's still dancing and singing. And our band accompanies the singing. I enjoyed myself immensely during the rehearsals. I felt like an actor in an opera house. The barracks has a fully equipped stage. We were arranged in front of the footlights before instrument stands, as is the practice. In the center was the conductor, to his right the flautist and clarinetist, and to the left, the brass. And, as is the practice, the bandmaster signaled to the choir and the actors. And, as one might expect, they sang mercilessly out of tune, and their timing was off. Besides the performance of *The Miller,* a ballerina will dance for these sweet soldier boys. Today there was a tryout. There were two ballerinas, one of them rather plump, and the other with dyed hair, a sealskin coat, a sharp nose—overall, rather catlike. They dance well, but there was nothing out of the ordinary. The mazurka, the *lezginka,* Russian dances. The officers onstage flocked around them as men will flock around women upon whom the magic glow of the footlights casts a spell of enchantment mixed with the promise of accessibility.

The soldiers stared at them like they were seeing the Crystal Palace, like something lovely and completely distant from them, almost unearthly. The actors and actresses from *The Miller* huddled around the corners of the stage. The bandmaster looked on with an expression of irony, as though he had seen it all before.

Yesterday the celebration of the Eighth Company took place. I felt very happy with it. And extremely surprised by it. It was a celebration in the true sense of that word—carried out in a foreign, not Russian, way. I was happy with the way it was organized. Everywhere I looked, I noticed an attention to detail. Everything had been anticipated and well planned. It was all very clean and orderly. The beds in their barracks had been shoved into one corner and covered with a green cloth. For the guests, there was a coat check, with hangers, numbers, and a rope barrier. There was a platform constructed of dining tables pushed together and draped with green kerchiefs around the edges. Everything was spacious, comfortable; different people were assigned to take care of every eventuality. It was evident that they had rehearsed their roles. When the concert was over, people appeared with tools in hand. Within two minutes, the platform was silently dismantled, someone rushed to wipe down the tables, someone else felt the edges of the tabletops to make sure there were no stray nails sticking out—and the concert hall turned into a buffet.

We played until four in the morning. Tonight we're going to play the whole night again. I'm just a bit tired. Tomorrow is the last holiday. All of this carries an aura of madness that no one seems to notice. Yesterday I read the papers for the last three months in the library. There are no reliable statistics, but as far as I can tell, the war has already cost at least five million lives; and it's impossible to even estimate how many wounded there are. At least twice that number, I should think. Despite this, the Entente refused the German offer of peace. Our life, the only life we have, which promises so much to us, is unfolding against a background of unrelenting global madness . . .

Your Jacob

33

Kiev–Moscow

(1917–1925)

acob, who got caught up in political activity during the first months after the February Revolution, became a member of the Kharkov Soviet of Workers' and Peasants' Deputies, but always felt somewhat out of place. The majority of the people around him were so backward and unenlightened, many of them illiterate, that he saw his primary task as one of education. Although he could have a conversation with each one of these people individually, when they came together in a crowd they turned into a raging, terrifying force of nature. His oratorical experiments quickly led him to the conclusion that, in this powerful revolutionary process, Jews provoked only irritation. His innate industriousness and energy constantly agitated people, and his desire to prove useful to his country in this hour of need, to rebuild its industry and reorganize its principles of management, inspired suspicion. Jacob tried to find a place for himself in all of this that corresponded to his ideals and his skills, but could not.

Ukraine reeled, shaken to its very foundations. The government in Kiev had changed seventeen times in the space of two years, and the inhabitants wanted something permanent, something that would remain once and for all. And something did. By December 1919, Soviet power was finally established.

Marusya, who was an enthusiastic supporter of the new dispensation, celebrated the victory over the bourgeois world. As early as 1917, when the Soviet authorities conquered power in Kiev for the first time, Marusya joined a group of politically engaged actors who were staging a Symbolist play called *Revolutionary Movements* under the direction of a young man from Galicia named Les Kurbas.

Immediately following this grandiose staging, which met with great success before large gatherings of people in the city squares, Marusya quarreled with Les Kurbas. She spoke Ukrainian fluently, but she reproached him for his excessive Ukrainian nationalism. She was certain that complete internationalism would reign in the new government, and that small national cultures would give way to a new, universal proletarian culture. This ended her career in the "Young Theater" that Kurbas directed. Who could have predicted that in 1937 Kurbas would be executed in the Solovki labor camp for his nationalist deviationism? Not to mention that, half a century later, culture really would achieve a certain degree of universalism—although its proletarian character would be forgotten, as though it had never been, because of the complete exhaustion of the Marxist notion of the vanguard role of the working classes. But Jacob was not with Marusya at that moment, and could not bring his conciliatory corrections to bear in the dispute. Indeed, Jacob himself, with his highly organized mind, was not given to such historical prognoses. He may have been ahead of his time, but not so far ahead as that.

When Jacob returned to Kiev, he dived headfirst into professional activity. Big changes were under way at the Commercial Institute. The professor who had insisted on his being appointed as assistant in the department left with the Germans. The docent Kalashnikov, who was scared to death, assumed his vacated position. A curious situation developed in which, in the eyes of the senior professors, Jacob appeared to be a revolutionary, and the people who were appointed by the authorities to run the Institute were astonishingly ill-informed professionally.

The authorities assigned the economists tasks that were formidable: nationalization of the economy, the halting of trade and cutting monetary ties, the introduction of a surplus appropriation system, . . . "military communism." Jacob despaired. Building some sort of new economy was out of the question.

The new way of life, organized along the lines of fairness and justice, dealt a direct blow to Jacob's family: the milling manufacture and transport along the Dnieper, which his father had built up at the turn of the century, was nationalized. The mill, which had worked punctiliously for nearly twenty years, was shut down. Jacob abandoned his budding career in the Commercial Institute and took a job in the Department of Statistics at the Ukrainian People's Commissariat of Labor. In the country's current situation, the only real task he could envision for himself was to document honestly the economic process as it unfolded. His energies now contracted to discussions within his immediate family, and his primary interlocutor was still Marusya, who was committed to the idea of building the grand future.

Little Genrikh shuttled between his grandmothers, each of them vying with the other for his attention. He didn't see much of his parents. They both worked with ardor and enthusiasm, and Marusya, as was her custom, found some courses for increasing the qualifications of her tattered education, and from time to time took part in theater and dance groups. The provinciality of Kiev was dispiriting to her, and she longed for Moscow, where her brother Mikhail had permanently settled. By that time, he had married and was engrossed in family life. Her brother Mark, along with his entire law firm, had relocated to Riga in 1913. Joseph, who had disappeared after his arrest in 1905, turned up in America, and wrote them the occasional confused missive. He had been a fiery revolutionary as early as 1905, but after the Bolshevik Revolution in 1917, he never returned to Russia. From his infrequent letters, his relatives were able to make out that he felt he was more useful to the cause of world revolution in America.

In 1923, Marusya's dream came true. Jacob received an appointment in the Central Statistics Directorate of the USSR Council of People's Commissars, and the small Ossetsky family moved to Moscow. They were given a large room in a communal apartment on Povarskaya Street, which was soon to lose its original name and be renamed after a Soviet diplomat, Vatslav Vorovsky. It would keep that name for several decades. They created a little space for Jacob's office. A desk was pushed right up against a window; a divan, which a carpenter hammered together any which way, was placed in the corner; and they bought a children's bed. The room also accommodated a dining table and a buffet, and bookshelves. A week later, Jacob dragged home an absurd but very useful object: a folding screen. The room was a large one—about 215 square feet. Luxury.

They enrolled Genrikh in school, and after school he went to a playgroup on Nikitsky Boulevard with an older German woman they found through an advertisement. His future wife Amalia also took walks on that very same boulevard. A Moscow childhood had begun.

Marusya again took up her studies in education and self-education. In her spare time, she taught Genrikh to read, to do gymnastics exercises, and to make things with clay. All this she did according to the Froebel system, which, though it had not been completely forgotten, had already gone out of fashion. The boy began spending more time with his mother, and the grandmas and grandpas from his former life in Kiev quickly faded from memory. He was a difficult child for his parents—he ate poorly, was disobedient and naughty, and on occasion stamped his feet or had tantrums and threw himself on the floor.

Jacob finished writing the book he had been planning to write in Kiev, called *The Logic of Management*. In it he elaborated an idea he had long held about the general laws of management, which are equally valid for the organization of capitalist or socialist systems of production. Marusya, meanwhile, tried to find a teaching position; but in the new system there was no demand for schools of movement and dance. Other people now occupied the places where she might formerly have been able to make use of her skills. The breadth of her interests came to her rescue, however. A friend of hers from the Froebel Courses, Vladislava Korzhevskaya, with whom she had worked in the kindergarten for domestic workers' children at the beginning of her career, introduced her to Nadezhda Krupskaya, Lenin's wife.

They talked for a long time, discussing the organization of kindergartens of a new kind. A Moscow architect, Armen Papazian, was engaged to develop the idea. The principles of preschool education, according to the thinking of Nadezhda Krupskaya, should be the same as those in the Young Pioneers organization—"like the Boy Scouts in form, but communist in content." Krupskaya was roundly criticized for taking the Boy Scouts as her inspiration when she was creating the Young Pioneers; but, though she publicly acknowledged her mistake, in her heart of hearts she held on to the idea stubbornly.

The conversation between Marusya and Nadezhda Krupskaya lasted more than two hours, and was replete with warmth and mutual understanding. They parted as kindred spirits, and Marusya was given the task of designing new toys for proletarian children's education, with the assistance of the ingenious Armen Papazian. The new designs would be implemented in one of the Moscow-area wood-processing plants.

Armen turned out to be a jolly Armenian fellow, not much taller than a child, but with a thick head of hair and a copious beard. He was an artist, a bona-fide artist. Within two weeks, the room on Povarskaya, to Genrikh's delight, was filled with construction sets, from which you could put together a hammer, a sickle, an automobile, and an airplane. The seven-year-old

Genrikh was completely absorbed in building and taking apart wooden and metal pieces, and there was nothing sweeter to him. His parents, observing his single-minded concentration, were encouraged by this early awakening of his engineering abilities. It was hard to drag him away from his activities. He cried and resisted, and even insisted on going to bed clutching some sort of metal connector that Marusya was afraid would poke into him and injure him while he slept.

On Sundays, his parents tried to expose Genrikh to cultural influences—they took him to museums and theaters. He was absolutely indifferent to visual art. In the theater, he fidgeted and demanded to be taken to the bathroom or to the buffet. Only when he saw *The Blue Bird* was he interested enough to forget about the refreshment buffet. But when the play was over, he dragged Marusya up to the stage: he wanted to find out whether the bird had really been colored blue with electricity, as he surmised. The only museum that he always wanted to visit, rain or shine, was the Polytechnic Museum. The trip to the museum on Sundays was ample reward for all the years when the boy was not allowed to walk through the city alone . . .

Jacob, who didn't have much faith in the abilities of the German nanny, tried to give German-language lessons to Genrikh, but his son was bored. The father sat him down at the piano, but it was a torment for both of them. One of the boy's unique character traits was his ability to fall sick on the occasion of any externally enforced homework. His stomach really did start to hurt each time Jacob insisted that he do a chore or task. He also complained of stomach upsets every time he didn't want to go to school.

Genrikh adored his mother and avoided his father. Whenever Jacob tried to force him to do something, he took refuge with his mother.

Marusya became overworked. She started losing weight again, suffered from insomnia, and coughed at night. The doctors diagnosed it as "nerves." When Genrikh finished second grade, Jacob sent his family to recuperate in the Crimea for almost two months.

34

Yurik in America

(1991–2000)

The surface of life had changed dramatically. At home in Moscow, Yurik had hardly noticed the way the days passed. They went by evenly, and movement through them was mechanical, automatic. He woke up, washed, had breakfast, went to school, came home from school, grabbed his guitar; and then life was all about music: everyday discoveries; intense, endless enjoyment. But here in America, there was a new home, full of small alien sounds, clean rain pattering outside the window; Martha, with her eternal smile plastered on her face; the silent Vitya; and English, which he knew almost solely from Beatles songs. The world of old habits collapsed, and new ones—the defense of the psyche against unfamiliar agitations—had not yet been formed.

Yurik's first days on Long Island coincided with the Christmas and New Year's holidays. Martha had planned to take Yurik to see the sights in the city, but she fell ill and had to cancel it. When Yurik tried to pick up his guitar and play, he couldn't concentrate—something stopped him. Vitya spent these Christmas holidays in the university lab. At the end of December, the university purchased a NeXT computer, the recent brainchild of Steve Jobs; he had been fired by that time from Apple and had started a new company that produced these new NeXTs with a new operating system, which laid the foundation for the future Mac OS X. Vitya couldn't tear himself away from this new toy. He invited Yurik to have a look. It was the first computer that Yurik had ever seen "in person." Vitya stroked the case and praised the black cube the way a dog lover praises the points of his favorite canine. He admired its power, its memory capacity, and the high-resolution graphics.

Yurik asked questions, and Vitya answered. When Vitya answered, Yurik asked him to repeat what he had said. And he grasped it. Four hours passed like a single minute. As they sat talking in the empty laboratory, Yurik began to understand that music wasn't the only interesting thing in life. They would have sat there all night, but Martha called to say that she was expecting them home for dinner. They went home under a fine rain when it was already dark, silent, each of them lost in his own thoughts. Vitya was thinking about the wonderful possibilities for modeling cell processes that the new computer offered, Yurik about how great it would be to unite music with this remarkable machine. He wasn't the first one this idea had occurred to, but he didn't realize it yet. Yurik had no idea that in a few years the computer would become an indispensable part of any musical process, from studying to recording to performing.

Vitya was a lousy communicator. He offered his thoughts, but there were gaps and lacunae, and he left out the important details that he considered self-evident. Yurik understood him, though, and knew how to negotiate his way through the holes in the conversation. He immediately grasped that Vitya's expertise lay in his ability to make the intelligent machine solve a problem that an ordinary person could also solve but would require far more time to do.

This was the beginning of the nineties, and the first experiments in the fascinating interdependence of the human and the machine, formerly a subject of science fiction, were now becoming a part of daily life. Programmers foresaw that the artificial brains created by humans could surpass the intellects of their creators, that the speed of calculation could engender a new kind and quality of intelligence.

Vitya had acquired a new audience for his ideas in Yurik; but Vitya did not become a new listener to Yurik's music. Their relationship did evolve, however. From the age of five, Yurik had been connected to his father through chess. Now, some ten years later, chess had been replaced by the computer.

On January 4, Martha took Yurik to enroll in the music department of a high school that specialized in the arts. Yurik had an interview about his knowledge of music. Since his English left something to be desired, they assigned him to an ESL class with a group of other foreign students. There were only four required courses: ESL (which, after two months, Yurik was calling "English for Slow-Wits," and he was transferred to the regular class), mathematics, the U.S. Constitution, and a vague catchall subject they called "science."

Of the many music courses on offer, Yurik chose four: music theory, classical and jazz guitar, and the foundation course in piano. There was also a course called Choir, which was mandatory for everyone who studied music.

The first day of school made a deep impression on Yurik. The four morning hours were devoted to analyzing a recent Christmas performance. The general choir of the school had sung a part of Händel's *Messiah*, and now the choir director, dissatisfied with the performance that the audience had raved about, was voicing his criticisms.

"Open to No. 22: 'Behold the Lamb of God that taketh away the sins of the world,'" the teacher's voice boomed out.

Yurik opened a homemade book of music and text. He found No. 22. All of them had these books. The teacher, waving his hand, looked more like a basketball player than a musician. His hands were like enormous shovels, and his arms flailed as if he were battling with enemy air.

To Yurik's ear, the choir sounded marvelous. There was no accompaniment, and groups of voices worked like different instruments. Yurik listened to them almost in a trance. He knew that the instrument could sound like a human voice, but that the voice could sound like an instrument—Yurik had never heard anything like it! The singing awoke a storm of feelings in him, an astonishing chaos he couldn't make sense of, but he felt on the verge of tears. Every now and then, the teacher stopped the singing with a gesture and explained to them where and how they had bungled it. It was remarkable, but Yurik understood him. The focus of his interests helped him in understanding a foreign language.

Fortune smiled on Yurik. He would finally have teachers who interested him in the subject, and he was able to escape from the dead end he had been stuck in at home. He understood that he was in the right place at the right time.

The best teacher of all was the one who taught music theory. He played strange Japanese music on the *koto*, an ancient Japanese instrument that had no definite number of notes per octave—not seven, not twelve, but as many as one wished. Instead of a scale, there was infinity . . . It simply boggled the mind.

His first jazz-guitar teacher, on the other hand, turned out to be a dry old curmudgeon, cut from a completely different cloth. A fat black man, a

Southerner, with a bald pate and a rich ring of hair circling it, he didn't even listen when Yurik played. He just pointed his finger at Yurik and said, "Practice scales!" This is what he told everyone, but the lessons in technique were individual, and Yurik didn't know that Mr. Kingsley taught everyone by the same method: he demanded that a student play 120 scales over two octaves in the course of ten minutes, and if the student made the slightest mistake he had to do it all over. The stress was such that Yurik even had a nosebleed during the second lesson. Kingsley wouldn't allow the students to play anything else. And he didn't let anyone talk, either. Much later, Yurik summed up this maniacal method by saying that there was not the slightest drop of joy in Kingsley's approach to music, only finger gymnastics. But Yurik already understood that if music brought no joy to the musician it wouldn't bring joy to anyone else, either.

The piano teacher was a charming elderly Frenchwoman. Watching her small wrinkled hands fluttering over the keys, Yurik experienced professional envy. Whereas the pianist uses the same mechanism of movement for both hands, a more complex coordination is required of the guitarist: the left and the right hands must live different lives, but stay in perfect sync. And, of course, the main advantage of the piano is that it allows one to introduce several voices simultaneously, and opens a whole universe of sounds that the guitar can't reproduce. In addition, there is an enormous amount of music literature for the piano—more than for any other instrument.

The classes in classical guitar, which he didn't like, expanded his abilities. The teacher, Emilio Gallardo, who happened to have the same name as, or was a relative of, the famous Spanish classical guitarist, showed his plucking technique on an excellent Antonio Sanchez instrument. Yurik began playing without a pick, and resorted to it only in special circumstances or when he broke a fingernail. Plucking the strings with his nails produced a completely different quality of sound. At the same time, Emilio Gallardo taught him how to treat his nails properly—how to grow them out and file them in a straight line, with the file held at a forty-five-degree angle to the nail. This was how the childhood trauma of nail cutting, the occasion of constant struggles with his mama, was resolved.

After his torments under Mr. Kingsley, Yurik transferred to another class with another jazz-guitar teacher, James Lovesky. Their tastes were more similar. Every day opened new possibilities, but he needed more theory. Before, Yurik had played the guitar as if it were something like a wind instrument; now he began to understand polyphony. It was in the jazz-guitar class that he acquired his musical literacy, and began writing his first ar-rangements of jazz standards. This turned out to be the most interesting as-pect of study for him.

Yurik attended the school for a year and a half. He played in the school jazz band, and was definitely considered to be a cool cat. He himself didn't doubt this. He considered his former infatuation with the Beatles to be just a phase he'd had to go through—though a necessary one, and he still cher-ished the memory of his first musical love. Now he played what the great jazz guitarists played—Wes Montgomery, Charlie Byrd, George Benson. He imitated them, biting the inside of his lip, tense and focused. Among his numerous new musical influences, Django Reinhardt, a Belgian Gypsy with two fingers missing on his left hand, occupied a special place. He was sim-ply beyond comprehension, the way a creature from another planet is be-yond comprehension. There could never be another like him.

In the first year of his American life, Yurik discovered New York on his own, and fell in love with the city. It was the capital of his music, and the musical life of the street in the Big Apple captivated him most of all. It was the city of a dream come true. When he got there, he was ready to fol-low the first street musician he came across, as he had used to follow cats through the neighborhood in childhood.

Every Sunday, he wandered through the city, either with other classmates or on his own. When he grew bolder, he began to take his guitar with him and join up with musicians playing in the subway, or in the squares. Some-times they chased him off; sometimes they let him play with them. But from that moment on, he never parted with his guitar. Wherever he went, the guitar went with him.

His relations with Martha were strong and positive, although she was often very worried about him, especially the first night when he failed to return from the city, staying overnight with a group of musicians and smok-ing weed with them. These all-nighters became more and more frequent. New York was so hospitable, so friendly . . . Long Island now seemed to him to be claustrophobic, like a village where nothing ever happened. This was not the case, of course—it had its own jazz festivals, its own in-crowds. But nothing could compare to New York.

Somehow or other, he managed to graduate from high school. He never learned to read Shakespeare in English, but his "home schooling" with Nora, her reading aloud, and the constant theater talk, in which Shakespeare re-ceived a lion's share of attention, gave him a strong enough background so he could get passing grades. The math teacher, who occasionally had to wake Yurik up during class, was irritated by his somnolence; but she knew that the math problems, which his classmates sweated over, he could solve better than they, even in his head, and more quickly. They taught math better in Russia; or maybe Vitya's genes had something to do with it . . . He had very good grades in his music subjects, and Martha, who had no ear for music, was excessively proud of his achievements and dreamed that he would continue his studies, perhaps at a first-rate music school, like Berklee.

At the end of his second year, Yurik had asked James, his favorite music teacher, "What would you do if you were me?"

"I would lock myself in my room for five years and play. You don't need to do anything else."

This suggestion was very much to Yurik's liking. The only thing that didn't appeal to him was the locked room. The city, which was everything but a locked room, beckoned to him. Life was lived to the hilt there, on every street corner. He wanted to learn by engaging in life, playfully.

Nora flew over for his high-school graduation ceremony. The plane landed early in the morning. She dropped her big suitcase off at Marina Chipkovskaya's and went directly to Long Island.

Yurik was glad to see his mother, but he greeted her as though he had just said goodbye to her yesterday, and not a whole year and a half ago. He immediately grabbed his guitar to show her what he had learned during that time, and played for four hours straight.

After the trans-Atlantic flight, Nora was a bit groggy and disoriented. She hadn't slept in two days. At first she was very happy about Yurik's music; then she started nodding off, and ended up in a strange state between sleeping and waking. In her head, some sort of light show was set in motion: northern lights of blue and acid-green, a hideous scarlet and orange, and she slipped into some parallel musical space, where dangers lurked, and from which she couldn't escape.

She stayed overnight at Vitya and Martha's house, in the living room. Martha was kind and welcoming toward her. It seemed that her adoration of Vitya extended to Nora as well—amazing. Out of the corner of her eye, Nora noticed how Vitya squeezed Martha's wrist affectionately, how he pulled the chair out for her when they were sitting down to dinner. Apparently, he had learned to see other people. Was it actually possible that a person who had taken a purely expedient view of other people his whole life had finally matured when he was in his forties? Could his love for a plain woman, no longer young, actually bring this about? It was also remarkable that Vitya never even asked about what was going on in Russia. Granted, what was happening there had no bearing on his professional activity, and he didn't perceive any difference between Gorbachev and Yeltsin, as he didn't perceive so much else.

The next morning, Nora and Yurik went to New York together. Yurik showed his mother around town, taking her to the musically hip spots that upstanding citizens and prosperous folk weren't even aware existed. He took her to the Lower East Side, to all his favorite places. Nora, who had explored the city quite thoroughly on her previous visit, with Tengiz, marveled at how multifaceted it was—it seemed to contain a whole host of disparate cities, independent and aloof from one another, but blending seamlessly into a larger whole. On one end of the street, you saw well-heeled, manicured people in business suits rushing to and fro; at the other end, brash, down-and-out tramps and dangerous-looking fellows in ripped undershirts were hanging out on the street corner.

They had not gone two steps before they ran into a black musician, who was snacking on a hot dog, sitting among a collection of pots and pans arranged around him, some of them standing on the ground, others hanging. Yurik greeted him with a warm handshake and clapped him on the back, and they exchanged a few words.

"My mother," Yurik said, pushing Nora toward the man. He held out his hand to her. For a plump hand, it was unexpectedly lively and mobile, like a small animal. The musician finished eating his hot dog and struck the hanging pot, which resounded with a surprisingly low sound. This was the overture. He let the sound fade out, then began tapping with his fingers, beating with his fists, and slapping with his palms, and in this way played his improvised drums.

"They call him 'Pots and Pans,'" Yurik said proudly. "A local genius. The only one of his kind in the world."

The City as Theater, Nora thought, still not having managed to explore all the little squares that deserved attention, its cozy, secluded stages and wings, utility rooms and workshops. Yurik did not just show her his favorite places, but revealed to her at the same time how the city accepted him as one of its own children, one of the multitude of players, dancers, the dissolute, the merrymakers. Nora didn't fully understand at that time the degree to which this atmosphere of freedom and flight was fed by the fumes of marijuana, hashish, and other intoxicating substances. And heroin would never have occurred to her.

Yurik invited Nora to his favorite hangouts—Performance Space 122 and Collective Unconscious. There were almost no people around when they stopped by at Collective Unconscious, only empty Coca-Cola bottles, bags, old bicycle parts, a dirty mattress, a sleeping bag, and a broken umbrella that represented the eponymous "collective unconscious" of the club. This was the very epicenter of lowlife revels and mad freedom, a place where people sang, drank, played, and shot up, all through the late evenings and into the night. She began feeling uncomfortable. They went around to several other, similar places. Yurik knew a few people, whom he greeted. He clearly felt proud of his connection to this underground world. Several fellows were sound asleep, wrapped up in sleeping bags. One old man, obviously drunk, woke up and crawled out of a pile of rags, asking for money. A human wreck.

"Give him a dollar, Mama." Nora gave it to him.

Yurik led Nora through town along a sinuous, meandering route. Although she had a map, she didn't want to refer to it, and she only approximately understood which way they were going. In this city, more than all others she was familiar with, there was an invisible compass pointing one toward the north, or toward the south . . . But they were in fact headed east, to the East River.

On Avenue A between East Seventh Street and St. Mark's Place, Yurik ducked into a place that was little more than a hole in the wall.

"Now we're going to have falafel. The cheapest in the whole city—a dollar twenty-five," he said. "All the Russians in town come here. The falafel is excellent. Akhmed the Cripple runs it."

Akhmed proffered Nora the thin dough pocket with its steaming-hot filling. She took a nibble and thought: If I were eighteen years old, I'd get stranded here for the rest of my life. I don't think I'd ever want to leave. It's a dangerous place, though. It's as though the sirens sing and call out, but don't devour you all at once; they suck you up gradually. But for now the shadow of danger only added to the charm of the place. Like a huge elephant, the city showed the inquisitive spectator first one side, then the other: now the tail, now the trunk.

Then Yurik took Nora to the Nuyorican Poets Cafe. At this late-afternoon hour, there were still not many visitors. The walls were plastered with photographs of famous people, of whom Nora could recognize only Che

Guevara. For the first time in his life, Yurik turned out to be better informed than she was. "Look! It's Allen Ginsberg." Under the photograph (his face was unprepossessing, to put it mildly) was a quote from the poet, in white letters on a black background: "The most integrated place on the planet."

Well put, but impossible to translate into Russian. An integrated place . . . But you could make sense of it—it was a place where people were equal, there was no segregation, freedom of expression was pushed to its utmost limits; a place where boundaries and limits of all kinds were suspended. Nora's literary imagination immediately started roaming to all the celebrated fin-de-siècle cafés she had read about: Les Deux Magots and the Café de la Rotonde in Paris; The Stray Dog in a Petersburg cellar; Els Quatre Gats in Barcelona. All of those places were the forebears, three generations removed, of this contemporary magnet for artists and literati; but this place was redolent not of Decadence or Futurism, not of Dada, but of social protest, revolution, and terrorism. Here was the modern-day, and even slightly dated, avant-garde. It was the front line of progress, of breaking with convention. There was music, and poetry, and performance, and none of it had anything to do with mainstream culture, with commerce. They were playing the music of some fantastic opera singer, and Nora stopped to listen. Yurik was quick to tell her that it was a countertenor. Such high male voices had been popular in Italy, and music was composed especially for the castrati. Now these voices were popular again. Yurik explained all of this, then said brightly, "You weren't aware of this before?"

"Yes, I knew about it, of course. But I had never heard it."

My word, Yurik. What an amazing place! she mused. Then she thought: I need to get him enrolled in some school or program as soon as possible. He could easily get stuck here for good.

She herself was completely enamored with it: a Rastafarian with a mass of intricate dreadlocks, and a parrot sitting on his shoulder; an anorexic-looking girl, bound up from head to foot like an Egyptian mummy. There was also a guitarist whom Yurik recognized. He almost fainted: "Mama, do you know who that is? It's John McLaughlin!"

The group sitting at the table next to theirs seemed to be playing cards. In fact, it wasn't a card game at all. A well-known fortune-teller was reading the tarot. In one dark corner of the room, a six-foot-five strikingly white person in an orange cape was sitting in the lotus position. An albino.

They walked to Bleecker Street. Nora was tired. The day was fast turning into evening. At the entrance to the subway, Nora went to buy a ticket.

Yurik glanced into the cashier's window and struck up an animated conversation with an elderly black man in a subway employee's uniform. Nora couldn't understand a word of their conversation. She walked away. The cashier opened up a side door and walked out of his little cage, pumped Yurik's hand, and clapped him on the back. Yurik told Nora that this aging fellow was a marvelous guitarist, an erstwhile hippie, who had taken on a steady job when the years started to overtake him. Everyone called him Gnome Poem. Yurik couldn't remember his real name.

They agreed that Nora would return to Marina's house in northern Manhattan by herself, and that he would hang out here for a while. He said he'd come back around eleven. He showed up at three. Marina had already gone to bed, and Nora was sitting in the kitchen, worrying about what she should do in these circumstances. Go looking for him? But where? Call him? Whom could she call? And, generally speaking, what should she do now, tomorrow, in a year?

Nora didn't make it to Long Island the following year. By this time, Yurik had left Long Island completely and put down roots in New York. It was a soft landing, however. Martha kept trying to persuade him to continue his studies, but Yurik considered that life in New York offered a better education than anything he could get at a university. By the middle of the summer, he had become so much at home in the Big Apple that it was no more possible to lure him away than it was to lure a worm out of the hard flesh of the sweet fruit. A few months later, he already knew dozens of other guitarists and drummers and horn players who had burrowed into the heart of the Apple, and they were all on a first-name basis with one another.

When he went to Long Island to take a bath and get clean underwear, Martha would lend him a few twenties and fifties. In the evening, sitting at the computer, Vitya showed his son new programs, marveling slightly at his slowness. Then they called Nora. The calls were expensive. Yurik couldn't allow himself such luxuries, and Nora could never find him at home when she called. Her strong and enduring connection with her son, which she had once feared might be a problem in itself, became more and more attenuated, and finally threatened to disappear altogether.

Vitya had never taken much interest in Yurik, and had no idea how he made a living. Martha took the burden of these trivial matters in life onto her own shoulders—she paid all the bills, bought all the food and clothing. Vitya had only the vaguest notions of what it took to get by in life.

In the first year after Yurik graduated from high school, Martha began to pay for his expenses as well, but she felt that what she was doing wasn't right. She came from a poor Irish family, and though she was Catholic, her views on life were completely Protestant. At the end of the first year of Yurik's semi-independent existence, she forced herself to tell him that she was not going to provide for him anymore. Yurik thought about getting a job.

An opportunity came his way through Ari, an Israeli friend of his who had been on an extended vacation in the United States after finishing his military service in the Israeli army. Ari had been born in Russia, and his family still spoke Russian at home, so he was happy for the chance to be able to chat with Yurik in their mother tongue.

The main topic of discussion was the army. Yurik, who had left Russia at the insistence of his mother to avoid military service, did not try to conceal this fact of his biography. To Ari's mind, this was immoral. Yurik considered military service itself to be immoral. He was well aware of the vagaries of Russian politics, and understood that, after Afghanistan, there had been other conflicts—Ossetia-Ingushetia and in Georgia-Abkhazia—not without the involvement of Russia. Now there was turmoil in Chechnya, too. All of this smacked of war, which his mother feared. Yurik didn't want to kill or to be killed. He wanted to play the guitar. Yurik's story about the Russian fellow who had hanged himself after serving in Afghanistan didn't make an impression on Ari. Ari's experience had been different: he adored the army.

"Before the army, I was just a piece of meat—an idiot with a guitar, and a source of shame for my family. After three years in the army, I became a real professional. I specialized as a radio operator, and I learned Arabic. The army teaches you how to survive, which is also a kind of science. The main thing was that I learned how to learn. I can teach you, too. I'll teach you how to be a furniture mover. Don't laugh—it's kind of like science, too. Not everyone can do it."

Yurik accepted the offer immediately.

The next day, Ari took him to a small moving company. The person who ran the operation was a Russian Jew with an Israeli passport and a checkered past. Around him revolved a motley assortment of people from all ends of the earth—losers, pariahs, and eccentrics of every stripe. The first crew he worked with was Israeli, and they taught him the tricks of the trade. They worked in a group of four: Ari, two more former Israeli soldiers, and Yurik. It turned out that a pack mule's endurance was more important than brute strength in this profession, and good mind-body coordination was more necessary than broad shoulders. He worked with this crew for three weeks, until it disintegrated because Ari and his friends went back to Israel. Then Yurik started working with a new crew: two Sherpas and another newbie, a towering African American hulk.

Both Sherpas—Apa and Pema—came up to about Yurik's chin, but their strength and stamina were the stuff of legend. Though they were unsociable at first, after a few days working together, watching Yurik toiling alongside them and trying to keep up, they grew very friendly and warm toward him. On the first day, the hulk cast disparaging glances at the Sherpas, but after three hours of work, he lay down next to the wall and didn't budge. Yurik and the Sherpas worked another ten hours before calling it a day, and the black giant never came back to work.

Yurik lived in an abandoned house. Alice, an aging alcoholic with a past in the theater, was the temporary landlady and self-appointed manager. She "enrolled" acceptable candidates and kicked out the ne'er-do-wells. She quelled conflicts, enforced sanitary norms, and negotiated with the municipal authorities, so that they would tolerate the existence of this illegal homeless shelter. She protected Yurik. He had lived under her roof for three years when the municipal authorities cleared the squat. Someone bought the building, and it was scheduled for restoration. Alice was offered a job with the municipality; she became an official.

Yurik also climbed up a notch on the social ladder: he rented an apartment. He and a friend, a thievish guitarist from Peru, split the monthly rent of three hundred dollars for a room in an apartment in which four other seekers after the American experience were living: an Arab girl who had run away from home, two Poles who were working in construction, and a Hindu preacher of some obscure offshoot of the religion. The Arab girl and one of the Poles inhabited the largest room, the Hindu and the other Pole lived in the middle-sized room, and Yurik and the Peruvian were in the smallest room.

Half a year later, the Peruvian underwent a miraculous change. To the bitter disappointment of the Hindu, he converted to Christianity. He stopped stealing, considered himself henceforth to be saved, and believed that in the coming months the Lord would summon everyone who had been saved, including himself, and that they would be ushered into the blessed beyond. He called himself a "born-again," sang hymns, and wrangled with the Hindu in the kitchen, until he set out for California, to meet even more blessed people.

Now Yurik was the sole inhabitant of the room. The bighearted Martha agreed to sponsor him, forking out the $150 a month that the Peruvian would no longer be contributing. His departure was very timely, because Yurik had found a girlfriend, one Laura Smith, and all his previous casual loves paled in comparison with her. Laura, who was just finishing high school, was the proverbial black sheep of an upstanding American family. They saw each other every day. She liked having a Russian guitarist for a boyfriend, and she went with him to all his gigs, whether in the subway, at clubs, or on street corners—wherever one of the two bands that invited him as a replacement was performing. Laura also had a dream of doing something creative. She wanted to be a belly dancer. She practiced her art constantly: at school, at home, in the subway, and on the street. A small girl, she undulated as she walked, swaying her boyish hips to and fro. She danced and danced . . .

Yurik's room became their love nest. And a messier room the world had never seen. It was a jumble of dirty socks strewn about the floor, sheet music, CDs, cigarette butts, paper plates, and half-filled cans of Coke. An old Hammond organ, left behind by former tenants, stood in the hallway, blocking half the entrance and leaving only a narrow space to squeeze through.

This was the room where the young couple broadened their knowledge of the world, from time to time ingesting substances that took them to other spaces and realities. But when Laura finished high school, and showed her parents the report card with grades that would never get her admitted into a decent college, she announced to Yurik that he had no prospects, and danced off forever. After leaving Yurik and giving him his first broken heart, she went to California. Then she flew off to the places where fearless and brainless enthusiasts of dangerous journeys fly to.

Yurik, his injury still fresh in his mind, wrote three songs, which the leader of a well-known band liked so much he added them to the band's new repertoire. For the first time, Yurik knew what it felt like to be a real songwriter. And he understood that new music arises from new experiences and sensations and troubles. That's what I was missing, he thought.

Since he had arrived, he had felt like a part of this city. Music, his music, rang out from every corner, from every nook and cranny. When he went to Long Island to visit Martha and Vitya, which he did rather infrequently, he began missing the city while he was still on the commuter train. The

Moscow of his childhood was so remote to him that thinking about it was like looking at a picture through the wrong end of the binoculars. Only Nora's visits reminded him of his pre-American existence.

Nora came for Parents' Weekend, as they called her yearly visits to New York. This visit disrupted Yurik's plans for acquiring new experiences. One week after his stint at the moving company, instead of the new experiences he desired, he was refreshing his old ones: he was walking through the city with Nora, showing her his favorite back streets and alleys. Nora was walking next to a completely grown-up man, handsome and tall, but not at all like the young people, students and actors, with whom she interacted at home. How was he different? In his absolute casualness, his lack of inhibition, his disarming childishness, and a kind of relaxed freedom.

No, Nora thought, trying to reason with herself. It's just that our life together has ended, and he is going his own way. His own way. I can't get him back. Why should I want to? And who am I to talk? I went off on my own at fifteen.

Nora had spent the evening before that with Martha and Vitya. The women understood that Yurik was having a hard time; Vitya nodded absently. They made the decision to encourage Yurik to study somewhere, study something. Nora didn't know whether she had any influence over him anymore; she didn't know what was happening to him. Was this just the way he was growing up, or was he becoming American?

In January, Nora had called him from Moscow to wish him a happy birthday. After a short pause, he said, "Mama, I'll never be a teenager anymore. It's sad."

They talked and walked, walked and talked. They were walking through Chelsea, perhaps the most stable and enduring part of town, the area most impervious to the ravages of time. The old mansions of the English inhabitants, symmetrical buildings with drop-down fire escapes, shabby walls, broken sidewalks.

"Here is an old Irish bar where they sell Guinness. Here's the hotel where everyone who was anyone stayed—Jimi Hendrix lived here, and all the major American writers, who were every bit as good as Dickens," Yurik said proudly, as though he himself were the owner of the hotel. Nora glanced into the entrance to the yard, where a single desiccated tree was standing. An old bench. It seemed as though the old man from the story "The Last Leaf" could have lived here, and in that apartment on the upper floor Jim and Della Dillingham, the main characters of the story "The Gift of the Magi," might have lived. Nora had so loved these stories as a child that she immediately recognized settings from O. Henry's stories. Nora stopped. Hell's Kitchen, the Garment District, the Meatpacking District—it was all here somewhere.

They stopped in front of a house where Yurik's teacher and friend Mickey lived, or, rather, was dying, of AIDS. He was quite a famous musician, a singer, who experimented in all kinds of ways with his voice. He had performed with all the jazz greats, but his name was connected for the most part with a marginal, noncommercial musical current—a driving mélange of funk and heavy metal. Now and then, one of the jazz masters, someone so great that Yurik had never seen him up close, would invite Mickey to cut a record.

Yurik spent a lot of time at Mickey's, and brought him the drugs he needed to survive. Now Yurik wondered whether he should tell Nora about this extraordinary fellow, about the tragic history of the gay man who had been banished from home at the age of thirteen; who, from being a homeless street kid, had become the owner of an apartment in one of the most famous buildings in Chelsea, which had been mortgaged, and remortgaged . . . At one time it had been luxurious, but it had fallen into disrepair and become a shelter for homeless cats and his down-and-out friends. No, it probably wasn't a good idea to tell her.

They continued walking west and ran into the Hudson. An old pier. Heavy, slow-moving water, boardwalks, abandoned coastal lands, boats lying askew on the shore, seagulls, some warehouses, abandoned factories . . . Silence. No one else in sight.

"What's over there?" Nora pointed to the opposite shore.

"That's Hoboken. It's in another state. I've never been there. They say it's cool."

Nora was wondering whether it was time to tell Yurik about the family decision, which was more like an ultimatum, that he needed to study something. When he heard it, he agreed without a second thought—though he did say that what he needed more than anything else was practice, and everything else would follow. They discussed the various possibilities. It ended with an explanation that the point in studying would be to allow him to earn his living not as a furniture mover, but as something for which he needed professional qualifications. Under pressure from the family, he agreed to enter the Sam Ash Music Institute, to train as a sound engineer.

Nora returned home, leaving Martha with money for the first semester's tuition.

After his mother left, Yurik actually did undertake to change his life. He quit the furniture movers, but he didn't go far. Using his music connections, he got a job with a music producer, an unsuccessful guitarist of about forty, and started transporting equipment, fine-tuning it, and doing repairs on it. In the fall, he did enroll in the sound-engineering institute, which turned out to be a rather sketchy establishment that prepared its graduates to be, at most, salesclerks in music stores. This is what Yurik reported to Nora, when he quit after a month of "studying." At the same time, he left the employ of the producer.

Meanwhile, Mickey's health had taken a turn for the worse. His last partner, a very femme young man from Malaysia with an everlasting smile, with whom Mickey had lived for five years, ran off, but not before withdrawing every last penny from Mickey's bank account. That was when Mickey asked Yurik to move in with him: "Not forever, Yurik; I won't be around for much longer."

Yurik gathered his belongings together and stuffed them into a large plastic garbage bag, grabbed his two guitars, and left his little room behind. He settled down into the dilapidated splendor of Mickey's house.

Mickey asked him to play, and he did, but on occasion Mickey would stir his gnarly, peeling fingers and repeat: "If you make a mistake, just keep playing until you get it right. Don't try to fix the mistake, just wait until your mistakes turn into something interesting." Sometimes he berated Yurik: "Why do you always say 'I'm going to, I'm trying to, I want to'? It's a way of doing nothing. Just do it."

Yurik kept thinking that something like this had happened to him before, music and death entwined, but he couldn't remember when or where. A captivating tremulousness surrounded Mickey like a cloud. With Mickey, Yurik got pretty well hooked on junk; sometimes he couldn't tell night from day, and sleep abandoned him altogether.

Throughout the dark, dank winter days, Yurik sat next to the slowly dying man. He dressed his festering feet, fed him, and got hold of the drugs without which Mickey couldn't have lasted another day. Yurik met with people who had been in debt to Mickey for a long time and pumped them for the money that Mickey was in the habit of lending freely. He became acquainted with dozens of dealers, and rushed around the city to score Mickey's heroin. The city took care of its sick, and gave away painkillers and sedatives for free, but this didn't suffice. They suggested that Mickey be admitted to the hospital and then into hospice care, but he refused: he wanted to die in his home. Yurik knew that he'd stay with him till the end. But it didn't work out that way.

On the first day of spring, when the air was saturated with moisture and the sun couldn't penetrate the heavy curtain of mist, Yurik was in the so-called Shooting Gallery, where a charming, jovial dealer named Spike had agreed to meet him. The Shooting Gallery was a place where drug addicts could get a fix inconspicuously, off the streets, without getting busted.

He had agreed to meet Spike at two, but it was already four and Spike hadn't turned up. Yurik started to get anxious. The landlady of the apartment, who was a very young girl, was pallid as death; people paid her for the use of this shelter for drugs. She hadn't left the house for a long time; she couldn't even eat anymore. A guy lying on a mattress handed her an ampoule—containing not what she needed, but something similar. Everything unfolded like a slow-motion movie. She spent a long time trying to puncture her arm with her shaking hand, sobbing and gasping, and finally ended up shooting up in a vein in her hand—there were hardly any others left to choose from. A minute later, she slumped over, her eyes rolling back in her head slowly. She had overdosed.

Just then, Spike appeared. He saw the girl lying in a heap and felt her pulse; it registered as only the faintest thread. He picked the girl up, set her on her feet, and ordered Yurik to walk her around the room. He himself ran out to score some cocaine to add to the other stuff he had on him.

Yurik tried to lead her around the room, but she could hardly walk. She dragged her scrawny legs across the dirty floor, like a limp rag doll in his grip. They walked, or shuffled, in this way for twenty minutes, and then for twenty more. Yurik forgot that Mickey was waiting for him. He was consumed by only one thought: was the girl still alive, or was he dragging around a barely living corpse?

Spike came back. Yurik thrust the girl at him, and grabbed the dose for Mickey, saying he couldn't stay a minute longer—Mickey was waiting.

Yurik never learned whether Spike had been able to bring the girl around. When he got back to Chelsea, Mickey was sleeping peacefully. Yurik didn't try to wake him. Mickey slept for another hour, then another. When Yurik touched him again, Mickey was not yet cold, but he was no longer alive. His face looked peaceful, his expression a bit mocking, and Yurik, after a moment of panic, felt a surge of calm acceptance, and relief. He grabbed his guitar and started playing, singing the words he still remembered from his youthful Beatlemania.

First he sang "I Want to Hold Your Hand," then "She's Leaving Home." Suddenly he remembered that he had sung these songs years ago, when his grandmother Amalia died and he was still a boy. How long ago it seemed! It was almost as though this had happened not to him but to someone else. And he felt a deep sense of loss, and mourning.

The entire New York music community came to say goodbye to Mickey. Everyone who was still alive, in any case. AIDS had reaped a rich harvest during those years, and drug addicts and gays were in the front ranks of its victims. Mickey's mother and sisters came to see the departed—a poor Puerto Rican family that had turned its back on him thirty years before. They showed up hoping that they would inherit something, but there wasn't anything to inherit. There was no money, and they didn't know that the apartment belonged almost wholly to the bank. They thought Yurik was Mickey's partner, but Yurik didn't care. Even if it had been true, it wouldn't have damaged his reputation in any way.

It so happened that Yurik got the most valuable inheritance of all from Mickey: his various friends. They were world-famous musicians, and street musicians, famous only on a single street corner or square in the Village, or at a particular subway station; they were DJs, producers, owners of recording studios, and the countless others who drive the wheels of the vast music industry. For the last year of his life, Mickey had seemed to want to vouchsafe all the people who visited him into Yurik's keeping, and at the funeral, which many of them attended, they greeted him and offered their condolences.

After the funeral, they went to a private club in Chelsea, where they drank and jammed the night away together—greats and nobodies alike. The slightly acrimonious, sardonic Mickey, a fan of folk and world music, would have been pleased. His Puerto Rican kin beat out the backbone of the music with their ridged wooden *güiro*, an elderly Indian man produced cosmic twangs and trills on the sitar, and a swarthy hunchback, most likely an extraterrestrial, drew forth psychedelic sounds from a wind instrument that resembled a sheaf of pipes, both diminutive and large. Yurik played, too, his own composition, which he had been working on for the entire year. In memory of Mickey.

For it was Mickey, who had lived so easily, so lightly, and had died so painfully, who had instilled in Yurik the consciousness that, in the highest sense, music had no authorship. It was a gift, and an ability to read the divine book, to transpose a universal sound that needed no notation into the language of paltry musical instruments, invented for the convenience and purpose of transmitting supremely important messages—messages that could not be conveyed in any other way . . . And the best ears, the best hearts and souls of this spiritual dimension called music, listened to Yurik's song that evening. And heard it.

That day marked another change of direction in Yurik's life. He received several tempting offers, and chose the one most interesting to him, though least promising from a financial perspective—an almost unknown band that performed funk covers from the seventies.

They rehearsed on 125th Street, on the outskirts of what was then still the "ghetto"—where, at the subway exit, a stream of Columbia University students headed in one direction, and a stream of African Americans headed in the other. The demarcation line was both visible and palpable.

Yurik detested racism, and white racists, but he and another guitarist, a Japanese guy they called Suzuki, agreed to be met at the subway entrance by Abe Carter. In this neighborhood, racism demonstrated its lesser-known reverse side. Abe, their black bass player, was their protector and guide into the interior, a rough neighborhood where Chuche, their singer, and Pete, their drummer, were waiting for them in a dilapidated apartment with boarded-up windows. After the rehearsal, Abe accompanied them back to the subway; there was less chance of their being jumped if they were to cross paths with a local gang.

They rehearsed for three months, almost daily, and at the end of it achieved a truly smooth, tight repertoire, not just a collection of random numbers. Yurik was giddy with delight, and felt like an athlete before the deciding match.

On the evening before a gig that had already been announced, their singer was killed in a street brawl. It was like a plane crashing during take-off. They spent a week in that wreck of an apartment, never leaving it, saying goodbye to Chuche: they drank, smoked, shot up, played . . . Yurik was badly shaken. First Mickey, and now Chuche . . . Death was hovering nearby, as though wanting to get to know him. The drugs these guys used were different, more potent and lethal. On the eighth day after the funeral, when days and nights in the decaying apartment had all blended into a single stream of swirling darkness and bright color, Yurik came to his senses and felt a rush of fear. He grabbed his guitar and went to Long Island—to save his own skin.

They didn't expect him. Martha was almost reconciled to the fact that the boy had gotten out of hand; but, from an American perspective, he was already grown up. His arrival was inconvenient. Another guest was staying in Yurik's room: Grisha, visiting from Israel. Yurik collapsed on the leather sofa in the living room, without even bothering to take a shower, and slept for nearly twenty-four hours. Before falling asleep, he managed to tell Martha that his friend had been killed.

"A trauma, yet another trauma," Martha said to Vitya, reminding him of the previous tragedy of Mickey. Vitya agreed absentmindedly.

Grisha, who had previously been very stout, had slimmed down over the last ten years and recovered his youthful slenderness. He was the father of six children of various ages. "Trauma," he said, "is an invention of that most unreliable of sciences—psychology. Everything is a matter of biochemistry and life experience."

Though Martha had worked in administration at the university for many years, she had been trained as a psychologist, and was surprised: why unreliable?

By now, Grisha had the answers to every possible question. "Because it's not even science! It's a delusion. There are precise, stable phenomena or systems: biochemistry, which is obvious, and not yet thoroughly understood, and the programmed behavior that corresponds to it. What does trauma have to do with it?" He ended by saying peevishly, "Everyone went crazy over Freud. Some sort of global delusion. Mystification at its worst . . . The chemistry of life, that's what it's all about."

Yurik was lying facedown. His tired hair, which hadn't been trimmed for more than two years, spread over the pillow in dank, heavy clumps. The clothes he had shed lay in a pile on the floor and stank. Martha gathered up the smelly heap and took it away to launder it. Before putting the clothes in the washing machine, she turned the pockets inside out. When she found two syringes in the pocket of his jacket, she recoiled in horror.

For two whole days and nights, with just a few short breaks, the conversation between Grisha and Vitya continued. They hadn't seen each other in three years, and corresponded infrequently; now Grisha was inundating him with what seemed to Vitya to be pure balderdash, in which he saw no meaning or logic. Grisha had played too big a role in his life for Vitya to be able to dismiss him out of hand, however. It was because of Grisha that Vitya had been able to relinquish his world of abstract dimensions and sets and devote himself to more concrete tasks, and he was happy and grateful for this. Now Grisha was the one spewing all kinds of abstract nonsense that was completely beyond the bounds of anything Vitya considered to be science.

"Vitya! There's one science. There's only one science in the world. We have to reject all the old thinking and retain only three disciplines: mathematics, biology, and physics. And the name of this new science is biomathics."

Vitya looked sleepily at the slightly agitated Grisha. What did he mean by biomathics? Why did he want to throw all the sciences overboard?

"Our world is created by God according to a single plan. The first pages of the Torah offer a modern scientific description of the origin of the universe, the earth, plants, animals, and man. It was not only the Torah that the Creator dictated. All life in the universe, on our planet, is the unfolding of a single grand text. We are all merely trying to decode it and read it. And the only purpose of man is to read this message."

"Grisha, these are just very generalized claims. They have no immediate bearing on human activity. They don't contain any revelations or discoveries. What's the main point, the essence of it?" Vitya said, trying to bring his friend back down to earth.

Grisha had already gotten a lot of flak about these very notions from their brethren in the scientific community, which Vitya could not have known. He had come seeking support from his friend, thinking perhaps he could recruit Vitya to his cause. By now Vitya had become the leading expert on the computer modeling of cells. In Grisha's mind, the two new tables of the covenant were the Text and the Living Computer.

Grisha sighed. The crowd, as everyone knows, does not heed prophets. They either mock them or stone them. In Israel above all. Especially in Israel! During recent years, he had expended so much energy wrestling with and trying to master the Text that he thought to be pre-eminent in the world, the Torah, and had come to the conviction that it was only a digest, just commentaries and references to an even more important Text. Grisha found no sympathy for his convictions among his fellow scientists, nor among his religious teachers. Only one mad Kabbalist from Tsfat, the head of a nonexistent school, welcomed Grisha's ideas. In Vitya, who was not in the mainstream of the scientific establishment, which Grisha viewed as science fiction, Grisha had expected to find a sympathetic listener at the very least. Instead, he encountered only perplexity. But he still didn't abandon hope.

"The thing is, Vitya, that the primary alphabet of the Text was discovered only in 1953—that was the four-letter code of DNA. Even Watson and Crick didn't realize they had discovered the ability to read the Divine Text. They had the most convincing argument in favor of the existence of God!" Grisha blushed deeply, raised his gaunt hands in the air like a street preacher, and exclaimed convulsively: "A conclusive argument! The ultimate argument. And they didn't see it!"

"Wait a minute," Vitya said, trying to pacify the overwrought Grisha. "Maybe Watson and Crick never needed this concept of a Creator? Actually, I never needed it myself. Not in the least."

"Vitya! You wait a minute! Do you really not see that our world was created by the One and Only God according to a unified plan?" Grisha blurted out, now even more incensed.

Vitya was sitting in a deep armchair, his knees nearly level with his chin. Yurik, one leg lolling on the floor, slept on the divan next to him, and Grisha circled around in the small space between the coffee table and another armchair, piled high with freshly laundered sheets that Martha hadn't had time to fold and put away in the cupboard.

"For seven years, I've been studying the Torah. I'm standing on the threshold of a discovery. Perhaps I'm one of the very few who are in a position to be able to compare modern discoveries in biology—the Science of Life—with the text of the Torah, which represents a paraphrasing of the genetic code of DNA. Today I'm convinced that many of the claims of the Five Books of Moses allow for direct experimental examination by modern scientific methods."

"Hold it," Vitya broke in impatiently. "I usually start from what I know. I can't follow your logic here. You're talking about things I know nothing about. I'm completely in the dark here. I've never in my life read any religious texts, and I have no desire to. Never have. You probably need to talk to Martha about this; she's a believer."

"That's exactly what I mean!" Grisha almost shouted. "This is one of the most important ideas. Today, at the end of the twentieth century, through the evolution of human consciousness, the speculative thought of the ancient philosophers coincides with religious thought. We are at a unique point in the evolutionary history of humanity. It is a new era. All the discoveries

338

in the fields of physics, chemistry, and science in the highest sense have no authorship!"

His final desperate yelp awakened Yurik, who couldn't quite figure out what was going on. But the words, sounded by a rather shrill male voice, seemed to be meant for him in particular.

"There is a Divine Text! And human evolution has only one goal, one task—to lead unfinished, incomplete Creation to a state in which man learns how to read it. All the alphabets, all the signs, all the numbers, music notes, et cetera, were invented by us so we might carry out this task."

Yurik dragged his head off the pillow. The shape of a button was imprinted on his cheek. The first thing he saw was an unfamiliar Jew in a yarmulke, with a graying, turned-up beard and a hand upraised.

Man, I'm tripping, he thought. When he noticed his father sitting behind the seething Jew, with a sullen look on his face, he was reassured. Okay, then, I'm not tripping.

Yurik propped himself up on his elbow, and sat up. The Jew stared at him in surprise. Grisha, who had already spent about twelve hours in this living room, had not noticed Yurik sleeping nearby on the couch.

"My son, Yurik," Vitya said dryly.

"My God! That's Nora's son?"

"Well, partly mine, too."

"Amazing," he said. "So you're here in the States, too? You're the spitting image of Vitya. No, no, you really look just like Nora. And I'm Grisha Lieber. I went to high school with your parents. Have they told you anything about me?"

Yurik suddenly felt good.

"I liked what you were saying just now about authorship," he said. "I also think that there's no real authorship. Music exists somewhere in the heavenly spheres, and a musician's job is to hear it and write it down. But since I'm a jazz musician, I know how much of the music stays out there, untranscribed, and lives only during the moments of improvisation."

Grisha was very glad to have received this unexpected moral support.

"Don't worry, it's in a secure repository. Everything has been written down. You see, you see, Vitya, your son immediately grasped what I'm talking about! The world is a book that we only learn to read letter by letter. We try, with the help of our alphabets, rudimentary sign systems, to read texts of enormous complexity, which exist beyond the limits of our own consciousness. Take Plato!"

At this point, Vitya, who hadn't read a word of Plato since the day he was born, lost all patience and shouted: "Martha! How's the dinner coming along?"

Grisha stopped importuning Vitya; he had found a marvelous listener in Yurik. He laid out his entire theory to him, offering Yurik a whole slew of new information—for the most part, all of it from the high-school curriculum. The school textbooks were dull, however, and the knowledge they contained was completely at odds with the things Yurik was interested in. So, recognizing that he had found an avid listener in Yurik, for three whole days—with breaks only for meals and a bit of shut-eye, right up to the moment he left—Grisha told Yurik, who was stunned by the plethora of information, thrilling things at which he could only marvel.

Beginning with the Law of Correspondences—the universe, the cell, and the atom are all constructed according to the same principle, "As above, so below; as below, so above"—advancing to the rhythmical character of the natural processes, from the rotation of the planets to the respiratory, circulatory, and other rhythms of the human organism, Grisha led him to the notion of informational energy and formulated the First Law of Thermodynamics.

"Let me remind you," Grisha said, in a voice slightly hoarse from his nonstop monologue, "that Lord Kelvin, in the middle of the last century, expressed the notion that the Creator, when he created the world, endowed it with an inexhaustible store of energy, that this divine gift would exist for all eternity. But he couldn't be more wrong!"

Skimming through the Second Law of Thermodynamics, Grisha reached the cell theory in its classic form, and, starting with Schleiden and Schwann, solemnly announced that now they had arrived at the most essential matter, about which the originators of this cell theory of all living things had no clue—that the cell was a molecular computer that functioned according to the DNA program created by God the Almighty.

"To be alive means, within the boundaries of the organism, not to increase the entropy throughout the course of the life cycle, in spite of all the possibilities the cell has at its disposal—in particular, reproduction. The cell is an immensely complex system. To understand how it functions, scientists create models that possess the characteristics of the living cell. And it seems that Vitya, your pops, is the world's foremost expert in this area. He's a genius, but he doesn't understand one fundamental thing, as is often the case with geniuses." Here Grisha again began waving his arms around and berating Vitya, who early that morning had ridden his bicycle to the lab to work—offering his son to Grisha as fodder for his training exercises in proselytizing. But, like a true devotee, Grisha was happy with anyone who would listen. All the more since he had now come to his hobbyhorse. "You know how a computer works, broadly speaking?"

Yurik nodded. "My father has explained the basics to me."

"The technical side of things, the hardware, doesn't concern us here," Grisha said dismissively. "We'll be focusing our attention on the organization of the information process itself. What is information exactly? Not long ago, it was considered to be a message that was transmitted from mouth to mouth, in written form, or with the help of some sort of signal, from one person to another. The theory of information was created—the transmission may occur not only from person to person, but from person to machine, from machine to machine. And there is an algorithm, a system of rules, according to which information is deployed for solving problems and tasks on different levels.

"Such algorithmic processes are also present in cells. And it is immaterial how we understand this process—whether as a means of communication between concrete, material objects, or whether we consider that the cell itself utilizes various material objects to realize its existence. The main idea here is that information and matter do not exist independent of one another. The life of a cell is revealed through the operation of its informational system.

"One can compare it to a symphony orchestra, in which a composer, a conductor, musicians, musical instruments, the score, and even the electricity that illuminates the sheet music, all take part. Yes, it's a good example; as a musician you would be predisposed to understand it. The composer writes the music—the algorithm for playing it—and transcribes it—programs or encodes it—in the form of a score with the help of notes—a special alphabet—for a long-term memory—that is, on paper or in the computer memory. The score contains information about the beginning and end of the musical composition, and about what and how each musical instrument should play at a given moment in time, during the course of performing the work. That's it!"

Grisha was beaming—with his eyes, his wrinkles, his swarthy pate, and every hair of his scraggly beard.

"That's it! Do you understand who the composer is here? The Creator! The score is written by Him with the help of the Text, by means of DNA.

Because DNA is the alphabet of the Creator. And now please explain to me why your father shies away from this simple truth, like the devil from holy water? It's so obvious. The Creator created the Law, but He Himself is subordinate to his own law. The universe is intelligent and multitiered. On every tier or level, understanding has its limits. This multitiered nature of things is described in various ways in all religious systems, and it is from this that the inherent intelligibility of the universe derives. If the universe is intelligible, it is possible to model it. Your father, who does computer programming, and does it better than anyone else, refuses to accept the Author of All Scores. It's incomprehensible! There is only one explanation for this: his work belongs to a higher level, but he himself is still on a lower one. And I can't force him to break through to the next one. Everyone must accomplish this on his own."

When Vitya returned home from the lab, Grisha redirected his attention to him. But no dialogue resulted: Grisha ranted and railed, and Vitya grunted occasionally, saying, "Hmm, interesting," while he ate a microwaved dinner that Martha had prepared for him and sipped Coca-Cola. Grisha's ardent inspiration made it impossible for him to accept that his friend couldn't hear what he was saying.

After three days of failure to elicit any sympathy from Vitya, and having exhausted his store of pent-up zeal on Yurik, Grisha flew back to Israel. Yurik saw off the agitated Grisha at JFK, boarded his favorite subway line, the A train, and felt that he had escaped from a bender without any withdrawal pains or other unpleasant consequences purely by means of intellectual exertions, the most powerful of his entire life thus far. He didn't remember the details of what Grisha had told him, but he was left with a sensation of soaring and flight.

He sat looking out the window of the train—it hadn't yet plunged underground—and listened to a melody in his head. He managed to remember what Grisha had said, that all music is written in the heavenly spheres.

Yurik transferred to a train going north and stopped near South Ferry. By that time the melody in his head had completely taken shape, with a strange hook at the beginning, then a repetition in which the hook straightened itself out, put out a little shoot, and then another . . . It could even have been depicted graphically, but it would have been better to play it first. When he emerged from the subway, he sat on the shore, took out his guitar, and played as much of it as he could, from beginning to end. The piece was as elegant and slender as a fish, as light as a bird, absolutely alive.

Toward evening, he arrived at Houston Street, and dropped in on old Tom Drew, the proprietor of a store and workshop that manufactured bar counters and other club furnishings. Tom Drew offered him a job. It was an excellent opportunity. Tom was an old hippie who had long since become a model citizen. His daughter Agnes, who had been born with severe hypothalamus syndrome, had set him on the straight and narrow. The mother abandoned them when the little girl was not yet a year old; from that time on, though still a hippie in his heart of hearts, he had worked like one possessed; he never drank or used drugs, and didn't even smoke. He was ready to do anything for his now grown daughter, who had turned into an unhappy, tyrannical hellcat. Still, Tom cherished a feeling of tenderness and disguised envy for hippies and musicians—his unfulfilled destiny.

Yurik stayed overnight in the utility room. He dreamed about Grisha, who talked about the Divine, then he turned into Mickey, wearing a stretched-out red T-shirt, cussing a mile a minute in Spanish, which was incomprehensible and for some reason very funny.

Life started rolling along as usual. Yurik moved heavy bar counters around, composed music, played with various bands, listened to world music of every variety, smoked weed, and for a while avoided all hard drugs. He changed jobs, lived here and there, but had managed to reform and become a decent young man before Nora's next visit. Every time, it was more and more difficult.

The drugs became a habitual and necessary condition of life for him—overdue credit that he would ultimately have to pay back. He understood this very well.

He wasn't able to keep a single job. He became a dealer, a drug peddler. And he was hooked on the stuff himself—there was already no turning back. Spike, a seasoned worker in the heroin trade, gave him one dose for every ten he delivered to various other addresses. At night, he cruised the city looking for a bonus dose of junk. During the evening, he played music wherever he could, sometimes on the street. Once, in a small square, he heard a busker playing *his* music. He sat down next to him and listened. The guy wasn't really any good. Still, it was amazing how the music came to life, independent of him.

Yurik was arrested twice for possession of narcotics. They let him go. The police understood perfectly well how the business was set up—that all the small-fry dealers were victims of a truly pitiless gang of big-time dealers, who reaped money from the deaths of young idiots. The judges were for the most part humane. They had one undeclared rule: they wouldn't nail a dealer until the third time he was caught. After being detained a second time, Yurik was getting used to the thought that, in his situation, prison wasn't the worst alternative.

The third time he was caught was at the end of 1999, right before the New Year. They busted him in the evening, he spent the night at the police department, and they took him before the judge the next morning. Everything happened very quickly. In the courtroom, he was with a group of young black men, half of whom Yurik knew by sight; one, a bass player, was someone he had played with about three years before. They were all looking at five or six years behind bars, and Yurik was trying to estimate how old he would be when he got out. He figured he would be at least thirty.

The cases were being handled individually at a rapid clip—ten minutes for each of them. Yurik was saved by the computer. When they typed in his last name, the prior offenses didn't show up. Dumbfounded by this stroke of luck, Yurik puzzled for a long time over the computer god that had intervened in his fate. Then he understood what had happened: he was saved by the alphabet. Or, rather, the transcription of Russian into English. He bore the surname of his mother, Ossetsky. There were a couple of spelling variants in English: Osetsky, Osezky . . . At the time of his last arrest, he hadn't been carrying any ID, and the officer wrote his name down as he'd heard it, not as it was officially spelled. So now they let him go. He left the building and sat down on the steps of the courthouse, without the strength to walk. And where would he go?

With great effort, he made it to Long Island. Martha grew terribly alarmed when she saw him, and called Nora in Moscow. Two weeks later, Nora flew back to New York.

35

Letters from Marusya to Jacob
Sudak
(JULY–AUGUST 1925)

JULY 24

Jacob, dearest! I'm writing you sitting on a suitcase on the floor. I'm in Tataria, as you well know—so the discomfort is easy to bear. But first about the trials and tribulations. And there have been not a few. Genrikh tormented me during the journey. He stuck his legs out of the train window, then hung out of it bodily. He ran to the platform at the end of the car and studied all the machinery, once almost managed to stop the train, etc., etc.

I got so worked up about him I nearly didn't sleep at all—and, on top of that, he started running a temperature. We arrived in Feodosia in the driving rain, at three o'clock. I was already exhausted. Then we had to lug all our things, dragging them through pools of water, to get to the boat, hurrying as fast as our legs would carry us, because it was already about to leave. We forgot our linens in the train, and so ran back to look for them, and so on. I am terribly indebted to a German couple who literally saved me. They took Genrikh in hand, helped me carry our belongings, and showed us a great deal of concern. We finally made it onto the boat, with all our things in tow. The natural scenery, which was completely new to me, quite took my breath away. It's almost impossible to describe. The only thing I know is that in the first few minutes, all the particles of my soul were transformed. A new blank space was filled out in its periodic table of elements. Through my own eyes, I saw the magnificence of the world. It was as though my hand had reached out to grasp it.

We arrived in Sudak at 11:00 p.m. (On the boat, Genrikh asked if there was anything to eat. I gave him a quarter of a chicken and some bread—he ate it all very quickly. The boat rocked quite a bit, and he grew very pale. But we made him put his head between his legs, and it passed.) A dark night.

At the mooring (just a small bridge, nothing more), we overheard rumors about a raid by bandits that had happened the night before. They cleaned out an entire boardinghouse—every last bit of it. My traveling companions and I began to look for shelter for the night. We wandered around Sudak in the dark. Every place we came to was already full; they wouldn't agree to any terms. We spent the night on the seashore.

We put Genrikh (very cranky, demanding we go back to Moscow) to sleep on the bedroll, and the whole night I watched over him—afraid that he would kick off the covers. This means I didn't sleep or change for three nights in a row.

The next day, we went searching again: NO ROOMS. Sudak is full up to the rafters. Many people are turning back, or going farther. I decided that it was impossible for me to drag myself from place to place with a child, without a destination. Toward evening, I found a room for thirty-five rubles. We went to fetch our things, and when we returned, this is what I find: "Apologies for mistake: room already let." I almost wept. There is no manager for the dachas (the dacha pension is a collective), and I went back down to the seashore to beg to stay the night in the sea transport offices.

The next day, I sought out the manager, and told him that I intended to occupy a dacha. I would sit in the front hall until they gave me a room; otherwise, I would call him to account, as the official in charge, for exploiting the rooms for personal gain. I threatened to send a telegram to my husband in the People's Commissariat. In short, I went on the warpath. The man turned out to be vainglorious and naïve. My voice was loud and commanding, my diction curt; but the main thing was that I was fully convinced I was in the right. In six days' time, I will be in my own room (and a very good one, at that). Last night, we slept on the floor. I haven't changed my clothes in all this time. Today a woman who is living here offered to let me live for a few days with her in her room, until her husband arrives.

In further news: I'm spending money like it's going out of style. It is not cheaper to live here than it is in Moscow. Prices are inflated with the influx of tourists, which is not at all usual here. For the time being, though, money isn't a problem. The amount I have allocated for living expenses for a month will suffice (with the fifty rubles I put aside). There isn't enough for a return trip, however.

Now for the good news. In spite of the torments I've gone through, I feel energetic and in good spirits. The Crimea is lovely, magnificent, full of marvels. Genrikh has come to life again. He's eating, he got deeply suntanned during these two or three days, and we haven't even sunbathed yet. I am unrecognizable (for your ears alone: I have become prettier). In spite of using my parasol, I even managed to get some sun; it looks quite nice, though. The air of the sea and the mountains invigorates me. I'm happy.

I'm tired, there are hardships and inconveniences, I work a lot, I'm always running back and forth to the bazaar in Sudak. But my eyes drink in the colors and light, my ears the rhythms; and I'm afraid I might become religious here. The effects of nature. A Tatar woman walks past with a basket of peaches balanced on her head. She doesn't even have to hold on to it. And all around is a symphony of mountains and sky. And I eat the Tatar with my eyes, swallow up the chain of mountains, and drink in the sunlight. And I love you. You are my one and only in this whole remarkable world. If your shoulder were nearby, I would cry from the wonder of it all.

A Tatar named Gustava (he's not pretending, it's his real name) treated me and Genrikh to some delicious shish kebab. Gustava loves Lenin: "I give him my great thanks," he says; and he wears a Lenin pin in his lapel. "Your Lenin is a good man." We take a long time saying goodbye, and the expressions of good wishes are elaborate and heartfelt. They are gentle, hospitable people. Passionate, proud. If they like you, they'll do anything for you. They like a good joke. They're quick to anger, and hate with a vengeance. I like talking to them. Genrikh and I ate a lot of shish kebab for lunch. We drank tea with lemon, and it all cost eighty kopecks. That's what we ate yesterday. Almonds cost twenty kopecks per pound. Pears fifteen kopecks. Genrikh devours fruit. We spend about sixty kopecks a day on fruit. I can't write anything more. Warmest hugs.

The sun here is so wonderful and burning hot.

Mar.

Address: Sudak, *poste restante*. Best to send via registered mail. We're in the middle of nowhere.

JULY 26

Well, we still have no room of our own. Genrikh and I are sleeping together on a folding cot, sharing the room with another person—it's inconvenient and awkward. I lost another room, the second, although I have a receipt for the security deposit. Both times, it was men, with their peahens and a trail of little ones following behind, who beat me out of the room. I'm almost beside myself with frustration. I can't live like this. It's been a whole week of ordeals, one after another. I run around all day long, hither and thither, and never manage to rest.

Today Genrikh nearly drowned. A wave knocked him off his feet—he fell, and started churning around in the water, gasping for air. I ran over and just managed to pluck him out. I'm not really sorry this happened: now he's good and scared, and it won't be so hard for me to watch out for him. I didn't get a moment's peace when we were at the seaside. I spent all my time shouting and chasing after him. He's such a difficult child. Very difficult. In Moscow, I have to make sure he doesn't fall out of a window. Here, in the Crimea, there are a thousand more things to worry about: the sea, wells, precipices . . .

Dinner is always a trial. Everyone sympathizes and reminds me that I'm not getting any rest. I don't need reminding about how difficult it is to look after him. Still, he's looking very well. And when my nerves are frayed and I'm absolutely weary, I look at his little round face, so fresh and alive, and see how happy he is, and I am reconciled to my own burdens.

I am very concerned about the financial side of our journey. We share one meal between the two of us; I can't afford full room and board. I prepare breakfast and lunch myself. I run around like a chicken with its head cut off. This is what a woman's vacation looks like.

The Crimea is marvelous, but I'll make good use of it in a year, when I come here by myself. For now, it's all for the sake of Genrikh. I can't even sunbathe properly. As soon as I shut my eyes, he's already sneaking off into the water; and the sea floor is full of holes and drop-offs he could fall into.

Now that you're in Moscow, I'm not as worried about you as I was. You're probably getting more rest there. If I knew better what our financial situation was, I would take a cure in the sea waters; but it's expensive—fifteen rubles. The baths would be very helpful for my leg, and for my overall health.

I spend three to three and a half rubles a day, living very, very modestly. The rooms cost thirty-five rubles. That's the cheapest kind; a good room costs forty to fifty. In a month, it will get cheaper. If Genrikh weren't such a handful, every hour in the Crimea would be absolute bliss. But he doesn't give me a moment's peace. I have to do the shopping, make meals, feed him, take care of him, bathe him, put him to bed, and in the evening I can't leave him alone.

Thanks to the fresh air, I have lots of energy and can get a lot done. I'm suntanned. It's a good thing I brought a parasol: the sun beats down without mercy. There are so many marvels here—but I'm not free to enjoy them. I'll have to wait. The fruits and vegetables are so juicy and sweet, it's no surprise the eastern peoples worshipped food and drink. You can't simply eat fruit like this—you have to savor it, partake of it. Every peach, every apricot is one-sixtieth, at least, of a pure heavenly blessing.

And the Tatar women at the fountain are the blessing in its entirety. I can't get enough of my dark, reserved, graceful sisters. I have already made a few friends. And we understand each other perfectly. We look into each other's eyes and smile. I hold their little ones in my arms—and we smile at each other. And we understand everything about one another. We're women, we love, we have children. I caress her child, and she dotes on mine. We nod to each other—then go our separate ways. It's wonderful.

Mahmed has a beautiful, quiet wife and two children. The large room is spread with intricate, colorful carpets, pillows. There are no chairs; everyone sits on the floor in silence, lost in thought. What an amazing existence! Here it seems that eternity, time, and these people are all of a piece, and flow together, on and on. Meetings, reports. Myasnitskaya Street, political and economic realities and confluences—what is the sense in all that? I embrace you, my dear one.

Mar.

JULY 28

Jacob, my best and dearest. Things are fine with me now. For the first time in my life, summer vacation is a joy to me. I am enjoying every moment of my existence here. Today I trekked over a hill to Sudak. There was a fierce wind. I breathed so fully, so deeply, and my heart beat so hard—I was bathing in the sun, the wind. Every time I leave the house—whether I'm going to the mountains or to the sea—feels like a momentous, lush experience to me. I look at Genrikh and it's a feast for my eyes! He's as brown as toast, with dark-red lips; his eyes are shining. We live here now in complete harmony. He's a gifted, openhearted child, and he makes life worth living for me. Today, at dinner, a sweet lady looked at him and said, "He has cunning eyes." Genrikh said, very seriously, "Yes, I have cunning."

Everyone here likes him very much. And for good reason. He's been eating well for two days now. I'm dreaming of the moment I can show him to you—our beautiful bronze boy. I look very fine, too, and am feeling well. My nerves are no longer on edge. And the air here, Jacob! I can't get my fill of it!

It's just sad that you can't take a vacation yourself, that you're so far away from all this beauty. But I'm truly indebted to you.

I received the money. I have everything I need now. Write me often. Send me about ten or fifteen sheets of blank paper. It's very hard to come by things here. And envelopes. There are still no grapes here. But the pears, the plums! And the almonds . . .

Kisses to you, Jacob.

Mar.

AUGUST 1

Genrikh is asleep in bed. A candle is burning next to us. The insects are bothering us. Mosquitoes, moths. He calls them *mouse*-keetoes. I've been living in a state of alarm for many days now. I haven't had any letters for a long, long time. I sent an emergency telegram; there was no answer. I received both a package and a letter the next day (one letter was in the package, another in the mail). But why was there no answer to the telegram? And again my nerves are strained to breaking, in a vicious circle. Today I sent another telegram (three days after sending the first). Tomorrow I won't go anywhere—I'll just stay here and wait for a reply.

The first flush of intoxication from the novelty of everything is gone now. The mountainous road into Sudak, the sea, the Tatars—they all seem mundane and ordinary to me. I admire their charms, but I'm no longer moved by them.

The Tatars like me. I have the feeling that they can't get enough of me. Their eyes watch me with open and naïve shamelessness. A Tatar named Mariv brings me fruit every day. He says that I am "a remarkable little madame." He offered me a huge peach and said that my eyes are just as large and sweet as this peach. I get into long conversations with the older Tatars. I feel a great deal of sympathy for these people. They are especially beautiful when they are in motion: they move with an almost majestic slowness. When he sees me from a distance, Mahmed bows respectfully but with great dignity, and raises his right hand in greeting. A fine gesture, almost hieratic. I smile warmly at every Tatar man and woman I meet. I love these unconsciously poetic and instinctive people. Gustava asks me for a favor: "Come down to the sea; there is a girl swimming there now, she is with her mother. I want to propose to her. Tell me how you like her."

I've spent a difficult night and day. I finally received your telegram today, Jacob. My wonderful one, my all . . . Everything ends there, where my anxiety about you begins. Everything seems unnecessary and trivial. Here today, gone tomorrow. The Sudak telephone and telegraph play havoc with the nerves of vacationers. I miss you desperately already. What this means, I will tell you in bed.

I'm sitting alone at a table on a terrace. In front of me is the sea—blue, sparkling quietly in the sun like diamonds. On the right are the mountains, with the Genoese fortress; on the left, a small group of young cypresses. Plantings. Where do I begin and end—what is me, what is not me? Such a beautiful world! And I've learned so many new things.

Yesterday Professor Uvarov and his wife visited me. He is a geographer. An old man who so resembles my father, it gives me a lump in my throat. I feel an insurmountable tenderness toward him. He has Papa's amiability, his sweetness, his equanimity. The only difference is that he is much taller than Papa, and has a different profession. He's a Muscovite. Our Genrikh will study his textbook when he goes to school.

About Genrikh. I can't get enough of looking at him; my joy knows no bounds. He's my sweetheart. He has become remarkably calm since we've been here. I don't have to raise my voice with him any longer. Braslavsky, a neighbor of ours from Moscow, is very impressed with him. The other day, when he was looking at Genrikh, he told me: "I believe in his future. He has an unusually good mind." The fact is that Genrikh beat Braslavsky twice in a game of chess, and Braslavsky plays well. He was astounded, very literally. Today he came to me carrying Genrikh on his shoulders. I'll tell you about both of them . . . when we're in bed.

I'm terribly afraid of betrayal—but I always try to display contempt toward any lack of freedom, and to be a freethinker about marriage. I'm afraid of someday encountering a malicious or pitying gaze. I try to pretend that, on the contrary, I approve of infatuations, and take a light view of betrayal, etc. You know this about me. Conscious thought says one thing—but the body says another. The idea that you might betray me is unbearable.

I long to be with you again. You know, my arms and shoulders are covered with freckles now. I look very dark. My body and skin are much stronger these days. The only problem is that I can't sleep.

I kiss you. Soon. M.

AUGUST 8

I am filled with rays of light, freshness, and love. Evening. The painful abscess of anxiety and worry about you has broken. I'm at peace now. Today I had a wonderful day. I lay naked on the stones by the edge of the water and enjoyed inspecting them. I turned over, with my back to the sun, then my breasts and hips, coming to life in the rays, in the salt of the sea, in the healing waters. I look at the years of my life in their physical aspect. My body has gone through so much! And how powerful, how resilient it must be, if it has survived.

In childhood, my body never knew water like this, never felt the air, or the sun. My whole childhood was spent without sun, in any sense of that word. Perhaps I would have been taller, with a more ample bosom, if I had lived differently as a child. In my youth, things were not so very different from my earliest years. The years of revolution and deprivation, without water, without the kind of food a young person needs, being subjected to physical stress and depression, and constant weariness—right up to the present day.

This is the first time in my life I've ever been to a resort. I remember my father saying that fresh air was bad for his health. I didn't even know what a resort was for! Only in the past few days have I gotten into the swing of things; and only now has my excitement at the novelty and the intensity of my experience finally diminished. And we're only in the Crimea—on the eastern shore, at that, which is not so very vibrant and dramatic. People tell me so much about the myriad charms and wonders of the world. And I have the urge to travel again, with renewed enthusiasm. I have the feeling that neither you nor I will be satisfied by just being homebodies any longer. It's not by chance I always hated dacha life. Dachas signify immobility, limitation. Here there are many inconveniences, but in spite of that it has been the best summer of my entire life. You'll see. You'll touch my hands, my breasts, you'll stroke my strong, smooth, hot skin. I can't wait until the moment we see each other again. I have so much to tell you! And so many kisses to give you.

Just be patient. Don't find someone else to give your impatience to. I am saving myself for you!

Genrikh's friend and partner, Braslavsky, is going to call on you. "What message shall I give your husband?" "That you saw us." "And what if I make something up?" "Of course you may; my husband knows how to appreciate fantasy—if the quality is good." This person lives at 31 Povarskaya Street. He's our neighbor.

After the beach. Genrikh and I were at the beach by eight in the morning. We sat under an awning at the shish-kebab stand. Fatma watches us with her gentle eyes. Her stern, thoughtful brow is furrowed. Genrikh eats his shish kebab hungrily. The Primus stove is broken, and this is already the fourth day we have breakfasted on shish kebab. It's Genrikh's favorite food. He tears at the meat with his teeth, drinks down hot milk, and for dessert he is offered delicious Tatar pastry with nuts. He's already begun eating grapes. Today he's already eaten two pounds, and he'll have as many more later in the day. Grapes are still expensive—twenty kopecks a pound—but delicious. Yesterday Genrikh said to me, "You're wearing a satin dress with two pink brooches." (I swim naked.) What do you think of that?

I spend a lot of time with the German couple, Emilia Werner and her very kind husband, Richard, who did me such a kind turn when we were all traveling here together. They are simply good, good people. Emilia is very maternal, and Richard is an exceptionally dear man. They make fine company for us. Genrikh and I get on beautifully together. He is a delight. We can be proud of ourselves, Jacob: we have a remarkable son. "In all the world, I have only two favorite people: you and Papa. I am very happy here in Sudak. But not completely, because Papa's not here." That's what he said. If you could only see how easily he leaps and hops about in the mountains. How kindly disposed other people are to him, because of his winning ways. They even think him attractive! That is the power of a winning personality.

Tomorrow we are going to Koktebel with Braslavsky. Max Voloshin's dacha is in Koktebel, and many people vacation there. A gliding competition is being organized. Someone will come to fetch Braslavsky in an automobile, and he invited Genrikh and me to go along. Our boy is over the moon at the prospect of this outing.

Mar.

AUGUST 12

I read sixty pages about Anatole France. And you are right—the disease put out its tentacles and began to wring out the nerves . . . I don't understand. I don't want to understand. Anatole France is dear to you? To me—no. He is the son of a country that has been eaten away by syphilis and thoroughly ravaged—how can I possibly care for him? Love? Yes. Without love there is no life. But what Anatole France is promoting has nothing to do with love. It can only be described by a crude, unprintable word. France's love is the underside of love. The back entrance of love. I don't need that. I don't want that kind of love. I don't want that kind of love for those who are dear to me. I don't want my sexual organs, wisely located in my nether regions, to take the place of my head, to strangle my heart. I will not allow the lower to govern the higher.

"Passion . . . sultriness . . . convulsions of lust." France's passion, convulsions, are what any rooster experiences. I read somewhere that at certain moments a rooster's feet begin convulsing uncontrollably. And this is what makes life worth living, according to his words? Only to seek out this kind of passion in life—everything else is trivial? It is Anatole France himself who is trivial and banal.

Devoid of character, devoid of ideology or principle, stuffed with the superficial brilliance of minds of millennia, a talented singer, rehashing the same songs that have been sung before by others, over and over, ad infinitum. A talented literary sensualist. Of what use is he to me? He's gone. Never mind. Others will come to take his place, new ones. They must answer our questions. I have no doubt that there are powerful experiences in life outside the sexual sphere. Lenin's Mausoleum on Red Square proves that a man lives not by the phallus (or penis) alone.

I am writing you in a state of agitation, because I have failed to receive any letters from you. The five-day rule in correspondence has been transgressed mightily by you. The postal service is not to blame. Everyone else is getting mail on a regular basis. The letters don't go astray; they simply never get written. Or is all your time taken up with an "old" lady, or a young one? I write and write . . . Do you even read my letters?

I won't write you another word. I am thoroughly disenchanted, and hurt to the bottom of my soul. If my recovery comes to naught, if my health suffers as before, I'm not to blame. Another week has passed. No letters. The mailman delivers reams of letters to everyone else—but not to me.

Goodbye.

Yes. I am beyond vexed.

Jacob! My life . . . Not a word from you in ten days. During all these days and nights, I have been preoccupied with a single idea. I cannot, and must not, hide it. We have never consciously lied to one another. I will say everything that is on my mind. My heart could not rest easy after I left Moscow. Anxiety continued to torment me. Clarity of thought eluded me, and I was haunted by a specific, unappeasable fear: I'm afraid for myself, and I'm sorry for you.

I don't quite know how to put this. I have lost faith in words and explanations. Numbers are stricter, more exacting. My last letter was neither a reproach nor an accusation, just the burning pain of an injured human life. When I first found out that you desired other women, I instinctively felt that it was the end. Life became a slowly unfolding torment. I fully comprehended your state of mind, and tried to reconcile myself to it. Your hands and lips wandered away from me, and were drawn to others, caressed others, your eyes delighted in others; and I stood as an obstacle, a stubborn obstacle, in your path. You struggled in me with yourself, and with me. And a clear and powerful certainty took root: Jacob doesn't love me anymore. I cannot fill him, complete him, anymore. I am not strong enough to fend off the images of others, to counter the attraction to others. And the meaning of love, its power and happiness, consists in the fact that, in loving one person, you are liberated from others, from attraction and longing for them. I am no longer a source of that peace for you. Neither of us is to blame for this. Believe me—I do not blame you with even so much as a sliver of my soul. And a difficult life "through common memory of the past" has begun for us.

You defended Freud—I hated him; you were enamored of Jung, with his psychology of the unconscious—I cursed him. And that's how it was with everything. We both struggled not so much for our own ideas, but for our own personal happiness.

I have a weak will and a weak resistance system. My character began to spoil, my personality to disintegrate. I began to blame myself for everything in life. And, truth to tell, this had never been the case before. I made my way in the world on my own strengths. I was never overwhelmed by fear or confusion. Unhappiness oppressed me. Yes, I began to blame myself, because I instinctively felt guilty toward you.

You write that you have "withstood" temptation, that you have not betrayed me. Well, what of it? Did that make things easier for either one of us? No. You have suppressed the temptation, and so have I, and now we both feel suppressed. Neither you nor I know how to make or accept sacrifice. What you wrote about "simple souls" is empty posturing. Anyone who is importuned by demands from all sides, as I am, becomes nervous, irritated, unhappy. I don't blame you and do not want to punish you. I am not an avenging angel, but a severe judge—of myself alone. I cannot, I am not able, to accept the sacrifices you bring. They are useless to me.

Now, it seems, you are struggling with yourself, tormenting yourself. Why? You will never forgive me for this, you won't be able to help punishing me for it; and still, at night, the images of your betrayal will haunt me, because it is in your blood, in your very existence. I experience everything that is in you with exceptional clarity and intensity. You say that you would tell me absolutely everything. I can also tell you absolutely everything about yourself.

You plead with me: Be my mother, my sister, my helpmeet. I cannot. I am a woman. And if our bond in love is destroyed, I am not capable of anything else beyond it. I do not blame you for your sexual desires. Please do not blame me for mine. You are, for me, a man. Beyond this, everything loses value and meaning. You are attracted by youth and beauty, and the attraction is powerful. This is your right. You did not love me for beauty, but fell out of love for me for lack of it. I cannot live beside you if I am not attractive to you as a woman, if I don't bring you joy through my way of dressing, my body, my kisses. I want to be loved. This is my right. It is not a demand. It is a necessity. Without this I cannot live, nor can you.

What to do? This is what we must do: end it. My blood runs cold when I say this. But it is unavoidable. You can and will live freely and happily. The world is open for you. It is full of beauties and joys. With me your life becomes duller, because that which brings you joy is outside of me.

I know you feel unrestrained pity for me, and that my unhappiness causes you suffering. But there is nothing I can do about it. One can't allow sympathy and pity to govern one's life. And listen, know, that death is not a disaster. It is happiness. To sever one's dependence on form, color, sensations—that is happiness. Do not be alarmed, though. That won't happen now, or anytime soon. The small, not yet fully fledged life of our child will not allow it. Perhaps the torment of life will become easier to bear with time. Perhaps these images of finality and departure will fall away.

Last night, I dreamed of you, too. An enormous bed. I was hiding away pathetically in a corner. You were standing on the bed, embracing a tall, naked woman. She had small breasts, but they began to grow, to fill out. You caressed her hips tenderly. Under your hands, her breasts were full and ripe. Quietly, with supple grace, you eased your bodies down, locked in an embrace. I woke up.

You see—my thoughts have been affected with malaise. It's not my imagination, not some unraveling of my nerves, but the cruel, insurmountable truth of life. Your daydreams have become mine. Do not blame me, as I don't blame you. And believe that I reproach you with nothing, nothing at all. There are laws of life, and we both suffer because of them. Both of us in our own ways, more or less, but no one is at fault here. Do not come here. Forgive me. If it is too difficult for you, I will do as you wish. Forgive me, my dear one, my good one, my loving one, my Jacob. I cannot tear myself away from this letter—I must tell you the truth.

I just got your letter. My dearest. You so want to help me. To behave "well." To make heroic efforts. My Jacob. But we cannot recover the past, as we cannot recover my youth. Love is possible only where there is youth and beauty. Love is a huge but primitive feeling. Its demands are primitive. A woman's most decisive value is her aesthetic value. I no longer have this—no, no, and again no. Literature, art, life—everything speaks of this. I feel the world is suffocating me. Genrikh whines and cries all day long. I am trying to make myself smaller, exerting myself. I want to overmaster myself—and am unable to. I must help him—but I have no strength. I overexert myself, and then feel weak with the effort. My head is spinning. Genrikh is as lonely as I am. There is no one by our side. I wander alone. No, I do not want your pity. I am shattered, and so I seem to demand pity. No, everything will pass. We must break with each other, no matter what the cost. It's unavoidable. Goodbye, my love.

Mar.

Postcard

AUGUST 28

The train arrives on the morning of the 30th. You will go from the station to your work, and I to Ugryumova, on errands. If you can't meet us at the station, don't worry. Send Manya to meet us. I kiss you and send you a strong hug, my dearest and sweetest one.

36

Lady Macbeth of the Mtsensk District

(EARLY 1999–2000)

The thought of Yurik never left her. Her previous visit to New York had been a failure. Nora saw Yurik only four times in the space of two weeks. He had a cold and a red, sniffly nose, and he was constantly rushing off somewhere or other. He was underdressed for the cold weather. She bought him a warm jacket. She couldn't figure out where he was living. He said he lived with Tom, but asked her not to call him there. He said he had lost his cell phone, along with his passport and green card. Or, rather, that he had been mugged. Nora insisted that he apply for a replacement of his Russian passport. Together they went to the embassy and filled out the forms for a new one.

He was always late for their rendezvous. One time he didn't show up at all, and she waited for two hours at Dante in the West Village, where he had agreed to meet her. She never made it to Long Island to see Martha and Vitya. Martha had gone to Ireland to attend the wedding of some cousin, eight times removed. Vitya spoke to her over the phone in monosyllables—yes and no—and she couldn't get any information from him.

She returned to Moscow. She felt wretched, her mood was lousy; but she had long since decided that the best mood she could expect for herself was none at all. At least that was better than a bad mood.

Nora taught in the theater college, having taken over Tusya's old position. She was constantly aware that she couldn't possibly fill Tusya's shoes—she didn't have her freedom, her command of the cultural sphere. The old guard of teachers was passing away, and the new generation couldn't measure up to the precedents of the old one. It seemed that the next generation of students would take another step down on the ladder. There were no interesting offers from the theater, either. Tengiz had been lying low for almost two years.

The mythical era of reconstruction, or "perestroika," seemed to have ended with the 1998 default of the ruble. Both Tengiz and Nora had understood, of course, from the very beginning, that perestroika had no relation to them at all. It turned out that neither of them had anything to "reconstruct" in order to achieve a correspondence between the newly permitted freedom of thought and their own matured thinking about the world, and their own place in it.

Since her high-school years, Nora had felt a high-minded contempt for collectivism, and she rejected the false dichotomy of a "social good" superior to the "personal good." In his patriarchal homeland of Georgia—from the age of thirteen, when his father went to fight on the battlefront during the Second World War—Tengiz had had to support his entire family by the sweat of his brow. He provided for his sister, his mother, his grandmother and grandfather, and his grandmother's blind sister, who lived with them her whole life. This early burden of responsibility shielded him from all kinds of foolishness and idiocy. His schooling was constantly interrupted, and only after his father returned was he able to make up for lost time, grasping at all the opportunities he was deprived of in childhood. He went to live with an uncle in Kutaisi, and attended the Institute of Culture. He transferred to acting school, quit, served in the military construction battalion, then worked evenings and nights—as a nude model, a cobbler, even as a cook—until he decided to become a theater director. He had had no time for being either Soviet or anti-Soviet.

The officially authorized freedom, or its shadow, made no impression on him. Nora didn't really notice it, either. She had always been so headstrong that willfulness had supplanted freedom for her from her earliest years. It was likely that Tengiz's independence and Nora's willfulness had struck a mutual chord in them. Somehow or other, both of them responded to the freedom they found in each other. It was a joy for them to work together. But their mutual endeavors—Nora had almost reconciled herself to this— had ended.

By the end of the 1990s, they had about two dozen joint stage productions under their belts. Even though the plays had not all enjoyed the same degree of popular success, they had received well-deserved professional and critical acclaim, a few prizes, and some international recognition. They had found friends in the Eastern European theater world, with whom they shared common views: a dismissively skeptical attitude toward politics, and an aversion to the coarser, cruder forms it took, such as the invasion of Prague in 1968 by Soviet troops and the recent American bombing of Yugoslavia, not to mention the secret killings, poisonings, and cloak-and-dagger intrigues.

It was just during these troubled times that a tentative, incoherent offer to stage a tried-and-true Russian classic came from their Hungarian friend István, the artistic director of a Budapest theater. He invited both Tengiz and Nora. Rise above politics! Theater for theater's sake!

Tengiz called Nora and said, "Well, are you on board?" She agreed without a second thought.

It was a turbulent year. The Caucasus was in a state of upheaval, but the trains from Georgia were running, and the planes were flying. Tengiz arrived in Moscow two days after his phone call. The set design was still the same—the view of Nikitsky Boulevard out the window, the same Kuznetsov china teacups on the table, the spines of the same books on the same bookshelves. The old Persian rug with bare patches from the legs of a desk that had long since been moved to another spot. The wall that bisected the molding—a reminder of the building's aristocratic youth, when the proportions between walls and ceiling were more commensurate, before the rooms were cut in half to accommodate more tenants.

The costumes were also the same—Nora in jeans and a man's shirt, and Tengiz in a baggy sweater and outdated, shapeless trousers. This play of life had lasted so long that both of them had managed to age, and their relationship, once intermittent and nonbinding, had grown into a bond as strong as any marriage.

The most important things in Nora's life had grown out of their combined efforts. She had learned to work without him, but always, internally, she consulted him on every new project she began. She corrected her course under his silent influence. Countless times during the past years, Nora had tried to break the chains of her servitude to him, but each time the chains seemed to grow stronger. Her fingers were callused and hard—and still she was not free.

"Take it easy," Tengiz had said, by way of comforting her, after yet another attempt to break out of this bondage. "Accept it as a fact. A fact of our biography."

This time, it was different. She made the bed in Yurik's room for Tengiz. He stared at her in astonishment.

"Is this the way it's going to be, then?"

"Yes," Nora said, nodding.

"But how will we work together?" Tengiz said.

"Otherwise, the same as always." And she closed the door behind her.

The next day, they went to visit Tusya, who had moved permanently to the dacha. They spent a long day there together. Tusya had grown decrepit with age, and was nearly blind. She read with a magnifying glass—memoirs of writers and cultural figures, to the exclusion of anything else. She admired Viktor Shklovsky, and Pasternak's correspondence with his cousin Olga Freidenberg, and waxed indignant about Dostoevsky and the correspondence between Chekhov and Knipper. She painted, using a housepainter's brush, on the back sides of old rolls of wallpaper, left behind after a renovation years since. Stripes, circles, spots . . .

"I just daub and mess around—but what a pleasure it is!" she said. And Nora smiled wryly; the drawings looked just like the work of the children in her art classes long ago.

The conversation then segued to their future work. They told her about the commission—a good Russian classic, above and beyond all politics.

"Chekhov," Tusya proposed. "Who else?"

Tengiz shook his head. He and Chekhov had parted ways back in the seventies.

Tusya took off her glasses and looked at them with her naked, red-rimmed eyes.

"I understand. Love and death. How young you both still are."

Young? Nora was already in her late fifties, and Tengiz was over seventy. Nora wanted to cite her favorite line from Brodsky: "From a mosquito's point of view, a human does not die," but she stopped herself short, because Tusya's life had been very long, and not only from a mosquito's point of view.

"The theater wants something very Russian," Nora said, smiling. "I don't know—Volga boatmen, river pirates, Cossack robbers . . . Any ideas, Tusya?"

"The most Russian of all stories is *The Captain's Daughter*. It has everything: the begging bag and prison. And love, to a certain degree. Pushkin didn't attach any significance to politics. It's all about human worth and dignity. A rare subject in Russia."

"No, no, Tusya, I can't take that on. Staging *The Captain's Daughter* . . . I wouldn't dare attempt it."

"Prison is a Russian subject. I'd suggest *The Gulag Archipelago*, but in our era Solzhenitsyn is still not a Russian classic. And his work is almost all politics—drenched in tears and blood. Leskov: *Lady Macbeth of the Mtsensk District*. That has everything."

She read my mind, Nora mused.

"I thought of Katerina Izmailova right off; but Shostakovich gave me pause," Tengiz said.

They exchanged glances. Yes, of course. Passion. Death. Infanticide. The begging bag and prison. Fate . . . Yes, of course.

"At first I didn't understand why Shostakovich threw out the infanticide. He was twenty-seven when he wrote the opera. He didn't understand that the murder of a child was a blood sacrifice. It's just that Katerina doesn't realize what she's doing. She is devoured by passion, and she throws everything into this fire—both Fedya, and her own child . . . She gave birth and she gave it away—take it! Take every single thing! As though she didn't even notice what was happening after the murder of Fedya. She's a far cry from Lady Macbeth. Her passion is fairly superficial—to wear a crown. But her conscience is alive. She goes mad, she can't wipe the blood off her hands. And she didn't even commit the murder herself.

"No, Nora, Lady Macbeth can't hold a candle to our Katerina. Our merchant's wife is blinded by her passion, blinded by it. Poor Katya! What a fate! And Shostakovich's music is pure fate. And we're working without this music. Nora, I want it all to be about fate; I don't want anything else to interfere. Horrible fate thrusts its finger into the genitals of an ordinary woman—not a sorceress-Medea, not Lady Macbeth, but a simple woman indistinguishable from a million others. And look what happens! Fate! How is she to blame? She has a petty soul, and an overload of passion—that's what fate is! She's not guilty! And all Leskov's prisoners—they're also victims of fate. A Russian fate, I'd like to note. It's the same—from the begging bag and prison . . . I want to show that fate and prison are one and the same; fate is a kind of prison."

The play took shape out of these inarticulate ramblings. This time, fate was woven from threads of about the thickness of a whole hand. An enormous, invisible spider ensnared the entire opening of the stage with dark filaments, a curtain of crude, shaggy ropes that lightly swayed and shivered. A spiderweb. The spider itself hid above it, in the rigging. The only things visible were its hairy legs. As they moved slowly, the ropes stirred as though they were flowing from the four pairs of legs. Across the proscenium, from left to right, filed the convicts—slowly, hunched over, singing a mournful song. They shuffled along in a continual cyclical movement, all of them alike, wearing long dark clothes, without faces, neither male nor female; and each figure seemed to be hanging from a thick black rope descending from the legs of the invisible spider.

The convicts filed offstage, and their lugubrious song faded away with them. Suddenly Sergei appeared, in his red shirt and black boots, holding an accordion, and shaking a curly lock of hair. He started dancing this way and that, squatting and throwing out his legs, and leaping to his feet again. Sergei, the lover . . . He danced his way back in the other direction—from the wings where the convicts had disappeared to the side from which they had appeared. Then a small platform with two levels materialized. On the upper level was Katerina Izmailova, with a distaff, a spindle. She impassively spun the yarn with her plump pink hands—fluffy white yarn . . .

"This structure, this set, can serve as a house, the police station, the prison, and the barge, without any transformation. We just have to decide about the water. The Volga River," Nora said, showing a sketch.

"Fewer words, fewer words," Tengiz said. "Incoherent, disconnected cries, cursing, fragments of musical phrases. We'll bring in some Shostakovich, I'll ask Gia . . . Or we'll find a composer in Budapest. Forget about Leskov's original text. We've thought everything through. We'll weave fate ourselves. And let Katerina be knitting some little socks—well, some large ones, even huge ones! With a red arrow up the sides. And in the first love scene, let her wind the yarn into . . . I don't know what it's called, you wind them on your hands."

"Skeins," Nora prompted.

"Yes, skeins. Skeins. The hands wind them and approach one another . . . I don't know, I don't know. You think up something," Tengiz said.

"Good, good. Winding the yarn is right. I think the entire first love scene is like a cocoon. The spider's thread winds around them. Let it be red, and the old man Izmailov comes and flings open the door, and the door breaks the thread."

"Now, *that* I'm not so sure about. But let's move along. I need the old man to be wrapped up in a shroud, and let's put him not in the basement but, rather, in the attic. We'll have this mummy hanging in the spiderweb up there on high. And some evil spirit or vermin, like a cat or a werewolf, is walking there above, and not below. How did Leskov manage to forget about witches? My God, it's unforgivable! They'd be perfect. They could hang from the hairy black ropes, and drop down."

"The attic—that means we need a third level. That's too much. There should just be two," Nora insisted.

"I don't know. I don't know. We can tackle the technicalities later. I need the dead—all four of them—to be wrapped in shrouds, in black shrouds."

"Wait a minute—why four? The old man Izmailov, Zinovy, and Fedya—"

"And the baby? Four! No, five! We forgot Sonyetka. She drags her into the water."

"Tengiz, this is frightening. Terrifying, even."

"And rightly so! It must be terrifying. This is not your everyday Ukrainian *Viy*! It's Russian. It is terrifying!"

"No, no. I can't do this. I don't want to!" Nora objected.

"Did you want a light at the end of the tunnel? Well, there's no light there. Everything is dark and dismal."

"And the boy? Fedya? The innocent boy, Fedya?" Nora said, grasping for some ray of hope.

"Fine, the finale is yours. Go ahead and do it. I'll watch and see what kind of heavenly kingdom you salvage out of this story," Tengiz said, agitated. "Come on! Do you remember Shostakovich's finale? You can't outdo him."

"That has no bearing on what we do. We're not staging an opera. Besides, I'm against the idea of using Shostakovich's music. Also, if you take three minutes of music, there will be no end of trouble over copyright issues. It would be far better to commission some up-and-coming young composer."

They argued for a long time over the finale. Right up until the moment when they had to submit the play, they couldn't agree on an ending. Their creative kinship had never been put to such a test before. Ultimately, they had to call upon the artistic director to make the final decision. And Nora's idea for a finale, with butterflies, won out. Tengiz accepted it, after much resistance. From a two-story structure—at Nora's insistence—the convicts emerge, into real water poured into flat zinc troughs. They wend their way down to the shore, all linked together by hairy black threads from the legs of the invisible spider, and, like black dirigibles, four cigar-shaped figures shrouded in black hang in the air from above.

The people look up, craning their necks, to see an enormous, iridescent black metal spider with a gleaming cross in the middle of its belly

364

and dangling bent legs, each with three claws on the end. Everyone freezes, attending to some faint, modulating sounds. One of the figures begins to crack. The sound grows louder. Out of the crack flits an enormous white butterfly . . . And another . . . A flute begins to play a tentative Eastern melody . . .

They stayed in Budapest for three months. The technical side of the play proved to be difficult. Tengiz rehearsed with a translator, pretty Tanya, the Russian wife of a Hungarian journalist. They ate together in a café during the breaks. Nora was jealous but refused to show it. From morning till night, she was in the workshops, making miracles. The head of the set construction department came to hate her. Old, conceited, hailing from some aristocratic family or other, not used to being prevailed upon like an inexperienced novice—first she needed this, then she needed that . . . But after the opening night, he went up to Nora and kissed her hand. Success. A great success.

Tengiz also went up to her afterward and told her to stop being an idiot: "You can't fool fate." And everything returned to the way it had been. In mid-December, they went back to Moscow. Nora didn't make up the bed in Yurik's room anymore.

He decided to spend the New Year—the year 2000—with Nora. The Second Chechen War was in full swing. The siege of Grozny began on December 26. Nora had not been able to get through to Yurik on the phone for three months. Tom kept telling her Yurik wasn't home. She got the impression that he didn't live there anymore. Martha, whom she called about once a week, had heard no word from Yurik, either.

Nora and Tengiz spent the New Year with a boisterous group of actors. The Vlasovs, who had never really recovered from their son Fedya's death—they carried their sorrow inside of them—were there as well. Every time Natasha Vlasov saw Nora, she seized the opportunity to whisper in her ear: "Don't let Yurik come back. I beg you, don't bring Yurik back here."

In the beginning, everyone made merry. Then the merriment gave way to political prognostication. Yeltsin, sitting in front of the Christmas tree, announced he was retiring. They argued about whether that was bad or good. They argued about when the war in Chechnya might end, and whether a war in Georgia would begin. They argued about whether the twenty-first century had already begun, or whether they had to hold out for another year. The new millennium had begun, but no one expected any good to come of it.

37

Uzun-Syrt–Stalingrad Tractor Plant

(1925–1933)

The boy forgot everything. The sea's elemental might, the ruins of the ancient Genoese fortress, the unprecedented taste of fruit and the shish kebab he would love for the rest of his life, the cypress trees, *cheburek* mutton pies, Tatars, Greeks, boats, horse carts—all of it paled in comparison with the vision of gliders floating above the long mountain of Uzun-Syrt in Koktebel. They didn't take Genrikh to see the gliders, however. Instead, they went to visit someone named Max. They all sat in a big room around a fat, bearded old man wearing a white sheet, his head bound up with a rope. They had a long, incomprehensible conversation. Another old man, gaunt, with a large nose, spoke about psychoanalysis, and the first fellow, the fat one, remained silent, sometimes nodding his head and smiling. Genrikh grew faint with impatience, because he had noticed the wonderful flying machines when they were entering the village, and now he wanted only one thing—to run as fast as his legs would carry him to the mountain that released them into the atmosphere. He tugged on the hem of Marusya's skirt, grabbed her by the hand, and, finally, crumpling over and wrinkling his face up like a little monkey, broke into silent sobs. Marusya stood up, excused herself, and, taking him by the hand, followed behind him.

Genrikh, letting go of her hand, almost rolled down the stairs and rushed toward the mountain from which the flying machines seemed to be taking off. Marusya ran after him, shouting for him to stop, but he couldn't hear her. He very soon tired, and slowed his pace. Marusya caught up to him and walked beside him, not saying a word. As a Froebel Miss, a specialist in childhood education, she felt herself to be a pedagogical failure. She had no choice but to follow after her son, however, without stopping. She understood that she shouldn't say anything at the moment—she was too annoyed and upset. Genrikh had spoiled the visit she had so long dreamed about.

Max Voloshin was one of those who a decade earlier—in another lifetime, which had passed away leaving barely a trace—had written with enthusiasm about Rabenek, about the studio of movement in which Marusya's curtailed career as a "barefoot dancer" had begun. Marusya very much wanted to turn the conversation back to those times, to allude to her own involvement in that refined art form. Instead of having the conversation she knew she would happily recall for the rest of her life, she found herself scrambling up a mountain to God knew where, chasing after her unruly and troublesome—yes, troublesome!—child, to see gliders.

It turned out to be quite far away. Marusya suggested that they return to the mountain the next day, early in the morning, but Genrikh did not intend to give up. He was consumed with excitement.

Yes, Jacob was right, a thousand times over, when he said, watching the repulsive tantrums accompanied by screaming, kicking, and thrashing about on the floor, which Genrikh had indulged in regularly since about the age of four: "Marusya, this isn't epilepsy, it's something completely different. It is a conflict between will and reality. He has an intense desire to realize some childish nonsense that we are preventing. When he is faced with a real problem or task, this energy will be invested in overcoming actual problems. Sublimation is a magnificent thing."

In their family, this word was repeated often.

It was very hot. The dusty, stony road was burning hot. She was so thirsty that even the back of her throat was dry. Marusya's head felt light, as though she might fall into a faint at any moment. But she couldn't allow herself that weakness, or luxury, and she steeled herself against it. Her son, limping a bit in stiff sandals that had rubbed his feet raw, walked on ahead, decisive and single-minded.

No one was waiting for them on the mountaintop, but there were a few dozen people there. They were all stroking and probing the glider, as a veterinarian does with a large animal. Genrikh melted into the crowd immediately. Though no one chased him away, they didn't pay any attention to him, either. A few other boys were hovering around, too. Marusya stepped gingerly around the dry wormwood bushes in the shadow of the tarpaulin hangar. A sharp, bitter scent wafted upward: wormwood, sage, thyme . . . She sat down on dry, odorous earth.

Everything swam before her eyes. She didn't lose consciousness, but dropped out of reality for a time. Then she opened her eyes and saw, yawning below her, a serpentine valley, Tatar hamlets clinging to the slopes, grazing goats, cliffs of the Kara Dag Mountain, and a glider, soaring in the clear blue air. And she was happy.

She approached a group of people who were watching the glider's flight and met the eyes of one of them—someone wearing civilian dress, but with a military bearing and the stern expression of an officer, and a mustache in the Caucasian style. She addressed him in an animated, upbeat manner: "Comrade! Could you help us to get back to Koktebel from here? We are so very tired, having climbed all the way up the mountain."

The comrade turned around.

"The flights are all finished for the day. Someone is coming to fetch us in half an hour. If you wait a bit, we can give you a lift."

Genrikh didn't see her. He had wormed his way into a group of local boys and was chattering away with them, waving his arms around with enthusiasm. Half an hour later, snorting and spitting, a dusty truck rolled up. The boys immediately forgot about the glider and crowded around the truck. Marusya pulled her straggling son out of the noisy crowd.

"Do you want to ride in the truck?"

Oh, joy! The plainly dressed military man proffered Marusya his arm, and she jumped lightly into the back. Marusya smiled seductively: "Could you drop us off at Max's?" The man's face broke into a broad smile; he had immediately guessed that the woman was one of their own, a kindred spirit. He was one of their own, too: the grandson of Ivan Aivazovsky, the great Russian artist. But Marusya didn't know this, and would never learn it. He got in next to the driver. About ten people packed into the back of the truck. Genrikh was about to make a scene, demanding to sit in the front seat, too. But here Marusya put her foot down, and calmly summoned up her dormant pedagogical skills. "We can always get out and walk. Is that what you want?" He most certainly did not.

Five days later, Marusya and her son were back in Moscow. Jacob Ossetsky met his family at the station. His reddish, neatly shorn mustache on a clean-shaven face, fresh haircut, proper suit from a former way of life, the bouquet of purple asters in one hand and his briefcase in the other, distinguished him from the rest of the slovenly crowd of welcomers. He had missed his family terribly, but on the whole was satisfied with the time away from them. During a month and a half of loneliness, he had written a handbook on statistics for communications workers and two articles for economics journals, and had begun to write a story about his life in the army, which he struggled to finish.

Marusya, wearing an elegant broad-brimmed hat and a linen dress with Ukrainian embroidery around the collar, appeared on the steps of the train. Wriggling out from under her hand, which had reached for a railing to steady her descent, a swarthy-looking Genrikh jumped down onto the platform first, swiveling his head with his newly long curls. When he saw his father, he made a rush for him, shouting: "Papa! We saw the gliders! Papa! I'm going to be a glider pilot when I grow up! Papa! Have you ever flown in a glider?"

Not wanting to put a damper on his enthusiasm, his father said that it was more complicated than he thought. It required not only physical training, but the knowledge of many subjects: physics, geography, meteorology . . . even foreign languages, because the first glider pilots were foreigners—Chinese and Arabs in ancient times, and, in the modern world, Germans and Frenchmen. And there were many articles he would have to read. And a lot to learn.

"For example, did you know that today, of all days, the pilot Gromov is trying to make the first flight from Peking to Tokyo? How many kilometers do you think he will fly?"

"A thousand!" Genrikh shouted.

"You're off by half. Two thousand," his father said. "I'll bring you today's paper, and we'll read about it. You can read it yourself."

Marusya stood behind her son, who was dangling around his father. Jacob smiled, nodded at her, and even winked slightly. After he had gently loosened Genrikh's grip, he embraced Marusya and whispered in her ear: "Silly girl, my sweet silly girl I love so much!"

He grabbed the suitcase and the portable bedding, and they proceeded to the square, where Jacob had hired a horse cab. Genrikh whined that he wanted to go in a motorized taxi, but there were none to be seen. He pouted, stamping his foot on the ground and digging in his heels, but his father scooped him up, lifting him slightly off the ground, then dropped him down again, saying, "Next time!"

During those years, the entire country was in the grip of an aviation craze. This was a reflection of government policy—overnight industrialization, and collectivization just around the corner—and swept the country like a storm. The best engineers and designers worked in powerful research labs and institutes, creating new models of airborne vehicles of all kinds. A paramilitary organization for the masses (the Society for Promotion of the Defense, Aviation, and Chemical Development of the USSR) was established, and later reorganized several times. Technology centers for children and youths opened all over the country, along with many model-airplane clubs. From nine years of age, like a little speck of dust, Genrikh was swept up in this current of mass enthusiasm. The boy succumbed to this wholesale mania for aviation, and, like a glider pilot, floated in its midst. This moment marked the fundamental renunciation of his search for an individual, personal path, which had been so important to his parents. For the first time, he felt the happiness of blending into the masses, of feeling at one with the surrounding world.

His former favorite toys—building blocks and construction sets, the results of the joint project between Nadezhda Krupskaya and Marusya, which had not borne fruit—now only irritated Genrikh. But, of course, the whole world was flying through the air, cutting turns and spirals and sideways twists, and he was still playing with children's toys. He dived headfirst into the mass hobby of model-airplane making, waiting for the time when he would be big enough to get behind the controls of a real flying machine. And, even better, the controls of a machine gun! To fly and to shoot—those were his two big dreams. The favorite dreams of an entire generation.

Jacob made great efforts to push his son's interests in a cultural direction. He lectured him on the first dreams of flying—from Icarus to Leonardo's inventions. He gave him books by Jules Verne to read, because balloon flights and trips to the moon also spoke to Genrikh's imagination. The boy began to get good grades in school, at least in the subjects that had something to do with his chosen profession. Jacob taught him German, and the boy didn't seem to mind too much.

Alas, his father couldn't impart to his son what he so stubbornly resisted—Genrikh was completely indifferent to the world culture that Jacob so admired and valued. Still, Jacob taught his son how to work in libraries, how to use the card catalogue to find the information he needed, and to discriminate between what was useful to him and what was superfluous.

By the age of fifteen, Genrikh had become fully defined as a person. He had outlived his interest in gliders and model airplanes, and had joined, and then quit, a parachuting club. Now he had his heart set not on a career as a pilot, but on the serious profession of engineering in the field of airplane construction. He was one of many thousands of such young enthusiasts.

Meanwhile, Jacob had been making a successful career in the VSNKh, the Supreme Council for National Economy. The problem of finding an apartment was resolved from the very beginning—the marvelous room on Povarskaya was a remarkable acquisition during the housing crisis of those years. They had bought a bookcase, a desk, and, finally, a piano—an old-fashioned upright with a wonderful sound—the last instrument in Jacob's life that he truly owned. In a very few years, he made a name for himself in the world of economists, scientists, and scholars, gave lectures, wrote articles, and changed jobs several times, in search of himself. He published the book he had written, *The Logic of Management*, which contained many penetrating and inopportune ideas and thoughts.

Marusya, who understood very little about sophisticated sciences, somehow sensed, with a woman's intuition, the danger the book posed for their lives. Jacob was oblivious to this. He was in charge of the Department of Statistics at the VSNKh, developing what seemed to be unprecedented subjects and fields—industrial geography and culture. He wrote descriptions of all the enterprises in the regions, their histories, their economic characteristics. In fact, this particular branch of economic geography had been all but forgotten for two centuries, since the time of Lomonosov. Jacob, describing and annotating already defunct manufactures, compared them with new enterprises with future prospects, scientifically developed and adapted to the ways of life in a small region, taking account of the specificities of geography and the local population. To give Marusya her due, her intuitions and her sense of unease about Jacob's interests did not mislead her; the entire country of the Soviets was walking in step, but he had strayed off somewhere into the sidelines.

By the spring of 1928, the Shakhty case was under way. More than fifty people who worked in the mines in the Donbass region and the Head Mining Directorate of the VSNKh were accused of "wrecking" or sabotage, and then of espionage. The trial lasted for less than two months. Of those accused, thirty confessed to the crime, and five of these were executed. Jacob knew one of those executed, from Kharkov, and couldn't believe he was guilty of such a crime.

Another event occurred at the time, in their own family. Jacob's father, who was working as a manager of the milling company that had once belonged to him, was arrested in Kiev. Although it had not yet been announced, this was the end of the NEP period.* Jacob considered this to be a precursor of economic catastrophe.

In the summer of 1928, at the plenary session of the Central Committee of the Communist Party of the Soviet Union, Stalin announced: "The greater our progress toward socialism, the more the class struggle will intensify." This pronouncement sounded like a theoretical construct, but Jacob, a Marxist, who had read the works of the writer not in translations for underground study circles for the proletariat, but in the original German, and already in his youth, had a low opinion of Stalin as a theoretician, although he acknowledged his skill as a politician. He also understood Stalin's words as a warning to the entire caste of the technical intelligentsia, who, despite pressure, were unable to carry out industrialization within the time stipulated by the official directives of the Party management.

Jacob was torn apart by conflicting thoughts. He lost sleep composing (in his mind) a letter to the Leader in which he tried to explain to him the misguidedness of his idea about the "intensification of the class struggle." It might, of course, intensify; only not in the broad expanses of the homeland, where the proletariat had won out, but precisely in the capitalist world, which had not yet matured to the point of accepting the idea of worldwide proletarian revolution. The Russian technical intelligentsia, on the contrary, was investing all its energies into building . . . and so forth. The other idea that kept him up at night was—escape. Escape from the field of economic statistics, which had become a dangerous science, and taking refuge in music. Why not? A teacher of music literature, music theory, director of a choir, private piano lessons, flute, clarinet . . . Wasn't that a dream worth having? Wouldn't that offer safety to him personally and to the whole family?

The attack on the technical intelligentsia, the search for wreckers and spies, was proceeding full speed ahead—and Jacob was too late. While he was analyzing the situation at hand, the next trial was already getting under way: the Industrial Party Trial.† Becoming acquainted with the trial transcripts, Jacob realized his own existence was in jeopardy.

---

* The New Economic Policy (NEP) was an economic policy adopted in Soviet Russia in 1921–28 with the goal of salvaging the national economy after the Russian Civil War of 1917–22.
† The Industrial Party ('Prompartija') Trial was the first of many show trials, culminating in Stalin's Great Terror of 1937, in which prominent members of the bourgeois intel-

Professor Ramzin, who was one of the defendants in the case, offered testimony that guaranteed corporal punishment to himself and his co-defendants, leading specialists in the State Planning Committee and the VSNKh. Although the execution was commuted to a prison sentence, Jacob realized he was still in danger. He would be next.

Wrecking was discovered in the economy, in mining, in forestry, in microbiology—everywhere. In 1930–31, the Special Council of the OGPU—the secret police—reviewed more than thirty-five thousand cases. One of those was the case of Jacob Ossetsky. He defended himself in a rather florid, elegant style; though he did not admit to wrecking, he repented of some of his mistakes. He was sentenced to three years of exile, serving in the Stalingrad Tractor Plant.

At the beginning of 1931, he arrived at his place of exile, and began to work in the STP planning department. This was better than any outcome he could have envisioned.

In the first letter he sent his wife from Stalingrad, Jacob reminded her that his first detention took place in 1913 in the Chelyabinsk guardhouse, and lasted fifteen days, which he now remembered as a happy period in his life. He asked her to keep her spirits up, not to languish, and to be strong for the sake of their son.

But things grew ever more complicated with their son. When Genrikh found out about his father's arrest—they had taken him from work, and informed Marusya twenty-four hours later—fifteen-year-old Genrikh, who had returned in the evening from his aviation club, listened to what his mother told him, turned pale, and slumped over. His jaw tight and his mouth compressed, he sighed deeply and said quietly, "A wrecker. I knew it."

He swept from the table all the teacups that had been sitting there since breakfast. He went to his father's desk, where there were two neatly stacked piles of books and two piles of paper, one blank and one covered with neat handwriting, and threw them off, too. After that, he went to the bookshelves and started to fling all the books, which had been carefully arranged by subject, onto the floor, shouting at the top of his lungs the word that was uppermost in his mind: "Wrecker! Wrecker!"

Marusya sat in the armchair, pressing her hands to her ears and squeezing

---

ligentsia, among others, and later Party officials themselves, were accused on trumped-up charges of sabotage and treason against the Soviet state. Many of the accused, though innocent, pleaded guilty.

her eyes shut. This was a genuine paroxysm of rage, and she had no idea how to stop it. When he had thrown to the floor every object he could lay his hands on, Genrikh collapsed onto the divan and began to howl. Several minutes passed. Marusya sat beside her son, and stroked his shoulders.

"Leave me alone! Leave me alone! You don't understand what this means. I'll never be admitted anywhere now! I'm the son of an enemy of the people! For always!"

His tears flowed thick and fast; his shoulders heaved. He thrashed around and kicked his legs and arms, just as he had done in childhood. Marusya did what she had always done—she went to the buffet and took a piece of chocolate from a bag she had hidden there, unwrapped it, and popped it into his mouth. He didn't spit it out, but didn't calm down, either. After thrashing and heaving for a long time, he fell asleep in his father's bed.

What has he done, what has he done? Marusya cried soundlessly. He's ruined everything! What will become of us?

38

First Exile
Stalingrad Tractor Plant
(1931–1933)

Jacob, it was likely, bore up under the misfortune that had struck him better than his family did. He knew how to begin again from scratch, but he took his entire previous life, his various interests and initiatives, with him into his new existence. Twelve large cities were now closed to him. He was transferred by omnipotent powers to the city on the Volga, where an enormous plant was being built according to an American design. He was appointed to work in the planning department. Though this wasn't particularly interesting to him, his knowledge of English improved his position. Within a week, he had received a tiny room in the director's office, where he translated American technical documentation. Two dozen girls hastily trained in the English language were not able to cope with the technical terminology. Jacob himself sometimes had to consult his American colleagues, of whom there were still quite a few in 1931.

Jacob liked the Americans. They were, for the most part, athletic fellows who dressed neatly and elegantly, and worked with gusto. In addition to the organization of production, their free time was also organized in a particular way—they had separate dining rooms, a restaurant, clubs, concerts for employees, and day care for the children. "As regards social achievements, the capitalists are ahead of us," Jacob was forced to admit. Or was all of this specially staged for propaganda purposes? One got the impression that their scientific organization of labor extended to social life and the life of the community as well.

Jacob was not the only one who observed these things. Soon he became acquainted with other exiles, working in different branches of general construction, specialists like him who had been sent to the STP for political mistakes and an erroneous worldview. All of them were more or less Marxists, more or less socialists, more or less communists, but their thinking was out of step, and the divergences in their opinions and views led to interesting discussions about nuances and details. They initially met just by chance, but later began to go out of their way to gather over tea. Within a few months, their meetings had turned into informal seminars at which they presented papers and read lectures. They exchanged opinions, feeling in no way guilty about it.

In November 1931, Jacob's son came to visit him. In the time during which they had not seen each other, Genrikh had grown half a head taller, his shoulders had become broader, and he had become a young man instead of an adolescent. Marusya did not come—she was burdened with work, ill health, a bad mood. They had a lively correspondence, according to an established scheme: they wrote letters every five days, beginning from the first day of the month, but no fewer than six letters a month; plus postcards, which didn't count, and, if necessary, telegrams.

Genrikh rarely wrote to his father.

Jacob received official permission to show his son the plant, and on one of the first days of Genrikh's stay, he took him around. The first thing Jacob did was to show Genrikh the American blueprint for the plant and explain the most unique aspect of it: it was conceived as a modular structure. Genrikh was thrilled. It was like his construction set! He recognized the similarity to his first toy, which had afforded him so much creative joy in his childhood. This entire plant was built as though some giant were putting it together out of blocks, only the blocks were much larger and more varied than the ones in his construction set. Jacob showed him on the scale model how the individual blocks were joined together, and how the same blocks could result in various structures. Genrikh observed the model, enchanted, a thought brewing in his head. Jacob enjoyed watching the eagerness in his son's eyes and the thought processes that the muscles of his face betrayed.

"Dad, it seems like each block is a letter, and when you put them together they form words, and even whole sentences?"

"That's a good way of looking at it, son," Jacob said happily.

Genrikh nodded solemnly—it wasn't often that his father praised him—and continued to think out loud. "I think that the whole world can be rebuilt out of letters just like this—now, that would be a real construction set!"

Jacob looked at his son attentively: there was certainly the germ of a serious thought in there, but in essence it was completely infantile. He needed a lot of polishing, a lot of polishing.

STALINGRAD–MOSCOW
JACOB TO GENRIKH
(LETTER TO GENRIKH PRIOR TO HIS VISIT IN
NOVEMBER)

MARCH 1931

Dear Genrikh, I met a person here that it would be good for you to get to know. You can't imagine all the professions that are represented in our factory. Altogether, there are 170! Would you imagine, for example, that there is a toy specialist? It turns out there is. A master craftsman who makes scale models for our museum. A superb worker who knows how to do metalworking, woodworking, as well as working with cardboard—everything that's needed. He is a joiner, a metalworker, an electrician, and a bookbinder. A master of all trades. His workshop is also like a play workshop—a little twenty-square-foot storeroom under the stairs. He has a tiny workbench, and his materials are stored on shelves suspended from the ceiling. He speaks quietly, thoughtfully. It's pleasant to have dealings with him. He always works alone, in silence.

I am now preparing a big exhibit on the tractor industry. When I'm finished, I'll send you pictures. Mama writes that it's very clean and tidy in your room. That makes it much easier to live.

I thought about writing a story about a family who lived in a very crowded and disorderly space. Everyone bickered and squabbled, and couldn't get on together. Then, gradually, they all picked up their rooms, introduced order into their lives, and began to live more peaceably. When I have some free time, I may write on this subject. Do you approve?

I send you a strong handshake.

Your dad, Jacob

NOVEMBER 8, 1931

Dearest Mama,

I've been here with Papa for two days now. When I arrived in Stalingrad, Papa wasn't at the station, so I went looking for him and got on the train to the tractor plant. On the train, I asked every person if they knew where Ossetsky lived, until I ran into Mstislavsky. Of course he said "No. 516." That's all I needed. When I got off the train, there was a very fine bus waiting there, and I was easily able to find No. 516, but it was locked. Papa wasn't home. Not getting discouraged, I took off my coat and my bag, left my belongings with the neighbors, and went to see the Volga. When I got back, my papa was at home, and he didn't even recognize me.

The next day, on the 7th, I went on a boat for the whole day with Papa, and in the evening we watched people dance the fox-trot (it's like they're just dawdling, not dancing). From my first visit there, I've really liked the American dining room. Yesterday Papa read some German (the *Nibelungenlied*). I like Papa's comrades, but not the Americans (they fight a lot).

With aviation-tractor greetings! A kiss, Genrikh

JACOB TO MARUSYA

NOVEMBER 10, 1931

Dearest friend, I'm late sending this to you by three days. Forgive me! I've been busy with Genrikh, and with the Great October Revolution holiday celebrations. He has grown—he's half a head taller than he was when I left him.

As for his general development, he hasn't made a lot of progress. Every day, I teach him a bit of German. From the very first days, I noticed he was no more diligent than he used to be.

His visit has been like a great holiday for me, but I must tell you frankly that a visit from you would be an even greater holiday. I'm concerned about his development. You must make an effort to counter his interests with others that are broader and deeper. He is too technically oriented, one-sided. After his aviation craze, his new obsession is military affairs and technology. When we were taking a walk in the mountains, he said, "This would be a good place for artillery." This is so unpleasant to my ears. He should stop attending that club for amateur snipers and gunners.

His studies seem to be going well, judging by his knowledge of trigonometry, which I checked. His knowledge of grammar is poor, and comes only as a result of much reading. We must encourage his literary interests. His innate taste and sensitivity to style will help.

Try to interest him in things that are far from him—an easy book on Darwinism, history, and so forth. The things we read at his age. I'm compiling a special reading list for him, if you approve of the idea. I'll look for the books in the catalogue here.

I'm reading Genrikh the *Nibelungenlied* in German. I found a place that you had underlined—"Love and suffering always go together."

I give you a kiss—a friendly, and even friendlier, one.

With all the passion of nighttime combat in which both come out victors.

FEBRUARY 8, 1932

My dear Marusya, I've fallen out of our regular rhythm of correspondence, because I can't meet the quota of evening studies. On February 10, I have to submit all expedited work, and I'll begin the cycle anew. And I'll keep up my end of our correspondence. Another significant date—the one-year anniversary of my tenure here. I've taken a liking to this work. The entire tractor project is American, and the first tractor is also being manufactured according to a successful American model.

For the time being, I think it will make you happy that I have received a prize as a model worker. Unfortunately, the reward did not take the form of a special ID, as I would have preferred, but a monetary prize. I don't know how much. I bought you galoshes, the smallest size, as you requested. If they don't fit, you have only yourself to blame. Tell me Genrikh's size—7 or 8? I'll soon be able to buy them. In addition, I was issued a premium bond for seventy rubles. We'll survive. And my lectures have been temporarily suspended. A pity. It kept me in shape to prepare every week. There are several top-notch economists here I like to socialize with. It's a narrow circle; we get together and discuss this and that.

The package is ready to be sent out to you. It will go out the day after tomorrow.

I kiss you, little one.

MARCH 10, 1932

My dearest Genrikh, it's hard for me to express my joy at your progress. You have achieved everything you wanted to, without any outside help. In fact, no one would have been able to help you in this. The Americans admire, above all, people who organize their own lives, on their own terms. They even have a term for this: a "self-made man."

If you want to, you can manage to organize your life in order to achieve what you wish. There are four areas of activity that should take priority for you: your technical studies, physical training, literature, and helping your mother. She wrote to me about your visit to the airport. It's too bad I couldn't have gone with you. I would have liked to hear your explanations. We haven't seen each other since last year, and now I can't even imagine when we'll see each other again. Let's hope and believe it will be soon.

I applaud your decision to leave school to study in the Workers' University. This is the action of a real man. If you get accepted for the subway construction project, it will provide you with a very good education. What profession are you considering now? Write me about all your new experiences and impressions, about your activities, about your new comrades. Where is the Workers' University, and how do you get there every day? I hope you have a book to read while you're en route. Always keep a book handy, so you won't waste time—a book you only read when you're en route.

I give you a firm handshake—your Jacob.

JACOB TO MARUSYA

OCTOBER 24, 1932

Well, Marusya, things are really looking up. At the moment, the money situation is good; and prospects for the future are also good. Yesterday I was very happy. Our first poster went to print. It's very impressive. Things are moving apace now. I am responsible for all the publishing work—it's far better than being in the planning department.

Today is a holiday. In the morning, I took an hour or two for my weekly general hygiene: washing in hot water, shaving, washing my hair, breakfast. An hour and a half to finish everything.

At ten, I'm already at my desk. The day is clear and sunny, but I'm under surprise attack. I have to edit a huge pile of manuscripts by the end of the day. Now, after four hours of work, I have two hours to catch my breath, take a walk, read the paper—then back I go.

The radio has been playing all day, but it doesn't prevent me from working. They played the waltz from *Eugene Onegin*, and I got up and danced around the room. Back and forth, from one side of the room to the other. Then I smoked a cigarette and sat down at the desk again to work.

By November 1, I will have written a chronicle of events, and I'll work on an exhibit the whole next month. I like this cooperation with American consultants. We have a lot to learn from them in the area of production organization. But I'll be freed up after November. I'm lagging behind in my reading these days—I want to read literature, economics, mathematics, and other things. Interacting with colleagues is terribly interesting. People of my status.

What about your article on Gogol, and why was he being commemorated? Was it an anniversary of some sort?

I want to emphasize again that you don't have to be a staff member— independent literary work is sufficient. Vigilyansky doesn't have a regular position. Try to get admitted to the Writers' Union, get involved with the activities of the House of Printing. They have a wonderful library there, where you can even borrow books to take home, and they have a good dining hall.

Marusya, I beg you to buy and send me a *Handbook of Labor in the USSR*. You will most likely find it in the store at the Communist Academy, which used to be located on Mokhovaya, opposite the university.

I kiss you, my dearest one. Soon I'll be sending you some extra money, so that you may eat well. J.

FEBRUARY 7, 1933

Two years have gone by, and it is eight months since the last time I saw you. Your visit, despite all the joy it brought me, left me with a feeling of sadness and bitterness. There is a crack, a fissure between us that seems to be growing wider. Only one thing will heal this fissure: you must come here again! For a week, for three days, for three hours. It is so important: looking at each other, touching each other . . . Marusya, a marriage will not survive on postage stamps alone. Come! I'm not only summoning you because I long for my beloved wife and girlfriend. Every life has some sort of foundation on which it stands, grows, from which it feeds. You are my soil, my foundation. But there is a sense of alienation emanating from your letters. And mere letters will not allow us to overcome this alienation. Sometimes I get the feeling that you either read only superficially the long letters I write, or you don't read them at all. Our correspondence is becoming chaotic, and keeps missing the mark.

Marusya, my love! Please come to me!

APRIL 18, 1933

My next postal money transfer will be delayed by several days. The book is nearing the end, but I can't seem to finish it. Don't be alarmed about my authorship: the book is truly a collective publication. I wrote to the publisher to make sure that the actual part of the work of each author was stipulated for each under collective conditions. I have learned something through this work. Several useful technical conventions have taken shape, and many new themes have suggested themselves, so work has played a big role. It can't come out under my own name, of course, and perhaps I don't even want that. One should write in solitude, not as part of a crowd. But the collective is on very amiable terms. There are several people with whom a serious discussion is possible. I hope that the publisher pays as they have promised to. I await with certainty good news from you. I kiss you, my friend. J.

APRIL 20, 1933

Your constant refrain—that the GTO physical-culture badge ("Readiness for Labor and Defense") carries weight, and we can't do without it—makes me wary. If you think carefully about it, this preoccupation with physical culture is really a replacement for culture, a substitute. You know that I have exercised and practiced gymnastics my whole life, and I believe that one must stay in good physical condition if one is to live a full life; but it isn't valuable in itself. Thinking this way is understandable in an adolescent, but you could analyze the situation more deeply: why are efforts made to promote mass physical culture instead of intellectual culture?

I often read in your letters: "Why am I going through all this? I'm a proletarian," etc. I can't write you about this in detail—we need to have a long talk about it—but this phrase is absolutely meaningless. Think about it. The question is much deeper and more serious . . . You need another label for your unhappiness. Neither you nor I belong to the proletariat. We come from the professional class, the class of master craftsmen—this is not our achievement, nor is it our fault. Of course, if you want to represent yourself as a proletarian, that is your prerogative. But you are an actress, an artist, a bohemian of sorts, an intellectual—and there is more truth in this than there is in your desire to be a proletarian. Nadezhda Krupskaya is not a proletarian, either. Teachers and specialists are crucially necessary to the government, and the proletariat can't move forward without specialists. But I love you, Marusya, despite whatever social portrait you choose for yourself. With what joy I would speak to you on this subject, hour upon hour. I kiss you, my dearest little friend. J.

SEPTEMBER 1, 1933

Dear friend, it's a pity you didn't accept the job offer at the toy magazine. You're making a mistake. It's applied, not pure, journalism. Whether you stayed involved in production would depend on you alone. Moreover, you would have a lot of free time there. You would be able to read and write. Working at some newspaper would be journalism without a particular subject; but a magazine with a very narrow application would be very much in keeping with your principles. Think about it, and weigh all the pros and cons again in your mind. I'm certain you're making a mistake. But the main thing is that you need time for thinking and reading. Otherwise, nothing will come of it. Writing insignificant, random articles doesn't add up to real authorship. If you work at a magazine, you'll be expected to do something bigger—a series of stories or a book.

A small circle of like-minded people, with broad interests, has taken shape here. Two more new comrades, besides Lavretsky and Dementiev, have joined. At our last meeting we discussed Mikhail Zoshchenko, and there was a doctor with some very interesting ideas about aging as loss. Our gatherings continue; we present papers, and occasionally small communiqués. It livens up our routine existence.

SEPTEMBER 25, 1933

Dear Marusya, things are close to completion. There is just a bit of time to wait. About myself I can say the same things I said in previous letters. I finished my work on the museum. I translated tons of technical literature, and I can truly say that I have become highly qualified. The collection of articles about labor under conditions of modern mechanized production has also been submitted to a publishing house. I am healthy, energetic; I am studying history and mathematics. I practice gymnastics every day, and take a cold sponge bath. Between studies, I listen to marvelous ancient

Cossack songs. My thoughts circle around folklore—it is an extremely undervalued source, and it contains great riches. No one studies it now! But it needs to be systematically studied and recorded.

All my anxiety concerns you and Genrikh. As soon as I return, I will immediately appeal to secure a reversal of my case. I would be disinclined to do this, but for Genrikh's sake I'll make the rounds of all those organizations. I hope the relatives won't deprive you of support. As soon as I get out, I'll take care of all the debts. I kiss you, sweet dear friends. Your Jacob.

(An unsent letter, expropriated during the search and arrest of Jacob Ossetsky on October 14, 1933.)

OCTOBER 14, 1933

With each month, with each day, the end of my term, and my release, gets nearer. Only twelve weeks remain from my three-year term. I am summing up everything in my mind. I am making plans for the future. I wrote several letters to colleagues, and I have asked them to describe the current situation. I have broadened my skills significantly. I am able to do serious translation work, as well as publishing. My participation in the organization of the STP museum has given me new qualifications. I didn't achieve terribly much during these two and a half years, but I haven't lost any of my former knowledge, either. I've followed all the scholarly journals—Russian, German, and English—that I could find in the library. I couldn't find any in French, but I've been able to keep up the level of my French through those two books by Anatole France that you sent me along with your disappointed critique. I truly long for music, and I haven't lost the hope of finding some work in Moscow connected to music, in addition to my basic professional pursuits.

Dear Marusya! I am full of faith and hope that we can recover that fullness we knew with one another during the time of our marriage. Believe me, I am not given to complaining, but my only source of regret is that I have caused you and Genrikh so much difficulty. On the other hand, thanks to my exile, characteristics have shown themselves in Genrikh that afford me real joy. I never expected such courage, dedication, and self-sacrifice from him. His going to work in the Metro Construction Project is also evidence of the seriousness of his attitude to life. It is already not only a boyish enthusiasm and revolutionary romanticism, familiar to us from our own youth, but a real presence and involvement on the construction site. He is deeper than I imagined him to be two years ago. This is truly the path of intellectual labor of the proletariat: the Workers' University, the technical college, and I'm certain he'll enter an institute with a good engineering program. And your affairs will improve, Marusya, I'm sure of it. Think—only eighty-four days left! And we will live happily ever after, forever and ever!

39

Yurik Comes Home

(EARLY 2000)

Nora recognized the chirping little voice immediately—she could have picked it out of a thousand others. It was Martha. As shapeless as a hayrick, as kind as a St. Bernard, with a voice like a windup toy.

"Nora! So glad I managed to get through to you. Come over as soon as you can. Yurik is on drugs; he's in a terrible state. Vitya and I don't know what to do about him." Martha spoke in English, but Nora understood every word she said.

"Where is he now?"

"In New York. He was here. Just left. He came to get money. He looks awful. It must be heroin or something like that. Hard drugs. Vitya is crying. He told me to call you. Please come as soon as you can!"

Tengiz was drowsing on the couch. He woke up and looked at her in alarm.

Vitya was crying? Unbelievable. Nora immediately dialed the last phone number she had for Yurik. It was Tom Drew's place, where she hadn't been able to reach him. But the stars were so kindly disposed toward her that Yurik had just stopped over at Tom's.

Without asking any diplomatic questions, Nora laid it all out for him: "Yurik, listen to me. Martha called me and told me you're on drugs. Listen carefully. This is what we're going to do. Here, in Moscow, there's a clinic. It's private, a very good one. The doctors are good friends of mine. I've already made arrangements. They'll get you out of this. No withdrawal—you won't have to suffer. You're going to be fine. I'm coming to get you, very soon, as soon as I buy the tickets. I have a visa already. There's just one thing you have to do—be careful. Be very, very careful. Stay strong until I get there. Don't give up. Maybe you should live with your father for the time being? . . . All right, all right, I understand. I'll let you know when I have the ticket. In the meantime, stay in touch with me yourself. Please."

Of course, there was no clinic where she had good doctor friends; but within three days, she had found one.

Nora didn't even ask him whether he wanted to return to Moscow or to escape the trap of addiction. They had never entertained the thought of his return until now. Nora had visited him once a year—she couldn't manage more than that. During her last visit, Marina, with whom she always stayed when she was in New York, had remarked that things seemed to be somewhat amiss with her son—his behavior was erratic, questionable. At that time, Nora had not wanted to hear it. She just shrugged it off, saying, "You just don't know him. He has always been a bit . . . different. Off in his own world." What had she done? She was the one who had sent him there.

Marina just nodded. She didn't try to explain to her friend that she was living in another time, in another country. In America, the rules of the game were different; there were other problems, other perils.

"I'll come with you. All right?" Tengiz said.

"Thank you," Nora said. She was glad.

But they weren't able to fly together. Tengiz made his visa arrangements in Tbilisi, and flew to New York three days later. Nora, as usual, stayed with Marina, who was rattled by all of this. She had long ago realized what was going on.

Marina Chipkovskaya's children, who had all been born in America and didn't speak Russian, were not thrilled about her mother's strange guests from Moscow. Her mother's friends, even the ones who lived here, émigrés, spoke English poorly, were not terribly successful, and generally irritated them. They didn't try to hide this. When she was still a child, her daughter had asked Marina, "Why do Russians have such bad teeth and greasy hair?"

Marina could have answered this question, but she chose to remain silent; there would have been just too much to explain, about how every culture has its own habits: Americans change their T-shirts twice a day and wash every time they come near a shower. But a Russian, from one generation to the next, washed once a week in the bathhouse, on Saturdays, and changed his underwear at the same time. Many of them lived in communal housing, where there was no bathroom at all. And she would also have had to talk about how every shabbily dressed Russian child at their age read as many books in a year as she and her brother were likely to read in a lifetime. And how every decent Russian adult knew as many poems by heart as a professor of philology in this country had ever known.

Marina said none of this to her children, because she wanted them to be 100 percent American, so that the cloying air of the immigrant would disperse as quickly as possible, in the first generation. Those newly arrived from Russia fell into two categories: the ones who taught their children Russian, so that they could read Pushkin and Tolstoy in the original and wouldn't lose touch with Russian culture; and the others, like Marina, who did not. What held true for both groups was that emigration brought enormous losses in social status, and very few were able to achieve the positions they had occupied in their homeland.

Vitya Chebotarev was one of the few who had managed to adjust painlessly to his new country. In Russia he had been an original, a unique talent, with no status whatsoever, and such he remained in America. Moreover, he had been overtaken by luck in the form of Martha, who had taken Varvara Vasilievna's place in running his household, and at the same time had become his truest friend, and later his wife.

In New York, it was some time before Nora could find her son. For two days, Tom answered the phone and told her Yurik wasn't there. On the third day, Yurik called her himself, and went over to Marina's apartment. Nora had prepared herself for the meeting with her son—she had to keep herself in check, not cast blame or reproach, suppress the horror that welled up in her. Yurik looked terrible. He was bedraggled and seemed very, very weary. They hugged. A stench of old clothes, rotting teeth, and death clung to him.

"Tired, old man?" Nora said.

Yurik looked at his mother in surprise. "Yes, that's exactly it. Tired."

"Well, I got here in time, then. We'll discuss everything later; it will all work out. Let's go into the city. We'll grab something to eat and buy our tickets."

"I can't buy a ticket, Mama. I lost my documents. I'm never getting out of here. It's the end for me."

His eyes were so full of despair that Nora felt she was being turned inside out. He understood everything. There was no hiding, and nothing more to hide.

"I didn't come here to bury you. I came to pull you out. But you have to help me—I can't pull it off without your help. Let's do it this way: you forget about yourself for a while, and help me save my son. All right?" Nora spoke quietly, calmly, in a voice that was almost steely, but inside she was howling and keening, being torn to bits.

"Mama, I told you, I don't have any ID. I lost everything—my green card and my driver's license."

So he didn't remember how they had gone last time to the Russian Embassy to get him a new passport. In order to do this, they had had to file a report with the police about the theft of the old one, and to have new photographs made. It hadn't been difficult. In the Russian Embassy, Nora had stood in line, and they submitted the application together. The passport was supposed to be ready within the month. Then Nora flew back home. Six months had passed since then. She realized he didn't remember, but she asked, just in case, "And your Russian passport?"

"My what?"

"We applied for one last time I was here. Did you lose it again?"

"No, I completely forgot about it."

Nora called the embassy. The passport had been ready for a long time, but it was only valid for him to be able to buy tickets to fly back to Moscow. Which was just what they needed.

They went together to pick up the passport. Tengiz was flying in on the same day, and Yurik promised to go with Nora to meet him at the airport. But suddenly he started hurrying nervously, claiming that he had urgent matters to attend to. He asked her for twenty dollars, and promised to come to Marina's in the evening.

Nora met Tengiz and took him to Marina's. The entire rescue operation was not at all to Marina's liking, but their long friendship bound her to the obligation of offering Nora and Tengiz refuge. Yurik didn't call that evening; he called the evening of the following day. When he showed up, he hugged Tengiz, and they ritually clapped each other on the back. And then Yurik immediately hurried off somewhere—on business. He asked his mother for another twenty. Nora gave him the money, realizing he needed it for a "fix." Everyone understood the situation. Nora said that she would buy the tickets the next day, for the following day.

"I'd rather wait a week," Yurik said.

But Nora objected. "No, Yurik. You wrap it up today. I'm buying tickets for the next flight. This is an urgent matter."

The next day, Nora and Tengiz went to buy tickets. They bought a new one for Yurik, but Nora's return ticket was, just by chance, for that very date.

A hundred-dollar fee allowed them to change the date on Tengiz's ticket so he would be on the same flight.

Nora asked Yurik to come over on the evening before the flight. Marina's nerves were so strained that she took the children and went to stay with a friend in Tarrytown. Yurik didn't show up that evening. Nora didn't sleep the whole night. She called Yurik every half hour at what she thought was his apartment—Tom Drew's, that is. Tom first told her that Yurik wasn't there, and then stopped answering the phone. If he knew where to look, he would have tried to find him, but no one knew. Yurik himself might not have known where he was.

To make it to JFK on time, they would have to leave home at four o'clock in the afternoon. Tengiz had hardly slept all night, either. He was gloomy and depressed, and went to take a walk in Central Park. He said he'd be home by two.

Nora stayed behind alone. She had never in her life felt so desperate and helpless. She counted her money—$830. It was clear that they'd have to rebook their existing tickets, because there wasn't enough money to buy new ones. She wondered how much Tengiz had on him. It would hardly be possible for them to buy three new tickets. They could go to the Aeroflot office and try to exchange them. But something stopped her—the faint hope that Yurik would show up in time. She wandered around the empty apartment. She found a bottle of whiskey in the kitchen cupboard, poured herself a shot, and drank it down. Vile stuff. But she immediately felt somewhat better, though not at all relaxed. She looked at the clock: ten in the morning. They still had six hours before they needed to leave the house for the airport.

She lay on the couch in the living room. One wall was covered with Marina's paintings, which had a tinge of the screams and anguish of expressionism. Marina had graduated from the Stroganovsky Institute of Industrial Art, but soon thereafter immigrated to the United States when her career in Russia was just getting under way. She had been one of the most promising students in her graduating class, but things didn't work out for her in America. Immigrants always land on the lowest rung of the social ladder, from which they need to start to work their way up again. Nora closed her eyes. Marina's pictures, which loomed before her, weren't making her feel any better.

Tengiz made his way to Columbus Circle and then into Central Park. He had no idea how enormous it was—this piece of Manhattan, with its granite boulders heaving up from the ground, overhangs, bare trees, snowy expanses, and frozen puddles. It was cold and sunny. The paths were peopled with multitudes of sweaty joggers, some with headphones and some without, bicyclists, and even horseback riders. No, Tengiz did not like America, although the park was wonderful. Something prevented him from taking a shine to it. Maybe, despite all its charms, it was still too big, too simple, too indifferent, this America; and our boy was being stalked by death here . . .

He went down to the big lake. It glittered with a fresh layer of ice. He sat down on a bench and felt as cold as the devil on a church pew. He lit up a cigarette. The bench was in a secluded nook, away from the runners and the walkers. Two black fellows were sitting on another bench not far away, one of them with a guitar. He was strumming quietly. A third fellow joined them—a young white man. It was Yurik. They shook hands, and exchanged something in the process. Holy shit, heroin! Of course, it was heroin. Tengiz was afraid he might scare them, but he couldn't let Yurik get away. So he started to sing. He sang a Georgian folk song at the top of his lungs. Yurik turned around and saw him, and his face lit up. He said goodbye to the others, who melted into the bushes immediately. Tengiz hugged Yurik, and they clapped each other on the back. Without withdrawing his hand from Yurik's shoulder, Tengiz announced joyously, "Let's go home, kid! We've got a plane to catch."

"What do you mean, Tengiz? I thought it was tomorrow."

"Why tomorrow? Tomorrow's today. Besides, what difference does it make? Let's go."

"Hold on, I have to collect my things, my guitar." Yurik tried to wriggle out from under Tengiz's grasp.

"What things, buddy?" Tengiz put on his most winning Georgian accent, the one he used for telling jokes. "What do you need that stuff for? An old guitar? Come on, we'll buy you a new one, and go to the airport."

Buying a new guitar was a dream Yurik had long cherished. He had sold his favorite instrument dirt-cheap several months before to a dealer, and his only other guitar wasn't worth beans. "Let's see. I know of this place with good prices, but it's sort of far away. Let's go to the Guitar Center; maybe we'll find one there."

By two o'clock, Tengiz, Yurik, and the new guitar all arrived at Marina's apartment.

Nora had already called all the ticket offices and agreed with one of the Aeroflot employees to rebook the tickets at the airport. She would pay a fee for these services to one Tamara Alexandrovna, who would meet her at the JFK entrance. How convenient it is to be Russian sometimes, Nora thought. Our bribery network functions the world over. The last vestiges of Nora's anxiety evaporated when she saw her men standing in the doorway. "Oh, Tengiz . . ." was all she managed to say. Yurik sat down in a chair and began to tune the guitar, as if nothing at all had happened.

Before leaving the house, Nora said something that mothers rarely have occasion to say to their sons: "Yurik, you do understand that we're going without heroin, don't you?"

"But I'll go into withdrawal."

"I know. So go to the bathroom and shoot up one last time."

But he shook his head and said he didn't need to yet. He would take his last fix at the airport, just before they took off.

"Are you crazy? What if they catch you?"

"Mama, I know what I'm doing. I have it hidden in my sock. And I'll already be clean when we board the plane."

Nora was the one losing it, not Yurik. Tengiz gripped her by the shoulder and said, "Be quiet."

They were traveling lightly—Nora with a small suitcase, Tengiz with a backpack, and Yurik with the guitar, with which he quietly carried on a conversation. Nora felt they had already made it to the last leg of their journey, but another surprise was waiting for them at the entrance to the airport. The baggage check took place not in the terminal, as she had come to expect, but right at the entrance. There were two policemen with a sniffer dog standing right behind the baggage conveyor belt. The dog wasn't a ferocious German shepherd, but a friendly setter that she immediately wanted to pet.

They stopped.

"Yurik, go outside and throw your junk away, into the first garbage can you find," Nora said quietly.

"I can't. I'll go into withdrawal in two hours if I do. You have no idea what it's like," Yurik said morosely.

"Have you lost your mind? Toss it out," Tengiz ordered sharply, the first time in all these days, and perhaps in their whole life together, that he spoke in such a tone.

Yurik's lips trembled, the corners of his mouth drew downward, and Nora understood that it was not a twenty-five-year-old man standing before her, but a fifteen-year-old boy who was gripped with fear. She hugged him tight, and whispered in his ear, "Don't be afraid. I have a sedative with me that would put an elephant to sleep. If you take it, you won't wake up for nine hours. Come on, throw the stuff away."

"You don't understand—once the withdrawal pains start, there's no way to stop them."

While they were negotiating, the dog fixed his intelligent eyes on his master and growled softly: he needed to relieve himself. The policeman with the dog left. Tengiz placed his things on the conveyor belt. Yurik was reluctant to part with the guitar and didn't want to put it under the X-ray, but he finally did. Nora thought again—fifteen years old, fourteen years old . . . Vitya, Vitya . . . The X-ray didn't reveal anything dangerous, and they walked briskly toward the terminal.

They had a bit of time for a snack, and sat down at a table.

"Well, it's time. Go to the bathroom and take what you've prepared," Nora said. And she thought, It's like a bad dream. Is this really happening to me? Like some B-movie . . .

"You know, I don't think I need to yet. I'll know when it's time. I'm okay for now."

They ate some sort of rubbery salad in a little plastic trough, and some plastic bread, and drank some American coffee that resembled dishwater in a paper cup. Nora recalled how she had liked all of this the first time she visited America. Where have we ended up as a result? This hasty, catastrophic departure from America, and his departure from Moscow to America nine years earlier, suddenly seemed to blend into a single event— damn, it was all her own doing. It's because she was so headstrong, it's because she wanted to take life into her own hands and mold it, organize the process to meet her needs and demands, to stage her own play . . .

A voice announced that their plane was boarding. They entered the plane, and there were no more checks. The plane was enormous and half empty. They sat down in the middle row—Yurik sitting between Tengiz and Nora. The plane took off. Nora, leaning over Yurik, took Tengiz's hand and kissed it. Tengiz didn't take it away, and even held it still for a moment; then he pulled her nose sharply . . . She laughed. A director indeed. He couldn't stand pathos. But she knew that, without Tengiz, she would never have been able to save Yurik.

It seemed to her that the worst was already behind them, and she fell asleep even before the plane finished its ascent.

An hour later, Yurik poked her in the side: "*Now*, Mama." She let him go, and he went to the bathroom. Five minutes later, there was an announcement that they had encountered some turbulence, and they requested passengers to stay seated and to fasten their seat belts again. The plane did begin to rock and shudder. Nora did, too—for her own reasons. Fifteen minutes later, Nora began to feel alarmed that Yurik was taking so long in the bathroom. Ten minutes later, she got up and went to the bathroom, then started to pound on the door, calling: "Yurik! Yurik!"

Silence . . . At that moment, Nora was gripped by panic. She banged on the door. A moment later, she heard him say: "Just a minute . . ."

He emerged, soaking wet from head to toe, as white as a sheet, enormous black eyes staring out—his pupils were so enlarged that there was no blue around them.

"What happened?"

"Nothing. I'm okay. The plane was shaking so hard it knocked the syringe out of my hand and the vein burst. Blood was spurting everywhere. I washed everything, and I had to rinse my clothes. I was covered with blood."

Much later, after a year or two, Yurik told his mother the details of what had happened, which she would otherwise never have known. "My brain had already switched off, and I didn't know what I was doing, Nora. I didn't have just one fix—I had four. I wanted to get good and high. If it hadn't been for that turbulence, I wouldn't have made it to Moscow alive."

He told her many things about his tenure in America, but the primary account of that experience was a thick notebook that he had filled almost completely during his six weeks in a clinic and then put away in his desk. Nora had opened it and wanted to read it, but she couldn't make out a single word. The handwriting was the same childish, uneven, crooked scrawl he had always written. This was part of the therapy: the patient had to disgorge everything he remembered about his past of drug addiction, not only in conversation with the psychologist, but also in written form. He had to reconstruct the whole history of his lethal experience. It was a text that had to be written and then excised from his life. Nora leafed through the notebook and put it back in its place—as part of the family archive.

40

From the Willow Chest–Biysk
Jacob's Letters
(1934–1936)

(En route to Novosibirsk)

APRIL 3, 1934

Dear Marusya! I'm not sure this note will reach you. A good man I met along the way promised to send it. For the last four days and nights, I have been full of the memories of our brief Moscow reunion—after two and a half years! I cannot begin to describe to you the joy it gave me—seeing your lovely but exhausted face—and how it grieved me to feel the estrangement and tension that emanates from you now. I will never forget our meeting in Moscow—I'll remember it till the very last. There was much I could not say to you in front of other people. They arrested and took away six of us, one of whom turned out to be a provocateur—Dr. Efim Goldberg, a convict like the rest. Half a year in a Stalingrad prison, heavy interrogation. The charge was anti-Soviet conspiracy. They accused me of being the most active member of a Trotsky-inspired anti-Soviet gang. This despite my lifelong aversion to Trotsky! I was sentenced to three years in exile by the Special Council—the most lenient sentence possible.

During this half year, I realized how misguided we have been, what kinds of illusions we have cherished. It seems to me I can put my finger on the very places out of which the illusions grew, the places where departures from the truth began. All of us will have to acknowledge what has been, and this realization will be the only thing that remains.

My dearest wife, the mistake in the Bible was that Eve was not made from Adam's rib, but that she was cut out of his heart. I feel this place in my heart physically. I am grateful to fate for you. Please forgive me for all the difficulties I have involuntarily caused the people I most love in the world—you and Genrikh.

Jacob

BIYSK–MOSCOW

JACOB TO MARUSYA

JUNE 19, 1934

My dear, marvelous, TRUEST (as you signed your letter) friend! Today I celebrate, because I received the first letter from all of you (express mail). It is the first letter I am able to read alone, without intermediary readers, in all these months. I'll try to write about everything in as much detail as possible, as you request.

After Moscow, the second half of the journey began. It was terribly sad to leave. My need to be with you had never felt so deep. Along the way to Novosibirsk, I read Gorky, partook of the delicious provisions you brought for me, and at the same time experienced conflicting feelings—sorrow for those I had left behind at the station, pleasure in my state of semi-freedom, the unknown future that beckons, and thirst, an enormous thirst for labor. We arrived in Novosibirsk in the evening. Although I was prepared for it, all the same I felt a strong sense of disappointment and deep sadness: it's like a repeat of Stalingrad, but a worse version of it. The worst thing of all is the dearth of books and cultured people. It was just by chance I had the book by Gorky, which I reread, but I realized I just couldn't read it a third time. During the hour of labor, I made a chessboard and pieces and played a game against myself. My only comfort is eating one piece of chocolate every evening from Eva's box. As they say, sweetness overcomes great sorrow.

I spent eight days in Novosibirsk. Only one interesting thing happened during this time—I met a young engineer, a former Komsomol member. He turned out to be a first-class chess player. I lost five games to him in record time, but there was compensation. For the first time in my life, I played a "blind game"—that is, looking at an empty board, with no pieces, you both call out your moves and write them down. I thought I wouldn't be able to play half the game. Imagine my surprise when it turned out I won! If Genrikh is interested, I can send him the move list with the moves explained.

In Novosibirsk, they gave me a choice of several places to settle, and I randomly picked Biysk. I arrived here at twelve midnight. After going through all the formalities, I walked along the sleeping streets to a hotel, which had received notice of my arrival by telephone from my supervising officer.

Today I'm sitting at work in the Fuel Plant, where I began work by writing a personal letter to you. I'll get three hundred rubles; but instead of distributing bread ration cards, they give you vague promises. Though they do sell commercial bread here, the lines are terribly long; the wait is too long for a solitary individual. I don't consider this work to be real work: it has nothing to do with my basic vision or goal.

Planning. En route from Novosibirsk to Biysk on the train, I thought for a long time about how to regulate my life so that I don't get sidetracked, but establish continuity with my former work in economics. I was a proponent of the idea of monographic research in industry. Now I must apply this idea to the regional economy. It is mandatory that I carry out economic research on "the Biysk region and its economy." In order to do this, I'll have to work in the Regional Planning Office. As soon as I arrived, I went there. I was received well, but the next day it became known that the budget is already exhausted and they can't take on a new person. I was doubly discouraged, since it seemed my primary goal was thwarted. I had to take another job; but not only did I refuse to give up on my plan, I actively started carrying it out. The library and museum are good here. In the Regional Planning Office, we agreed that I would transfer there in a few months. Now all my efforts are directed toward finding a room. There's a little hovel, and if nothing better turns up tomorrow, I'll have to move into it temporarily, because the tourist hostel has eaten up all my finances.

My work on the book is fascinating. I'm already contemplating with pleasure the different parts or phases of the work. I think that it will be unique in economic literature, something between economic research and a feature story or essay.

Biysk is a small town. The Siberian Biya River is cold, and the waters are ample. It is probable that there are few cultured people here. I am expecting solitude and intensive work. There are occasional tourists. I play the piano in the tourist hostel, and remember my entire repertoire. The city is built on a plain. The high Altai Mountains are nearby, which is where the tourists go. But the Biysk region itself is not mountainous—it's flat—and it is not a very rich subject for an economic monograph. However, the scantier the subject matter, the easier it is to expand it in different directions. It must be exhaustive—that is my task. I have about six to eight months to complete it.

Well, those are the details you requested. Also exhaustive, it seems.

Tell Genrikh that I love him just the same as I always have and as I always will, no matter what he does or where he gets accepted, whether he writes to me or not—none of that has the slightest bearing on the deep affection and tenderness I feel for my son, who is also my friend. Let him study wherever he sees fit; he will always be my pride and joy.

Goodbye, my dear friend and wife; be strong and good. The motto of our life is: "The times of unhappiness will pass."

I embrace you, my dear. J.

OCTOBER 12, 1934

My sweet, dear, wondrous wife!

Your letters are arriving regularly—the long one with your description of women's matters, and the postcards—everything has arrived.

(1) How have you prepared for the winter? Why hasn't the glass in the windows been repaired? Have you seen any mice? Why don't you try to get rid of them when I'm not there? When I was there, I managed to drive them out completely—remember, I caught about forty of them, and after that they disappeared. Genrikh has to take my place, in large as well as small matters. I beg him to take over this task for me.

(2) When you happen to mention your past literary commissions, you always speak of them very warmly and positively. But now that they are offering you the possibility of devoting yourself to writing completely, you beat the retreat—"I want to have a profession; that isn't a profession." Incoherent and puzzling. It will give you more leisure time, and more satisfaction. Please, elaborate on your position. And send me some of your writings that are ready for publication, or something that has already appeared in print.

(3) Why did you need to join a Party-history study circle? All you have to do is read a book about it. All these little "rehashing" groups of the Party-history variety are unbearably boring and dreary, and a waste of time. I recommend you stay away from the group; just learn about it on your own if you must.

(4) About my health—you often ask about it. I am as strong and healthy as a longshoreman. I stopped smoking. I exercise in the morning. My hands are clear; the eczema has disappeared once and for all. I never considered it necessary to share all the details with you, but now I find I need to tell the history of my condition. When I was combing my memory, I realized that I had experienced the first symptoms in 1913. I had it treated by the doctor for the first time in 1917 in Kharkov. The disease spread, and I tried very hard to have it cured: X-ray treatment in Kiev; and, in 1924, Asya Smolkina referred me to the National Institute of Physiotherapy, for a course of d'Arsonval's electrotherapy treatment. After that, I consulted neurologists (I was under Dovbnya's care for a time—half a year). Then I had a relapse and was treated by Dr. Nechayev, using hypnosis again—to no avail.

In Stalingrad, I also received treatment, which didn't work. But I found a good skin doctor there who recommended the simplest treatment of all: tar, diluted in a special way. However, the tar stained my papers when it dripped off my fingers. At that time, the cure almost succeeded. For the first three months in prison, I was completely healthy, but then I suffered a relapse, and there was no tar. It grew very bad. But since I arrived in Biysk, the symptoms of my "leprosy" have disappeared. I sleep like a baby. There is no itching. And so, after twenty years of illness and constant treatment, stubborn and unrelenting, I have achieved my goal. I have been cured, in part by the Dovbnya method, and in part by the Zoshchenko method—that is, experimenting on myself. I realized long ago that your very presence is the best medicine for me, that you free me from this illness. And not in a physiological sense, but in a more elevated one!

How long we have lived apart from one another! As it turns out, such a long period of abstention is not only possible, but not terribly difficult. Very occasionally, I lapse into physical unwellness, but usually I am fine. Because I live a rich intellectual life, there is certainly a transfer of energy, and sublimation takes place.

During the past three or four weeks I have read:

Eddington. *Relativity Theory of Protons and Electrons.* A book on physics. I copied out the whole book.
Shklovsky. *Theory of Prose.* I copied the book.
Kataev. *Time, Forward!*
Articles in journals on animal husbandry.
A Course in Animal Breeding. (I gave up.)

A book of poems by Bryusov.
Several issues of the magazine *The Frontiers of Science and
Technology.*

Sasha, Rayechka's husband, sent me the Eddington, for which I am
deeply grateful. It's an astounding book. I devoured it. I don't understand
everything in it, but I have understood enough to be enthralled and excited
by it. It's impossible to paraphrase it, to sum it up. It's also hard to charac-
terize the boldness of the physicists (Einstein, Dirac, et al.), their fearless
thinking.

Shklovsky's book is good in another way. He's also a sharp thinker. And
I don't understand everything he writes about, either. I can't achieve sufficient *"defamiliarization"*! When I met him in person, he didn't strike me
as such a deep thinker. I didn't recognize him for what he is!

I work quite intensively, but even so the days and evenings are not packed
absolutely full, and valuable minutes fall through the cracks.

The stack of books on my desk that I want to read keeps growing. The
books enter my room by the ton, but their residue is nearly as light as air. If
it takes three hours to read a book, to reread it and take copious notes on
it takes another five. It's a finicky, arduous method, but the results are
worth it.

Write me about Genrikh. I don't demand that he write me back (I've
already reconciled myself to the fact that he won't), but tell me how I
should understand it—is it a sincere and principled decision, or just a strategy required by external circumstances? Is he interested in my life? My
letters? What glider accident? What is the goal of these studies, if he does
not plan to become a pilot? Where is he working? What is he reading? Does
he keep a diary? Sometimes I reread the letters he wrote me in the Stalingrad prison.

I embrace you, my sweet friend, with a strong Siberian hug.

J.

NOVEMBER 15, 1934

I'm still thinking about why you took up Gogol. It's not customary to do
that sort of thorough preparation for writing a newspaper article. Have you
not tried to submit this piece to the journal instead? The article must contain some central idea that I have not been able to fathom yet. You must find

it. Maybe this idea would work: Writers die, but their work survives in the coming epochs; it also ages, and dies, and is then resurrected. The Revolution re-envisioned and recarved not only the present, but also the past—all of history, literature, and bygone epochs.

All the extremists from the past were revived and came to life again—the ones who perceived and felt things very intensely. This is why Turgenev and Goncharov receded, whereas Gogol and Dostoevsky seemed to return to us. People began to read and study them more. Their rich and saturated forms spoke to us. The Revolution likes what is hot, what shouts and screams, and it refuses to tolerate what mumbles and prattles, what is lukewarm. Only Tolstoy speaks for all time.

All of this concerns the form. Now, as regards the content:

Gogol's world is the greatest foe of the Revolution: the provincial petite bourgeoisie. What Gogol described is not as cruel as Gorky's town of Okurov; it's just a limitless bog. He gathered up all the most painful phenomena of Russian history, experienced them himself, and held them up to view for the entire Russian people, with astonishing power and insight. He created an image of surprising precision, and at the same time conveyed the hopelessness of his world. What to do about it? Gogol doesn't tell us. The Revolution supplied the answer: destroy it, don't leave a single stone standing. In this way, the theme will become topical.

It's evening. Still, I began rereading *Evenings at a Farm near Dikanka* and completely forgot about my analysis—of course, the main thing about Gogol is his divine use of language.

JACOB TO GENRIKH

NOVEMBER 17, 1934

My dear boy, your letter crossed in the mail with mine—the one in which I took you to task for your silence. Everything in your letter makes me happy. Of course, instead of reading about the November celebrations of the Revolution, I would have preferred to read about you personally—still, it was a fine letter. I would like to note that it's the first letter without a single grammatical error. A big milestone for us both—author and reader alike! You have scaled the grammatical heights and reached the top.

Your choice of a future path, I think, should lie in the direction of a technical school. I still haven't completely understood why you decided to drop out of school if they didn't expel you. The factory apprentice school is certainly out of the question. Tell me in greater detail about your technical school and the Workers' University—send me the curriculum for both of them, if you can. Only by comparing them can you really decide. The technical school is better because it belongs to the Aerohydrodynamic Institute. The Workers' University could suddenly decide to assign you some very narrow specialization, and you'd end up not knowing how to cope with that. The technical school is better, but find out more about it. Tell me how you intend to get accepted there. Who will give you a recommendation? And where is it easier to get admitted?

I bought you a suit and a coat of light summer cloth. I'm trying to find someone who will be able to pass the package on to you.

I have learned how to darn socks and mend sheets and underwear. I want very much for you to learn how to do this, too. When you learn how, you will start to be very careful with things. You won't allow a single large hole to appear, and you'll repair your underwear as soon as it starts to show wear and tear. Let me know how you manage with it.

Do you take cold sponge baths in the morning? I do, every day. And I often do exercises to the radio. I play volleyball when I can . . .

You don't say much about Mama. I know there's been some conflict, if only a small one. You should tell me about it. Who are your friends? Tell me about them, and what their interests are.

I press your hand warmly.

Your J.

JACOB TO MARUSYA

NOVEMBER 25, 1934

You ask about my household affairs. I'll tell you. First, I buy commercial bread, not subsidized. You can buy it here easily now; there's no standing in line. It used to be hard to come by. When there are interruptions in the supply, I have a stash of dried bread that the landlady made. There was such a shortage recently, and I ate dried bread from my sack of provisions for a whole week. When it was almost gone, they opened the bakery. Now I'm building up a supply of dried bread again. Moreover, I was given eight kilos of flour at work, and this will also become part of the emergency supply, in case of shortages. I eat in the House of Workers' Education. The first course costs 60–80 kopecks, and the main dish, with meat, costs 1.50 to 1.80 rubles.

I've been working in the Butter Trust for nearly a month already, and I still haven't received my salary. They promise to give it to me tomorrow. I eat breakfast and lunch at home—bread with the same butter they give me at work. All in all, I eat quite well. I still don't have any electricity. I'm waiting for them to give me my pay.

My room is very warm. I'm sitting here writing you wearing only a shirt. The windows in Biysk are made without any ventilation panes, but I have an air vent in the wall. After an evening of work by the light of the kerosene lamp, the air is very bad. It will be much better with electricity.

In the last issue of *New World*, there is an excellent article about a modern family in Germany. You would relish reading it as much as I did. It addresses all the issues that especially interest you, and the approaches of all the various schools of German educational ideologists are cited here, too. Among them you will find many who share your own views. It will be especially interesting for you to discover these faraway kindred spirits.

The article contains a long bibliography on this issue (in German). Read Kellerman as soon as possible, for advice about further reading.

I will send you this issue. There are many things I could add to what the author has said. The article gave me an interesting idea—to write a book about women's labor in various countries. If you would like to take up this theme, I am ready to offer you my secret co-authorship.

I read your review in *Our Achievements* about the partisan collection. I would like to see a more detailed explication of the book itself. Reviews seldom inspire one to read a book; they often end up as substitutes for a book, and for this reason should be more detailed and exhaustive.

I embrace you, my marvelous friend. J.

JANUARY 30, 1935

Yesterday I received your letter of January 22 about Genrikh's illness. His heredity isn't bad, so his body will be able to cope with it. Our financial situation will improve, and with it his diet. I'll be sending you butter now every month—eight or ten pounds of it. I already sent you two shipments: one on January 16 with ten pounds, and another on the 26th with four. I'm afraid the first shipment might get lost in the mail: it was not registered, and I had to send it without declaring the value. The second will reach you: I sent it registered with a declared value of sixty rubles. If I get a notice that it has been received, I'll send you the next shipment. I have sixty rubles set aside for the next one. As of the beginning of February,

I'm going to be working as the choir director at the social club. I requested two hundred rubles. They apologized, but could only pay me one hundred, saying they would supplement it in some other way. I tentatively agreed. I think I'll be earning what I am worth. In addition to the butter, I can still send you a hundred rubles a month. With this support, I think we will be able to help Genrikh recover very quickly from his illness. Write me and tell me what condition the butter is in when it reaches you. Altai butter is considered to be the best. Tell me what kind you like most—sweet, salty, or clarified.

I already wrote you that nothing came of the English lessons. I was told that whoever had given permission for the classes later withdrew it. But how wonderful it would have been to give a language course in the library!

My monthly budget breaks down like this: Dinner is expensive (three rubles a day). Bread costs one ruble a day, and the rest of the food for one day costs another ruble. Thus, about 150–160 rubles a month go for food. The room is twenty rubles; heating, twenty rubles. The wash, bathhouse, kerosene, and other incidentals come to about thirty rubles a month. It all adds up to 220–230 a month. My salary is supposed to be 350, but in fact it is 310.

Tell me about where you eat, where Genrikh takes his meals, how much lunch costs, what kind of nourishment you are getting.

I've started taking a keen interest in history. I'm reading a wonderful book by Mehring: *The History of Germany*. I regret that I didn't discover this book years ago. I delight in every line. In his analysis of the Middle Ages, the papacy, and Christianity, there is an enormous breadth of generalization.

My incidental reading is four volumes of the tiresome *Jean-Christophe*, the curious French writer Giraudoux (that is who Olesha takes his cues from), Masuccio Salernitano (a contemporary of Boccaccio), and Schopenhauer on the essence of music. Interesting, but somehow fails to elaborate on some very important points.

I work on my story "Man and Things." It's expanding, much to my chagrin. It's already nearly a novella, about forty or fifty pages. The work is going very slowly. I polish word by word, phrase by phrase. Every day I read it ten times over—no, countless times. The plot has already assumed its final shape; now I need to work on the details, the characters, who must be revealed in passing, through precise, incisive traits. The erotic scene came out very well, I thought.

Adieu. When will I finally get word that you have received the butter? I can't wait. J.

You write that my political evolution estranges me from you, that the fissure that has been present all these years is deepening. That is because we cannot have a deep and serious conversation. I await the time when we can converse and be together again, not only in letters but in person. I would be able to allay many of your anxieties. You understood me wrong when I said that there was no sense in attending the Party-history study circle. If you have decided to take up that study, you by all means should. There is nothing wrong with that. There cannot ever be anything wrong in learning new things. The current level of teaching is not up to par, in my opinion. I could be wrong, of course. When you begin to study, write and tell me whether it is interesting.

Forty-five years old is nothing! Now it is already clear that even at sixty-five I will be the same person I am today. With the years, you mature, your capacity for work increases, and, to be honest, you become smarter. We'll live to be at least seventy.

. . . books on literature. Four volumes of Kogan. *The History of Modern Russian Literature.* I took it only because of Bryusov, who has become a beloved poet of mine, but I ended up reading the whole book. I am learning a great deal that I should have learned long ago. Kogan's study is not deep, but extremely packed with material and even ideas that he has evidently borrowed from others.

And Lunacharsky's *On Literature and Art* is lying on the table, waiting its turn. I try to keep myself in check—otherwise, I would have another enormous stack of books about natural history, about physics. Nonetheless, *The History of the Continents* (about geography) is already on my desk, waiting to be read. History will occupy me at least until spring, or maybe even summer. I'm in the Middle Ages, and there is still Russian and modern history to go. I'm in a terrible hurry, as though I don't have much time to live, or as though exams are coming up. And from every book I read, something remains in my notes.

I liked very much the part about the dispute over whether Gorky is a proletarian writer or not. Lunacharsky writes that you can't create a standard of measure for a proletarian writer and apply it to every individual to see whether he fits. Gorky is an enormous phenomenon in literature, and in fact you have to do the opposite: with Gorky as your point of departure, construct your profile of a proletarian writer. It's not standards of measure that create things, but things that give rise to standards of measure.

I once read Andreyev, and Sologub, and Bryusov, and Balmont, and only now, when I'm reading this book, do all the disparate impressions arrange themselves into some coherent system. The system emerged because all of them—the former—are now illuminated by the light that the searchlight of the Revolution throws on them.

Did you receive the letters with the passage by Sterne on the erotic relationship, the description of my morning ablutions, how I am wearing socks with holes in them, with an insert of rough sketches with Greek phrases, a poem by Selvinsky, a tender letter in which I wrote about the aroma of poverty, a long political letter that ended with Goethe's line *"Alles ist gesagt"*? I cannot come up with a system—perhaps I should begin to number the letters again, as we used to do once upon a time?

Let me know which of these names is most fitting for a story:

> The subtitle will be: "A Story of Doing."
> "Man and Things"
> "Things and Man"
> "Things: Masters and Slaves"

You wrote nothing about Genrikh!

I would write more, but it's already five o'clock. I'm hurrying to the club to practice with the choir. It's the third week they have invited me to lead it. I embrace you, my dear. J.

JACOB TO HIS SISTER EVA

FEBRUARY 14, 1935

My dear Eva! Your letter made me very, very happy. From it I was able to gather that the dark clouds have dispersed somewhat. I write Mama, knowing that she will share everything with you. But, of course, there are things I don't share with Mama. I know from her about your home affairs, and I assume that you don't quite share everything with her. The withholding of information has been hanging over our heads, as close as we are, for many years already.

I'll tell you about myself in a few short words. I had many difficulties with work. I changed jobs many times in the space of a year. I had no idea how adept I was at running an obstacle race! I worked as an accountant, an economist, a music teacher, a singing teacher, and I even taught accordion, which I had never laid eyes on before in my life. Now I'm the pianist in a dance class and have become a specialist in the foxtrot, all the waltzes (Boston, English, American), tango, and rumba. I can bear witness to the fact that the "foxtrotization" of Biysk is happening at a remarkably quick pace. Entire offices and organizations, from couriers to chairmen, have signed up for dance classes. People as respectable as the chairman of the Butter Trust, the local public prosecutor, and the chief of the local police all do the foxtrot! Soon, most likely, the banks will get on board. Respectable people hide their embarrassment behind the pretext of collectivity—the whole collective dances, and it's awkward being left out.

I was recently at a party held by some acquaintances. The hostess, who was celebrating her name day, invited me. The dinner was unbelievably sumptuous, with twenty different kinds of hors d'oeuvres, including such exotic dishes as pickled cabbage, pickled pumpkin, and beets. Provincial amusements are very limited. There is a great deal of bad wine and food, and loudness is a surrogate for good cheer and merrymaking. The louder the merrier. It's difficult to refuse an invitation to drink, but I was staunch in my refusal, and stopped after two small glasses. Do you remember the Kiev cherry brandy that Dunya used to make? I recall that it was the best of all drinks—in color, taste, aroma, strength.

They danced the foxtrot, and I played on a dilapidated old piano. They danced in furs, with the fur turned inside out. They sang and shouted out such masterpieces as "From a Far, Far Land," "The Days of Our Lives," and other examples of musical paleontology. I played the dancers an impossible mishmash of melodies, whatever came into my head.

At three o'clock, with enormous pleasure, I returned alone to my room. I never suffer from boredom except on those evenings when I'm expected to have a good time. Then I feel I've fallen into some late-nineteenth-century mediocre Russian novel. These are the Russian provinces—and it's as though nothing has changed since the time of Ostrovsky. But I'm running off at the mouth, as my habit has been with you from days of old . . . And it's been so long since we talked—oh, how long. I don't know whether you saw it, but there was a poem in the newspaper that went: ". . . work gave me knowledge, and that's not all; my brain seethes with Marx's *Das Kapital.*"

Although there are fewer pressures in my life in Biysk than there were in Stalingrad, I recall the STP as a very interesting time, but I feel indignant about it. I did much valuable work there—an economic report about the reconstruction of the plant for a new model of tractor, the STP No. 3; a city planning project for a settlement; I wrote an article for an industrial journal on the popular economic significance of the STP (calculating the effects of the STP on the popular economy); an essay on the initial phase, etc. Being exposed to the American style of working turned out to be interesting and useful.

But, for the most part, I have become disenchanted with economics. I read many books in new disciplines, and each time I regret the specialization I chose. I became disappointed in it even before it became disappointed in me. I recall with distaste the economic Mount Olympus that I was so enamored of in 1928 and '29. I remember the battles in the State Planning Committee, the leading lights of the political philistines, who, during those years before the storm, understood as much about the political outlook as blind puppies. The country was about to take a giant leap into the unknown, which demanded courage and decisiveness, and they answered everything with their splendid "abstaining from voting." Now they are all silent, not only because they have no political language, but because they have absolutely nothing to say.

Long before the events in my own life occurred, I acknowledged my old mistakes; but I still can't consider myself to be one of the nonpartisan Bolsheviks, following Marusya, who tries to pull me in that direction with all the passion of her nature. I regret that I'm unable. It would be easier if I could march in step with the times, with society, with my family. It's unfortunate that I could have been able to work fruitfully, for the good of the country, but that under the circumstances I'm unable to do anything. From time to time, there is a false note that grates on my ear. It's sad that almost none of the people with whom I could talk as easily and get along with as naturally as you are left on earth.

Be gentle with Marusya, and don't judge her harshly. All her unhappiness, and many of Genrikh's problems, were caused by me. I always feel guilty that I could not have provided them with a peaceful and dignified existence. I bow down before your husband, whom I always underestimated, though now I understand the depths of his nobility, and wisdom, and self-sacrifice, and all those qualities that are lacking in me.

JACOB TO MARUSYA

After work, I went skating. It was the third time I've been out on the ice, and after the mishaps of the first two times, I felt so confident and strong today that I did ten circles around the rink. I had tea at home, and all evening put together a chronology of the music of the Middle Ages. I am in desperate need of books.

The last two postcards were so unpleasant, and upset me so much, that I immediately decided not to answer right away, so as not to give expression to rash feelings or ill-considered thoughts. Now enough time has passed so that I am able to answer calmly, and, possibly, in a humorous vein . . .

Judge for yourself. Here's what you wrote: "You're smarter than everyone else, aren't you . . . stubborn as a mule!" (I can't even believe you would use such a phrase.)

". . . Your obstinacy . . . If you don't want to, you don't want to!

"Your insurmountable obstinacy . . .

"And I've become stubborn as well . . ."

There was another one, a letter, long before these postcards. The letter with the "necessary cruelties." I read it, and my pride and self-esteem were sharply injured. But I struggled against this bitterness and pretended I hadn't received it. After that, I wrote everything in the same even tone, with equanimity.

Dear friend, please understand me. Every remark you make to me is valuable and instructive, but you have more effective words at your disposal than those you have used. That is not the style, or the tone, that will reach me and evoke the desired response. A straightforward, friendly tone is all that's needed. Not this "stubborn as a mule," "pigheaded," etc. That language is not in keeping with your style, and it is not worthy of our (I say with bold certainty) exemplary spousal and amicable relations.

I wanted to write in a gentle tone, in order to protect your sense of self-worth and dignity, and in order not to offend you with some sharp nuance or careless turn of phrase. If you truly find my words to be affectations, unwanted impositions, understand that it is only due to stylistic awkwardness on my part. Don't take the letter as it came out, but as I wanted it to be. This one time, judge me not by the results, but by my intentions. I am certain that my closing salutations will not give rise to dissonance when

I write that I embrace you heartily, and kiss you deeply, and still long for a true and authentic relationship with you. J.

My dear one, I received the postcard in which you write that your bad working conditions are causing you great anxiety. What can you do if your high qualifications, your extensive knowledge, are not valued or required? The fault does not lie with you; it's because the government has little interest in culture. More specifically, it demands culture that is truncated, "pragmatically oriented," "useful" to its own needs. This is understandable: the government is seeking new cultural forms, and this is a difficult process.

In March, I may send you at least as much as I sent in February, so keep this in mind when you're looking for a new job. I already wrote you about my new earnings. If nothing changes, my affairs are going superbly, and I will be grateful my entire life for the fact that the Butter Trust first hired me, then fired me six months later. All the more since I've continued to do some paperwork for them in exchange for butter rather than money, and I sent it immediately through the mail to you. My life here is ideal—there are no other words for it.

In the morning, I get up and read. I work at least five hours. My job starts in the evening. I've arranged things thus: the club pays two hundred, and the two technical schools pay 250. If everything stays the same . . . But my circumstances are subject to change. If I hadn't taken up music, I would never have found work here at all.

About my studies. I am delving into Darwinism, into biology. I have learned remarkable things, very significant. I move along at a rapid clip—I read a single thick scientific work in one morning, and during the next two I reread it and take my copious notes. And on to the next one.

About letters. Fewer and fewer people I was once close to, even the nearest and dearest, answer my letters now. I tried once more to write to Miron—I sent him Tchaikovsky's Violin Concerto. A month has passed, and still no letter. Is he avoiding me? Write me if you have any news of him. Perhaps I should stop trying to contact him?

When you receive a parcel, please confirm it to me not in vague terms ("I received both the butter and the money"), but very specifically—how many pounds and on what date; there are several packages and transfers on the way at the same time, and I need to know which of them you've received.

I beg you, do not forget to do this for me. And although I am reprimanding you severely for your lapse, nevertheless I conclude with some lines from Selvinsky's *Fur Trade*:

My little source of love and mirth,
How marvelous that you agreed
To spend your precious time on earth.

J.

MAY 2, 1935

My dearest, my little one, what has happened? There has never before been such a long disruption in our correspondence. You wrote me your last letter on March 25; then there was a telegram that your letter would be delayed—and that was the last I heard. I have a presentiment of some sort of mishap or misfortune that you want to conceal from me. I left the most vulnerable part of my existence behind in Moscow—I never forget that.

I went to send a telegram several times, but every time I decided against it—I didn't want to distress you any more than you already are. I write you regularly; instead of a letter, on April 7 I sent you greetings (with money) through Konstantinovsky. I don't know whether the money reached you.

A month without news of you is so hard! And, as if by coincidence, I haven't heard from the rest of the family, either. I'm very concerned—has something happened? I miss all of you terribly. The thought of Genrikh is painful to me, and in the last letter, when I gave way to this feeling, I wrote several words I shouldn't have.

My dear, wonderful friend, what should I write you? I feel that dark clouds have covered my existence again. What is happening with you, with Genrikh? I feel so lost and alienated in the Siberian expanses, and I am conscious of being absolutely helpless. Moreover, my longtime friend eczema has returned. I have the feeling that it returned because I so long for your touch.

I embrace you, my girl. Please, write me more often.

Your J.

NOVEMBER 23, 1935

Working in a bank . . . It's not terribly hard, in fact. I've never worked in finance, and if I was able to master all the skills necessary for the job within

411

a month, it means it isn't a real profession. Any half-intelligent person could do the same. And this is a pity. I would like to sequester myself from dilettantes and nonspecialists through my profession. In recent years, I've become professionally disappointed.

A departmental economist is a clerk, an educated pencil-pusher. When I entered this profession, I thought about economic research, and writing about it, in an academic environment. This did not work out, for both general and personal reasons.

I beg you, find a free minute and go to October 25 Street (I don't know the real name), Bldg. 10/2, Literary Consultancy of the State Publishing House, and find out whether the contest has already ended. If not, please pass along my three stories to them in an envelope.

NOVEMBER 28, 1935
. . . Now, about the parallels you see between Ehrenburg and Ostrovsky. In his book about Dostoevsky, André Gide expresses indignation at people who reduce writers to one thesis or idea, when the best thing about them is their complexity. He is delighted with the contradictions and intricacies in Dostoevsky's writing. The best thing in life is complexity. In N. Ostrovsky's case (*How the Steel Was Tempered*), it's impossible not to see that, as literature, the book is weak and insubstantial, and that the style is a mixture of tastelessness and lack of culture. Ostrovsky is a miracle of will, of self-aggrandizement, let's say—a genius at overcoming misfortune. That's the best thing about the book. This is the only way the book captures the attention and sympathy of the reader. The rest of the book is very, very poor. The strongest thing in the book is its autobiographical dimension. His second book, with an invented plot, will be weaker. And how could someone who never had time to learn write a good book in the first place? When another such novice—the baker Gorky—began to write, he had already managed to digest an entire library. He was already inundated with literature. Writers are shaped either by life + books, or only books; but never life without books.

You don't have enough objectivity to evaluate Ehrenburg. I know that you evaluate him in light of one White Guard phrase about the national flag on an automobile, which he wrote in the Kiev Whites' newspaper in a passing fit. After that, you refuse to countenance anything he writes.

This is not right. Ehrenburg is a great writer. Both *The Second Day* and *Without Pausing for Breath* are superb, masterfully written books. And such was the unanimous opinion of the Soviet critics. Ehrenburg is a writer of real complexity. He has internalized the technical skills of French literature, and he has introduced traditions of literary treatment of the written word into the Soviet literary tradition—which were always weak in our literary tradition, and wholly lacking in Ostrovsky. Ostrovsky doesn't really write at all . . . It's interesting to note that Ostrovsky finished writing his book in the evening, and in the morning sent it off by post. What naïveté!

And read Ehrenburg's poetry. Poetry doesn't deceive. He's a poet of great sensitivity, a true one.

DECEMBER 28, 1935

My dear friend, I am forcing myself to sit down to write you a detailed letter. It pains me to have to write it. This postcard information exchange is so ice-bound, so slippery (in addition to being irresponsible).

But in the last postcard you informed me that you had already written a long letter, with an "analysis of our relations," which was, moreover, cruel, in the tradition of "necessary cruelties."

If you have not yet sent it, please do not. I do not need it; nor do you.

We have had a quarrel, a married couple's quarrel. I want to resolve it, to end it, to put it behind us, to expunge it completely from the record. But you, on the other hand, want to explain things, to "teach me understanding." I take everything back; I repent.

My unfounded apprehensions about you, my vain interrogations, my inappropriate advice—let's assume I didn't write any of it. They were empty words and phrases. But, please, I beg you, let's leave behind the unpleasantness.

What was it that happened? In fact, it was trivial—something that in our former existence would have been resolved and forgotten momentarily. But here, at a distance, with miles and years interposed between us, a paltry thing becomes a large grievance.

But now it is gone, all is forgotten. Let's begin anew. We will write to each other about ordinary, daily things, about the details of life; about joys, and our small tribulations, and the joys of our small tribulations (as Rolland would say).

JANUARY 19, 1936

My sweet friend, today I got up early, before eight, when it was still dark. I hurried out into the morning frost, under urgent physiological stimulus. I met up with the dog Roska, the unfortunate Roska. Every morning she is locked into a dark kennel, and in the evening they let her out. She never sees the light of day. She throws herself at me in greeting, and twists and twirls joyously. I always whisper the same words to her: "Poor dog, poor Roska." If I come home late, she senses through the closed gate that it's me and doesn't bark. While I'm making my way over the fence, she again launches into her hysterical show of friendship. Once, in the darkness, she didn't recognize me and started barking with hostility. When she got close enough to recognize me, she felt compunction and wanted me to understand that it was a mistake, that she didn't mean it. She did her little somersaults and twirled around yelping and whining twice as much as usual. I whispered to her, "Poor little dog, poor little Roska, it's all right, I'm not angry."

I stand in the yard a long time, watching the predawn sky, which I usually don't get to see. I know the evening sky well. I can pick out the constellations easily; but I don't often see the morning sky. The Big Dipper is situated differently, almost showing off its rear end, right above my head. The stars shine with a particular morning brightness. You can see how the entire bulwark—the vault of the sky—shifted over half the sky during those eight hours when I wasn't watching. What a magnificent book it is for those who know how to read it! One of the first books that humanity learned to read, before hieroglyphs and alphabets were invented.

Yesterday morning, I took part in a weekend concert broadcast on the radio. It was devoted to contemporary Soviet poetry. We have a well-educated consultant from the library here, a literary critic. They read the work of poets I don't know well: Antokolsky, Petrovsky (a LEF writer, reminiscent of Khlebnikov), and others. Some of the poems were set to music, which I played. And since it was impossible to choose the pieces beforehand, I boldly improvised. My musical accompaniment to Bagritsky's poem "The Lay of Opanas" was very apt, in particular the gloomy melody I hit upon for Makhno. I still can't get them out of my head. After the concert, there was a meeting about organizing musical programs for the radio. I was offered the position of music director, which I very eagerly accepted; but I'm not sure whether anything will come of it. Whatever I do, wherever I find myself, I am above all a "*Kulturträger*," a culture bearer; I am very ardent and energetic about such matters, and if nothing gets done, it is not my fault.

In Fedin's *Brothers*, there is a marvelous passage about German culture. I will cite it here from memory: "This musical culture achieved such heights because whole generations of unknown conductors, musical directors, and choirmasters, brick by brick, constructed the foundation of knowledge out of which the masterpieces of Bayreuth and Düsseldorf grew. And Nikita wanted to return to the native soil of his Chagin, where he had known his first love and his first hate, in order to put down his bricks."

I'm not very good with bricks. At the STP I set down a brick, but here in Biysk I haven't managed yet. Perhaps it will happen on the radio.

JANUARY 24, 1936

My dear friend and wife, your last letter, in which you write about celebrating the New Year, is a fine letter, from start to finish. Every line sings, beginning with the chintz garters, and ending with the tears you shed over pages of the newspaper. At last you've told me the issue in which your own work was printed. I immediately dashed down to the library. In two libraries, the entire set of *Our Achievements* had been sent off to be bound, so I'll have to wait. In the third library, they don't subscribe to it. And the fourth—I'll visit tomorrow.

I read Rolland's *Musicians of Today* and returned to an old idea: to write a textbook on the history of music. A textbook for schools, clubs, and radio listeners. I set to work with enthusiasm, although there's precious little literature devoted to this subject. If you happen to come upon any music books from my library, send them to me. You don't have to make a special effort, but anything you come across might help. The local library here has ordered a few dozen books from Moscow for me.

I'm already working on the first three chapters: (1) folk music, (2) European music which Vitya could not have known before Bach, and (3) Bach. The draft of the book will be ready by the end of this year. When I am able to use the big library, I'll spend a few months making additions to it. The first chapter, on folk music, is virtually finished. I haven't hit upon the proper style yet. My literary style surpasses my scholarly style; it sounds very dry at present. But I will revise it many more times. I like this task. No other such book exists yet. For me it is more than just another literary pastime. The Biysk library has initiated an inter-library-loan subscription with the Novosibirsk library, which receives a copy of every single book published in the Soviet Union. They arranged this especially for me. When it begins to function, I will be provided with all the books that come out, and I'll be able to work more quickly and efficiently. The radio should also help—I need to listen again to dozens of composers. On my desk I have the radio

415

program of all the concerts for the month. I've underlined the ones I need to hear.

Along with the history of music, I am writing (in short bursts) a novella. This is the fifth one I've written, following "The Gifts of Need," "A History of Beauty" (this one is about a woman who suffers from her beauty, from the unwanted attentions of men, and marries a blind man), "Life Is Too Long" (about two sisters who begin an independent life when they are already nearly old women, after the death of their despotic parents), and one about a girl who is in love with an old man who is a photographer. I seem to be suffering from "graphomania." It's rather absurd to write for the desk drawer, without any readership, appreciation, or even criticism. But, patience, patience . . .

You write that Genrikh is studying English. I have a wonderful book for him. Have you heard of the *Basic English* system of Professor Ogden? He has reduced all the rich diversity of language to 850 words, and only sixteen verbs. If you master this bare minimum of words and know how to use them, you can read the literature that this same Ogden publishes: Swift, Dickens, etc.

A Russian publisher has already released the book *Step by Step* by Ivy Litvinov (wife of the people's commissar); it costs two rubles and forty kopecks. I acquired it even before Stalingrad—look on the lower shelf of the bookcase, where the dictionaries are. The Basic system is a wonderful idea. Such a system for other languages will no doubt follow. Learning a language according to this system (simplified language, of course) requires only eighty-eight hours.

I wish you a very happy January 23 birthday (again)—if you wish to live according to the calendar of Pope Gregory (of Rome), and survive on pounds rather than kilograms. I kiss you. J.

FEBRUARY 19, 1936

I spent the whole of yesterday in a haze, as though I had been smoking opium. All morning, I read a book by a German biologist, *Secrets of Nature*, and then prepared the midday meal for myself. (It takes all of fifteen minutes to put on the soup, and another hour of stirring it now and then.) After my meal, I went to the library to read newspapers, and the whole evening I read *The Good Earth*, a novel by the American writer Pearl Buck, with a foreword by Tretyakov. A marvelous book about life in China. You must borrow it from the library—it appears in the journal *International Literature*. Buck is a missionary in China, no longer young, who all of a sudden decided to write this wonderful novel. And immediately acquired an international reputation. When I read the book, I perceive her as a reader, as a literary technician, as a writer, as a rival. I read her lines, and observe how the lines are made. How the plot drifts around huge obstacles and backs up on itself, and how the subject is resolved at the end. That's probably the most challenging part—the resolution of the subject. I read somewhere that French playwrights write a play beginning with the fifth act, with the dénouement, and if it is powerful enough, it is adopted as the groundwork upon which the first four acts are built. You must read Pearl Buck. It is an exemplary novel, in my view: real training for the beginning writer. No doubt, the general structure of narrative, as well as of music, in the highest sense, can be captured in some general formula . . . But even Shklovsky doesn't write about this!

MARCH 8, 1936

Nothing came of my involvement in radio; they changed their minds. Today, though, I was offered the possibility of teaching music to an eight-year-old boy, and we met for the first time. This happened after my first pupil played a sonatina on the radio, to great acclaim; and I hope pupils will be beating a path to my door now. That is, I hope all eight children from the good families of the city of Biysk will be standing in line for lessons from the maestro!

Today I spoke with the bank manager about a raise. He promised to do what he could, so things are developing in a satisfactory way. For this reason, I even had a radio installed in my room. And that is where my big-spender ways will end. I have furnished myself with electricity, a radio subscription, laid in a supply of firewood, had my shoes repaired, as well as all my clothing.

JUNE 19, 1936

I'm sitting at the table, reading about forestry. The radio broadcast Tchaikovsky's Fifth Symphony, and the sounds of bitter grief are still ringing in my ears. Everything is getting mixed up together: your letter of yesterday, and Gorky's death, which was announced over the radio, the rain beating against the windowpane, and the passionate refrain of the symphony . . .

About your essay. I read your literary portrait of Tretyakov five times over. The article made me very happy. It's beautifully rendered, and the quality far outstrips the average for the journal. The language is good—in a word, brava! This is your first article of the kind, and the next ones are sure to be even more powerful.

I can take delight in an article that expresses ideas I don't agree with—neither with their conclusions, nor their assessments, not even with the structure of the piece. Nevertheless, I praise it without reservation. If I am permitted to express myself on this subject and offer criticism, tactfully, without any dogmatic sermonizing, I would say the following.

A literary essay should not give an appraisal at all. The critic is not an evaluator. He is a commentator, an opponent, a proponent, or a sociologist of the ideas that move the writer. Above all, one should not overpraise. And you give way to this in your essay when you write: "His mind is perfectly poised . . . a rich and resonant voice . . . an unusual writer"—twice—"full of significance . . . exceptional mastery (!) . . . wonderful essays . . . a writer of all genres . . ."

Is this all true? In a cup of tea there are five pieces of sugar. If he is indeed a writer of all genres, I would respond that, though he is great in his genre, his genre is too insignificant. Tretyakov is a useful writer, but, if one must sum him up, I would say: he is a typical second-rate writer, a mediocre talent.

His main shortcoming (and that of many other writers) is that he has no ideas of his own. You cannot name a single idea or thought that would immediately bring Tretyakov to mind. He is diluted in the epoch, produced by it; he studies it but doesn't enrich it. He takes and doesn't give back. He doesn't have enough extremism and self-limitation for this.

"Mastery lies in limitation" (Goethe).

Tretyakov is an essayist skimming the surface of many ideas, but none of them is memorable, none stands out above any others.

Enough about him—now about you. You write that there were roads and crossroads, victories and defeats, but he found what was most important—"and the road was found"—essays on German writers. What is unique about them? It's a literary device of significant details and trivia. Is that all? That's very little. And "the victory and the road" are not convincing. The engine of enormous (is it really enormous?) power turns the coffee grinder—this is the epigraph it deserves, the only epigraph that would ring true.

Trivia:

(1) The piano imagery doesn't work. If the "upper lid of the piano is the height of Tretyakov," he is very small of stature—a regular dwarf.

(2) "His gesture is fluid, his thought lightning-quick" (!)—and immediately Pushkin comes to mind: "His eyes / Shine. His face is terrible. / His movements are quick. He is magnificent. / He is like divine thunder."

If I were to write a critical essay on the writer, I would do it differently. The path of the writer is a social phenomenon, and not individual. In this case, the author himself is a matter of secondary importance. I would take a single idea of the author's (if he has any ideas at all), and I would adopt it as the title and central thesis of the essay. I would talk about the author (if possible without evaluation) only as an example of this idea.

The essay would then be devoted not to the writer but to his ideas, and it would be independent of the writer himself. What is the governing idea of this writer? That in our time "life is more important than literature, writing is a side effect of the deed." "In the beginning was the Deed," then the word appeared—this is how he sums up the time we live in. What are the deeds of Tretyakov himself? His own deeds are small, insignificant, and he does not write on a grand scale, by any means. And his own point of view ("literature as the refuse of life") is not checked against life itself, and doesn't ring true; it doesn't stand up to scrutiny. Literature is a self-justifying value.

Then the essay would be more "finished," and it would have a general thesis; its claims would be independent of second-rate examples. These are the thoughts that your essay suggests to me.

Nevertheless, in spite of my remarks, it is an essay of a very high order. Yesterday I read *Our Achievements*, but it was no more than dull, inartistic daubing. Written not with a pen but with a spade, a stirring rod, a housepainter's brush—a disgrace. I know the one who appears alongside you and writes such a vapid essay about Paris. During a difficult moment at the end of the twenties, I fed him a meal of my paltry crumbs. Then it turned out he didn't deserve this.

Your writing is the best in the issue. If there are any good minds on the editorial board, they should not let someone with your talents slip away. Reading your article was a real feast for me. Write, write—write and don't stop. Stay strong and active.

I kiss you and shake your hand,
with a literary greeting,

with a spousal greeting,
with a friend's greeting.

AUGUST 1, 1936

... I received all the postcards you sent. Thinking about our correspondence during the recent past, I realize that our separation has had palpable results. Soon we will have been apart for six years, and I have sorely missed your closeness and the friendship of my son. We are separated by miles and years, and other less notable but still real divergences of paths. Divergence of paths, and the difficulty of mutual understanding.

For the time being, I have felt this in your letters; perhaps you have sensed the same in mine?

There are questions you refuse to answer. If I insist, I get a short reply: Don't be anxious or nervous, be patient. It is difficult to survive in ignorance. I understand how much effort is required of both of us in order to reconnect again, to find our former selves in those we have now become.

Our next reunion is approaching. I'll be honest with you: I am apprehensive about how this meeting will go. You write me that when we see each other again I will find you and our son just the same as when I left you, and there is no need to be anxious. But nothing ever returns to the same place, and I know that a great deal has changed, though I can't really envision how. I am trying to solve this puzzle, to anticipate the future, though I admit I'm as yet unable.

Your letters, in fact, are very cold and informative, but in your last letter you suddenly gave vent to reproaches that had built up over the years. The pain scorched me when I read it. Can't we accept one another with "open hearts"?

For me, Genrikh is a sphinx, a mystery that is unlikely to afford me a happy surprise when it is uncovered. All of this I now have to consider, to think and feel through, and I must prepare myself for it.

Marusya, I love you deeply. I am no longer young, but I am not ashamed to repeat the words of our first meetings. At our age, such words are often avoided. The emotional expressions of our youth are now absent in our letters, and have been absent a long time—those sweet intimacies that filled our correspondence at one time in the past.

Please send me a picture of you. It's silly to say you've aged, you're no longer attractive. I'm not interested in a picture of a fresh young beauty. I

420

need *your* picture, a picture of *you* exactly as you are now. I've aged, too—by as many years as you have. Send me a picture.

I'll end this letter with the refrain that always fits the bill—but I hope it sounds fresh this time.

I kiss you. Deeply and tenderly, as I did in those moments when I wanted, and was able, to reverse your bad or sad mood. I embrace you—"along every line"—if you remember what this once meant to us. J.

SEPTEMBER 26, 1936

It's rather difficult for me to write just now, dearest one! You ask me whether I know anything yet. No, not yet, but what usually happens is that everyone who has served his term here gets a passport and a free train ticket to any destination he wishes. It will probably be the same in my case. It's up to the Moscow police whether they will allow me to live there and give me a residence permit. Most likely, they will not. Actually, this depends on random local circumstances. Gerchuk, my old friend, went to live in Moscow after his term of exile, and has been living there a long time; other friends of mine are not given permission. In any event, I'll come home for a few days and decide what to do after that.

I've never been confronted with so many unknown factors in my life as I am now. Nothing in the future is clear to me—neither my legal status, nor even my family circumstances. I'll have to do a new inventory of the household goods—what remains, and in what condition is it?

But, for the time being, I'm busy with trivial predeparture matters. I bought a suitcase, had my shoes repaired, had trousers made, and finished my dental work. I need to reread my archive and bring it up to date. The time of accumulating knowledge is past; it is time to bring things to fruition.

OCTOBER 2, 1936

Dear friend, I've just been listening to a concert performed by Oborin that was broadcast on the radio from Novosibirsk. The headphones are on a long cord, so I can move around the room wearing them, walking from one corner to another. Whenever they broadcast a long concert, I listen and sew at the same time. The whole concert I spent repairing my trousers. My memory carried me back to the past, to those distant years when I first heard these pieces. There is so much sadness in the remote depths of my past. But I don't wish to dwell on that now, but on something else—on how music has defined our relationship. Tchaikovsky and Rachmaninoff introduced us to each other. Schumann brought us closer together, and other composers seduced us. It's rare that I hear a concert that doesn't bring back such warm memories. Yesterday, I listened to Schubert's "Der Doppelgänger," today Oborin played Schubert/Liszt's "Barcarolle," Liszt's "The Hunt" étude, and Schumann's *Carnaval*. I listen to broadcasts from Moscow of guest appearances of the Ukraine Opera, that same Kiev opera theater from which I received my musical education in the twelfth row of the balcony for thirty kopecks a ticket.

I recall with gratitude the people who helped awaken my musical tastes, and try to trace that chain of events that alienated me from music. How sad it all is.

It's so strange that in Moscow I became completely estranged from it, whereas in Biysk I grew close to it again. I don't think I will ever again abandon it seriously, and for a long time.

It's hard for me to imagine that we will enter the Main Hall of the Conservatory again . . . On the very first evening, I'll buy tickets at the door.

NOVEMBER 16, 1936

. . . to clarify a few important details. Please obtain the following papers before the day of my arrival:

(1) certificate of your employment
(2) certificate of Genrikh's employment
(3) certificate from the Housing Committee stating that I lived there from 1923 to 1931

When I arrive, I will submit a request to the NKVD for permission to live in Moscow and to be registered there. I might postpone submitting it until the end of November, when the new Constitution is adopted, but I'm not sure. I was informed that a general amnesty was being planned for that day. Although according to my documents I was released earlier, these circumstances may have bearing on my situation, too.

Send me a postcard when you receive this letter, and let me know your phone number, and the number at Ostozhenka Street. Most likely, the old number, 1-94-13, has been changed to a direct one; and I've forgotten Eva's.

The NKVD told me that they will not delay me even one extra day. It will take a few days for the police to give me a passport. I anticipate that I will be home by the end of the year. It is possible, however, that administrative complications will keep me here for another few weeks. Judging by others' experience, no one has ever finished the term on the stipulated date.

Well, that's about all. I sense how hard our correspondence has become for you to maintain, and not only because there isn't enough time. In general, our communications have grown weaker—six years is a long time. And it has become difficult for me to write you as well. Sometimes I sit over a letter for a long time, and nothing comes of it.

It's a good thing that the bad recedes into the past.

I kiss you.

—J.

41

Letters from the Willow Chest

War

(1942–1943)

SVERDLOVSK–MOSCOW

GENRIKH TO MARUSYA

Checked by the Military Censor

FEBRUARY 3, 1942

My dearest mother! I haven't heard anything from you for a long time—
why? If you only knew how necessary your letters are to me, you would
write more often. There's not a single person here I can share my thoughts
and worries with, not a single person from whom I could expect to hear a
kind word. And only now have I come to understand how much I need that.
Mother, dear, best in the world, I curse the hour when I had to leave Moscow. I so want to be with you, and I could put up with the hardest circumstances if only we could endure them together. My comrades? They're all
good people, to a greater or lesser degree, but living together, seeing the
same faces day in and day out, hearing the same things over and over . . .
Well, you understand what I mean.

I'm not eating very well. This is what they feed us: I try to get up as late
as I can. After that I eat three and a half ounces of bread and drink boiled
water. At one in the afternoon, I go to the dining hall, where I have the midday meal and seven ounces of bread. At seven or eight in the evening, I get
seven ounces of bread. Before, we used to get commercial bread, but now it

has become hard to find, and you have to stand in line for it just to get eighteen ounces. But what is eighteen ounces for me? Still, I try to keep my spirits up. I received news from Tomsk. Students from my Institute who were evacuated to Tomsk are going to Moscow soon. How we envy them!

Mama, why don't you tell me anything about yourself? This silence can be interpreted in various ways.

It's better to write the truth than to keep silent. I understand very well that things are hard for you. If you wish, make inquiries at my Institute about the possibility of my return—but that's a pipe dream that is not likely to come true. The most difficult thing about my situation is prospects for the future. I'm awaiting a job assignment, which will happen when I graduate from the Institute (mid-July). Either I'll remain in Sverdlovsk and undertake something important, or I'll have to go out to the boondocks (Lysva, Chusovaya, Beloretsk). Moreover, there's no guarantee of being able to work there long. And dreaming about Moscow . . .

If possible, send me my skating boots, canvas shoes, underwear, and my old suit coat, plus a few shirts. And write me letters, and more often, please, my dear mother! I go to the post office nearly every day and try to find a trace of you—but you're not there. The post office is rather far away, and it closes early. I don't always make it in time.

It's better to write directly to my address than to the post office:
Genrikh Ossetsky
Student Dormitory 1, room 417
Sverdlovsk, 9 Vtuzgorodok, Ural Industrial Institute

I send you many, many kisses!
Genrikh
P.S. Did you find Jack Rubin?

Checked by the Military Censor

FEBRUARY 8, 1942
Dear Mother,

I have been thinking over what I have lived through during the past week. I feel that during those days I experienced a sharp turnaround. The first three days of February were very difficult, and my mood was dark. The

425

change in diet was just an impetus. I thought about many things during this time, and suddenly there was a breakthrough. It became clear that I had lived my life without achieving anything. Recently, I turned in a design project for machine tooling, and got the highest mark for it; but this didn't make me happy. I felt indifferent to it. I am now carrying out a special commission for which I'll be paid and which will count as a design project for the cutting-instrument course. Now the chance to earn a bit of extra money has turned up, but I can't take advantage of it, because I am under constant pressure with the various design projects I have to submit. There are a lot of them!

. My dear mother! It hurts me so much that you don't tell me anything about yourself, but toss off these postcards that reveal nothing. You don't answer any of my questions, and it ends up being not a correspondence but an exchange of greetings—nothing more. In all this time, I have received only one letter, dated January 2! I can imagine how tired you are when you come home after work and collapse on the divan. You haven't told me how you like your new job. Have you really become a person who just punches in and out at work? I can't imagine it!

I've become used to my new diet here.

Now that my health has recovered a bit, I can inform you: I had Pityriasis rosea, a very uncomfortable rashlike condition. Now I'm completely cured.

In the *Ural Worker* newspaper, there are often essays by Lyudm. Alex. They are completely without redeeming qualities. And you magnanimously opined that she still had time to learn. It's too late for her to learn.

That is not at all what I wanted to write you, though. I'm unable to determine my own state of affairs. Perhaps with time everything will become clear. I'm feeling easier in my soul these days, but my situation is uncertain as I have begun to be aware of my own feelings, I have begun to find myself. I don't know whether you will understand me. My dear mother, I have one dream for which I am willing to sacrifice everything—that is being together with you. Often, when I'm doing something, or making some decision, I ask myself, "What would Mama say?" Although I'll soon be twenty-six, I sometimes feel like a little son, even helpless, and it's very pleasant.

Sending you many, many kisses, your Genrikh. Excuse the jumble of thoughts in this letter; but what else could I do? That's what I'm like now.

FEBRUARY 10, 1942

My dear Mother!

Hooray! Today I received your registered letter from February 1 and was very, very glad. It's the second letter (registered) that I've received from you. Soon it will be four months since I left Moscow, but it seems like yesterday. Time flies, and it's impossible to make up for every hour lost. That's something I realized only recently. I'm working here at full tilt, and work is one of my few sources of comfort.

Your letter disturbed me. I can so clearly imagine your life, and I wanted so much to be there with you, to lighten your burden at least a little bit. I can see that it is not easy and that it is grounded in your clearly defined character and your enthusiasm. Mama, I want to be there with you! It's so wonderful how you describe going to the theater and remember things that happened ten, twenty, thirty years ago. But for me, memories hold no interest whatsoever. Everything is in the future. I want to achieve something big and useful, and, to be honest, something that will bring fame and respect, and all that sort of thing. For the country, and for you. It won't be easy, with my family legacy, but I'll make it, you'll see!

Write me and tell me whether you received my birthday telegram on January 23, and the money transfer of a hundred rubles that I sent you on the 20th. Right now I'm snowed under with work from my classes, and I haven't managed to earn any more money—and, added to that, I have many expenses (paying for the studies, war tax, and repairing my felt winter boots). But I have provided for myself in advance for the next one and a half months. I will help you if I can. My dream is to be able to help you regularly. In a month, I'll graduate from the theoretical courses of the Institute. Then only the applied part of the course and my thesis will remain to be completed. I'm almost an engineer.

I recently saw *Enough Stupidity in Every Wise Man* at the Red Army Theater. I went there because of the buffet (here they call even the local opera and ballet theater "The Theater of Opera and Buffet"). My hunting expedition was successful. I bought eighteen sandwiches and five buns (the first time since leaving Moscow that I've had white bread). I wasn't accepted into the Military Academy program, for reasons that had nothing to do with me. But I still stand a chance, since there will be a new round of admissions in May. I'm afraid that the academy is not for me. All my life, aviation, the dream of my childhood and youth, has eluded me. The admissions committee didn't accept Kolya F., either. They refused Egor Gavrilin, and he had to get into the academy, since his studies at the Institute are in an abysmal state. He took only two exams, and he hasn't even begun his project. The fellow got lazy. But they agreed at least to consider him in the next round of admissions.

It is now one in the morning. I just returned from the post office. All the other fellows have gone to bed, and they certainly foul up the air while they're sleeping—that's a result of the diet. I changed my schedule a bit. Now I study until three or four in the morning, get up at eleven or twelve, and eat my midday meal immediately. In that way, I allay my hunger and save time simultaneously. Mother, tell me more about what your day is like. What's it like at home in the apartment: Is it cold? Is there gas for cooking?

Where is A. Kostromin? What do you hear from Uncle Mikhail? Does he write at all? Whom do you meet with, who are your friends? Write me about what my beloved Moscow looks like. And tell me how things stand with your food supply—I'm very worried about it.

The stipend will be disbursed pending the results of sixteen exams. I passed six of them already, and got four A's and two B's. I still need to get good marks on at least three more. It will be hard. I don't attend lectures, but work only with my books. With few exceptions, the lecturers aren't well qualified. I'm putting all my efforts into passing the exams early. Write me if you've heard any news about Osip Shapir and Sergey Prasolov. Sasha Volkov and Boris Kokin were killed near Leningrad. I was very upset by the news. And one of our students, Zhenya Pochando, received the decoration of Hero of the Soviet Union. Good for him! I bitterly regret that I'm not at the front.

Mother, write me more often. I desperately need your letters.

Send my greetings and a big kiss to Uncle Mikhail and the family. Thank you for the envelopes, by the way.

If you have the chance, send me socks, a darning needle and thread, some underwear, my skating boots and canvas shoes, a few shirts, a suitcase if at all possible, because I have nothing but a gunnysack. And please send me a suit as well. But the most important things are a slide rule, a pencil box, and pencils (drafting pencils—they're in the desk drawer).

I send you many kisses (8,888 of them), Genrikh

P.S. I didn't want to write you about it, but I can't help myself. At the end of December, just by chance, I met my former classmate Amalia Kotenko in town. Do you remember her? You must—she got married to our classmate Tisha Golovanov as soon as she finished the tenth grade. You certainly remember him. He came to our house in the seventh grade and we played chess. He died in the first month of the war. I feel terribly sorry for her. We've started to meet each other occasionally. She was such a bright, happy girl, and now her light seems to have gone out. Cursed war. I'm trying to cheer her up a bit; she is "thawing" out bit by bit.

SVERDLOVSK–MOSCOW
EGOR GAVRILIN TO MARUSYA

FEBRUARY 15, 1942

Hello, Mrs. Ossetsky!

Genrikh let me read your last letter, and it touched me so deeply I wanted to write you a few warm and friendly lines, not by way of comfort—you are not one of those people who need that—and there's probably nothing to comfort you for, but simply out of an excess of feeling, as they say. When I read your casual remarks about Moscow, about daily life there, about the working conditions of ordinary people, I get a sense of the reality of war and the front line. Here you don't feel it at all. People know about it, and talk about it, but nothing more. At first, this seemed strange to me, but, gradually, even we who smelled the gunpowder, on earth and in the sky, out of the corner of our noses, so to speak, got used to it; so it's not surprising that the people in Sverdlovsk have that reaction.

For this reason, it's not surprising that the news of missing relatives or abandoned apartments, and many other things that are so natural for us in Moscow, and inevitable in wartime (especially this war), inspire indignation here. And you are absolutely right when you say that we live in a kind of paradise here—only we don't appreciate it, and, I'm certain, if you were in our place you wouldn't appreciate it, either. And that's why you, more than anyone else, can understand why Genrikh is so eager to get to Moscow. We are sitting on pins and needles here, and we are very nervous, and we can't feel at home. That very Sverdlovskian complacency irritates us, as does the fact that, on the very day when Lozovaya was recaptured by our troops, some students—yes, students!—got into a fight in the buffet over a salami sandwich. What does the man in the street here think about on such a day? How to snatch another person's portion, whoever he might be. But the people who have experienced the war firsthand (and there are many such people here), refugees from Ukraine, Belorussia, Leningrad, Moscow, and the western regions, turn on the morning news as soon as they get up, and after that stand over the Soviet map arguing for the next few hours.

You describe a passage from *Peer Gynt*—the death of Åse. You are right, Mrs. Ossetsky, that it is perhaps the most powerful part of Ibsen's play, and Grieg's music.

Much has been said about a mother's love, about its power and endurance, by all the great masters of the word—Romain Rolland, Gorky, Chekhov, Maupassant, Nekrasov, Heine, and many others. But this short scene of a mother's quiet death in the arms of her estranged son, who has come to shut her eyes and to comfort her in her hour of death, surpasses almost everything in its laconicism, its emotional restraint, its power.

Truly, when the war ends, our Soviet Union will become stronger and more cohesive, all the wounds will heal, everything that has been destroyed will be reborn, life will gush forth like a spring, women and girls will find themselves new husbands and lovers—but who will heal the wounds of thousands of mothers? Who will answer for their suffering and irreparable grief? Yes, who besides the mothers themselves can understand their suffering? For it's impossible to tell it. You are right a hundred times over. Every letter I get from my mother, in which she tries not to show her terrible anguish because she doesn't want me to worry, enters the tiniest particles of my life and awakens such a storm of indignation and sorrow that I can't tell where the indignation ends and the sorrow begins. But, reading your letter, I am convinced that all mothers feel the same, or at least very similar, anguish about their sons. The only thing that remains is to hope that all the sons feel the same love and gratitude toward their mothers that Genrikh and I feel.

But I am an optimist, Mrs. Ossetsky, and I know that you are, too, more so than many, and for that reason we will hope that very soon we will all be together in Moscow, and we will raise a toast in honor of the victorious finish of the war and all the good that lies ahead.

I send you my warmest, warmest greetings,
Egor Gavrilin

Postcard

FEBRUARY 15, 1942

Mama! Sasha Figner has not heard anything from his parents in more than one and a half months. He asks you to call phone number D2-24-47, or inquire at his parents' address: 6 Novinsky Boulevard, apartment 13, to find out whether everything is all right.

Some marriages are made in heaven, but the war made Amalia and Genrikh's. They were never friends during high school. Genrikh looked at Amalia from afar, but she was surrounded by an impenetrable wall of friends, both boys and girls, and at the time when Genrikh left school, Tisha Golovanov, who was in love with her, was always by her side. Amalia and Tisha married right after they finished tenth grade and graduated, and the whole class celebrated the first wedding among their classmates. Genrikh didn't attend the wedding—by that time he was already living the life of an adult, working and studying, and he rarely saw his former classmates.

He and Amalia didn't meet again until December 1941, in Sverdlovsk, at the bazaar. Both of them had been evacuated—Genrikh with students of the Institute from which he was supposed to graduate that year, and Amalia from the design bureau where she worked. They both worked for Uralmash, which at that time was launching self-propelled guns. Genrikh worked in the project design department, and Amalia in Design Bureau 9, on the other side of town.

They delighted in each other's company—as fellow Muscovites, neighbors, former classmates, with a great many common memories and common friends. During the first months of the war, four boys from their class perished. The first "killed in battle" notice was about Amalia's husband, Tisha Golovanov, at the end of July 1941. Amalia took her bereavement very hard. The last stage of their relationship had been difficult: Tisha had begun to drink heavily, Amalia was ashamed about his drunkenness, they quarreled for an entire year, and Amalia's mother, Zinaida, having suffered enough from the drunken behavior of men, lit a match to the fire so Amalia would kick Tisha out. He went to live with his mother; but now, after his

431

death, Amalia couldn't forgive herself for the falling out. Why couldn't she simply have put up with it? It was especially painful to her that she and her husband hadn't even managed to say goodbye, she had never written to him, and she hadn't received a single letter from him. Amalia, as his wife, was given the news first, and had to go inform Tisha's mother, who wailed and keened and then chased Amalia out of the house.

Amalia suffered not only the loss of her husband, but the loss of herself. She was used to living in peace with herself. The world smiled at her, and she liked herself well enough—what she didn't like, she just didn't look at. Instinctively, she preferred to avoid complications, not to multiply them. After Tisha's death, she couldn't return to her old habits of mind and her peaceable accommodation with the world. She was haunted by a feeling of guilt toward him, and tormented by what she thought was her own sinfulness, overcome by despair and loneliness, without a shadow of hope. Her own life seemed doomed and worthless to her.

She was happy to be evacuated—Moscow had become unbearable—but Sverdlovsk turned out to be worse.

Work was hard. It began at eight in the morning, and ended at various times, but never before eight in the evening. She left work every day with a swollen face and blue-tinged fingers, shivering with cold. In the room where the drafting boards were set up, where she worked, the temperature never rose above fifty degrees Fahrenheit.

The food supply in the city was meager. Food rations had not yet been introduced, and people lined up at the stores from early morning to buy a portion. A single person with a job had no time to stand in line. If it hadn't been for the cafeteria at her workplace, she would have starved. On the last weekend before the New Year's celebration, Amalia made her way to the market to buy some food—potatoes and rutabagas. Right in the middle of the vegetable stands, Genrikh appeared. She didn't recognize him at first. Genrikh recognized her right away, by her blue eyes and her white fur hat—which she had worn since high school—with two earflaps and a pompom on the top.

They grabbed each other's hands and embraced warmly. Genrikh picked up her bag and carried it for her—two kilograms of potatoes and a kilogram of rutabagas. Amalia also wanted to buy milk, but she didn't have enough money; it had already become very expensive. Genrikh had a bottle of vodka to barter. They exchanged it for two loaves of bread. He gave one of them to

Amalia. People were already hungry, but that was only the beginning of the deprivations they would experience in the coming year.

They celebrated the New Year in Genrikh's dormitory, with his fellow students. Amalia was acknowledged to be the prettiest girl there. The contestants were few: Dilyara, a typist from the dean's office, sweet, with slightly bulging eyes caused by Graves' disease; and Sonya, the librarian, with an elongated nose, narrow face, and slightly protruding ears. From that evening on, Amalia became Genrikh's girlfriend.

Genrikh met Amalia after work to accompany her to her dormitory, and then returned to his own, an hour's walk through the dark, deserted city.

They got married in the spring of 1942. Now they lived not in dormitories but in a room in the family barracks. It was partitioned by a curtain; the second half of the room was occupied by a couple that had also been evacuated—engineers from Minsk, reticent and unfriendly. It was easier, and warmer for the two of them, to live together in the luxury of half a room. Still, they were hungry.

At the same time, Marusya was rushing around Moscow, which was becoming empty of residents, trying to find a decent job. She had been dogged by disappointment for a long time now: after the high hopes and expectations of her youth, the star that had lured her had begun to set. She had not become an actress, or a pedagogue; and she had not been able to break into journalism, either. The apex of her career was an occasional publication in the newspaper *The Factory Whistle*. It was comforting to know that wonderful writers appeared in the publication—Ilf and Petrov, Yuri Olesha, Paustovsky . . . and Marusya. There was also *Pioneers' Pravda*, where Marusya managed to publish her articles devoted to children's arts, gesturing subtly toward the Froebel principles of pedagogy. Her favorite journal, *Soviet Toys and Games*, to which she had been recommended by Nadezhda Krupskaya herself, had already closed down before the war. How interesting it had been to work there! They created new Soviet games and toys with new ideological content . . . But it was in the past, it was all in the past.

Marusya did not give up, however. She wrote, and ran around from one editorial office to another, offering them her work, and suddenly her efforts were met with unexpected success. A chance meeting, an offer that it would have been impossible even to contemplate—she was invited to work at the Moscow Theater of Drama as assistant to the artistic director in the Literary Section, and, if the occasion arose, to work with the actors. The other theaters had all been evacuated, but this one, organized by a director named Gorchakov, had elected to stay in Moscow in 1941.

Oh, joy! Marusya again breathed in the air of the theater and the dust of the footlights. They staged a play the public needed—*Russian People*, by Konstantin Simonov. It didn't matter that the play was somewhat clumsy, and that daily life was hard, and shortages unavoidable. Marusya had the luxury of creative work, which was dearer to her than that most essential thing, bread. She flew through the darkened streets of Moscow, reborn, and dead tired. She wrote Genrikh occasional cheery letters and worked unflaggingly for the welfare of the country.

Amalia and Genrikh worked quietly behind their curtain, and their silent lovemaking brought forth fruit. What had not happened in five years of married life with Tisha came about now: Amalia was pregnant. She didn't realize it for the first few months. Her period stopped, but during that hungry year, many young women stopped menstruating. Nature resisted conception. Amalia attributed her symptoms to exhaustion and malnourishment. She visited the doctor for the first time during the sixth month of her pregnancy, when the baby had begun to kick, announcing its existence. Her belly had begun to round out a little, some yellow spots had appeared on her face, and her lips were swollen. But she didn't need to adjust a single button on her clothing—she herself lost weight, and all her nourishment went to the child. Her gait changed; she rocked as she walked, leaning back a bit like a duck, in her fear of falling.

The summer was unusually cold and rainy that year. It passed by almost unnoticed, and an early winter set in. The biggest trial was not the constant hunger, but the outhouse, which one had to visit every day, whether one wanted to or not. A long trench was dug, with rough boards resting on top like the walls of a temporary shed. Inside, by the wall, was a kind of battered platform covered with frozen urine and steadily increasing piles of excrement. Every trip to the outhouse was like a double balancing act. The natural boundaries of shame collapsed. Gripping her husband's arms, in the darkness cut by the light of Genrikh's flashlight, Amalia planted herself above a terrifying hole. Tears flowed down her face as blood squeezed out of the hemorrhoidal knots in her rectum. Genrikh could hardly keep from crying himself, seeing his wife's suffering. With passion that surpassed that of the three Prozorov sisters by many degrees, the couple echoed Chekhov's words: "To Moscow! To Moscow!" Because of the war, this was virtually impossible.

At the beginning of 1943, the Stalingrad Tractor Plant, well known to Genrikh from his visit to his father, was closed down. Uralmash increased its production of tanks at an expedited pace. Genrikh worked on a design project that facilitated one of the most labor-intensive processes in high-precision metalworking. After finishing his work ahead of schedule, he received a prize. On the basis of this achievement, he asked the chief of his department, Abuzarov, to write him a letter of reference for an appointment with the director of the plant, Muzrukov. The director's secretary, Dina, toward whom he was kindly disposed, was Abuzarov's sister . . . Abuzarov laughed and refused, saying that it was impossible to make an appointment with the Lord God Himself. There had never been a case when the director agreed to receive a paltry engineer. Genrikh refused to back down, however.

"But why is it so urgent for you to see the big boss?" Abuzarov said. "You received a prize; what more do you want? They still won't give you a room to live in."

"Ask Dina. As a personal favor. I have to send my wife to Moscow," Genrikh told him. "She's been driven to exhaustion, and she's going to give birth soon."

Abuzarov scratched his scaly cheek with his scaly hand. "I'll ask Dina, but it isn't likely to work. If it does, you owe me one."

"Three, if you want!" Genrikh said.

The meeting did take place, and the results were very positive. The director assumed that the greenhorn would request a separate room in a dormitory—but the housing issue was very tense. The scrawny-necked youth, who didn't look a day over eighteen, asked for a permit for his pregnant wife to return to Moscow. This took Muzrukov by surprise—he's not asking for housing?—and he called Design Bureau 9, where Amalia worked. Though they were even more surprised to receive a call from the big boss, they agreed to let Amalia leave for Moscow under the circumstances.

During the entire conversation, Genrikh stood at attention before the director's desk, astonished at the ease with which decisions were made about issues that were insoluble for ordinary people.

The entrance permit into Moscow was wangled in a particular way, by a complex procedure. Muzrukov called the first secretary of the Sverdlovsk Regional Party Committee, Andrianov, and the issue was resolved definitively—a permit to go to Moscow to reside was ordered and duly received.

Three bottles of vodka, purchased on the black market at half the sum

Genrikh earned from his prize, were given to Abuzarov. Abuzarov was happy. His father was trying to finish rebuilding a cowshed that had fallen into disrepair. Building materials were hard to come by, and vodka had been used as a currency of exchange for any goods since time immemorial.

The second half of the prize money was sent to Marusya. At first, Amalia was offended that Genrikh had sent the rest of it to his mother, but then she reconsidered and realized that he had not yet quite grown used to being a husband.

In the beginning of 1943, during a raging blizzard, Genrikh took his wife, who was heavily pregnant, to the station. He had to search and search to find the train, which was standing half a mile from the platform, and he propelled Amalia in that direction. He managed to stuff her suitcase into the car of the train, but the bag with scanty provisions for the trip stayed behind. The train started moving away. Thus, Amalia traveled for nearly four days and nights almost without eating. She was ill with flu, racked by pain, and bleeding. Her mother met her at the station with their lame neighbor, Pustygin, whom Zinaida had asked to carry the suitcase.

It was cold and dark at the station in Moscow. A blizzard was raging there, too, but not of such prodigious proportions as the one that had seen Amalia off in the Urals.

A few days later, Marusya, Amalia's mother-in-law, visited. The first visit was very cordial. Her mother-in-law talked about Genrikh; she was cheerful and witty. Amalia recalled their classmates, whom Marusya remembered, too; she even mentioned Tisha. They counted the dead. They grieved, and they found reasons to be glad as well.

"It would be good if the baby were a girl," Marusya said before she left.

"Everyone says that it will be a girl. Mama says that girls suck away the mother's good looks, and I've become so unattractive since I got pregnant."

"It will pass, it will pass," Marusya said magnanimously.

In the beginning of March, in the Grauerman Maternity Hospital, where she herself had been born, Amalia brought into the world a four-pound-four-ounce girl. They called her Nora, on Marusya's insistence. Amalia would have preferred "Lenochka," but it was not Nora's fate to be a Lenochka. The doctor delivered the baby and tied up the hemorrhoids that had plagued Amalia the entire second half of her pregnancy. They never troubled her again.

At the end of 1944, Genrikh returned to Moscow. The war had turned into victory—Stalin's Ten Blows ushered the Red Army into Europe. Victory was already hanging in the air, but the "killed in battle" notices kept coming.

Of all the boys in their class, only two remained alive after the war: Genrikh himself, and Jack Rubin. Jack came home with no legs. From the class of '41, there were also only two who survived. One of them was Daniel Mitlyansky, who subsequently became a sculptor. In front of their school, a statue commemorating these boys still stands, a statue made by Daniel at the beginning of the 1970s. But that time was still a long way off.

42

Fifth Try

(2000–2009)

Liza and Yurik saw each other for the first time in the rehabilitation clinic, on the day Yurik was discharged. Liza came to pick up her cousin Marfa, who had finished her rehab treatment on the same day. A group of people who had been waiting for more than an hour for official stamps on their documents, which had been locked in the desk drawer by a secretary who had gone to lunch, consisted of Nora, Tengiz, and Yurik in one cluster, and, in the other, Liza, Marfa, and Liza's fat aunt Rita, as crushed by the misfortune of it all as a 250-pound hulk, holding a tiny infant encased in a towel—Marfa's three-month-old son—could possibly be. Marfa, who could hardly be said to exist at all if not for the evidence of her penciled-on eyebrows and large, brown-painted lips outlined in a darker-brown lipstick, had somehow managed to give birth, having barely been aware of her pregnancy or the labor itself. For the whole previous year, Marfa had been in a constant drug-induced stupor, and had only a fragmentary recollection of what had happened. Marfa and Yurik were the only ones in the group who talked to each other. All the other relatives of those who had finished their six-week treatment were cautiously silent. They were used to living with a shameful secret that demanded nondisclosure by all concerned. Yurik and Marfa discussed a fellow who was staying behind in the clinic, and even censured him for his overbearing behavior.

Liza, who had spent a great deal of effort trying to drag her cousin out of her narcotic haze, regarded with sympathy another family who were fighting for the life of their child. Nora and Tengiz left to smoke every ten minutes. The first time they went out, Tengiz motioned to Yurik to come with them to smoke.

"No, no, Tengiz. I don't smoke . . . for the time being," said the curly-haired drug addict, laughing. "Just give me two or three days."

"Damn, you're one tough dude, Yurik!" Marfa praised him.

"If you had brought the guitar, I'd sit down to play right now . . ."

"Your guitar is in the car. I brought it," his mother said.

"Nora, you're amazing."

Maybe they're not his parents, since he calls them by name, Liza thought to herself. But the fellow called after Nora as she went out, "Mama, the six-string, I hope?"

"Naturally," she said, nodding.

Nora brought in the guitar. Yurik took it out of the case and stroked the strings with his hand. They responded the way a dog responds to the touch of its master—with eager warmth and devotion. And he played something familiar, tender, and cheerful. His face changed: he pressed his lips together, and his eyes stared in front of him with intense concentration, seeing clearly what was inaccessible to others. His head nodded slightly in time with the music.

How could they have spent an entire month and a half without books, without music, without any interaction with others besides themselves? Liza mused. A strange rehab program. Some American system from Massachusetts, without medication, relying only on soul-saving conversations with psychologists . . . Well, as long as it helps. Poor Marfa, and this guy Yurik, too; poor things.

She liked him. The expression on his face, the way he played . . .

He has a happy face. How strange for a drug addict, but he has a happy face. Marfa, on the other hand, has always been inclined to suffering, Liza thought.

Then the secretary came in and took out the stamps, and the two families gravitated apart, in order not to mingle.

Fate attempted to unite Yurik and Liza a second time in the fall of 2006. By this time, he had become steeped in the history of jazz, and in music theory that lay beyond the realm of the purely academic. He had lost interest in performing with bands as a guitarist, and had mastered a profession that seemed to fall into his lap: he had become an interpreter. His English didn't equip him for the task of literary translation, but it was just what was required for film, especially modern American blockbusters, featuring criminals, policemen, gangs, and prostitutes galore. This was the language of the ghetto, the African American and Latino ghettos in particular, a language in which he was absolutely proficient, and which was not taught in foreign-language institutes or universities. Naturally, he was invited to the "AmFest," the first Russian-American film festival. He dubbed three films a day. The working schedule was frenzied, but he easily kept up with it.

"The path from my ear to my tongue is short; it bypasses my brain completely," he said. "My brain gets to take a breather."

In the break between screenings in the Horizon Theater, where the entire Moscow elite was gathered, especially the more disheveled variety, Yurik went to drink some coffee and ended up at the table where Liza was sitting. He didn't recognize her. But Liza recognized him, and hesitated—was it worth reminding him that they had met? She asked him whether he remembered when he and Marfa were released from the clinic together. His cup froze in his hand.

"Marfa died four years ago. I was at her funeral," he said.

"Yes, I arranged the funeral. She was my cousin. It was not the right occasion for getting to know someone, of course. But I don't remember seeing you there."

"That year, three of the people who were in treatment with us died. Marfa, Mustafa, and Slava. There were twenty-five people in the group. Two of them, as far as I know, pulled themselves together and stayed clean; about eight people started shooting up again; one person was killed; and I don't know anything about the rest of them. During the first year, everyone got together regularly in meetings, but, little by little, everyone stopped going. That's in keeping with the statistics, actually. I've got to go now."

It was their second try, and it failed miserably. This rather plump girl, with long hair and a face that looked a bit feral—like that of a fox or a wolf cub—had reminded him of things he wanted to forget. And he promptly forgot about the encounter.

Liza berated herself—what a little idiot she had been! As if she couldn't pick a better topic. But she liked Yurik still more than she had at the rehab clinic. There was something indefinable in him that she had never sensed in other people, and the commonalities that other thirty-somethings of her acquaintance shared were completely lacking in him; she couldn't quite put her finger on what the quality was.

After Marfa's death, Liza adopted her nephew, Timosha, as her own. He was born with a cleft palate and lip—or "harelip," in the vernacular. This birth defect did not affect his mental development, but it certainly made his own life, and that of his relatives, miserable. Liza spent a great deal of time with the boy, arranged for consultations with doctors, paid plastic surgeons, and became very emotionally attached to him. Her aunt was only too grateful that she had taken him under her wing. Liza gave up journalism and went to work in a travel agency, as a full partner. Business started booming, in large part thanks to Liza's talent for talking on the telephone. In addition to the gift of gab, her affable nature, and her sociability, she had a remarkably pleasant voice.

In short, everything was going swimmingly. She had more than enough money. She exchanged her small two-room apartment in the back of beyond for a three-room apartment in a stately Stalin-era building in an old Moscow neighborhood. She arranged for Timosha to undergo four surgeries, after which he was as pretty as Marfa had been in childhood, but much smarter. By the time he was six, all the required surgeries had been performed. The surgeons did not rule out the possibility that he might need more cosmetic surgery as an adult, when his face was fully formed. Timosha was a wonderful child—clever, affectionate, with a sound character. His black Asian hair was the only thing he had obviously inherited from his unknown father.

On the surface, everything was good. But Liza longed for another child. To carry, to bring into the world. Ideally, a girl. If there was one thing lacking in her otherwise prosperous and happy life, it was that she had never been married. She did not experience any great social discomfort because of this. She was surrounded by many unmarried, divorced, lonely people; and there were still more who were tormented by family life, constantly complaining about their husbands, former beauties desperately awaiting lovers. It was a commonly known fact that it was easier to chance it and get married when you are nineteen than to solve this problem at thirty, when you already understand the qualities a real partner should have. By that time, all the men who are worth their salt are already married. The only ones who are not taken are dyed-in-the-wool bachelors who are disinclined to family life, or those who have been rejected despite the meager supply of partners.

Liza's last romance, with a married man who was very compatible with her, fizzled out by itself: they went their separate ways. After that, she got involved with Pasha, a young manager at her company—a biker, and a fan of some kind of otherworldly sport that involved scaling roofs. Liza became pregnant from him. Contrary to expectation, he was delighted. He immediately proposed to her, and in the most traditional form—with a bouquet of flowers and a ring in a red box. Liza was deeply touched, accepted the ring—but didn't marry him.

The next attempt by fate to unite Liza and Yurik was also very clumsy. Liza was in the final stages of her pregnancy. They met at her travel agency by the Nikitsky Gates, where Yurik had come with Nora to buy a package deal to Croatia or Montenegro. Nora had suddenly been seized by the idea of such a trip, and within fifteen minutes she and her son were stopping by the nearest travel agency.

Liza was sitting at her desk, talking on the telephone. She waved to them and said, holding her hand over the receiver, "I'll be with you in just a moment."

A year had passed since their last meeting at the film festival, and this time Yurik recognized her. By her voice—rather low and husky, with a marvelous timbre.

Liza advised them not to buy a package deal. She offered to book them a hotel in Dubrovnik and suggested they buy plane tickets instead. From Dubrovnik they could take a trip to Montenegro for a day or two, by bus. It was cheaper, and they wouldn't feel so constrained. Nora laughed: "But what about your premium? I don't quite understand."

Liza laughed, too, and said, "I don't always understand myself. But I think you'll like this option better."

She drummed on her large belly with her long fingers like a trained hare in a circus, and booked the hotel for Nora.

After that, they didn't see each other again for two years. Both of them were busy with their own affairs. Liza had a baby—a little girl she had named Olga. Timosha was happy. Liza could never have imagined the brotherly tenderness and delight that Timosha felt for his newborn sister. During Liza's pregnancy, Pasha helped her a great deal. Now powerful paternal emotions had been awakened in him, and he moved in with her. It was a wonder how a fellow who was fairly unsophisticated, fairly rough around the edges, could be capable of so much tenderness and awe. After a month, when Liza was ready to hire a nanny for the children and go back to work, Pasha implored her to let him beg off work for good and stay home with the children. Timosha and Pasha had already formed a close bond. Liza decided to try it out. When Pasha had left his job and was staying home to take care of the children, Liza spent most of her time in the travel bureau; during her absence, the business had begun to go to rack and ruin. She threw all her energy into picking it up off the ground again.

Pasha, with just as much enthusiasm, threw himself into raising the children. They rented a dacha for the summer, and he took care of the little ones. His mother, who in the beginning had greeted Liza with hostility, gradually melted. Of course, Liza was too old for him—eight years his senior—but when all was said and done, she was without peer.

Pasha had grown up without a father, and family life, as he was now experiencing it, was very much to his liking. He liked Liza, too. None of his biker buddies had ever had such a remarkable woman—beautiful, calm, educated, and practical. Pasha was used to working off his emotions by driving fast and scaling roofs. Though he wasn't given to strong passions, he valued having a good relationship. In short, everything was as fine as it could be. Liza came to the dacha on Friday evening and stayed until Tuesday morning, sometimes Wednesday. In this way, she managed to keep the business going, and the children were completely happy.

Still, summer was high season for the travel bureau, and Liza couldn't abandon the office altogether. Whenever she wasn't there, slips and blunders tended to happen. On a Tuesday in August, Liza was driving out of the entranceway of a residential building next to her office, where she parked her car, when she saw Yurik standing there with two guitars, trying to hitch a ride with a chance passerby. Stopping in this spot, in front of an entranceway on Novy Arbat, was forbidden, and he could have stood there for a long time without having any luck. Liza drove up to him and shouted: "Quick, get in!"

Yurik hopped into the car, and only recognized Liza when he was already sitting next to her. This was fate's fifth try, if one counted Marfa's funeral, where it was only by chance that they had not run into each other. But this didn't occur to Yurik. Liza was the one who counted.

"Where are we going?"

Yurik named the address of a club that was popular among young people.

"Do you have a gig?"

"Something like that. I'm giving a lecture," he said, smiling. "A lecture series. About the history of jazz. Tonight is the first one. I have no idea how it will turn out."

"May I stay and listen?"

"Sure. That would be great. I'm not even sure if anyone will show up. So I'll at least have an audience of one."

There were about twenty people in the audience. Yurik sat at the head of a long table, assembled out of eight small ones, and asked Liza to sit opposite him. He knew from his experience in music that when you don't know the public, it's good to find someone in the crowd to perform for. He began the conversation about jazz like a good teacher showing the first letters to a group of first-graders—giving them a sense of discovery, something happening before their very eyes.

"Today we're not yet going to talk about jazz, the parts of which came together during the course of twenty or thirty years. We're going to talk about the musical realities that existed before it, that had always been there, that flowed together and spurred the development of a single huge current that falls under the general moniker 'jazz.'"

He began to talk and to demonstrate to Liza all kinds of things she had never known before. He played the guitar, and tapped out rhythms on a small drum, and sometimes sang a musical phrase or two. He played the blues, the music of the American slaves, and excused himself for the banality he couldn't avoid when he told the audience the already classic definition of the blues—"The blues ain't nothin' but a good man feelin' bad," in the words of Leon Redbone. He played and showed and sang lines in English, then translated them, then sang some more. Then he came to the subject of black gospel music, which had its roots in the singing of praise songs, of the Psalms, and of what came to be known as "spirituals." After this, he interrupted himself, saying that he had gotten carried away and hadn't stuck to the plan of his lecture at all, but that he would continue the lecture at exactly this point in a week. In parting, he played the most popular and well-known spiritual in the world, "Go Down, Moses."

After the lecture, Yurik went up to Liza, who was clearly moved, and thanked her for being there so he could talk "to her" during the presentation, because her face was so intelligent, and also empathic.

"I don't think we say that in Russian—an 'empathic face,' but I like it. It was a wonderful lecture. Incredible!" And Yurik took Liza by the hand and they went to the bar, where they drank a glass of orange juice each, because they both had their own reasons for avoiding alcohol.

Then they got into the car and left. Each of them was thinking at that moment: Where are we going?

And they simultaneously answered the question. Liza said, "Your place?" Yurik said, "My place?" And they went back to Nikitsky Boulevard. Nora, very conveniently, was in Chelyabinsk, or Perm . . .

The windows of the old apartment building on Nikitsky Boulevard looked out on Liza's office, if rather obliquely. Yurik's family had lived here for four generations already, more than one hundred years. This apartment remembered the blind precentor, his unhappy wife, the unhappy marriage between Amalia and Genrikh, the happy love of Amalia and Andrei Ivanovich, Vitya and his school notebook with literature notes, and Nora and Tengiz, who had been locked in a lovers' struggle for the better part of their lives. The apartment had accepted them all and accommodated them graciously. It was good here, and no ghosts haunted the premises.

A long conjugal life lay in store for Yurik and Liza, which they both immediately sensed. It was foolish to ask which was more important, the spirit or the flesh—and, indeed, it never occurred to them to ask that question. Their intimacy was full and boundless, a kind rarely encountered in anyone's life.

They took a hot shower together. Yurik admired Liza, and Liza Yurik, as if they were seeing with the eyes of Adam and Eve in the garden, who had just come to know . . . what was it again? They were both about the same height. He was skinny, his shoulders sloped, and his legs were slightly bowed. She was fleshy by today's standards, with breasts that sagged slightly under their own generous weight, and curvy hips somewhat resembling jodhpurs. In the thick, steamy heat, their bodies turned pink, and the shower stand rose up between them like the Biblical Tree of Life.

Then they sat in the kitchen, eating red apples. There was no other food in the house. Liza bit off an entire half of a small apple and said, "I like green apples best, though red ones will do."

"I'll have to disappoint you. It's unlikely I'll be able to buy you green ones. I'm color-blind."

"No matter. I can buy as many as I need for myself."

He was thirty-four, and she was thirty-two. They had both been in love before, had had relationships, both happy and unhappy; but both of them had the same feeling, that the past had receded and was no longer significant. They were like the only two people in the world. They didn't know each other well yet, but the most meaningful thing was resolved without words. She accepted his past as a drug addict—although there are no former drug addicts or KGB agents, as they say. She accepted the artistic chaos of his life and his rejection of that stability that Liza herself valued and maintained. And he accepted her—with her children, her family problems, Pasha and his indeterminate status in her life, her Aunt Rita, and the travel bureau.

43

Family Secrets

(1936–1937)

A marriage will not survive on postage stamps alone. Come!" Jacob
had written to Marusya. He was probably right. During his six years
of exile, she came to see him only once, at the beginning of his ordeal, in Stalingrad. That was in 1932. His second reunion with his wife took
place at the train station in Moscow just over two years later. This time, he
was on his way from the Stalingrad prison to Novosibirsk, via Moscow.
His sister and her husband had come to see him off, too, but they had presented no obstacle to renewed declarations of love. Jacob had only thirty
minutes in which to change trains. Jacob and Marusya had to run from
the Kazan station to the Kursk station, and talk in the presence of an elderly, weary captain of the local Ministry of State Security, who issued Jacob his ticket to Novosibirsk. One of the dubious privileges of exiles and
prisoners was a free ticket from their place of residence to the destination
where they would serve their term. The words Jacob and Marusya exchanged in haste, literally on the run, were insignificant, but the eye saw
more than words could say. Marusya looked tired and depressed. She had
dark circles under her eyes, and her usual leanness—she always complained of losing weight—inspired in Jacob a sense of guilt for inadvertently
causing his wife to suffer.

It wasn't only these visible signs of suffering that oppressed Jacob. He
felt much more deeply Marusya's disappointment—in him, her husband,
who had promised her so much in life and who had constantly let her down.
She looked very unhappy. The differences in their inward dispositions were

clearly manifested here. To be happy, Marusya needed constant external signs of success and recognition. When Marusya was able to admire Jacob, to be confident in their brilliant future together, her own strength was amplified. But her strong, passionate temperament went hand in hand with an inner fragility and weakness, and the vividness of her desires with volatility. Her soul balked when it had to cope with the blows that life dealt. She grumbled, blamed the circumstances, and fell into despondency.

The sense of being unhappy was alien to Jacob. He did not permit himself the luxury of such feelings, and was ashamed when such thoughts occurred to him. Even in the most vexing circumstances, he tried to derive joy from the small, quotidian gifts of life: the sun peeping out, a green branch outside the window, a pleasant person he met along the way and chatted with about this and that; and, most important, good books. Marusya also knew how to derive joy from small things, but for this she needed Jacob to be beside her. Joy did not come easily to her if there was no spectator to witness it. An actress always needs an audience.

Jacob was certain that he could conquer Marusya's despondency with his masculine authority and power, with that rare and wonderful intimacy that had always enhanced their conjugal life: to smooth away, caress, kiss, and bring her to the peak of mutual pleasure, and even beyond, into a realm of pure bliss that left the joys of the flesh behind.

But, despite his virtuosity with the pen, and however deep and tender his letters to his wife may have been, his physical absence was an insurmountable obstacle for them. He felt this in her letters to him, in the irritation that broke through, in the jabs and reproaches, and, mainly, in the increasing expressions of ideological protest on her part. She called herself a "nonpartisan Bolshevik," and accused Jacob of political myopia, of floundering in a petit-bourgeois swamp. She had become irreversibly alienated from him.

He knew Marusya's impressionability and the enthusiasm with which she always adopted new projects—her infatuation with pedagogy during her studies at the Froebel Institute; pedology, the rejected sister of pedagogy; the new religion of "movement" in the Rabenek studio; followed by theater, then journalism . . . He was moved by her touching conviction about the "higher good" when one infatuation replaced another, and then hoped that her enthusiasm about Bolshevism, in its nonpartisan variety, would not give way to Party membership. In fact, they would not have accepted her, anyway—the wife of a "wrecker," an enemy of the people.

There was still another obstacle, one that lurked in her own character: a boundary that Marusya would not have been able to cross. She was essentially bohemian in nature, and any kind of orthodox discipline, strict Party discipline in particular, was anathema to her. It was Jacob who had reported dutifully to work from a young age; until the end of her life, Marusya was never willing or able to tie herself down with routine work. Her worst fear, the greatest bugaboo to her, was punching in and out—that is, showing up on time for work every day, and leaving at a certain hour, and registering one's arrival and departure on the time clock.

There was one other thought that alarmed Jacob. He knew Marusya's susceptibility and suspected that she might have fallen under the spell of a new, different kind of infatuation. With a man. Jacob was not jealous, although when they were young Marusya had unconsciously provoked him with stories of important, interesting men who had sought her out. She conveyed this primarily in letters. Yet Jacob had actually been inclined to feel some pride in these reports. He completely understood the men who showed an interest in his fiancée, then his wife. Her attractions were such that Jacob could not even imagine comparing her to other women. She surpassed all others in her charms. Even in the fits of jealousy to which she was prone, she never lost her fascinating appeal.

Her jealousy was unfounded: Jacob never betrayed his wife. That is not to say that Jacob didn't like other women. He did; he liked them very much. When he was young, he had been desperately in love with a fellow student named Lydia, but she preferred another to him. Back then, at seventeen, he went through the experience of rejection. Even before that, he had liked very much the daughter of the family's neighbor, the architect Kovalenko; he had been attracted to the sister of one of his friends, and another girl he knew, who attended college. Later, when he was already married to Marusya, he was enamored with a nurse, Valentina Beloglazova, who had given him glucose injections when he was stationed in Kharkov; he also liked Nadezhda Belskaya, secretary at the People's Commissariat of Labor, where he often found himself. She liked him very much, too, and she gave him to understand this. It was not his eyes, but another organ greedy for pleasure that gave him a signal, which he immediately refused. He kept his own body under control, and didn't let its demands overmaster him. All in all, accepting the postulate about the primacy of matter and the subordination of the spirit to it, the couple made wonderful mutual use of the body for promoting conjugal happiness, while still considering the Seventh Commandment to be sacrosanct.

Yet, on this particular issue, Marusya experienced some sort of psychological or emotional malfunction. For some reason, it was terribly painful for her to feel that her husband was attracted to another woman. He never betrayed her, or gave in to his desires—this he swore to her—but if he was attracted to another woman, and only refused to give in to his desires out of moral considerations, what was this morality, then? Was it not purely spiritual? Was it not higher than the flesh in that case? At this point Marusya grew weary, and began to cry. But, at the same time, she insisted on complete honesty in their relations, and constantly tormented herself with the confessions she forced from her husband about how his body reacted to this, that, or the other woman.

Now this had all receded into a realm of Jacob's memory that only called up a sad smile in him. Since he could not change his wife's mood, he postponed the clarification and restoration of their good relations until such time as he could put his arms around her thin shoulders, and chased away the jealous suspicion that someone else was occupying Marusya's feelings and thoughts, embracing her small shoulders, and doing with her all the mundane things in which there was no beauty, no mystery, but only mutually coordinated movements. Small details seared his imagination—her head thrown back, the blue vein in her neck, the grayish mother-of-pearl of her eyes looking out from under the half-closed lids, and the elongated dimple in her chin. Jacob chased away these thoughts and memories and devoted all his energies toward what he called "productive life." He went to work, invented all kinds of extra sources of income for himself, such as private language and music lessons; he arranged and settled his life, and sent money and parcels to Moscow, though it was customary for such "care packages" to travel in the other direction—from Moscow to Biysk, to those in exile.

The letters from home were not comforting. Marusya dredged up all their disputes, artistic or political, and invested them with new energy. Jacob tried to explain himself, which added fuel to the fire; everything became a pretext for new reproaches, until Jacob understood that Marusya simply wanted to pick a fight, no matter the reason. His replies became more reserved, and the intervals between letters grew longer.

At the same time, his eczema flared up again. His hands and feet were covered with a dry crust that erupted in tiny wet pustules, and it itched, burned, and made him generally miserable. During the day, he kept himself in check, but at night, when he was asleep, he scratched himself until he bled. He would wake up from the pain, then fall asleep again, reaching some strange state of semiconsciousness in which he came to an agreement with the unbearable itching: I'm sleeping, and in my sleep I can scratch the wounds . . .

The subject of health became one of the safest in their correspondence. He once wrote his wife that the eczema was playing up to such a degree that it freed him from all the sad thoughts that would otherwise preoccupy him.

A few days after she received this letter, Marusya's wrists began itching. The connection between herself and her husband turned out to be much stronger and deeper than she would have liked. Jacob was to a certain degree correct in his surmises. She wanted to free herself from him, but was unable to do so, and she was unconsciously seeking masculine authority and power.

She was no longer the young, bewitching actress with an undefined and exciting future ahead of her; older men no longer turned around to look at her. But she was not seeking a man so much as an idea that would free her. The ideas about emancipation that had long preoccupied her stalled at this point: the bearers of ideas, Marusya's protests and objections notwithstanding, were men.

Jacob, with his intelligent love, knew how to quell the mixture of pride and uncertainty that created a room-sized hell in her soul, but she was not alone. Their son, Genrikh, was also in need of support. Like Marusya, he, too, was preparing for flight, but in the most concrete terms: gliders, airplanes, air, the sky . . . Yet life had deposited him in a place that was the polar opposite of his dreams: the Metrostroi, construction of the subway system. Yet even underground he managed to find the communist romanticism that was so dear to him. Marusya supported him in any way she could, but she had her own problems to deal with.

Then Ivan Belousov reappeared. A person from the past, from her Kiev youth, a friend of her brother's, who once was desperately and hopelessly in love with her. He had spent summer evenings in the courtyard of her family's home, at a long wooden table with a small table adjoining it for the samovar. Incidents seemed to follow Ivan all the time: He would burn his fingers on the samovar, or overturn a glass of tea on her father's duck-cloth trousers. Once he stepped on an old dog lying beneath the table, and it bit him. It was probably the first time in its entire life that this dog had bitten anyone, and more out of fright than pain. Everyone laughed at Belousov constantly, and there was no person on earth who was more good-natured about the jokes and jibes leveled at him by Marusya's brother Mikhail.

Belousov, unable to conceal his feelings for Marusya, watched the sixteen-year-old girl like a child staring at candy. Though Marusya pretended to be angry, she was really flirting with him, always flirting. Several times, she went with Belousov to the theater, and felt uncomfortable and disproportionately small next to him. At six feet six inches, he was twice her size. When he took her by the arm, she yanked it away and advised him to bring a collar and a leash next time—that would make it easier for them to walk together. His excessive height inspired mockery in the Kerns, who were all rather small in stature. He was embarrassed by his height, his long thin hands, which stuck too far out of the sleeves of his shirts, and his enormous boots, which were specially made for him by an Armenian cobbler who charged him for one and a half pairs instead of just one. Ivan turned red, then bunched up his handkerchief in his sweaty hands and rubbed his forehead and his prominent nose, with its large nostrils. To all appearances a mild-mannered, gentle, awkward fellow.

Meanwhile, Ivan Belousov was a genuine revolutionary, one of the few Bolsheviks in Kiev who knew how to write leaflets. The first one he wrote was about the death of Tolstoy, very cocky and self-assured, summoning people to band together "under the banner of the Social Democratic Labor Party, to struggle for the overthrow of the government of robbers and thieves, against the violence and tyranny of the Tsar's henchmen, against the deadly etc. evils and of the disintegrating bourgeois-capitalist system." Tolstoy would hardly have approved.

At first, Marusya didn't see him as a real activist. In the fall of 1913, however, when Kiev was reeling from the Beilis Affair, he brought her a leaflet from the RSDRP with a call to protest against the oppression of the non-Russian peoples of Russia, and to strengthen the international union of workers of all nationalities, and informed her that he was the author of the text. That was the moment when Marusya began to regard him with seriousness and respect. But nothing more. She was already eternally, as she thought then, bound to Jacob.

At about this time, Ivan Belousov was expelled from the university, became a member of the Kiev committee of the RSDRP, and ran a propaganda study circle to which he invited Marusya. He was no longer comically in love with her, although he still blushed and bunched up his handkerchief in her presence. She visited this semi-underground gathering several times, but her enthusiasm for the Froebel movement outweighed her interest in revolutionary politics.

Shortly before the start of World War I, Ivan disappeared. Marusya didn't think about him anymore. Twenty years later, in 1935, when she attended the courses on the history of the Communist Party for journalists, in the Institute of the Red Professorate, she met him again. The lecturer, a large bald man in a gray service jacket, was one Comrade Belousov, a professor.

He began his first lecture with a quote from Lenin: "You can only become a communist when you have enriched your memory with the entire wealth of knowledge accumulated by humanity." He went on to discuss Marx and Engels, whose ideas Marusya knew already but now listened to attentively. Ivan spoke distinctly, clearly, with careful diction. The only thing lacking in him was artistry, and Marusya had something to compare him to: she had attended lectures by some world-class pedagogues at the Froebel Institute.

After the lecture, Marusya approached Professor Belousov—not to renew their acquaintance, but to ask him about the program of study. And to get a good look at him . . . and . . . just because . . .

"Marusya? How did you end up here?" He blushed, took his crumpled handkerchief out of his pocket, and mopped his brow.

There he was, Ivan Belousov himself. It could not have been said that she liked him in his new guise; rather, he interested her. He walked her home. From the Strastnoy Monastery they walked along the boulevards to the Nikitsky Gates, then turned toward home. He didn't hunch over to talk to her, as he had before. On the contrary, Marusya strained her long, graceful neck to look up at him, and it seemed to her that he was looking down at her tenderly. They said goodbye at the entrance to her building. From then on, they renewed their friendship and saw each other regularly. Talked about things. Discussed politics. Marusya valued his proletarian rootedness in life—that which was lacking in her.

At the beginning of March, Marusya's cousin Asya Smolkina, whom she rarely saw, called her and asked whether she could drop by for a minute. It was inopportune, but Asya said she was already in the neighborhood, and Marusya had to agree. Among her many cousins, Asya had a reputation as the kindest and the stupidest. It is likely that these two qualities share a common core; but perhaps people who are intelligent and unkind yoke them together only to justify the absence of goodness in themselves. Be that as it may, Asya showed up, both good and stupid. Since childhood, she had looked up to Marusya, extolling her many talents, authentic and imaginary; her beauty, which had faded somewhat by now; her intelligence; her education; and, of late, the bitterness of her lot. But, for all her admiration of Marusya, she held Jacob in even higher esteem.

Her relatives didn't appreciate the selfless and unquestioning help that Asya bestowed on all of them, distant and close, without exception. They took her empathy and altruism for granted. Only once had Asya received a sign of gratitude for her invisible exploits and deeds—lancing abscesses, giving injections, preparing poultices, and administering enemas to old ladies on their deathbeds. Her whole life, Asya had remembered how Jacob, after returning to Kiev from Kharkov during a three-day furlough, came to her house with a bouquet of flowers, a nearly forgotten sign of gratitude, kissed her hand, which was desiccated from constant exposure to alcohol (the hand of a surgical nurse), and thanked her for saving his son's life, and his wife's breasts, with her healing arts. But where had he managed to get hold of flowers during the harsh privations of 1916?

"My goodness, Jacob, what do you mean? You're exaggerating. I'm only glad I could help," Asya murmured, feeling as though she had received a decoration. From that moment on, she had considered him to be the noblest person she had ever met in her life.

During the rare celebrations when all the relatives got together, Asya usually sat at the far end of the table and devoured Jacob with her eyes, unaware that the other cousins were winking at one another and exchanging glances at her expense. She didn't consider her raptures over Jacob to be anything like being in love, because since childhood she had been certain that no man would ever marry her, and that it wasn't even worth dreaming about. The best thing she could do was to serve all the people who surrounded her, without exception. The notion of people who were "near and dear" was unknown to her. She did not suspect that she had taken a kind of monastic vow, and she didn't even know she was making sacrifices. Well, is that not what others would call stupid?

She entered Marusya's house, smiling her bland, foolish smile. She had tender hairs on her upper lip that promised to become more mannish with the years. Her close-set eyes shone. When she smiled more broadly, her long mouth opened to reveal perfect, white, evenly spaced teeth that looked as if they had been intended for someone else. In her hands she was holding a paper bag with pastries. Marusya boiled the teakettle on a hot plate she had in the room—she tried to avoid going into the communal kitchen if she could help it. Drinking tea and eating éclairs, they discussed the relatives. Marusya didn't mention Jacob. When Asya asked what news she had of him, Marusya told her about the eczema, which had grown worse. Asya opened her arms wide in a gesture of surprise, exclaiming: "Really? But what a co-incidence! Vera's Annechka also has eczema."

Marusya just shrugged. Which Vera was she talking about? Who was Annechka? What was she so thrilled about?

"I mean that I'm happy because my colleague Vera discovered some old lady in a village near Moscow, an herbalist or some such person. And she gave Annechka, her daughter, some kind of poultice. It stank to high heaven—black stuff, God knows what's in it—but it helped. It worked wonders! Two weeks later, she didn't have a single spot. It was just recently. If you want, I can find out about it, and get some of it for Jacob."

Marusya promptly forgot about this herbalist and her miracle cure, but a week later Asya called her on the phone. Brimming with excitement, Asya informed her that she had managed to get hold of the potion, that the old woman was simply remarkable, that she lived in the village of Firsanovka, that her whole house was covered with icons. The woman was a fervent believer, but not slow-witted—very sensible and wise, and even rather well read. She had books on botany . . . A genuine herbalist, and her own grandmother had been an herbalist, too. So folk medicine really was better than any newfangled treatments; Marusya should make sure to get this potion to Jacob, and right away! Otherwise, within two weeks it would go bad and lose its healing properties.

Marusya asked her to send the remedy by mail. Asya was at a loss for words. When she recovered her composure, she said yes, she could send it by mail, but by the time it got there it wouldn't work anymore. Besides, would they even allow her to send a bottle through the mail?

Politely, without any spite, Marusya told Asya that she had no plans to go to Biysk in the near future, and that if Asya considered it necessary she was free to go herself—today, if need be.

Asya, thrown off guard, and living up to her reputation, said, "But I don't even know where Jacob lives."

"The town of Biysk, 27 Kvartalnaya Street. Please excuse me, Asya, I can't talk right now." And Marusya hung up the phone. My goodness, what an idiot, she thought to herself.

Asya went to the train station and bought a ticket for the city of Novo-sibirsk. They told her that she could only reach Biysk by a local commuter train. By the evening of the next day, she was sitting on a train to Siberia, traveling to a place that Marusya would never make it to.

In her suitcase, encased in a canvas covering, Asya was carrying a care-fully wrapped half-liter bottle of a viscous dark-amber liquid, and, just as carefully wrapped, foodstuffs—two bottles of homemade jam, two kilo-grams of flour, and two kilograms of millet. She looked out the window, and enjoyed watching the fields and forests slip past; she hadn't gone on va-cation in three years, and everything she saw delighted her.

Since her youth, she had spent the greater part of her time in hospitals and clinics, among doctors and the sick, and twice she had been called upon to assist famous surgeons. One of them was killed in a field hospital during the war, by a random shell. The second, an old country doctor, died of a heart attack while he was operating. Admiration was a requirement for her rapturous nature, and the surgeons she worked with now did not inspire respect. One of them accepted gifts from the patients—bribes, in other words. Another had a reputation as a ladies' man, and surrounded himself with a flock of pretty nurses, with whom he amused himself in convenient nooks and corners of the clinic. For shame, for shame . . .

Asya was unable to find her ideal in her immediate surroundings, but Jacob, to whom in her youth she had assigned the role of ideal man and human being, still existed in some far-off place. The dark-amber liquid in the bottle that she had brought from the back of beyond was intended to allay his suffering. This was her mission—it was not the ordinary journey of a distant relative to an exile banished to a remote realm, somewhere deep in Siberia. What a pity that it was she and not Marusya on that train—a visit from his wife would have brought Jacob far greater joy!

While the crazy Asya was journeying toward the Altai Mountains with the miracle potion in her suitcase, Marusya was also thinking about Jacob. The reason for this was Ivan Belousov, with whom (not simply out of the blue) she had renewed her relations. The history of the Party was the main topic of discussion, and Marusya tenderly recalled the time when the curly-haired, clumsy Ivan had tried to take her by the arm.

Ivan walked her home now after classes. He took her by the arm with-out any hesitation, was friendly but reserved, and did not transgress any boundaries. But their conversation, starting with the main topic, Party his-tory, somehow flowed smoothly into the memories of their youth, and at one point he squeezed her arm above her elbow—not very firmly, but not too weakly, either; with just the right degree of pressure. At that moment, Marusya felt that she was betraying Jacob. Yes, she wanted to betray him . . . After she got home, she weighed every word that Ivan had said that evening and realized that she agreed with him. Jacob would not have agreed with him: he would have said something sharp and critical! And she experienced a surge of irritation toward her husband.

She had to admit that Belousov, ridiculous and awkward in his youth, had now become a kindred spirit. He was educated, but in another way from Jacob; and, like Jacob, he was also a writer, but in a different vein. How easily his dyed-in-the-wool proletarian origins won out over Jacob's bourgeois complexities!

Their walks after classes lasted longer and longer, and Jacob was a constant presence, somewhere in the background. Marusya felt she was carrying on a conversation with two people: with Ivan out loud, and with Jacob in her head.

Asya had to wait for the train to Biysk for three hours, and she managed to send a telegram to Jacob to let him know she was coming. He didn't meet her at the station. Late in the evening, with a suitcase and a handbag, in boots with little heels that sank into a deep layer of freshly fallen snow, as soft and light as feathers, she wandered around for a long time in search of Jacob's house, though he lived only ten minutes by foot from the station.

The telegram was delivered while Asya was groping through the darkness next to the house where Jacob rented a room. She couldn't imagine the intense surge of happiness Jacob felt when he took the telegram and read the words "Meet me." For years now, these words had been connected with the dream of a visit from his wife. Nor could she have imagined how deep was his surprise and dismay when he saw that the signature on the telegram read "Asya." He didn't immediately understand who this Asya was that was coming to see him. It occurred to him it might have been some sort of mistake. He put on his overcoat and went out onto the porch, and a moment later was greeting his visitor. He pressed the frozen hand that she worked out of her sleeve, grabbed the suitcase, half buried in the snow, and led her into the house, nearly weeping from sad disappointment.

After helping Asya take off her coat, her headscarf, her boots, he put the kettle on for tea. Asya smiled and began rubbing her red hands together— intelligent, skillful hands with fingernails clipped nearly to the quick, and with a permanent outline of iodine around the rims.

Jacob didn't even think to wonder why she had come. He assumed that she had affairs of her own to attend to, that she was on some sort of business trip, or whatever it was called in her line of work. While she tried to get warm, he placed a mug and a glass on the desk (he had no other table in the tiny room) and poured out the tea. They ate black bread and butter and drank bitter tea. Asya regretted that she had not thought to buy good tea (and would not have had time, anyway) at Eliseyevsky's delicacy store. At first their conversation revolved around the family, but Asya had no information to convey about the daily affairs of Marusya and Genrikh. She saw them seldom, and couldn't add anything to what Jacob already knew. He began to question Asya about her work, and she eagerly, even fervently, informed him about the hospital where she had been working for ten years. She told him about how she had gotten the job, and which prominent surgeons she had assisted, on which occasions.

She glanced furtively at his hands; they looked terrible.

"If you don't mind, I'll have a look," Asya said.

Jacob placed both hands on the top of the desk. They looked as if he were wearing crimson fingerless gloves. His long, white fingers, which bent slightly at the last joints, were clean, but from the knuckles upward, and running under the sleeve of his sweater, was one big scab. She turned his hands over and began examining his palms. The skin was healthy up to his wrists, but above them it looked like a sleeve made of some rough red fabric.

Jacob smiled through his mustache and said, joking, "Asya, did you come here on account of this?"

"Yes, of course! Didn't Marusya write you about the wonder-working potion? My friend"—here the scrupulous Asya corrected herself—"the daughter of my friend, that is—was cured in two weeks. And she had already tried everything; they even took her to the Military Academy Hospital in Leningrad and gave her X-ray treatments, but nothing helped."

Asya rushed over to her suitcase, still in its canvas casing and standing in a puddle of melting snow. She started peeling off the soaking layer of heavy fabric. Jacob tried to help her, but she said no, no, she would do it herself. Finally, she pulled out the sacred bottle, removed an outer layer of newspaper, then the thick black paper in which it was wrapped, and plunked it down on the table.

"There. For you."

How touching, how sweet this Asya is, thought Jacob. She'd carried this ridiculous bottle all the way from Moscow to Siberia.

"Thank you, Asya, I will certainly give it a try. There have been times when the rash cleared up completely, but then it came back. I don't think they have invented a medicament that will cure eczema once and for all. But I will definitely try it."

"Let's try it right now, so as not to waste any more time. Annechka already saw a difference in her condition by the third day. You know, Jacob, I have a return ticket in only eight days. I took a leave of two weeks, but the traveling time takes nearly seven days. So let's start right away. I'll apply the poultice and then go to a hotel. Is there a hotel near the station?"

"Asya," Jacob said. A wild suspicion seized him. "Did you come to Biysk on a business trip, or . . . ?"

"No, no. Didn't Marusya tell you? I got hold of the medicine, thinking that she would bring it to you herself, but she was busy, so she gave me the address, and . . . here I am."

This was some sort of madness. Asya here, and some old lady, a poultice . . . And *this* is why she came all the way to Biysk?

Scratching his hand, Jacob suggested that they postpone the first treatment until the next day, but Asya insisted: Right now! No waiting. He firmly announced that it was too late today and that he needed to go to bed, because he had to go to work early the next morning. He settled Asya on his narrow cot and made a pallet on the floor for himself—a sheepskin coat covered with a sheet. There was no hotel to speak of in Biysk, but he'd have to go to the police to register her tomorrow.

In the morning, Jacob went to work at the bank. When he returned, Asya was sitting at the desk, crocheting white lace with a tiny hook. She was embarrassed.

"Everyone says it's silly and bourgeois, but it's so soothing." She quickly folded away her handiwork in a knitted bag.

In the evening, the first treatment took place. At the same time, there was a fall from grace. He didn't even get the chance to start liking the woman. In all her forty years, no man had ever liked her, even in her youth. But her firm and gentle touch on his hands, and his legs, and his groin, which was also covered with the small, fiery-red spots of eczema, was so arousing that it happened in a flash, almost unconsciously. The prolonged male hunger and the professional sympathy of a woman's hands came together and quickened the flame of passion.

Asya had no wish to seduce someone else's husband, especially the husband of her revered Marusya, but everything happened so fast, so spontaneously, for both of them.

They lay on a white sheet spotted with brown herbs from the potion, themselves smeared with the herbal sludge, pressed closely together—and they both cried. It was an upheaval, and a great corporeal celebration, and a terrible shame, which receded when Jacob again entered the heart of the world, the depths of the body of a woman to whom he was not bound by anything except perhaps gratitude. And so, until morning, they both struggled with shame, and came out victors. Almost victors. Devastation, then tenderness, and again gratitude.

They spent the whole week with hardly a break in their nighttime embraces. Then they parted—a decision they had made mutually—forever. Jacob accompanied Asya to the station. The March snow had not ceased falling since the day Asya arrived. She brushed the snow from her eyelashes, and lifted her boots out of the drifts, in which they kept getting stuck. Jacob carried her suitcase. With a certain sense of relief, Jacob kissed Asya, pushed his hand under her coat, and stroked her heavy breasts, destined for nourishing a multitude of children but preserved in barren virginity. They had decided between them that they were not guilty of anything, and that fate had presented them with a holiday they would keep secret for the rest of their lives. And Marusya had nothing to do with it. As for the main purpose of Asya's visit, it had not been achieved. The wonder-working brew had absolutely no effect on Jacob's eczema.

Moscow had experienced the same heavy snowfall as there had been in Altai. Ivan Belousov waited for Marusya by the entrance on Povarskaya Street, and when she came downstairs—wearing a black coat with a lambskin collar and a lambskin muff, and with her slightly reddened eyelids lowered, Ivan suddenly embraced her and kissed her. Nothing like that had happened before between them, and the kiss was more like one of childish ecstasy than mature, masculine delight.

Marusya had been spending a great deal of time with Professor Belousov for half a year already. They no longer limited their time together to walks down the boulevards. They attended lectures at the Polytechnic Museum together and went to various concerts and performances. This time, Ivan had invited Marusya to the première of the opera *And Quiet Flows the Don*.

Marusya was agitated. For one thing, whatever would she wear? She had no appropriate garments for an opening night. Second, going to the opera like this was an open challenge, and an admission. A challenge to those acquaintances she might meet in the theater, and an admission that Professor Belousov had the sort of relationship with her that allowed him to invite her to the theater. In twenty-five years she had never been to the theater with any man other than her husband. In fact, though, Ivan had also invited her to the theater when they were even younger ... But the main question was, what should she wear?

When she was able to think more seriously about it, Marusya told herself that one's attire, in this case, was completely insignificant. This was proletarian art, and it would actually have been awkward to dress in silk and velvet for such an event. Moreover, she didn't have any fancy attire; she had only old dresses that had long since gone out of fashion and were completely worn out. So never mind!

They took their place in the orchestra seats—Ivan in his everyday service jacket, and Marusya in her blue dress with a striped sash and striped cuffs, modest but stylish, and listened to the music of Dzerzhinsky—not the notorious founder of the Cheka, the secret police, who was already dead, but his namesake.

The music didn't impress Marusya as being very good, but it wasn't bad, either. It was strange music—in some places it was crude, in other places strains of folk music could be heard. One thing Marusya understood unequivocally: this was not Shostakovich. It didn't have the power, the novelty. But Shostakovich had been hauled over the coals without mercy in *Pravda* for his *Lady Macbeth of the Mtsensk District*. It would be interesting to see how *And Quiet Flows the Don* fared. And Jacob, who could have explained whether the music was good, and in what way, was not with her . . . The voices were marvelous, although Smolich's staging seemed somewhat lacking.

Their evening at the Bolshoi Theater changed something in their relationship. All of the preliminaries had been taken care of. Jacob hardly existed anymore in her life—or so thought Ivan, gathering this from Marusya's own words. He himself had long lived in a semi-divorced state from his wife, who had moved with their daughter to Kiev, and whom he seldom saw. Ivan considered the marriage, which had lasted about ten years, to have been a mistake, and he hinted to Marusya that he had loved only one woman in his life, and Marusya knew who she was. When he looked at her with his devoted eyes, her memory of that absurd Kievan Ivan Belousov was immediately awakened.

In the Institute of the Red Professorate, Ivan taught courses on the history of the workers' movement, historical materialism, and Western European philosophy; he led study circles in factories, wrote brochures, read and remembered a great deal, studied German his entire life, but read Kant and Hegel only in translation.

Marusya recalled how Jacob disparaged these translations, claiming that translating the German philosophers into Russian was futile: since Russian had not developed philosophical terminology, the translations were unintelligible and abstruse. He also said that, strange as it might seem, Kant was more accessible in English. He spoke about the grammar of language, about how it was linked to the national character, and that it had not been determined whether the language conditioned the character of the people or the other way around. He knew everything, everything, and he had a theory about everything, Marusya thought with irritation. But he was never capable of a simple "yes" or "no." It was all devilish nuance and complexity! Ivan is simple and straightforward, she thought, and how refreshing that is! A healthy proletarian foundation removes all the confusion, all the fruitless play of the mind that prevents one from achieving goals. Ivan's goal is simple and noble—creating the new man, preparing cadres for the future, giving the youth what is necessary and sufficient. Jacob has always been interested only in what was superfluous. He doesn't know how to cut away these superfluities. And this is his tragedy. Woe from Wit! And this is the source of his endless conflicts with the authorities, with the proletarian government, than which nothing better has ever been invented in history! And Ivan is right on this point, not Jacob. In a matter so grave and so grand, one needs to pay attention not to the mistakes, which are inevitable, but to the achievements. Here again, Ivan is right. We are tainted by our families. Ivan's father is a railroad worker. Ivan forged his own road, but Jacob was educated by hired teachers—language teachers, music teachers. A bourgeois environment. And I so wanted to break away from my petit-bourgeois home, from the milieu of small craftsmen, storekeepers, the strictures of that airless Jewish stuffiness. And where did I end up? In a wealthy home, at a formal dining table with a bourgeois papa at the head and a white tablecloth and a pink-and-white dinner service with a cook and a chambermaid. And I wanted only simplicity, purity . . .

All these thoughts drew her closer to Ivan. No, there was nothing sensual in the attraction, but something upright, something enviably direct. Without any refined, intellectual moaning and groaning.

461

The end of Jacob's term of exile was approaching, and Marusya thought with anguish about how he would soon return home—and again she would be racked with internal conflict, and would always lose out to him; and again her work would seem secondary and insignificant compared with his important scientific pursuits. Would they even give him a residence permit in Moscow? If they did, would he be able to find a job? And if they didn't register him in Moscow, he would leave again for some far-off realm, and she would live in the same way, bearing the stigma of rejection, with papers in which every personnel officer, every cadre, could see her social stain. Divorce was the only thing that could save her from this.

But she had Genrikh to think about. He was twenty years old. The spoiled and capricious child had disappeared, and in his place had emerged a completely new person, practical and single-minded. He lived a difficult and demanding existence, and he coped with it well. He brought home his paycheck from work to his mother, leaving for himself only what he needed for transportation and a midday meal at work. He had been accepted into the Komsomol, and he was proud of this. When he finished at the Workers' University, he entered the Technical College and was just as enthusiastic about his studies as he had been about his construction set when he was a child. He had spent the most difficult years of his adolescence without his father, consciously turning away from his father's precepts and admonitions and cultural values, and even feeling a certain degree of contempt for them. The sole thing that interested him was science and technology.

Genrikh was the only one with whom Marusya shared her new thoughts. She was nervous before the conversation, but, much to her surprise, her son encouraged her to decide on that course of action. "I think you're right, Mama. Perhaps you should have done it sooner. In Stalingrad."

And so she made the decision to carry out her intention. She didn't have to appear in court; it was very quick. In the hallway were three other women waiting for the same decision. The court dissolved all the marriages, and all it took was fifteen minutes for the four of them together. This was a common practice during those years. Although the NKVD memorandum about divorce from imprisoned spouses had not yet been published, the employees of the Marriage Bureaus had already been acquainted with the directive concerning the granting of one-sided divorce of spouses who were incarcerated or in exile; it was not necessary for the absent spouse to fill out any forms or sign any papers. Marusya received the document granting her divorce in August 1936. Only two people knew about this: she herself and Genrikh.

Marusya did not write to Jacob about the divorce; she kept postponing it. Their correspondence continued, though it was rather strained. The nearer the time for her husband's release, the more certain Marusya was that she wanted to live alone. It had been Marusya's fate to live her entire youth as the wife of her "one-and-only husband." Emotionally and intellectually, she was a free woman in a new era, emancipated, though outwardly she adhered to established bourgeois expectations. This was the way it had happened. Jacob completely occupied her feelings, and she had never longed for anyone else's embrace. Theoretically, she completely subscribed to the "glass of water" theory of absolute sexual freedom, which had been propagated by Aurore Dudevant (George Sand), Alexandra Kollontai, and Inessa Armand. In practice, something had always stopped her. Marusya even kept her open admirer at a distance, though they were already on the verge of intimacy. Ivan was either noble or perhaps timid, or else he was waiting for an overt sign from her. Everything came down to the fact that the time had come to free herself from the unbearable authority of an old love. Cast it off! Cast it off!

At the end of November, Marusya received a letter from Jacob with a list of official papers he would need to get a residence permit. He didn't know that there were already papers that would doom all his efforts to failure—the divorce papers. Marusya was filled with confusion, but the divorce had been finalized, and she had decided. She would not allow Jacob to be registered as her husband, so that she could keep . . . no, not her apartment, but her independence, her individuality.

Ivan also made an important decision. After all, he was no Mr. Greenhorn. He had been courting her for so long, it was time to resolve the matter. Marusya never invited him to her home; indeed, it wouldn't have been possible, since she had a grown son. Ivan also hesitated to invite her to his tiny room in a communal apartment, stuffed with boxes overflowing with file cards, quotations, alphabetically ordered clippings—an enormous collection of Lenin's excerpts and dicta about everything under the sun. Ivan was an acknowledged expert on the texts of the leader, and not even the card catalogue in the Lenin Library was as abundant as his collection. But he could hardly invite Marusya to his dusty lair, to share a soldier's iron cot, on torn sheets . . .

Ivan found the solution: he called the Central Commission for the Betterment of Living Conditions of Scholars and requested two vouchers to the sanatorium in Uzkoye, a wonderful spot just outside of Moscow. The great scholars and scientists all vacationed there. The academics who ran the sanatorium did not particularly like the Red Professorate, but the Academy of Sciences had not long before merged with the Communist Academy, and spots had been allocated to them. They promised a place to Belousov as of December 1.

"Marusya, we're going to a sanatorium. We need a vacation," the soft-spoken Ivan announced firmly.

"When?"

"The first of December."

This offered the best possible resolution of Marusya's agitation and disquiet. She simply wouldn't be in Moscow when Jacob returned. In this way, she could at least put off a tormenting, painful explanation. As for Ivan, she would just have to see how things panned out. Radical? Yes! It *was* a desperate, mad act.

The December morning was damp and seemed darker than usual. Marusya rocked back and forth in the automobile and felt slightly sick to her stomach. She almost always suffered from motion sickness, and berated herself for agreeing to come on this trip. By the time they reached Uzkoye, it was already light. They entered the tall entrance gates, and an avenue of old trees opened up before them. Beyond was a house with a portico and columns, and a church, with a service in progress. When they entered the main building, her heart skipped a beat. Everything was orderly, formal, restrained, and refined. Her back seemed to straighten up of its own accord. Her chin lifted higher, and her former posture and gait, which had been lost in the humiliations of life, were restored in a single moment. The noble furnishings inspired equanimity and confidence in her, and a sense of her own dignity and worth. A lady with gray curls gathered on top of her head led them along the corridor and showed them their rooms.

"We usually settle most of our guests in the wing, but this room happened to be unoccupied. If you please . . ."

They didn't attend lunch, but they did go down for dinner. There were few people in the dining room, primarily elderly and even aged men, with vaguely familiar faces. They were most likely all academics. Marusya recognized one of them—Fersman, a geochemist.

Marusya was wearing a dark-blue suit and a modest but brightly colored

464

blouse decorated with an Egyptian motif on the sleeves. She immediately felt that she was in her element, and thus felt perfectly at ease. Besides the waitress, there was only one other woman among the guests in the dining room. She was large, with a birthmark that covered half her face, probably also an academic. She was eating and reading a newspaper at the same time.

After dinner, Marusya settled down on an uncomfortable Voltaire armchair in the small dining room with Céline's novel *Journey to the End of the Night*. The novel had been published a few years before. She was reading, not the French original, but a translation by Elsa Triolet. Marusya picked it up after reading a recent scathing review in *Pravda*. The author of the piece railed at Céline for his "aesthetic of filth," which was, moreover, the filth of capitalistic society, the filth of the bourgeoisie. Marusya enjoyed both the novel and the translation, and at the same time she admired the paintings, the mahogany furniture, and the view onto the park. She perceived the advantages of aristocratic life over grasping bourgeois decadence.

The first three days, they walked through the huge park after breakfast: ponds, tree-lined avenues, a birch grove, lime trees. It was very pleasant, but a bit wearisome: as they talked about social and political subjects, the conversation was strained. Ivan, tired of walking around in circles, lost his self-confidence. Too bad. He left Marusya, intending to sit down to work on his never-ending *Bulletin of the Institute of the Red Professorate*, which he had maintained almost single-handedly for the past five years.

On Sunday morning, December 6, the papers arrived bearing news of the Stalin Constitution. Ivan had already known for a long time that the great event was in the offing, and here it was. The newspaper announced that socialism had been built, and that the dictatorship of the proletariat had accomplished its mission. Professor Belousov would now have to modify his syllabus to accommodate these new achievements. To celebrate this remarkable turn of events, Ivan took a bottle of Kagor, monastery wine from Moldavia, out of his suitcase. He had been keeping the wine for just such an occasion, and he invited Marusya to spend the rest of the evening in an intimate setting, in his room.

Ivan succeeded in luring Marusya into his love net in the short interim between the second and third glasses. She was not aware of much, since alcohol, even such a pious variety, had a rapid and violent effect on her. She smiled, and laughed; then the walls started reeling, and she clutched Ivan's sleeve so she wouldn't collapse. Belousov grabbed her and did not waste any time—and five minutes later exulted over his blitz victory, while Marusya ran off to the next room, where she threw up the thick red wine. She felt very sick.

When Ivan knocked on her door about twenty minutes later, she was lying on top of the covers, pale, in her decorated blouse, her chest all wet. Ivan ministered to her gently, carrying out her every wish. He put a hot compress on her head and made some tea; she asked for more sugar. Then she vomited again. Ivan nearly cried from tender sympathy: sweet, fragile girl . . . He took care of her as he had taken care of his own daughter when she was sick with scarlet fever. Marusya was touched. He was a warm person—a caring, warm person. And the most important thing was that he had clear positions, solid and benign, with no intellectually refined twists and turns of thought.

Jacob sent a telegram when he was leaving Novosibirsk. Neither Marusya nor Genrikh was there to meet him when he arrived. On December 4, he went to Povarskaya Street. The neighbors opened the door of the communal apartment. The door of their room was locked; he didn't have a key. He went to his sister's.

In the evening, he managed to get through to Genrikh by phone. His son said, "Congratulations on your release. Mama's in a sanatorium. I'm not sure which one."

Jacob found out about the divorce that had already been officialized when Marusya returned from her holiday. By this time, he already understood that he would have no Moscow residence permit; nor would he have a wife or a son. He would have nothing that he had been counting on. He did find a job, however, outside Moscow, in the Yegoryevsky District, in the planning department of a paltry little factory.

Before he left to start his new job, he sought out Asya. They met by the Novokuznetskaya metro station. Pink, touching, wearing a little beret, with an expectant expression in her eyes, Asya asked him how his eczema was. "My eczema is feeling just fine," he joked. She invited him to her house— she lived nearby, on Pyatnitskaya Street. Jacob declined. They walked down Ordynka Street. When they were saying goodbye to each other, Jacob, in an old-fashioned, gallant gesture, kissed her hand.

Marusya and Ivan did not continue to see each other much longer. He was straightforward and reliable—politically competent, and morally steadfast. But in April he was arrested. The trial was carried out quietly, drowned out by other, more celebrated cases of that fateful year. When Ivan's house was searched, among the catalogued drawers and boxes full of quotations from Lenin, excerpts from the French newspaper *L'Écho de Paris*, with a review of Trotsky's last book, *The Revolution Betrayed*, were found. Marusya, whom Ivan had asked to translate the article, had underlined in red pencil this shocking phrase: "Without wanting it himself, the Georgian with the low forehead has become the direct heir of Ivan the Terrible, Peter the Great, and Catherine II. He destroys his opponents—revolutionaries, true to their infernal faith, who are consumed by a constant neurotic thirst for destruction."

Ivan honestly denied having a knowledge of French during the interrogation. He did not name the person who had marked the passage—firing-squad words—with a red pencil.

Two months later, all those involved in the case were executed as Trotsky-ites. Ivan had never been a Trotskyite. Though he was a true Leninist, this had no bearing on the matter. It was 1937. Surviving the year would be difficult. But people survived. Some of them.

44

Variations on a Theme

Fiddler on the Roof

(1992)

Tusya was aging beautifully. She thinned out, became smaller. Although her back, which had been disfigured in childhood by osseous tuberculosis, became still more bent, her hands were not affected, and her wrinkles lay on her face like a beautiful geometric grid. Her vision gave out, but she had acquired a large magnifying glass, which she became adept at using, and assured Nora that reading this way had its advantages: you missed nothing, as though not only the letters were magnified, but their meaning as well. She was pushing eighty. Physically, she had grown decrepit, but her clarity of mind and her wit had remained intact. Nora occasionally took her to theaters. She came to pick her up in the car, sat her in the back seat, and led her to the staff entrance of the theater. Leaning on a polished black cane with a silver sheep's head as a knob, Tusya waited while Nora parked the car. Then they walked arm in arm, two genuine leading lights of the theater world, venerable connoisseurs, and visitors to all the significant theatrical events.

Tusya's students didn't forget her, and invited her to all the premières and guest performances that were worthy of attention. She attended with pleasure, dressing up theatrically, piling big Asian rings with turquoises and cornelians onto her thin fingers. For Nora, every such outing was a holiday. The years had not been able to dim the excitement of a première for her, and Tusya's presence always heightened this feeling, independent of whether the play was good or just so-so.

The theater they went to on this occasion was not a favorite of theirs.

Although the director enjoyed acclaim far and wide, he was, in Tusya's opinion, mediocre. The playwright, who had adapted the voluble Sholem Aleichem's works for the stage, was talented and much sought after, but his work still carried the aura of the student skit. One of Tusya's best students, a set-and-production designer, had invited them. They were staging the story of Tevye the Dairyman, and Tusya didn't have very high expectations of it. She still remembered when Mikhoels played the role in 1938.

In the audience, the air was charged with happy anticipation. When the comedic actor—an actor beloved by all, who specialized in playing bewitchingly honest simpletons—took the stage, for some reason against the background of a looming eight-armed cross, the audience howled with delight. To begin, the actor announced: "Here, in our village, Russians, Ukrainians, and Jews live side by side . . ." What followed was a mixture of nauseating gobbledygook about the friendship of the peoples, presented with the intonations of a Jewish joke, good-natured and bittersweet, and lowbrow literary clownery, which made Tusya ever more dismal and gloomy, and the audience ever more giddy and cheerful. At the end of the first act, the Jewish wedding gave way to a pogrom, carried out by the peaceable Russian neighbors on the convincing grounds that "it's either thrash them, or get slapped with a fine by the authorities ourselves!"

The Cossack sergeant was torn by the contradiction between a sense of duty—enforcing the pogrom ordered from on high by the powers-that-be—and a neighborly compassion for the simple Jewish peasants, sympathy toward the Jewish dairyman. According to the playwright's view, the pogrom was instigated by one villain, a kind of local Ilse Koch, anticipating by many years the gas chambers organized by other bad people of German extraction.

The pogrom was successful. Tevye walked out onto the proscenium carrying his bleeding youngest daughter in his arms, and then left a red imprint of his enormous bloodied workingman's hand on a white wall. The bells started tolling; the pogrom thugs broke into a Cossack dance; the well-intentioned sergeant asked him to stay calm; the good priest opened his arms; Tevye howled to his Jewish God, who had failed to intervene, thereby awakening the young and enlightened Jews to revolutionary action. Sholem Aleichem had already been laid to rest in his grave in a Jewish cemetery in Queens more than seventy years before, and his soul spoke the long-buried language of Yiddish with the souls of six million European Jews who had formerly occupied a country with indefinite borders that was called Yiddishland.

Thunderous applause.

"Unbelievably base and trite," Tusya whispered to Nora.

"Base? Why?" Nora was surprised.

"If you don't understand, I'll explain later."

They stayed until the end of the play. Then they left to go home, in the middle of a stormy ovation, repeated bows from the actors, the director, the playwright. Nora hadn't seen Tusya in such a despondent state in a long time.

The elevator in the apartment building was broken, so they had to climb up four flights of stairs. They wended their way up slowly, stopping to rest on every landing. Tusya was silent. Nora refrained from asking any questions.

They ate whatever there was on hand—pasta, served with grated cheese. Tusya found a bottle of wine in the cupboard. She drank in the European way, without toasting. Several times she seemed to be on the verge of saying something, then decided against it. It was already after one in the morning, and their conversation still hadn't gotten off the ground. Nora went home, the unsaid words still hanging in the air. Tusya usually came up with such brilliant analyses . . .

It's possible that they would never have returned to this subject had Tevye the Dairyman not come up again in a telephone conversation. This time, a proposal came not from Tengiz but from Efim Berg, a director from the provinces—a person with a reputation as a troublemaker, who had mysterious connections. He was, in fact, not really from the provinces; he had studied in Moscow, staged plays in Leningrad, and for five years worked as the head director in one of the oldest theaters in Siberia.

The first thing Efim asked Nora was "What is your ethnicity? Are you a Jew, by any chance?"

Nora was taken by surprise. In her passport, she was identified by the ethnicity of her mother—Russian—but she had never concealed the fact that her father was Jewish.

"Half, on my father's side," she said.

"You will do, then," Efim said, and invited Nora to take part in a staging of *Fiddler on the Roof.*

As it later turned out, his offer had an interesting history. The fact was that the designs and sketches for the stage set had already been made, by the extremely well-known artist Kononov, and they had even been accepted, but Efim rejected them at the last minute. Kononov, a recipient of many national prizes and distinctions and a favorite of the authorities, had never worked in theater before. His reputation had been built on portraits of government officials and enormous patriotic canvases on heroic-historical subjects—from the thirteenth-century Battle on the Ice to the routing of the fascists at Stalingrad. Kononov was an ideological anti-Semite, which everyone knew very well, and Efim Berg was surprised, to say the least, when Kononov received the offer to design the stage sets for the Jewish play *Fiddler on the Roof.* His name alone, appearing on all the posters announcing the performance, would guarantee the interest of the broader public and the indulgence of the ministry heads.

Swiftly, in a realistic style, the monumental Kononov drew the crooked little houses of the Jewish shtetl, and they were ready to start constructing the sets—the sketches had been passed on to the set-building department already—when all hell broke loose. Right before leaving, the director and the artist sat down to drink a glass "for the road." Both of them relaxed and let their guard down, and Efim, in a fit of drunken gratitude, admitted that he had always considered Kononov to be an anti-Semite, but he was glad that he had turned out to be a "regular guy" and was committed to staging the Jewish performance. Kononov began defending his reputation, and his right to take part in this production:

"You Jews are so aggressive and pushy, you always try to move into others' territory. Your painter Levitan paints our landscapes; your Chagall introduces his Jewish fantasy into our space; Pasternak and Mandelstam use our language as their own; you taint our Russian art, injecting into it the spirit of cosmopolitanism, destroying Russian integrity and purity. Anti-Semitism is our only protection, because, if we don't wall ourselves off from you, if we don't create impediments for you, you'll infect the whole world with your Jewish ideas. And this whole avant-garde, from Malevich to Shostakovich"—here he was mistaken—"are the result of this Jewish disease, absorbed by the Russian people merely through proximity to you. Yes, I'm an anti-Semite, but I'm prepared to help you stage your Jewish play if only you will agree not to muscle your way into our Russian world with your destructive ideas. Yes, let a hundred flowers grow where they will, but no one wants hybrids and mongrels; therefore, I will fight for the purity of Russian art.

"Go ahead and stage your Sholem Aleichem. I will even help you; but don't touch my Chekhov!" announced Kononov with a good-natured smile.

At that very moment, shrieking the words "*Your* Chekhov!," the diminutive and springy Efim leveled a punch at his interlocutor, striking him on the jaw. Kononov, who had a significant advantage in size, floored Efim with a single blow. Efim, in turn, after somehow managing to struggle up to his knees, grabbed from the table a paperweight that had found its way into the theater four directors ago, even before the war, and only the fact that the producer and the assistant just happened to be nearby prevented a murder. They dragged Efim away bodily, stuffed the artist in a car, and sent it off in the direction of the airport.

After recovering from his upset, which was more moral than physical, Efim turned over in his mind all the set designers of Jewish descent he knew. Unfortunately, David Borovsky was engaged for the entire year. Mark Bornstein, an acquaintance from Leningrad, also declined. Then Efim remembered Nora.

Their acquaintance was also marked by a conflict, which had transpired five years earlier. At that time Efim had been appointed head director, and he had invited Tengiz, many of whose productions he was familiar with, to stage Dickens's *A Christmas Carol*. Tengiz accepted the offer, and arrived with Nora. Time was short: the play was due to be performed before the start of the school vacation. Everyone was in a rush; they were all on pins and needles. Finally, Efim and Tengiz quarreled about something, the cause of which neither of them could remember afterward. Now Efim was asking Nora to stage Sholem Aleichem with him.

Nora laughed. "I was just at the Moscow première, and the applause at the end nearly brought the house down. That will be a hard act to follow."

"No, I'm not talking about that play, I'm talking about *Fiddler on the Roof*. It's a brilliant musical—a Broadway play—it's been performed all over the world. The script is by Joseph Stein, and the score is by Jerry Bock. I have two voices in the theater now that would make Topol go green with envy."

At that moment, Nora had no idea which Topol it was who would soon turn green, but she said that she'd take a look at the material. That evening, she went to see Tusya. Tusya was unexpectedly glad. She found an American LP on the shelf and put it on the record player. The music was enchanting—sadly happy, happily sad, lively, and carrying inside it the impulse to dance.

"It's klezmer music, a wonderful modern arrangement," Tusya explained. "Small klezmer orchestras wandered through Eastern Europe before the war. Nowadays there are vestiges of the music in a few pop renditions. But this is klezmer at its best."

They listened to the record from beginning to end.

"I've never heard anything like this," Nora said.

Tusya was surprised. "I didn't teach you very well, then."

From that evening on, a new subject—Jewishness—became part of Nora's life. A circumstance that had previously not really concerned her at all, and had not seemed significant in any sense—the Jewish half of her—began to mean a great deal to her. And, as was usually the case in her life, this new knowledge came through the theater. It was the last realm of knowledge her old teacher personally inducted her into.

"You see, Nora," Tusya said, "at the end of my life, I've been forced to examine my relationship with Jewishness. For Russian Jews of our fathers', and your grandfathers', generation, it was a very painful issue. It was the problem of assimilation. They were ashamed of their Jewishness, and put great effort into pulling up these roots and becoming part of Russian culture, as seamlessly as possible. They had to struggle against enormous resistance within the Russian milieu. The same thing happened in Europe. It began earlier there, though—at the end of the eighteenth century. Look it up in any encyclopedia. Under the letter 'A,' for 'assimilation.' Look up 'Austro-Hungary.' The first volume." And she gestured toward the bookshelf.

"In a nutshell: In the nineteenth century, educated Jews became the leading cosmopolitans of Europe, and created a new intellectual universalism. There was an enormous explosion of intellectual energy. With wild enthusiasm, Jewish youth broke away from the *heder* and began to pursue secular education. They made great strides in science, art, and literature. And, it goes without saying, in economics. At the same time, they began to lose what would later be called their 'national identity.'

"Simultaneously, another movement got under way, completely contrary to the first. This was Zionism. The goal of Zionism was to create an independent Jewish state, which had not existed for almost two millennia. In spite of historical precedents, this state was created—but at an enormous cost: the six million Jews who died in the gas chambers. My late father would lose his mind if he heard me say this. These are the thoughts I think in my waning years. Why were Jews so enamored of Soviet power? Because, in the initial years, it replaced 'national identity' or ethnicity with 'internationalism.' Many Jews hoped in this way to free themselves of the burden of being Jewish."

It was remarkable. When Tusya was present, the mundane chatter around a dinner table quickly turned into an intellectual conversation of the highest order. When she led a seminar on set design, the primary topic of discussion had become literature, dramaturgy. A decade later, when she began to lecture on the history of theater, she led her students beyond the boundaries of theater into the realm of psychology and philosophy. Every subject she broached immediately became too narrow, too confining, and she spoke of the adjoining areas, what lay beyond, about things that at first glance did not seem directly relevant—but it later turned out that what was most interesting lay precisely in these marginal spaces. Nora had long known this about Tusya, and now, listening to her spontaneous lecture on the fate of the Jews, she thought about how far Tusya had come from Tevye the Dairyman, with his mundane, and at the same time ponderous, questions.

"I'll try to explain to you why that play so irked me, but it's not easy. It's saccharine and mendacious. There's no more 'Tumbalalaika' anywhere in the world. That is a cheap, cookie-cutter stereotype, a cartoon. There is a Jewish people scattered around the world that introduced contemporary morality harking back to the Ten Commandments. There is an image, very fraught intellectually, of the two-thousand-year existence of the Jews, banished from one country after another, a small people who miraculously survived, and who want to retain their Jewish identity and live on their own land—and have a right to do so, as do all other peoples. Alongside this is the image of a mighty power that to this day wants to destroy them. I have nothing against Sholem Aleichem, but we need to retire Anatevka to the museum; things have moved far beyond that. Not to mention that it no longer exists, and never will again. I wanted to be able to say all these things before you begin your production. And I would never dare say any of this to you if I didn't believe that the theater today is still capable of saying things that are impossible to articulate, to express, any other way."

"But this musical doesn't allude to any of the things you are telling me—nothing I could discern, anyway," Nora objected.

"Nora, you have to know how to unearth meanings. It's very often up to you to extract them not from the work at hand but from yourself."

This turned out to be the most difficult of all Nora's projects. She wrestled with the text. What helped her most was the splendid premiere with the bells tolling in the finale—she didn't have the right to trespass on that territory in any way. Efim Berg came to Moscow on business. They met and spent a wonderful evening with Tusya. Efim, usually garrulous and disinclined to listen in a conversation, was reticent and attentive this time. They spoke about the merits and shortcomings of musical theater, about the gradual transformation of the genre of high opera into the democratic genre of the musical, about the two revolutionary American musicals, Bernstein's *West Side Story* and Webber's *Jesus Christ Superstar*. Tusya again surprised Nora with her thoughts about possible trajectories of development in the theater: about the broadening of the space of theater thanks to cinematographic devices; the use of street scenes, drawing the viewer into the action on-stage; about the carnivalization of life; and about the return of theater itself to its ancient mystical roots.

"All of that was tried in Russia just after the Revolution, but it was squelched. And very quickly it returned to its conservative forms, and the Russian avant-garde, which promised so much, was silenced," said Tusya, folding her arms over her chest in a cross, like a corpse.

Then, when it was already night, Efim took Nora to visit a theater friend of his at his house. There, on a new VCR brought back from America, Nora watched the film version of *Fiddler on the Roof* for the first time. Though it had long since become a relic, it had never lost its riveting appeal. Now Nora knew that, from this generally accessible spectacle, so sweet and appealingly humane, without changing a single line, she would have to extract something much more essential than the playwright had communicated. Efim couldn't sit still—he sprang up to his feet and galloped around, tapping and stamping his feet, clapping his hands—but he had already fallen under Tusya's influence, and the play appealed to him more and more.

Nora was already coming up with ideas and drawing them on big sheets of Whatman paper. She drew the small box of a stage hung on the inside with long strips of colored fabric, alternating red, brown, and dark blue. Small human figures rushed around inside this compressed space, chaotically, hither and thither. A horse and a cow seemed to appear, then disappear again, filling the box with living creatures of the land. She drew a rope with rags hanging from it, and then took a fresh piece of paper and peopled it with other figures, old women and children, and again changed everything in this constricted world. Then she drew a leaning table platform and placed on it a pot, with bowls, and again drew an empty box. She couldn't figure out whether all these outward signs of an impoverished, benighted rural existence were necessary, or whether they were superfluous details that would distract the eye. Finally, she scrapped it all except the platform leaning downstage.

This wrapped up the preliminary work; now it was time to consider the actual staging. Nora was not sure whether Berg, a talented but capricious and ambitious man, would accept her fully formed vision. In addition to everything else, she proposed that the stage dimensions be diminished, creating a compressed space that would open up only in the finale.

She made three mock-ups, and laid them one inside another. They differed only in the color of the curtains that constituted the "body" of the set. On fourteen poles hung three layers of fabric. In the center of each section of cloth was a small vertical slit, invisible when the fabric was hanging.

The first layer was thick red, ceremonial and disquieting. At the end of the "Sabbath Prayer" scene, Tevye would pull a curtain from the pole and put it over himself like a mantle, placing his head through the slit in the fabric. All the other actors would also put on these improvised red mantles, and sing a Sabbath song, which Nora already knew was not a real Sabbath song, but commonplace, ordinary music, an ingeniously interwoven medley of religious and local folkloric melodies.

Now Nora removed the outermost mock-up and revealed the next layer of curtains, the brownish-ocher ones. When the next scene was performed—with the matchmaking and the wedding, which seamlessly blended into the pogrom—these curtains would be pulled down in turn, and transformed into overcoats, traveling garments. And again, on the proscenium, the crowd of shocked and agitated Jewish villagers would sing the prescribed mournful melody, and under the layer of brownish ocher would be revealed the last layer, the dark blue.

Nora removed the second mock-up, leaving only the last. This was where the finale would play out. The Cossack sergeant informed the Jews that all of them would be expelled from Anatevka, and from the rigging a ladder descended. One could interpret this as one willed, in accordance with one's awareness of Biblical texts. It could be viewed as Jacob's Ladder—the villagers would yank the final layers of fabric from the poles and throw over themselves these garments the color of the nighttime heavens, then ascend the stairway and disappear there, in the gridiron. On the darkened stage, in a black room, only the poles would remain—not a single human being. An empty world, from which all people were gone.

And while they ascended the stairs into the heavens, they would sing their little ditties and songs, and snatches of conversation would be heard: "Did you forget the frying pan? And the rug? Where's the pot, the bridle, the candlestick holder?" And this would be even better! Because the contrast between the trivial details of the daily round of life, with its matchmaking and its marriages—its Friday hustle and bustle, and a sick cow, two-cent cheating and two-bit guile—and the great drama of life of the human being, the end of human existence on earth and the complete collapse of the failed plan of the Lord God, would be all the starker.

From on high, out of the darkness of the heavens, let not only these unpretentious folkloric strains be audible, but the sixth, the seventh, the eighth, and the seventeenth, and the thirty-second preludes and fugues, fragments of *The Well-Tempered Clavier*, those magnificent musical texts, music for all time—let that music resound. Because, ultimately, all these mad and evil games of rash and mindless people led to the dress rehearsal of the end of the human world, to the Holocaust.

On the stage, all that would remain were the black poles, and emptiness, and silence . . . Oh, and about the costumes . . . What will they be? Leotards, and on top of them some loose-fitting smocks or tunics, garments without shape or color, and no ethnic allusions—no embroidered vests or headscarves tied above the forehead—nothing of that sort.

And, please, no applause. Only ancient fear and the presentiment of absolute finality, of wholesale death. Go home, ladies and gentlemen, into the darkness and into the silence . . .

"Good, Nora! Very good. We'll do it. There's just one thing I don't understand. What is this Jacob's Ladder you mentioned?"

Nora glanced at Berg in surprise. "You don't know? The dream of the patriarch Jacob near Bethlehem. He dreamed of a stairway with angels going up and down it, and at the very top of it, the Lord God says to Jacob something like 'The place where you are lying asleep, this land, I will give to you and your descendants, and I will bless you and them, and I will be with you and all your peoples.'"

"Amazing dream. For some reason I didn't remember it."

"I would have missed it, too. Tusya pointed me in the right direction. Don't worry, Efim. The most important thing for us is that the Lord God bless all peoples through the Jews, each and every person. And if the Jews are hounded out of this world, it is not certain whether the blessing will be preserved," Nora said, laughing.

With Mikhoels

(1945–1948)

They were the same age, Jacob Ossetsky and Solomon Vovsi, but Jacob entered the Commercial Institute a year earlier. Jacob's friend invited him to a literary evening where this very Solomon was reading a long and unintelligible poem in Yiddish to a group of admirers. Jacob remembered his striking outward appearance, which verged on the grotesque, and his artistic expressiveness and passion. This was in 1911, and by 1912 neither of them was at the Institute any longer.

Many years later, in 1925, when they had already moved to Moscow, Jacob and Marusya chanced to be at a play in the Moscow State Yiddish Theater. By that time, Marusya had parted with the theater for good, but her youthful dreams about a career as an actress still rankled her.

Marusya was agitated about the play, *A Night at the Old Market*. On the one hand, she liked the tradition of farce, but the story about corpses that come to life was unpalatable to her. She had become disenchanted with mysticism at that point, and had also outgrown her theatrical past and rejected "disengaged" art. She sought a political meaning in everything, and it disturbed her that this otherwise compelling play had no ideological underpinning. The language itself, Yiddish, called up associations with bourgeois nationalism. The content of the play was flimsy, even trifling, but even so the play was magnificent. Professionally, the direction and set design were of the highest order. The acting was stunning—the delivery of the lines was sharp and light, with remarkable concordance of intonation, the movements were beautifully choreographed, and the music was superb.

In short, Marusya suffered from artistic-ideological discomfort; nor could Jacob fully enjoy the play. He kept feeling he knew the actor in one of the main roles. He snatched the program from Marusya's hand, but couldn't make out in the darkness the name of this marvelous jester who combined provincial humor, which was directed at himself, and the manner of the Italian piazzas, which at the same time made fun of the public.

As soon as the lights went up after the first act, Jacob looked at the program to see the name of the actor.

"Marusya, do you know Mikhoels? His face is so familiar, I'm sure I know him from somewhere. He's extraordinarily talented."

"Yes, he is," Marusya said sourly, as though Mikhoels had deprived her of her calling. "It's a stage name. His real name is Vovsi."

"Ah, Vovsi! Now I remember. He studied at the Commercial Institute with me, in Kiev. Then he disappeared."

"Jacob, you and I are the ones who disappeared. Vovsi never went anywhere. He's made a name for himself; they've begun writing about him. Often."

"You didn't like him? I think he was superb."

"This play, this spectacle, is for philistines, Jacob. Look around you—all you can see are Jewish dentists."

Here Jacob realized that he had made a blunder and touched a sore spot in Marusya. But at that very moment, someone took him by the arm from behind. He turned around. It was a doctor he had visited for a consultation a year before. A dermatologist, though, not a dentist.

"Well, what do you think of Mikhoels? He's my cousin! What a pair! Mikhoels and Suskin!"

"Abel Isaakovich, meet my wife, Marusya. Marusya—Dr. Dobkin, a dermatologist."

Marusya could hardly contain her laughter, but she managed to get out: "Oh, I thought you were a dentist!" And they all went to the buffet together.

There was an endless ovation at the end of the play. Then they stood in line at the cloakroom with Abel and his wife, and when the audience had almost dispersed, and Abel's wife was struggling with her gray felt boots, which she couldn't get to buckle all the way up, Mikhoels—small of stature, with a large head—emerged from a side door. He was looking for someone, and when he saw Abel, he came up to him, patted him on the back, and kissed him. Then he looked at Jacob, who hadn't taken his eyes off him, and smiled inquiringly.

"Jacob Ossetsky, right? Ah, how grateful I am to you! You know, in your younger years, it's very important when people give you pointed criticism."

"I don't remember offering any criticism at all. Now I feel I should apologize . . ."

"No, there's nothing to apologize for. At the time, you expressed yourself with great civility. I'll remind you: 'Clearly, a great talent—just not in the realm of poetry!'" And Mikhoels guffawed, turning his homely face, with its protruding lower lip and flattened nose, toward the others. "It was a terrible poem! Let's go. We're having a small party tonight. I'd like to invite you."

Then a tall woman, somewhat advanced in years, appeared. Mikhoels followed behind her to the cloakroom, and all of them, in a large group, peeling off the winter coats they had already pulled on, fell in line behind him.

After that, they met up with one another on occasion—outside, by the Nikitsky Gates, sometimes at the conservatory, or for concerts at the Gnesin Institute of Music. The Moscow they inhabited was quite circumscribed. At their last prewar meeting, not long before Jacob's first arrest, they met by chance on Malaya Bronnaya. They shook hands, and Mikhoels invited Jacob to a play.

"Maybe this evening? *The Court Is in Session*, by Dobrushin. A contemporary play."

This was in 1930, and Jacob had never seen the play. A few months later he was arrested, and he observed the subject of the play not from the point of view of the audience, but from the defendant's dock.

The next chance meeting took place fifteen years later, after the war, in 1945. By this time, Jacob's long peregrinations through the provinces had already ended. The best years of his life were under way: freedom, books, music, pleasant proximity to film, while teaching statistics in the Economics Department at the Institute of Cinematography.

On that day, Mikhoels had a business meeting at the Institute, where he had been offered the opportunity to teach an acting workshop. They ran into each other in the cafeteria. Mikhoels embraced Jacob like an old friend. Then they ate pea soup—the cafeteria had already run out of the main course—and had some tea with bread.

Mikhoels's face was homely, but his hands looked as if they had been sculpted by the Lord God Himself. Jacob couldn't take his eyes off the large supple fingers clasping the dim glass of tea. The conversation was lively and touched upon the Jewish Anti-Fascist Committee, which had interested

Jacob for a long time already. Mikhoels, seeing the lively interest his inter-locutor took in the matter, suggested he visit him to discuss it further. They exchanged phone numbers.

Jacob was a bit abashed by Mikhoels's hail-fellow-well-met attitude toward him, which didn't correspond to their long, but no more than nod-ding, acquaintance. But he found an explanation for this cordiality—and Mikhoels confirmed his surmise in later meetings. During the fifteen years that had passed since they last saw each other, before the war, so many people had disappeared, gone missing, died of starvation, or perished at the front that every familiar face seemed to belong to someone newly returned from the land of the dead.

Thus began a rather intense interaction. Ossetsky was interesting to Mikhoels. The actor did not often socialize with people who were so scho-lastically inclined, with such erudition and finely honed logic. In addition, during his years of exile, Jacob had learned the art of reading newspapers. Through the structure of the phrases, the subordinate clauses, even through the punctuation marks, Jacob knew how to excavate the subtext, the implicit message, the undisclosed intentions and latent tendencies. Mikhoels sensed this.

It was a transitional period, vacillating and uncertain. Things that had seemed clear-cut and comprehensible somehow grew turbid and blurry. The Jewish Anti-Fascist Committee had done a great service to the homeland during the war when, in '43, even before the opening of the second front, it completed its tour through America, Canada, and Mexico, collecting money for equipping the Red Army. Now, however, after the victory over fascism, the committee was faced with a new, vaguely defined task—to demonstrate to the world the pro-Israeli and at the same time anti-British policy of the Soviet Union with regard to the creation of a Jewish state in Palestine.

Mikhoels very delicately described the situation the Jewish Anti-Fascist Committee was in today, more complex than it had been during the war, before the opening of the second front. He had already caught indirect signals that the people at the very top were dissatisfied with the activities of the committee. Jacob reacted immediately and, with the precision of formulation characteristic of him, put into words exactly what was filling Mikhoels with alarm: the deep discrepancy between the logic of the exter-nal and internal policies.

"Yes, yes, something of that nature," Mikhoels said, nodding.

"With Europe, things are more or less clear. The new borders have essentially been determined. But there is a global geographic map, and new borders are being formed there, too. Now the real question is: Who will Palestine belong to after the war—the Arabs, and the British who back them, or the Jews, and the Soviet Union, which in turn supports them? And will the Jewish state be patterned on a socialist or, better yet, a communist model? This is a very thorny issue. On the one hand, Zionism, as a variety of nationalism, is a bourgeois current or trend; on the other hand, European Jewry is completely permeated with the spirit of communism." This was how Jacob outlined the situation to Mikhoels, who listened attentively, his head cocked to one side, like a bird.

Mikhoels, who had received many letters from Jews, in particular from those who had fought on the front line, expressing a readiness to fight to conquer Palestine for the Jews, suspected as much. How should he answer them? He was in a quandary. He understood that Israel was not the same as Spain. And he didn't pick up any clear signals from the government on this issue.

"I don't think Soviet Jews will be allowed to leave for Palestine," Jacob ventured to say.

He is certainly well versed in this political mathematics, Mikhoels concluded. And, before long, he enjoined Jacob to write overviews of the Western press on the Palestinian question for the Jewish Anti-Fascist Committee. Jacob would work under contract as a consultant.

For Jacob, this agreement meant not only supplementary income but also the satisfaction of interesting reading, a new domain of knowledge, and deeper understanding of all these burning issues. In postwar Europe, there were hundreds of thousands of Jews who had been spared extermination, who wandered around from pillar to post, dreaming of their own state. They were not allowed into Palestine. Their fate was an insignificant chip in the game of the victorious powers, which had not yet completed the postwar division of the world, its borders, cultural values, oil, grain, water, and air.

Jacob agreed to take the job, with the caveat that, along with his examination of what was happening currently, it would be necessary for him to assess the Palestinian political situation at least from the time of the Balfour Declaration. This historical context was indispensable.

Mikhoels agreed, and immediately gave Jacob a book by Richard Williams-Thompson that had just been published in London, titled *The Palestine Problem*.

This was how Jacob began his work with the Jewish Anti-Fascist Committee.

His greatest difficulty in the job was the limited—in effect, closed to nonspecialists—access to the American and British press. The sources that Jacob used at first were generally accessible—newspapers published in "fraternal" countries, or communist publications from Western countries. But, in spite of his skills in squeezing the necessary information from newspapers, he still lacked comprehensive source material.

He recalled the now-distant past when he had had a reliable personal source for Western newspapers—the Englishwoman Ivy Litvinov, wife of the former people's commissar for international relations. Their acquaintance dated back to the end of the 1920s, when the Litvinovs' daughter, Tanya, and Jacob's son, Genrikh, were in the same class in school. Later, Jacob even took English lessons from Ivy. In those days, he often took home with him a pile of newspapers from the Litvinovs' house. This is how he learned the particular language of newspapers, which differed from the literary English he was acquainted with.

But his contact with Ivy Litvinov, as with many other former friends and colleagues, had been broken long ago. He passed by the government residence where the Litvinovs had lived before the war fairly often, but he wasn't sure whether they still lived there. From newspaper notices, he gathered that Litvinov had been dismissed from his post. In other words, he had fallen into disgrace. But disgrace has many gradations, from quiet retirement to quiet annihilation. Jacob, of course, could not have known that the renowned people's commissar, onetime close collaborator of Lenin, lived full-time at his dacha and kept a handgun under his pillow, awaiting arrest. No, he would never again get any English newspapers from Ivy Litvinov. But he had great need of them.

During those days, there were only a handful of places in Moscow where one could find the British and American press, and they all required a special permit, the right of access to special collections. Mikhoels set to work and managed to get hold of such a privilege for Jacob. A month later, Ossetsky, as a consultant for the Jewish Anti-Fascist Committee, received permission to work in the library of the Ministry of Foreign Affairs. Once a week, on Tuesdays at 9:00 a.m., he went to the library—a seven-minute walk from his house—and spent two hours there, poring over the week-old papers. Then he went home to drink tea and muse over the new information.

The most difficult task for Jacob was the first report he had to write. He submitted it at the beginning of 1946. He had to find just the right language and tone of exposition. As a result, he developed a new genre of scholarly narrative, a blend of political analysis, historical research, and essay. This was his favorite threefold form: the present, the past, and a possible scenario for the future.

Life, which had heretofore contorted its aspect into a grimace, now began to smile upon Jacob. After many years of hardship and ordeals in the provincial towns, doing the practical work of an economist that did not inspire him with any enthusiasm, he was finally able to write and undertake the scholarly work that was closest to his heart and his inclinations. His efforts to get a residence permit in Moscow finally paid off—he was able to register at his sister Eva's place. He lived with her family, had a strong friendship with his brother-in-law, and was close to his two nephews. Exile and war were behind them now, and things were so good that even his trusty foe eczema left him in peace. The only thing that cast a shadow over his life was his long-lost wife and his estranged son, who had married and now had a child of his own, whom Jacob had never met.

Jacob managed to accomplish a great deal—in part through the commissioned work he was doing. But such was his cast of mind; he didn't know how to limit himself, how to draw boundaries. He threw himself into new interests as they arose, and they arose before he had exhausted all the possibilities of the old ones. Abandoning yesterday's, he took up tomorrow's—research on Palestine, its history and projects for a future that remained uncertain. He was particularly interested in the history of Palestine after its exit from the Ottoman Empire. This period, after Great Britain had received a mandate to govern Palestine, had been thoroughly explored in English publications after the First World War. These took the form of memoirs and political, archaeological, and cultural studies that were available to the public in several large libraries. It was precisely at this time that he produced an overview of the political forces in the region for the Jewish Anti-Fascist Committee, analyzing the various parties involved: socialists, communists, workers, Arabs, Jews, nationalists, and internationalists. At the same time, he examined the labor movement. The picture was frighteningly diverse and replete with explosive compounds and combinations.

At a certain moment, Jacob felt an urgent need to learn yet another language—Hebrew. So he set about mastering it. Now he recalled with gratitude his late father, who had hired a tutor to teach Jacob the languages of Jewish culture, Hebrew and Yiddish. This modest foundation was enough to allow him fairly quickly to begin reading publications in the ancient, but rapidly adopted and renewed, language of the future Palestine. Now a rather detailed picture of Arab-Jewish relations in the Middle East was taking shape in his mind. He believed that the best resolution of the situation would be the creation of a single Arab-Jewish state, without the division of Palestine. This was the outcome preferred by Zionists of both socialist and communist persuasion. But, in the final analysis, the future of Israel would be decided by only one person, who was sitting in the Kremlin.

Ossetsky's reports were sent from the Jewish Anti-Fascist Committee to Stern, an adviser in the Ministry of Foreign Affairs, and on up the ladder. The final destination was the table of the Soviet working group of the United Nations. In the spring of 1947, Arab-Jewish tensions had become so sharp that the question of creating a Palestinian state was in urgent need of resolution.

Jacob worked like one possessed. As usual, he formulated a work plan for the week, the month, the year. He adhered to this schedule, and was distraught when circumstances prevented him from carrying it out. His two years of collaboration with the Jewish Anti-Fascist Committee finally bore fruit: Jacob was already laying plans for a future book on the history and geography of this region. He signed a contract with a publisher.

He did not abandon his scholarly research on demographics, either. He always had a reserve of ideas, enough for several years in advance. Jacob delivered his final report to the secretary of the Jewish Anti-Fascist Committee, Heifetz. Mikhoels was absent from Moscow, on tour, for almost all of December 1947.

The tragedy occurred on January 12, 1948. According to the official version, Mikhoels was hit by a car in Minsk. He had been there for several days to meet with the directors and actors of the Belorussian Jewish Theater. The entire Jewish community, depleted in numbers a hundredfold after the war, flocked to him. They performed *Tevye the Dairyman* in his honor, regaled him at concerts, fêted him in restaurants, and invited him to actors' residential dormitories. They adored him, showered him with adulation, and surrounded him with a protective human wall, from which he broke out only once, on the eve of his return to Moscow. Golubov, the Moscow theater critic who was accompanying Mikhoels on the tour, kept pressing him to come with him to visit his Minsk friend, but Mikhoels was so busy the entire week that he didn't manage to make the visit until the last evening of his stay in Minsk. He never returned to his hotel. They found his body early in the morning on the 13th, with many fractures and a crushed skull.

Jacob found out about this accident on the following day, over the radio. The funeral took place several days later. So many people attended the funeral that Jacob had to wait an hour to reach the coffin to pay his last respects. The head of the deceased was mutilated, but his face was recognizable—bluish gray and stony. Next to him, on a small table, lay his broken spectacles.

Jacob left the theater where the body was lying in state. It was frosty, and the light was extinguished quickly, as in the theater. From Malaya Bronnaya, he turned automatically in the direction of his former home, on Povarskaya. Then he brought himself up short, turned around, and walked along the boulevards to Ostozhenka. The past never disappears; it only sinks into the depths. Most likely, the memory is submerged in some deep layers of the cerebral cortex, where it slumbers. Jacob had no doubt that it was a political murder, an assassination. What was Mikhoels thinking about, what did he remember, when they killed him?

Give up everything, abandon it all, and go to the provinces—to teach children music theory, or piano, or clarinet, to read Dickens, to learn Italian and read Dante . . . If I have time . . .

46

Reunion in Moscow
(2003)

fter Vitya's departure for America, Varvara Vasilievna began to love
Nora. This about-face seemed to be the result of some unknown variety of tectonic shift that took place in her psyche; Vitya certainly played
no role in it himself. From the moment Martha began taking charge of
Vitya's life, he sent his mother money. Although sending money to Russia
was no simple procedure, Martha managed to organize an intermittent but
regular method: she sent the money through Nora. Now and then, Martha
even managed to force Vitya to write a letter, but often he simply signed his
name to a brightly colorful postcard, and Martha had it mailed to Moscow.
Varvara, a person of unexpected decisiveness and unexpected, sometimes
idiotic, ideas, in the meantime transferred her longtime hatred from Nora
to Martha, although the wedding photograph of her son and his second wife
hung above her bed.

This unexpected love for Nora bore a weekly character—on Saturdays
she visited Nikitsky Boulevard, bringing with her a blackberry pie and a parent's blessing. Nora served tea, cut the pie into slices, nibbled at it politely,
praising it, then put it aside. After her mother-in-law left, she gave the pie
to the neighbors.

From exotic esoteric beliefs, Varvara Vasilievna moved on to the more
traditional Russian Orthodoxy. She no longer drove off evil spirits or puri-
fied her karma. When Yurik returned to Moscow, Nora's problem—what
to do with the weekly pies—was easily resolved: he ate them whole. Nora
was used to spending Saturday mornings at home. She never made any

appointments for then. She received her mother-in-law precisely at ten, took the still-warm pie from her hands, and woke up Yurik, so that his grandmother could see him take the first bite. After this, Nora handed her fifty dollars; Varvara Vasilievna preferred the U.S. currency to that of her homeland. Then, more than satisfied, she took her leave. Although Nora continually emphasized that Vitya was the one sending the money, Varvara was absolutely certain that it was Nora's beneficence she was receiving. Her reasoning was simple: if Nora gave her the money and didn't keep it for herself, it was a mark of her virtue.

This financial-gastronomic interaction continued for several years, until Nora noticed that for two Saturdays running her mother-in-law had not shown up. She didn't answer the telephone, either. Nora decided to go to her house. No one answered the door, but the neighbor told her that Varvara Vasilievna was in the hospital. Through the district clinic, Nora soon found out that her former mother-in-law had been hospitalized after suffering a stroke. Nora and Yurik took turns visiting her, first in the hospital, then, after a month, in a rehabilitation center outside the city. Nora smiled wryly to herself. Who would have thought fate had such wit? The elderly woman who had hated her for so many years had fallen under her care.

Nora was sorry for the old woman, naturally, but she had no idea what past transgression she was paying for. Perhaps she was making a down payment for a future transgression, just in case?

Unlike Nora, Yurik fulfilled this filial duty without protest or complaint. He came to see his grandmother and took her for walks in the park in her wheelchair. Then he sat beside her on a bench and played the guitar. What did he play? The Beatles, of course. Varvara Vasilievna's speech was slurred, but from her mumbling it was clear that she was very pleased with Yurik and his music. Nora did not catch the moment when Varvara Vasilievna had ceased to doubt Vitya's paternity. Perhaps during the years when Yurik began playing chess with his father . . .

Varvara Vasilievna returned home two months later. She had become a complete invalid, though it was hard to distinguish between the symptoms of her senile dementia, her damaged speech, and her physical infirmity. The neighbor, who was a pensioner, agreed to look after the sick woman. Nora compensated her for these services, and put a checkmark next to the box: "Varvara—care."

Yurik made a convenient ramp leading from the room onto the balcony. For half the day, Varvara dozed outside on the balcony, and the neighbor fed her and changed her diapers. A year and a half later, at the beginning of July, a few weeks before her eightieth birthday, Varvara fell asleep on the balcony and didn't wake up.

Vitya and Martha, who had planned to visit Moscow for her birthday, ended up at her funeral instead.

Three years had gone by since Yurik left America. For three years, he hadn't seen his father or Martha. For Nora it was longer. The last trip, when she and Tengiz had evacuated Yurik, she had never made it to Long Island. Vitya had not seen his mother in more than fifteen years. He hardly recognized her in the deceased woman with the crumpled stranger's face, and began to cry. Then Nora, who had competently, without any fuss or bother, taken care of all the funeral arrangements—the visit to the morgue, the requiem service in the church, the gravesite at the cemetery—was so moved that she began to cry, too. For so many years, she had considered Vitya to be devoid of normal human emotions, but either she had been mistaken or he had stopped being completely self-absorbed. Martha must have removed the spell from him. Huge, hulking Martha, as big as a house, who was pouring out tears on Vitya's shoulder.

They all got into Nora's car and went to her house, the four of them. Nora drove, and didn't try to enter the conversation. They all spoke English in Martha's presence. Just as they were entering the apartment, the phone rang. Nora didn't make it to the phone before the answering machine picked up. She heard: "Nora! It's Grisha Lieber. I'm here for a few days, to see my granddaughter. Kirill had a daughter. I wanted to see you. Give me a call."

He didn't have time to say the number before Nora grabbed the receiver, exclaiming: "Grisha! Grisha! Vitya and Martha are in Moscow. Come over!"

Half an hour later, the doorbell rang. Grisha was staying in his childhood apartment on Malaya Nikitskaya, a ten-minute walk from Nora's. At one time, it had been the grand residence of a famous surgeon. Then it had been occupied by Grisha's parents, physicists, and now Grisha's first wife, Lucy, who had never agreed to go to Israel with him, lived in it. The apartment was stuffed full of new residents—Lucy's second husband, their small daughter, Grisha's son Kirill, with his wife and newborn granddaughter, as yet nameless. Grisha, the former legal occupant of the grand apartment, was relegated to the kitchen, where he slept on a folding cot. The whole family was very amused by this, especially Grisha. In Israel, he had fathered another five children; one son lived in Australia, another in America, and all of them estimated how many folding cots in various parts of the world he would be sleeping on when he was an old man.

A little old adolescent man, with a tanned bald pate resembling an acorn and a scraggly beard, in a black yarmulke, wearing shorts, and holding a bottle of vodka in his hand. Nora, hardly able to suppress her laughter, announced as she greeted him: "We're just back from a funeral. We buried Varvara Vasilievna today."

"Oy oy oy! *Baruch dayan emet*, as they say in Israel. The Lord gives, and the Lord takes away. May she rest in peace."

Grisha put his bottle down in the middle of the table and stood next to Vitya. They no longer resembled Don Quixote and Sancho Panza. Vitya had expanded in width, and therefore seemed shorter, and Grisha had turned into a scrawny little old man, with not a hint of his former rotundity and paunchiness. No one was in a position to judge this but Nora, however.

I have changed less than anyone, Nora thought. But no one notices.

Suddenly Vitya said, "Grisha, look at Nora! She's the one who hasn't changed a bit."

Unbelievable. What's happened to Vitya? He never even noticed people before, Nora mused.

"It's no surprise, Vitya. It's no surprise. Because of our metabolism, you and I long ago exchanged all our material composition—you consist completely of matter of the New World, and I of matter of the Holy Land. And Nora renews her body by virtue of the molecular structure of local matter. That's why she doesn't change," Grisha said, laughing heartily.

"I doubt that atoms carry that kind of information," Vitya said, translating what Grisha had said to Martha, and asking everyone to speak English so Martha could understand. Self-absorbed no more.

"All right, but let me say one more thing. There is a DNA program that arranges molecules and atoms in a certain order, and this order includes—"

Here Nora interrupted him and invited him to sit down at the table. Yurik poured them each a shot of vodka. They poured the ritual glass for the deceased and covered it with a piece of brown bread. Only Grisha drank the vodka. Nora took a sip, for propriety's sake, then drank no more. Vitya, Martha, and Yurik didn't touch alcohol. They raised their glasses, filled to the brim, and set them back down on the table. With this the funeral rites came to an end. And the duet between Grisha and Vitya, which had lasted fifty years, with frequent interruptions, began again.

Grisha had progressed a long way in his molecular-Biblical research over the years, and had completely abandoned experimental science—never relinquishing his beloved notion of the quantum computer, however. He had immersed himself in areas of speculation completely unacceptable to Vitya, always relying on the latest achievements in molecular biology to back up his ideas.

Nevertheless, it was still a funeral repast, and at first they all observed the laws of decorum, without any special effort.

Grisha, as always, was drawn toward the higher spheres. He raised his glass, saying, "How happy I am that I can see you all, even though it is such a sad occasion. And what I would like to say is this: Death is not a glitch in the program, it is contained in the program itself. Nothing slips from the Creator's grasp. Every human life is a Text. And this Text is necessary, for some reason, to God."

"I'm not sure what sort of text my mother, Varvara Vasilievna, could communicate to God that He didn't already know. It seems to me, Grisha, that you're exaggerating a bit."

Grisha downed another shot of vodka. "Vitya! Vitya! Every human being is a Text. The mysteries are being unraveled. The twentieth century resolved half the eternal questions that plagued humankind; people just don't realize it yet. Everything that lives is a Text that has been written over the course of three and a half billion years, from the first living cell to my own granddaughter, born just one week ago—in fulfillment of the command to 'go forth and multiply.' And this is the only way of reading and producing the Divine Text. By *realizing* it. All the information collected by a human being throughout his life becomes part of a general repository—the memory of the Lord God. Varvara Vasilievna gave birth to you, and that was her part in the great work of enduring Creation. Grisha wiped the sweat from his forehead, sighed, and knocked back another glass of vodka.

"All right, all right, just leave my poor mother out of it," Vitya said, laughing.

Yurik laughed, too. Nora didn't quite get the gist of what Grisha was saying, but she didn't feel like questioning him more closely about it. She understood very well, however, that a sense of humor, of which she had never seen any evidence before, had awakened in Vitya. Martha had never impressed her as much of a wit before, either. Did this mean that Vitya, like a sunflower in a field, had bloomed in proximity to his wife, from good light and beneficent watering?

Grisha drank another glass, sighed deeply, and ate a piece of brown bread. Nora pushed a fried chicken leg toward him—"Bush's Legs," as they were called at the time, since the foodstuff was an American import. He refused it: he was much more interested in talking than in eating. Besides, he had just consumed a piece of cheese, which was not permitted in combination with chicken, according to Jewish law.

"You see, no one eats those legs but you," Yurik whispered to her.

It was true—these chicken legs had caused a scandal. People suspected they caused some infection or disease, which the Americans had injected in them. But Nora didn't care; she wouldn't turn up her nose even at these dubious legs.

Grisha went on: "The best computer ever made by the Creator is the living cell. It's impossible to improve on it."

Vitya jabbed a chicken leg with a fork and picked it up. He had no prejudices about the moral incompatibility of meat and dairy. Anyway, there was nothing in the world he preferred to white bread with his favorite kind of salami.

"Grisha," Vitya said, "it *is* possible to improve on it. It's possible to make a computer that works faster—and they're already being made, you know that as well as I do. If a program is written well, a computer can solve problems at a far greater speed than the human brain will ever be capable of. All the more since computers are now self-learning, and they learn much faster than a human being does, too. The human consciousness is hampered by far greater limitations than a computer is."

Grisha jumped to his feet. "The brain is not made from a network of neurons, basic elements, but from a network of molecular supercomputers. This alone completely defeats your notions. But I'm talking about something else. Human consciousness is the only place in the universe where texts can touch one another, interact with one another to produce a new text, new thoughts! This is what 'in the image and likeness' is all about. The human being resembles the Creator precisely in this—in the ability to generate new texts." Grisha knocked on his head rather resoundingly with his fist. "Right in here! This is the only place."

"Are you quite sure that's the only place?" Vitya countered, somewhat lazily. "Are you sure that at this stage of evolution a new generation of people won't emerge, superhuman people, who will represent a sort of hybrid product? Martha's mother has been living with a pacemaker for ten years; our neighbor Jeremy uses his artificial hand to put drops in his eyes; and I don't have to tell you the kinds of things that robots are able to do nowadays. The future is taking shape as we speak, and I don't like to make predictions, but the world has entered a new stage: hybrid evolution is already under way. You understand that human consciousness, allied with the computer, is a qualitatively new product."

Grisha, who had now finished off half the bottle of vodka, was growing more and more heated.

"Vitya! You fail to understand the most important thing. Excuse me, but you are a technician, a technocrat. Any text is a form of existence for information. Life on earth must be understood as a text. The Divine Text, which is not written by us. The Creator is information. The Divine Spirit is information. The human spirit is a fragment of information. The 'I' is a fragment of information. Life is not a means of existence of protein bodies, as Engels thought, but a means of existence of information. Proteins become denatured, but information is indestructible. There is no death. Information is immortal. But this American struggle of yours, the race for speed, leads in the final analysis to a world that belongs to the ones who have the fastest computers. And the instinct for consumption lies at the heart of this race. And self-destruction. Modern-day humankind cannot curb itself, rein itself in. It hungers for dominion, it thirsts for war. It wants to devour everything in its path. Whether America, or Russia, or China. This is a false path. Open your eyes. You're working for war. In this slaughterhouse, only the Tibetan hermits, and other like-minded people, will survive. A new generation of people will arise out of them, and it will be a new branch in the evolution of *sapiens*, not amid mammoths and saber-toothed tigers, but amid rusty computers and in the presence of high levels of radiation . . ."

Here, finally, turning to Vitya, Martha put in her word: "Vitya, he speaks like a prophet."

In a gesture very familiar to Nora, Vitya rubbed his clean-shaven chin.

"Martha, he's talking like a Jew. It's the Jewish passion for reading into a text something that wasn't there to begin with."

"What do you mean?" Grisha shouted. "It was written! It was written in very straightforward, down-to-earth words: 'Hammer your swords into plowshares'! You have to read the texts!"

"I didn't understand the reference," Nora whispered to Yurik. "Translation, please."

He translated.

The more agitated Grisha became, the calmer and merrier Vitya looked.

"Grisha, I did read that text you're talking about. A long time ago. My wife, Martha, wanted very much for us to get married. I must admit, to this day I don't understand why it was so important to her. I assumed that it meant putting on a black suit and tie and going to her favorite church, and losing a day's work for going through the ceremony. But that's not how it worked out. The priest demanded that I go to catechism classes before we got married. In short, it took loads of time, and I read the Bible. Perhaps for the Hebrews it was the Divine Text, but it seems to me to be a completely archaic document in the present world. Too much cruelty, too much illogic, too many discrepancies and contradictions. It's not just by chance that for three thousand years Jews have been writing commentaries, interpreting and reinterpreting texts, and turning them inside out, trying to get rid of these contradictions. It seems to me that the proverbial inclination of Jews to scholarship derives precisely from this ancient nitpicking."

"You don't know how to read it," Grisha bellowed. "Jews are the models or exemplars of the human being. As with any exemplars, there were simplifications. All people should, in a sense, strive to become Jews. Adam Kadmon, the original, the first, human being, was the spiritual appearance or manifestation of the human essence, the proto-image of the spiritual and material world. But today we understand that 'spiritual' is a synonym for 'informational.' And the human being is created, according to Rabbi Akiva (and I fully agree with him), in the image of Adam Kadmon. In other words, this was the model that was realized in the framework of the Creation."

"Mama, I don't think I understand any of this all of a sudden," Yurik whispered to Nora.

"It is very interesting, nonetheless," Nora said.

"That's true," Yurik agreed.

They sat there quietly, trying to follow the intellectual theater that was being played out before them by these two former schoolboys who didn't seem to have grown up yet, though they were both already sixty. However surprising, Vitya seemed to be the older and more mature of the two.

Nora caught herself thinking that she actually liked Vitya. She had never liked him before, but now she did. He displayed a natural reserve, an economy with words, even a gentle tact in coping with Grisha's verbal onslaughts.

It's strange, but I never thought about it before, Nora thought. We really have ended up in a completely different world. Vitya is probably right—yes, they both are. Humanity has crossed some invisible boundary that the majority of people simply aren't aware of. We were taught that there is a material world, that the human being is the crown of Creation; but he's not a crown, not a ruler—he's a child. A child of nature. Two hundred years ago, the theory of evolution was a scandalous idea. Today the human being has not only discovered the mechanics behind it, but has himself become not only its product, but its engineer. What a good thing it was that they told me this; I would never have suspected it myself. And how great—and what a coincidence—that Vitya is the father of my child. It might have been better if it had been Tengiz; but nature saw the matter differently.

Grisha still argued with Vitya for a long time. Yurik ran off to attend to his own affairs. Nora was tired of their conversation and stopped trying to understand it. Martha was dozing in an armchair; she should put her to bed.

Nora opened her appointment book. There was a to-do list for the week—go to Varvara Vasilievna's apartment with Vitya and Yurik to find out whether there was a will, meet with a lawyer, go to the bank to pay the bills—so that she could mark it all as finished and get on with her own life.

47

Theater of Shadows

(2010)

I t was the same disease that killed Amalia. Many years had passed since
her death, and although they had not found a cure, they had learned how
to prolong life. Sometimes the patient lived long enough to die of another
illness, with a more pleasant name, or even of old age.

Nora had already survived Amalia by twenty-odd years. Each time she
celebrated another birthday, she remembered to add another year to that
number. In the sixty-eighth year of Nora's life, the defect, hidden away in
some gene, handed down to her from her mother, manifested, and the diagnosis was the same. Ironically enough, the Theater Workers Polyclinic,
which was renowned for its otolaryngology and its phoniatrics departments,
but not for its oncology, managed nonetheless to diagnose Nora's illness at
a fairly early stage. They sent off a urine sample to be tested, found some
sort of protein, and immediately got on the ball. She underwent the usual
course of treatment, and after a year and a half the quality of her blood was
restored. They discharged her and recommended regular checkups, blood
tests, and testing for markers of the cancer cells.

After six months of treatment, Nora had become reconciled to the idea
of her untimely death. Now that she had received a respite for an indefinite
period, she experienced an unprecedented surge of vitality. All her senses
were sharply honed. Life, which she had never before experienced as a gift,
now became a moment-by-moment celebration. Each tiny detail, all the inconsequential trifles, seemed to glow from within and afford her delight—
her morning cup of coffee, water spurting out in the shower in a powerful

stream, a line drawn in pencil across a piece of paper, a glimpse of a clump of grass working its way out from under a rock. Music that was once merely pleasant became an event, as though she were having a personal conversation with Bach or Beethoven. Trivial things that had once annoyed her—banal talk, foolish disputes—now ceased to bother her at all.

She felt sheer joy at living, with an intensity that had suddenly increased a thousandfold. Even telephone conversations that had once distracted her, which she had felt to be a waste of time, gave her pleasure—the voices of friends, not necessarily terribly close ones, suddenly surfaced out of the distant past: a classmate she had nearly forgotten; a dressmaker from the sewing workshop of a Siberian theater in which she had staged a play twenty years before; a call out of the blue from Nikita Tregubsky, her first devastating heartthrob in the eighth grade . . . What did he want? He was visiting from Canada, where he had been living for a long time, and wanted to see his old friends. He realized that, more than anyone else, he wanted to see Nora. Funny, absurd, and completely unnecessary. David, a Georgian actor who had left Moscow to settle back in his historical homeland, called from Tbilisi, and asked her to come for a visit.

"I'll think about it," Nora said. "Leave me your number."

She mulled it over for a while. Even before the phone call, she had been considering some sort of journey. A trip to Altai, or to Perm, perhaps to Irkutsk—to the cities where she had once worked. Tbilisi was the one place she hadn't considered. The shadow of Tengiz, which had almost left her, seemed to stir again and come to life in the corners of her apartment. They hadn't seen each other for ten years. He made the decision, and they parted. She hadn't heard anything about him in a long while. She had read that he was staging productions in France and in Portugal, that he had received awards at various festivals, that he was teaching. Then he returned to Georgia, and the notices about him in theater publications ceased. He was fifteen years older than Nora. Eighty-three? Eighty-four? Is he even alive? Oh, what the hell, I'm going anyway, Nora decided. I've always loved traveling.

The war with Georgia had already become chronic. Everyone was used to it, the way one gets used to bad weather. The weather was, however, glorious. It was April, replete with all its promise. There were direct flights to Tbilisi about once a week. Nora bought a two-way ticket; she would spend a week there. As someone who was used to traveling on business trips, she packed her suitcase deftly, grabbed a book of reminiscences about Tusya (written by her students after her death), bought some chocolates to give as gifts, and flew off, with a long-forgotten feeling of ease and lightness, a readiness to encounter both difficulty and adventure.

The airplane landed. The design of the airport had changed, but the people looked the same. Even the customs officials smiled. The crowd waiting in the arrivals area was a sea of black headscarves on Caucasian widows and the ageless, ubiquitous flat black caps of the menfolk. David, now bald but still very youthful, stood just to the side, holding three blue irises for her. They embraced. He took her to the empty apartment of his aunt, who had also left on a trip. There was a loaf of bread wrapped in a napkin, a piece of Sulguni cheese, and a bowl full of raisins. There was also a bottle of wine. It was already late in the evening.

"I'll come by tomorrow morning, and we'll go for a walk," David said.

It was a marvelous week. David was unemployed, and lived alone. Nora had never figured out exactly how he was able to make a living. He seemed to earn something from moonlighting as a gypsy cab driver in his old Toyota. In any case, he had long ago parted ways with the theater. On the first day, they went up Mount Mtatsminda, a de rigueur destination for tourists. They walked along its slopes, scattered with primroses, white and yellow. The buds on the trees were ripe to bursting, and on the highest sundrenched spots the trees were already covered in a light-green lacy mist of newly opened leaves. A tree she couldn't identify, which had taken the lead, was already shedding sweetly scented blossoms. David was the ideal guide for Nora. He hardly spoke, but when Nora asked him a question, the answer came, in words both spare and precise. They descended, not by the lift, but on foot, and then stopped by the ancient Church of Mamadaviti.

It was a wonder to behold—a clean, beautiful space, with old brickwork, perfect and even, and just as perfectly imperfect monuments and statues in the necropolis—Vazha-Pshavela, Sergo Zakariadze, and Ekaterina "Keke" Geladze Dzhugashvili, Stalin's mother. The finest monument was the one dedicated to Kote Marjanishvili. His grave resembled a round, stagelike platform. If only they hadn't added the sculpted bust . . . Her grandmother Marusya had worked in his theater troupe in Moscow for a time, if Nora remembered correctly. A nice little tie with the past. But it was remarkable—such a dynamic, theatrical, artistic people—and such dreary Socialist Realism, pathetic and simplistic, against the background of the ancient, impeccable architecture. But what a tender, somehow weightless land it was—the green veil of emerging leaves, the scent of living soil, currents of thick, wine-laden air ascending the slopes, everything growing clean and pure, dissolving in light. How good it must be for a Caucasian to be living in his own land, in a world of mountains and valleys . . .

For three days, they walked through the sparsely populated and silently hospitable city. Then David said that the next place they must visit was the David Gareja Monastery in the desert, but he had no money for gas.

"The gasoline is on me," Nora said, and thought: Poor guy, it's clear he's hard up, or he never would have mentioned it.

Nora had never heard anything about a monastery in the desert, but in the morning, David came to pick her up, and they set off. They drove for quite a while. The view of the landscape from the window was captivating. Such a small and diverse country: mountains, foothills, vineyards, villages, but no desert that she could see. They left the car in a parking lot near the monastery. They walked a bit, then came upon scattered buildings, the monastery grounds. The monastery itself, built upon cliffs, had been founded in the sixth century by Syrian monks. Carved in the mountainside were dozens of caves that had been occupied by the early Christian hermit-monks who had arrived from the East, from Syria, in the sixth century. Here was one more page of a great culture that she had not yet come into contact with. And time was so short. It's all because my life was lived entirely through the theater, Nora thought. I have missed so much. And that door does not allow you entry everywhere. A great deal remains sealed off.

First they stopped in the monastery shop—paper icons, crosses, tourist trappings and trinkets. David bought two bottles of local wine. They glanced into the monastery itself, then began walking up a path. A beautiful, somewhat circumscribed vista opened up to them. There was a valley that extended nearly to the horizon. A desert. But in April it was green, carpeted with tiny, nearly invisible blooms. Mountains loomed blue on the horizon. Strange, alien, tantalizing.

"This is the border with Azerbaijan. The desert is Azerbaijan. And those mountains are already Armenia," David said, gesturing vaguely with his hand.

From this vantage point, one could see churches in varying states of disrepair, caves here and there . . .

When they were walking back from the monastery to the parking lot, they heard singing in the church. Nora stopped. The singing was different from what she was used to hearing in Russian churches. She recalled the folk ensemble that she had worked with long ago for a time. This was something absolutely different, completely different . . .

They returned to Tbilisi toward evening. She still had one more day left, and David said he planned to take her to a rather distant village, toward the region of South Ossetia. It was the site of a fairly recent border skirmish, a military confrontation between Russia and Georgia. But it also held a working monastery, with a school; and there was an auditorium in which theater productions were often staged. Tengiz was the director of the theater. Excellent! She had not made a single move toward him of her own volition. The matter had arranged itself. She nodded: We're going!

The next morning, they set out again—and again she fell under the spell of the roads, the landscapes, the motion itself. They drove slowly. The road was uneven and pitted, and they were in no hurry to get to their destination. They had left early enough to have time to spare. Mountains, plains, vineyards. Half-ruined villages—signs of the recent war. David stopped the car and got out. Nora followed behind him. The road wound through a blackened vineyard, which had been burned down in the autumn, before the harvest. David broke off a cluster and placed it in Nora's palm. When she touched the grapes, they crumbled into dust. A shadow of the wine that was not to be . . .

Will I really see Tengiz? How strange that we're still alive, Nora thought, without the least bit of agitation or excitement. Perhaps it's because I've outlived my own death and reached old age. How wonderful old age is, what freedom it holds! She smiled, recalling how her heart had beat in her throat at the sound of his voice, how she nearly fainted at his touch. It's not his fault that I was so madly in love with him. Only now can I understand what an emotional burden this must have been for him. Poor Tengiz! But what unrelieved gloom I felt when he told me he was going to marry again! He was already getting on in years, and I believed the remainder of his life belonged to me . . . I was such a fool! Nora smiled to herself, because the cancer was a blessing from God, and had completely liberated her from the habit of possessiveness.

"We're going to be a bit late, after all," David said.

Again, a church, a courtyard, monastery buildings. Bright and clean— inside and out. A long stone structure. Old, but the period from which it dated was unclear. The masonry was crude, and the stones had not been smoothed or finished. They opened the door.

They entered a darkened room. The darkness was thick and palpable. They stood by the door, pressing themselves to the wall. They could just make out the soft sound of a high-pitched, insect-like droning. A screen—

fairly long, not very tall—flickered with light. Vague, unidentifiable shadows passed over it in waves—perhaps water, perhaps grass, like an image under the lens of a microscope. Beautiful, incomprehensible—but no explanation was necessary. Then the shadows merged to form two figures, a male and a female. They moved together in mutual response and harmony. Suddenly they were not whole figures, but hands that approached each other, and touched; then the screen seemed to shatter in an explosion of shadows.

There was no music in the conventional sense—only, from time to time, tentative ripples of sound that vaguely recalled music. Plants emerged out of nothing, out of nowhere, strange flowers bloomed and faded, and it was impossible to tell how this was accomplished until the hands appeared: a road, mountains, a landscape; a church on a mountain, a river. Absolutely unfathomable how it was done.

The shadows were thick but also completely transparent. Fish swam past—schools of them. Then, instead of a multitude of small fry, two of them loomed into view, enormous, one a real monster. It wasn't a struggle, but a dance. The screen glittered; there was nothing except shadows—and strange animals—some very familiar, dogs and rabbits, bears and elephants, and others, walking octopuses and interlaced snakes . . . An intricate, perfect, eventful process of life was unfolding, only the events were indecipherable. There were only hints, gestures, surmises.

And mysterious sounds—a musical instrument, or a human voice, or an animal emitting some signals . . . They enchanted, bewildered, bewitched. Now the shadows clung to each other, they merged together and flowed over. And a baby appeared, a baby held on the palms of a pair of large hands . . . It was impossible to identify what sort of substance it was made of . . . There was no substance—it was a theater without matter, without substance. An Ideal Theater, in which there was nothing but shadows; neither was there music—just shadows of sound.

Tears streamed down her face. There had never before been such a space on earth, never. It was a world that Tengiz had created completely from shadows, and the content of the world could not be expressed in any language. There wasn't a single word to accompany it. There was, in fact, nothing at all . . . It was Creation. Not a *story* about Creation, but Creation *itself*. It almost made sense: why he had rejected the corporeal and substantial theater, why during the past years he had become weary of the crudeness of theater, why he spoke about the hypocrisy and insincerity of the theater, the lies of words, the deception of theatrical décor and props, costumes, makeup, the constant overreaching of gestures, the inadequacy of the points of departure, and the impossibility of reaching a goal that in itself wasn't worth the effort . . . How could he reject that which formed the sine qua non of the existence of the theater—the actor? How did he find a theater troupe in which the performers agreed to renounce their need to reveal themselves onstage? The anticlimactic finale . . . What a wholesale retreat from theater! What was the use of Stanislavsky, of Meyerhold? What did Brecht matter, who was Grotowski? Tengiz had transcended substance, taken flight to a place where nothing but shadows existed anymore.

Suddenly everything on the screen changed—there were easily identifiable bears and rabbits, giraffes and swans. As they played out funny little scenes, the audience began to smile, then laugh. Was he making fun of them? Was he putting the self-important spectator in his place, bringing him down a notch? Pulling the wool over his eyes? Indeed, just then, a shadowy goat (not a sheep) with horns and a fat udder appeared. Amusing . . . Nora didn't even notice her own tears. They flowed freely down her sunken cheeks, and all the while she was smiling. Oh, Tengiz! We were young together, and I didn't know then what you knew. Or perhaps you didn't know it, either? Is this really the reason I suffered so because of you—so that in old age I would understand that only shadows remain? They are the only thing that is real, the only thing that can be said to exist . . .

The lights came on. The room was rather small, and not all the seats were occupied. People clapped. There were many children in the audience, but still more adults. They spoke in Georgian, and she didn't understand what they were saying. Then a heavyset old man with a crutch came out onstage. He had a large shaven head, a bright face. He waved his hand—and those who had created the shadows came out onstage, too. Nora smiled—the shadows of the shadows, seven young men and women.

David pressed his hand lightly on Nora's shoulder: Shall we go up to greet him?

Tengiz gestured toward someone—a single, powerful gesture. A young woman joined him onstage. She was large, stout, with curly hair. He embraced her and patted her buoyant ringlets. She slightly resembled Natella, his late wife. She had a good smile. They looked at each other tenderly. No, Nora didn't tremble inside. The shadow of love was stronger than love itself . . . And more pure. Shadows are not possessive.

"Let's go say hello. He'll be happy," David whispered. "Come on."

"No, David, let's leave. Let's go back to the car." And Nora slipped out the door.

David followed her to where the car was parked. They didn't speak, just got in the car and drove to Tbilisi. It was shortly before sundown, the last hour of daylight, when the day reveals everything it is capable of, all the beauty and sadness and tenderness that it has accumulated in its brief span of life, from dawn to sunset.

Darkness fell suddenly. The road was poor, but nearly empty. Once in a while, the sliding cones of headlights seemed to uproot sparse roadside bushes or occasional buildings from the darkness. Nora felt as if she were half asleep. When they were already getting near the city, she said, almost as though she were talking to herself, "Tengiz's young wife is very pretty; they make a good couple."

"What wife, Nora? That's his granddaughter, Nino's youngest daughter. After Natella's death he never remarried. He's a widower. He never found another woman who could match him."

"Oh" was all Nora said.

Why did he tell me he was going to get married, then? Nora thought. Did he decide to free me from himself? Or free himself from me? No, to set me free, of course. It doesn't matter anymore.

The next day, she flew back to Moscow. If anyone loved long-distance flights, it was Nora. She loved it when you found yourself nowhere at all—in a sort of abstract space and an indeterminate, vacillating time, when, all of a sudden, all obligations, all promises, cease. Everything is put on hold—telephone calls, the mail, requests, offers, and complaints—they all stop short, and you hover, you fly, you soar between heaven and earth, between the earth and the moon, between the earth and the sun. You fall out of your ordinary system of coordinates. You fly . . . as Tengiz, my soulmate, had; the only one I knew who had burst through all the boundaries of this world alive, and had learned to inhabit another world—the world of shadows . . . Tengiz . . . Love beyond touch, love outside of time.

48

Liberation
(1955)

Jacob's final prison camp was a special one—the Abez camp, for invalids. It was the place they sent the sick and the weak, the convicts exhausted by work in the Inta mines, as well as the rest of the goners from all over the Komi Republic. It was a barracks settlement with whimsical, eccentric structures—workshops, barns, two retired steam engines whose boilers worked to heat only the administrative headquarters. From the hangar that had grown up around the steam engines, monstrous pipelines wrapped in hairy black insulating material loomed over the heads of people from all sides, like the malignant spiderweb of a concealed arachnid.

At first, after the prison officials had glanced at his documents and determined his level of competency, they sent him to an elite technical department in the accounting office. But there he had a falling out with the boorish boss, also a convict, who wrote a memorandum with contents that Jacob was not privy to. First they threw him in the lockup for five days and nights, and then appointed him to work in the library in the Culture and Education Section, where he was more a watchman than a librarian.

Prisoners convicted for espionage and slander against the touchy Soviet authorities settled in the town. Read: Russians from every part of the country, Lithuanians, Poles, Jews, and other people of every possible description. An enormous graveyard of nearly four hectares had grown up on the outskirts of the camp, beyond the drainage ditch, in a place that never dried out, either because a stream flowed through it, or because a swamp festered there. Makeshift bridges made of railroad ties were thrown over the ditch;

beyond, stretching to the very horizon, were the same kinds of ditches, only they had been dug to serve as graves. In the winter, the snow mercifully covered the common graves, which had been dug in a timely manner before the first snowfall—each ditch to hold fifty corpses. In the spring, when the snow melted, earth was strewn over the thawing corpses. No pickax was capable of breaking up that earth after the frost set in, especially since the people who were still alive to perform the task were weak and sickly. Thousands and thousands of bodies of exhausted foes and admirers of the authorities, the illiterate and the highly educated, the stupid and the wise, the world-renowned and the completely obscure, lay side by side in these ditches. Under pegs to which numbers were affixed.

Jacob knew a secret that a casual friend, the field doctor Kostya Govorunov, had divulged to him. Somewhere in these ditches, among thousands of others, lay the Orthodox philosopher Karsavin, until recently a professor at the University of Vilnius. A Lithuanian doctor, also one of the convicts, who had performed the autopsy, had secreted in the stomach of the deceased a small dark-glass flacon containing a piece of paper with the philosopher's name written on it. Kostya was present during the procedure, and saw it with his own eyes. This doctor hoped that the time would come when the exhumation of bodies would begin, this note would be found among the remains of the nameless bodies left there to rot, and a monument would be erected to the philosopher.

For a long time already, Jacob had been trying on for size the intolerable idea that he would be buried here, near the Arctic Circle, in a common grave under a peg. This had been the fate of many in his immediate and extended family, of his people. They lay in a common grave in Kiev, at Lukyanovo cemetery—his murdered younger brother, four of his girl cousins . . . Altogether, twenty-nine blood relatives. And all over Europe, many millions he was not directly related to.

It was the second year that he had been living in Abez, after his left leg had refused to work and he had been able to walk only on crutches. The camp was the worst of all those he had been forced to live in, and he now recalled his previous years in exile as paradise. Meaningful, solid years, shot through with hope, full of plans, a variety of projects and ideas, work. The only thing that Jacob didn't feel he was lacking here was company. Human interaction. The camp was populated with members of several generations who had been plucked out and earmarked for annihilation. Scholars, scientists, poets, artists—the flower of the Russian intelligentsia, branded by the founder of the Soviet government as the "shit of the nation." Among this multinational "shit," Jacob found several very precious acquaintances. His neighbor in the barracks was an elderly hydrogeographer, Richard Werner. Conversations with him were an inspiration and a pleasure. They read German poetry to each other. He introduced Jacob to Rilke, whom Jacob hadn't known, or appreciated, before. After they had been acquainted for about three months, they began talking about Sudak, where Werner and his wife had vacationed earlier. Word by word, Marusya and little Genrikh were drawn out of the depths of Werner's random recollections. In the camp, a fleeting moment or coincidence, a long-forgotten crossing of paths, acquires great significance. Richard suddenly became like a long-lost relative to Jacob, and was a source of joy. Half a year later, Richard Werner died of pneumonia. Then Jacob began to gather material for his future work. He had not thought of a title, but he had subject matter in abundance. It would be a demographic analysis of this labor-camp "shit"—the most erudite, highly educated members of society, whose lives ended in Abez.

Being a librarian was very much in keeping with his scholarly interests. He had at his disposal not only the card catalogue, but also the personal library cards of all the readers, on which his predecessor had scrupulously written their professions and titles. He had finished the demographic analysis in two weeks and then ran out of material. He hit upon the idea of a special educational index and envisioned doing the same for the camp authorities and wards, but there was no material whatsoever on them. This demographic of the camp population did not visit the library; they read their own newspapers for political education.

His post as librarian, which was in some sense the nadir of his life, was among the safest and most secure in the camp. The library holdings were more or less rubbish. They consisted primarily of books confiscated from convicts. The best of the collection was the second volume of Alpatov's work, devoted to the Renaissance, and sent to the camp to Nikolai Nikolayevich Punin. The book survived with Punin for a year, but ultimately ended up in the library. Jacob put a stamp in it, appropriated the inventory number, and gave himself over to the Renaissance for several days, all the while lamenting that the Northern Renaissance was so poorly represented, and that the Italian Renaissance was so clearly valorized. He was already mentally developing an idea about the differences in perception of the human image in paintings of the Italian and the Northern Renaissance; but, recalling the death of the manuscript of his novel when he was convoyed to Abez from his previous camp, he stopped himself. In his heart, he had abdicated from his favorite pastime—writing.

Since he didn't know how to exist without big projects or tasks, he began studying Lithuanian. It proved easy for him; besides its being an Indo-European language, he was surrounded by many native speakers he could consult.

He was already sixty-three years old, and old enough to start contemplating the years he had lived with the benefit of hindsight. *The Boustrophedon of My Life*—he laughed to himself. But there wasn't even anyone to share this with. Marusya . . . He still wanted to write letters to her, but she had imposed a ban on correspondence, even one-sided, with him. Warming his frozen hands with his breath, by force of habit, he composed letters with no addressee, and categorized them under the empty term "Texts."

Everything changed in the space of a single day. The copy of *Pravda* that reported the Leader's illness, dated March 4, 1953, reached the camp, as usual, one day late—on March 5, when the radio was already announcing his death. Kostya Govorunov rushed over from the dispensary to tell Jacob, "Stalin is dead!"

A commotion started up, quiet but widespread. The workday was in progress, but people spilled out onto the street, hobbling out as though they had been called to a task.

Agitated by the announcement, Jacob even limped over to see Samuil Galkin, a Jewish poet whom he had gotten to know in the Jewish Anti-Fascist Committee in 1947. He had to discuss the astounding news. Galkin waved his hands. "Be quiet, Jacob—hold your tongue. Don't jinx it." And he commanded an interlude, as usual, by reading a poem in Yiddish. He valued Jacob as perhaps his only listener who didn't need a translation.

But Jacob was unable to listen: the prospect of return held him captive, tantalizing him. Was it really possible that he would make it back, that he would be able to see his sisters, his mother, his cousins—his heart quaked—perhaps even Genrikh, and his granddaughter, whom he had never met before? Here his thoughts faltered, and he was brought up short.

He didn't sleep that night. His leg, as usual, ached, as did all his joints. But his head felt as clear as a bell. Of course, he should begin writing letters to all the appropriate organizations, and he tried to go down the list, deciding whom to write, why, about what—a review of his case; rehabilitation; pardon? Then his thoughts turned in another direction. His demographic theory found a practical application. The death of Stalin should serve as a point of departure for the birth of a new generation. No matter how the history of the Soviet Union unfolded in the future, the era that began on this day would be known as "post-Stalinism," and the children born in 1953, after the death of Stalin, would no longer be called "postwar," but would be known as the "post-Stalin" generation. He wouldn't live much longer, his days were numbered . . . but how fascinating it might be, what a turn things might take! Yes, I have an idea how this research project should be organized. I'll ask Urlanis, Kopeishchikov, Zotov . . . Hold on, I'm getting carried away.

On March 6, they were not marshaled to go to work. They sat in the barracks, expecting some sort of sea change in the routine of life—if not today, then tomorrow. They talked very little. At night, on the 7th, they erected a crude rostrum out of slabs of wood. The quartermaster, a former priest, whispered that all the black fabric from the depot had been commandeered, on the orders of Bondar, the camp's warden. No one knew who sewed the banners that night—perhaps the officers' wives—but in the morning, red cloth panels with black funeral lining were draped over the main gates and above the rostrum. Work was again called off, and all the inmates and residents of the camp were assembled on the parade grounds. Music started pouring out of the loudspeakers in the damp gloom of the dull northern morning.

From the first notes, Jacob recognized the dear, familiar sounds of the finale of Tchaikovsky's Sixth Symphony. He had not forgotten a single note: the main section of the fourth movement begins with the same theme as the secondary theme of the first . . . And it emerges and builds, and suffers, and threatens, then transforms itself into a requiem, into the adagio lamentoso . . .

Jacob started weeping at the first sounds. How long it had been since he had heard music, how he had longed for it! Ibrahim, a mullah from Samarkand standing beside him, looked at him curiously. Valdis, a Lithuanian nationalist who was standing on his left, smirked. What was he crying about? But Jacob didn't notice. His eyes were closed, and tears ran down his cheeks—the strangest tears of all the tears shed all over that huge country. But Jacob's tears did not end here, because after a short pause, almost a splice, the seventh movement of Mozart's Requiem in D minor, the Lacrimosa, started up.

At the very same moment, Nora, Jacob's twelve-year-old granddaughter, stood in her school's auditorium before a plaster bust of the Leader, his head hardly visible above a mountain of flowers, suffering from a terrible sense of loneliness, alienation, and her inability to share in the common grief of her classmates and teachers. For the life of her, the tears just wouldn't come.

Meanwhile, on the camp rostrum, things were not going as planned. Captain Svinolup and Lieutenant Kunkin had taken their places long before, but the warden was nowhere to be seen. The middle of the rostrum, the traditional spot for the warden Bondar, remained vacant, and proceedings could not begin without him. It was cold, and the situation was alarming and incomprehensible. Everyone was already frozen stiff, but, apart from the music, nothing at all was happening. At this very moment, a doctor, shaking with fright, was administering drops of valerian to Bondar, who had suffered a mild heart attack. Forty minutes later, pale and bloated, Bondar appeared, and the music stopped. The event got under way.

Stalin was dead, but on the surface it was as though nothing in life had changed. The camp, which was intended to hold five thousand people, in fact accommodated more than eleven thousand. All of them had a burning interest in politics. They followed the newspapers avidly in search of deeper changes. Strangely, the changes that promised to transform the country after Stalin's death reached them only very slowly. Again, a circle of "clever ones," people fond of political debates, of launching new concepts and ideas, developed around Jacob. The primary instincts and penchants of the intelligentsia were rekindled. They wrote letters to secure their release. And they waited.

At the end of March, the Gulag was transferred from the jurisdiction of the Ministry of Internal Affairs to the jurisdiction of the Ministry of Justice, and this reassured them. A year passed; the Gulag was again placed under the auspices of the Ministry of Internal Affairs. Again the prisoners wrote all manner of letters to all possible addresses, and again they waited. Jacob sat up until late in the library of the Culture and Education Section. He had formulated for himself a plan of life again, with points, sub-points, and commentaries, and life took on new meaning, which had almost been extinguished in the "Abez Hole," as he called his existence there. Along a circuitous route, through one of the camp's hired civilian employees, and then through his sister Eva, he managed to send several letters to colleagues of his, conveying scholarly concerns and proposals. He wrote one other letter—to Marusya. He wrote this one after his discharge, when he was already wending his way back toward Moscow.

It was the final letter of a correspondence that had lasted from 1911 to 1936—a quarter-century of love, friendship, and marriage.

LAST LETTER FROM JACOB TO MARUSYA
INTA–MOSCOW
JACOB TO MARUSYA

DECEMBER 10, 1954

Dear Marusya,

We haven't seen each other in what seems like an eternity, and we most likely won't be seeing each other again. We are both old now, living our final years, trying to tie up loose ends. It is natural that one's thoughts hark back to the past. I'll begin with the most important thing: I was happy throughout my youth, all twenty-five years of our marriage. After we met, the first years we knew each other, and the first years of our marriage, enveloped us in such limitless joy, such deep—and I say it unequivocally—happiness, that even the reflected light of these years should have illumined the later ones, should have helped soften the inevitable rough corners and edges.

It was always interesting for us to be in one another's company. We never experienced boredom in our marriage. My first impulse and desire was always to report my fresh experiences and impressions, all my joys and sufferings, all my new thoughts or creative efforts, to you. This practice has become so deeply rooted in me that, even now, though we long ago parted ways, I have not broken the habit, and I have to struggle against the desire to share something with you. This is not only the content of a marriage, but its very essence, its pride, its gem.

And the world of art, through which we lived our life together? To this day, the radio has not ceased to stir me, to move me. Whether I hear Rachmaninoff's Second Symphony, which brought us together, or Schubert's "Barcarolle," which I so often played to accompany you, or Glinka's "Doubt"—all these charming pieces of our youth—as of old I repeat to myself, "These sad times will pass, and we will see each other again." But will we? Is it still possible?

The harshness of my fate prepared a difficult biography for me. Blow after blow, without respite; years of constant moves, one after another. A husband and wife must live together; marriage cannot survive on postage stamps alone. And now it is clear to everyone who is responsible for destroying my family. I am surrounded by thousands of others just like us.

Stalingrad; Biysk; then the mine; Yegoryevsk; Sukhobezvodnaya, where I was horrified, seeing my approaching fate (oh, how little you understood then!); and then Abez. What sort of family could have survived such trials? It would have had to be made of steel. But now this is all *Plusquamperfectum*. I am now free. I am in Inta, and in a few days I will get a certificate attesting to my freedom, then travel to Moscow. Judging by the experience of my comrades, they are hardly likely to give me a resident permit—a "right to live" (remember this term from our youth?) in a large city. But Moscow is where I will receive the assignment for a city of residence.

I am now a cripple, and I walk with a crutch. My life is approaching its end. My dream is to see you. We will not weigh old grievances and sorrows. I have never loved anyone, ever, but you.

I can imagine the bitter irony of your reaction. However, someone who took the decision to divorce in absentia, someone who did not wish to hear either a confession or a defense, has no right to irony. This is absolutely true. In my situation, neither disingenuous avowal nor belated pretense is of any use. I have made many attempts at reconciliation—all for naught. At first there was simply distance, then alienation . . .

If you agreed to meet me, or at least to send me a friendly word or two, it would afford me great relief. I would be able to shed a burden I have borne for many years. I would like to be able to kiss your hand in farewell. Or, if nothing else, a letter written in your hand.

Thank you for my past, our past.

I would be happy to see you when I am in Moscow. Eva lives in the same house on Ostozhenka where they came to arrest me six years ago. You know the address and telephone number. If you wish, you can get in touch with me through her.

Jacob

There was no reply to the letter.

———

Jacob arrived in Moscow at the end of December 1955. The room on Ostozhenka, which had been sealed on the day of his arrest, had been given to the yardman. Jacob decided not to stay at his sister's. His situation was the same one the authorities always forced on him: he was banned from entering Moscow, but the paper that would assign him a new place of residence, which was almost like a sanitized form of exile, he could only receive in Moscow, from the public prosecutor's office.

Asya, who still lived in her communal apartment on Ordynka—where there was no watchful yardman, and where other residents were few in number, beaten down, and disinclined to denounce people to the authorities— took Jacob in. In the apartment there was an elderly Jewish lady whose daughter was a famous poet, with a Stalin Prize under her belt and a note in her passport pointing to her ethnicity (the infamous "fifth paragraph"*). She had been trained by her daughter into weak-willed, approving silence. There was also a middle-aged couple who, for their entire lives, had concealed their aristocratic origins, their observance of their Orthodox faith, their education, which they had received abroad until 1917, as well as a new circumstance— their only son was in jail for robbery. These neighbors pretended not to be aware of the nighttime presence of a guest without proper registration papers or a residence permit in their apartment. They didn't ask a single question.

Jacob held in his hands a wonder about which he had not even dared dream—a pair of large white breasts, youthful, silken, only a trifle pendulous—objects of Marusya's jealousy and envy. He hid his face in them and breathed in the scent of a woman's skin. Asya stroked his head with her small, skillful hands, which could lance a boil, puncture a vein with a fat needle, give blood transfusions, and many other things. It was exactly as it had been in '36, when Asya had come to visit him in Biysk, even before the news of the in absentia divorce. And it was even better than after the war, the first three years before his next arrest, when they were together for the second time. This was the third and final time Jacob had been with the woman whose love had embarrassed him in his youth and later, in Biysk, had inspired him with a sense of awkwardness and guilt because he couldn't respond to her feelings in kind. Now her lifelong love, which for decades had been unsolicited and inconvenient, turned out to be the only anchor in

* The "fifth paragraph" was a line in the Soviet passport identifying the ethnicity (or "nationality," as it is called in Russian) of the bearer, thus sanctioning discrimination on ethnic grounds.

his broken, unmoored existence. She was prepared to abandon everything, to retire from her job in the polyclinic and follow him anywhere—to Vorkuta, to Chita, to Magadan . . .

Five days later, Jacob received the necessary papers and instructions to reside in the nearby city of Kalinin. Banished to the boondocks, the back of beyond. A day before his departure, he called his son's apartment. Amalia, his son's wife, answered the phone. She gasped when he said his name. She had never seen her father-in-law, even though she knew he was in the camps. Genrikh had hardly ever mentioned him, and she didn't ask. Amalia invited him to visit on any day, though she asked that he warn her beforehand so she could prepare a festive meal. But it was now or never—he had to leave the next day for Kalinin, and today was his last day in Moscow.

When Jacob came out of the Arbat subway station, he was drawn, as though by a magnet, in the direction of Povarskaya, to Marusya's, and his own, house. But this destination and the route to it were now closed to him forever. With a heavy heart, he turned toward Nikitsky Boulevard. He had never been to his son's apartment—only ten minutes away from their former home.

Amalia was unable to warn Genrikh beforehand of his father's arrival, and they converged at almost the same moment—Genrikh five minutes earlier. They embraced and kissed each other. The table was set in the larger room. Jacob was seated at the head of the table. He leaned his crutch on his chair. Nora emerged from the side room. It seemed to Jacob that the girl slightly resembled Marusya, though she was homelier. She sat down in her place without saying a word, and glanced furtively at her grandfather. Her glance alone told him she was a clever girl. He also guessed that Amalia didn't love Genrikh. He didn't sense that fleeting but deep eye-contact that fills the interaction of lovers; they didn't address each other at all, as though they were quarreling. But they weren't quarreling. This was simply their life—without commonality, without intimacy, and with Andrei Ivanovich waiting on the sidelines. They divorced a year later. The girl, gloomy and silent, sat looking down at her plate.

"What grade are you in?" her grandfather asked.

"Fourth," she said, her eyes still lowered.

Reserved, unsociable. Not a very happy little girl, Jacob thought. "Do you like it?"

"What, school? No, I don't like school," said the girl, looking at him for the first time.

Her eyes were gray, circled with a dark fringe, like Marusya's. Her neck was long, and her hair was light chestnut, parted at the top of her forehead and falling down in two waves, like Marusya's. But her mouth and her cheekbones are mine, Jacob thought . . . Genes, genes . . .

Amalia was sweet and cordial, but she looked at him with abashed curiosity: he was one of the first "newly freed" ones, and her eyes were full of unasked questions. Genrikh was tense, and also reluctant to ask questions. Instead, he tried to joke. Nora blushed at his jokes, though they didn't in the least merit this reaction. Genrikh laughed at his own attempts at humor, and Jacob felt anguish inside, knowing that he would never ask his son the question that had tormented him for so many years.

After tea, Jacob left. When they were saying goodbye, he stroked Nora's head, patted Amalia's shoulder, scratched the gray cat Murka behind the ears, and shook Genrikh's hand. They never saw him again.

The next morning, Asya accompanied Jacob to the station. He carried a rucksack on his back. In his right hand he held his crutch; in his left he carried a small suitcase in a canvas casing. They kissed each other on the platform. Asya's little face was homely. Her gray, unkempt hair stuck out from under her beret, but under her heavy black woolen coat, under a rough woolen vest, under her white blouse, in the two ample linen pouches of her women's undergarments, lay her wondrous breasts, which had awakened in Jacob his slumbering sensuality, and her love—he knew—was firm and enduring, and was sufficient for all the days of his life that remained. A life without Marusya . . .

Two weeks after the New Year, and after finishing the matters she needed to attend to in Moscow, Asya arrived in Kalinin. He led her to a wooden house, relating to her the history of the city as they walked, telling her what a marvelous town it was, independent, recalcitrant. It had fought against the Golden Horde, had forged a friendship with the Lithuanians. The first generation had settled here before Moscow was founded, and the princes had been worthy and decent. He talked about the felicitous geographical situation of the city, about the river Tvertsa, which they simply must try to navigate in the summer, sailing from the mouth of the river to its source. About the wonderful local library, which they never seemed to weed out— he had discovered such remarkable ancient gems of literature behind its doors. About the possibility that he could continue his work, at last . . .

The house was an old, dilapidated wooden structure, but the original porch with its finely turned wooden pillars, and the ornately carved window frames, had all been preserved. The room was large and clean, and the hospitable landlady was a quiet woman. The windows were too low, because the old house was sinking into the earth; but the four-poster bed, with metal knobs atop the posts, was too high. With his bad leg, it was difficult for Jacob to climb onto it. As soon as she arrived, he informed Asya that he had already found a carpenter who would hammer together a broad, low divan on which they could place a mattress.

In a wonderful notebook in a wooden binding, which he had bought in a stationer's shop on his first day back in Moscow in December 1955, Jacob managed to fill up several pages with his beautiful, but somewhat characterless, script. He decided to begin this fresh notebook in the New Year, and the first page was dated January 1, 1956.

Below the date was a list of eighteen points. This was a to-do list for his professional affairs. On the second page, household matters, there were fewer points, and several of them were already checked off. Number one was a teakettle, and the kettle—sturdy, enameled in acid-green—was already standing on the table.

"What a splendid green!" Asya ventured to say, touching the gleaming side of the new teakettle and smiling.

"Asya, I'm color-blind. I was sure the color was a tranquil gray."

The eighteen points laying out his professional goals represented the project to which he planned to devote the remainder of his life. He no longer wished to return to the manuscripts that had perished in the Lubyanka, the secret police headquarters. The Abez prison camp had given him the kind of experience that in part canceled out, in part simply devalued his prosaic exercises—it was good that nothing had been preserved. Whatever would he do with it now?

His scholarly research could have been continued. He felt it had a certain degree of social relevance—not today, not just now, but perhaps in ten years' time. The only thing he was sure he wished to return to was music. The three-volume textbook on world musical culture, which he had begun to write in Altai, could even now be useful to a number of people—those trying to further their educations, or to broaden their culture horizons. Yes, yes, being a *Kulturträger*, a "culture bearer"—that was the right path for him now. But he decided to begin with that marvelous work that he had embarked on in the military, when he conducted the soldiers' choir, an amateurs' orchestra.

As was his custom, as a person who thrived on organization, he began carrying out his plans by investigating the local libraries (check), and visiting the local Houses of Culture (check, with the name of the director beside it: Morgachev, Pavel Nikanorovich). At the bottom of the page was a short list of sheet-music titles that he would have to order in the regional library. There was no check after that entry.

Jacob died eight months later, at the end of August, of a heart attack. Asya had gone to Moscow to pick up her pension, and when she returned, she found him lying on the mattress, dead. On his last desk there were two newspapers from the previous day, a pile of freshly written pages of cheap gray paper, and four library books: a Lithuanian language textbook; Lenin's *Materialism and Empirio-Criticism*, the pages densely covered with penciled notes; Einstein and Infeld's newly published *The Evolution of Physics*; and the prerevolutionary score of Händel's oratorio *The Messiah*.

Written on a sheet of dull paper stuck between the pages of the book by Lenin were these words:

Always lags behind in his reading of scientific literature. Writes about the existence of matter in space and time in 1908, already after the discovery of the theory of relativity. Calls the transformation of matter into energy "idealism," at the same time that, in 1884, John Henry Poynting demonstrated that energy, as well as the mass of matter, is localized, transferred by a field, and its flux has measurable density.

Such were the last happy months of Jacob's life.

49

The Birth of a New Jacob

(2011)

This time, too, Liza demonstrated her abundant organizational skills. She found places for Timosha and Olga in nursery schools. She hired a housekeeper, a fifty-year-old Georgian woman named Victoria, who was the sole support of her family in Kutaisi and needed to supplement her earnings. She had bought (notwithstanding the Russian superstition that counseled against doing so before the birth) a newborn's layette. Her children were so eager for the birth of a sibling that they were practically glued to her belly. They tapped on it gently and chatted with their little brother, who, to their delight, they could sometimes feel answering back.

The child's first attempt to see the light of day occurred on New Year's Day but he reconsidered. This was just as well, since it would have been most inconvenient. Victoria was off for the holidays, and dishes and pots and pans were piling up in the sink. Either because of the warmth in their home or the sense of impatience hanging in the air, the Christmas tree had prematurely shed half its needles. Yurik suffered from an allergy whose cause was unknown. He itched and scratched like a mangy mutt, and, out of the depths of his long-lost childhood, the panicky fear of infection that had gripped him at the age of five, when Nora drew him a picture of some germ-monsters, came back to haunt him. This time he was not afraid for himself, however, but for Liza and the children. For several nights in a row, he slept on a narrow couch in the kitchen. Liza's belly, which after all these months had grown used to Yurik's nighttime embraces, felt forlorn. Liza was perplexed.

For the past two years, she had fallen asleep and woken up alongside her husband, like a single indivisible being.

Immediately after the New Year, the children also came down with Yurik's inexplicable rash. Timosha was especially uncomfortable with it. Liza didn't call the doctor, and she didn't bother to take him to the polyclinic, since the holidays were still in progress. People hung around in their courtyards, exhausted from drinking, not knowing what to do with themselves; they were tired of the never-ending vacation. Buses seemed to be running at whim, the polyclinics were operating haphazardly, and it was not easy to reach them, since the roads were nearly impassable. Heavy snowfall alternated with thaws, and the Tajik migrant workers who usually cleaned them were idle, since they weren't paid to work during holidays. Liza decided independently on a course of action—she gave everyone suffering from the condition antihistamine tablets—and the ghost of the evil germ vanished.

On the morning of January 4, the little one sounded the alarm that he was ready to make his appearance. Labor pains began. They went to the maternity hospital to see their obstetrician, Dr. Igor Olegovich, who was straightforward and brusque and didn't suffer fools. This was how he had won Liza's heart when they signed the contract with him for delivering the baby. Yurik didn't like him, but Liza defended her preference, saying he was as sharp as a whip, not some wishy-washy pantywaist. She herself was inclined to be straightforward and brusque, so it was all fine with her.

The brusque Igor Olegovich probed the surface of her belly, then put on a glove and poked his iron finger into her soft, fleshy depths. He told Liza to come back when the labor pains were so intense that she wanted to "tear the radiator from the wall." Besides, according to the calendar, she wasn't due until the 9th, and disturbing doctors without good reason was bad manners.

Liza meekly submitted to his orders. Her pregnancy had so softened her that she held her tongue, and didn't respond with the kind of reply the doctor deserved. To be honest, the labor pains had stopped of their own accord. Tired out by the expectations and the results of the false alarm, the couple slowly wended their way along the banks of the Moscow River. They were both thinking only about the upcoming events, but they talked about everything else except that.

"It's nice when a city has a lot of water. The windows of my favorite apartment in New York faced the East River. There were three of us renting it, and each of us had our own little room. But I was the only one with a view of the river. And I liked Staten Island a lot, too. There's so little water in Moscow. In New York, I always tried to live close to the water."

"Tell me about it," Liza said.

"Ask Nora. She loves telling people how she came to see me in about '94 or '95. I don't remember exactly. I was living in my first apartment. Not alone—with a whole group of people. There was a black guy who played sax; an English girl, the granddaughter of some famous writer, either Iris Murdoch or Muriel Spark, I don't remember. The place was so trashed that it took Nora two days just to clean the kitchen. And after that she threw out four garbage bags of rubbish from my room alone. She never said a word. Well, she asked only one question: 'Yurik, how did you end up with two left shoes, both of them worn out?'"

"Yes, Nora's amazing, of course. I would have raised such a stink if I had been in her place!"

"No, that's not her style."

"Were you already hooked by then?"

"No. Just a bit. But not like later. I mean, I didn't realize I was already hooked yet. I thought I was just experimenting. Nora was staying at her friend's house in Manhattan, a wonderful lady. I borrowed money from her the first year. I tried to pay it back, but I didn't always manage. Her nickname was Chipa. I forget her real name. She had a window that overlooked the water, too—a view of the Hudson. I tried so hard to throw away that piece of my life that it seems I've even forgotten what I never intended to forget."

A taxi approached, and Yurik pulled Liza into the back seat. They went home and started waiting until January 9, which they referred to as "Day X." On the morning of the 9th, Liza called the doctor and asked whether it was now time to give birth. The doctor casually told her to wait another week.

"Doctor," Liza said, "I've had labor pains for a whole week. I mean, they're not evenly spaced, true; they come and go, sometimes often, sometimes less so. But they're absolutely real. Shouldn't we do an ultrasound, at least, to see what the little one is up to in there?"

"Fine. Go pay to have an ultrasound, if you so desire," the brusque doctor said.

They traveled to the outskirts of the city for the ultrasound, and sat waiting their turn for an hour. A woman with greasy hair examined the sonogram and diagnosed a double nuchal cord. Liza's spirits sank; she felt she had run out of strength. The children whined all evening, squabbled, and howled before bed in two-part harmony. Yurik picked up his guitar to play, but even this tried-and-true calmative was ineffectual.

In the evening, Pasha, Liza's former lover, called and asked whether they needed his help. They certainly did. Their angel-nanny Victoria had come down with the flu and gone away to stay with her relatives for several days to convalesce. Pasha came over an hour later. The children clambered all over him. Yurik, with whom they had long been on the best of terms, asked Pasha to put them to bed for him, and he sat with Liza. She just wanted everything to be over as soon as possible, and she drank some sedative—to keep from crying, and to keep from thinking about anything. The sedative had very little effect on the labor pains, and she simply couldn't sleep. Toward six in the morning, Liza made the decision that it was time to give birth. Immediately. Yurik tried to joke: "Are you thinking about the radiator?"

But the labor pains, which were not evenly spaced but coming as nature deemed fit, now turned into one long corridor of pain. Pasha was sleeping in the nursery, on a cot. At a quarter to seven, Liza and Yurik closed the door quietly behind them and got into a taxi. Two traffic lights later, Liza realized that the baby was on the way. At just after seven, they arrived at the maternity hospital. The entrance gate was closed. The guard's booth looked deserted. There was no time to see whether the guard was inside. It was easier to go on foot to the reception desk.

Liza climbed out of the taxi and stepped right into an icy puddle. But she was unable to walk. Not a single step. Everything was like in a bad movie, the only difference being that it was impossible to slow it down or stop it. Standing nearly up to her knees in the icy puddle, Liza gripped the handle of the taxi door tightly; the taxi driver shouted that it was time for him to leave and that they needed to pay up immediately. Uncoupling herself from the door with difficulty, Liza gave Yurik precise instructions about what to do next: "Run to the reception desk and tell them that you need a doctor and a gurney—your wife is having a baby. Tell them I've gone into labor!"

Yurik hadn't experienced such fear, and such a complete break with reality, since his dangerous narcotic trips. Nevertheless, he behaved very reasonably. Nearby, a small, frightened Tajik streetcleaner was trying to break up the ice on the frozen sidewalk with a crowbar. Yurik grabbed him by the scruff of the neck and said to him sternly, "Hold her up." And he ran off to the reception desk.

The Tajik knew only two words in Russian that might be appropriate in this situation: "girl," and "fuuuuuck . . ."

"Girl, fuuuuuuck," he said to Liza, stroking her back.

Liza leaned against the crowbar, which in some unknown way had ended up in her hands. The pain, which had already been powerful, now overmastered her, so that nothing was left of her but pain. At that moment, she seemed to turn into an animal, operating only on instinct. And her instinct told her: lie down and give birth.

Liza threw her coat off onto the snow and said firmly to the Tajik, "Right now!" And she got down on all fours.

"Girl . . . fuuuuuck . . ." the Tajik whispered. Crouching down beside her on his haunches, he began praying, quietly and rapidly. Then Yurik came back.

"Liza! Liza, wait—they're on their way. Stand up—what are you doing?" he cried in horror.

This was the most terrifying scene he had ever witnessed in his life. He bent over to help his wife up, but when he saw her up close, her teeth bared, he started reeling. At that moment, a blonde woman in a faded green lab coat ran up to them.

"Stand up. Come on, try to stand up," she said.

Liza answered her with a sound that resembled "*RRRuunnhhh.*"

"Come on, now, stand up," the midwife commanded, and tried to lift Liza up by her shoulders.

"I won't make it," Liza insisted.

The midwife let her go, and thrust her hand into Liza's trousers, where she fished around, and, simultaneously with the Tajik, said, "Fuuuuck . . ." Then she added: "Totally fucked."

Then, for some reason, they all got distracted and looked over at the guard's booth. Meanwhile, the baby made one last sprint for the finish.

"Help me, for God's sake, the baby's coming out!" Liza commanded all of a sudden, very soberly. Apparently the child had given her a breather, and was building up his strength for the next onslaught.

All of them—Yurik, the Tajik, and the midwife—after looking around, raised Liza up and led her to the booth. The gurney had gotten stuck somewhere along the way.

Lyuda, the midwife, threw open the door of the booth; the guard was there, having sex with a naked woman.

"What the hell!" the midwife said, dumbfounded.

The naked woman didn't take her words too seriously. She simply dressed herself rapidly and freed up the little booth, grumbling: "Big deal, she's having a baby. Everyone does."

"Please, just don't have your baby on my bed!" said the fastidious guard, although it was too late to do anything about it: Liza was already in his bed. Yurik was taking off her shoes.

Then the waylaid gurney rolled up. They dragged Liza onto it. Half naked, wearing only her sweatshirt, her hips and nether regions bared, their paleness gleaming festively for all the world to see, no shoes on her feet, her hair damp and matted, fastened by her daughter Olga's brightly colored hair clips, Liza was wheeled toward the reception hall on the ramshackle, hobbled gurney by the Tajik, the guard, the midwife, and the random person who had brought the gurney out of nowhere, with Yurik at the head of this crazy procession. They pushed it along through the melting ice puddles, over the hummocks and potholes, up the stairs, along the tiled floor. "The baby's coming!" While they were rolling along, Liza tried to explain to the midwife about the double nuchal cord.

"That's the least of our worries right now," the midwife said gloomily. They finally made it to the delivery room.

Yurik had absolutely no desire to attend the birth, but he ended up there anyway. There were three people present: the midwife Lyuda; the nurse on duty, who had managed to get hold of the gurney, and who rushed up with a cup of tea in her hands; and Yurik. Neither the brusque doctor nor any other doctor of any description was anywhere to be seen. They were all, apparently, still celebrating the New Year.

In the delivery room, Lyuda asked Liza to be patient and to keep the baby in for another minute, at least giving her time to prepare the medical equipment. The metal instruments clinked, and liquid burbled. The nurse pulled on her gloves, with rubbery squeeches and sharp snaps. The pain was now too much for Liza to bear.

"Scream out, then, scream!" Lyuda told her. Liza wanted very much to scream, but wouldn't allow herself to let go. Somewhere in the distance, Yurik hovered, very pale, on the brink of fainting.

"Okay, now push like hell!" Lyuda commanded gaily.

The baby boy slipped right into her hands—en caul, in his bubblelike amniotic sac. The first thing she did, even before taking him out of the bubble, was to unwind the umbilical cord from his neck. She said, her voice now soft and low, "Here he is. A frisky little man! And he's already wearing a shirt!"

She offered to let Yurik cut the cord. But he didn't even hear her. He just kept repeating: "Liza! Liza! Jacob is born! All the terrible things are behind us!"

It was January 10, 2011. Marusya's birthday. A day Jacob Ossetsky honored and observed his whole life. The centenary of the correspondence, preserved in the willow chest.

50

The Archives

(2011)

I n 2011, unexpectedly, old age caught up with her. No, it wasn't that she was in her dotage. It would be more accurate to say that youth ended, never to return. She had managed to overcome her congenital cancer, at least temporarily. Yurik and Liza made her happy, with the equanimity and delight that radiated from them. Nora had never experienced this kind of familial happiness. Even Amalia and Andrei Ivanovich, with all their enveloping mutual affection, suffered from a lack of fulfillment—they left no direct progeny. Yurik and Liza had a son, Nora's grandson, who brought with him a completely new kind of happiness. Nora scrutinized the little fellow and was able to descry the intermingled legacy of previous lives, of his predecessors—Amalia's rounded eyebrows, Genrikh's small, neat mouth, Vitya's fingers, and Liza's light-brown Asiatic eyes—a gift from her Buryat grandmother. All of this went deep down, far and wide, back to a time when the depiction of faces with the help of silver salts had not been invented, in the pre-photography Mesozoic Era, when only artists—with varying exactitude of vision, varying gifts and habits of the imagination—were able to leave lasting images. There were no portraits of forebears in Nora's family. After Genrikh's death, what remained was a sheaf of photographs.

The haste in which Nora had lived her entire conscious life ceased. Her journey to Tbilisi had helped her to arrange things in her mind and heart, to put everything in its proper place. She had not been mistaken; she had not gone astray. Not only did Tengiz not disappoint her, but he ultimately turned out to be the very person who pushed her, who led her, in just the way she needed to be led in order to arrive at this quiet and meaningful point. The storms of love that she had experienced with him left neither bitterness nor pain—only vivid and rich memories, and slight perplexity: Why had these hormonal surges, these flashes and flickers, taken up such a great part of her life? Was it just the way the female body worked? Ultimatums of her genome? Laws of biology that ensured the propagation of the species?

By this time, Nora had written a book about the Russian avant-garde in theater. The very same year, it was translated into English and French. She devoted herself more and more to teaching—seminars on the history of theater and stage design in the theater school, the same seminars that Tusya had once taught. And, just as Tusya had been, Nora was now the idol of her students.

She was happier than she had ever been in her life. The only thing that worried her was a number of unfulfilled tasks. She made a list of things to do in the near future, beginning with the household affairs. She replaced the bathtub with a shower stall; bought a new stove; acquired two antique Swedish bookcases at the antiques store on Malaya Nikitskaya; and got rid of the old, warped homemade shelves. She weeded out her overgrown library. And when, finally, all the entries on that to-do list had been crossed out, she took the bundle of letters that had been passed down to her from her grandmother Marusya out of the desk drawer. She hadn't opened the bundle since her grandmother's death, but she remembered that on the top were letters from her grandfather Jacob, dating from 1911. She unfolded the oilcloth in which they were wrapped, now disintegrating with age. The delicate letters had survived for a century, and Nora realized that she was the only person on earth who remembered these long-dead people: Marusya Kerns, whom she had so loved when she was a child and then fallen out of love with, and Jacob Ossetsky, whom she had seen only once in her life, when she was a girl, not long before his death, when he visited them on Nikitsky Boulevard after one term of exile was over and before the next one began.

The letters were neatly arranged by year, all of them still in their envelopes, with stamps, dates, addresses, and inscriptions in the sort of handwriting that no letter on earth would ever be written in again.

It took her a week to read all of them, almost without a break. She cried, she laughed, she was perplexed. She was filled with delight. In the same bundle, she discovered several notebooks that Jacob had begun keeping as an adolescent. The story of a great love, the story of a search for meaning, creativity as a way of life, and an unquenchable passion for knowledge, for trying to understand an unruly, disheveled, mad world. Many family secrets came to light, but questions arose as well—questions for which there were no answers.

Nora arranged the old photographs—Genrikh's legacy. There were quite a few of them. Some of them were signed, and these Nora put aside. Many photographs depicted people she didn't know: relatives and friends whose names it was no longer possible to recover. At the turn of the twentieth century, amateur photography was virtually nonexistent; all of these were taken in a studio by a professional, and affixed to a piece of cardboard bearing the address of the studio, and often the name of the photographer. The earliest photograph was dated 1861. It was a picture of an old man with a large beard, in a yarmulke. Most likely Marusya's grandfather.

A strange, powerful feeling gripped her, as though she, Nora, the one and only Nora, were floating down a river, and behind her, like a fan opening up, were her ancestors, three generations of them, imprinted on pieces of cardboard, with familiar names. Behind them, in the depths of these waters, was an endless line of nameless predecessors, men and women who had chosen one another through love, through passion, through convenience, or by arrangement of their parents. They produced and protected their progeny, great multitudes of them, and they settled the entire earth, and the shores of all the rivers. They had propagated and multiplied, in order to produce her, Nora; and she to bring forth her only son, Yurik; and he to produce still another little boy, Jacob. It is an endless story, the meaning of which is so hard to discern, though it always beckons, as the most fragile of threads.

All the work of generations, all the games of chance—all so that a new child, Jacob, would be born and become part of this eternally meaningless, meaningful current. This play has been performed for thousands of years, with insignificant variations: birth-life-death, birth-life-death . . . So why is it still interesting and exciting to float down this river, watching the landscape change? Is it not because someone, at some time, dreamed up an intricate little bubble, the sheerest of membranes, to enclose within delimited boundaries each living being, each "I" floating down the river—until it bursts, with a dull moan, and pours back into the waters of eternity? These ancient letters, preserved by some miracle, are the everlasting contents of this "I," the trace of existence . . .

Why did I wait so long to read these letters? Nora asked herself. Out of fear. I was afraid to discover something terrible about Jacob, who lived in exile and in labor camps for at least thirteen years; and about Marusya, who was always hiding something, and constantly almost revealing secrets, and then maintaining a deafening silence again. I was afraid to find out about the fears and passions that devoured them, and about those base acts that fear pushes people to. But the letters explained a great deal.

Now there was just one thing left to do—to find out about what happened beyond what the letters revealed. That was Nora's final step. She visited the KGB archives.

The archives were located by Kuznetsky Bridge, five minutes by foot from the dark heart of the city, from the Lubyanka. Nora said she would like to see the papers on file for the case of Jacob Ossetsky, who was released from prison at the end of 1955. The archival assistant asked Nora whether she had any documents attesting to her relationship.

"I have the same surname, and I have my father's birth certificate, which bears the name of my grandfather."

"No problem, then. Leave your phone number, and we'll order the file of your grandfather's case and call you within the next two weeks," said the very forthcoming archival assistant.

Two weeks later, she called to inform Nora that she could come to acquaint herself with Jacob Ossetsky's case. Nora went to the archives.

The woman delivered a folder, on the cover of which were these words:

Case. OSSETSKY, J. S.
Opened: 1 December 1948.
Closed: 4 April 1949.
Submitted to archive R-6649
KGB Archive No. 2160

The folder was thick. There were large-format sealed envelopes inserted between the yellowing pages, sewn together. The archival assistant warned her that the envelopes must not be unsealed. It was also forbidden to photograph, scan, or photocopy the contents, but she was permitted to take notes and copy extracts. She found a photograph in an unsealed envelope. Jacob Ossetsky, on the day he was processed, in profile and full face—with a shaved head, a small mustache, and a firmly compressed mouth.

The face took her breath away.

Nora placed a plain notebook she had brought from home next to the case file. The first three pages of the notebook had been filled up with Yurik's handwriting in 1991, not long before he left for America; she hadn't been able to find a fresh notebook at home, and the stationer's store was closed. She turned the page with Yurik's chicken scratch, and began to take notes:

Born . . . studied . . . served in the army . . . worked . . .
First arrest 1931: 3 years exile (Stalingrad Tractor Plant)
Second arrest 1933: 3 years exile (Biysk)
Third arrest: December 2, 1948

Nora had already read about the first two terms of exile in her grand-father's letters. About the last term, she knew only that he had been imprisoned in 1948 and released in 1955.

Her eyes came to rest on a sheet of thick, fine-quality paper on which was written, in wonderful prerevolutionary clerk's script: "Arrest Warrant from December 1, 1948." And a fingerprint!

On the other pages—yellowing, dog-eared—was written the entire history, in an awkward, unlettered (in every sense) hand. Nora barely noticed these shortcomings, however.

The search was carried out at the place of residence of his sister Eva Samoilovna Rezvinsky at 41 Ostozhenka Street, Apt. 32, who works as a teacher of French and German in School No. 57. During the search, his sister E. Rezvinsky and the yardman and building janitor Soskova, M. N., were present. The witness was Chmurilo, A. A.

What followed was a long list of his belongings, which Nora began to copy down, though she stopped before reaching the end of the list.

DESCRIPTION OF PROPERTY:
1. Iron bed
2. Bookstands, two pieces
3. Telefunken radio set, imported

One page of entries was missing. The list began again with:

17. Plywood suitcase
18. Abacus
19. Safety razor
20. Slide rule
21. Men's overcoat, mid-season, herringbone, used
22. Men's overcoat, summer-weight wool
23. Men's suit, wool
24. Black two-piece suit—old
25. Men's jacket, wool
26. Shirts, 3 old
27. Undershirts, 2 old
28. Long underwear, 4 pairs, old
29. Underwear, 4 pairs, old
30. Towel, cotton

In her mind, Nora arranged the bed, the two bookcases, and a table in a narrow room. She distributed some of the "used" objects, and realized she was already staging a play . . .

DURING THE SEARCH, THE FOLLOWING ITEMS WERE CONFISCATED:
1. Dissertation of J. Ossetsky, *Demographic Notions of Generations*, 3 volumes, 754 pp., 1946–1948
2. Brochure by J. Ossetsky, *Statistical Data on the European Economy*
3. Journal, *Thought*, issues 6–11 from 1919, Kharkov
4. Materials in draft form, *British-Palestinian Handbook*, 577 pp.
5. Notes on economic statistics, 314 pp.
6. Letters, 173 items, numbering 190 pp.
7. Newspapers in various foreign languages (English, German, French, and Turkish—according to J. Ossetsky), 18 items
8. Reports for the Jewish Anti-Fascist Committee on the Palestine question, 4 volumes, typewritten, with an inscription on each volume: "Mikhoels"
9. Report on the Palestine question for the Ministry of Foreign Affairs of the USSR (with an inscription: "to B. Stern, adviser at the Ministry of Foreign Affairs")

There were sixty-eight entries altogether. Following this was a list of books, also lengthy:

BOOKS:
1. Pokrovsky, *Rus. History*
2. Martov, *History of Russian Social-Democracy*, with notations
3. Urlanis, *Population Growth in Europe*
4. *History of the Jewish People*, Mir Publishers, 1915
5. *The Jewish Encyclopedia*, prerevolutionary edition, 17 volumes
6. L. Rosenthal, *About Uprisings*, with notations
7. Yu. Larin, *Soc. Structure of the USSR and the Fate of the Agrarian Population*, with notations
8. Karl Marx, *A Contribution to the Critique of Political Economy*, with notations

Nora glanced at the end of the list—980 entries, half of which were in foreign languages.

During the search, also confiscated were 34 large-format notebooks, 65 folders and 180 notepads on the history of literature and music, and a savings-account passbook to the tune of 400 rubles.

There was also a receipt, No. 1807/6, from the internal prison of the Ministry of State Security, dated December 2, 1948, and a list of what he carried with him, from pillowcases to cuff links.

On a separate piece of paper, twenty pages later, Nora discovered the following decree:

Decree of March 21, 1949:
The enumerated materials are to be destroyed by means of burning.
Signed: Major Ezepov

On the following page was a report on the "fulfillment of the decree to destroy by burning in the Internal Prison of the Ministry of State Security–KGB, in the presence of Major Ezepov." With the signature of the major.

The experts had studied Grandfather's book and papers for three months, judging by the dates, before they were condemned to fire.

At this point, Nora was overcome with nausea, broke off her note-taking, handed the "Case" back to the kindly archival assistant, and left. She returned on the following day and kept coming until the end of the week, copying out excerpts of the case into a notebook, not really understanding why she was doing this. The notebook was already half filled, but Nora couldn't stop.

Medical files and records. In one, "chronic radiculitus"; in another, more cultured, in Latin—"*eczema tybolicum*, chronic case." And, the conclusion— "able-bodied and fit for physical labor."

Nora glanced down at her wrists. During the last few years, her eczema had abated. The only reminder of it was the thin, shiny layer of skin that covered the formerly affected parts. And the newborn baby, from his first days, had allergic contact dermatitis. Evidently a congenital condition. Genes . . .

Protocol of interrogation from December 2, 1948.

Twenty-four handwritten pages. At the end, the signature: Lieutenant Colonel Gorbunov. And another one: Ossetsky.

It was a mild interrogation, neutral. Question-and-answer.

Q: Among the material evidence in your case is the work *Can the Bolsheviks Retain State Power?* Did you have any doubts in this regard?
A: The work in question was written by Lenin. It was written in September 1917, and we were discussing this article in 1931 or 1932 . . . I don't remember exactly.
Q: We, meaning who? Identify them by name.
A: That was more than sixteen years ago. I don't remember exactly.

At first, Nora copied everything down in sequence; then she began to cull excerpts—parts that were underlined in red pencil.

—Denies anti-Soviet activity (propaganda) . . .
—Denies taking part in the Soviet of Workers' and Soldiers' Deputies in Kharkov in 1918 . . .
—States that his father, Samuil Ossetsky, was an employee at a mill before the Revolution . . .
—Admits to being acquainted with the chairman of the Jewish Anti-Fascist Committee, Solomon Mikhoels, and the secretary, Heifetz . . .
—Admits to taking part in the work of the Jewish Anti-Fascist

531

Committee as a hired consultant, carrying out literary work on commission.

Following this was a list of places he had been employed, remarkable in its length and diversity:

1919: Municipal labor exchange, statistician, Kiev
1920: People's Committee of Labor, head of statistics of the labor market, Kiev
1920–1921: Head of statistics, Union of Workers' Cooperatives, Kiev
1921–1923: Office of the Tsentrosoyuz, Kiev
1923–1924: Central Statistical Administration of the Sovnarkom, Moscow
1924–1931: Supreme Soviet of the National Economy, economist, Moscow
In 1931: arrested, charged with sabotage. By the decision of the Collegium of the Joint State Political Directorate, banned from residence in 12 controlled-access cities of the USSR.
1931–1933: Economist at the Stalingrad Tractor Plant. Arrested in 1933, 6 months under investigation. Sentenced by the Special Council of the People's Commissariat for Internal Affairs of the USSR (NKVD) to 3 years exile. Resided in the city of Biysk until December 1936, after which he returned to the Moscow region.
1937: Yegoryevsky region, mines, head of the legal department.
1938: Civilian head of the planning department in the Unzhinsk corrective labor camp
1939: Returned to Yegoryevsk, gave private music lessons
1940: Kuntsevo, Krasin Pencil Factory, head of production group
1941: Scientific Research Institute of Municipal Transport, head of the planning-contract department
1941, October: Ulyanovsk, planner in the building-and-assembly administration
1943, May: the organization re-evacuated to Moscow
1944: Research fellow at Timiryazev Agricultural Academy
1945–1948: Instructor in statistics at the Economics Department of the Institute of Cinematography
From September 1, 1948: No specific occupation

She went back to the beginning of the file, examined the transcript from the first interrogation, paged forward to the next one, and started to compare them. The second interrogation transcript was half as long. The questions were the same, but the answers were different. Why the answers had changed, and what had happened to Ossetsky during the interval of six days between the first and the second interrogations, was anyone's guess. Nora felt sick. She didn't understand why she was copying out these excerpts, without rhyme or reason. But she couldn't stop.

J. Ossetsky is exposed as guilty, according to the deposition of Romanov, V. I., of using "malicious and obscene language when describing the leadership of the Soviet Bolshevik Communist Party and government," as well as the deposition of Khotinsky, O. I., accusing Ossetsky of spreading rumors about starvation in Kuban during the period 1932–1933.

J. Ossetsky denies "the possibility of [him] using any malicious and obscene language when describing anyone and admits to his participation in spreading rumors about starvation in Kuban."

J. Ossetsky acknowledges that before the Revolution his father, Samuil Osipovich Ossetsky, was a merchant in the first guild, a purveyor of grain, leaseholder of a mill, owned a ferry on the Dnieper, and was in possession of his own barges. In 1917, all the property was nationalized. During the NEP years, he carried on petty trade. In 1922, he was prosecuted for concealment of gold.

J. Ossetsky acknowledges that he greeted the "bourgeois-democratic revolution positively, then worked in the Kiev Social Revolutionary–Menshevik Soviet of Workers' and Soldiers' Deputies, and shared the views of the Mensheviks. [He] worked in the Soviet as an instructor in the legal department until October 1917. [He] greeted the October Revolution with hostility, carried out agitation that aimed to undermine and overthrow the Soviet authorities. In 1918, [he] finally renounced [his] Menshevik views, because this party ceased to interest [him]."

"I acknowledge that in 1931–1933 I entertained hostile views toward the policies of the Soviet Bolshevik Communist Party on issues of the collectivization of agriculture, and expressed these views to people with whom I was in communication."

"Be informed that I made the acquaintance of Mikhoels on my own initiative, with the goal of offering him my services in drawing up reports on the question of Palestine . . . I submitted four reports, numbering 150 to

250 pages, to the Jewish Anti-Fascist Committee. The reports were approved, and I received payment amounting to more than 3,000 rubles. I expressed a pro-British bourgeois-nationalist point of view on the question of Palestine."

Q: With whom else did you communicate in Mikhoels's circle?
A: With the head of the Middle Eastern Department of the Ministry of Foreign Affairs, a former Menshevik, Stern. I was tasked by these persons to elaborate the so-called political problem, and provided them with slanderous bourgeois-nationalistic materials with a pro-British bent, which I adopted from foreign sources.

This was an "openhearted confession," and from this moment on it was already clear that he was doomed. It was only a matter of whether he would be sent away with the first echelons, all of whom were executed, or with the second, who received reduced sentences, starting at ten years.

Then they produced Ossetsky's telephone book.

Q: Tell us about your relationships with the people in your phone book. Alphabetically . . . Abashidze? Nikolai Atarov? Dmitreva? Gerchuk? Krongauz? Levashev? Litvinov? Lukyanov? Naiman? Polovtsev? Polyansky? Potapova? Shklovsky? Shor? Urlanis? Viktor Vasiliev?

Dozens of surnames . . .
Answers: Colleague . . . never heard of him . . . I don't have his home address, never visited his home, no information, don't remember the house number . . . a neighbor, used to walk his dog in the courtyard . . . I don't remember the apartment number, never visited his home . . . a chance acquaintance from Kiev . . . member of the editorial board . . . colleague, we didn't communicate . . .

Q: Who is Mikhail Kerns?
A: An acquaintance from Kiev. We haven't met since before the war. He died during the war.

Kerns was Marusya's brother—Nora remembered this perfectly well. She

534

knew his granddaughters, one of whom, Lyubochka, was an artist. Jacob didn't say a word about his being Marusya's brother. He protected her. He protected everyone. About Marusya, he said that he had cut off all relations with her in 1931. He had had no communications with her, and no information about her.

On the fourth day of her research, Nora discovered some documents in the file that astounded her. It was a statement filed by Genrikh Ossetsky to the Party Bureau of the Institute where he worked, dated December 3, 1948, two days after his father's arrest, and another, similar one, from January 5, 1949, addressed to the minister of state security at the time.

Statement by Genrikh Ossetsky, head of the laboratory of the All-Union Toolmaking Scientific Research Institute, 49 B. Semenovskaya St.
I informed the Party Bureau of the Institute where I work about the arrest of my father, Jacob Ossetsky, by the Ministry of State Security. The arrest took place on December 1, 1948, by order of the Ministry of State Security No. 359.

During the examination of my statement at the meeting of the Party Bureau on December 24, 1948, I was asked to recall whether there had been any hostile expressions or actions on the part of my father. Since I have not lived with my father since 1931, I interact with him very seldom. However, I did recall one fact, which seemed suspicious to the Party Bureau, and the Party Bureau requested that I report this to investigative bodies.

At the start of the war, in about September 1941, I met my father on the street by chance. We talked about the situation at the front. My father suggested that within a short period of time the Germans might reach Moscow and occupy it. (I don't remember the precise wording of this phrase, but that was the gist of it.) At the time, I didn't pay any attention to what he had said, and only later did I judge his views to be reflective of a defeatist attitude.

In carrying out the decision of the Party Bureau, and asking you about this fact, I request you to consider that henceforth in this case, if you are in need of my testimony, I will provide it to you not as the son of a prisoner, but as a member of the Bolshevik Soviet Communist Party, since I put my political convictions above my filial sentiments.

In the event that my father is declared an enemy of the people, I will renounce him without hesitation, for the Party and the Soviet authority,

which have nurtured and educated me, are dearer to me than everything else.
January 5, 1949

After this there was a page with the transcript of the interrogation of Genrikh Ossetsky. Her head ached terribly. She felt sick to her stomach, and her mouth was parched. A migraine, which Nora had not had for a long time, flared up. The last excerpt Nora copied that day read: "Bound for the special camp of the Ministry of Internal Affairs of the USSR—sentenced to 10 years for political agitation and propaganda, and being in possession of counterrevolutionary literature."

She closed the file and took it to the counter, where a new archival assistant was on duty—somewhat older, also forthcoming and kind—and turned around to go. But before she went, she committed a theft. From an envelope that was lying in the file, she pinched a book, *The Revolt of the Angels* by Anatole France, with this inscription:

Binding made from a stolen folder, socks, and bread.
Bound March 4–6, 1934, in the most trying days of my sojourn in cell no. 2 in
the Stalingrad prison.
Resigne Toi, mon Coeur,
Dors, mon soleil!

How it had ended up in here, and why it hadn't been destroyed, no one would ever know.

The rain, which had been pattering gently for two days, had stopped. A late-afternoon sun, weak and uncertain, came out. Nora remembered that she had an emergency pill, which she never took out of her handbag. She found the pill, but, having no water to wash it down, she put the bitter medicine in her mouth and chewed.

She walked to the Lubyanka and stopped opposite the gray monstrosity. The tall doors of the entrances were dead—no one went in or out. From inside this hellish abomination, which pretended to be just an ugly, featureless building, came the vile, putrid smell of fear and cruelty, baseness and cowardice; and the gentle afternoon sunlight was powerless to combat it. Why didn't a heavenly fire pour down upon it? Why didn't pitch and brimstone envelop this cursed place? Poor little Sodom and pathetic, insignificant Gomorrah, refuge of depraved lechers, had been burned down; why was there no divine punishment, and why was this hellhole still standing in the middle of this indifferent, vainglorious, self-involved city? Would it stand here forever? No, nothing is forever. The Prolomnye Gates were gone; the Vitali Fountain was no longer on the square, nor was the Rossiya Insurance Company. Even the monument to Dzerzhinsky had disappeared. Nora turned around and walked toward the Teatralny Passage.

Her headache hadn't let up, and the same thought kept pounding in her brain—"Poor Genrikh!" Kind, somewhat dull-witted, laughing at silly jokes, harmless and easygoing Genrikh. Why had he rushed to repudiate his father on the very next day after his arrest? Why had he denounced him, thus justifying himself and burying his father once and for all? Was he protecting his career, his place under the stunted, sickly sun—or perhaps his family? Mama and me? Poor Genrikh . . .

What kind of rot and decay was this? What kind of curse? Fear, cowardice . . . or perhaps he knew something that I'll never know.

Nora walked homeward by a random, circuitous route. She passed Kamergersky Lane, and walked by the corner house immortalized by Pasternak. The house where "a candle on the table burned, a candle burned . . ." Antipov was renting an apartment there, and Yury Zhivago, caught in the lacy intricacy of an as yet unfulfilled fate, rode past, noticing this meaningless little flame in one of the windows, and committing it to literary eternity.

Then Nora turned into Stoleshnikov Lane. Before, there had been people she knew living in almost every house, but many of them had been resettled, had moved, or were already dead. When you live your whole life in one city, it is filled with points of memory, as though ineradicable memories are nailed to every gateway, to every corner.

In the Church of Cosmas and Damian, the bells started ringing. Before, this building had housed the printing press of the Ministry of Culture. Once, Nora had come here on business—to print some playbills or performance notices, she could no longer remember.

Walking past, she heard wonderful singing coming from the open window of the church. She stopped to listen. Beggars swarmed around the entrance. Inside, it smelled of apples and candles. There was a long table on the side where apples, grapes, and other fruits were arranged. The singing mingled with the air perfumed by the apples, and the sound was sublime. Nora sat on a bench right by the entrance. Next to her sat two old women and a mother with a sleeping child, a little girl of about two. It was impossible to make out the words that the choir was singing, but it didn't matter.

All of a sudden, Nora started to cry. She was not at all religious. Russian Orthodoxy had no special meaning for her; nor did any other religion. But her heart responded to the sounds. My God, she thought, this is my other grandfather, Alexander Kotenko, the precentor, sending me a sign—this is his music, his life. I know nothing about him, absolutely nothing; he tormented his wife, he was evil and blind, as Amalia told it.

Why did this music move her so? Was it really a signal of some kind? They had all been so musical—both her grandfathers, Alexander and Jacob—and Genrikh . . . Genrikh . . . And from her heart a deep lament rose up and choked her, and it was as though it wasn't she crying, but Genrikh in her. Little Genrikh, intolerable little child who threw himself on the floor and thrashed his arms and legs, who wanted to fly a glider or an airplane, whom they barred from his beloved profession of aviation—yes, of course, because his father, Jacob, was an enemy of the people and ruined everything. He was robbed of his dreams, his hopes, his shining, beckoning future. Oh, poor Genrikh!

Nora cried together with him, this boy, her future and former father, who had not been given the chance to live the life he dreamed about. He sobbed and gasped for air, then grew tired and moaned quietly, then howled again, and started throwing a tantrum. Nora just wiped away the tears. How awful! Would his grief never end? Would it never burn out, never die? Would it torment him, and Nora, and the newborn Jacob, who had only just arrived and was not guilty of anything at all? Is it possible that the evil we commit never dissipates, but hangs above the head of every new child that emerges out of this river of time?

She left the church. It was the eve of the Feast of the Transfiguration of the Lord. "As always, a light without flame shines on this day from Mount Tabor . . ." Yes, of course! The light without flame . . . The light has already waned, but the holiday has not yet ended. Suddenly she felt buoyant and weightless, as though someone had taken from her the whole burden of this day. She had crossed a frontier.

Almost next door was Aragvi, a restaurant that Nora and Tengiz used to frequent. She smiled, remembering this. The theater of shadows, which he had shown her without knowing it himself, was an intimation that what was beyond their corporeal existence, so full of fear and shame, was something else, something that, from here, was visible only as beautiful dim shadows.

Nora crossed Tverskaya Street through the underpass, then came out on Tverskoy Boulevard, which she saw with a kind of double vision—the way it looked today, and the way it looked after the war, lined with old trees, with the Pushkin statue at the head of the boulevard, a drugstore on Novopushkinsky Square, the wall, visible from here, of the ruined Strastnoy Monastery, and the long-gone music school in the courtyard of a long-gone building, where they had taken her in childhood to tap on the keys, in the spot where the present-day box of a building of the *Izvestia* newspaper was located.

She walked along Tverskoy Boulevard, remembering people she knew who had lived in the surrounding houses—her mother's and her own classmates and friends. She passed the house where Taisia, who had died long ago in Argentina, had once lived. She crossed Tverskoy to Nikitsky, making a small detour around the rerun movie theater where she had received her introduction to art without being aware of it. She glanced in passing at the House of Polar Explorers, at the final refuge of Gogol, and Vitya's first apartment, on the semi-basement floor, from where he came to see her, running across the boulevard—Vitya, her lawful husband and the father of her only son . . .

It grew dark, but the light without flame still warmed the sky. "Poor Genrikh!" Nora sighed one last time, and entered the house where she had lived her whole life. She didn't bother taking the lift, but walked up to the fourth floor, glad that she could make it without undue weariness. And all the way up to her apartment, she thought about how everything had in fact worked out for the best; she still had time to take care of all the loose ends, and to think some things through about which she had a vague suspicion, but certainly could not be said to know. Perhaps she would arrange old letters and write a book, the sort of book that either her grandfather had not had time to write, or, if it had been written, had been burned in the Internal Prison of the Lubyanka.

But who is he, my protagonist? Jacob? Marusya? Genrikh? Me? Yurik? No. No one, in fact, who is conscious of an individual existence, of birth and an anticipated, and unavoidable, death.

Not a person at all, one might say, but a substance with a certain chemical makeup. And is it possible to call a "substance" something that, being immortal, has the capacity to transform itself, to change all its fine, subtle little planes and angles, its crooks and crevices, its radicals? It is more likely an essence that belongs neither to being nor to nonbeing. It wanders through generations, from person to person, and creates the very illusion of personality. It is the immortal essence, written in code, that organized the mortal bodies of Pythagoras and Aristotle, Parmenides and Plato, as well as the random person one encounters on the road, in the streetcar, on the metro, or in the seat next to you in an airplane. Who suddenly appears before you, and calls up a familiar, dim sensation of a previously glimpsed outline, a bend or a curve, a likeness—perhaps of a great-grandfather, a fellow villager, or even someone from the other side of the world. Thus, my protagonist is essence itself. The bearer of everything that defines a human being—the high and the low, courage and cowardice, cruelty and gentleness, and the hunger for knowledge.

One hundred thousand essences, united in a certain pattern and order, form a human being, a temporary abode for each and every person. This is, in fact, immortality. And you, a human being—a white man, a black woman, an idiot, a genius, a Nigerian pirate, a Parisian baker, a transvestite from Rio de Janeiro, an old rabbi from Bnei Brak—you, too, are just a temporary abode.

Jacob! Is this the book you wished to write, and could not?

Epilogue

Everything ends well: death follows the happy ending. Everything, at
long last, is accepted—the destruction of a people; the funeral of one's
only child, who has died of leukemia. The old Jacob is reading otherworldly books in otherworldly libraries, and listening to otherworldly
music. The little Jacob is learning to read, pecking on the piano keyboard,
and attending to the clear sounds.

Marusya has finally found herself—look how the clouds move, changing their aspect from moment to moment, at will, not submitting to
any logic. She moves in concert with clouds, and with sounds; and this
is joy . . .

At the end of her life, Nora begins to resemble Tusya. She wears Tusya's
large rings on her bony fingers, and teaches theater to aspiring young
artists.

Vitya receives the Major Prize, which he fully deserves, and which
Grisha secretly dreamed about.

At the end of the 2030s, Grisha dies, an old, old man, in Jerusalem. At
his grave, his innumerable children and grandchildren place a slab on
which, according to his will, is carved not his name, but a URL: "www . . ."
If the curious follow the link, they can read an ecstatic missive about
the Divine Text, addressed to Grisha's heirs and at the same time to all humanity. His text is as long and convoluted as it is remarkable.

Yurik, like his great-grandfather Jacob, is immersed in music. Not the clarinet, not the piano, not the guitar—he is trying to hear the music that pours through the cosmos. And it is not in the least important whether he became a professional composer, or remained that same small boy, who used to say:

"Mama, remember how I sang in your tummy?"

Author's Note

Excerpts from letters in my family archives and excerpts from the file of Jacob Ulitsky have been included in this story. (KGB Archive No. 2160)

Acknowledgments

With thanks to my family and friends

This book would never have been written without the help and support of my family. To my husband, Andrei Krasulin—thank you for your patience and indulgence; to my sons Alyosha and, especially, Petya Evgeniev—thank you for all kinds of support, including technological; to my cousin, Olga Bulgakova—thank you for preserving the ambience of our family, of which almost no one remains.

To my friends—Nikita Shklovsky, who devoted so much time to conversation and discussion of the biological questions the book touches on; and Vladimir Andreevich Uspensky, who enlightened me in the parts of the book concerning mathematics. You are in large part coauthors of this book.

Special thanks to Katya Gordeeva for her brilliant participation and contribution—while I was giving birth to this book, she gave birth to her son Jacob, which lent authenticity to the whole of this partially invented story.

Thank you to my dear friends Lika Nutkevich, Ira Shchipacheva, Lyuba Grivorieva, and Tanya Gorina, for their care, patience, and support when my spirits fell and I came close to despair; and to Dianochka, who helps me in that department of life which is particularly difficult for me.

Thank you to my first readers and editors: the publisher Elena Shubina; Elena Kostioukovitch; Yulia Dobrovolskaya; and Sasha Klimin (he, more than anyone, gave his all and sweated over every page of the book!). I thank all those friends who sheared off sizable chunks of the text; to Dima Bavilsky, who opened my eyes to the use of possessive pronouns and a few obtrusive verbs; to Ira Uvarova and Alyona Zaitseva for sharing their expertise on theater; to Misha Golubovsky for scientific consultation. Thank you to my dear Alexanders, who have accompanied me throughout my life: Alexander Khelemsky, who explained things to me that I had spent my whole life trying to understand, with varying results; and Alexander Gorin, who advised me on questions of computer programming. Because of both of them, I now know a bit more than I did before I began. To Bondarev and Smolyansky, for their meticulousness; Okun, for his support at a critical moment; Varshavsky, for his indulgence; and Borisov, who prayed I would survive.

And to all the equally dear friends who helped me by not hindering me . . .

I thank all those whom I've forgotten to mention in these notes. In truth, I should go through my alphabetical index file and thank all my beloved friends from all the stages and ages in my life, some of whom are already gone . . .

This would be fitting, but there would be no end to it.

And one more, very special, expression of thanks. When I had already finished this book, my dear friend Katya Genieva died. I was able to say goodbye to her, and the dignity, intelligence, and grace of her leavetaking reconciled me to the necessity of parting from this remarkable, wonderful, and at times terribly difficult world we still live in.

I thank you all.